NATURAL CONSEQUENCES

ELLIOTT KAY

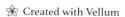 Created with Vellum

WARNING

Natural Consequences contains explicit sex, explicit violence, explicit expletives, violent misuse of office equipment, nudity, perfidy, disruption of public transit services, polyamory, theft, arson, open relationships, trespassing, heterosexual foreplay, lesbian sex, depictions of beings of a divine and demonic nature bearing little resemblance to established religious or mythological canon, cell phone hacking, contempt of court, flagrant violations of civil rights, dangerous use of alcoholic drinks, infidelity, public sex, bras, panties, murder, attempted murder, blasphemy, atheist rationalizations, cannibalism, decapitations, gossiping, defenestration, exsanguinations, tax evasion, oral sex, multiple threesomes, sexual harassment, ancient Babylonian marriage customs, horse-poisoning, stalking, selfies, bribery, assault under color of authority, fantasy depictions of sorcery and witchcraft, highly sexualized Halloween costumes, assault and battery, stabbings, excessive handcuff play, mayhem, explosions, existential discussions, controversial topics of sci-fi fandom, living room sex, home invasions, mind control, conspiracy, cohabitation outside of marriage, multiple references to British science fiction literature and television, bad study habits, government surveillance, donuts, discharge of firearms on Federal property, spousal abuse, interrogations, even more explicit sex, guys from Eugene, sexual harassment in the workplace, classroom misconduct, sexual misconduct, divine misconduct, general misconduct, voyeurism, reckless driving, murder of Federal agents, poor firearms safety habits, misuse of a swimming pool for gladiatorial combat, insanity, immolations, public endangerment, sexual promiscuity, consistent contempt of vampires (screw 'em, they suck), disorderly conduct, kidnapping of police officers, kidnapping of Federal agents, underage drinking, dismemberment, abuse of authority, still more explicit sex, electrocutions, destruction of private property, escape from Federal custody, barbering without a cosmetology license, World War I, betrayals, slavery, mild dom/sub play, cosplaying, a high school flashback, infidelity, reliable predictions of eternal damnation, destruction of a nice Zoot suit, nutshots, party fouls, littering, domestic violence, lengthy foreplay, abbreviated foreplay, disrespect for authority, falsification of records, prostitution, public indecency, impersonation of police officers, obstruction of justice, biting, clawing, hair-pulling, trash-talking and a general and willful disregard for traditional Western family values.

All characters are over the age of 18.

For Val,
who gave Rachel her voice.

ACKNOWLEDGEMENTS

Several people helped me out significantly with this book. I owe sincere thanks to Matt Y., Matt S., Miguel and Randy for their professional legal advice regarding numerous plot points. I did not set out to write an entirely realistic and fact-checked book about demons, werewolves and secret courts, but I prefer to at least know how the real world works when I decide to go off the rails. Their input meant a great deal to me.

I owe a lot to Erica for the countless times I babbled to her about what I had written or what I planned to write. Every gaming geek knows that "Let me tell you about my character" is normally the kiss of death, but somehow Erica has let me tell her about my characters ad nauseum and yet she's still with me.

I want to thank Lee Moyer, Venetia and Val for making my books look so good, and again to thank Jesse Means for helping me get my first book off the ground.

Numerous friends helped me via long and ridiculous Facebook conversations about love, dating, chapter titles, the proper handgun for causing explosive cranial catastrophes and the great debate over whether it's better to behead one's enemies or set them on fire. Both Matts, Jenny, Beth, Wolf and everyone else who beta read my book also deserve my thanks.

And as a matter of academic honesty and giving credit where it's due, I want to thank Herodotus for telling me about the Babylonian Marriage Market in his *Histories*. Turns out that's a really good book.

PROLOGUE

"T his is the case of the United States of America versus Raven Sebastian Winterhome, AKA Sir Julian Storm, AKA Lord Marcus Etienne Ravenscar... birth name Marvin Kowalski," the judge added with a cynical frown. His eyes glanced up from the papers in front of him. "Are you Marvin Kowalski? Or any of these other aliases?"

The chamber bore greater resemblance to a bunker than a courtroom. The furnishings and layout were all present—tables for prosecution and defense, a judge's bench and witness stand, even an American flag in one corner—but the concrete walls had been left unpainted. Heavy steel doors fit for a naval ship lay closed and locked at either end of the room. The digital clock embedded in the wall noted an hour far too late for any ordinary court proceeding.

The judge sat in black robes at his bench. The prosecutor and defense attorney both wore suits, as did the man and woman in the gallery. Three uniformed bailiffs stood at the ready. All attention fell on the deathly pale, young-looking man with black hair, frosty blue eyes and the bright orange jumpsuit of a prison inmate behind the defense table. Thick chains connected his manacles to a similarly thick bullnose ring imbedded in the floor. He could stand and sit, but not much else.

"Fuck you, chum," the pale man said. His Cockney accent and defiant tone contrasted sharply with the calm, business-as-usual demeanor of the judge.

"This ain't no real cour'room. Why'nt you tell me wot the fuck you lot 're doin' an' knock off the fucking charades, eh?"

"Mr. Kowalski," murmured the suited attorney to his right, "speaking to the judge like that won't do you any favors."

"Piss off."

The judge was unmoved. "I am Judge Eduardo Castillo. Mr. Kowalski, you've been charged in an indictment with the murders of Caroline Morris, Raymond Wong, and Douglas Kramer. You are also charged with three counts of kidnapping, twenty-three counts of aggravated assault, assault on federal agents, resisting arrest, misprision of felonies and tax evasion." He lifted his eyes toward the defendant. "Do you have a copy of the indictment?"

"Fuck yourself wi' your indictment. Stick it up your crusty arse!" The defendant tugged at his chains, struggling as if he had every reason to believe they might break. "Let me the fuck ou' of 'ere! You sacks dunno wot you're dealin' with!"

"It's here, your honor," said the attorney beside the prisoner.

"Very well. Mr. Kowalski, let me inform you of your constitutional rights. You have the right to remain silent. You don't have to say anything to anyone. Anything you say can and likely will be used against you. Do you understand your right to remain silent?"

"Fuck you. That's what I understand."

The defense attorney leaned in and hissed, "Mr. Kowalski, do you understand that this is quite probably a capital case?"

"Oh, piss off, mate! These fuck'ead Feds jus' jumped me in the parking lot of a fucking 'otel three hours ago! Even if this is a real court, all o' this is bollocks an' they know it! So either quit the fucking farce an' tell me wot's goin' on, or give me my phone call so I can get a real fucking lawyer!"

"Mr. Kowalski, *they know what you are.*"

Taken aback by the warning, the defendant asked, "Wot?"

"Your fangs are showing," advised the attorney.

Kowalski's eyes widened in fear. "There's no law against that!"

"You're not on trial for that. Read the indictment."

Judge Castillo continued. "You also have the right to representation by a lawyer with appropriate security clearances. Counselor Lopez, who holds proper clearance, currently assists you. Do you have a different lawyer with top secret clearance you would like to use?"

"Wait, clearance?" the defendant blinked. "Wot the fuck you talkin' abou'?"

"Mr. Kowalski, this court operates under top secret Federal orders pursuant to national security. You will make no phone calls. You do not get to pick any old attorney off the Internet. So again, do you currently have on retainer an attorney with top secret clearance? If not, I will appoint Counselor Lopez to continue to represent you. The court will cover all expenses in such a case."

"What the—wait, this is ridiculous!" the defendant spat. "I want a real fucking court with a real fucking lawyer and a real fucking judge! Don't give me this 'top secret' bullshit!"

"Very well," Castillo conceded. "I will remand you to the Federal District Court of Los Angeles. Your arraignment will proceed at 10 am on Tuesday, October the 22nd."

Marvin's bluster ground to a halt. So did his phony accent. "Wait, what?"

"10 am, Tuesday, Los Angeles," Castillo repeated.

Marvin blinked nervously. "Ten in the morning?" He swallowed, looking to Lopez on his left. "They can do that to me?"

Lopez gave a bit of a nod. "The regular courts run on regular schedules. This is the only court in the nation that accommodates supernatural conditions."

"None of the other courts fucking *know* about supernatural conditions!"

Again, Lopez nodded. "It's a problem," he sniffed.

Marvin looked from the judge to the lawyer and back again. "Uh, Judge... I think... I think I'll take this court. And, uh, this lawyer."

"Understood. I hereby appoint Michael Lopez to represent you. Is defense counsel prepared to proceed with the arraignment?"

"Yes, your honor," Lopez answered.

"Are you correctly named in the indictment? Would you like me to formally read the indictment into the record?" He took his cues from Lopez's short, quick replies. "How do you plead?"

Lopez glanced at Marvin, who looked back at a complete loss for words. "Your honor, my client pleads not guilty," Lopez announced.

Castillo's attention turned to the prosecution's table. "What is the government's position on detention?"

"Your honor, the defendant struggled violently against arrest, assaulting several Federal agents," the prosecutor explained. "His health conditions require the ingestion of warm blood, and he has shown every willingness to commit assault to attain it. He has also demonstrated extraordinary strength, speed and stealth, and is largely unharmed by most weapons carried by police or the general public. It is the government's position that he is a severe flight risk."

"Very well, Counselor Oswalt," Castillo nodded, "Mr. Kowalski will remain in Federal custody until trial."

"What?!" Marvin burst. "That's it? That's my bail hearing?"

"Yeah, they always screw my clients on that one." Lopez glanced at his watch. "Look, you'll get two liters of fresh chicken blood every night."

"Chicken blood?!"

Behind him, the suited man rose and turned for the door. He was a trim man in his early thirties, tall and clean-shaven. He held the door for the younger woman who followed him out while Kowalski unleashed a torrent of worried questions on his attorney.

"That one's gonna be a slam dunk," said Agent Paul Keeley.

Agent Amber Maddox was not so comfortable with all this. It showed on her young, pretty face. Her pantsuit did little to show off her athletic figure, but that was how she preferred it in these environments. It was hard enough to be taken seriously when she looked even younger than she really was. Waiters and bartenders routinely double-checked her driver's license. Dressing in anything but the most conservative styles at work typically drew the same reactions. Tonight, at least, she could accessorize with the small gauze pad taped over her temple. Kowalski's arrest had not gone as smoothly as anyone had hoped, but in the end the Bureau got its man.

Kowalski had been her first supernatural encounter. Up until now, she had focused purely on learning the ropes within the task force, building an airtight case and making the arrest. Thoughts of what would come after that had to be put on hold, but now those concerns were front and center. "What makes you say that?" she asked. "I mean, Kowalski is obviously not all that bright—"

"Dumb as a box of rocks," interrupted Keeley with a wry grin, "if you want to be charitable."

"—and his defense attorney might not be the most energetic I've seen—"

"Lopez knows how to pick his battles," Keeley shrugged. "He's good at his job. Knows a shit case when he sees one. Not all those charges will stick."

Amber paused, wondering if she should say something about being allowed to say her peace. To his credit, Keeley caught onto her understandable frustration immediately. "Sorry," he grunted, "it's late. Go on."

4

"Like you said, not all the charges will stick," Amber said. "I mean, he gets a full jury trial, right? You said this is done by the book, secrecy notwithstanding?"

"Well," Keeley shrugged, "they're *entitled* to a jury trial. Doesn't mean it actually happens. Remember what we told you about the loyalty oaths? Swearing fealty when they're given the big bite and such? Secrecy is the most important aspect. Every vampire is brought in promising to keep their existence secret, even at the cost of their lives. They enforce that on one another brutally.

"The second a vampire realizes he's been made, he starts sweating bullets. Having to go through a trial like this is some scary shit for them, because even if they get out, their vampire buddies would be all over them to know if they slipped up even just a bit... and they wouldn't be here if they hadn't already slipped, right?

"A jury is twelve more people who know the truth. That's twelve more screw-ups on the vampire's part. So usually they waive their right and opt for a bench trial. Lopez argues that the trial isn't legit, because it violates the defendant's Sixth Amendment right to a public trial; Oswalt says the defendant just waived that right by opting for this court over a regular public courthouse, and Castillo agrees, so that settles that. And then we move to the bench trial."

Not for the first time this month, a small part of her kicked herself for waiting until now to ask all this. It wasn't as if Keeley or the other agents on the Kowalski case had held anything back. "And if they want a jury?"

"Then we give it to 'em," answered Keeley. "Twelve U.S. citizens, fluent and literate in English, with no previous connections to the case, who all hold top secret security clearance. And yes," he added, "Lopez objects to that wrinkle, too, and points out that this creates a jury that is naturally predisposed toward the government. Castillo overrules and life goes on."

Amber walked beside him, unsure which question to ask next. That had more or less been the story of her life for these last few weeks. "So is this how it always goes?"

"For the vampires, yeah, pretty much," said Keeley. "We've had a couple curveballs, of course. In the beginning, everything seemed so crazy that there'd never be a normal. But you start to see patterns. The werewolves have their own goofy habits. And then there're the other weirdoes," he grunted, "but we haven't caught enough of those other kinds to establish any baselines."

Amber's next question had been on her mind for some time. Amid all the cloak and dagger procedures and the grim confidence of the task force, it had seemed almost naïve, but now she had to ask. "What are you gonna do when one of these cases ends in an acquittal?"

Keeley came to another door. He paused before he opened it to look over his shoulder at the young agent. "I don't know," he smiled. "I'll tell you when it happens. 'til then, we keep moving on to the next case. And this one's a bit of a problem."

Amber followed him into a conference room dominated by a long table and a white projection screen opposite the door. The room's four occupants had all gone for loosened ties and rolled-up shirtsleeves. She saw Chinese take-out boxes, bottles of soda and a good number of manila file folders. One wall of the room was covered with suspect sketches.

"You ready for us, Joe?" Keeley asked as they entered. "Arraignment's all pretty much finished anyway."

Standing taller than the rest was a blond man with football hero shoulders, a square jaw and something just shy of a flat-top. The sight of Keeley and the other man together immediately made Amber think, "Good cop, tackle cop."

She met Agent Hauser briefly when she was first recruited onto the task force. He hadn't said much at that meeting. Now, he acknowledged her with much the same grunt as then, but this time he spoke. "Agent Maddox," he nodded, "it's good to have you here. Congratulations on your first arrest with the task force."

"Thank you, sir," Amber mumbled.

"Everyone," Hauser said to the others present, "this is Agent Amber Maddox. Received her high school diploma *and* her Associate's degree at age 17 through Washington's Running Start program. Graduated University of Washington with double honors degrees in chemistry and physics, age 20. Worked for three years in the Bureau's Applied Sciences lab, then went to the Academy in Quantico and served in C.I.D. for a year before she signed on with the task force three weeks ago."

Amber glanced around at the others: one woman, two men, plus Hauser and Keeley, all staring at her. "That's a bit more of an introduction than I usually get," she said. Five minutes from now, she'd come up with something much wittier.

"Everyone here has at least ten years on you, Amber," Hauser explained. "I don't want anyone wondering why you're here, least of all you. You've kicked a lot of ass to be here." He paused. "Plus I needed to see if you'd blush."

"Did I?"

"No. Have a seat, everyone."

Amber felt many eyes still upon her as she took up an empty chair. "I only did the honors program in chemistry," she confessed. "Physics is hard."

"Amber, these are Agents Doug Bridger, Matt Lanier and Colleen Nguyen," Hauser began as the lights went down and the projector mounted in the ceiling flickered to life. "They've all been on the task force for several years. You'll be working with us for the foreseeable future in your hometown of Seattle."

Amber blinked. She knew relocation was a potential factor in this transfer, but thought that train had left the station. "I'm not staying with the LA office?"

"No," Hauser said. "No, that was just your audition. We had to make sure you wouldn't freak out at the first encounter with a supernatural. Some people don't take too well to seeing those kinds of abilities." He paused, offering up a wry smirk. "Most people don't respond by tackling the perp to the ground."

She felt grateful the lights had gone down. It was a pretty sure bet she'd be blushing by now. She paid attention to the map of the west coast on the screen and its red, blue and green circles here and there.

"The west coast is something of a hotbed of organized supernatural activity. We've got large vampire societies in LA and San Fran and a couple of distinct werewolf packs spread out across the southwest. The vampires organize themselves in a somewhat feudal structure. There's no discernible consistency of who claims what titles, but there are chains of allegiance. Many of those chains lead to this woman, Lady Anastacia Illyana Kanatova of Seattle."

The slide changed, offering up a detailed sketch of a thin woman of regal beauty. She was blonde, with Eastern European features and a haughty, elegant look. "We have no idea of her original name or how old she might be, but she clearly dates back centuries. As far as we can tell, she's the best-connected vampire on the west coast, with allies across the country. She's in charge of a group of at least sixty other vampires in the Seattle area, which is one of the largest populations we've identified.

"They all vanished last month. We haven't picked up a trace of them since."

Amber blinked. Hauser shifted to the next slide, which showed multiple views of what must have been a large house—perhaps a mansion, judging by its footprint—that had burned down to the foundation. She had to wonder how long it had been burning before the firefighters in the pictures arrived. Even much of the grass had burned within an acre of the house, maybe more.

"We know that in mid-September, Kanatova held some sort of major party at this house in one of Seattle's northern suburbs. We don't know what the hell happened at that party. The fire burned so hot we can't really piece together any physical evidence. Property records are suspiciously sketchy. We've matched several abandoned vehicles nearby to known vampires in the Seattle metro area. We're sure at least some of the vampires survived, but they've gone to ground.

"Local authorities found one still-unidentified woman in the tree line with her head twisted almost in a full turn, and ashes from two vampires, along with their dresses," Hauser said, clicking the slideshow along, "but that's pretty much it. No human remains. No shell casings. Nothing.

"We've got wire-taps on vampires from here to New York and Miami, and everything indicates they haven't a clue what happened, but they're extremely concerned. They suspect it was a hit by another supernatural faction, but hits this size don't happen.

"About a week before this incident, a similar fire destroyed a cemetery chapel in Seattle," Hauser continued, shifting to a new spread of pictures. "Again, cause undetermined. Someone inside called 911, but left the phone off the hook without giving any info. No human remains were found. Nothing but ash."

Hauser leaned forward on the table. His voice held steady, but his frustration couldn't be missed. "Years of investigations. Thousands of hours of surveillance. Research. Solid cases, just waiting for a safe moment to nab the suspects. All gone up in smoke, without an explanation. And now we have vampires all across the country and probably beyond on a hair-trigger to retaliate."

Amber glanced around the table. The expressions worn by her fellow agents confirmed that they all knew the whole story already. This briefing was specifically for her. "So we don't have any leads at all?"

"One," Hauser grunted. He clicked to the next picture.

She saw a typical cell phone self-portrait: bathroom mirror, sink in the foreground, towels on a rack on the wall behind the subject. The guy in the picture might barely be old enough to drink. He was skinny, with short, wet brown hair, a pale, mostly hairless chest and a towel wrapped around his waist. His thug-life posture looked so comical that he couldn't possibly have taken himself seriously. In one hand, he held his cell phone. In the other, he held what appeared to be a wooden stake and a necklace of fangs.

An inset photo beside the youth's face provided a blow-up of the fangs, with markings to denote their likely legitimacy.

"His name is Jason Cohen."

1

AND IT'S ONLY TUESDAY

"This picture's all over the place," Alex teased. He held his phone in one hand, both his elbows on the restaurant table. "I mean, you've got fangs in your hand, posing like you're about to bust out some terrible nerdcore rap, but all this lens flare makes it look like you've just joined Starfleet... I don't know if I'm supposed to think you got these fangs from vampire Klingons or vampire Tupac, y'know?"

"Oh, like you're the guy to critique anyone's photography," retorted Jason. Baskets of half-finished gyros and Greek fries sat between the pair. "Didn't you burn down a church the last time you busted out your camera?"

Alex cringed. "I've taken pictures since then," he said, his voice dropping. He wore a blue dress shirt and black slacks, having come over for lunch from work. "And it was just a funeral chapel. Anyway, you know we didn't take out all the bad guys that night. Why would you want to ask for more trouble?"

"Dude, nobody's listening to us. It ain't like any of 'em are gonna eavesdrop on us at this hour," Jason said, jerking his thumb toward the window. Though Seattle's skies were as overcast and its streets as wet as in any other October, it wasn't exactly dark. "Lorelei said those guys are like supernatural bottom feeders, right? So what's the big deal?"

"They aren't a big deal to her or to Rachel," Alex corrected, "or to Molly and Onyx. But I—"

"Yeah, have you called them lately?" interrupted Jason.

Alex winced. "No."

"Why not? They seem awesome."

"They are, I'm just... can we stay on topic? Look, there are more of those guys out there. They knew my name and how to find me, so they must know how to use computers. I deleted all my social media shit, but we both know all that stuff stays out there anyway. How hard do you think it'd be for them to figure out who my friends are?"

Jason gave a bit of a scowl. "You're that freaked out about it?"

"*We* are, yeah," Alex nodded. "Jason, I'd be dead right now if it wasn't for you. Twice, at least. And I don't want to think about what would've happened to Lorelei. She almost pulled out of her thing with the conservatory board today to come talk to you about this. I don't think you know how much you mean to her, man."

Sighing, Jason pulled out his phone. His fingers tapped through his password and called up the web page out of muscle memory. Jason barely had to look. "I was just fucking around anyway," he muttered. "Not like I thought anyone other than you two and the guys would get what's in that picture."

"Yeah, that's what I figured at first. Lorelei convinced me otherwise. She's dealt with these assholes before. She says they're hard-core about their secrecy stuff and so it stands to reason that they pay people to cruise the Internet and check for anything that might be about them. Even dorky bathroom cell phone pics."

Jason rolled his eyes. "It's gone, okay? Already off my profile pic. I'm deleting it from my pictures, see?" He tilted his phone to show the webpage. "Wasn't even up all that long."

"Thank you," Alex said. "Although that brings up the other question— where in the hell did you get those, anyway? Those were real fangs?"

"Yeah, they're real," Jason said. "I picked 'em up just after the fight. They were just sitting there in the piles of ashes. I guess not all of them crumble up all the way. We wanted to pick up all the incriminating evidence, right?"

"So you could post it on your profile page?" asked Alex.

"Hey, it's gone, alright? It's gone."

"Thank you," Alex sighed. "And you won't show those to anyone, right?"

Jason sighed back, more dramatically than before. "No," he grumbled. "Nobody'd know what they really were, anyway."

"Hopefully."

"Unless Lorelei knows any demon girls who are single," he added. "If that sort of stuff impresses them."

"I kinda doubt it. What about Britney and Brittany? How's that going?"

"Uh. Well, that wasn't ever gonna work out anyway," Jason said, scratching the back of his neck. "I mean, I don't think I'm ready to settle down yet, y'know?"

"Fucked it up?" Alex asked.

"You might be right about me blabbing too much online," Jason confessed. "Less said about all that, the better. Anyway, I'm back on the market."

"Don't worry about it. Just give it some time. You'll find someone new, or she'll find you."

"Easy for you to say. You've had women hanging all over you ever since all the crazy started."

"That's not all a good thing," frowned Alex.

"Oh, whatever. It's only not a good thing for you because you're..." Words failed him. He waved his hand at Alex. "You're *you*."

"Jason, the one thing that I learned from all the crazy was that I wasn't getting anywhere with girls because I wore all my angst and loneliness like a neon t-shirt. Nobody wants to get with that. Fact is, you're a good catch, and you know why. Just relax and don't worry about it."

"Is that how you work it?" Jason said, trying not to sound sullen.

His friend grunted, wanting to avoid that topic entirely. "Hey, I gotta head back to work," Alex said.

"Yeah, I've got another class soon myself. Should probably get going."

"I've got the bill," said Alex, leaving cash on the table. He stood as Jason stepped out of his seat. "Everybody still on for pool tomorrow night? I'm gonna be late, but I'll be there."

"Sure," Jason said. "See you then." With that, he headed out the door.

Before he left, Alex pulled out his phone and sent out a text message: "Mission accomplished. Everything's cool." He didn't expect a response from Lorelei anytime soon. Fundraising for the arts required a lot of schmoozing and charm, neither of which would be helped by poor cell phone etiquette.

He looked up from his phone to find one of the restaurant's servers standing in front of him at his table. "You know you don't have to hurry out of here, right?" she asked, smiling up at him with dark eyes and darker hair. She gestured to the mostly empty tables beyond his. "You kinda came in after the lunch rush was over, anyway. If you want to hang out, it's not like we need the table...?"

Alex smiled back reflexively, and then saw from her stance that she read it as an encouraging sign. He realized then that perhaps he shouldn't have let his eyes drift over to her so many times while he and Jason ate, and that he'd gone out of his way to be polite and friendly... perhaps too far out.

"Sorry," he said, "I've gotta get back to work. Going to lunch this late was an exception as it is."

The waitress just shrugged. "Come back anytime."

He felt her eyes on him as he passed. His strongest urges made it difficult to walk out the door, but his willpower won out in the end. Tempting as it was to stay and flirt, Alex preferred instead to keep his job—which presented plenty of its own similar challenges.

SOME DAYS WERE EASIER than others.

This afternoon would be tough. He could feel it in the elevator. He had only three hours to go after his late lunch, and knew he'd tremble through probably half of them.

Half of him hoped he would find Kat filling in at reception in her tight sweater, or perhaps Stephanie and her white, form-hugging dress shirt with the top buttons ever so innocently popped open when Alex came around. The other half of him told him to keep it in his pants, to avoid Stephanie entirely this afternoon, to stop thinking about sex and to focus on his work. He had a lot of filing ahead of him. Three hours of decent, reliable, utterly chaste filing.

Alex couldn't claim his hair-trigger arousal didn't feel good. Allowing himself even harmless fantasies made real opportunities hard to resist, though —and living under the "curse" of a succubus seemed to ensure those opportunities would come his way. Moreover, his natural charm and confidence seemed to grow in leaps and bounds under Lorelei's influence. Once shy and wary of coming off as a creep, Alex now had to make an effort *not* to flirt.

At least he had no issues working beside Kat, despite her perfume and her eye-catching figure. The work dynamic between Alex and Kat was rife with innuendo, but there was never any chance she'd cheat on her boyfriend, or that Alex would tempt her toward that. No matter how much they teased, Kat served as a reality check on his magnetism. Not every woman was interested.

Kat was safe. She was great eye-candy and great company, but no one's self-control seemed ready to crumble there.

Stephanie was another matter entirely. Alex's attraction to the party-girl copy room clerk had originally been one-sided, but as his confidence and experience grew, so did her interest. He didn't know if he could deny another overt advance from her today.

He stepped off the elevator to find Shirley back from her lunch break and at the front desk once more. He smiled and waved at the grey-haired receptionist. No temptation to be faced there. Just a warm greeting and a wave on through into the law offices of Keating & Rose.

Alex took the long way around to the file room so he wouldn't have to pass by the copy room. He turned the corner and found two of the company's sharpest attorneys in an office doorway. Whatever conversation Susan had been having with Trinh stopped immediately. His stride faltered. Both women glowered at him, then stepped inside Susan's office and shut the door.

Oh no, he thought. The last time he'd been in that office, Susan threw him up against a wall, kissed him hard... and wasn't happy at all to hear that he was seeing someone.

Alex scratched his head and wondered how he could mend that fence as he wandered to the file room. Kat wasn't back from lunch yet. He sat at his desk and rolled the mouse to bring his monitor out of screen saver mode. He entered his login and password, found it rejected and tried again. No luck. He wondered what he was doing wrong. Was the caps lock on?

"Alex?" asked a cool, confident female voice. He looked up to see Olivia—pretty, older, dark-haired office manager Olivia—standing in the doorway. "Could I talk to you in my office, please?"

"Uh, sure, Olivia," Alex shrugged. He rose from his seat to follow and found he couldn't help but look at the sway in her hips as she walked. That skirt wasn't too short to be professional, but wasn't long enough to be conservative, either. He liked the stockings, too. And the woman wearing them.

Stop it, he reminded himself. *Stop thinking about that. Try something else. Think about math. Motorcycle maintenance. No, baseball! Baseball isn't sexy! Except for all the innuendos about getting to bases. Dammit!*

Olivia shut and locked the door behind him. Her hand came to his chest, gently pushing him backward. The smoldering look in her eyes made her intentions plain.

Aw hell. Not again. Not today. I can't handle this today.

"Olivia, what—wait, what's going on?" he asked. The couch snuck up on him, taking his legs out from under him at the knees. He fell back into a seat.

"I think you know," she murmured. Olivia sat sideways in his lap, bringing her legs across his, not waiting for anything resembling permission. She kissed him hotly, slipping one hand behind his neck and up to grab a little of his short black hair. "I'm all about grabbing opportunities while they last."

He was stronger some days than others.

When she kissed him again, he didn't resist. He couldn't. Justifications filled his mind: She was an adult. She knew what she was doing. This was completely within the bounds of his relationship rules. Somewhere out there, a demon who loved him silently urged Alex to tear Olivia's clothes off. At least one angel probably had similar wishes with more vulgar expressions for them.

Olivia looked great with her hair down like this. Felt good up against him. Alex's hands roamed up her sides, leaving him curious about the lacy bra he felt underneath her top.

He didn't initiate this. He never did. Alex hadn't even ever flirted with his boss like he had with Stephanie, or Susan...

Wait. No. Susan. Stop. "Stop," Alex managed to say in the middle of their kiss, then repeated, "Wait, Olivia. Stop for a second."

Olivia's hand in his hair took a firmer grip, tilting his head back so she could lick his neck. "Can't it wait?"

"Did Susan say anything to you today?"

She pulled back. His shirt was already half unbuttoned. Her blazer was off. "You really want to do this now?" Frustration and annoyance replaced the tone of lust in her voice.

"Do what now? What happened?"

"What happened? Oh, nothing, except that Susan found out that you've been fooling around with Stephanie."

"What?" Alex blinked.

"Stephanie left her cell phone out on a countertop in the copy room with a message to you showing. Susan decided that wasn't okay with her."

"But I didn't fool around with Stephanie. Nothing actually happened."

"Hm. Well, I told Susan that what she saw didn't sound like conclusive evidence to me, but in the end it doesn't matter. What does matter is what Susan believes and what I'm left to deal with."

"Susan filed a complaint?"

"She talked to me as a first step, yes. Next step if I don't resolve it is to take it to the partners. Can't have that, can we?"

He didn't even know what to say. "Then this—what is this? This here? You and me and... what the hell, Olivia?"

"*This* is nothing anyone will ever be able to prove, because I'm not careless enough to leave evidence lying around," shrugged the office manager. "Now, I know you've got a girlfriend. I don't expect what happens here to leave this office. The real question is whether or not you'd like me to fix this for you."

"For me?" he blinked. "Is Stephanie in trouble, too?"

"She's gone. Talked to her just before you went out to lunch. She's already packed up and out of here."

Suddenly he felt awful. "Olivia, why did you do that?" he demanded.

"Because Susan has a lot of loyal clients, Alex. Business contacts. Wealthy people. If she leaves the firm, she'll take them with her." She got off him and retrieved her blazer from the floor, putting it on as she sat behind her desk and straightened her hair. She seemed shockingly calm about all this. "And I think I can see where this is going. I'm sorry, Alex, but the firm can't tolerate this sort of behavior."

"What?" he burst.

"You've been a good worker and everyone likes you, Alex. But this sort of sexual harassment is unacceptable."

His jaw hadn't closed yet, so it had no farther to drop. He stood from the couch. "You're *firing* me?"

Olivia looked him over and gestured absently at the impressive tent formed by the crotch of his slacks. "Unless you can give me some reason I shouldn't?"

His response didn't come out right away, jammed up as it was by a dozen other shocked and disgusted replies all trying to escape his mouth. "Go to hell!"

The office manager sighed. "I was afraid you'd get self-righteous about this."

"Self-righteous?" Alex sputtered as she reached for the phone. "You—"

"I'm calling building security now," Olivia said flatly. "They'll have someone up to watch you collect your belongings and escort you to the parking garage."

There was nothing more to say. Nothing to debate. No defense he could muster. Alex stormed out of Olivia's office without another word. He headed back into the file room, buttoning his shirt back up as if it mattered.

"Wow," said an amused female voice, "that shit did *not* go the way I expected." Alex found her lying atop the long counter that made up his and Kat's desk, lounging with her head propped up on one arm. The radiance of Rachel's halo seemed a bit toned down, perhaps for his benefit. The slender, youthful beauty's broad white wings mostly faded into the wall behind her.

Usually, Rachel's mere appearance gave him an immediate thrill. He saw her almost daily, but never at predictable moments. Given her responsibilities, the angel could not spend as much time with her lovers as any of them might wish.

Alex had responsibilities, too. Fewer of them now. It didn't feel good.

"Were you watching?" he asked, keeping his voice low. He could still count the number of people who'd ever seen her on his fingers. Fired or not, Alex didn't want anyone walking in to see him talking to the wall. Somewhere out there was a security guard on the way.

"Yeah, most of it. I felt her coming onto you. Figured as long as I was gonna get vicariously boned, I'd come get the visuals to match." she grinned.

"Sorry about that," he muttered. "I feel like such an asshole."

"Why? Your boss is the asshole here," Rachel shrugged. Her voice dropped to a whisper. "Between you and me, Olivia's guardian angel says she's always been like this. You're not the first guy she's hit with the fuck-me-or-you're-fired bit."

"So you don't think this I brought this on myself?" he fumed.

"Oh, sure, 'cause you come to work dressed like a slut, right?" the angel deadpanned. "Doesn't matter how hot you are or if you flirted with her or not. If the genders were reversed, you wouldn't even question who was in the wrong."

"Still. Women never even hit on me before Lorelei came along."

"Hah! You mean you didn't notice. Alex, your *eau de succubus* just advertises what a great lay you are," she said with a melodramatic gesture. "It doesn't turn anyone into a slobbering drone. There are four other chicks in this office who've fantasized about fucking you into the dirt, but they handle attraction like rational adults. You don't see them tying you up and stuffing their panties in your mouth."

Alex blinked. "Freudian slip much?"

"Maybe," Rachel replied with her sweet, naturally innocent grin. "But still. As much as Stephanie wanted to jump you, she kept it under control, didn't she?"

"Ugh. Yes, and I feel awful for her. I don't even have her phone number or her email. Can't even apologize."

"It's not on you to apologize. I'm telling you, this is about Olivia being a crazy bitch. Shit happens. You can't make it all about you."

"Doesn't mean I don't feel bad."

"Fair. Hey, I'll talk with Stephanie's guardian. Maybe we'll bend a couple rules about interventions to make it up to her."

Alex nodded and slumped down into his chair. He knew he should set to clearing out his desk, but fuck it. He was entitled to a few minutes for this to sink in.

"Anyway, screw this job," Rachel said. "You don't actually need it. You can't tell me filing all day long was a thrill a minute."

"I liked having this job," he scowled.

Rachel made a face. She looked at the file racks and the pile of papers in his in box. "For fuck's sake, why?"

"Because after the way all my other opportunities coming out of high school fell apart, it felt good to at least have an adult job. This might not be exciting, but it beats working a register or standing behind a deep fryer. That's all most people my age can find." He paused and added, "It felt good to have a job to go to after all the other craziness in my life, too. Helped keep me grounded. Made it feel like I wasn't just sponging off Lorelei."

"You don't *need* to stay grounded, love. What you need is a long, sustained stretch of party time. No, seriously," she said as she saw the objection rise to his mouth. "You've had life after life of hard knocks and sacrifice. I know you don't remember any details anymore, but it weighs on your soul. I see it."

"Other lives. They weren't *me*."

"Yes, they were, dork-ass," Rachel sighed, reaching out to nudge at his heart. "It's all the same soul. It's *who you are*." The thought gave her a bit of a frown. "Nobody should have that kind of consistency, but there it is. You made all those choices. You carried all those burdens. It's time to dump 'em. Relax. Have some fun with this life."

His eyebrow rose. "You don't think I have enough fun with you and Lorelei?" he asked, his lips hinting at a grin despite his stress.

She mimicked his expression. "You could have more," she suggested. "I'm kind of surprised life isn't all strippers and sex clubs for you and Lorelei yet. You're under a succubus curse. If you try to deny it, you'll go nuts. You've gotta manage it, and that means letting your freak flag fly sometimes."

"That's what I'm saying, though," he said as his grin faded. "You and Lorelei are incredible. Shouldn't that be good enough? More than enough?"

"It's not a question of 'good enough,' lover," Rachel answered patiently. "For either of you. It's a curse. It's not supposed to be fair."

"No, but *I* should be."

Rachel let his statement hang in the air before she spoke again. "Y'know, this isn't the only open relationship in the world. We didn't invent the term. The others don't come from demonic curses, either. The *healthy* ones just get there through a whole lot of honesty."

"Yeah," he nodded. "Yeah, I've been working on that."

"I know," she said. Rachel sat up on the counter, gracefully sliding over to put both her feet on the arms of Alex's desk chair. "I should probably get back on the job. Still got things to deal with in the bay. All kinds of nasty tentacled shits trying to move in down there. Ugh. So fucking gross. I'll come back to you when I'm free again. You gonna turn into a mopey emo bastard on me?"

"This happened like two minutes ago. Give it a chance to sink in, okay?"

"It's just a job," she reminded him evenly.

"It is," Alex sighed. "I'll get over it."

"Go home. Talk it out with Lorelei," the angel nodded. "She loves you. So do I." She leaned in to kiss him softly. Then she was gone.

Alex opened his eyes to find a scowling security guard looming over him. His nametag read "Lambert." The man pushed an empty trash bag in his hands. "Two minutes, creep," said Lambert. "Get your shit and get out of my building."

GATHERING his belongings didn't take long. Alex wasn't one for pictures or trinkets, but like anyone in an office for almost two years, there were a few things he wanted to save. He had a good pocket knife, a coffee mug, an iPod dock with speakers and a few holiday cards. His daily LolCat calendar. The small blue police box pencil sharpener that Kat gave him last Christmas.

Frustratingly, the guard hounded him out the door before Kat got back. He didn't get a chance to say goodbye to her or anyone else, though he caught a vengeful glare from Susan on his way out.

"You don't plan to keep that roll of tape, do you?" asked Lambert. The guard watched as Alex secured the trash bag of belongings to the back seat of his motorcycle in the parking garage. Sadly, he had neither saddlebags nor a back-pack today. This was as good as it would get. But it would've been easier to make sure he didn't leave tape residue on the leather seat without Lambert pressuring him.

"Is that why you followed me out here?" Alex asked. "Seriously? The roll of packing tape?" He kept working, eager to just make his exit.

"Yeah. That and making sure you don't find any other women to harass on the way out." Lambert had a few years on Alex, along with a few more pounds —both muscle and otherwise. With a blond buzzcut, thick black-rimmed glasses, a torso spreading slightly over his Sam Brown utility belt and a canister of pepper spray on his hip, Lambert was somewhere between mildly intimi-dating and sadly comical. Alex couldn't decide which.

"Dude. This is the fifth floor of the parking building. I'm not gonna harass anyone out here."

"No, you're not," Lambert glowered. "Because I'm gonna watch you ride your little scooter out of here and never come back."

Alex bristled. He understood Lambert's hostility. The guy thought Alex was a creepy, woman-groping bastard, and Alex had no chance of convincing him otherwise. It wasn't even worth the attempt. But willfully calling his motorcycle a scooter wasn't so forgivable.

He tossed the roll of tape down on the ground behind Lambert. "I'd ask what kind of self-respecting hipster gets a job as a security guard," Alex scowled, "but self-respecting hipster is an oxymoron anyway, so the hell with it."

"Least I've got a job," Lambert countered.

He had a point there. Alex didn't have a comeback for that.

"Alex," said a woman's voice behind him. He didn't recognize it and didn't want to stay and talk to anyone anyway. Alex retrieved the helmet off its hook on the side of his bike. "I've been looking for you."

That earned more of his attention. Alex turned around. She stood only a few feet away, dressed a long tie-dyed skirt and what Alex subconsciously labeled as a hippie hoodie. Her brown hair was tied back into a ponytail, revealing bright blue eyes and a strong, lovely face. She stood to his same height, perhaps even slightly taller. He didn't recognize her immediately.

And then he did.

Oh no, he thought. *Seriously?*

"We had a terrible first meeting," said Diana, "and an even worse parting."

"Ma'am, this guy's being escorted off the premises," said Lambert. "Turns out he doesn't conduct himself well around women."

Diana ignored the security guard. So did Alex. "That was a pretty shitty night for me," Alex frowned.

"Yet you accomplished all you set out to do," Diana nodded. "I didn't think you could. I underestimated you, and your friends. I didn't even know you had friends there."

"I've got lots of friends."

"I can see why." Diana took a step forward, offering a cool smile.

"I can't," Lambert chimed in.

"Shut up," Diana told him without so much as a glance. Alex took a step back. She followed. "You're brave. Intelligent. Handsome. Loyal. Deadly."

"Yeah, I try not to focus a lot on that last bit," he replied guardedly. He shifted his grip on his helmet, now holding it low by the chin guard so he could use it as a weapon if necessary. He didn't find the hungry look in her eyes comforting at all.

She struck an appealing image. The modern hippie look usually did little for him, but Diana made it work. Unfortunately, he remembered their first meeting all too well—and, in particular, her presumptuous offers and the fact that behind that pretty face was a towering furry rage monster that could tear his motorcycle in half and beat him to a pulp with it.

Now here she was, a month later, cornering him in the parking lot at his job.

Somewhere out there, Alex considered, was a campaign or a charity that worked to protect women from stalkers. They had just earned at least half of whatever he had coming to him in his last paycheck, *because this creepy shit right here just sucks.*

"I haven't been able to get you out of my head since we parted. As soon as I recovered, I began searching for you. And now here we are."

"Yeah," he swallowed. "In the parking garage. At my job."

"Had I a phone number, I would have used it."

Alex paused. That sounded reasonable.

"I retrieved your home address from your office the other night," Diana went on. "Your office manager didn't even lock her door. But when I went to your home, I found no one lived there anymore. So I waited for you here."

That didn't sound so reasonable.

"Well," Alex swallowed, keeping his voice calm and steady, "how about you give me your phone number... and I'll give you a fake one, and I won't call you, and you'll get the hint and leave me alone?"

"Oh, Alex. Don't you see? I didn't do all this to let you go now."

"Ma'am," Lambert spoke up again, "it's time for him to leave and for you to—"

Diana backhanded him across the face, sending the guard staggering back. "I said shut up."

"Hey!" Alex snapped. "Leave him alone. It's cool. There's no call for that."

"Lady," Lambert huffed, snatching for the pepper spray on his belt, "you're under citizen's arrest!"

Diana's eyes flared. She seized Lambert's throat with one hand. She snatched his wrist with the other, turning it until he dropped the pepper spray. Displaying surprising strength for her admittedly fit frame, Diana lifted Lambert by his neck.

"Aw, shit," Alex grunted. He shoved the motorcycle helmet down on his head. Not for the first time in his life, Alex wished he had a better plan, but there wasn't time to think one up.

Alex drew back one gloved fist and planted it as forcefully as he could into Diana's back, right at her kidney. The blow forced Diana to grunt and step forward to maintain her balance. She dropped Lambert to the concrete floor, turning to look at Alex with frustration plain on her face.

"We could talk this out..." she growled.

"Run!" Alex shouted at Lambert, already backing away.

"...if you would just *listen to me!*" Diana finished, showing sharp, fearsome teeth as she rushed forward. Alex caught only a glance of the suddenly feral look in her eye before he turned to flee.

He didn't get far. Three, perhaps four steps at the most separated them for only a heartbeat, and then he felt her catch his arm. Diana flung him against the trunk of a parked car. She shoved him back against it with one hand on his chest before he could fall or dodge away.

"Now then," Diana began again.

Alex caught her square in the cheek with a right hook.

The hand on his chest clutched at his jacket. She heaved him up and slammed him back into the car several times. "Stop hitting me!" Diana demanded.

Jostled and hurt by the brutal treatment, Alex gasped to breathe again. Were it not for his helmet, he'd have been hurt even worse. Diana took a quick, heavy breath as if to calm herself. "I enjoy a little rough play," Diana told him, "but not so soon. Don't make me be like this."

Alex glanced off to his side. Lambert wisely took off—either for escape or for help. Knowing what Diana was capable of, Alex hoped it was the former. He didn't see what good more security guards would do. Regardless, he needed to buy the guy a little more time.

"I'm in a relationship, alright?" he grunted. "A serious, committed, permanent relationship."

"You are under the sway of a demon." Her hand kept him up against the car.

"She's a good demon," he countered, then winced. "Okay, that's not true. That's just stupid. But she's not a threat to me."

"I am no threat to you."

"Could've fooled me!"

Diana tilted her head thoughtfully. "You bring this on yourself."

"You were hurting that guy!"

"No one of consequence," Diana shrugged. "I'm sorry if I frightened you, but you'll learn not to take such things so seriously." Her voice dropped somewhat, becoming almost playful. Flirtatious. Intimate. "We both know you can defend yourself. You are mortal, but far from ordinary. I would not desire you so had I not seen you in action."

"I'd be happy to avoid violence altogether if it's all the same to you."

"It is not. You feel lost. Weak. Vulnerable, despite your victories. I can smell your fear." Her face drew in closer to his. "I would make you stronger, Alex. Faster. Deadlier. Powerful, like the wild. Like me. *With* me."

Alex tentatively reached out to take her shoulders. She allowed his touch, smiling. Then he slammed his helmeted forehead down on her nose with a crunch. Blood burst from her nostrils as cartilage fractured under the blow. The raised plastic visor of his helmet cracked and shattered as he swung his own head like a flail against her skull.

With a half-feminine, half-animal roar, Diana lifted him off his feet and hurled him away. Alex landed several parking spaces away on the concrete, tumbling as best he could but mostly just getting hurt. He didn't stop to assess the damage he'd done. He just scrambled to his feet and ran for the stairway exit.

The door opened inward; Alex pushed his way past, then slammed it shut again and stepped beside it rather than rushing down the stairs. His hand reached inside his jacket, hoping to God that Diana had more reason to stop Lambert from pulling his pepper spray than a concern for what it would do to her perfume.

He couldn't take her in a fight. She was plainly going easy on him despite her anger. He couldn't hope to outrun her, either. It was either this or hope to survive until Rachel popped in on him again, and that might not be for hours.

Only a second passed before the door flew open again. Alex caught it and slammed it shut as hard as he could once again, catching Diana with it before she crossed through. He stayed low, avoiding the arm that flung out sideways to retaliate, and let loose his pepper spray in a wide, panicked burst. Much of it hit the wall behind her, but more than enough wound up in her bloodied face to do the job.

The overwhelming fumes from his weapon had an effect on him, too. He choked despite trying to hold his breath and barely kept his eyes open. Diana swung around blindly, but didn't fall.

Alex placed one leg between hers, caught her wrist and twisted. His free hand came up against her shoulder and pushed with all his strength. Disoriented, off-balance and without leverage, Diana went straight over the handrail and tumbled head-first over the stairway railing.

Tears welling up in his eyes, Alex threw himself back through the doorway. He blinked as quickly as he could to clear his vision as he got to his bike, his hands fighting to draw the keys from his pocket. He'd had dreams like this as a child: someone chasing him, escape nearby, just a matter of getting his keys, only to find it impossible to get them out of his pocket, or impossible to insert in the ignition or the door or whatever symbolized escape, and then the killer or the monster or whatever would get him. Déjà vu did nothing to calm his nerves.

The bike roared to life, never sounding so beautiful or reassuring as now. He backed out without even looking in the mirror, realizing his mistake only after luck allowed him to get away with it. Alex kicked it into first gear, twisted the accelerator and swung around to head down the wrong way out of the parking garage.

She'll hear this, he realized. *She might already be up again. Might be waiting for me. Might jump me again before I get out of here.*

He cursed his luck, knowing he had no other option. It wasn't like he could hop onto a bus or call the cops. Alex swung down around another level, accepting the honking horn of an SUV and another from a Prius and wishing they'd just shut the hell up so he could get away.

On level two, he spotted the wolf. Its brown fur matched Diana's hair, and the blood trailing from its nose and the anger in its eyes surely fit. Alex couldn't help but notice how big it was—and how angry. The thing waited beside a car in a crouch, ready to leap out at him. Alex tilted his handlebars toward it, only for a split second, and flashed his high-beam while honking his horn.

The wolf turned its head, wincing and blinking, and then Alex was past. He swept on through to the first level, and then he was out onto wet, open streets.

He spared a glance in his mirror and saw the wolf lope out of the garage to watch him go. Then he had to turn his attention to traffic around him.

The straight shot to home took him to I-5, and then to downtown. At this hour, it would take him only fifteen minutes at the most.

Instead, Alex rode to the 520 bridge across Lake Washington, rode all the way to Bellevue, and then back again toward Seattle across the other bridge on I-90 before he went home, hoping all the while for a rain shower to eliminate his scent and wondering if it would matter.

THOUGH THEY HAD no rent to pay, Alex contributed as a matter of principle. He covered utilities and association dues. Those alone amounted to his fair share in terms of his financial means... which, on their own, would never have taken him anywhere near ownership of a luxury condominium in downtown.

The absurdity of it all sank in as he sat at the black marble-top bar of their spacious kitchen, staring at the depressingly short section of job ads in the newspaper. He had bigger concerns, of course, but at least unemployment was a mundane problem. He didn't need supernatural help to find a job.

Alex hadn't been out of work since he was sixteen. It was all part-time stuff, and living under his mother's roof meant that he hadn't exactly faced homelessness or bankruptcy, but the mitigating details didn't make much difference. He couldn't hope to land a job that would bring him to Lorelei's financial level, and that didn't bother him... but the thought of having no job at all rankled him deeply.

The front door opened and closed. Alex heard heels click along the tile at the foyer, but didn't look up from the newspaper. He figured he could get to the end of the page before conversation distracted him. It seemed crazy to him that the want ads section was so short in a city this big.

"Hey, are you home early from work?" asked a familiar voice—and not one he expected to hear. Alex winced. No matter what his body had to say about it, he was not up for what would inevitably come of this.

"Hi, Cindy," Alex replied, still not quite tearing his eyes away. His mind sought out both answers to some of the acronyms and abbreviations on the page and for a way to dial things back with the part-time maid. From the state of the apartment, he figured she'd already come and gone.

"Is Lorelei home, too?" she asked as she came up close behind him.

"Not yet," he answered. "Probably still out doing her fundraising thing." Alex turned on his barstool and found exactly the sort of naughty grin on Cindy's pretty face he expected. Mischievous eyes looked out at his from under red locks. Her top showed off a little more cleavage than the last one she wore, but his eyes came back to those lips once again.

He felt her hands slip up to his thighs, but she seemed to catch on to his mood even as she touched him. "Are you okay?" she asked, putting aside her obvious plans for the briefest of moments.

Alex gently put his hands over hers to stop them from roaming. "I'm fine," he said. Desires rose in him, reminding him of how much fun they'd had the last time she came by while Lorelei was out. More than half of him wanted to go for a repeat, but not with so much on his mind. He shut his eyes to block out the distraction of those appealing lips long enough to get a sentence out. "Listen, Cindy, you're awesome, but I don't know if we should keep going with—"

"Alex. Look at me."

His eyes opened. Lorelei stared back at him intently. Startled, Alex jerked upright in his seat. Her hands stayed on his legs. "What—holy shit, Lorelei!"

"Forgive me, love," she said calmly. "I did not expect to see such stress in your eyes, or there would have been no subterfuge."

"Subt—is that what you call this?" he blinked.

"Are you angry?" she asked.

"I'm... no." Alex looked at her in exasperation. "Cindy's" racy top was long gone, replaced by Lorelei's stylish blue dress. Cindy was more than pretty enough to catch Alex's attention, but she wasn't as stunning as Lorelei. Few women were.

His mind caught up to the implications quickly. "I'm not mad, but what is this? Have you been Cindy all along?"

"You never exactly saw us together, did you?" she shrugged with the mildest hint of guilt, or at least admission. "I thought it harmless. It seemed a safe bet that you would laugh once the truth came out. We've both had our fun."

"Wow," he huffed, shaking his head. "You plan to do this to me often? Pretend to be other women to seduce me?"

"*You* seduced 'Cindy,' love, not the other way around," Lorelei reminded him with a soft smile, "much to my delight. You've held back on other opportunities these last few weeks. I enjoyed creating at least one exception. And I'll only continue such games if you continue to enjoy them. But maintaining the façade seemed trite compared to the cares on your face," she finished, touching his cheek with her fingertips. "What troubles you? What happened?"

Shifting topics required a little effort, but Alex pushed the issue of "Cindy" out of his mind. "I got jumped by a werewolf today while leaving work. After I got fired."

Lorelei's expression turned grave. She led him from the bar stool over to the living room couch. "Was it the same woman from our abduction?"

"Yeah," Alex sighed. "Diana. She showed up in the parking lot and said she'd been looking for me, that we're meant to be together. Building security had a dude there to give me the boot, and I wound up having to protect him from her. Between her attacking the guard and us smashing up a couple cars, I'll be lucky if I don't hear from the cops."

"Was she alone?"

"Far as I know. I just bought time for the guard to bail and then I took off."

"Did you come directly home?"

"No. She said she doesn't know where I live. I rode across the lake and back."

"Good," Lorelei nodded. "Why didn't you call me right away?"

"Pain in the ass finding a pay phone in this town to begin with, but I didn't know the number at the conservatory, anyway. I went by, but the lady at the desk said your meeting had broken up for drinks or something."

"You could have called my cell."

"Your which?"

"My cell phone?"

"What's a—?" Alex blinked. Then he remembered. *Oh God*, he thought. *How can I be* remembering *what a cell phone is? It's right in my jacket pocket.* He looked over to the countertop and the newspaper want ads. *Why didn't I just go online to look for jobs?*

Lorelei caught it, too. Her expression changed. Alex saw her concern. "What's wrong with me?" he asked.

Her hand came to his cheek again. "I have my suspicions. *Put it aside, love*," she said, allaying his rush of concern with a measure of supernatural suggestion. "Focus on the matter at hand for now."

Alex shook his head. "She said she went looking for me at my old address, Lorelei. Mom's in New York right now, but what if Diana finds her new place?"

"Do not worry about others," Lorelei said with a shake of her head. "She is fixated on you. Proxies would only be in danger once she has you in her control. The werewolves are quite dangerous. Only a fool would face one alone. Flight was the wisest course of action." She tilted her head thoughtfully. "Is she attractive?"

"She's pretty, yeah," he shrugged.

"Alex, as encouraging as I am of whatever trysts you might wish, this one—"

"Hey, no. She's pretty, but I'm not attracted to her. I do not want to go there. The whole thing freaked me out."

"Ah. I felt whatever moment of sensuality and pleasure you had earlier. It did not seem familiar to me. I thought it might be her."

"No," Alex sighed. "That was Olivia trying to play sexual harassment training video with me. I didn't play along, so she fired me on the spot. She fired Stephanie while I was at lunch, too, because Susan didn't like us flirting. Someone *else* who couldn't keep her hands off me," he added sourly.

His words elicited only the tiniest flinch. He saw it in her eyes and in the tension in her jaw. Beyond that, everything about her remained placid. Were they not so close, he doubted he would've noticed. "You blame me for this," she said.

"No," he shook his head. "No, I don't."

"You believe you are more attractive to other women because of me, and that is in fact somewhat true. You still don't accept how little of that is due to mystical influence rather than natural confidence and experience. You worry that women are under some sinister spell, when they are free to—"

"Lorelei, stop," he interrupted. Then he took a breath. "I'm sorry. I didn't mean to snap. I don't blame you for Olivia."

"And the others?" she asked. "I know your desires, Alex. I know how you feel about all of these women, and others. You know your freedom, and yet you do not follow your urges. Is that not because you fear there is some clouding of consent?"

"No. I mean I did, but I kind of understand now. It's more that..." His voice trailed off

"More that what?"

Alex mustered his courage. He had to address this, for both their sakes. "Lorelei, do you want other men?"

Her answer was calm, quiet and straightforward: "Yes."

He felt it hit inside. Thankfully, she continued.

"You asked a direct question, and you deserve a direct answer. Alex, no one will ever replace you. You have not failed or fallen short in any way. I could never enjoy anything that brought you harm. I will not tire of you. Quite the contrary—you and I will never have enough of one another, regardless of the sorcery and the curses that bind us.

"When I was made into a succubus, I became a creature of desire, of lust and hedonism. You and Rachel satisfy me, you excite me... but it would be a lie to claim that I would not enjoy others."

"Is this because—" Alex started to ask, and then stopped. "No. Not because. Is this *why* you wanted me to be with other women?"

"Partially," confessed Lorelei. "I receive both pleasure and power when you give in to your desires. Our direct intimacy and that which you share with Rachel is always the most fulfilling. Your other dalliances do not bring the same ecstasy, but they are still wonderful.

"Yet I also hoped that your freedom would help you eventually understand my point of view and my urges, and the security we have together." Her voice fell a notch. "I did not expect to have this conversation with you so soon. Not for years. But I knew it would come. I knew this double standard would trouble you long before I began to chafe."

"Yeah, I guess I kind of knew, too. That's why I haven't been fooling around. It just didn't seem right when you couldn't."

Slight amusement brightened her face. "We haven't exactly had a complete restriction. I've had my fun."

"Oh, I'm sure," Alex rolled his eyes, "but I imagine only being able to get with other women isn't the same."

"You should not underestimate how much pleasure I take from women."

"Still," he shook his head. "The more I think about it, the more the only reason I was okay with other women but not other men was just... ego."

"You're allowed to have an ego, Alex," Lorelei smiled.

"Yeah, but I'm saying... you and Rachel are serious. You're in love. It's not a Penthouse fantasy. So if I'm okay with that, why should the gender matter?"

"Every relationship must find its balances. Again, I don't want you to force yourself on this. I am not burdened. You'll note I've never brought the subject up."

"Okay, but... what *do* you want?"

Lorelei shrugged. "I cannot imagine wanting to be with another man when I could have you, but the two of us are not together at all times—nor should we be. I would enjoy the freedom to play when we are apart, should interest arise... and it inevitably will. Context also plays a role; often my desires are born more from a situation than by attraction to a given individual. Sooner or later, I will want to play through on such circumstances."

"One night stands can turn into something bigger," he observed soberly.

"They can," nodded Lorelei, "and we must both recognize that. But Alex—can you imagine falling for anyone the way you have for Rachel and I?"

"Seems a little far-fetched, given who we're talking about there," he frowned.

"Do you think that I am any less in awe of you and her?" Alex looked up to her eyes. "You have been with several women since we came together. None of them changed anything for you and I. Do you think that my love is not as deep?"

Alex let out a long sigh. He stared at the coffee table. "I know what I'm gonna say," he grumbled. "It's just a big step. I'm not the type of guy who fantasizes about his girlfriend screwing someone else."

"I know all of your desires," Lorelei nodded. "You aren't that type. Alex, I would never disrespect you or our love, or tolerate such from anyone else. If I have ever held anything sacred, it is what you, Rachel and I share. Now more than ever," she added quietly.

It only reminded him how much she amazed him. "I just... I don't know if I won't get jealous, you know?"

"You may," she conceded. "It happens. My love and respect for you and Rachel is paramount. We will work through anything else."

"You could fall in love."

Lorelei nodded slowly. "It seems unlikely...though you and I seemed unlikely at first, too, yet here we are. Again, all our bonds aside... I know that I will never love or desire another as much as you and Rachel. Only time can prove that."

"Just like every other relationship in the world, huh?" Alex asked.

"I suspect you find that far more comforting than any mystic binding."

"Yeah, I would," he nodded soberly. "Okay. We'll need to work out some details, but..."

"But what about you?" Her voice dropped to an intimate hush. She crept forward, guiding his shoulders back onto the couch. "Will you allow yourself to indulge in the opportunities that come your way?" She slid one leg between his as she crawled over him. "You turned down satisfaction today. For all your troubles, you still carry that arousal."

A single, deft hand loosened and slid off his belt. She unbuttoned and unzipped his pants, relieving him of the tension of fabric against hardening need.

"I share your desires, my love. I have carried this arousal, too... with no danger or great concern to distract me."

"No distractions?" he asked with a grin. "How'd the conservatory board meeting go?"

"Fine," she shrugged dismissively. "There will be high-end fundraisers soon. I will charm considerable money out of wealthy people for the sake of the arts. Except for a few stodgy old men, the board is quite taken with me, as you expected. It's hardly the sort of thing on my mind right now."

"I'm interested in your life, Lorelei," Alex said, though his tones grew heavy with arousal along with hers.

"I am interested in your pleasures, Alex," she countered. "You must learn to accept them as they come, both from me and from others." Her hair fell around his head, creating a familiar curtain of intimacy that she knew he loved. "I want this for you. I love you. I would *drown* you in a sea of lust if I had my way," she told him softly. "Over and over, until the world ended."

Her mouth came down on his, pushing his head back against the cushion as she kissed him deeply. Alex slid his hands up her legs and then along her back. He untied the knot of fabric holding her dress up behind her neck.

Lorelei knew Alex loved a good show. She leaned back briefly, allowing her dress to cascade from her shoulders to reveal her breasts. She smiled with approval as he slid the fabric up from her hips and aided him in bringing it the rest of the way over her head to toss it aside on the coffee table. Then she moved in again, resuming their deep, hungry kiss.

His pants were gone literally before he knew it. She unbuttoned his shirt without him even noticing. He loved that trick.

She slid against him, leaving him trembling with pleasure at the sensations of her skin on his. One hand remained around his neck. The other traced down his chest once more, down his stomach, fingers curling around his erection and slowly stroking him.

"I live for this," he confessed.

"You do. Your lust defines you as much as your conscience. We merely have to find a way to balance them."

He let out a soft moan as her hand brought him between her legs, teasing him with her moist, welcoming flesh. Their eyes fluttered open together, staring back at one another for this moment as they so often did. His hands on her hips urged her down onto him, and as she took him inside her they shared a heavy breath.

Lorelei smiled broadly, grinding her hips against his to revel in the intimacy that would consume their whole night together. Establishing her control, Lorelei set a slow, savoring pace. His hands slid up her sides to cup her breasts. Before they met their goal, Lorelei squeezed him within her and ground against his groin, leaving his eyes rolling back as he gasped.

When his eyes opened again, he found his succubus staring back with a haughty grin. Her smooth, perfect skin turned red. Her horns and wings were now on full display. He felt her tail slash against his legs. It left him feeling all the more naked, and all the more intimate.

"Shall we bargain, mortal?" the demon asked, proud and wicked and loving. "Do you trust me?"

She never let up on him, claiming him within her mercilessly. It made it difficult to talk, as she knew very well. He remembered the first time she asked him this. "With my life," he exhaled.

"You offer me great freedom," she said, her slow grind driving him wild. She took his wrists in her hands and pinned them over his head. "Surely there is some price."

She wasn't bargaining. She knew there were no conditions. This was just another game. Immobilized and loving it, Alex watched his demon lover as she rode him and grinned. "I could stand to see more of this look," he suggested.

"So little a thing?" Lorelei taunted. Her voice sounded out notes of ecstasy, but her composure didn't waver. "Merely that in exchange for such a gift?"

Her tail snaked between his legs and along his thighs again. She waited patiently for an answer, enjoying the slow ride as much as Alex. If he gave in so far as to forget her question, so much for the better.

"I will grant you any pleasure you wish," she offered, "all night long, for ten nights or more. Wear anything you like... or any face. Indulge in any game."

His mind swam. She'd do any of that anyway, and they both knew it. Lorelei consumed his nights, his weekends, and so much time in between. What more could he want?

He finally answered with a shaking breath: "Use your imagination."

The beauty above him was almost frightening. She had him close to release, and was near to it herself. It would be the first of many. He looked forward to more, but now she held him there. Tortured him with it.

Loved him.

"That may come to more than you expect," she warned.

"Deal," he said.

Whether it was her triumph or the pleasures of his release that soon set her off, Alex couldn't tell, but Lorelei's climax was as beautiful as anything he'd ever experienced.

DESPITE THE RACKET of his own horse, Skorri heard the one behind him collapse with a shriek. Both of its riders cried out. Skorri looked back over his shoulder, but naturally saw little more than darkness and trees.

"Gunnar," Skorri said to the man sharing his horse, whose belt he gripped with one hand, "Unferth and Bjorn are down."

"Don't do it, boy," warned Gunnar. "They're bastards anyway!"

You can't just leave them behind, said a voice in Skorri's head.

Skorri looked back again. He couldn't see their two fellow raiders—nor the scores of angry Danes closing in pursuit. In the opposite direction lay the sea, and escape, and survival.

It isn't right, said the voice. You'll never forgive yourself.

Skorri grunted. That voice had told him to go on this stupid raid in the first place. It had not gone well. The Danes had started this feud. Skorri and the others came to end it, but slaying a rival chief was one thing. Getting away from his angry allies was another.

He should have stayed home with Halla.

The younger warrior lifted up one leg and rolled off the back of the horse. His

34

landing was unpleasant, but he ignored the pain and scrambled to his feet. Gunnar shouted something after him as he continued on.

Skorri was glad Gunnar kept riding. The brothers really were bastards. Abandoning them wasn't right, but neither was risking more than one life for their hides.

Some of the Danes rode with torches to supplement the light of the full moon. Others rode with spears in hand. Two lead riders spotted Unferth as the bearded raider struggled to free himself from his fallen horse. Bjorn lay stunned and disoriented nearby. The one with the spear leveled his weapon at Bjorn and urged his mount into a charge. Unferth cried out to him, but with his leg pinned and his axe out of reach he could do nothing to help his blond brother.

Skorri's sword lay among fallen warriors in a field miles from here, but he had one last axe and a good throwing arm. He hurled his weapon as he ran, striking home to knock the Dane from his saddle. The horse trotted past Bjorn and then Unferth and his ruined mount, plainly uninterested in fighting on anyone's behalf.

Sure enough, the other rider closed in on Skorri, swinging his torch. Searing pain erupted across Skorri's left shoulder, but thankfully not his head. Stepping back and away bought the raider time as the horseman turned his mount around again.

Skorri rolled his left shoulder. It hurt like hell but seemed to work fine, though he often underestimated his injuries when the rage took hold like this. At least he could still think this time.

His eyes darted left and right. Unferth was finally free, limping over to his brother. Bjorn rose to his hands and knees, his long blond hair dangling over his face.

The other Danes hadn't caught on to this struggle yet. They could all still make it out of this mess alive.

The Dane charged in at Skorri once more, intent on running the raider down with his mount this time. Skorri dodged to one side and then grabbed for the rider's leg.

Naturally, the Dane tried to batter Skorri away with his torch. Skorri grabbed at his wrist with both hands and then lifted his feet off the ground, pulling the Dane from his horse in a tumble.

Skorri recovered first. He also had the torch. He leapt upon the Dane, pinning his shoulders to the ground with his knees, and then brought the flaming end of the torch down on the Dane's face with brutal force.

"Crazy bastard," Unferth said as he helped Bjorn to his feet. He wiped blood and spittle from his ragged red beard. "I thought we were both dead."

"We may all still be," Skorri half-growled and half-grinned. "Better that than to tell Halla that I left men behind." He rushed to the riderless horse, grabbing its reins and tugging it over.

"More of them," Bjorn gestured breathlessly into the darkness beyond. "Right on top of us!"

"You're both hurt," Skorri said. "Take the horse and go. Hold a boat for me. I'll be right behind."

Neither Unferth nor Bjorn hesitated. They both mounted up and rode down toward the fishing village beneath the hill without a backward glance.

Skorri found the fallen spear amid long, thick tree roots and then looked toward the approaching torches and the sound of hooves. He needed a horse of his own, and the other raiders needed time.

THEY ONLY MADE it to the village before dawn and ahead of their pursuers because of Skorri. Everything had gone wrong on this raid, culminating in the death of Thialfi and the seizure of his longship. Skorri was not a leader of men—he was too young and wild—but his spirit helped keep the band moving. His ferocity staved off disaster more than once.

He nearly caught up in time. He saw fishing boats rowing out to sea as his horse burst from the tree line at the edge of the village. Most were halfway across the bay already. One last boat lay close to shore. Skorri recognized Unferth's big red beard in the boat and Bjorn's long blond hair.

Skorri rode for his life. Several other horsemen followed close behind, but Skorri had enough of a lead. He could make it.

"Row!" Unferth commanded. His loud voice carried across the water to the shore. "Damn it, row!"

"Unferth!" cried Skorri. "Wait!"

"Row!"

Skorri's horse crashed into the cold water, and he with it. He let the mount go in favor of swimming under his own power, a talent he had nurtured as a child when the water was warm enough.

Skorri had a wife at home. He couldn't winter here with the Danes, not with all of them after every raider's head. He couldn't leave Halla alone to wonder.

He kept swimming. The Danes did not pursue. They had no bows with which to threaten those in the water. Skorri's boots and his clothes dragged him down, but he kept swimming. He only needed a minute's pause to catch up.

Unferth and his men kept rowing.

· · ·

HIS ARMS FLAILED ABOUT in the darkness, mostly upward, reaching for something to hold onto. Panicked huffs and grunts came from his throat. His eyes opened wide. The water clung to him like bedsheets, tangling his arms and his legs.

He felt nothing but desperation and fear.

Strong, feminine arms came around his naked chest. "*Ssshhh, love, you are safe,*" Lorelei told him urgently, whispering close to his ear. "*Relax,*" she commanded, unhurt by the way his elbows and head bumped into her before his thrashing lessened.

"You are Alex Carlisle," Lorelei told him, "You are home, in bed, with me." She kissed the back of his neck, then his shoulder, caressing him to calm him down. "Whatever life you dreamt of is over now, and can hurt you no more."

His eyes darted around. A spacious bedroom replaced the bay. The bed seemed vast in the darkness. It was larger than king sized, bought with a humorous, indulgent smile that promised thorough use. He heard the rain fall against the bedroom windows. His skin was soaked with sweat, but not water.

An angel appeared through the open bedroom door, seeming to illuminate the room merely with her presence. She rounded the bed, sat down beside him opposite Lorelei, and gently kissed him.

Calming under Lorelei's influence already, Alex soon felt his body relax. Fear and desperation melted away with Rachel's touch. She smiled at him, her eyes as full of comfort as Lorelei's arms. "21st Century, lover," she said. "Your life's awesome. Drop the baggage. We're here. Go to sleep."

His eyelids felt heavy. Lorelei eased him back down again. "*Sleep,*" she urged. His breathing quickly grew steady once more.

"Worse tonight, huh?" Rachel asked.

"Yes. He was accosted today. I'll explain later," Lorelei added as Rachel's eyebrow rose, "but the stress seems to have worsened this. His memories confused him even during the day. Were all of his lives so violent?"

Rachel hesitated, biting back her first answer before she spoke. "Yeah," she said. "Yeah, pretty much. They always were at the end, anyway."

"I understand little of such things, but I know that isn't natural."

The angel sighed. "No, it's not. I can't get into it. I'm sorry." She gestured to their younger partner. "This is why mortals aren't supposed to know too much."

"I only listen to him," said Lorelei. "I offer counsel only with great care. But he cannot be left to suffer like this." Rachel looked to Lorelei without speaking.

The succubus nodded in understanding. "So be it. I understand. My hands are not tied like yours. I have at least one prospect in mind." Her head tilted curiously. "How long have you been home?"

"Literally just blew in through the window," Rachel said with a shake of her head and a smile. "Don't think I'd be fucking around out in the living room if I could be in here with you, do you?"

"I should hope not," Lorelei replied mildly. "You don't seem one to waste your opportunities for free time."

"Yeah, well. City's a supernatural shithole," the angel shrugged.

"What romantic imagery." She gave her lover a thoughtful look. "You know you need only ask for my help."

"I figured cleaning up the town wouldn't be your style."

"Perhaps not, but you know where my loyalties lie. You have dreams. I would be a terrible lover if I did not help you realize them."

"I'll keep the offer in mind… but it means a lot to hear you make it."

"Come now, you're an angel. I must lull you with a façade of benevolence and demonstrate my eagerness to amend my evil ways. Only once you've lowered your defenses can I truly defile you."

The angel rolled her eyes, but smiled. "You have no idea how often I hear that exact same thing from… well. Bitches, really. Of every gender."

"I never expected that initial outpouring of support for our relationship would last," said Lorelei.

"Nah. Plenty of that was genuine, but what people applaud in front of all their peers isn't necessarily what they'll support in private or in smaller groups. Angels are people, too," Rachel shrugged. "But you know that, don't you?"

"Yes. I make no apologies for what I am, or how I came to it."

Rachel shook her head. "I don't ever want you to."

"My offer stands. If I can help you, I will."

"I'll keep it in mind. It means a lot that you'd offer," she said. Her eyes drifted toward Lorelei's legs. Her hands followed her gaze, reaching out to explore. Rachel leaned in close, her lips brushing against the side of Lorelei's neck. "That bit about defilement sounded pretty good."

"I am happy to accommodate," Lorelei taunted. She waited for Rachel to shift closer in, slipping her fingers under Rachel's soft white dress only after the angel's kisses and her breath conveyed rising needs. She coaxed Rachel to rise on her knees with gentle, teasing fingers. Rachel shuddered and clung to her, the angel nearly buckling under the pleasuring touch of the demon's tail that snaked between her legs. "How can I resist when you willingly throw your-self at me like a wanton, shameless harlot at every opportunity?"

Rachel let out a tiny whine. Lorelei could be vicious with that tail. "I've got some shame," she protested weakly. "Makes it hotter when I give in to you." She held to Lorelei as the succubus manipulated her, bringing her to a first, small, appetizing orgasm. Lorelei held Rachel in a supporting embrace as her partner rode out the spasms of pleasure.

Rachel's lips split into an eager grin as her tremors faded. She pushed Lorelei onto her back with a playful shove and crawled over her with her eyes shining. The succubus deftly slipped Rachel's white dress from her shoulders and then down her hips. Lorelei's hand slid between her legs, cupping her sex and holding still. The sensation sent Rachel's eyes rolling back into her head. Moans escaped from her throat as Lorelei began to slowly, gently move her hand against Rachel's already wet lips. The angel felt Lorelei's mouth on her pert breast, teasing her with further arousal.

Their mortal partner slumbered peacefully beside them as they made love through the night.

2

WELCOME TO OUR MADHOUSE

D*on't be afraid to take it slow. Learn the lay of the land. Hold off and observe. Get him used to seeing you in his life. Nobody expects miracle results right away. First contact is always tough.*

Warnings, encouragement and advice reverberated in Amber's head as she walked to class. She kept her textbook and notebook close to her chest, head down with her newly auburn hair dangling over one side of her face as she walked toward the lecture hall. She couldn't help but worry that she would be recognized.

Matt Lanier ran a check on literally every class roster from both her high school and the university just to be sure. There were some hits, of course, but none of them came near her class schedule. Nothing set off any warning bells.

Plenty of alarms went off in her head, though, over how quickly Lanier could acquire, sort and analyze all that data. Still more unsettling had been Hauser's advice: "Exploit any opening you can find. The rulebook for this task force isn't very thick. CIA deals with more red tape than we do. Short of committing a felony yourself, you're free to improvise all you want."

Amber tried not to read too much into Hauser's choice of words. She reminded herself they were all on the same side.

Students filed into class without ceremony. With most of her college pre-req classes completed while she was still in high school, Amber hadn't spent much time in UW's big lecture halls. She checked in with one of the TAs to provide her transfer paperwork.

Without fuss or suspicion, Amber joined the roster of Topics in Sociology. She wished, not for the first time, that she could've taken a real science course and not some bullshit class like this, but her target dictated such concerns.

Amber looked out at the audience of students for an open seat and, more importantly, for her suspect. Target. Mark. She couldn't pick an appropriate term for him, since he wasn't suspected of a crime yet. Amber considered not worrying about it too much just yet. Settling into her cover would be enough work for day one. Still, it would be negligent not to at least try to get near the guy and watch him.

She spotted Cohen as he entered with his headphones on and his backpack slung over one shoulder. He wore a Green Lantern t-shirt, a plain unzipped hoodie and jeans. Cohen moved up toward the seats in the back without worry or stress in his stride. He seemed to look out at the crowd, at the students taking their seats, and even at those still milling about near the lectern. Amber watched, finding his gait marginally curious, and soon discerned the cause of it.

He was checking out the girls. His gaze didn't linger long on any one of them, and he took care not to stumble or bump into anyone, but within seconds she found herself drawing imaginary straight lines between his eyes and that girl's cleavage, and then that girl's ass, and that one's legs... She stopped staring when he looked her way, breaking her gaze just late enough to note that he, too, broke eye contact when he realized he'd been busted.

Ordinarily, Amber wouldn't have known whether to be flattered that he'd been looking her over or to roll her eyes. Today she called it a bonus. Her impression from Cohen's profile was that he might be shy and reserved around girls—much as she'd been in high school and college with guys. She figured she'd have to be the one to initiate contact. If he thought she was cute, he'd be more receptive.

Several seats in his row remained open. The spots in the row behind his were taken, which spoiled the chance of looking over his shoulder. Sitting right down next to him would look weird, but taking up a spot a few seats down seemed reasonable. Amber considered all the advice of her much more experienced colleagues, weighed her options, and decided to trust her gut.

She didn't look up at him as she ascended the steps toward his row. Best to look like she was minding her own business. She set down her books on an empty chair beside hers, pulled off her jacket to reveal her Blue Sun t-shirt, and settled in for class.

Amber fished a pen out of her pocket. Thumbed her notebook open to a blank page. Turned off her phone. Realized that Cohen had stood from his seat and stepped a little closer.

"Y'know," he said in a "hey grrrl" tone that he couldn't *possibly* be serious about, "your coat's kind of a brownish color."

She looked up, not at Jason but at the projection screen noting the class's agenda, and restrained herself from grinning quite as broadly as she wanted. "It was on sale," she answered nonchalantly. *Exploit any opening*, she thought. *Geek culture for the win.*

"Mind if I take this spot?" he asked with a far more reasonable voice.

"Sure. Can I look at your notes? I just transferred in."

He sat down beside her. There was, she decided, enough room with the seats and the armrests for this not to be too forward—but only just. "I'm Jason," he said.

"Amber," said Amber as he dug his notebook out of his backpack. She looked at the clock, noted that she had made contact in less than two minutes, and tried not to laugh.

———

"NOTHING worse than an ex who won't leave you alone," Jason nodded sagely. He downed another chip, realized the cheese sauce had dripped onto his chin and possibly onto his shirt, and quickly tried to recover.

Amber watched with mild amusement. "Had that happen to you often?"

"Never," Jason admitted, finding a napkin amid the clutter on their simple table, "but it's happened to friends. I've only ever had girlfriends cut me off cold turkey. Probably better that way."

"Well, I went to the trouble of rearranging my whole class schedule to get away from him, and now I find out he dropped out of school entirely. Feels like half the quarter's shot and I've got nothing to show for it. All the friends I've made out here—'scuse me, *thought* I'd made out here—are part of his social circle. I feel like I don't even know what people do around here for fun."

"That sucks," Jason nodded. Amber glanced up at him, saw his eyes wandering, and considered prompting him with more. Before her mouth opened again, though, she saw the light bulb go off. "If you'd like to come out and play pool sometime, I know a great place."

"I dunno," she mused, not wanting to look too eager too soon, "I mean, I'm just getting out of a relationship. I'm not completely sure where my head's at."

"You don't have to consider it a date," Jason shrugged. "I'm there a lot with my friends. You'd like them. They'd like you. I'm just sayin', you want to go out and be around nice people, I know some. I'm not trying to hit on you." He smiled. "Unless that would work. But I'm guessing it's too soon, right? Too soon? Yeah. That's cool. I'll be all sensitive and zero-pressure and stuff."

She couldn't help but smirk. The obvious self-awareness in his tone and expression made his non-flirtatious flirting amusing, but not particularly effective. "You don't ask girls out a lot, do you?"

"Not really," he admitted with good humor. "Mostly it's just been girls falling in my lap."

"How often has that happened?"

His eyes narrowed thoughtfully, and then he held out his hands as if to offer up two ranges of distance. "What sort of sample period are we talking? Like, just recently, or all the way back to puberty?"

"Whatever works to your advantage," Amber granted.

He narrowed the space between his hands to a couple inches. "Constantly," he declared.

Amber got a good laugh out of that. She couldn't deny that he was funny. He was perhaps more than a little awkward, too, but funny and confident in his own way. Nothing about him seemed criminal, though, or even dangerous. Amber remembered the picture of Jason and his necklace of vampire fangs, and knew how deceiving appearances could be, but she couldn't picture Jason doing anything more violent than playing video games.

"Listen," Jason went on, "I'm not gonna hard sell you on this. You sound like you could use some good company. If you're not interested, no worries, but I'm goin' out tonight anyway and I'd be happy to bring you with. No whining about 'friend zones' or any bullshit like that. I just think we could have a good time together."

That she would accept the invitation was a foregone conclusion, but not for the reasons Jason believed. Yet she had to admit that she liked his pitch. For all his goofiness and self-deprecation, he seemed quite comfortable in his own skin. It was something she envied.

"Okay," she nodded. "I'm interested."

THE GAME between Drew and Wade ground to a halt. They stood on the same side of the pool table, looking at Amber after Jason's introduction without betraying a hint of emotion. They just looked on, not quite staring, leaving Amber feeling a little awkward in the silence.

She said hi already, and wondered now if it was worth repeating. The other customers, their games and the Foo Fighters song on the speakers weren't so loud that one had to shout.

With several hours between lunch and the evening meet-up, Amber had plenty of time to prepare. She worked with the task force to establish back-up calls, got to know the immediate neighborhood around the pool hall and firmed up her cover story. She also had time to review Jason's online presence, which given his youth and enthusiasm was considerable. Drew and Wade appeared many times in his photo album.

They more or less lived up to their online images. Drew was a tall, well-built and good-looking young black man, dressed in stylish slacks and a blue and black striped shirt. The tall white Southerner beside him seemed somehow even more unlikely as a friend of Jason's, his heritage on display through his faded blue jeans and John Deere ball cap.

Amber quickly found herself feeling self-conscious under their stares. She'd given serious thought to making the right impressions. She went with black jeans and a flattering white top, wanting to make sure she looked good without obviously going all-out. Nothing she had said could possibly have been insulting or odd. She glanced at Jason to find an equally perplexed expression on his face.

"Is something wrong?" she ventured.

"Nothin'," Drew answered evenly, giving a slow, brief shake of his head. Wade sighed. Drew held out a hand toward him, not looking away from Amber. Wade fished out a billfold, peeled off a twenty and handed it to him. "Nice to meet you," Drew smiled as he put the bill in his pocket.

"Likewise," she replied slowly.

"The fuck was that?" asked Jason, his brow furrowing and his eyes on Wade as the other man stepped around the pool table to get back to his shot.

"Bad call on mah part," Wade shrugged. His eyes were back on his game, but his tone was perfectly friendly.

"Did you just lose a bet?" Amber pressed, her lips quirking in a grin.

"Yup. So Jason didn't mention you b'fore. How'd y'all meet?"

"We just met today," Jason answered, a mild touch of irritation evident in his voice. "Amber's still new in town and I thought it'd be nice to bring her out to meet some cool people. You guys happen to know any, maybe?"

"Ah might've met a couple before," grinned Wade. He sank his shot and rounded the table to line up for his next.

"Where you from, Amber?" Drew asked. He moved over to one of the tall chairs by their small table for drinks, pulling his jacket off to make room for her. His tone and smile became considerably warmer.

"I'm from Oly," Amber said, taking him up on his invitation to sit at the table. "And yes, we met in class today. You two go to UW?"

"I don't start 'til next quarter," said Drew. "Just been workin' since I got out of high school."

"Ah'm at North Seattle Community," Wade answered. "Ain't yet decided when ah'm gonna transfer."

Amber already felt much more welcome. "Where do you work, Drew?"

The Bureau taught her to be observant. She noticed the quick, questioning glance Drew threw at Jason before he answered, though not Jason's wordless response, whatever it had been. "Here, lately," Drew said. "Mostly day stuff, helping with inventory and the records. I'm kind of on hold for actual service work 'til I turn twenty-one next week. Alcohol laws and all that, y'know?"

"Oh, that's awesome," Amber smiled. "Big birthday plans in the works?"

"Think I've got one person or another takin' me out to dinner every night that week, but we usually save the birthday party for Halloween. We've got another friend who was actually born on the day, so it should be a big thing. Got a big costume ball in the city we're all going to this year."

"Is Sherri coming?" Jason asked. "Are you two official now?"

"Officially over," Drew shook his head.

"Aw, what happened?"

"I guess I was too much of a distraction from her school work. That's what she said, anyway."

"Callin' it," announced Wade, who had been on a roll while no one else was looking. "Side pocket." One stroke of his cue stick later, Wade smiled up at Drew with a triumphant look, then glanced to the others. "Who's next?"

Amber looked to Jason and shrugged. "Anyone else likely to show up soon? Should we wait?"

"Nah, they can wait us out," Jason decided. "Two on two?"

"All good," said Drew as he racked up the balls. "Amber, you wanna break?"

"I can do that," she accepted. Amber picked a cue stick off the rack on the wall, then moved around to the end of the table. She waited for Drew to clear out. Set up the cue ball. Lined up her shot. Glanced up, once, at movement on the other side of the table. Spiked the ball in shock as her brain registered what she saw.

The dark-haired stunner on the other side of the table caught the flying cue ball without the slightest break in her composure. Amber's mind nearly went blank as she just stared. The newcomer smiled gently, rolling the cue ball back across the table to its starting point.

"Hello," the woman said. She glanced to the young men around the table. "Gentlemen. Who's this?"

"Lorelei, this is Amber," Jason spoke up. "She's a classmate of mine."

Amber blinked. She couldn't believe that Jason or the others could speak so comfortably with her. Why weren't they just as awed? Hell, they were guys, and young ones, too—why weren't they *more* awed?

The woman rounded the table to offer her hand. She looked noticeably older than the rest of them, perhaps around thirty, though with unfairly perfect skin and a figure that women would kill for. Amber slowly took the woman's hand, shook it, and mumbled out a greeting. She couldn't tell if Lorelei didn't realize how taken aback she was or if the older woman was simply too gracious to draw any attention to it. Amber suspected the latter.

As she shook it off, Lorelei asked, "You said you're here with Jason?"

"Yeah-huh," Amber nodded.

Lorelei's cool smile remained. She slipped over to stand next to Drew. He didn't look her way, but he waited with his hand out and a smug smile as she fished a twenty from her purse.

"YOU DON'T NEED to play your cards so close to the chest, you know," Lorelei told her as they got to the bar. "They're trustworthy. They like you already."

Not for the first time that evening, Amber found herself taken aback. A dozen replies came to mind, none of them honest. She chose the most non-committal: "What do you mean?"

Lorelei favored her with a quiet, sly grin. "You ask much more than you tell," she observed. "I can't blame you. They're an interesting crowd. Yet I can't help but think you hide things about yourself. You need not."

"Am I that obvious?"

"No," Lorelei replied. "Not obvious at all. You're good." Her tone was so cool and knowing that it made Amber nervous. "They are all sharp young men—I would not spend my time with them otherwise—but they haven't caught on just yet. I'm a little more practiced at reading people. You needn't be so guarded, Amber. You might be surprised at how accepting they are."

"I bet everyone's accepting of you," Amber huffed. It hadn't taken long for her to get over her initial shock, but she'd spent the last hour trying to piece together why a woman like Lorelei hung out with these guys. That her boyfriend was part of the circle of friends was perfectly clear; that she had great affection for all of them was also obvious. Yet even so, the casual socializing just didn't seem to add up. Who the hell was this woman, and just how much did she suspect?

"That's a loaded topic. Ahmed, hello," Lorelei said to the older man behind the bar. "Gin and tonic for me, and for my friend...?" She looked to Amber.

"Guinness," answered the younger woman. She paused to choose her words as Ahmed moved off to fill the order. "I dunno. After everything that happened with my last boyfriend and all that, I guess I'm a little gun-shy."

"I don't think that's it, no," Lorelei mused, thoughtfully looking her over. "You haven't decided whether you're attracted to Jason or not, but you find him intriguing and you enjoy his company. You suspect there's much more under the surface, and you're right about that."

"I am?"

"He's not suave, I'll grant, but he's honest with himself about who he is. He's a strong soul. Witty. Resourceful. Exceedingly brave and loyal." Lorelei leaned back on the bar, looking to the group of young men. "You'll have to earn the stories," she added with a smile. "He's also quite intelligent. He knows that bringing you out to meet his friends runs the risk that you'll find one of them more attractive."

Amber nodded. She wasn't naïve. "Then why did he invite me out here for tonight if he knew that?"

"I imagine he felt that alleviating your loneliness was more important than getting laid." Her eyes turned to Amber's again. "You worry that they will discover something about you that will drive them away from you. Something scandalous? No," she seemed to think aloud, analyzing Amber as they stood waiting for their drinks. "Deceptive. Unforgiveable."

"Well, when you say it like that, I might get worried," Amber chuckled.

"You might be shocked at what those young men can forgive."

"You sure about that?"

Lorelei nodded. "I've had personal experience."

"What did they have to forgive you for?"

"All that I am," Lorelei murmured, accepting the drink from Ahmed with a smile. Her first response wasn't meant to be heard, but Amber caught it. The second came out clearer: "We didn't meet under ideal circumstances."

"But you're seeing one of Jason's friends, right? That's how you met them?" asked Amber. "How did that come about? I mean, I haven't met him yet, but you seem like the kind of woman who could grab any man she wants."

"That is more of a story than I think we'd care for tonight, but if you want the simple answer? I can talk to him as I had never been able to speak to any other. Alex has wit and courage. I liked the look of him. He overcame every obstacle that life offered. There are of course a dozen qualities of relevance. But if you ask what first made me give him a chance, and what keeps us together from day to day? He listens to me, as he did from the start. He accepts me for what I am, and has never asked me to change."

Amber chewed on that, glancing back at the guys again. "That's what makes him stand out? I mean judging by his friends, you probably don't come from the same social circles."

"Not remotely."

"You don't think another man might have all those qualities?"

"Surely there are others," nodded Lorelei. "They missed their chance."

"Hey, Lori, back again," came a male voice. The two looked up to find a tall, muscular man looming behind them, his smile not quite as broad as his chest. He had to be proud of both. His teeth were laser white. His shirt spread unbuttoned at the top, showing off both his gold chain and the dark chest hair threatening to explode from his pecs. She caught an accent that she could not immediately place as the handsome stranger said in a great voice, "I've missed you so much. Why do you never come around anymore?"

"I was here only last week, Emir," Lorelei answered. "You don't remember?"

"Ah, every night without you is like an eternity," he said, so smoothly Amber guessed he must have practiced it. The next line was dismissive rather than grandiose: "Besides, you were with that boy you keep hanging around with."

"We are rather fond of sharing our time together," Lorelei smiled patiently.

"Sure, but you could maybe share a drink with me, eh? Maybe let me take you out some time? He's not here now. How serious could you and your boy be?"

"Quite serious. I don't think I'll take you up on your offer, Emir."

"What's the matter?" he scowled, though trying to maintain a cheerful tone, "you afraid you'll like it? Or maybe you're afraid he won't?"

"Emir, I'm not interested, and that alone should settle the matter. But since you asked," Lorelei smiled sweetly, and then stepped closer, putting one hand on Emir's chest, right over his heart.

Amber leaned in to hear what Lorelei said, but it all came out in a different language. *Is that Arabic?* Amber wondered. *Turkish?* Regardless, her words took the wind from Emir's sails. His eyes went wide with disbelief and even fear.

He stepped aside. Lorelei walked past. Amber followed. They weaved through the aisles of pool tables. As before, Amber knew that most every man watched Lorelei pass. "What did you say to him?"

"Emir obviously grew up believing that women don't know their own minds," Lorelei shrugged. "Were I interested in investing the time, I'd correct his error. I find him annoying, though, so I put things in terms he'd understand."

"What was that?"

"I told him that the last time a man wouldn't leave me alone, my love followed him into his home and stabbed him in the heart. Right in front of all of his friends."

Amber almost tripped. "Is that... wait, really? He believed that?"

Lorelei grinned over her shoulder. "Why shouldn't he? Don't you?"

NOT FOR THE FIRST TIME, Alex regretted putting his photography class ahead of his social life.

"In contrast to modern American policies, photographs of the dead were not forbidden or banned by the Allies during the Great War," droned the lecturer. Above and behind him, black and white photographs of hospital scenes and lifeless soldiers laid out in rows flashed past.

"Plenty of examples can be found in the archives, from the war's beginning in 1914 right through 'til its end." The lecturer clicked through more black and white tragedy. Alex cringed.

His photography professor pitched this as a study of the growth of camera technology, and a way for students to earn some extra credit. The various sign-in sheets in the lobby and the bodies packing the auditorium suggested that plenty of classes from other schools had similar interests. Alex had all his assignments in, but his attendance had grown spotty as of late. He needed the points.

He didn't need the First World War. Somehow, nobody thought to note that little detail in the lecture title. His professor conveniently glossed over that.

"Naturally, photographs of the action as it happened on the front lines were difficult to arrange," said the lecturer. "Equipment was clumsy and not particularly quick to operate like cameras today. Naturally, you don't see many views of the battlefields at night. Flash photography could cause all sorts of potential problems among armed, jumpy men," he added with a chuckle.

"Laugh it up, ye fookin' cunt," Alex heard someone mutter bitterly. He blinked, turned his head this way and that—and found the people on either side staring at him.

The girl to his left leaned in across the empty seat between them. "Hey," she smiled, "are you Irish?"

Alex looked back to the screen. He saw more devastation, of course. This had all started out with photos of parades and men in dress uniforms—just like the war itself, he remembered, though the photos lacked the full color of memory.

Chelsea fawned over how he looked in his uniform before he shipped out. She said all he needed were some medals.

Alex rubbed his eyes. Who the hell was Chelsea? An image flitted through his mind, but it was of a photograph, not the memory of a face. He saw Chelsea's wedding picture by the light of an overhead flare, lying in some mud. He smelled dead flesh.

The lecturer droned on. Alex raised his head to try to follow. Disjointed as his thoughts were, he couldn't tell what might be real and what might be imagined.

Then he recognized the shattered hillside, the broken and dead remnants of a forest, and the ruined walls of a house that inexplicably stood while everything else had been blasted away by artillery.

51

Soft light swept into the auditorium as a door opened in the back. He cringed out of reflex, almost ducking behind the seat in front of him. Then the door fell shut with a loud slam, and reflex took over. He squatted down in front of his seat and threw his hands over his head.

"Woah," said the girl to his left.

"Hey, what the hell?" hissed the guy on his right.

Alex looked up. No one else ducked. There were just people sitting around his trench without helmets or guns, all looking at him like he was mad.

No. Not a trench. An auditorium, at the UW.

Oh shit, Alex finally realized. He looked to the screen to see a landscape of mud and craters filled with water. He felt himself drowning.

He had to go. This had been a mistake. Just like signing up with the BEF. Just like transferring to the infantry after Hooge chateau. Just like the whole stupid war.

Alex stumbled through the crowd—rudely, but if the fools didn't know by now to keep their heads down, it was their own stupid fault. Served them right if a sniper took them out. Several protested, a couple even shoved back at him, but he had to get out.

His body shook with fear. He had to get out.

"Stay here, ye daft bastard!"

"Sergeant, it's a mess out there," Alex grunted.

"Man, get the fuck off me!"

"Help me! Someone help me!"

"Ow! Watch it, asshole!"

"My leg... I need help..."

"I can't move. Don't leave me here!"

"Don't even think about it, Shanahan!"

Alex broke free into the aisle, stumbling to his hands and knees in the darkness. Everything was wet from the rain, but at least he could move. He hustled to his feet and ran.

Sergeant Tinney called after him, telling him to get back under cover, but he'd never liked Tinney, anyway. He stayed low as he rushed out of the auditorium. He didn't ask where the door came from. He just pushed his way through it.

Neither the bright lights nor open, welcoming space of the lobby registered in his mind. He saw only darkness and mud, felt only the rain on his skin and the weary ache of his muscles, and heard the silence shattered by an artillery shell as the door behind him slammed shut again.

He flung himself to the ground and covered up. It was just a single shell. He waited, heard nothing more, and rose into a crouching position to continue toward the voices.

Everything was mud and darkness and more mud. There was precious little light to see by, as the flares never stayed in the air long. Back in '14, all this artillery would have left more than a few things burning. Three years later, there was nothing left to burn.

Aidan crept and crawled along, heading out to the closest cry for help. At the bottom of a watery crater he found a fellow trooper lying in the mud. The man must've been wounded, though in this light Aidan couldn't see how. The water was already up to his shoulders. It seemed all the man could do to sit mostly upright. "Can you move?" hissed Aidan.

"I've one leg shot, but the other's fine... just stuck in the mud to the knee," the man said. "Trapped." His words came out haltingly as he fought through pain. "I can move if I get unstuck."

A flare went into the sky, offering Aidan a clearer look at the crater. He thought better of rolling in. A man could easily sink both legs into that sort of bog. Jumping straight in would only leave two men trapped in the mud. "Half a moment," Aidan warned, and crept away looking for wiser of options.

Soon, he found a couple planks of wood amid the remains of a wagon. Aidan crawled back over with them, wishing there was more in the way of cover or shadow out here as he waited out the flickering light of another flare.

The fellow in the crater stared down at something white and grey in his hands. "Hey, I'm back," Aidan hissed. "Hey! Chum!" Aidan wondered how rattled the man was. He seemed absorbed with his little photograph. "Look here! I'm going to get you out!"

The man looked up. Aidan saw another flare go overhead, cursed at their frequency, and hugged the ground. That was when he recognized his company commander. "Captain Westerbrook?"

The captain just shrugged and looked down at his photo. "Captain," Aidan whispered urgently, "snap out of it, sir! I've got these boards. Put them by your leg so I'll have something to stand on. We'll dig you out."

No response. Aidan fumed, then tossed the boards down into the crater and slipped inside after them. Several times the mud threatened to envelop his foot or his hand, but Aidan trudged through it.

"Captain?" he asked.

"Shouldn't have come," the other man mumbled.

"Aye, you and me both, sir," Aidan agreed, his cheerful Irish accent contrasting with the captain's morose tones.

"I was married before I left," Westerbrook continued. "Should've stayed."

"That her?" Aidan asked, not bothering to look as he fished out the boards and set them around Westerbrook's trapped leg.

The captain sniffed. He nodded, though Aidan didn't see. "Chelsea."

"Huh. That's funny. I've a girl named Chelsea, too," Aidan grinned, probing for the captain's leg with his shovel. "Londoner like yourself, actually. Met before the war. Alright, sir, I'm gonna give this a shove and try to get your foot some slack, y'see?" He heard the hiss of a flare above them.

"Got to stay quiet, sir," Aidan warned, glancing up at the flare as it soared overhead, then down at the captain, and the captain's wedding picture.

It was dark and wet. Shadows and light danced across the photograph as the flare carried on into the night, but Aidan would have known that smile anywhere.

"Son of a bitch," Aidan murmured. He stared down into the blackness that followed when the light disappeared from the crater. The captain sniffled.

You can't leave him here, said a voice in his head. He's too important. More important than you.

Aidan fumed and fought with himself, but he didn't lash out. He didn't strike the other man in the head with his shovel, or unsling his rifle and shoot him, or accuse him of stealing Aidan's girl while he was off to war and Westerbrook was still in school. He thought about doing all those things, of course, but the voice in his head was half right. Westerbrook wasn't more important than Aidan; he was just another stupid officer. But Aidan couldn't leave him here. Despite his sins against Aidan—and hell, knowing Chelsea, Westerbrook probably hadn't a clue—the man didn't deserve to die out here like this. No one deserved to die alone in a muddy pit.

He leaned in on his shovel, dug into the ground along the side of Westerbrook's calf and ankle, and fought to give him some space to pry out his foot.

The rain kept falling. Another flare went up. "Move, damn you, sir," Aidan grunted and shoved. He put his shoulder into the other man's ribs just to snap him out of it. "Move, for Christ's sake! You want to see her again or drown out here?"

Westerbrook regained his wits. He put his free foot on Aidan's other board, leaned over Aidan's shoulders and struggled to pull his leg out of the mud. Together, they felt him come loose.

"Alright, I'll give you a boost up and out," Aidan huffed. He staggered over *to the edge of the crater with Westerbrook, wondering absently where he'd find the strength to do this for the next man in the next crater. He put his hands together to give the captain's mud-soaked good foot a boost and heaved upward. Westerbrook pulled himself up and over, flopping down onto the ground outside.*

The rain had picked up. Even standing at the edge, it was almost waist high. Aidan dug his hands into the mud, working to climb his way out as another flare passed overhead.

Aidan didn't hear the sniper shot that struck him in the small of the back. The pain overrode his other senses. It was more as if he'd remembered hearing the rifle shot rather than actually registering it as it happened. His eyes, squeezing shut in the instant of impact, opened to see Westerbrook shuffling away into the night, looking back once but not stopping to help.

Aidan sank down along the crater wall. He hurt too much to move his legs at first, but as he breathed and focused and tried to overcome the pain, he realized there was more to his inability to move than just the shock. That bullet had hit him quite near the center of his back, and exited out, he now realized, through his gut.

The rain kept falling.

He gasped, struggling to breathe, looking up at the darkness above. Another flare went out. He glanced around the crater, wondering if there was something, anything he could hold to pull himself out.

Chelsea's wedding picture floated by his eyes more than once as the water rose.

He flailed, shaking uncontrollably and gasping for air on a hard, cold tile floor under bright lights. The incongruity between the surface under him and the water and mud became too much for his confused mind to ignore. Alex found his fight for air get easier to win with every breath, yet he still fought. The jumble of sensory information left him trying to synthesize perception and memory.

He was at once in dire danger and basically safe, falling apart for no reason in the empty lobby of an auditorium that kept returning to a battlefield. Alex knew he couldn't explain this to anyone who might see. No one would understand. He crawled and then staggered toward the bathroom nearby and shut himself inside. He reached for the lock without thinking about it and then curled up on the floor.

The silence helped, as did the lights and the reassurance of a solid floor. He stared at the pattern in the tile. Workmen had laid this out years ago. Hell, maybe it had been a woman who did it. Maybe he'd been black, or Asian, or

Latino. He wasn't in Europe, and it wasn't 1917. He felt himself calming down again.

Then the door slammed outside, still too loud to ignore. Alex jerked into a fetal position, covering his head and neck with his hands. The door slammed again and again as people emptied out of the auditorium. To Alex, it was too much like an artillery barrage. The footsteps echoed in his mind like charging boots.

He lay shaking on the floor all alone until he heard only silence again. In his brief flashes of lucidity, he wondered when his past would leave him alone.

IN LIFE, Don Geraldo Rafael de Leon had been a servant of the crown, a hero to his people and a slayer of pirates. He had sailed repeatedly between Spain and the New World, braving storms and hostile natives and all the spawn of the Devil that lurked beneath the sea.

He died in the deep end of an empty swimming pool in Malibu.

Witnesses crowded all around the pool's edges. Some cheered for the Spaniard and his band, others for his opponents. Were it not for the floodlights hung from the palm trees just for the party, Don Geraldo would have seen more witnesses on the balcony of the extravagant mansion that rose above the shallow end. He knew they were there, though. Were it not for their presence, he never would have agreed to this fight.

Don Geraldo and his five companions dressed for the formal occasion that the invitation had described. They wore silk breeches and hose, fine jewelry and shirts with delicate lace. Naturally, they each carried their ornate rapiers, as befit their stations. That did not mean the Don and his men came looking for a fight, as they were happy to tell anyone... but they also carried their pride, and would not lay that down for any challenger.

To their surprise, a challenge came over a dispute spanning the nights of two centuries. Don Geraldo could not evade the confrontation through diplomacy. His host knew all along that this would come. Indeed, it was likely the reason that the challengers received invitations.

Don Geraldo's men willingly put themselves between their liege and danger as their opponents—both of them—charged in with a bloodthirsty howl. Some in the crowd mimicked and echoed that howl; others gave voice to cries of their own.

Spanish rapiers turned out to be poor weapons against vampires. Stabbing blades did little against men and women whose vital organs no longer served much purpose. Yet to their credit, the line of Spanish vampires held their ground with blades drawn and gave battle, slashing and stabbing with fierce elegance. Their rapiers cut through leather and flesh. For a brief moment, Don Geraldo entertained a brief glimmer of hope.

Then he saw the heavy blade of an axe cleave through Rodrigo's neck in a single blow. Enraged eyes hidden behind an iron helm and an inelegant, savage red beard glared at him as Rodrigo's headless body fell, soon to crumble to ash. The enemy dressed in a mismatch of modern clothing and armor made in old styles but with modern technique. Don Geraldo saw black leather and black denim, but also bracers and a mail shirt. None of that mattered to him as much as the bloodthirst in the Viking's eyes. Don Geraldo's men closed ranks before the muscular Viking could advance.

Fighting continued. So did the cheers. Bass-heavy dance music boomed over speakers set throughout the wide pool patio, but the melody could hardly keep up with the pace of a battle between vampires. Don Geraldo watched his men give battle, come up short, and quickly fall.

The last of his men, Esteban, was not even given the dignity of death by the blade. He was seized at each shoulder by the other Viking, whose blond hair hung to his chest, and hoisted off his feet. The Viking bit savagely into Esteban's neck. Blood sprayed everywhere as the larger man gnawed at the flesh of his screaming victim.

The bearded one stalked forward, leaving his brother to feast. "You have had a long time to pay this off, Geraldo," he seethed.

Proud to the end, Geraldo refused to show fear to a barbarian like this. "I have always paid my debts, Unferth," he said with a defiant twitch of his chin. "If you had a legitimate claim, yours would have been paid honorably."

His hand reached into the folds of his black silk cape. He had one chance at this. It would not likely kill Unferth outright, but a proper blow would at least stun him for several minutes. Geraldo would then have to take on Bjorn, but he could at least evade the other Viking's sword long enough to stab out his opponent's eyes. Then he would have the rest of the night to deal with them both. As long as this worked…

Unferth kept coming. He had to recognize the trap, but he was too arrogant to care. With practiced speed and precision, Geraldo drew his black powder pistol and leveled it at Unferth's head.

Moving with surprising speed, Unferth slapped the pistol up and away. It went off, sending its lead shot up at the crowd. A mortal brought along as refreshment took the shot across the face. He died instantly, swaying backward and then pitching forward into the pool, a trail of blood flowing in his wake.

The crowd laughed.

Don Geraldo and Unferth moved together, though not by the Don's consent. He brought up his rapier; Unferth brought down his axe, severing Geraldo's hand at the wrist. Geraldo stumbled back. Unferth kicked him hard, applying enough force to the Spaniard's gut to lift him up and send him flying the last two feet before he hit the back wall of the pool.

Don Geraldo's eyes opened just in time to see the blade of Unferth's axe come straight down into his head, and knew that rather than being his end, this was just a final cruelty. His skull split under the axe, but Don Geraldo was a vampire. Pain and disorientation overwhelmed him, but he did not die until the axe came down again, this time on his neck.

Cheers and applause from vampires in a vast array of clothes greeted Unferth and Bjorn as they emerged from the pool. Some guests wore faithful reproductions of the garments of their breathing days. Others dressed in more modern fashions that nevertheless bore the mark of their centuries-old sensibilities. Modern fashions could be seen, too. They provided a way to differentiate guests from food.

The brothers ignored the praise and cheers. They had business here. On their way back to the house, though, Bjorn made a detour to walk up to a set of tables covered in modern electronics equipment. Behind the pile of gear stood a pale-skinned man of apparent youth. His pallor marked him as a vampire, but his headphones and constant dancing motion indicated that he was quite new.

Bjorn swung his broadsword in a wide arc across the table. With a single mighty blow, he swept nearly all of the gear and computer equipment from its surface. The music stopped instantly. The young vampire on the other side of the table turned and looked on his unexpected critic with shock.

"We care not if others find entertainment in our battles," snarled Bjorn, "but I will not perform like some animal at a circus!"

"Okay, dude! Okay! Chill! Holy shit, dude!" the DJ balked. "Sorry you didn't like the music! Should've asked if you had a request! My bad, bro! My bad!"

"Bjorn," called Unferth. "The others will be waiting. Let's go."

The other Viking gave the DJ one last glare, then turned and left as he sheathed his sword once more. He joined his brother at the entrance to the mansion. "I hate this city," Bjorn grumbled. "It is too warm, and everyone we meet here is a sycophant."

As he entered the house, a pretty mortal servant girl knelt before him with a towel in hand and a wordless offer on her face. Bjorn motioned absently to her. She rose and wiped the blood from his shirt, his bared arms and his face. A second servant, this one a slender young man, came forward with a bowl and more towels.

The slaves of vampires learned quickly how to clean up spilled blood. Bjorn eyed them as they worked. He felt like devouring them both just because he could. At least they were fresh. Drinking from a fellow vampire was an effective combat technique, but the blood of the undead always tasted stale.

"Not everyone, I hope," someone voiced in the Queen's English. He stepped up to them with an entourage of vampires and mortal servants. His darkly-colored suit came closer to modern fashion than the clothes of most of the vampires present, but its style and wool fabric were at least a century and a half out of date. He walked with a cane that he did not need and a polite smile.

"Wentworth," nodded Unferth.

"You will address him as Lord Mayor—" objected one of the newcomer's retainers, but the leader interrupted with a casual gesture of his hand.

"There's no need for that," he said. "Unferth and Bjorn are honored warriors. The least I can do for them is forego the lofty titles."

Bjorn snorted. "Yours is less pretentious than most. The whole practice is ridiculous. Claim a city, claim a title based on nothing but a whim. We met the Marquess of San Francisco an hour ago. I hear Hawaii has a shogun, for fuck's sake."

Wentworth tilted his head in deference to Bjorn's disdain. "The pace of the modern world encourages a bit of creative license, but I do prefer humbler titles."

"Nothing like our host's," grunted Bjorn.

"Yes, well. Let's not bring that up in his presence, shall we?"

"He has a millennium on us as well, Wentworth," frowned Unferth. "No one has dared challenge him since before Bjorn and I last saw the sun. We didn't survive this long by being stupid. It's just too bad that this mess didn't turn up on your side of the continent instead of *hers*."

"Let's hope it's still her side," put in Bjorn. "If not, we may have to leave this coast for saner territory."

Unferth nodded. "As I say. You may be young as lords go, Wentworth, but at least you aren't raving mad."

Wentworth's clipped smile twitched a bit as if to convey his thanks. "I'm sure we'll be able to resolve this mess with your help. I will try to mitigate our host's... eccentricities." He spotted a servant at the top of a broad, open staircase nearby. "Is he ready for us?"

The servant nodded. "Lords and ladies, honored guests, your attention, please." He spoke loudly enough to break into every conversation within earshot, but with a tone that dripped with respect and subordination. "Gaius Cornelius Vaspasianus, sole Consul of the Republic of Los Angeles awaits his most honored guests to take counsel with him in his audience chamber. He bids you attend at your convenience."

Unferth and Bjorn shared a glance and a roll of their eyes, but only Wentworth saw it. Even they did not want to directly insult their host. Cornelius was mad, but powerful in a great many ways.

Arriving in the audience chamber, the guests found faux-Imperial Roman décor and the usual assortment of vampires wearing outfits that spanned centuries of fashion. At the center of the room on a large oaken throne sat Cornelius himself in a red toga and laurel crown. Never a noble or even a leader in life, Cornelius ruled now through awe of his age. It was hard to find so old a vampire anywhere in North America. Few wanted to test his prowess.

Only one vampire kept him from claiming the whole of the West as his own... and no one knew if she still walked.

"Unferth! Bjorn! So good to see you," Cornelius smiled. He rose and crossed the room to clap them both on the shoulders. They felt the great strength of his hands—surely the only reason he made such a gesture—and nodded politely, but did not return his smile. "I witnessed your victory from the balcony. The outcome was never in doubt."

"We thank you for putting us in the same room as the Spaniards," said Bjorn. "Finally."

Unferth wanted to cuff his brother for daring to hide a veiled complaint in his words of gratitude, but he decided not to bring attention to it. "This night has been a long time coming for us, Lord Cornelius," he nodded.

"Yes," Cornelius smiled, "I know it has. I am glad your dispute is put to rest. Far graver concerns await our attention. I'm afraid I must ask you to repay my favor more or less immediately."

"You have a lead?" asked Unferth.

"I do," nodded Cornelius. He stepped back from them and looked briefly to Wentworth. "Lord Mayor, if I may?"

Wentworth bowed. "You are the host, after all, sir. And the one responsible for locating this vital information."

"Thank you. My lords and ladies," Cornelius said, holding his arms out wide, "as you all know, I have searched tirelessly for our vanished friend and ally to the north and her court. From across the continent, Lord Mayor Wentworth offered his aid, and together we have labored to find answers. We now have the scent of blood, and we will follow its trail."

He gestured grandly to a lovely young Latina woman in a white toga beside his bed. Her skin was still flush with warmth. Only a mortal slated to receive the gift of eternal night from the host himself would be allowed in such private counsel. She raised a small plastic remote to one wall and pressed a button, causing the wall panels to slide back and reveal a large, state of the art flat screen television.

The image that flickered to life was of a scrawny, bald, broken man. His hands were cuffed to the arms of his chair. Not all of his fingers remained. The evil eye tattooed at his neck and other symbols on his skin suggested much. Dozens of small scars covered his head, neck and shoulders, all of them looking to be fresh but at least sealed.

"This is Kenneth," explained Cornelius. "He was a member, though junior in rank and likely not valued, of a group of sorcerers in Seattle that called themselves the Brotherhood of Apollo."

Murmurs broke the silence of his audience. Cornelius continued. "As you may or may not be aware, it is difficult for mortals to cast spells without fingers. It also requires a certain precision of speech," he added with a smile, waving one finger around his own mouth. "Please forgive Kenneth's lisp. He had only recently lost his front teeth when this video was made. But I bid you pay close attention. He tells an interesting story."

"So Jason turns up at mah place the next night, right? An' he's got this bewildered look on his face like he's jus' come outta combat or somethin'. He's got every inch of his arms covered with stuff in pink marker, like hearts an' X's and O's, an' ah swear t' God one hand is marked 'shock' an' the other says 'awe,' an' his neck is jus' covered in hickies..."

"This is so not cool, man," Jason grumbled.

"The hell it ain't," chuckled Drew. He slapped Jason on the back as he rounded the table again to make another shot.

"Now you know how Alex felt when he first introduced me to you," smiled Lorelei.

"No, no, I'm interested," Amber pressed, leaning her butt against the pool table as she listened. She waved for Wade to continue despite Jason's objections.

"So ah'm like, 'Whut the fuck happened to you?' An' Jason says, 'Hey, can I crash here for a night or two? Mah momma jus' threw me outta the house.'"

"I want to point out that I didn't sound like a hick," Jason interrupted.

"An' ah said, 'What inna hell did you do?' Well, Jason jus' walks inside, dumps his bags right in the hallway inside mah door. He slumps down on mah couch, an' stares off into space, an' then he finally says, 'It's true what they say, man. It's all true. Pimpin' ain't easy at all.'"

Laughter burst from Amber. She noted that the story had not yet gotten old for Drew or Lorelei either, given their smiles. "So wait," Amber said, turning to Jason, "you said you've got your own place now, right?"

"Yeah, I was only on Wade's couch for like two or three nights. I mean my parents went back and forth on the whole 'exile' thing, but after a week of not knowing where I'd be sleeping on a given night, I said, 'Fuck it,' and I got my own place. It's small, but at least it's mine and there's no bullshit."

"No roommates either, right?" Amber asked. She ventured a wink.

"Hell no," Jason said, giving a cocky shrug. "Cramps my style."

"But you say you don't have a girlfriend. Or, you know, plural. So was this just a one-night stand?"

"More like a couple weeks. Everyone was cool at first. I mean I'm not gonna say it was all just, uh, sex," he grunted as if reluctant to say it out loud, "but in the end we didn't have all that much in common. I don't think either of them was hoping for a white picket fence."

"I imagine not, if they were trying to share you," Amber said. The whole thing seemed more than a little unbelievable, but here stood other people swearing to the whole story. "That sort of thing doesn't sound like it could last. I mean, two girlfriends?"

"Polyamory has more in common with monogamy than you might think," Lorelei countered mildly. "They both require communication. Honesty. Commitment to the rules of the relationship, whatever they might be. Ultimately, the relationship works until it doesn't. One can say all the same for traditional dating and marriage."

"Been there, done that, huh?" smiled Amber.

Lorelei nodded. "I am."

"Oh? How so?"

"Yeah, Lorelei, how so?" Jason agreed.

"Hey, you aren't off the hook yet," Amber told him, shaking a finger at him without looking. She waited for an answer from Lorelei.

"Aw, man," he grumbled.

"Yeah," Drew agreed, "she's still gotta hear about the Great Open Teamspeak Mic incident that ended your run on My Two Shorties."

"Teamspeak?" Amber asked. "What, you mean like on an MMO?"

"Oh Jesus, really?" Jason sighed, "Do we really have to do this?"

"Greatest total party kill story ever," Wade nodded sagely.

"You weren't even there!"

"Ah've seen the YouTube."

"There's a YouTube?" Jason exploded.

"Okay, wait wait wait," Amber chuckled, "I want to hear this, but don't change the subject yet. Lorelei, what did you mean?"

"As we mentioned, I was introduced to our friends here through my partner, Alex. He and I share a second partner named Rachel." Her eyes swept the faces of the young men around them as if to convey a soft reminder. "She likely won't be here tonight. I had thought Alex would join us by now, though," she muttered.

"Wait, you 'share' another partner?" asked Amber.

"We are all equal parts of the same relationship, yes," Lorelei nodded. "Some would call it a triad, though I care little for labels."

"Wow. I can't say I've never heard of the idea, but I've never actually met anyone with that kind of, um, arrangement." She paused. "I imagine you get a lot of dumb questions about it?"

"We don't exactly advertise. I wouldn't tell you of it, but for the likelihood that it will come up," she said, eyeing Jason with a bit of a smile. "Rachel doesn't get out with us much. If others perceive Alex as my only partner, she doesn't mind. She is not one for fretting about the opinions of others.

"But yes, I have some experience in relationships outside of traditional models. I would suggest that Jason's recent entanglements fell apart not because it was inherently flawed as a model, but because of the individuals involved." She threw a calm wink to Jason to take any potential sting from her comment.

"I suppose that's fair," Amber said, though skepticism colored her voice.

Drew gave a bit of a nod over Amber's shoulder. "You could always ask Alex his take on it, too," he offered.

Amber turned to look as the newcomer arrived. With her mind split between acting natural and thinking like an investigator, she made assessments quickly. She found youth that fit with the guys around her, but immediately recognized a degree of sex appeal and good looks that somewhat justified Lorelei's interest. She spotted the leather jacket and the helmet in one hand marking him as a rider. Yet she also noted a slightly breathless, amped-up look in his eyes and his stride that seemed a bit out of place for a night at a pool hall.

"I was afraid I wouldn't catch you before you left," Alex said as he moved in to embrace Lorelei. Amber caught the lilt in his voice—and the reactions of his friends. "I'm not even sure what time it is."

"It's almost eleven," answered Drew with a frown.

"Ah, so late, but not too late, I'd say," Alex smiled. He turned to the rest with Lorelei's arm still around his shoulder. Amber caught his eye. "Who's this, then?"

"Alex, this is Amber," said Jason.

Amber stuck out her hand with a friendly smile. "Hi," she said. "So at the risk of sounding dumb, I'll just ask now: are you from Ireland?"

The question stopped Alex in his tracks. He blinked and looked to his friends. "No," he answered with a flawless Irish brogue, "I've lived in Seattle all my life."

"Bro, you feelin' okay?" Drew asked.

The others waited while Alex hesitated. Amber detected a shared look of concern on everyone else's face. Finally, Alex said, "No. No, I'm not." He swallowed hard. "Wade, have you ever... have you ever had a flashback to... you know, fightin'?"

"Can't say ah have, but y'all don't look right," said Wade. "Where've ya been?"

"Over at the U," answered Alex, his brogue still strong. "And, uh... Ypres, I think. I dunno. I was at the lecture, and then I was in the mud, and... and I locked myself in a bathroom."

"Oh Jesus," breathed Drew, "did you get on your *bike* and come here? Why didn't you call us and have one of us pick your ass up?"

Lorelei closed her eyes with a soft curse of frustration. "Alex, do you trust me?" she asked.

Though out of sorts, Alex answered easily, as if the only oddity were that she would even need to ask. "With me life," he nodded.

"My friends," she said, "there is much to tell you, but I didn't expect us to be in mixed company. I am sorry."

"It's okay," Amber spoke up. The last thing she wanted was to be excluded now. "Don't worry about me."

"I must," said Lorelei, stepping closer. "I am sorry." She reached out to slip her hand around Amber's neck and looked deeply into her eyes. "*Forget the awkwardness of these last few minutes,*" she said. "*You found nothing worthy of suspicion here tonight. You found companionship and acceptance. Nothing more.*"

Amber almost swooned. She leaned on Jason, nodding, finding his presence comforting. He was a nice guy. They were all nice guys. Whatever bothered her must not have been a big deal.

"Woah," Jason blinked. He'd been at Amber's side all along, and heard every word. "I didn't... what did you do?"

"What I had to, Jason," Lorelei explained. "I do only what I must. She will be fine, but you should see her home."

"Oh, I'm sorry," murmured Amber. "Is it time to go?"

"It is for us," Lorelei replied. "I'm sorry to cut this short. Alex is not well. He should not ride. Can either of you follow us on his motorcycle?" she asked Drew and Wade.

"Yeah, I got it," nodded Drew.

"Ah c'n follow," Wade spoke up. "Drew hitched a ride here with me anyway."

"Thank you," said Lorelei. She kept one hand on Alex's arm through the brief conversation. "Jason—"

"No, I get it," he shook his head. "I mean, with him," he added, gesturing toward Alex.

Lorelei nodded with gratitude, but her controlled urgency remained. "Amber, it was a pleasure, and I hope to see more of you."

"Um. Sure?" Amber shrugged. She gave just a little wave as the older woman led Alex and his friends toward the exit. Then she turned to Jason, who seemed to be working up some sort of apology. "I like your friends," she declared happily.

3

IT'S WORSE THAN IT LOOKS

"I swear it's not normally this weird with them," Jason said as he pulled up outside the apartment building. "Or with me." He paused. "And by 'normally,' I mean frequently. I mean for most of us. Weird shit seems to happen to Alex lately."

"Hey, I had a good time," Amber shrugged. "Your friends were all nice. They seem like cool people." It was honest enough. She saw no reason for him to feel guilty or freaked out. Hell, she was of half a mind to just tell him she was an FBI agent and to ask him point blank about the vampire fangs. Nothing she'd discovered in the last few hours led her to believe there was anything suspicious about Jason or his friends.

"Cool," Jason nodded. He thought about turning off the car and walking her to her door. Or not. He thought about asking her if he could call her later. Or not. Asking if she wanted to do anything Friday night, or Saturday, or just trying to kiss her right now... or not. How far was too far? How much was too much? If he didn't do anything to say he was interested in more than just friendship, would he quickly lose any chance of something more?

"Thanks for bringing me along," said Amber, breaking him from his momentary internal struggle. "I'm glad I came."

"Cool," he nodded again.

Amber paused. Regardless of her allayed suspicions, she still had an investigation to run, and had only one lead. No sense risking it floating away. "I'd like to hang out again sometime."

Jason smiled. "Cool."

"See you in class?"

"Yup," he nodded as she stepped out of the car and headed to the front door. Jason waited, waved at her from the car once she had the door open, and pulled away as she closed it behind her.

Amber climbed the stairs to her apartment, opened it and set down her jacket and purse. There wasn't much to the one-bedroom affair besides a smattering of cheap Ikea furniture. Not a poster or picture decorated the place. It fit in with her "ex-boyfriend trashed all my stuff" story and the task force's budget. Amber had hardly even seen any of it; Matt and Colleen had handled her move-in for her while she was at school.

She had just enough time to hit the restroom before there was a knock on her door. Amber found Hauser, Colleen and Doug waiting for her. "Hey, I was just coming upstairs to report in."

Hauser and the others walked inside, closing the door behind them. "What did you find out?" Hauser asked.

"They all seem nice," she shrugged. "Just a night out. All pretty mellow."

Hauser's eyes turned to Doug, who scowled, sniffed her, and then pulled a crystal out of his pocket. He held the crystal up to his eye, muttered something and stared at Amber through it.

Amber gestured to Doug and asked Hauser, "Is he serious with this?"

"Something's wrong," Doug grunted. He put the crystal back in his pocket, fished out a tiny leather bag from the same pocket and poured what looked like sea salt crystals from it into his hands.

"What are you doing?" asked Amber. "I mean I get that you're the cult expert here—"

"Occult expert," Hauser corrected. "Let him work."

"Uh," Amber mumbled. She didn't resist as Doug took her hand and placed a rounded bit of obsidian in it.

"Close your eyes," Doug advised.

"...okay?" She did as he asked. She heard and felt the puff of his breath, and the hundred tiny impacts of sea salt crystals on her face. Amber made a face, taking half a step back in reflex, wondering why Doug didn't just use a whole cream pie... and then blinked. She stared at Doug. The others waited. "Okay, wait," she said, her eyes not tracking much of anything as her memories of the night became clearer. She remembered details, and suspicions, and emotions.

"Oh hell," she murmured, "it's all real."

"It is of course wise to be on your guard, but I doubt you have much to fear as yet," Lorelei emphasized. "It is Alex she wants, not you. At most, if she follows you, it will be as a means to find him."

"Gotcha," Wade said. His hand rested on the doorknob. "An' she really won't go nuts if somethin' happens in public? You said she won't go wolfie or nothin', but can't she just pull out a gun and start shootin'? Ah mean, it don't take bein' a monster t' cause a lotta trouble."

"This is true," nodded Lorelei, "and there are never guarantees. I have seen their kind fight with weapons in the past, but such is rare. I believe the urge to hunt comes more from the animal within than the man, and thus they eschew using tools for such purposes. But they have human minds, and can think outside such boxes." Lorelei gave a little shrug. "We shall have to be cautious."

"We'll go tell Jason right now," Drew assured her. "Even if he's already in bed. We'll wake his ass up and give him the lowdown."

"Thank you for everything," Lorelei said. She hugged them both before they left her apartment, her eyes lingering on them as they walked to the elevator down the hall. Lorelei then returned to the living room, where Alex sat staring off into space on the couch.

"We're normally in bed by this time," he observed, "or at least naked somewhere." His weariness colored his voice, but he simply wasn't ready to sleep yet. Better to sit up awake than stare at a dark ceiling.

"Do I detect an apology?" she asked with a gentle smile as she curled up against him. "Our habits are driven as much by need as affection, but I can survive without sex. It would appear such things aren't on your mind right now, either."

"I wish they were, actually. It means a lot to me. Sometimes I think more than it should. Y'know, curses aside and such. I wasn't exaggerating yesterday. I really feel like I live for it. Sometimes I wonder if it's more than just a high sex drive, or your influence, or..." Alex shrugged. "I wonder if I'm not just trying to distract myself."

"I would know it, if that were the case," said Lorelei. "I've known many with such a motive. The truth is that you and I both long to make up for lost time. Lost lifetimes, even," she added. "Rachel, too."

"Do you think this is just my karma?" Alex asked, clearly looking for the right word. "I don't know how to say it. Maybe that's just how my life is meant to be?"

"Speaking of Rachel," Lorelei noted, rolling her eyes a little.

"Oh. Right. 'Man Was Not Meant to Know' stuff, huh?"

"It is something she takes seriously." Lorelei paused. "Alex, I have seen precious little to lead me to believe that anything is 'meant to be' in the lives of mortals. Heaven and Hell and forces outside of both might steer individual events or people. Yet I have seen almost three millennia pass, I have encountered many angels and been a closely prized servant of two of the mightiest lords in Hell... and I am no more aware of a single grand design than you or any mortal you know." She noted the tilt of his head as she spoke. "What is it?"

"'Almost three millennia?' And the other night you mentioned you became a succubus, which implies you were something before."

"I was."

"Can you tell me about it? I never asked because it seemed like something you'd rather leave behind, but you've dropped a couple of hints lately."

"If I did so, it was entirely by accident," Lorelei smiled ruefully.

"We can leave it alone if you want. I've always been curious, but it just seemed... rude to ask."

"It is not rude. You know what I am, and at least in the abstract you know the things that I have done. I feared for a time that such details would drive you from me, but I know better now. Still, the story would not lift your spirits. You are already haunted by your own tragedy. Leave it for another night," she said, molding her body against his.

"Where were you from?"

"Babylon," she answered, her voice dropping to nearly a whisper. "Babylon, and closer to what Herodotus described than I think even he knew."

Alex shrugged. "We can leave it for another night."

"We should. It is... painful. No. Ugly," she corrected softly upon reflection. "The tale is quite ugly."

"Smell that," said Billy, holding his index and middle fingers out under Jimbo's nose. Sparks from the fire pit floated up between them into the night sky.

The bearded man grimaced, tilting his head back while slapping Billy's hand away. "The hell's that for?" Jimbo scowled. "Tryin' to impress me or somethin'? You think I ain't smelled pussy before?"

"Yeah, but that's gen-yew-wine Fresno hooker right there," Billy pressed. He spit some of his chew out into the fire pit, offering up his fingers again as if the flannel-clad man beside him might change his mind. "Natural redhead, too. Fresh one. Didn' taste a lick of meth or crack on 'er."

Seated in a camping chair by the fire, Red watched the two with a chuckle. "Always count on Billy to appreciate the finer things in life."

"You want a piece of her, Red? Anyone?" Billy offered, looking up at his score of companions. "She's still in the back of my truck. Most of 'er, anyway. We can prob'ly still warm her up good enough. Hardly a day dead. Kinda like reheated chicken, I know, but it don't look like anyone else brought goodies to this shindig tonight."

"Disgusting," grunted another of their number. Eyes turned in the darkness toward a tall, broad-chested man in denim and worn leather sitting atop a cooler. "You wallow in your own shit like a pig."

Billy seemed stopped in his stride by the comment, but only for a moment. He blinked, assessed, and then resumed his easy smile. "She ain't shit, Jared! She's leftovers! Clean for a hooker. Healthy, too. Gave 'er a good run out in the desert before I dragged her back to my truck."

"Do you think this impresses anyone?" Jared asked. "The difference between you and the rest of us is that we finish our business and our kills and then move on. You make a show of it. By now you should've realized no one cares. You're still a mongrel to the rest of us."

Again, Billy blinked. He squinted at Jared, looked at his other companions, then back once more. "What did you just call me?"

"A mongrel," said a tall, slim blonde in leather riding chaps and black Harley tank top. She came to stand beside Jared. "It means you're a piece of shit, and you were born that way. I guess that means maybe we shouldn't hold it against you since it's not your fault."

"Hey, I'm not takin' any shit from newbies! You better shut that mouth before I shut it for you, bitch," Billy snapped. Jimbo and Red got a good chuckle out of it.

"The only bitch here is you," said Jared, blending a firm tone with matter-of-fact simplicity.

At that, Billy began to bristle—literally. Black hairs all up and down his thick arms stood up on end. He stepped forward, his breath turning to a huffing snarl as his lips curled back. His nails began to stretch into long, dark claws. With a single jerk at the button of his jeans, Billy began to step out of his pants as his legs lengthened and grew fur. He took less care of his t-shirt, which tore and split as his shoulders broadened.

Jimbo and Red stayed as they sat, but several of the others backed off with concern. Jared and Sally watched and waited calmly.

"Knock it off," ordered another voice. Billy's head snapped to his left, looking past the campfire to the imposing figure beyond. He stood a full head taller than Billy, with long, dirty blond hair falling out under a beat-up cowboy hat and a similarly scraggly beard. He wore little more than faded flannel and denim, seeming for all the world like a homeless drifter.

That was exactly what he was, except he was also much more. "I ain't interested in watchin' you fight or waitin' for you to heal up any more than I'm interested in hearin' you whine. Sally, quit teasin' Billy for bein' a retard. Jared, you, too. Billy, you calm the hell down right now an' go clean out that dead hooker mess in the back of your truck."

At first, Billy looked as if he would ignore the older man's advice. His stance remained tense, arms wide and legs at shoulder length as if to pounce. Yet his growth in height and mass slackened, then reversed, and his hair went back to looking normal rather than growing into a scraggly mess. He stood wearing only the tattered remains of his shirt and his socks. "But Caleb—!"

"Billy, don't make me repeat myself. Git!"

Like a hurt puppy, Billy's head bowed low. He snatched up his discarded jeans before he walked back to the rest stop parking lot, where his truck and its gruesome contents awaited him.

"Caleb, why in the hell did you choose him?" Jared asked.

"Same reason I chose you for my child. Same reason you chose Sally. He was a killer and he fit the bill."

Jared turned to Sally beside him. "I didn't choose you because you're a slob or a retard," he said.

"I know, daddy," Sally said in a tone that wasn't remotely familial. She slipped her arms up over Jared's shoulders, holding to him much as a daughter wouldn't.

Caleb tilted his head as he conceded, "Didn't exactly have the kind of fun with him you had with Sally, though. Went more like it went with you. 'cept Billy was a bit sloppier. But you make investments, you know? Gotta see 'em through. He might be less sophisticated an' charmin' than the rest of you—"

A long, loud belch interrupted him. Jimbo put down his beer can. "Sorry," he muttered guiltily.

"—but that don't mean he ain't worth his place at the table. Or the camp-fire, as it happens. Just remember, we're all family here. We're a pack. Do what you want when you're out wandering, but when we come together like this, we're all on the same side."

"Seems less like family when we're missin' someone," noted Red. He didn't look Caleb in the eye as he spoke, nor anyone else, gazing instead into the fire. "Been almost two months now."

"Now, Red, you know I'm worried about Diana just like the rest of you," Caleb told him.

"Are you?" Red asked. "I'm startin' to wonder. Been three months we been stayin' clear of them dead little bitches, all the way from Tacoma to Everett, just to keep them happy, and ain't one of us done shit to get her back 'cause you told us not to. Said you'd handle it."

"I am handlin' it, Red," Caleb assured him. "I'm surprised you care so much. Last I checked, you an' Diana didn't exactly get along."

"I care enough to wonder if this is how you'd handle things if it was my ass got snatched away," countered Red. "She's pack, right? Family. You always said so, weird as she was."

"What's weird about Diana?" wondered Sally.

"She talks funny," answered Jared.

"Course she talks funny," snapped Caleb, "she was a goddamn poetry an' theater major when I found her! And a Canadian!" He turned his attention to Red. "Goddammit, boy, I told you before, we ain't got no way of just bargin' in there an' gettin' her back when we don't even know where they're keepin' her."

"We could *look*," Red shrugged sullenly.

Caleb stormed over to Red, pushing Jimbo out of the way before slapping Red out of his folding camper's chair onto the ground, sending his beer flying. "That's enough outta you!" Caleb snarled. "I'm the father of this pack! Me! You think I taught you all to be like family so you could turn on me?"

"No, father," came a calm voice from the shadows beyond the fire, "you taught us to be family to prevent that."

Heads turned. Downwind and obscured by the conversation, Diana managed to sneak right up on the group undetected. Spotting her in the darkness was no trouble for the others now that they knew to look. She walked into the light of the campfire, her eyes moving from one adopted family member to the next. From one shoulder hung a backpack; from the other, a tie-dyed hobo bag. Tucked in her hair just over her ear was a big red flower.

"Did I hear your name was Sally?" she asked. "You're with Jared?"

"Yeah," the other woman nodded. "Are you... are you Diana?"

"I am," Diana nodded. "I'll endeavor not to sound too weird. Welcome to the pack. Hello, Jared. Red. Jimbo. Everyone."

Grunts and mumbles of greeting from the others filled the silence for only a moment, but soon all they heard was the crackle of the campfire. Everyone watched as Diana and Caleb stared at one another.

"You got out," observed Caleb.

"I did."

"What'd you give 'em?"

"Nothing at all," Diana shook her head slowly. "Just like you."

"So, what, you escaped all them vampires all on your own?" he asked. "You know I've always had faith in you, but that seems a might unlikely."

"I did nothing to buy my way out," Diana said, "nor did anyone pay ransom for me. They didn't release me. I found an opportunity, fought and escaped."

Caleb's mouth spread into a grin. "I imagine you've got a story, then."

"I do. And an agenda."

"Oh?"

Diana nodded. "I've found a mate. I will claim him and make him one of us. The pack will help."

"You've decided that for us?" Caleb scowled. "For me?"

"I have, father."

"You know you don't give the orders around here. That's my job."

Again, she nodded, and dropped her backpack and purse at her feet. "You're right. I agree one hundred percent. You're in charge. I'll have to kill and eat you."

Not a sound was heard after that; it was as if even the crackling fire had gone silent. The world continued to turn around the makeshift family—burning wood split, insects chirped, cars rolled on down the highway past the rest stop—but not a single one of them noticed any of it after that. As far as the others were concerned in that moment, the entire world was comprised of Caleb, Diana and the challenge she had just leveled.

He was equally angered and stunned. He opened his mouth to speak, but Diana calmly interrupted him. "I owe you everything. You are strong and proud and you have taught us well, but you abandoned me to our enemies. You will not talk your way out of this."

Caleb charged. He exploded into towering muscle and fur as he moved, shifting so quickly it surprised the youngest among his adopted "children." Claws swept out to either side, ready to slash into the woman before him. His jaw opened wide, revealing sharp, frightful teeth.

The single second it took Caleb to cross the ground between them seemed to happen in slow-motion for the others, because Diana hardly moved. She placidly waited to be demolished. Her hand shot out at his snout as the monster closed in, releasing a handful of a fine white powder. How she could do this and also slip down and around him fast enough to get away, none of the others could follow. In one instant, she gave him a face full of powder; an eyeblink later, she was down low, one leg outstretched, tripping him and sending him sprawling down on the ground.

Caleb quickly recovered, or at least tried. Nothing about the move or his fall left him stunned, but as he spun he seemed to wobble and swoon. He snorted once, then again, his head turning this way and that as if unable to see. Diana swung a wide left hook directly into his nose.

Though by no means a small woman, her move seemed comical when performed against such a huge foe. Yet Caleb clearly felt it, reeled slightly, and swung back with his wide claws. Again, he missed, for Diana had already stepped back. Caleb slashed around and around, left and right, moving forward, turning and snapping his jaws at nothing, trying to catch her.

The moment repeated itself: Caleb sniffed and Diana punched, hard enough to make him feel it despite the discrepancy in size. This time, though, Caleb swung back quickly enough to bat her away with his forearm. Diana fell under the powerful blow, grunting in pain before she landed on her back. Caleb's other arm slashed down on her, tearing downward across her shoulder, chest and abdomen. Diana let out a cry of pain.

Caleb roared, reaching back with both arms to bring down a killing blow, and left himself wide open. Diana lurched forward as she became a similarly frightful beast, clawing up into and through his groin while she tumbled between his legs. Caleb's triumphant cry turned into an animal shriek of pain as his knees buckled.

She recovered behind him, bleeding but still formidable, spun and leapt upon his back. Her clawed hands slammed down on his ears, digging in mercilessly until they came away with rent flesh and fur. Caleb made no secret of his pain as he howled and thrashed.

Partially blinded, largely deafened and unable to smell anything but the powder in his nose, Caleb could hardly fight. For all Diana's impressive strength, the older werewolf was larger, stronger, more experienced... and none of that helped him. She stayed out of his reach, striking whenever she found a vulnerability.

Diana knew her final opening when she saw it. She lurked behind him, watching his strength wane, and leapt forward to clamp her jaws down on his left arm just below the shoulder. She caught his right with hers and kept chewing through muscle and blood. When he fell, little kept his arm attached other than exposed bone.

She rolled him over onto his back and slashed at his face a few more times out of sheer viciousness before her clawed hands began to dig into his massive chest.

The entire audience was comprised solely of killers and sinners. Wanton acts of savagery marked each of them as candidates for "adoption" in the first place. Such deeds became second nature once they had been initiated into the pack. The werewolves were monsters in contrast to both animal and man; normal wolves killed and ate out of hunger. Werewolves did so out of enjoyment.

The others looked on with discomfort as Diana's snout pushed into Caleb's shredded, broken chest... but also with envy. Much as Diana had said, they all felt a great debt to Caleb. He had made them stronger. Tougher. More than human. But to see their mentor and father figure laid low and mauled in such a way inspired an arousal none would freely admit. Blood spurt in every direction from Caleb's chest. Diana's jaw closed on her goal, tearing it free while her audience watched with heavy, hungry breath.

Billy came rushing back, slower and clumsier in his human form than his other options thanks to his girth. He stopped at the edge of the campfire's light, huffing, "What's goin' on? What'd I miss?"

Diana straddled the broken and mangled wolf-man that had brought them all into their power. She returned to her natural form, naked and covered in blood. As she chewed on the mass of muscle in her hands, blood spilling all over her, the terrible lesions left in her by Caleb's claws began to slowly close.

"You gotta be kiddin' me," Billy breathed.

"Someone please take a walk and make sure no one comes to check out all the noise," Diana asked. Her eyes swept the group to ensure they did not confuse her command for a request despite her polite tone. "I would rather not be disturbed while I'm eating."

"THAT'S THE ONE. ALEX CARLISLE." Amber leaned back from the computer screen to rub her eyes. It had been a long day and a long night. Neither school nor her evening at a pool hall were physically taxing, but doing it all while maintaining a cover created plenty of mental stress.

"Funny how he deleted his whole profile page the week after the mansion fire," noted Matt Lanier. He'd had to work to dig up caches of Carlisle's online life, but the Internet was an archive. It wasn't like Carlisle could truly erase himself.

"No link to the girlfriend, though?" Hauser asked. He sat on the couch, reviewing info on his own laptop computer.

"Nope," Lanier shrugged. "Even the stuff he had posted was pretty guarded. This is someone who paid attention to Internet safety lectures in school."

Hauser grunted. "Presuming he's a real boy in the first place."

The whole task force—all six of them—sat in the apartment's living room. Empty pizza boxes, discarded soda cans and laptops abounded. The apartment one floor up from Amber's lodgings was minimally furnished with cheap chairs, couches and a couple of coffee tables.

"You think he's a vampire?" Amber frowned. "He didn't seem pale enough, or... I dunno. None of them did. Something I can't put my finger on."

"Not douchey enough?" offered Keeley from the kitchen.

"Yeah," Amber said. "That."

"Doesn't mean much," Hauser shrugged. "But this woman doesn't fit with these kids. Not at all."

"Boss," Lanier said, "check your email. Sent you the records sweep on Reinhardt." He busily tapped away at his keyboard, muttering, "Running one on the Carlisle kid now."

Hauser nodded. He said nothing right away, though Amber immediately saw their leader's eyebrows rise. "What is it?"

"Gimme a second to digest all this," Hauser murmured.

"Be nice if we could just talk to the local cops to see what they know," sighed Colleen Nguyen. She had more or less sunk into the couch, her head tilted back with a soda in her hand. "Kind of ridiculous having to skulk around like this."

"Why can't we?" asked Amber.

"Vampires generally make a point of getting their hooks into local police departments," she explained. "It's useful in covering up all their bullshit. One of them slips up, kills a victim or whatever, it helps to have the cops there to make it all go away, y'know?"

"How bad does that get?"

"Bad enough," said Keeley. "Sometimes it's straight bribery or intimidation. Other times they use their woojy supernatural mind tricks on people to bring 'em in line. Even the ones in LA and San Fran don't own whole departments or anything, but all it takes is one dirty cop knowing that the FBI is in town snooping around. He calls up his vampire sugar daddy and suddenly the whole batch scurries underground."

"But we had local cops in LA helping us," Amber pointed out.

"Hand-picked," Keeley nodded. "Every one of them learned about the boogeyman on their own. It happens. Usually the ones who know the truth feel all alone and just shut up about it rather than getting checked into a padded cell. I like to think there are more of them than there are dirty ones, but..." he shrugged. "It's not like we can take a survey."

She shook her head, troubled once more by the whole thing. The Bureau encouraged its people to work with local authorities, not hide from them. So much of this assignment was all about unlearning everything she'd ever been taught.

"Wow," grunted Lanier. His eyes didn't come up from his screen.

"What?" Hauser asked.

"Sending."

"Christ," grumbled Colleen, "you two are like a couple kids passing notes in class. Why don't you just speak up?"

"Gimme a second," Hauser said.

Amber heard the toilet flush and water running from the sink in the bathroom. Doug Bridger stepped out then, drying his hands with a paper towel. "Anything yet?"

"Joe told us to sit down and shut up," Colleen answered.

"No, he didn't," Keeley corrected.

"I said gimme a second," Hauser repeated.

"See?" Colleen gestured to Hauser. "That's Hauser-speak for 'sit down and shut up.'"

"Figured," nodded Doug. He sat down beside Amber. "Still feeling okay?"

"Shouldn't I be?"

He shrugged a bit. "I've only done that a few times. Have any of your recollections changed? Any of your impressions?"

Amber considered it, then shook her head. "No. Jason seems like a decent guy. Friends seem like that, too. Lorelei... I didn't find her threatening or frightening, but something about her isn't normal."

"You said that Lorelei was incredibly attractive."

Amber frowned. "I've never been attracted to women. I don't think it was that. More like I knew she was attractive without actually being attracted to her, y'know? Like seeing a hot movie star on screen and knowing she's sexy."

"Never been able to see male movie stars that way," Doug shrugged.

Amber rolled her eyes. "Of course not. You're a guy." She ventured the question that had been on her mind ever since she got back: "So are you a wizard or what?"

"No," he said, shrugging again, "I'm a nerd. I went for my masters in ancient history and got researching superstitions and mysticism. I came at it from the standpoint that maybe it wasn't all silly nonsense, just to get some insight into the people who practiced it. Then I figured out it was for real, and that I could actually use some of it."

"So you joined the FBI?"

"I recruited him," Colleen said, still looking up at the ceiling. "Everybody has a story for how they got here."

"I don't," muttered Lanier.

"Okay," Colleen conceded, "Matt doesn't. We just needed a computer guy, so we recruited him from the white collar crime division."

"Time to focus, people," Hauser spoke up. "All these guys were good school boys right up through graduation. Drew has been arrested a couple times, probably just for being black in the wrong neighborhoods," Hauser scowled. "Past that, they're all perfectly clean… except every one of them has some little bad ass quality about him. Cohen's the mildest—he's listed on the rolls for a bunch of NRA-certified shooting courses at a local gun shop. Drew Jones has a black belt in kung fu. Wade Reinhardt graduated a semester early from high school to enlist in the Army. Looks like a nice record of service, but some of it's classified… and for a kid with eighteen months in the airborne, that just doesn't wash.

"And then here's Alex Carlisle. Last month, he and some girl escaped being kidnapped by gang bangers. Carlisle put two of them in the hospital while getting shot himself, but it was a miraculously light wound. And he's allegedly this Lorelei woman's boyfriend."

Hauser looked up from his screen then, sweeping the room with his eyes to look over each of his agents. "Reinhardt's had his own place since he was discharged in September… but the others have all just recently moved out of their parents' homes.

"Mystery woman surrounds herself with a bunch of young, malleable bad-asses of limited financial means, and then all of Seattle's vampires just up and disappear? Yeah. I'd say we're gonna be in town for a little while."

4

DUE DILIGENCE

Amber sat in her white graduation gown, her hat still on her head, wishing she had someone to talk to or laugh with while the principal droned on. She ought to have been surrounded by friends. Everyone else was. Instead, she sat surrounded by classmates, which was not remotely the same.

Some of the hats around her were decorated with paint and glitter and glued-on shimmering beads. The boy to her left, who had been suspended three times this year alone for fighting and who regularly insulted his teachers, had a makeshift lei of candy hanging around his neck, bought for him by parents who apparently felt graduating high school was some huge accomplishment. The girl on Amber's right hadn't looked up from her cell phone since they'd sat down. Amber remembered sharing an essay with her in freshman English, just to show her how the five-paragraph format was done, only to be confronted by their angry teacher who couldn't help but notice that the same essay had turned up twice in his in-box, once in Amber's name and once with the other girl's.

The girl texted to a friend, "Sittin next 2 skankula," and never once turned to her left to look Amber in the eye or say a thing to her.

A boy and girl seated in front of her alternately held hands and hugged and giggled through the ceremony. When names of fellow students were called, they frequently shouted out "I love you" or cheered or whistled with great affection.

One of them had asked Amber in class, point blank and in front of everyone as if it *wasn't an insult, if she was a dyke and that was why she never had a boyfriend. The other had literally pushed Amber down a flight of stairs between classes and only barely acted like it was an accident.*

None of the obvious explanations for the petty, pointless cruelty of children applied. Amber was not at all ugly, or overweight, or queer or disabled. She did not have low social skills. She didn't smell bad or dress funny. Nothing aside from academic achievement set her apart from her peers, and surely others who'd achieved more suffered less derision. Sometimes students would treat her decently, or at least with indifference, but it seemed only because they sometimes forgot to be mean. Teenagers couldn't be asked to be consistent. Amber never knew why her classmates shut her out.

The cheers continued. Amber's row was called. They walked to the front of the field as they had during rehearsal, many of them waving and receiving call-outs from the stands. Amber looked up to the bleachers, wondering if Dad had his camera ready. The only reason she had to go through with this whole ceremony was to get pictures for her grandmother. Otherwise, she'd have skipped it, just like she skipped the end-of-the-year carnival for four years running, and the homecoming game, and the prom. It wasn't like she'd ever been asked to any dances, except once on account of a dare.

The boy with the candy lei got a huge pop of cheers and applause from both the stands and the assembled graduates when his name was called. Amber waited, and heard her name, and then heard nothing. Her father was doubtlessly too focused on getting the picture to shout out anything.

Running Start had cut her time in that hellhole in half for her last two years. She traded three hours of her day with snotty teenagers to instead be with older students —adults—who had more important things to do than socialize with a teen. She made no real connections, but never regretted the choice. At least nobody at the community college used her as the butt of a joke.

Amber accepted her diploma without a smile, and wondered—not for the last time —what it was like to have friends.

"Joe, there's something else I've been meaning to say. I haven't been sure how to bring it up, but I figure I'd better just come out with it."

Hauser didn't look away from the road. He merely continued up 45th, trapped between an overly-optimistic bicyclist and a bus as they crawled up the short hill. "So come out with it," he grunted.

It was more or less the response she'd expected. Amber felt less like an FBI agent and more like the daughter of an irritable father. It was a ridiculous comparison, of course; Hauser hardly resembled either of her parents with his strict, almost military demeanor. He was demanding and firm like they were, but the flavor was all different.

She had to suck it up. This wasn't about daddy issues; this was about her job.

"I think Jason—Cohen—is attracted to me."

Again, Hauser grunted. "Figured he would be. You're a girl and you're into all the same nerd stuff. He probably doesn't find much of that."

Muscles in her jaw clenched up. Her hand balled into a fist. Something in her stomach rolled around, wanting to get out, and it wasn't her breakfast. She stomped on her instinct to retaliate. *He's a goon*, she thought. *He doesn't even realize how many ways he just insulted me. Don't let this turn into a thing.*

"I'm pretty sure I can keep it to 'just friends' and he'll still want to hang out with me," she continued, "so I don't think it'll blow the connection—"

"But you probably won't get as much info that way, and not as quickly," Hauser finished for her.

"Yeah," she muttered.

"Agent Maddox, we've already gone to a lot of trouble and expense to establish this cover. You didn't see this as a potential problem in the beginning?"

"Before I made contact, we thought he was seeing those girls in all his pictures on Face—"

"But he's not anymore. He's a nineteen-year-old guy. What do you think he's interested in more than anything else? It damn sure doesn't seem to me like it's football. Like I said before, we don't have much of a rulebook for this task force. We need every edge we can get. Do you think you can do this job?"

Amber tried not to seethe. Bad enough that he wouldn't give her a straight answer, but being interrupted just made her angrier. "That's not what I'm saying, I just wanted to know what I'm supposed to do if—"

"You don't commit any felonies. You don't commit any other crimes that aren't necessary to maintain your cover. Past that, the only question is how much you can handle." He turned into the north entrance to the university campus, steering for the first available parking lot. "This is an inherently dangerous assignment, Agent Maddox. We're all exposing ourselves to worse things than bullets here, and you most of all. Every one of us knows that. But we're here and we're on the job, and we're all gonna have to take some risks and make some sacrifices.

"This is the real deal, Amber. This is what we do. The question is whether or not you're up for that?"

He pulled around a section of parked cars, making no effort to find a space for himself. This was only a drop-off. Amber would have to walk the rest of the way across campus in the rain.

It was only then that he looked at her. "You made contact ahead of anyone's expectations. You've already dug up matters worth investigation, and you held your cover together even after that woman monkeyed with your brain. That's all outstanding work. But we're gonna need more and we're gonna need it soon. Are you ready to do what it takes?"

Once again, Amber instinctively bit down on her first reply. She didn't know which made her angrier: that Hauser clearly considered a fake romantic entanglement to be well within the bounds of reasonable expectations—regardless of how Amber felt about being the one involved—or that Hauser pointedly didn't give explicit instructions one way or the other. Or his passive-aggressive way of daring her to accept whatever came her way.

She could ask him point blank, she knew, but she had no reason to expect anything more than another non-answer. "I'll handle it," she said, hoisting her backpack as she stepped out of the car. "Don't worry about me."

"Page us with updates when you can," Hauser reminded as he drove away.

"It's called 'texting,' asshole," muttered Amber.

The walk to the lecture hall didn't do much to lift her spirits. She trudged through the constant drizzle, thinking back to earlier years on this same campus, in this same weather, and wondered if it was just her lot in life to be here. That she would always love her alma mater was never in doubt, but there were reasons why she left her hometown. LA wasn't like this; when it rained, it rained, and then the sun came out again. Morning clouds usually all burned away by the afternoon. Hell, it was still warm down there, too.

People didn't patronize her in LA, either. She encountered the random tact-less supervisor or co-worker, but it hadn't taken long to establish herself in the lab. Her first year as an actual agent went well. She'd taken her lumps. Paid her dues. Didn't need anyone telling her what was the 'real deal' as if she thought someone had given her a cover identity and an apartment to just fuck around with.

She glanced toward Bagley Hall and remembered her father asking her if she had reconsidered pushing on with graduate studies and becoming a *real* scientist. Because, again, nothing she had done up until then was anything but fucking around, right? All her double major did was qualify her for the next step up.

The way Dad's eyes spun when she told him she'd been hired on by the Bureau's research lab...

A growl rumbled somewhere in her throat. Okay. Fine. Maybe daddy issues couldn't be completely written off. Whatthefuckever.

She loved the university. This place opened up the world for her. It ushered her into adulthood. Opportunities. Freedom. Her first decent friendships since middle school. None of that meant she wanted to come back, let alone so soon. And certainly not to take Composition for Topics in Social Science.

Amber drug herself out of her grumbling thoughts as she arrived at her class. Thankfully, Jason caught her eye and waved. He sat in the back here just like he had in the lecture hall. That was good. There was also an empty seat beside him, which was excellent. Amber went through the same introduction with this professor—scratch that, with this grad student instructor—as she had with the TA the day before. Again, she found few objections.

Get your head in the game, girl. He's right there.

At least he's a nice enough guy so far.

Finished with her introductions, Amber shuffled to the back of the classroom, dumped her bag and slumped into her seat. She glanced up at Jason and muttered, "Hi," before she turned around again to dig out her notebook and a pen.

"You look like you just got out of a shitty conversation," he observed. Amber looked up, finding nothing but a sympathetic smile in his eyes.

"What? No," she chuckled. He kept his gaze on her, waiting for her to say more. "No, I just—it's nothing, I mean—what?"

"Nothing," Jason shrugged. "I'm listening. I don't want to interrupt."

Amber blinked. He'd meant that. It wasn't a cheap line or a ploy. He meant it. He was a genuinely nice guy. Lorelei's words echoed in her head: *He listened to me.*

"Is it obvious?" Amber asked.

"Shot in the dark. I don't know you well enough to guess what might be bugging you, but I figure most people have parents."

She held back her grin long enough to look away. He was still looking at her.

Unbidden and unasked for its opinion, a tiny voice within her admitted that she liked it.

"I had a nice time last night," she said.

His reaction wasn't what she expected. He seemed chagrined, embarrassed, pleased and amused at himself all at once. "Yeah, that didn't quite go how I hoped," Jason muttered.

"It was fine." They heard a noise at the front of the classroom as their instructor got set up and ready to go. Amber considered, with a sinking feeling, that this assignment could go on for a while. She might well need to maintain her cover faithfully for the foreseeable future. That meant actually following the course material and doing the assignments. *Like writing research papers and essays. Great.*

"What other classes do you have today?" she asked.

"Just one, right after this."

"Welcome back, people," said the instructor, who then began to drone on about something or other.

"You wanna hang out later?" Amber hissed.

"Well, I don't want to seem all clingy or needy, but hell yeah."

She grinned, nodded back in confirmation, and then turned her attention to the instructor and his PowerPoint slides. Waking up had been rough, as had her commute. Thus far, Jason's eagerness to spend more time with her was her sole accomplishment for the morning. Now Amber needed a way to keep herself awake through Mr. Grad Student and his lecture.

Three minutes in, a tiny slip of paper appeared on her desk. She glanced over to Jason, who completed his stretch as if nothing untoward had prompted it. She turned over the note. It read, "Such a bullshit subject. I'm going back to real sciences next quarter. Quarks or GTFO."

Her heart jumped. She pushed it back down. Just because he said and did all the right things didn't make him any older or any less of a person of interest in a Federal investigation.

She turned to a fresh page in her notebook and wrote in big letters, holding it up to him when she was finished so he could read. "Notes in class? Really? Don't you have text messaging?"

Jason gave his best rapper's shrug, patted his chest, and flashed her two letters in sign language: "O.G."

Amber couldn't bite down on her laugh fast enough to avoid an annoyed glance from Mr. Grad Student.

"Boom!" Amber shouted gleefully. Jason's wrestler went over the ropes and onto the concrete. "Suck it, noob!"

"This is bullshit!" Jason moaned, twiddling his controllers while his opponent bounced around happily next to him on the futon. "Aw, you're gonna blow my streak! I—holy shit, how'd you program your girl to do crotch-chops? Is that even in the options menu?"

Amber's triumphant laugh continued. She brought her custom female wrestler out of the ring and put Jason's avatar through another health-bar-punishing piledriver. She quickly went for the pin. "Falls count anywhere, biatch," she cackled.

"Aw, man, that's it," he sighed. "I'm down. Crap."

"What? Hey, don't give up, fight out of it!"

"Why?" he asked, but worked the controller anyway at her behest. "I'm not gonna recover in—see? You got the pin."

"It's sweeter if you keep struggling," she grinned.

"You put in cheat codes while I was in the bathroom, didn't you?"

"Just the one for the crotch-chops," Amber confessed. "We can start over and I'll trash you again on a fresh character if you don't believe me."

"No, no, I believe you. Wow. That was ugly." He noticed right away that Amber's bouncing had brought her shoulder to shoulder with him. The closeness felt good. Her head turned to look at him, revealing her triumphant grin and her glittering eyes. That felt even better.

His mind went into warp speed.

Is this a good first kiss moment? Pro wrestling on a console? Really? It'd be funny at least. Maybe sweet. We're bonding regardless. She's so close. She's looking at me. Wait, she's slowing down here, like she's wondering if I'm gonna go for it, should I? Oh God I don't know, I want to but our shoulders are both in the way and if she I go for it and she turns away I'm gonna—no. She turned. Okay. Well. Damn.

He didn't know whether to be annoyed or relieved that he didn't try it before the moment was gone. He opted for the latter. *Nothing romantic about pro wrestling video games anyway.*

Amber took a deep breath, managing to keep her smile up as she put her initials into the game's record of champions. *Thought he was gonna go for it.* She did not allow herself to consider whether she actually wanted him to or not.

"Okay, how often do you play this at home?" he asked.

"Often enough, but usually just against the computer. It's not like I've had a lot of live opponents lately."

"I have a hard time believing you can't find people to play with."

"Well, not people I really like, anyway," she huffed, "and that's the problem with finding real live friends, right? You can't just turn them off. They have drama or needs or low social skills. Or they won't go home when you want them to, so you can't bring them to your place. Or they don't pick up after themselves or clean their bathrooms, so you don't want to go over there." Amber shook her head. "People are complicated."

"I'm sorry, I have a hard time believing it's tough for you to find friends," Jason pressed, nudging her with his shoulder. "You're too awesome."

Her smile faded a bit, though not because the sentiment displeased her. "You'd be surprised," she said. "Besides, even if it's not a problem with me, often enough it's a problem with them. And then I wonder if I'm just being a bitch, or if no, I really shouldn't put up with them... it's tough to find people I like who like me." She gave a little shrug. "I like you."

Shit. I shouldn't have said that. Now he really is gonna kiss me.

Damn. That's a signal, bro. You gotta go for that. Don't be a pussy. "I like you, too," Jason said, ignoring the childish voice in his head. It might have been dead-on, but he saw the slight, sudden flinch in her eyes. "You're about the coolest woman I've ever met."

Amber blushed. She fought her smile, holding it down to just a smirk, and opted to back out of the danger zone. "We both know that's not true."

"Oh, you think I'm just throwing out random flattery?"

"What about your friend, Lorelei?"

Her bid to reduce the tension worked; Jason rolled his eyes, turning toward her but scooting back on the futon to lean against the armrest. Amber did the same, cutting the volume off on the console.

"That's a special case, there," Jason said. "I mean I don't want to sound like I'm into making crass comparisons or anything."

"It's okay," Amber assured him. "Believe me, I get that she's not just a random college gal or anything. She's not even in college at all, anymore, is she?"

"No. Nah, she's just slummin' it with us. Hell, I don't even know if she ever went to a college. Probably. I dunno."

"She makes quite an impression, though."

"Yeah, she does. Makes you feel like you're the only person in the room that matters when she talks to you, right?" Jason asked. "Only if you hang out with her long enough, you realize she does that with everybody. At least, everybody she puts any effort or interest into."

"Well, you guys all grew up with her boyfriend. It stands to reason she'd want to get along with you."

"Sure, but she doesn't have to come play pool with us while he's busy. I mean that's how you know when someone really wants to be friends, right? They initiate hang-outs rather than making you do all the work."

Amber smiled wistfully. "Must be nice."

"I'd have to have your phone number or your email to do any initiating," he suggested.

She patted around the coat hanging off the side of the futon to find a pen. Then she scribbled the numbers and letters onto the first random receipt within reach.

Score, Jason thought.

She offered it to him, then snatched it up out of his reach and held it high. "Do not—do *not* start playing 'maybe I should wait two days before I call so I don't look desperate' bullshit with me," she said. "I'm not into that." He nodded. She lowered the paper, then snatched it up again as he reached. "And don't just hang up on my voicemail."

"Fuck, what am I, a dolphin in a waterpark?" he chuckled, snatching the slip of paper from her hand.

"Okay, so what's the deal with them, though?"

"Them who?"

"Them. I get that Lorelei's like the cool older woman you guys all hang out with—and I like your friends, by the way—but I didn't really get to meet Alex. He was feeling crappy when he showed up, right? But what's their story?"

Jason paused. Amber noticed. *He knows,* she thought, suddenly feeling a pit in her stomach. *He knows I'm not supposed to remember.* She kept up her comfortable, mildly curious expression.

"Uh. Hrm. I'm gonna be honest and say I'm not sure what to say here, 'cuz Lorelei's like, kind of private, y'know?" he fumbled.

"Lorelei said I'd have to earn this story," Amber noted.

"Kind of, yeah, but I should let Lorelei tell it," Jason said, adding silently, *because she's a way better liar than I am and Alex would probably fuck it up worse than I would.* "Like I said. Kinda private."

"Well, she was open enough to mention their other girlfriend," Amber grinned. "It's none of my business, I know, but that's still curious, isn't it?"

"Hey, it's not exactly unheard of," he reminded her dryly.

"Yeah, but your thing with those girls lasted what? Two weeks? And were they into each other?"

"Mostly just for kicks, I think. Not seriously. Lorelei and Rachel are for real."

"That's like every guy's dream, isn't it?"

Jason shrugged. "Yes and no, I guess. Maybe. Depends. Plenty of drama to go with it. Don't go judging someone's life when all you get to see is the high-light reel, right? I forget who first said that, but there you go."

"That's kind of interesting," Amber mused. She saw a curious look on Jason's face as her thoughts trailed off. "But you wouldn't want that?"

"I'm sayin' it ain't for everyone, and you shouldn't presume it's all porn and roses," Jason said. "And no. Probably not me."

"Not again, anyway." She grinned widely. "I still like Drew's term. 'Adventures in Britneyland.'"

Jason groaned loudly. "Okay, do not judge me on that."

"But I can still judge other people, right?"

He conceded that one with a nod. "Maybe not the women, but Alex is kind of a tramp, yeah. You go ahead and judge him all you want. We all do."

"Heh. Wow. Lorelei's ex-boyfriends must kick themselves now, huh?"

"Oh, I dunno," Jason said, his eyes widening knowingly. "Can't imagine it ever ended well from the perspective of any of her previous guys."

⸻

"SHE *FUCKED* 'IM TO *DEATH*. KNOWWHATI'MSAYIN'?"

"No," Agent Keeley answered, "I don't know what you're saying. At all."

The skinny, blond convict thumped his hands down on the black table. "I'm sayin' she took my homie up to his place an' fucked 'im 'til the motherfucker *died*, man. Damn. Shit ain't complicated. Just banged away on him 'til he ain't got nothin' left in 'im."

"Mister Koblitz," Keeley said, making an effort of will not to slap the pale-skinned moron across from him, "do you have any evidence of that? Any way to prove that at all?"

"Nah, man. Shit. What evidence would there be? Motherfucker probably died naked on his bed with a big fuckin' clown-face smile, that ain't evidence enough? Can't someone do some CSI shit on his dick? Oh, no, probably too late for that, and nobody cares when a brother from the 'hood dies under mysterious bullshit, right? No bullets, no crime?"

"Mr. Koblitz, did you actually see this woman during or after your fight in the parking lot?"

"No. No, man, that's what I'm tellin' you. We just grabbed Carlisle an' the underwear salesgirl an' then there was the fight an' you've read about all that already. Only other bitch we ran into was the blonde that knocked me out. I still say she must've been holdin' a brick or somethin'."

"So you don't know her name?"

"No. You don't see it in the police reports, do you? Any of the legal papers? I read all that shit after I got here. I picked up a dictionary an' all my papers an' started readin' 'em like Malcom X an' shit, and ain't nowhere in 'em does that chick's name show up. Man, I still don't even know what it is. Now you wanna tell me that ain't suspicious?"

"Not if she wasn't part of the crime or one of its victims," Keeley shrugged. "She was not a direct witness. She saw nothing and had nothing to report."

"But she was *there*, man!" Tony snapped, slamming his hands down on the table again. "She was still a part of this! You tell me how a half-dozen cops an' the prosecuting attorney just ignore that shit! Like they ignored Damon getting fuck-murdered!"

"Mr. Koblitz," Agent Hauser grumbled, "in your altercation with Alex Carlisle, would you say he demonstrated great fighting skill? You said he was unarmed. You had him outnumbered. Neither you nor your associates are smaller than he is. Did he seem to be trained for combat?"

"No," Tony fumed. "He didn't know no kung fu or boxing or any of that other bullshit. He didn't throw a punch like a girl or nothin', but it wasn't like he went all Jackie Chan on us. It was just a street fight. He suckered us an' the girl kept messin' with me, but mostly it just turned into a mess."

"And then the blonde showed up, and knocked you out—"

"Yeah, with a brick or somethin'—"

"—and you woke up in police custody. You never saw any of them again nor had any contact since, correct?"

"Yeah, man."

"And the same goes for your associates?"

Tony's frown turned sullen. "Yeah, man," he repeated. "Far as I know."

"Damon Curtis?" Hauser asked, writing it down. "Died this past New Years'? Thank you. We'll look into it. Mr. Koblitz, if any of this leads to a trial, are you ready to testify that this woman was the last person seen with Curtis before his death? Okay. Mr. Koblitz, one last question: all of your observation of this woman took place during the evening, correct? You never saw her during the daytime?"

Koblitz made a face. "What, you think my eyes aren't so good?"

"It's important to establish a pattern of behavior is all."

He gave it a little thought. "Yeah, it was already nighttime when shit started with the whole mall thing. An' the New Years' party. It was daylight while she was fuckin' Damon, though."

"But you didn't actually see her during those times?"

"I heard her," asserted Koblitz, "but naw, man, I ain't bargin' in on a dude when he's tappin' ass."

"Thank you." Hauser stood. Keeley rose with him.

"Hey, so what do I get out of this?" Tony asked. "They told me this would get me some good behavior type points!"

"We'll be in touch," Hauser said. He knocked on the door to be let out by the guard. The agents ignored Tony's demands as they walked away.

"That doesn't tell us much," grumbled Keeley.

"It's more than we had before we walked in. His statements are consistent with what he said after his arrest. We'll pull all the case files and have Lanier look up this Curtis guy. My bet is there was no autopsy, so there's no telling how much blood he had in his body when he was found."

Keeley shrugged, then blinked and looked back at the closed door to the prison conference room. "So you're taking him seriously?"

"I think he's a pinhead, but he saw what he saw. Who'd make that shit up? The corpses seduce their victims all the time, and that involves sex often enough. Look, if we see this Lorelei woman out and about in the sunlight, that'll eliminate the possibility. Until then we keep an open mind about what she really is. I just hope we can pick up on Carlisle's trail today. Mighty convenient moving out of his mom's home without changing a single address in any of his files."

"Well, it usually takes me awhile to get around to it," Keeley shrugged. "Can't call it that suspicious."

"You don't live with a woman who doesn't even exist," snorted Hauser.

"I've got faith in our people," Keeley smiled. "They'll find him."

"SOMEDAY, all this stuff we've done will come out into public light, and we're all going to look horrible for it." There had been a time, back when Matt Lanier first joined the FBI, when he looked forward to not sitting at a desk staring at computer screens all day. Now he got to stare at a computer screen while sitting in the back of a car. He wondered if he could call that progress.

"Only to some people," Colleen shrugged. She sat at the wheel, marveling at how much trouble people here had in driving on wet roads when this was allegedly one of the wettest places in the nation. "We play a lot fairer than the guys going after the terrorists. I figure when it all hits the fan, most people will wonder why we ever bothered to get search warrants."

"Yeah, all from the same judge," muttered Matt. "I mean we got this one in less than five minutes."

"We're passing the college on the left here," said Doug Bridger, watching the map on his phone from the shotgun seat. "Pull off the freeway and be ready to make a left." He leaned back in his seat, tilting his head over his left shoulder. "So what did he check out of the library again?"

"Couple psych books on dreams and dream control, looks like," Matt answered. He scrolled through Carlisle's school computer account. "Looks like he downloaded some journal articles on that recently, too. But I'm looking at his transcripts and his schedule and it doesn't sound relevant to his classes."

"We'll be lucky if he's still on campus by the time we get there," grumbled Colleen. She honked twice as she exited the freeway and pulled onto the surface street. "God, these fucking drivers..."

They knew it was a longshot when they piled into the car. Carlisle spent most of the day completely off their radar. Only in the late afternoon did he turn up on any of Matt's open trace programs. He had already logged off before they made it to the campus. Hope of picking up his trail dimmed with each passing minute.

"Colleen, there!" barked Doug, pointing to the road up ahead. "Coming toward us, black motorcycle, leather jacket."

"Does it match the—shit, does it match the plates? Dammit!" Colleen didn't wait for a reply. She cut off the driver on her left to shoot into the turn lane.

Matt sat up in his seat and looked as the bike cruised past. "ZTN-123, that's our boy," he announced. "Doesn't look—ulp!" Matt threw his arm out as Colleen executed a sharp U-turn. Horns honked all around her, but she ignored them all. "Jesus, you don't fuck around."

"Secret Service defensive driving school, buddy," Colleen grinned, quickly bringing the car to a smooth pace in pursuit of Carlisle. "Counterintel division puts you through all kinds of fun training."

"Ssssooo," Doug ventured, "won't we catch his attention by driving this aggressively behind him?"

"Nah, I'm slowing down already, see?" Colleen assured him. She did not, in fact, slow down by any measure that either of her companions could notice. "This is a bland car. It's getting close to rush hour and everyone else in this town drives like an asshole, too. We'll be fine. Still can't figure out why everyone acts like the speed limit means something around here, though," she grumbled.

Doug stole a glance over his shoulder at Matt, who gave a little shrug. "She's from LA," he explained.

Minutes later, their quarry arrived at his destination. Colleen passed him by as he pulled into the garage of a motorcycle repair shop, cursing her luck. "Dammit, he might be putting the bike in for repairs," she muttered. "Doug, jump out here at the curb and pull out your phone."

"Huh?" Doug asked.

"Jump! Call me and I'll explain! Go!" She hit the brakes at the corner. The agent scrambled out of the car as instructed, and an instant later Colleen pulled away again and turned up the block.

Without looking, she pulled her phone from her jacket and tossed it back to Matt. He'd still been looking back toward Doug; the phone thumped against his chest, bounced off his laptop and fell onto the floor. "Grab it, he's gonna call," she said.

"What—Colleen, what the hell—?"

"I'm not gonna talk on my phone and drive at the same time," Colleen said. "Seriously, don't you know how dangerous that is?" She glanced in the mirror, allowing herself an amused smile once she saw Matt busily fishing for her phone as it rang.

Finally getting hold of the thing, Matt sat upright again and answered the call. "Doug, you're on speakerphone," he announced, holding it toward Colleen.

"Colleen, can you hear me?" Doug's voice asked. "What the hell?"

"Doug, are you watching the shop?"

"Uh—yeah."

"Okay. Can you see Carlisle inside the building?"

"Um... no?"

"Fine. Doug, I want you to take off your jacket and your tie, right now."

"Why?"

"Hold on. Matt, see if you can find a list of bus stops nearby."

"Colleen," Doug pressed, "where the hell are you going?"

"Right now I'm looking for a parking spot. There weren't any on that street. Doug, take off your jacket and tie. Watch the motorcycle shop to see if Carlisle leaves on his bike or if anyone picks him up. Otherwise you might have to follow him on foot and tell us what bus stop he goes to."

"...'kay, why am I taking my jacket and tie off?"

"So you can put them back on later if you have to tail him on a bus or on foot. Right now he'll just see a guy in a blue shirt. This way you can be a guy in a full suit later. And put your sunglasses on."

"What sunglasses?"

"What kind of FBI guy doesn't always have sunglasses?" Colleen asked. She saw Matt's head bowed in his task. Again, she allowed herself a smile.

"What am I supposed to do about my weapon and my holster?"

"Wrap 'em up in your jacket, silly!"

The phone let out a plaintive tone. "It's Hauser," said Matt.

"Speakerphone, conference call it," Colleen instructed She found a parking spot half a block back from where she'd left Doug.

"Joe, can you hear us?" asked Matt.

"What's going on?" Hauser asked.

"Carlisle came up on Matt's radar," Colleen explained. "I'm teaching the boys how to run a tail."

"How's it going?"

She sat up in her seat, looking out over the other cars. Doug held his phone up, pretending to be lost and looking for directions. "They've got some promise."

"Colleen," Matt murmured, "we can see everything from here, we could pick him up—"

"Ssssshhh," she replied. "Let him learn."

"Shit," Doug grunted, "he's out of there already, coming my way. He doesn't have his helmet, so I think he's—"

"Doug, shut up and play dumb!" Colleen hissed. The line went silent. She watched as Alex jogged across the street, walked straight past Doug and ducked into another storefront. "What is that?"

"It's a florist shop," Doug said. He fell silent. One minute stretched into the next. "He's picking up two bouquets of roses," Doug observed. "What's a guy get for buying his girl two bouquets?"

"Such *lovely* breasts," Amber taunted, revealing them with a flirtatious smile. "Firm. Plump. Healthy." She tossed the package down onto Jason's kitchen counter. Then she opened his refrigerator and drew forth a small cardboard carton. "*Huevos*," she said in her best telenovia pout. "We ladies like a man with *huevos*."

"That's a great accent," smiled Jason. "You took Spanish?"

"Always wanted to move to California," Amber smiled, rising again and closing his 'fridge with her foot. "Had to take one language or another. Seemed like the thing to do."

"Anything else we need?"

"One thing," she breathed, then threw herself up against the refrigerator as if she loved it, staring at him, sliding one hand up its smooth, solid front, and grabbed the box of corn flakes sitting at its top. "There's just no way to make corn flakes sexy," she cooed, managing to stay in character for roughly two seconds more until she couldn't help but laugh.

Jason shook his head. "I'm impressed."

"Me, too. I've never seen a casserole dish in a bachelor pad. Pretty fancy for a college boy."

"It came with the set," he said. "Not like it's quality."

"You're living on your own. It's a step up from most guys." She put the package of chicken on the cutting board, pulled his sole kitchen knife from its holder and slid them over to him, along with a suspicious grin. "Or is this all just more burdensome college debt?"

"No, tuition and books and all that are college debt. I got some scholarships, but nothing like a full ride. The apartment is, uh..." His words faltered. She said nothing in the silence, waiting quietly as she went about her end of preparations for cooking dinner. Eventually her eyebrows rose, wordlessly encouraging him to finish his sentence. "I guess you could call it inheritance money?"

"I'm sorry to hear that."

He set to trimming the chicken. "Wasn't anyone close at all. Kind of a— well. Anyway. Yeah. Less said about it the better."

"You don't have to talk about anything you don't want to talk about," Amber assured him with just the right tone.

"Kinda promised I wouldn't," Jason said. "I don't want to give the wrong impression."

"Don't trust me, huh?" Amber smirked.

"If you don't see me keep my word with other people, why would you expect me to keep quiet when you trust me with something?"

She couldn't fault his logic. "You've got me there," she said. "I mean it, though. I'm not trying to pry. Sorry if it seems that way." She felt like apologizing for lying about that, too, but that wasn't exactly in the cards.

Silence crept in between them. Amber ran the chicken through the beaten eggs, then rolled it in crushed cornflakes and set it in the casserole dish.

"Does this feel awkward all of the sudden?" Jason asked after rinsing his hands off.

Yes. Absolutely. You don't even know. "What do you mean?"

"Well, it's just..." He waited for her to look up at him again. Then he leaned in, saw her eyes widen as she realized what was about to happen, and continued on until their lips met.

Her eyes closed. He was gentle. Soft. Sweet. His hand on her shoulder didn't squeeze or hold firm or do anything except offer a reassuring point of reference when every other sound and sight of the world fell away until there was nothing but a first kiss.

He wasn't her first. She dated in college and afterward. Yet she hadn't gotten to a point where first kisses were ever casual. She let his lips linger, and kissed back, and if her lips were timid on his they still didn't pull away.

Amber's eyes fluttered open only a breath before his. They stared quietly. She saw a confidence in his smile that hadn't been there before. "I had to clear that up," he said.

One corner of her mouth spread out away from the other. "Not the moment I thought you'd pick."

"I didn't want you to feel cornered or trapped." His hand slid down her shoulder, then her side, and finally fell away. "Plus if you run away screaming now all I need to do is put the dish in the oven."

Amber let out a snorting laugh, covered her face in instant embarrassment, peeked at him through her fingers and laughed again. Jason took it upon himself to open the oven and slide the dish inside. "Man, check me out. I'm domestic *and* suave," he said.

The stupid, bashful grin on her face wouldn't go away. Not when she reminded herself that they were five critical years apart instead of the two she claimed as part of her cover. Nor when she reminded herself that she was, indeed, here undercover.

She felt guilty about that, and worried, but it all seemed far away, and none of it diminished her smile.

"How long does this need to go?" he asked.

"About twenty minutes," she replied. "Maybe twenty-five."

"What do we do in the meantime, then?"

Amber knew there were a hundred things wrong with this. She couldn't let this go too far. Whatever the ambiguity in her instructions, there was something very wrong in initiating all this.

A small part of her brain pointed out that she hadn't initiated it at all. Jason did that. Adrift in a storm of concerns hidden behind a shy smile, Amber said, "I dunno. Got any ideas?"

"I've got a pretty comfortable couch," he suggested, slipping his hand in hers.

She didn't initiate that. She wouldn't initiate what she knew would come next, either. "Okay," she said.

UNEMPLOYMENT STILL DIDN'T SIT WELL with Alex, but he couldn't claim that having a weekday off from school and work had no advantages. His long and torrid morning at home with Lorelei made for a great start to his day, but eventually he had to come up for air. There were matters to attend to and a world beyond their apartment.

He got his hair cut by an old barber who complained about liberals and taxes. Rode over to the college for a few hours at the library, mindfully doing all he could to avoid female attention. Dropped off his motorcycle for overdue maintenance. Hit a florist's shop on the way home for two bouquets of roses.

Boarding the bus, Alex had to shuffle his bundles around to pay the fare. "You in that much trouble with your woman you need two bouquets?" smirked the bus driver.

Alex smiled back, "I'd be in trouble if I brought home roses for only one of 'em."

Eventually he gave up his seat for an elderly man, again having to rearrange his burdens to make room as he stood with many other commuters. The flowers naturally caught wandering eyes. Alex took it in stride. For all its oddities, Alex would never claim his domestic life was anything less than awesome. Far from tranquil, to be sure, but definitely awesome. *Hell yeah, I need two bouquets to get the job done*, he thought with a grin. He had a great deal to be thankful for, and never forgot it.

Fumbling for his keys outside the door to the apartment after the long elevator ride, Alex heard laughter from within. Several voices, all of them female. He paused. One of them sounded like Lorelei. The others didn't sound like Rachel.

She hadn't mentioned any plans for company before he left. Several scenarios and possibilities ran through his mind. Lorelei knew plenty of people outside his social circle, and she could charm virtually anyone at the drop of a hat, but thus far Lorelei seemed content—even preferred—to restrict the invitations to their home to Alex's tight group of friends from high school.

He carefully balanced his pair of bouquets in his left arm and unlocked the door, which refused to open quietly.

"Alex," he heard Lorelei call, "I'm glad you're home. Come join us." The other voices fell silent. He shut the door behind him, threw the deadbolt, and walked in toward the open living room.

Lounging on the couches with wine glasses in their hands were Lorelei and her guests. The couches were arranged in an "L," with one of them facing directly away from him, yet he recognized the occupants. His heart stopped.

Sitting by herself on one couch, Molly looked up at him with a grin. The fire engine red color of her lipstick matched her short hair and contrasted with the dark colors of her torn-up jeans and VNV Nation t-shirt. Beside Lorelei on the other couch sat Onyx. Her curly black locks obscured her face from his view at first, but she slowly turned her head to regard him with sharp blue eyes and an arching eyebrow that spoke volumes.

"Oh," Alex blinked. "Hi."

"Nice flowers," Onyx said before turning back away from him.

"I didn't—"

"Very thoughtful of you," Lorelei said. "I was afraid you hadn't gotten my text about inviting Molly and Onyx over."

"Nice save," Molly murmured into her wine.

"Hush, you," Lorelei replied under her breath without the slightest break in her smile.

Alex just bit his tongue. *I should've bought four bouquets*, he thought. *Wait. No. That would've been stupid. And I'd still feel like a jackass.* He opted to play it straight. "I forgot to turn my phone back on after I left the library," he admitted.

Lorelei sighed a bit. "It's fine," Onyx told her quietly.

"I should. Um. Yeah," Alex mumbled, walking over to the kitchen counter to deposit the flowers.

"I'll take care of those later," Lorelei assured him.

He set his burdens down and took off his jacket before he walked over to face the music. "So I haven't seen either of you in a while."

"Yeah," Onyx said, her eyes on her glass. Alex tried not to be distracted by the sight of her, but it was hard. Had it not been for his crush on Molly and the girl in the black lacy dress and knee-high Doc Marten boots, his life would be nothing like this. Her next comment assured him that he was, as he suspected, in more than a little trouble with her: "Almost like you've been avoiding us."

Lorelei looked from one guest to the other. "You'd like to talk."

"Yeah," Molly nodded.

"Please?" Onyx asked, her tone friendly and polite toward Lorelei.

"Of course," Lorelei said. She scooped up a yellow legal pad covered in notes and a pen along with her wine. Her grace never waned as she slipped between the couches and the sleek glass coffee table to pass by Alex, pausing for a light kiss. "I'll be in the study," she said, then sauntered off.

He didn't know what to say. Molly looked him dead in the eyes, an expectant grin playing at her lips. Onyx kept her gaze on her wine glass. He tried to collect his thoughts as they all ran away from him. Alex grabbed onto the most honest one. It seemed important. "So are you two, um... y'know, protected?"

"Yes," answered Molly, "Lorelei warned us your magic fuck-me cooties might be on full blast right now."

From down the hall behind him, Alex heard an uncharacteristic snort of laughter just before Lorelei closed the door to the study. He came over to sit on the opposite end of Onyx's couch so he could see them both. Onyx turned and looked at him with eyes so expressionless that he couldn't help but project his guilt onto them.

"I'm sorry," he began.

"For what?" asked Onyx.

"For avoiding you."

"So I wasn't imagining it." Her disturbingly placid expression remained. "Why did you avoid us?"

"There's, um... okay, there's no way for me to explain this without feeling like I'm a complete asshole, so I just want to state that up front."

"I won't object to your feelings," Onyx deadpanned.

He winced. When his eyes opened, he looked to Molly. The hard-edged redhead looked on with mild amusement. The unshakeable loyalty between her and Onyx was evident as always.

That was, ultimately, why he stayed away. "You mean a lot to me. You both do. I've gotten worried that I'll cause problems for you or get between you."

"How would you come between us?" Onyx asked.

Suddenly everything seemed pretentious. He felt bad for even presuming Molly or Onyx liked him at all. "Did Lorelei say anything about this?"

"No. Lorelei invited us over to talk business," Onyx replied. "We barely talked about you at all."

"She said you'd want to handle this part yourself," Molly chimed in, "when you were up to it. But she figured that might be tonight since we're here."

Alex nodded. That fit. "Okay, well... you said you wanted to keep seeing me. Dating, more or less."

"Casually, yes," Onyx nodded.

"Both of you."

"Sure," conceded Molly.

He took a deep breath. "Full disclosure?"

"That was always my one condition," said Onyx.

"I haven't been ready to trust myself," Alex shrugged. "Onyx, it's like I told you originally—"

"Originally you didn't tell me at all, and I forgave you for that," she broke in smoothly. "But go on."

"Okay. Fair. Anyway, I just lost my job because my boss wanted to screw me and I wouldn't cooperate. I had two other co-workers get a lot more than just flirty with me before that happened. Not really sure how I turned 'em down, but I did. But I keep finding myself in these situations, and I just... I just don't know if it's smart to get involved with someone who's already involved in a relationship, y'know?"

Molly snickered. Onyx ignored it. "What about your 'friend,' Taylor? Are you still seeing her, too?"

"No," Alex shook his head. "We had one more hook-up after all the craziness, but she started seeing another guy and I didn't want to mess that up, so I've cooled it."

"By cutting off all contact?"

"No. Just by cooling it."

"Ah," Onyx nodded, "so what I'm hearing here is that you *can* control yourself. What was it you told me? 'I'd rather be your friend than your bed buddy. But I'd much rather be both.' I seem to recall doing everything I could to show I was down with all that." She paused to let that sink in. "Who else?"

He swallowed. "The, uh, real estate agent who sold Lorelei the condo. That actually went all the way."

"How'd that end up?" Onyx asked, and when he hesitated, she reminded him, "Full disclosure."

"Kind of ended up right where Molly's sitting now, actually," Alex blushed. Molly couldn't help but snicker at that. "It was practically a ridiculous scenario out of a porno movie. Cliché dialogue and everything. I think she's jumped clients before me, though."

Onyx smothered a laugh. The confession threatened her composure, but in the end her willpower triumphed. "So in the four weeks since you first agreed to keep seeing me, *and* Molly, and with all of us acknowledging and accepting that you had this..." she twirled her pinky at his groin, "little problem, you've had sex with *one* other woman, and *one* last fling with Taylor. I imagine your sex life here with Lorelei and Rachel is gonzo insane every night, right?"

He felt like he should qualify that somehow, but instead he just nodded. "Rachel doesn't come home every night," he elaborated, "but... yeah."

"Alex, without all this—if your life hadn't become an endless letter to Penthouse—would you want to date either of us?"

"Yes," he answered honestly. "You're amazing. Both of you. I just... like I said, sometimes women just get irrational with me. I didn't want that to happen to you."

"What, you don't know any guys who get irrational about attractive women?" Onyx frowned. "Alex, right now I would absolutely not fuck you, no matter what, and I'm not the least bit protected."

He blinked. "What do you mean?"

"I thought you might still be worried about that, so I wanted to test it out. You said it's not mind control, and you know what? You're right. It's nowhere near it. I'm not happy with you and it doesn't matter how sexy you might seem or how long you spent in bed with Lorelei last night or this morning."

"She mentioned you'd had the day off and we did the math," Molly put in, making a lewd gesture with her fingers.

"Hell, this is my third glass of wine and I'm not any nearer to jumping you. And so if that's the case," Onyx said, her head tilting somewhat, "I think the reverse must be true, too. Lorelei might make it easier, but you weren't a leper before she came along. You've doubtlessly learned a lot from her and your other flings that has nothing to do with curses. I think Dumbo can probably fly just fine without his magic feather."

She let that sink in, turning to refill her wineglass before she looked at him again. "You need to stop second-guessing Molly and I. We told you before. It's not about your cologne."

"So... you really want to give this another chance?"

"Were you really avoiding us just so you wouldn't cause us problems?" Molly countered. "Not because you were trying to make time for seeing any other floosies?"

Onyx blinked. "Did you just say 'floosies?'"

"Oh, shut up, we're not any better."

"It wasn't about the time," Alex shook his head.

"I'd like to talk directly to Lorelei and Rachel about it eventually, just for the sake of open communication and peace of mind," Onyx said. "But as it stands, they've already given their blessing, right?"

"Yes," Alex nodded. "They both take for granted that a closed relationship isn't really in the cards. I'm the one looking for a way to keep myself in check."

Onyx gave a little sidelong nod. "Here to help you, buddy." Then she gave him a warning look. "But not tonight, so don't get any ideas."

He couldn't help but grin. "You're sure?"

"You've still got time to serve out in the penalty box. I'll take my arousal out on her when we get home, thank you very much," she said, jerking her thumb at Molly, who smiled eagerly. Finally her expression softened. "We missed you. It's not just the flirting or whatever. We don't *have* other friends who know the truth about us. We even missed just having you in photography class. Molly and I talked this out a lot. We want a good guy we can get crazy with once in a while, and we like you. Can we not do this again?"

"I can't promise I won't try to seduce you both all the time," Alex warned with a grin. "In fact I can promise pretty much the opposite."

"Oh no. Not that."

Alex moved closer then, slipping his arms around her and holding her close. "No ideas tonight," she said into his shoulder, sniffling a bit. "Penalty box."

"Okay," Alex agreed, releasing her. "What about Molly? Can we—?"

"Yes!" Molly burst, playfully jumping onto his lap.

"No!" Onyx snapped, smacking her on the shoulder.

"Dammit!" Molly grumbled.

"Bad lesbian!" accused her girlfriend.

"We're not *entirely* lesbians," Molly grumbled further. She released her hold on him, but pointed to him, then to herself, and gave an openly lecherous "aw yeah" nod before she sat down beside her lover opposite Alex.

"So Lorelei said she didn't call you over to make this happen?" he asked.

"She seems like the type to have a layered agenda," Onyx mused.

"She is," Alex nodded. "It's true."

"She wanted to hire us for a job," Molly explained. "Security stuff. She told us about your stalker problem and how she wants to make sure this place safe for the two of you. Three of you. Whatever," she smirked. "I still wanna hang out with your angel sometime, if she's not pissed at us."

"I'm a little scared of how well you two might hit it off," Alex said. "What are you gonna do to the apartment?"

"Defenses and wards and stuff," Onyx asked. "We've done the same for our home, but we couldn't afford to do it all at once. Lorelei wants the whole nine yards."

"Well, thank you both," said Alex. "I wouldn't have thought of this."

"You're not a demon," shrugged Molly. "If we'd known you had trouble, we'd have come over to do it for free. Except for the materials, anyway."

"No, if this is work, it's work," Alex shook his head. The thought made him curious. "Um. What's the rate for magic, anyway? You guys have a union wage or something?"

"We sorta destroyed most of what amounted to a sorcerers' union around here, remember?" Onyx smirked. "Anyway, no. Your girlfriend suggested it was at least as valuable as hiring a good lawyer and offered comparable rates," she explained, and more or less gritted her teeth while glancing at Molly as she added, "and we're gonna shut up and take the money and say thank you."

"Is that a fair rate? I mean I can't imagine there are anywhere near as many, uh, sorcerers as there are lawyers."

"Witches, Alex," Molly corrected. "We're witches. And yeah, maybe we're not so common, but you know how when you close your eyes you see a whole big black nothing? That's about as much money as we've ever made on our magic. Lawyer money sounds pretty good to us."

"Especially as she's talking about keeping us on retainer."

"So... that's not gonna be weird, what with us--?"

"Alex, do you want your home security set up by two skilled witches?"

"Yes."

"You still hoping to sleep with them?"

"Yes."

"Then shut up," Onyx told him, and reached up to give him a brief, soft kiss on the lips. "Now. Full disclosure, okay?"

"Okay...?"

"Tell us about the dreams."

"Yup. Seventeenth floor. Not the penthouse, but close. I don't know what the market's like in this town, but no way did that go for less than three mil. Whoever decorated it has nice taste, too."

"Colleen, where the hell did you even go?"

She chuckled at the perfectly clear tone of exasperation over her earpiece. "I'm in the tower across the street," she said, keeping her camera up to her eyes. She stood at the window of a completely dark office, watching her subject with interest.

"Wait, most of those floors are dark!" Doug burst. "How did you get in there?"

"Stick with me, kid," Colleen said. "I'll teach you all you need to know."

"I've been *trying* to stick with you," he grumbled.

"Keep trying. I have faith."

"How'd you find which floor they're on? The resident entrance is locked up from the outside. We can't even get to a directory or the mailboxes."

"I just started looking and ignored the windows with the drapes pulled. I got lucky and found one with two brand new bouquets of roses on the kitchen counter."

"Anything interesting going on there?"

"Yeah," Colleen murmured. "He's got some very friendly female company, but neither of them are that Lorelei woman. I think they're about to leave, actually. I'm gonna stay up here for now and keep watch. You get ready to follow. We've got two girls: one redheaded punk-type, the other's some Goth princess. Can you tail them?"

"Uh. I don't think so, no."

"Why not?" Colleen asked urgently. "What's wrong?"

"I think I'm being towed."

She sighed. "Better handle it quick." She kept her eyes on the apartment through the camera lens, watching the two young women collect coats and shuffle through a lingering farewell. Carlisle and his guests were plainly fond of one another and flirty—and then joined by a third woman.

"Huh," Colleen murmured. She knew now what Amber had meant about Lorelei's physical appearance. A woman with that face, that body and even a shred of acting talent could make a fortune in Hollywood.

Carlisle seemed too young for her. That much was obvious. He was good looking, sure. In decent shape. But her posture, her elegant stride and that sleek blue dress just didn't match with the community college kid in jeans by her side.

The other two women accepted her chaste kisses on the cheek as they left. Colleen's eyebrow went up, though, as the redhead kissed Carlisle full on the mouth, and then her brow rose as far as it could when the other girl followed suit. He seemed only a little surprised. Were they the recipients of the roses?

No. No, they're leaving, she thought. *Nobody's even giving the roses a glance. He's holding the door for them, nice guy, we're all friends or maybe a little more than just friends here. Goodbye, goodbye, okay, now we're all alone and—wow.*

Colleen all but froze as she watched Carlisle and Lorelei slip together, wrap their arms around one another, and kiss like they'd been waiting for it for weeks. She watched them grow fiercer and hungrier. Lorelei took hold of his t-shirt at the neck and tore it right down the middle.

He wasn't brawny, but he was clearly fit and had great definition in those muscles. Though he didn't do any tearing, Carlisle wrenched Lorelei's dress off as if greedily unwrapping a present. He got just rough enough with her that an onlooker might grow concerned, but for the way Lorelei initiated this and the smile that grew under the locks of her hair as he shoved her against the wall, groping her freely and burying his face in her neck.

For all the strength she'd just shown, Lorelei all but hung from his shoulders. Colleen watched as Carlisle manhandled her against the door. One hand pushed her dress down over her shapely hips. The other seemed to claim one of her breasts, causing her to tilt her head back and breathe heavily. Colleen saw hints of a garter and stockings as the dress fell away, but her view wasn't perfect.

The phone vibrated. Colleen all but jumped. She blinked away her reverie and keyed the earpiece again. "I'm here," she said, and had to repeat it again because her voice shook.

"It's Hauser. What've we got?"

"I've got Carlisle and I'm pretty sure Lorelei. Long as they stay in the living room, anyway."

"Got some pictures?"

Pictures! Right! "Yeah, we're good," Colleen said. She captured a few more images of the two kissing, then remembered she needed facial shots. She waited for them to part and was soon rewarded.

She remembered the first time her husband looked at her like that.

"...gonna have a briefing as soon as we hear back from Maddox," Hauser said, or at least that's what she thought he said. Colleen remained somewhat distracted. Lorelei stepped back from Alex, gave Colleen a couple of good shots of her face... and then unfastened Carlisle's pants. Somewhere in the mix, he'd already lost his shoes.

"Boss, I gotta go," Colleen said, entirely because his voice was ruining the moment.

Carlisle's hands fell to Lorelei's hips. He pulled the drawstrings on her panties and let them fall at their feet. Lorelei said something flirtatious and taunting that Colleen couldn't read on her lips. They stared at one another for a heartbeat, and then Alex swept her around him to bend her over the couch. Once more, Lorelei grinned eagerly through what might otherwise have been much too rough. Colleen had just a brief full view of Alex from the front before he pressed in behind Lorelei. He claimed a fistful of her hair, drawing her back toward him.

Colleen couldn't see the moment of penetration from this angle, of course, but she could read it in the ecstasy on Lorelei's face. He had Lorelei wildly turned on.

She wasn't the only one.

Colleen pulled her cell phone from her pocket, keyed two buttons, and waited.

"Hello?"

"Don?" she asked.

"Hey, Colleen, how are you? I didn't expect to hear from you after it got past—"

"Don, I need you to do something for me. It's important. You love me, Don?"

"I—you know I do, Colleen. What's wrong?"

Colleen's mouth quivered as the couple across the street picked up the pace of their rutting. She couldn't hear anything, but she saw Lorelei cry out under the power of her possessive lover. Carlisle clearly had some technique. Hearing her husband's strong, confident voice only heightened Colleen's arousal. "I need you to get yourself up to Seattle for the weekend and get a hotel room."

"Are you okay? What happened?"

"I'm fine, Don, but I need you to do this for me."

"Okay, okay," her husband assured her, "I will, but what's wrong? I mean I guess the kids—"

"—are both out of middle school now and they can throw a party and burn the house to the ground for all I care right now, I need you up here," Colleen said breathlessly.

"Honey, what's wrong?"

"...I need a man, Don," she grinned. "I need one real bad."

DINNER PROVIDED ONLY the briefest of interruptions. It led to a cooling off period of coy smiles and good-natured frustration, but not a single spoken acknowledgement of what had preceded it. They came up with side dishes quickly. Sorted out their meals. Discussed the relative merits of different Starfleet captains. Cleaned up. Shared a questioning look.

And then found themselves intertwined on the futon again.

His hands drifted across her shoulders, her back and her sides. His fingers slipped under her shirt occasionally, or across her bared waist, but never more than that. Amber remained slightly more chaste, satisfied with this much and unwilling to encourage more for many reasons.

Jason's fingers eventually began to run through her hair, trailing gently across her scalp. She let out an approving purr.

"You have no idea how many points you've racked up today," she smiled. "Tonight. Whichever."

"What'd I do?" he asked innocently.

"It's what you haven't done."

"Oh. Huh. Y'know, I actually thought about goin' for your bra before, but I don't think I can manage that one-handed. My arm fell asleep about twenty minutes ago," he joked.

She let out a snicker. "Can't have that," she said, nudging him around until she lay on her back and he mostly on his side. "Problem with cuddling on a couch is there's usually only room for three arms at the most. Someone's always got the superfluous limb with nowhere to go."

"Seriously," he agreed, and kissed her again. "Lots of points?"

"Tons."

"Do I get a free level?"

"You one-upped the last player—um," she stopped herself, and blushed. "Sorry. Not bringing that up."

"Too late," Jason said, unperturbed. "Now I know you've made out with other guys. I'm gonna have to blog about that." Amber rolled her eyes and accepted his next kiss without objection. "That's all that stuff nobody's supposed to talk about on a first or second date but you know everyone actually does, right?"

"Pretty much," Amber said. Her fingers played with the collar of his shirt. "I'm not... ugh!" she grumbled and grinned in spite of herself. It was dangerous territory, but she was already here. The best she could do was run with it. *Use what you know*, Colleen had advised. *Use the truth when you can. It's easier to remember.*

"I've dated mostly Type-A overachiever guys," she explained. "Figured, 'Hey, I'm running with this crowd, no reason for me to settle for an average guy.' Shoe-ins for six-figure incomes, smart, good-looking... trouble is, they all know it. And they get used to it. Used to winning. The last guy... well, I don't wanna talk about the last guy, but the guy *before* him was his prep school valedictorian. And a star athlete. The whole deal.

"Pretty soon you realize there isn't a whole lot of room for you in the car when you've gotta squeeze into the shotgun seat with your boyfriend's ego," she mused. "Trophy girlfriends aren't always just smiles and a nice figure. Sometimes they're like me. Doesn't mean they're aren't trophies."

She looked up at Jason, still enjoying the fingers in her hair. "You didn't let me win at all those games. But you didn't freak out when I beat you."

"Uh... they're just games," Jason shrugged.

"You'd be surprised. It's not like that ever ended a relationship for me, but I can tell when it bothers a guy. You weren't bothered."

"I've got things I'm good at. You've got things you're good at. Maybe you're better than me at some of my talents. Maybe not. What's the big deal?"

"That's not something I'm used to. Not in anyone I find attractive."

"See, I knew there was a reason you wanted to hang out with me."

"Yes. Dork. I wouldn't be here on your futon otherwise. You aren't *average*," she said. "I've seen plenty of evidence to indicate otherwise."

"You're incredible."

"Don't—don't rush into anything," Amber cautioned him, placing her hand upon his chest without pushing him away. "I mean it."

"I'm trying to go slow," he assured her, and leaned in to kiss her again.

Once more, she allowed it. She kept allowing things. Kept justifying it all to herself. She had a job here, and things to be suspicious about... but he also seemed like such a genuinely great guy. Young for her, but special. Real. His easy smile, his lips, and his pressure-free way of drawing down her defenses muted the alarm bells that rang in her head.

She felt things click with Jason from the beginning. It was why she tried to take up the conversation with her boss this morning. She expected to be told to stick to the usual restrictions, and that would help her cool it. Conversely, had Hauser explicitly told her to take this approach, she'd have told him to go to hell, task force be damned... yet he gave only ambiguous bullshit, and left her to her own judgment.

Amber wouldn't make out with a guy on a couch unless she wanted to make out with him. Nothing else could justify this, and she knew it.

Her hand on Jason's chest fell away, hanging over the edge of the futon. For no reason at all, it swept underneath the frame and thunked into flat metal. "Hm."

"What?" he murmured.

It was hard to talk while they chewed on one another's lips, but she managed. "What's this?" she grinned.

"Um. Shoot. So I don't want to freak you out, but that's a gun case."

Her interest rose immediately. "Why would that freak me out?"

"Oh, you know. Some people just don't ever wanna be in a house with guns."

"Why do you have so many guns you need a case?"

"One's enough to need a case," he shrugged. "I'm safe. They're not loaded."

She grinned a little. "Show me."

"I wanna point out that I'm the guy and you're the girl and yet you're the one who wants to stop with the romantic make-out so you can look at my guns."

"I'm curious!" she protested. "Show me. What, you don't trust me?" She regretted it as soon as she said it. She felt even guiltier when it worked.

"Nah, it's cool, we're good," he said, rolling off her to slide the case out. "This stupid case didn't fit on any of the closet shelves, so it had to go out here."

Amber watched Jason roll in the combination and pop the locks. He opened up the lid to reveal a shotgun and pistol, along with a couple of boxes of bullets. A small cut-out space in the foam lining held some other loose bullets.

"So that's a 12-gauge, and that's a Beretta."

"Ninety-two, yeah," Amber murmured.

Jason blinked. "Uh. You know guns?"

She realized her flub and looked up at him with a bit of a shrug. She thought fast. "Dad liked guns. I liked knowing boy stuff. I've gone to the range a few times."

"Huh."

"Hey, why do some of your bullets have these red rings on them?" she asked, picking one up from the small compartment.

"Uh," Jason blinked, "no reason? Not that I know."

She let the lie slide. "I'm keeping your bullet," she announced, forcing a smile as she stuffed it in her pocket.

"That's... okay?" Jason frowned.

She matched his expression. "Something to bring back next time. The clock over there says I gotta get going," she said, gesturing over his shoulder. "Stuff to do before school tomorrow."

"Oh. Right. Sorry, didn't mean to keep you here too long."

She smiled at him. "I don't mind. I'd stay longer if I could. Like I said, I'll be back. I have to return things now."

His head twitched slightly. "You realize that's a live bullet, right?"

"I'll be careful with it," she nodded.

He shrugged and closed up his gun case. "Lemme grab my jacket."

Amber kept her hand in her pocket, reminding herself that the bullet didn't match either gun in the case... and that Jason, for all his good vibes and warm, easy manner, clearly had a lot to hide.

Then again, Amber had just let her undercover behavior with a person of interest get romantic. She couldn't even begin to come up with a way to tell her team about that. Jason and his friends knew things they simply couldn't begin to explain to others. Amber knew the feeling.

5

FREAKS HAVE MORE FUN

Everything aligned with his careful research. The boots fit. The black pants worked. The navy blue v-neck t-shirt matched several episodes. Most importantly, the leather coat was *perfect*—not cheap by his personal standards, but perfect. He'd get plenty of use out of it after tonight, though. He could wear that jacket every day and feel like a cheerful, goofy bad ass. It was pretty much all he'd ever wanted to be when he grew up.

Alex stood in his faded blue bathrobe looking over his costume pieces on the bed—all of it ordinary street clothes, but anyone who dug good sci-fi would recognize the ensemble immediately—and couldn't get the smile off his face. As a small child, Halloween bothered him. He didn't care for skeletons and ghosts and spiders. He didn't like being scared by monsters. He certainly didn't like demons.

Then he grew up and found a demon that he liked more than just about anyone else in the world.

"You're sure about this?" asked Lorelei, leaning on the doorframe in a purple silk robe. She could make even the hair clippers in her hand work as an accessory. "I cannot make your hair grow back if you change your mind. My magic has limits."

"I think it'll be fine," Alex nodded. "You have a number four on there, right?"

"Yes, love," she smiled coolly, "just like the fan club website said."

He paused. This costume plan pre-dated their relationship. The coat had hung in his closet since summer. "You find this amusing, don't you?" he chuckled.

Lorelei shrugged. "Only a little. The clothes look good on you. And no, I'm not saying that to make you feel better. At least I don't have to talk you out of wearing a bow tie or a suit with sneakers like the other versions."

"Thank you," he said.

"For what?"

"Helping. Being with me. Everything."

His lover's smile turned sinister. She stepped forward, taking him by the collar of his bathrobe and buzzing the clippers under his neck menacingly. "Happy birthday, lover."

"Okay, let's get this over with," he laughed. "I'll need a shower and you need to get ready and whatever."

"Don't worry about me. I'll change once we're there," Lorelei assured him.

His phone buzzed before they got to the kitchen, where a barstool, towel and scissors awaited. Alex pulled the phone from his pocket to look at the message.

"Costume fail," it read. "Gonna b l8 if I'm lucky. Date will b here in less than 60. So fucked."

"What is it?" Lorelei asked, noting the concern on Alex's face.

"It's Jason," he mumbled, hitting the speed dial. "Something's wrong with his costume, I guess." He waited. "Jason, what's up?"

"Holy shit, dude," Jason answered breathlessly. "There was fucking bleach in the washing machine and I didn't even know."

"What?"

"No, seriously. Some other stupid tenant in the building was halfway set to do her wash and then walked out of the laundry room when she heard her kid cryin' and left the machine loaded with bleach. I didn't even know 'til like just now."

"You were washing your costume just now?" Alex frowned.

"No, like an hour ago! I've been freakin' out trying to think of something since then! Dude, I am so screwed. Amber's comin' over in like an hour, and—"

"Jason. Chill. It's okay."

"No, it isn't, Alex!" Jason snapped. "I finally got something real going on with a girl and I've fucked up the first real date before it's even on! What the hell am I gonna do to find a costume now? It's Halloween and the sun's down already. The only thing I'm gonna find at a store now is whatever stupid gorilla suit nobody else wanted."

Alex hardly even heard the last words. His mind raced for a solution. Though generally quite bright, Jason had clearly placed too much pressure on himself to think through his options.

His eyes went to the bedroom. "Jason. Chill. I got this," he said. "Sit tight. I'm comin' over. I've got a costume for you."

Lorelei stood beside him, understanding his intent instantly. Her expression softened with a slight shake of her head.

"What, you've just got spare costumes layin' around in your fucking apartment?"

"Well, yeah," Alex replied. "You know my girlfriends are into some freaky shit. Hope you like wearing leather. I'm on my way." With that, he cut out the phone and turned his eyes to Lorelei. "I gotta go."

She nodded. "It's good that he called when he did, I suppose," she said, putting the clippers down on the counter.

"Yeah," Alex agreed. He headed to the bedroom, stopped, turned and grabbed the clippers. "I've got an hour," he declared.

"This is the girliest shit we have ever done," frowned Jason. "Ever."

Alex stood behind him in the cramped kitchen, his brow knit in concentration. He pressed the clippers to Jason's neck, shaving off more hair and hoping to God that this would turn out looking okay. "I don't remember us ever doing much girly shit," he muttered.

"I'm just sayin'. You don't breathe a word of this to Drew or Wade," said the skinny, shirtless young man in the cheap Ikea chair.

"Wouldn't dream of it," Alex assured him. "Last thing I wanna do is take responsibility for this fucked-up haircut."

Jason's eyes went wide. "Oh shit, you—"

"I'm kidding! I'm just kidding. It's fine."

"Taking you long enough."

"Yeah, well, now I understand why people go to school to learn to do this. You could be a little more patient."

Jason let out a tense breath. "Sorry," he said. "I'm sorry. I know you dropped everything to come help me out on your birthday. I'm just nervous about Amber."

"Nah, it's cool," Alex said. "Nobody wants to dress up as the Bleached Lantern. Rachel and Lorelei get me spun up all the time, too. I know how it is. Anyway, I only got to meet her for like two minutes after I had a flashback. I kinda don't know a lot yet. How serious have you gotten?"

"I dunno. I'm serious about liking her. Hung out with her almost every day since we met. I mean, she says she doesn't want to jump into anything serious right now 'cause she's still burnt from her last relationship, but then she initiates the make-outs just as much as I do."

Alex stepped in front of Jason to check his sideburns one more time. "So you're at the making out stage just a few days in? That sounds like progress."

"Oh, that's rich, coming from you," Jason said. Then he blinked, and his eyes focused on his friend's. "Dude!"

"What?"

"*Seriously* girly shit! What, aren't we supposed to share some ice cream now? Rent a fuckin' Sandra Bullock movie or something?"

Alex laughed. "Hey, you're the one with a wardrobe crisis. Anyway, I'm done. We're good. Brush all that hair off yourself and get dressed."

Jason nearly shot out of the chair. "Thank you," he grunted, his gratitude still overwhelmed by his tension. Alex paid it no mind.

His helmet and saddlebags sat on Jason's living room futon. Alex pulled off his shirt and stuffed it into the empty bag with a sigh, then bent over to remove his shoes. "Hey, you're gonna give me a ride, right?" he called to Jason. "I mean I don't want to be a fifth wheel for you two, but I don't want to have to get to the party and change there."

"Yeah, it's no big deal," Jason said. "At first I thought you were coming over with Lorelei, but it's cool. You can ride with us. We'll have room. Long as you don't mind leaving your bike here."

"No worries," Alex said. "I think Lorelei wants to wait on Rachel, anyway."

"Rachel's gonna be there? I figured she'd be out saving the city from freaky cultists or some bullshit tonight."

"She just said she wouldn't miss my birthday party for the world."

He was mostly dressed in the pajamas he'd bought on the way over when he heard the knock on the door. "I've got it," he called for Jason's benefit. Thinking little of his state of dress, Alex reached for the door and threw it open.

He'd never seen green fatigues and black web gear look so good. "Wow," he blinked. "I. Um. Wow."

Amber cocked her head. It was encased in a green helmet, complete with dents, scarred paint and black microphone piece. "Hi," she said. "Hey, you're Alex, right? We only met in passing the other night. I'm Amber." She slung her huge black sci-fi machinegun and offered her gloved hand.

"Right. Yeah, I'm Alex. Hi."

She grinned. He grinned back. Neither realized at first that they were staring.

Then Alex blinked away his reverie. "Wow, that's an awesome costume. Even the patches look cool. 'course now you're gonna have people quoting *Aliens* at you all night."

"Yeah. If it gets annoying, I'll just shoot 'em."

"Sounds like a plan," Alex chuckled. He looked back toward the apartment's bedroom. "Hey, Jason, your infantry support is here!"

Amber laughed as she slipped inside, coming closer to him than she needed. "I'm sorry, was this supposed to be a sleepover? I totally forgot my pajamas at home."

"No, no sleepover here. Not for me, anyway. Sorry," Alex replied, stepping back to allow her inside as he buttoned up his pajama shirt the rest of the way. He wasn't sure if Amber was staring or not, and gave it as little thought as he could. *Woah, boy. Jason's date. So off-limits.* "Just a sudden change of plans."

"Should I let you and Jason be alone?" she asked suggestively.

"Nah. He likes you better than me. I had a last-minute catastrophe and came rushing over." Alex pulled his bathrobe out of his saddlebags and threw it on. "I never really did get the hang of Thursdays."

"Hah! Now I get it," Amber smiled. "Nice literary choice. It just took me a second. Where's your towel?"

"Shit, I knew I forgot something important."

"Hey!" Jason said, walking in on the two. He had intended to show off, knowing he looked good, but stopped dead in his tracks. "Holy shit, Amber, that costume kicks ass!"

"Aw, thanks. Turns out I had a few things safely stored away after all. And look at you! Number Nine," Amber said immediately, her smile only brightening as she looked him over. "Very nice. Gosh, that leather coat is perfect. If I'd known you were both going so British, I'd have tried to come up with something to match."

"I like what you've got on now," Jason told her.

"Uh. Hey, Jason, I need you to rescue my costume one more time," Alex said as much for Amber's benefit as anything else. "You got a towel I can borrow?"

"YOU CAN'T JUST SLAP a bunch of gears on your old cowboy outfit and say it's steampunk," asserted Wade's critic. He had to shout to be heard over the music and the crowd, but that seemed reasonable to him. This was important.

"Oh, but buyin' BDUs an' a toy raygun makes you a space ranger or whatever y'all are?" laughed Wade. "Besides," he said, tugging on the bit of black leather and glass around his neck, "ah got mah goggles. Don't that make me legit?"

"Those are welder's goggles!"

"Yeah? And?" Wade shrugged. He couldn't be bothered to get upset about this. He also couldn't be bothered to be tactful. Spinning up nerds was far too funny.

"So those don't count!"

"They don't? That's not what the internet said." Wade took another sip of his drink. He'd have preferred it stronger, but at least they accepted his hand-stamp and his wristband as proof that he was over twenty-one, instead of checking his driver's license—which said, explicitly, that he wasn't legal just yet.

The space ranger's eyes lit up behind his thick glasses as if he'd hit paydirt. He raised his gloved finger to drive home his point. "So you went online to research but didn't notice that just gluing gears on it wasn't good enough?"

"Meh," Wade smiled. "Ah jus' didn't *care*. Anyway, if flyin' the steampunk flag correctly is so important to you, why aren't you doin' it?"

"I'm here with friends," answered the space trooper. "We've got a theme. We all come from the same legion of the Imperial Guard!"

"Aw, that's cool. Mah buddies an' ah got us a theme, too!"

Sensing a bad joke but unwilling to cede the issue yet, the other man asked, "Like what?"

"People who ain't gettin' spun up about unimportant shit," Wade said as if it were a great joke his debate partner would actually appreciate.

The bearded space trooper sputtered. "It's people like you that ruin sci-fi fandom!" he said before he turned and dove back into the dark crowd of costumes.

"The hell was that about?" asked a voice behind Wade. Drew appeared behind him dressed in a sharp black suit and sunglasses.

"Apparently ah'm ruinin' sci-fi, f'r everyone," Wade answered as he turned. Then he paused. "Drew," he asked, "izzat a phone number on your cup?"

"Huh? Oh, yeah," Drew nodded. "I guess it is."

A lithe "alien" in a black bikini and green body paint sauntered by Drew, reaching out her arm to trace around his shoulders and then throwing him a sultry look as she passed. Wade's amused but accusing glare remained.

"You wanna pick up girls?" Drew asked smugly. "Wear a suit to a nerd party."

Wade shook his head once more as the two set to weaving their way through the crowd. The Emerald City Halloween Ball had become a big event over its few short years, now to the point of renting out the convention space of a downtown hotel. Tickets were no longer cheap, nor were other little details like parking or coat checks. Yet for all the opportunistic price hikes, attendees to the event still felt like they got what they paid for.

The event sold out months in advance. Scalped tickets went for three figures. At those prices, Wade and Drew gave up on attending this year—until one of their newest friends learned of her lover's interest. Gaining tickets for the event had impressed all of Lorelei's friends; getting them put on the guest list to speed them through check-in and security went above and beyond their expectations.

They walked past store-bought ensembles, homemade costumes and serious cosplayers that put everyone around them to shame. Many times, they found themselves surrounded by space explorers, by sci-fi heroes and a great many aliens, all in keeping with the year's "Not of This Earth" theme. There were also plenty of people outside the theme: hookers and pimps, doctors, nurses, ninjas and cops.

A great many of the women at the ball fully embraced the racy freedoms of Halloween. Neither Drew nor Wade found anything wrong with that at all.

LORELEI OBSERVED the main entrance from a rooftop across the street. She listened and inhaled deeply as her eyes scanned the crowd. She planned in advance, taking numerous precautions before this point, but last minute assurances were still worthwhile. It was one thing to take chances. It was another to take them stupidly.

Had any demon claimed the venue as its own, the succubus would surely have suffered the pain of violating their territory. Anyone less powerful than Lorelei would have a hard time escaping her notice. Anyone more powerful would not likely bother to hide.

Seattle's supernatural population was simply not what it had been. Rachel's first order of business upon achieving Dominion over the city was to begin actively hunting any demon that dared show its face. The vampires and the most belligerent sorcerers—those who survived the recent conflicts, at least—had all either fled the city or gone to ground to evade fellow survivors. Werewolves detested crowds like this. Ghosts had similar problems with large numbers of the living. And if nothing else, so many mortals meant for a fair number of guardian angels on hand at any time—and Lorelei had a good connection there, too.

The night brightened around her as Rachel faded up through the rooftop. She seemed distracted. The tremor in her lips was quite obvious. For a brief moment, Lorelei grew concerned. Then Rachel stepped closer, and Lorelei recognized the look in the angel's eyes.

"Yes, love?" she asked.

"He's checking in now. He *reeks*, Lorelei," Rachel explained breathlessly. "He reeks of selflessness and friendship. HolyfuckingshitIwannafuckhim," the angel laughed, grabbing her lover by the arms and pulling her close. "If I had panties, they'd be on the floor already."

"He gave Jason his costume?"

"Yeah. On his birthday, too. I mean how sweet is that? Seriously, we need to drag him into a broom closet or something. He's just in a bathrobe and pajamas. It's not like getting him undressed is gonna be complicated."

Lorelei's lips spread with mild amusement. "I can see how this would arouse you madly," she mused.

"Pff. You don't."

"I do," Lorelei assured her.

Rachel made a face, but it faded quickly. "Lorelei," she said, "you know I'm not... it's not like I play favorites or—"

"Shh, love, I do not doubt us," Lorelei shook her head, stepping in to caress

Rachel's cheek. "What better time would there be for us to both dote on him than his birthday?"

Rachel let out another aroused breath past Lorelei's ear as the succubus lightly embraced her. "By dote you mean fuck him out of his mind, right?"

"We may drive him mad well before it gets to that, but he'll be grateful, I'm sure. Do you believe this place is safe?"

The angel flashed a naughty smile and nodded. "Coast looks clear to me," she confirmed. "Swung through the place twice. Plenty of everyday dirtbags around, but nothing we need to worry about."

"Then you feel you can go through with our plan?"

Rachel nodded again. "Yeah. I think I can hang around for most of the party. Never know if I might have to leave unexpectedly, but..." she shrugged. "I'm game."

Lorelei lifted the broad paper shopping bag. A set of fake white angel's wings peeked out from within. "Then let's get changed."

"How's he even know which one he's dancing with?"

"What?" Alex shouted over the music and the ambient noise of the crowd. It was hard enough to talk at the edge of the dance floor; conversation further in was even tougher.

"I said, how's he even know which girl he's dancing with?" Amber asked. She had to lean in a little closer. She didn't mind.

Alex peered through the crowd on the dance floor—one of several at the ball, but surely the largest—and made out the form of Drew, along with several women in various costumes. "Pretty sure he doesn't care," Alex chuckled. "They're probably just happy to find a guy who can dance."

"I know the feeling," smirked Jason. He had to stand close to the pair to hear and be heard. He also didn't want his date forgetting him. Jason had thought nothing of it while they were in the car on the way over. Amber seemed to have many questions for and about Alex during the drive, but he was the last of Jason's closest friends she had to meet. Unfortunately, once at the party she still stuck to Alex like glue.

Twenty minutes into their night at the Ball, Jason felt ready to face great, longstanding fears to keep his date's attention. "C'mon, Amber, I promise nobody's watching you," he said encouragingly, taking her hand. "I don't care how you dance. It's not like I'm wonderstud, either."

"No, wonderstud's out there with the Working Women of Aurora Boulevard," Alex chuckled, gesturing towards Drew. Several women in fishnets and big wigs competed to rope Drew in with their feather boas.

"I dunno, Jason," Amber replied. Her feet felt rooted to the floor. "I don't go out dancing a lot." *Or at all*, she corrected silently. *Ever.* "I'm happy to just hang out. Besides, we'll lose Alex."

"Oh, I'm good," Alex smiled. "Don't worry about me."

In a quieter setting, everyone would've heard the rumble of Jason's frustrated breath. Here it was thankfully masked by booming music. At least Alex didn't say or do anything to encourage her. "Amber," Jason said, stepping in closer, "you're not worried about what *I'm* gonna think, are you?"

"There's a correct answer to that and an honest answer."

"Listen. I don't care how you dance," he smiled. "I bet I'll look sillier out there than you will, anyway. I don't care if you've only got one move and you do it over and over again and I don't care if you lose the beat or just sway back and forth. I'd just like to dance with my date."

Amber bit her lip. She had more than one reason to stand her ground on this, but more than one reason to give as well. In her brain, a little girl left standing against the cafeteria wall at a middle school dance told Amber to quit being such a chicken. "You really don't care?"

"Not if you don't care how bad a dancer I am," Jason shrugged. "It's not like I do this a lot. But if you don't care and I don't care, what's to worry about?"

"Everybody else?" Amber asked.

Jason shook his head. "You're at a costume party," he said, and reached up to pull down the black visor on her helmet. "Nobody here knows who you are."

He couldn't hear her choke. The music was too loud. *Oh God, if you only knew*, she thought.

He took her hand. "Got anything else stopping you?"

"What if everyone points and laughs at me?"

"You've got a gun," Jason reminded her. "Just shoot everyone."

He saw the smile under the black-tinted visor. "Okay," she said, slinging her prop machinegun over her back.

Jason kept hold of her other hand, pulling her along as he stepped backward into the crowd. Naturally, he soon bumped into someone. He apologized, bumped into someone else, and laughed it off as he and his date got the hang of weaving through the crowd to create a little space for themselves.

Amber looked over her shoulder only once to find that Alex had already disappeared from view. It was bound to happen, but it frustrated her to lose her chance to talk more with him. Too many of the core questions of the investigation seemed to revolve around him and his older girlfriend to pass up any opportunity.

As she turned back, though, finding herself alone with her date amid a crowd of strangers, Amber set those troubles aside. The FBI had taught her focus. It had taught her to block out distractions and to manage different sources of stress. The investigation would have to wait. Her team wasn't there. Hauser wasn't there.

There was just Jason, and those smiling eyes, and her two left feet.

She swayed with him. Tried to find the beat. Felt silly. "I have no idea what I'm doing," she confessed.

"Me, neither," he said. Jason at least had his arms out a bit, and seemed to be picking his feet up off the floor as he moved. She'd have to try that.

Like he said, she could always just shoot anyone who laughed at her. For the first time in her life, she conceded that maybe the inflated self-esteem brought on by being armed wasn't entirely a bad thing.

ALONE IN THE CROWD, Alex moved off to make sure Jason had Amber to himself for a while. He could see why Jason liked her so much. She was smart, friendly, pretty... and the geek in him couldn't get over her sharp costume. That had to have been a real investment, unless she'd had a real job at some point and not just the small-time stuff most college students swung. He knew she was older, but not by how much.

She wasn't too much older to be into Jason, apparently. He wished his friend luck with that. He roamed around the outskirts of the dance floor, checking out the crowd and their costumes. Lorelei and Alex went dancing— or, more to the point, went to dancing classes for his benefit—several times, but the ballroom styles she preferred were a far cry from this sort of thing. None of the confidence and enjoyment Alex derived from those nights applied to this dance floor. He had complete sympathy with Amber. For that matter, he knew Jason wasn't much into it, either, but he was trying.

He contented himself with a few minutes of people-watching. The costumes were great. More than a few of the women would have been quite eye-catching in any situation, let alone Halloween.

Spotting Drew wasn't difficult at all, given the spectacle made of him. Drew caught sight of his friend, flashed a hand and a grin and then was roped back to the attention of his new ladyfriends. Wade was in there somewhere, but Alex caught only glimpses.

"So are you supposed to be Hugh Hefner in that?" someone asked.

"Yeah," added another voice, "where are your bitches? Or ain't you got none?"

Alex turned around. He found four guys in fake fur coats, huge hats and oversized sunglasses. Their bling stood proud. Their canes, clearly cheap costume pieces, all matched.

"No, it's from a book," Alex shook his head. He tugged on the towel over his shoulder. "I'm Arthur D—"

"Is that Will Smith wannabe a friend of yours?" one of the pimps asked, pointing out at the dance floor.

"Oh, he's not trying to be Will Smith," replied Alex. "The whole myth of the 'men in black' is older than those movies. That's where the original idea came fr—"

"He's looking to get his little metro ass kicked," another pimp warned.

Alex blinked. He looked out onto the dance floor again, and specifically at Drew's dance partners. They all seemed to be of the same general college age as the pimps in front of him. Then he took another look at the collection of pimps. "Wait, really?" he asked.

"Really what?"

He looked back and forth one more time. Very pretty women having a good time. Skinny, ratty-looking guys with peachfuzz facial hair looking put out over it. "I've seen this before," Alex said, and then it clicked. "Hey, do you guys go to U of O?"

The frowns deepened. "Why?"

Alex couldn't take this seriously at all. "I mean you see pretty girls hook up with douchey guys sometimes, but with a sample size like this—"

"What the fuck?"

"You're all from Eugene, aren't you?" Alex finished.

"Oh, you think you're fuckin' funny?"

"Well maybe a little. Look, why are you mad at him and not your dates? What sense does that make?"

"Who are you calling a douchebag, Hef?" another one of them asked. "I don't see you standing out here with your date. She run off with someone, too? Or did you even come here with anyone?"

Turned toward the gaggle of pimps as he was, Alex had his back to the dance floor. He was oblivious to the gradual change of mood among the crowd, or the shift in its density behind him. "What's wrong with coming stag? Seems to have worked out fine for him," Alex said, jerking his thumb over his shoulder. "Anyway, I told you before, I'm not Hugh Hefner. I'm Arthur De—okay, what?" he asked.

The pimps looked past him in awe. Two of them stood with their mouths agape. Alex turned around.

The crowd parted as dancers made way for the angel and demon walking across the floor. Men and women alike stared at the two winged women, distracted by their shapely bodies and scanty outfits.

The angel's wings and halo were plainly store-bought, but of good quality. Her tiny white skirt and top showed off a bare midriff and plenty of skin besides. The demoness wore even less than that, relying on a black leather bikini-style top, a loincloth and tall black boots to satisfy the barest requirements of public decency. She bore wings, horns and a tail that had to have been put together by a professional make-up artist. Her red body paint had to be a professional job, too.

A handful of guys in the hall knew better.

"Wow," Alex murmured. The distraction lasted only a moment for most of the crowd. Men and women turned their attention back to the music and to their dance partners, though stolen looks aplenty came from the dance floor.

Lorelei and Rachel smoothly leaned up against Alex, one on each side, and softly kissed his neck. "Happy birthday, lover," one or the other of them said. He couldn't track which. His arms came around their hips.

"You are an honest man forced to hide so much," said Lorelei. "The truth is we are not normal. Your life is not ordinary. Just for tonight—this of all nights —why not let down the pretense?"

"Don't worry if your ego swells a little tonight," Rachel grinned. "We think pretty highly of you, too."

Her words reminded him of his surroundings. He looked back to the pimps.

"I'm not Hugh Hefner," he said. "But I *am* a shallow, adolescent male fantasy. You guys have fun being cranky."

. . .

"I can't believe they did that," declared Jason.

"What do you mean?" Amber asked. "Do you know those two?" She had her arm on Jason's shoulder, with his hand on her waist, but their dancing faltered just like most of the rest of the crowd. They didn't get back to it quite as quickly.

"Yeah. That's Lorelei and Rachel."

"Really? Wow! Oh, wow," Amber blinked. Her mind went into overdrive. Both of her primary subjects were now present, along with their 'other girl-friend.' "That's some serious costume coordination."

"Yeah. Guess you could call it that," Jason mumbled. He'd seen demon horns before—right as they were pried off an enemy's head. Rachel wore fake wings and a toy halo, but he doubted Lorelei wore even a pinch of make-up.

"Should we go over and say hi?" asked Amber. She regretted it almost as soon as she said it. Two songs after Jason lured her out onto the floor, she only now loosening up and having fun. So was he. She had a job to do, but... "I mean I'm not in a hurry or anything, but if you want to?"

"Maybe we oughta leave 'em alone for a bit?" Jason suggested. "It's their first birthday together. They went to the trouble to make an entrance."

"Yeah, they did," grinned Amber. "Guess you're right. No sense rushing over there so you can drool, anyway."

"Hey, I'm not drooling!"

"You're not?"

"Not over them, anyway," he shrugged.

"Okay, stop," Amber told him. "You're making me self-conscious."

"You'll just have to get over that."

———

"Is this safe?" Alex asked, still happily occupied with a lover on each arm. "I'm not complaining, I just... um... wow." His words trailed off as lips came to both sides of his neck, nuzzling up under his ears.

"As safe as we'll ever be," Lorelei told him. Her hands roamed over his body, not quite lewdly but more than friendly enough to leave him trembling. Rachel did her part as well, though the angel was a little more direct with her touch. She had no shame about grabbing his ass.

Bound together through sorcery, both women enjoyed all the same physical pleasures he received. They draped themselves against him, making no effort at showing off for others but caring little for modesty, either. If envy consumed outside observers, none of the three cared.

He meant to say something, but lost it in the shudder of breath forced from him as Rachel's fingers ran through his hair. "It's your birthday, lover," Rachel whispered into his ear, blocking out all the music and the noise of the crowd. "You have to let us spoil you tonight."

"I have to?" he smiled.

Rachel turned in on him to bring her chest against his. "Spoiled rotten," she said as she kissed him.

As always, his worries crumbled at the touch of her lips. He felt energized, and awake, and happy. He felt loved.

Their lips parted. The music faded back into his ears, growing louder as the room around him grew dark once more. Vibrant, flashing lights in dozens of colors and a broad range of costumes created an exciting backdrop.

"Aren't angels supposed to lead men away from temptation?" Alex grinned.

"Hah! Fuck that noise," laughed Rachel. She backed into the dance floor, pulling him along by both hands. "I'm here to drag you into it with me."

Lorelei effortlessly stayed close behind. "I am with you. No one will notice anything inappropriate."

Not far into the dance floor, Rachel pulled herself up against Alex again. Her arms came around him. Her legs slid against his as she pulled herself into a slow, sensuous grind. Lorelei rested her arms against his back and laid her head against his shoulder. "Trust in us," she told him. "No one will notice."

"Notice wha—ohh," Alex sighed. Rachel opened his bathrobe and pressed her body against his, letting her hands roam freely under his pajamas. The buttons on his shirt didn't stay fastened long, nor did the drawstrings on his pants remain tied. Embraced both from the front and behind, Alex could do little but return the caresses and let the women have their way.

"We love you, Alex," Rachel grinned against him, her leg sliding down his and her breasts up against his chest. "We know what you live for. And we approve."

"We need this, Alex," Lorelei murmured. "All three of us. Now."

Rachel's fingernails scratched softly down his back, outlining the shape of Lorelei's body pressed against his. "I know what you did tonight," she breathed heavily, growing anxious and hungry right along with him. "Brotherly love.

Humility. You know how much that turns me on. You're a *very good boy*, Alex," she said with almost sinful delight.

"You're a very bad girl, Rachel," he countered.

"I know," she grinned. "There's gotta be a couple dozen other angels in here... and not one of them can see me doing this with you now."

She may as well have been giving him a lapdance. Alex felt her flesh slide across his. Lorelei's dextrous hands helped Rachel along, smoothly relieving her of her drawstring panties without the slightest disruption of their foreplay.

Rachel teased the head of his cock with her wet labia, sliding along his length as she purred and nibbled on his neck.

Lorelei's lips came against his ear again. "Be a good victim, love," she whispered with a teasing smile. "Just for now. Allow us to dote upon you. Tend to Rachel's passion, and to my hunger."

The music changed. The crowd danced. Shielded by Lorelei's enchantments, the three lovers found privacy within the mob. Casual glances revealed just another trio of dancing people, and nothing more.

Not a soul outside their embrace knew a thing as Alex lifted Rachel's thigh to his hip and slowly probed the wetness between her legs with his cock. Rachel's eyes fluttered and she gave off soft little breaths of gratitude and need as she hung from his shoulders. She was light as a feather against him.

He slipped his other hand along her opposite thigh and lifted that, too. Rachel moaned with joy as she slid fully onto him. She squeezed his hips with her thighs and ultimately hugged both Alex and Lorelei with her legs as she accepted him into herself.

Lorelei moaned with her. Her breath and voice against Alex's ear was as sensuous as a kiss. "Give in to your lust, Alex," she goaded him as he lifted Rachel and then brought her back down on himself again. "Embrace it as you embrace us. We belong to one another. Let yourself go this weekend."

Further moans overcame anything else she might've said. Alex took their words and actions to heart. He thrust into Rachel, holding her up, using her body for their mutual pleasure and drinking in the sounds of her joy. Lorelei's involvement restricted their movement slightly, serving to control their pace and prolong their coupling rather than obstructing it.

The music and the dancers carried on. Swirling colored lights and a thumping beat made for unique scenery, but for all the sensory input as one song blended into the next, Alex only paid attention to his partner's cues and the pleasures of her flesh.

"Yeah, lover," Rachel grunted. Her voice wavered as climax drew close for them both. "Hard. Unh. Hard as... you want. Oh. Take... me... oh!"

Their shared orgasm left them both trembling. Lorelei clung to Alex, shuddering as she experienced his pleasure and reveling in the renewal of her power as her victim indulged his lust. She helped him remain upright as he gave in to release.

Rachel slid down off him, but the three remained close. He felt his clothing again. Lorelei smoothly pulled his pants back into place, ensuring that no one —not even Alex himself—would sense anything out of the ordinary. His breathing returned to normal. Alex came back down to Earth with everyone else.

His arousal calmed but remained. He was the victim of a succubus. He always wanted more. At times that bothered him. Now, it seemed like a gift.

"It's your birthday," Rachel repeated as she leaned against his chest. "We know you're a horny bastard. We love that about you. Have fun with it tonight."

He felt Lorelei give him an extra squeeze. It reminded him of his bargain with his demon lover. Alex let out a happy breath. "How would I argue with that?"

"THE ONLY RATIONAL thing to do with the money is to buy ourselves out of debt. We can splurge later."

"Molly, you're preaching to the choir," said Onyx. She walked slightly ahead of her partner, eager to take advantage of the apparent lull at the security check station in the hallway.

"I'm just saying," Molly pressed, "I know there's a lot we could do. We made a lot of sacrifices to stop backsliding—"

"I agree," Onyx tried to interrupt.

"—but even so, we're still treading water on the stupid credit cards. We could kill that all now. We could put the money we're spending on that bullshit to better use, y'know?"

Onyx stopped in her tracks. The folds of her black and crimson Renaissance skirt whirled along with her as she spun around. Faced with the need for a costume and little time to put together anything elaborate, she decided to go for "sorceress" and festooned her RenFaire garb with pentagram jewelry. She even tied a fake newt to her belt. If she couldn't go with the theme, she figured, she'd go with the snark.

Molly, conversely, tackled the challenge of costuming with all the ingenuity borne of years of theatre experience. Small barnacles and starfish decorated the fishnet draped over her shoulders and hips, with a tattered but flattering black dress underneath. With a greenish hue to her exposed skin, she arrived at the party looking equally eerie and slinky.

"We're good," Onyx declared, biting down on her irritation. "Molly, I haven't gone shopping for fun in a year, because you're right. I haven't suggested we go out to dinner in all that time, either, because you're right. We didn't realize how tight things would get, but we've adjusted, and we're cool, and I'm comfortable with how we live. If we have to stick it out for a while longer, that's fine. I don't expect anything more. Okay?"

Holding her hands up in a gesture of peace, Molly also had to chomp down on her stressful reactions. Though happy-go-lucky about most things in life, financial issues got under her skin. "I'm sorry," she said, trying to let it go. "I just don't want to get carried away with having a little success."

"We talked about that already," Onyx reminded her.

"Yeah, I know. I wasn't thinking about it until we got here." Molly gestured to the costumed partygoers passing by them in different directions. "We haven't been able to spend money on anything fun in a long time."

"That's not true. We go out."

"Yeah, to cheap stuff," Molly rolled her eyes.

Onyx shook her head. "Spending money on it doesn't make it better." She heard her lover snort, and then sighed. "Okay, that's totally not true. But still. It's not like I haven't been happy, right? Or you? So we've been poor. Fuck it. Maybe that taught us discipline."

"It held us back," Molly countered.

"No," Onyx replied with a much lower voice, "competing with the influence of a single giant group of other sorcerers held us back."

Molly let out another long breath. Onyx was right. Working magic was easier with fewer Practitioners in the city. "Point," she conceded.

Onyx took her hands. "Things are turning around for us," she predicted. "This is just the beginning. We're gonna be livin' the dream, Molly. Working witches, you and I. Now are we good? Because me feeling carefree and you being wound up like we're in Bizarro-world hurts my head."

"I'm good," Molly relaxed. "I'm good. I want a drink or something, but I'm good. Let's go."

Check-in turned out to be much as they expected. Both women were patted down and had to open their bags—or, in Onyx's case, her belt pouches—but none of the security staff raised any objections. It wasn't as if they knew legitimate magic wands when they saw them.

"Think the main dance floor is this one," Molly said, guiding Onyx along through the crowd. They slipped inside the ballroom, quickly immersed in booming bass and flashing lights. "You wanna look for him the old fashioned way?"

"Hell no," Onyx snorted. "Why would I do that?" From her belt pouch, she produced a tiny vial—plastic and modern, rather than a period piece—and wet her fingers with the water inside. Then she gently placed a drop on the side of each eye, murmuring a spell in Greek.

Solely in Onyx's vision, the crowd shifted to grey and then began to gently fade. Silhouettes and faint features remained, but she saw through people and obstacles as her gaze swept the room. Her eyes disregarded unimportant details, helping her see through all distractions until she located the subject of her thoughts. Magical perception had always been a particular talent for her. She read auras with almost casual effort. Even formidable illusions rarely fooled the young witch.

She stopped. Gasped. Clamped a hand down on Molly's, looking on with wide eyes and a slight choke.

"What?" asked Molly.

Onyx pulled her in close, whispering another enchantment into the redhead's ear: "*Share this with me.*"

Molly watched as the spell woven by her lover took over her vision. She turned her attention in the direction indicated by Onyx and watched with a surprised grin.

Alex stood on the dance floor in an open bathrobe, with an angel hanging from his shoulders. Her legs, wrapped around his hips, helped her grind up and down against him. The succubus lingered at his back. The witches saw all the colors and lights of their emotions. They read the trio's body language. There was simply no mistaking what they saw.

Neither looked away. Silence held between them as Rachel slid off Alex and the two women brought him back down to Earth once more.

"Wow," Molly breathed.

"I know, right?" Onyx agreed loudly enough for Molly to hear over the music.

Molly frowned. She squeezed Onyx by the arm. "You okay?"

"Yeah, I just... didn't expect to see that."

"Are you bothered?"

"I can't decide if I should be or not. That's the problem."

"Like you said. It's complicated. We don't have to be anything but friends," Molly reminded her. "Or is this a competition thing?"

Onyx shook her head. "It's not that," she frowned, making sure she was honest with herself as she spoke. "It's just... they were fucking in public."

"Yeah."

"All three of them," Onyx said, waving her hands. "I mean it's not like we didn't know, but we hadn't actually seen it."

"I don't think we were meant to, love," Molly pointed out. "I don't think anyone was reasonably supposed to see that. You've got better eyes than anyone I've ever heard of."

"I suppose so."

"We knew they had to be pretty kinky," added Molly. "Let's face it: succubus. For all we know, that was tame." She waited for Onyx to respond, and found she couldn't get a read on her partner's thoughts. "He'll tell us if we ask him. He'll tell us everything. Those are the rules, right?"

"They are."

"And he'll play by the rules. We know that."

Onyx nodded without an answer.

"You okay?"

"I'm fine," Onyx shrugged. "I just want to make sure I know how I feel about all this before it goes further."

Molly waited to hear more, and finally gave her a tug. "They're still friends and it's still his birthday. We can do that much without the complications, right?"

"Yeah. I'm good. We're fine."

Molly led her girlfriend through the crowd and then stopped. "So are you gonna be weirded out if I still go for it?" she joked.

Onyx swatted Molly's arm, laughing in spite of herself. Alex sorted his clothes out again by the time the witches made it to him. He and his lovers looked calmer, though Onyx saw plenty of swirling colors of passion in their auras. Lorelei's enchantment faded. Onyx allowed her spell to lapse.

His arms still around Rachel, Alex opened his eyes to find the witches standing behind her. "Hey!" he blinked, smiling at them. Rachel released him to allow for welcoming hugs. "You both look awesome." He had to fairly shout to be heard over the music, but at least no one in the crowd jostled them.

"Thanks," Molly chuckled. "We like your costume, too."

"Yeah," agreed Onyx with a grin. "Very practical."

"Well, it's comfortable enough, but originally I was gonna... um... oh." The smile on his face faded as the one shared by Molly and Onyx grew. "Oh no."

"Yeah, we didn't know there would be a floor show," Molly pressed before she and Onyx stopped holding back their laughter.

"Oh god," Alex groaned.

"You sounded differently when you were yelling that a second ago. Hi, Rachel. Lorelei," Onyx smiled.

"Lorelei," Alex asked, "I thought—?"

"They are quite skilled," shrugged the demon. She gestured to the dancing partiers surrounding them on all sides. "No one else noticed."

"Yeah, but... I just... wow," he sighed, looking at the ceiling and smiling in spite of himself. "Just kinda feel like there's egg on my face now."

"Aw, there's nothin' on your face, lover," Rachel consoled him. "I didn't think you'd be okay with getting oral on me here."

His eyes went wide. Molly and Onyx burst out laughing all over again. Lorelei slipped in and took his arm to offer a rescue. "Ladies, I'm going to be selfish and claim him for a dance before the night runs away with us. We've got a table reserved over by the wall there if you like. Wade wanted to have a toast."

"Gotcha," Onyx nodded.

"Toodles," grinned Molly, who slapped Alex on the ass as he moved into the crowd. Then she turned back to see the angel staring at her, and her grin faded. "Uh. Hi," she said.

"Hi," Rachel nodded.

"So."

"Yeah."

"It's nice to see you again?" offered Onyx, hoping to sound more genuine than awkward.

"You two kidnapped me a month ago and now you wanna ride my boyfriend like a rodeo bull," Rachel deadpanned. She waited while the witches shared a glance filled with trepidation. Then she jerked her thumb over her shoulder. "Buy me a drink and we'll call it even? I don't carry cash."

"So you should know that I have to stick to certain rules on dealing with mortals," Rachel said over her drink. She stood at the corner of their bar, cradling her whiskey and coke in her hand. "You'll probably think it's patronizing as fuck, and anything I could say in defense against that would also be patronizing as fuck, so the hell with it.

"Anyway. There's a whole list of no-go topics. Me and Alex and Lorelei being together is a giant case of special dispensation and mitigating circumstances. I'm on a need-to-know basis with all of you, twenty-four-seven. I can only even tell you this much 'cause me meeting you wasn't my fault."

"Okay," nodded Molly. She, too, had a drink in hand. Onyx stood close at her back, easily within earshot but still waiting at the bar for hers.

"Mortals need to work shit out for themselves. Angels aren't supposed to give you the answers. I can't tell you what God's like at dinner. I can say God exists, but so could that asshole over there in the cow outfit, right? I can't tell you which religion is right or if they're all wrong. I can't even tell you if you're living your lives well, and I'm absolutely not allowed to tell you whether or not witchcraft stains your soul and damns you to hell for all eternity or if that's just hysterical, misogynistic Satanic-panic bullshit."

"That makes sense," said Molly as she brought her drink to her mouth.

Rachel leaned in. "It *is* all hysterical, misogynistic Satanic-panic bullshit," she said, and barely cracked a grin as Molly choked on her drink. "Seriously. I think you two are great."

Molly had to pause to wipe her mouth. Onyx looked over her shoulder. "So you're not mad at us?"

"Well you *did* pull a massive cock-block on one of the best nights of my life," Rachel smirked. "But it all worked out better than I could've wished for, honestly. And you meant well. You stuck your necks out for someone you barely knew. 'Greater love hath no man' and all that, right? So we're good there."

Her drink finally in hand, Onyx stepped around Molly to take her place by her side. "You're sure?" she asked.

"Yeah. Hey, I'm an angel," Rachel shrugged. "I'm practically made of forgiveness and benevolence."

Before her sentence had concluded, a third party joined the conversation.

The stranger slipped around Rachel's store-bought fake wings, clad in a pirate outfit and flashing his most charming grin. "Baby, you're also made of—"

Rachel put her hand on his face and pushed him away without even looking. The stranger stumbled and fell into the crowd with his pick-up line unfinished. "Ask Alex," she continued, "I get wet every time he gives money to a panhandler."

The shriek from the pirate on the floor interrupted whatever reply Molly or Onyx might have offered. "My hand!" he shouted. "You're stepping on my hand!"

"OhmygodI'msosorry!" blurted Snow White as she lifted her foot.

"Aw, fuckin' Christ I think it's broken," whimpered the pirate.

"Don't blaspheme," grunted Rachel. She raised her cup to her lips, then brought it back down and looked to her side. "Hey! Don't give me any shit," she fairly snarled, seemingly at nobody. "He's insured! You were gonna have to stop him from driving home drunk and mowing down some trick-or-treating kids, anyway, and you know it! Now he'll dry out in the ER all safe-like, so get off my ass!"

The fratboy in the Starfleet uniform directly in front of her held his hands up innocently. "Woah, why you yellin' at me?" he asked.

"I wasn't talking to you!" Rachel snapped at Starfleet guy. She glanced at his date. "Wow, you are seriously ovulating, chica," she warned Snow White. "I'm not sayin' you shouldn't take this guy home, but do some family plannin' shit before you get nasty, 'kay?" Then she looked back at the Starfleet guy—or rather at the air right in front of him. "What?" she asked indignantly. "I'm helping people!"

"Uh, Rachel," Molly broke in, daring to put a hand on the angel's shoulder, "who are you talking to?"

"Co-workers," Rachel grumbled. "Anyway, we all got our drink on? We should bounce. C'mon," she gestured, leading the witches away from the bar and moving toward their table.

"So, look, I know what you wanna talk about, and there's nothing to it," Rachel explained as they moved. "I don't suffer from jealousy. I can see right into his heart, and yours. I'm not worried about losing him. I knew going into this that he's doomed to freaky sexcapades. I'm not even bothered. Honestly, if my responsibilities didn't keep me here, I'd say he and Lorelei and I should move to LA so he could get a job making porn. He'd be great at that."

Her audience glanced at one another and burst into laughter. The suggestion itself was one thing, but Rachel's utter sincerity was another.

The angel was not bothered. "I can already tell looking at you how committed you are to one another. I'm not worried about either of you deciding that he's your One and Only True Love and you have to have him for yourself."

She stopped. She turned to face them. "There's no such thing as One and Only, either," she told them. "There are seven billion people on this planet. You can find more than one person who's right for you." She paused. "I'm not supposed to tell you that, either, but fuck it." The angel turned and led the stunned young women on toward the tables.

"Anyway, you've got to remember that he's committed, too, and that neither of his commitments are with normal chicks. Lorelei's got her needs, and it's not all freaky sex stuff. I've got my needs, too. The worst part for me is that my job means I can't keep anything close to a regular schedule, so I just drop in on them whenever I can. But my biggest need is for trust... 'cause like I said, there's a mountain of shit I just can't say or do or keep him from doing, ever."

"So does that mean you can't tell us, either?" Onyx asked.

"Pretty much," Rachel shrugged. "Anyway, I'm not the one you need to negotiate anything with."

Onyx turned her head suspiciously. "Do we need to negotiate with Lorelei?"

"You might," Rachel warned.

Onyx shared another wary glance with Molly. "Any advice on that?"

Rachel's mouth tightened. She looked the women over. "Promise not to take this the wrong way?"

"...okay?"

"Fuck her," the angel shrugged. "I did."

"So you're twenty-one now," Amber said, looking sidelong at Drew.

"Yeah," he confirmed.

"Like for really-really," Amber pressed.

"Like my ID actually matches my birth certificate," Drew nodded, and then cast an accusing, sarcastic glance at the other two men standing around the table. "Unlike *some* dudes here," he added.

Amber's eyes turned to Wade. He merely shrugged. "Underage drinkin' don't even rate a mention on my list of crimes," he said before having another sip.

"So this is an even bigger birthday for you than it is for Alex, right?" Amber asked Drew. "Lotta guys would be set on getting completely plowed tonight."

"Well, I might later, but, uh..." His words trailed off as a couple of women in not-so-realistic police costumes walked by, their eyes on him as they passed. "There are better things to do at a party like this than just getting drunk."

"My guys!" yelled out a female voice. Drew and Wade staggered slightly as a blonde angel leapt upon them from behind, throwing an arm around the shoulders of each tall young man. "How the hell are you?" Rachel asked. She planted a sloppy kiss on Wade's cheek, and then another on Drew's. "And happy birthday, sexy thing," she added, hugging him tightly.

"Hi, Rachel," the guys said simultaneously.

"Hey, Rachel," Jason began, "this is—"

"Jason!" Rachel yelled happily, hugged him, and then pushed him back. She nudged him with the same hand that held her half-consumed drink. "Now you remember the rules. No theological trolling me, 'kay?"

"Okay, deal," he agreed. "Anyway, I wanted you to—"

"Oh, shit, before I forget," Rachel interrupted, "you guys remember Molly and Onyx, right?" She gestured back between Drew and Wade at the pair of young women standing behind them. Murmuring polite hellos, the two quietly took up spots around the table. "Molly just told me the most badass thing ever," Rachel said with excitement. She jabbed her finger at Wade's chest. "Did you guys know they make strapless dildos now?"

Molly bit down on her lips and tried not to laugh out loud as Onyx turned and buried her head in her companion's shoulder. In spite of all he'd seen and done and survived, Wade found it in himself to blush.

Amber tugged at Drew's sleeve. He and Jason leaned in together to hear her ask, "Is she drunk?"

Both men snorted. "Nnnoo," Drew whispered slowly, shaking his head. "She's just being herself."

"I cannot fucking *wait* to get one," Rachel continued.

"Rachel!" Jason tried again.

"Yeah, hon?" she asked, turning to face him. Her brow furrowed. "Hey. You look different."

"Rachel," he said, gesturing with one hand to the woman in combat fatigues beside him, "this is Amber."

"Hi," waved his date. "It's nice to meet you."

Rachel's mood faltered. "Hi," she said, fairly staring at Amber.

"I'm here with Jason," said Amber, offering her hand.

The angel shook Amber's hand, locking onto her with a guarded stare. "Right," Rachel said. "Jason's... date."

Amber noticed. Anyone could. "Is something wrong?"

"No," Rachel answered, shaking her head, though her tone and the tiny frown on her lips said otherwise.

"You sure?" Amber asked.

Rachel blinked quickly, realizing now how she stared. The crowd distracted the others, but both Jason and Amber had Rachel's full attention. "No, it's... don't worry about me," she said. "Nothing I can explain anyway. Just weird." She frowned again, tried to fight it, and only half succeeded. "Welcome to the party," she managed. "Jason's awesome."

"Yeah," Amber said, smiling at him. "I'm getting kind of sweet on him."

"You are," Rachel confirmed.

"Hey! Birthday boy!" Drew yelled out.

"What up, birthday boy?" Alex answered. He arrived with Lorelei on his arm, though he released her so he could share a hug with his best friend. Lorelei looked on appreciatively, though her gaze soon settled on Rachel.

The angel's face set in a somber mood unfit for celebration. Lorelei questioned her wordlessly, offering a simple tilt of her head. Rachel frowned and waved it off.

Wade banged on the table. "A'right, now that we've got y'all here," he began, ensuring he had everyone's attention. "Ah know better than to give a long speech or expect ev'ryone to stay together at a deal like this. Y'all got better things to do than to listen to me."

"Kind of an interesting exercise, actually," quipped Molly. Onyx swatted her arm, but Wade took it with a grin.

"Mah people have a tradition," declared Wade with feigned gravitas. He raised his cup.

Alex gave Molly a conspiratorial nudge. "This tradition is like two minutes old," he said loudly enough for everyone to hear.

"Shuddup," Wade countered without lowering his cup or relaxing his deliberately puffed-out chest. "It's a tradition among mah civilized, cultured Southern brethren—"

"Hillbillies!" coughed out Jason.

"—who are taught somethin' called *manners*, unlike y'all heathen savages of the Pacific Northwest."

"You were born in Tacoma!" protested Drew.

"Hey!" Onyx countered. "Don't be mean."

"Thank you, miss," Wade bowed, then resumed his stance.

"Nobody deserves to have something like that aired out in public," Onyx finished. She flashed Wade a comforting smile. "Don't worry, Wade. It's not your fault."

"Are y'all quite finished?" Wade asked. His eyes swept the group, settling on Rachel. "Okay, I *know* you got somethin' to say."

The angel tore her eyes off the newcomer leaning against Jason. "No," she shook her head. "No, go on. Your people have a tradition."

Standing behind Alex with her arms draped affectionately around him, Lorelei found herself far more concerned with her other lover. Their eyes met. Again, Rachel just shook her head.

"Yeah. A tradition y'all could've been done with five minutes ago an' gone off to dance or get schnockered or whatever the hell y'all got in mind, if y'all hadn't kept interruptin' me." Wade held his cup high and puffed out his chest once again. "But here we are now. We ain't even gotta talk about what we been through lately. Ain't gotta say thank yous or your welcomes. 'cause we're all pals. Old an' new," he added, nodding to Onyx and Molly, and then to Amber.

"An' so ah just wanted t' make sure we all got t'gether for a couple minutes to give a toast to both Drew, turnin' twenty-one finally as of yesterday but who gives a shit about details as long as he's legal here," Wade said, gesturing to Drew with his cup. "A fine gentleman who's still gracious enough t' slum it with folks like us even though he could surely find more sophisticated company."

An uncoordinated but happy round of "Happy birthday, Drew" came from the others, their cups raised as Drew accepted it all with a smile.

"An' we also wanna say happy birthday to Alex, who for some fuckin' reason thought he could be born on goddamn Halloween an' never ever have anything creepy or spooky or weird happen to his ass," Wade grinned. Alex hung his head in mock shame. Wade then added, calling out loudly above and beyond the group to a crowded hall of disinterested partygoers, "An' Alex is *totally* twenty-one today in case any state, local or Federal authorities might be listenin'!"

Amber winced, but she drank the toast along with everyone else. She felt Rachel's gaze and hoped she hadn't somehow given anything away. Wanting to hide from it somehow, she turned to Jason and asked the first thing to come to mind: "When's your birthday, anyway?"

"Two days before Christmas," he grumbled. "And yes, that still sucks even though I'm Jewish."

"Aw, poor thing," Amber chuckled. She leaned in to kiss him on the cheek.

"Babe, I gotta go for a bit," Rachel told Alex, abruptly putting her emptied cup down on the table. "Duty calls."

Alex tilted his head curiously. "Everything okay?"

She shrugged. "Can't say." She moved off, only to find her arm caught by Lorelei not five steps later. "Please don't," Rachel said.

"You are troubled," Lorelei observed quietly. "What is it?"

"Leave it alone, Lorelei." Her voice dropped and her shoulders sagged. "Please."

"What bothers you?" She watched as Rachel's distress flashed across her face. "Is it Amber? You were staring."

"I can't talk about it. I just can't."

"You don't have to shut me out, Rachel," Lorelei pressed gently. "You can tell me anything. I am not mortal."

"No, but everyone else here is," Rachel countered. "It might be okay for me to tell you what's up, but you turning around and interfering doesn't make it any less my fault if…" She shook her head. "I'm sorry, Lorelei. That's not fair. It's not even about trusting you. I do. I love you. But I've got my duty."

Lorelei watched Rachel for a long breath. "What am I to do?"

"Just carry on?" Rachel asked. "Don't worry about it. The sun's still gonna come up tomorrow and we'll all still love each other. Let me do my thing and I'll be back when I can. No drama. It's his birthday," she shrugged. "Trust me. Anyway, you need to talk to the witches."

"About?"

"I dunno," Rachel said. "You're all hot, bi and partially available. I'm sure you'll think of something." With that, she turned and disappeared into the crowd.

Lorelei scowled, naturally dissatisfied with Rachel's lack of answers. She stood alone on the dance floor, considering the situation.

Trust what? Lorelei wondered. *Trust her judgment? Trust her ability to handle whatever is wrong? Or trust her to follow Heaven's ethics of allowing mortals to stumble and fall on their own?*

That Rachel's concern had something to do with Amber seemed reasonable, but Lorelei couldn't be sure. Rachel's reaction neither confirmed nor ruled out Lorelei's suspicions. She knew Rachel's could read people at a glance, but she also knew that such information was often incomplete or seemingly random. Rachel's heart was every bit as big as one might imagine of an angel, too. For all Lorelei knew, Rachel saw some family tragedy in Amber's recent past, or an undiscovered health defect... or something dangerous to Lorelei, Alex and their friends.

Trust did not come naturally to demons.

Love and the ritual binding them both to Alex compelled Rachel to defend him if he faced true danger. Lorelei had faith in her own abilities. She could never call Alex helpless, either. Her jaw set firmly as she fought with herself to put her love over her instincts, and found she could not entirely do either.

Lorelei had to trust Rachel to handle this, whatever it was, and to wait until she explained herself... and until then, Lorelei could at least expand her options and her resources. Rachel had just encouraged exactly that, whether she knew it or not.

"No, really, Alex," Onyx goaded him, "you should totally tell Amber how we first met." She leaned in toward him from across their table. Her grin said all sorts of teasing things.

"Oh, this sounds good," Amber smirked.

"I did!" Alex protested. "We met in a photography class. That's the truth."

"Yeah, but it's not the whole truth, is it?" Molly countered.

"C'mon, Alex," pressed Onyx with wide, innocent eyes, "you can tell the story. It's not like you did anything silly. Or desperate. Or middle-schoolish."

"Aw, tell me!" Amber asked.

"Yeah, Alex," Jason agreed.

"Seriously?" Alex frowned at his friend. "You, too?"

"Well, it's not like I knew you were gonna do what you did," shrugged Jason, "otherwise I might've told you it was dumb to begin with."

"I'm not telling that story."

"I know you're not," Onyx teased. "I just wanna hear whatever lie you plan on telling people instead."

Lorelei slid in with the group. "My love, do you require a rescue here?"

Alex looked up with hope in his eyes. "Yes! Yes, I do!"

"Very well. Ladies," she said, looking to Molly and Onyx, "shall we go powder our noses?"

"Sure," Onyx said after a wordless query to her girlfriend. "Probably about that time for us."

"Wait, what?" blinked Alex.

"Girl talk," said Molly, sticking her tongue out at him. "Amber, you coming?"

"I'm good, thanks," she answered.

Thinking of Rachel, Lorelei forced herself to let Amber stay behind. She led the two other women through the crowd.

"I thought all you women were supposed to go to the bathroom in a pack?" Jason asked.

"I never fit in with that," she shrugged. Her head tilted. "Alex, what's wrong?"

He turned to look in every direction. A frown grew ever deeper on his face. "I just lost my dates," he complained, more to himself than anyone else. "*Both* my dates. How the hell did I manage to lose *both* my dates?"

Behind him, Wade tugged on Drew's sleeve. As they leaned together, Wade asked, "Y'all notice the two different guys on opposite sides of us who keep taking pictures with us conveniently in view?"

"Uh. No," Drew admitted. "No, I haven't."

"Ninja at eight o'clock. Spider-Man at two o'clock."

Drew smiled broadly and waited a beat before glancing in that direction, doing his best to be subtle about it. "Sure you aren't being paranoid?"

"Nope," Wade shook his head. "Of course, ah'd ask maybe one of our supernatural buddies t' check it out, but they all just took off."

"Ninja looks like he's leaving now," Drew said, noting how the two both turned their backs to head out. "You wanna follow? Or talk to Spidey?"

"Let's follow the ninja," Wade said. "This turns out all wrong, ah'm gonna feel terrible for punchin' out a childhood superhero. Hey, Alex," he called, "Drew an' me are gonna go check somethin' out."

Alex blinked. "Okay?"

"Stay with Jason an' Amber," Wade advised as he and Drew headed out. He had no time for anything more than that.

Alex watched as the pair disappeared. He turned to Jason and Amber, who stood just out of earshot. "Where'd Drew and Wade go?" Jason asked.

"Bathroom or the bar, I guess?" Alex shrugged. "This party broke up fast."

"Aw, don't worry," Amber assured him. "We'll stay with you."

Jason winced. As soon as Amber looked away, Alex held out his hands in a plea and mouthed out, "Sorry!"

RACHEL DIDN'T GO FAR. She only needed to ensure no one would see her fade out of sight or touch from mortals. Then she immediately spun 180 degrees and stomped back through the crowd, literally passing through people on her way.

No angels blocked her path. Most of the guardians hovered above the crowd, watching their charges for as long as they could spare, then flying off to look in on other charges in other locations. Others lingered. A given guardian angel had to split his or her attention between many charges, and had to prioritize appropriately. Some guardians took a hands-off approach. Some guardians intervened more than others.

A few guardians were wet blankets. "Daniel!" Rachel snapped as she found him looming over Jason and his date.

"Oh, now she wants to talk," huffed the other angel. He folded his arms across his chest and frowned to show his indignation.

"Now? What the *fuck*, Daniel?"

His brow knit together in further disapproval. "Must you be so coarse?"

"Yes. Suck it up. Daniel, you could've come talk to me at any time. Anyone can. You know that. Open door, like I told everyone when I got the job. What's with the fuckin' attitude all of a sudden?"

"You might have been a little more pro-active."

"I'm pro-active about all sorts of shit! Daniel, my job is to watch over the city as a whole, not tell you guardians how to do your jobs. Every fuckin' one of you has more experience at your job than I've got at mine. Besides, is my management style what you want to talk about right now?"

"Perhaps it is," came the other angel's sour reply.

"Oh, get off my ass," Rachel scowled. "I know damn well you can't be comfortable with *that*." She pointed to Amber without even looking at her. The young woman had her arms draped around Jason's neck, fingers knit together as she pulled him away from the group's table. Alex followed.

Daniel glanced at his mortal charge and huffed again. "Yes. Well. I can't say

I didn't see anything like this coming after everything your mortal boyfriend and that hussy you've shacked up with have already put my Jason through."

"Wha—! What the shit, Daniel? Are you gonna explain what's up or just take cheap fuckin' shots at me all night?"

He grumbled and shifted his stance and fought with himself over what to say. "It's the sort of thing that we must leave to mortal hands."

"Spill!"

"She's an undercover agent. Jason represents a lead on her case. She's posing as a classmate to get close to him and his friends."

"Yeah, I got that much from just looking at her, thanks," fumed Rachel. "Who's she work for? Jason's not even dirty enough to have gone anal on those bimbos he was with last month—"

Daniel's eyes fairly bugged out of his head. "Can we please not discuss such things?"

"—let alone commit crimes, so what's she after? And who's her guardian?"

"I am," came a voice to Rachel's side. She stood almost a head taller than Rachel, with dark hair hanging to her shoulders and a stern, proud look in her eyes. The angel looked Rachel up and down, giving no hint of approval with her expression. "Theresa," she said.

Rachel stopped herself, taking a breath to control her emotions. "Sorry we're meeting like this."

"Indeed," nodded Theresa. "I was told that you do not require guardians to meet with you upon entering your dominion?"

"No," Rachel shook her head. "I don't micro-manage. You guys know what you're doing."

"Excellent. I'm glad you understand this."

Rachel blinked. "Okay, I don't want to read you wrong, so I'll just ask: are you unhappy about something here?"

"You seem quite unhappy yourself."

"What, apart from my friendly banter with Daniel?"

"Huh. Friendly banter," Daniel repeated sourly.

"I've heard a good deal about you," said Theresa. "I haven't liked much of it."

Rachel's jaw slowly clenched. "Oh, for the love of fuck. Please tell me you weren't spreadin' 'em for Vincent, too."

"Hardly. I've more sense than that," Theresa replied. Rather than wait to see if Rachel caught the veiled insult in her comment, she continued. "You know full well that your actions are not lauded by everyone, regardless of the opinion of your council. I am happy to know good things arose from your fiasco. I am not entirely comfortable with the way in which that happened... or how certain vital standards have been allowed to slide in your special case."

"Nice," Rachel sighed. "Well, welcome to Seattle and all that bullshit. Guess we can skip trying to be friendly. What the fuck is up with your girl?"

Theresa's gaze turned on Daniel just long enough to stare a few daggers at him. "I'm sure our associate here has told you more than enough already."

"Like fuck he has. Who does your girl work for, and what's she investigating?"

"I'm not sure it's best for you to know, Rachel," Theresa replied. "You are quite close to the situation. Your direct involvement has compromised these mortals enough already, hasn't it?"

Rachel's eyes flared. "Oh, holy shit, you're gonna walk into my city and piss all over everything that's happened in the last month before you even take a look around? Is that your plan? I am way more careful with my involvement than you are with your fuckin' attitude, stranger. Tell me what's going on."

"Is that an order?" Theresa asked. Her cool tone relaxed somewhat, but not so much as to signal an apology.

"No," answered Rachel. She forced herself not to growl. "Call it a request for professional fu—courtesy. Professional courtesy," she repeated, though her glare showed nothing of the sort. "I'm worried about Jason 'cause he's my friend and I care about him, and I can see plain as day how mixed up about him your girl is. But that's *her* emotional train wreck to live through, and yours. I wanna know if this is small-time bullshit or if it's something serious."

Theresa held her gaze, but again, her tone stepped down a notch. "You will hold your interference to what is in Heaven's interests?"

"Chica, I want my guys to live their lives and go to Heaven when they die just like everyone else here," Rachel said, gesturing to the angels floating up above. "If they gotta fall down and go boom, I'll fucking weep, but I'll toe the line and let nature take its course just like every other angel's gotta. Even with Jason. Even with Alex."

She stepped in closer, her stare growing deathly cold. "But if this situation brings in a whole bunch of vile supernatural bullshit into this city that I've been busting my ass to clean up, and if I find out you could've warned me but didn't, I will pull every feather off your wings and cram them up your ass one by fucking one."

6
_____

PARTY FOULS

"**S**o thanks again for getting us tickets to this, by the way," said Molly as they slipped through the crowd at the ballroom entrance. Plenty of partygoers occupied the hotel's passages, but not so many as to make movement through the hallways difficult.

"It is my pleasure," Lorelei shrugged. The demon leaned in and said, "Please stay close to me and do nothing to draw attention. We can speak with one another, but keep a thought toward being unobtrusive. I have some talent for hiding in plain sight as long as no one does anything unusual."

"Is that how you make it through a crowd when you look like that?" asked Molly with a bit of a smile.

"Normally I prefer to be noticed," Lorelei nodded, sharing her grin. She reached out to touch her two companions, both on the hand and only fleetingly, but the two witches both sensed the enchantment. "I draw pleasure and some small energy from the lust of others, but my interests are not on random strangers tonight. You have my full attention. I am glad to have yours."

With that, she turned and led them away. Onyx nudged Molly forward, making the redhead blink away her reverie. Molly turned to find a knowing smirk on her lover's face. "She knows we're both staring," Onyx murmured.

"Yeah. Well." Molly took Onyx's hand, squeezing it as they followed Lorelei. Her eyes went straight to Lorelei's swaying hips. "There's a lot to stare at."

Onyx didn't reply; she just squeezed back and nodded.

Lorelei felt their stares and their lust. She knew better than to acknowledge either... yet. "The ladies' rooms will doubtlessly be occupied," she said, turning toward the elevators. She pressed the button to summon one. "Fortunately, I'm the sort to plan ahead."

"You rented a room?" Onyx asked. "You live less than a mile away."

"I always prefer to keep privacy readily available," Lorelei smiled. Once inside the elevator, Lorelei ushered her companions inside and pressed the button for the fifth floor.

"I must ask," Lorelei said now that they were truly alone, "are the two of you on your guard tonight?"

The witches shared a serious glance. "Our defenses are up, yes," nodded Molly. "They don't exactly confiscate wands as weapons here, either. We're prepared for trouble if it comes up. You think there's going to be any?"

Lorelei shook her head. "Nothing immediate or violent, no," she frowned. "No one who would harm any of us would expose themselves in such an open environment, and we should see them coming, anyway. But I thought I should ask."

Molly's eyes slid toward Onyx. The other young woman shrugged. "I kinda figured I should have my eyes open extra-wide. Most supernatural types would stick out in a crowd to me tonight. Magic, werewolves, all that. I never make guarantees, though."

"Of course. I have perfect faith in you," Lorelei assured her. The door opened. She led them to a room close to the elevator. "Did anything about Amber seem odd to you?" she asked, slipping the card key out of her top.

"Jason's date?" Onyx asked.

"Only that her costume looks bad ass," Molly said as Lorelei brought them inside and closed the door. She turned to see the demon looking her up and down, and felt her breath catch under that gaze.

"Not to sound catty or put her down," Lorelei said coolly, "but if we're to talk of costumes, I *much* prefer yours."

The redhead in the sea witch dress blushed. She looked down at her tentacles and her fishnet skirts. "Thanks, but I want hers, too."

Onyx had never seen Molly blush before, let alone made it happen. It would have given her a tiny stab of jealousy, had the moment come from anyone else. Instead, Onyx just grinned at Molly's reaction and logged it as something to tease her about later, and opted to stay on Lorelei's chosen subject. "What's on your mind?"

"She's inquisitive but shares little about herself," Lorelei explained. She crossed the room to take one of the seats at the small table near the window. "While that alone would not raise my concern, she seems quite guarded. Careful. Always aware of her surroundings."

Molly leaned against the dresser. "Has she known Jason long? Was she friends with anyone else in the group before they met?"

Lorelei shook her head. "He has known her for only a week. He clearly wants to push things further along with her. I would be happy for him, but the events that brought us all together aren't exactly matters I'd want him to share with someone when they haven't moved past casual dating."

"Kinda have to run that risk with all of those guys, though, don't you?" suggested Onyx. "Molly and I know enough to keep supernatural stuff quiet, but... You *have* talked to them about that, right?"

"Of course. Moreover, they all have some inherent sense of it. They know how hard it would be to explain certain aspects of their lives. No, I am less worried about Jason deliberately revealing too much, and more that Amber suspects something. It would explain her wariness."

"I want to like her. I can see why Jason is attracted to her, and she seems to get on fine with everyone, but..." Lorelei's voice trailed off. "Trust does not come naturally to me. I am quite practiced at establishing a friendly atmosphere, and at maintaining a friendly tone, but actual friendship is... new. I am unused to it."

Onyx broke the silence that followed. "We've never talked about that. The other night at your place was nice and all, but that was all small talk and business. Nothing personal."

"No," Lorelei agreed.

"So, on that note," Molly spoke up, trying to smile through her trepidation. "Onyx and I want everything to be above-board. All of it. We dig Alex, he's said you're okay with fooling around, but..."

"But there is a difference between hearing that from him and establishing an understanding with me," Lorelei finished, "and presumably Rachel?"

"We already talked to her," Onyx nodded. Molly snorted, and then the two both found themselves giggling. "That was an experience."

Lorelei smiled knowingly. "She always is. I trust she was as reassuring as she was jarring."

"Yeah, you could say that," Molly smirked.

"But you wish to know where I stand, and to hear it from me directly."

Lorelei paused. "Unlike Alex, you have some understanding of supernatural matters. You have embraced them. You know that not everyone or everything lives within ordinary mortal sensibilities."

"Ordinary mortals don't always do that, either," frowned Molly.

"No, indeed," Lorelei smiled warmly. "I have very few friends. I wish dearly to count you among them—regardless of what passes between you and Alex."

Onyx felt her girlfriend's eyes on her. Though Molly shared many of her concerns, the redhead took things as they came. Ultimately it was Onyx who needed everything out in the open from the start. "What if it gets serious?" she ventured.

"I am inclined to say that is likely," replied Lorelei. "So far you've only discussed this as a casual exploration. As a matter of adult play. If that is all that comes of it, I don't believe anyone will be disappointed... but I don't believe it will end there. You all mesh too well for that. Onyx, I *felt* the two of you make love. I trust he has told you that is part of our bond? Yes. Full disclosure, of course," she nodded. "I would not presume to compare my experience to yours, but it was wonderful."

"Is that why you want this?" Molly asked. "Because it's good for you? I mean, you're not just 'okay' with Alex seeing us. You actually want it, don't you?"

"I do," Lorelei admitted. The briefest of smiles played at her lips. "Full disclosure is no more natural for me than friendship or trust. I have laid my soul bare only to Rachel and Alex, and there are sureties there..."

The younger women listened. Onyx sat down on the edge of the bed facing the demon. Molly came over to sit beside her, slipping her hand in her lover's. Always the more observant of the two, Onyx noticed how Lorelei's words slowed and her voice dropped. Whether Molly had caught on or not, Onyx couldn't tell, but it hardly mattered; both young women felt increasingly aroused by Lorelei's natural allure.

"Alex is my lover, my friend *and* my victim. His natural appetites are strong even for a healthy young man, but mine are well beyond natural, and we are bound together. If I truly had all I wanted of him, all to myself... he would be worse for it. We would become disconnected from the mortal world, to say nothing of the eventual damage I would do to his health and well-being. Involving others goes some way to mitigating that. It takes the edge off, so to speak. It helps to satisfy the curse without putting him directly at the mercy of my needs.

"This is no sacrifice or chore for me. I want him to indulge with other women because I enjoy it. I share his sensations, I draw power from his dalliances, and I find him all the more attractive for his success with other women. Call it a kink or call it an instinct; either way, I am drawn to these habits. Most succubae are. What made me different from the rest was that they encouraged their victims to employ deceit and treachery to satisfy their desires. They relished the strife and chaos wrought by selfish promiscuity."

"But you didn't?" asked Molly.

"I was indifferent," Lorelei shrugged. "I will not pretend to have ever been a whore with a heart of gold, but... I didn't change for Alex. I *wanted* to change long before we met. He and Rachel provided an opportunity that I never had, and indeed had never imagined, but they did not do so intentionally.

"Make no mistake: I am still a succubus, and Alex is bound to me. I care nothing for this society's inhibitions and its harsh judgments regarding sex. Temptation and lust will find Alex even if he does not seek it out, and I will gladly enable his indulgence. I mean to show him pleasure as *I* define it... not as it is defined by the prudish sensibilities of this era.

"You wanted full disclosure. Accept this as part of who he is. Alex would lock himself in a prison and throw away the key rather than cause harm in pursuing his desires. I mean to show him that such denial is not necessary."

The demon cracked a wry, soft grin. "I do not tell you this to rationalize or justify my desires, or his. Alex carries genuine feelings for you. His desire for this—for you—is real, and so is mine."

Molly waited for Onyx to chime in again, but heard nothing for a few beats. She decided to take the initiative. "So if we're all fine, do we need to talk boundaries, or... or..." Her voice trailed off as her attention was drawn to her side. She saw Onyx staring at Lorelei with wide eyes, her mouth slightly open and her breathing heavy.

Then Molly felt it, too. Her appreciation for Lorelei's beauty and sensuality had been there all night long, of course—and every other time they'd inter-acted—but now things changed. Lorelei was no longer an abstraction out of arm's reach.

The demon rose out of her chair. She slowly stepped up close enough to touch.

Molly found her voice, and understood then what had left Onyx stunned. "You really said that, didn't you?" she asked.

"I asked if you were guarded in part so that you would know your feelings are your own," Lorelei said softly. "I wouldn't want you to think I have used some supernatural power of compulsion upon you. As I told you, I can read desires. I draw power from them. I have felt yours all along... and shared them."

Her hands slowly reached out. One gently traced along Molly's chin. The other glided down Onyx's black curls. "Alex is my prey, but it is not only through him that I find pleasure or satisfaction."

Onyx all but lost her voice. Butterflies took over her stomach as Lorelei knelt in front of the bed between the two young women. Onyx felt Molly's presence beside her, and thought back to all the offhand conversations they'd had about the undeniable sex appeal of their new associates and hall passes and what they'd do given the chance... but that had all just been idle talk until now.

"I thought..." Onyx tried, and swallowed, and tried again. "I thought we came up to talk... uh..." That hand came down her curls again, only now Lorelei's fingertips trailed across her collarbone. She shivered.

Lorelei's other hand was on Molly's thigh. Onyx saw it out of the corner of her eye, and found it every bit as exciting as the one that touched her now.

"We came here to establish an understanding between us," Lorelei smiled.

"Uh. Thuh," Molly blinked away her shock, and felt like a fool for stammering, only to open her eyes again to see Lorelei looking back without the least bit of reproach or mockery. She liked the way the demon looked at her. "The party?"

"We don't have to be long," Lorelei assured her, "but you brought up boundaries. You should know mine."

EVENT SECURITY diligently checked guests in and out. They patted people down as they entered and reminded costumed partygoers about stamps and re-entry when they exited. They also ensured that nobody left with a drink in hand. Passing through the security guards posted at the bridge between the hotel and the parking garage across the street, Wade and Drew negotiated said check with little difficulty or concern.

The security guard raised an eyebrow when Wade reached into the garbage can beside him and pulled out an empty red Solo cup, but saw no reason to stop him. Anyone outside the event was simply not security's problem.

Wade's odd behavior, though, was something of a concern for Drew. "The hell are you doing?" he asked. He kept walking, trying to keep an eye on the guy in the black ninja outfit ahead of them. Neither he nor Wade wanted their quarry to be out of sight for long, but they simply couldn't catch up before the ninja rounded the corner into the garage without looking suspicious.

"Just fixin' a drink," Wade shrugged. As he walked, he slipped his hand down his pants and pulled out a silver flask.

"...the fuck?" Drew blinked.

Wade smoothly spun the cap and opened the flask and upended it into the cup. "Y'know how it is. Can't always be sure th' bars at a thing like this will have what you want."

"Of what?"

"Everclear," Wade muttered. "Hadda drive all'a way ta Portland for it."

"You've been carrying around a flask in your junk all night?"

"Naw, it's only been by my junk t' get in and out of the party," Wade corrected. "I ain't some pervert, y'know."

Drew wanted to pursue his line of questioning, but lacked the time. The ninja had already made it around a corner. He and Wade picked up the pace. "So what the hell do we say to this guy?"

"Reckon ah got an idea," Wade grunted. "Follow mah lead."

Drew nodded. He glanced at the windows to either side before they hit the corner, and caught sight of a new concern in the reflection behind them. "Shit," he murmured. "Spider-Man at six o'clock. Now I *know* somethin's up."

They had already turned into the parking garage. "Y'all wanna back off?"

It was an honest question. "Might be a good idea."

As he spoke, though, they both realized it was too late. The ninja stood beside a black van, facing them with his arms folded across his chest. Only once within conversational distance did the two see the pair of small teardrop tattoos beside the ninja's left eye.

He wasn't alone. Two of his companions wore normal street clothes—baggy jeans, untucked shirts and blue bandanas. The third, though, looked quite out of place if only by virtue of his markedly pale complexion and his sharp, authentic blue zoot suit.

"You got a problem, homes?" asked the ninja.

Wade blinked. "Ah'm sorry? Problem?"

"You been followin' me," the ninja pressed, tilting his head toward the hotel bridge. "I'm not a fuckin' moron."

"Well, yeah, but that ain't 'cause we got a problem," Wade shook his head, holding his hands up—one still holding his drink—in a show of innocence.

Drew, too, shook his head, following Wade's lead. It wasn't the first time; all through high school, Wade had always been the guy to come up with the quick plans. Though he was quite used to making decisions on his own, Drew had complete faith in his friend, and he knew how to be part of a team.

He also knew an ugly situation when it stared him in the face like these guys did. As he glanced around, knowing exactly what to look for, he found that the reflections in the car windows and windshields around them failed to show the guy in the zoot suit. He hoped Wade would notice, too.

"So you are following me," the ninja said. His friends stepped to his left, forming an arc around Wade and Drew. The pale one in the zoot suit stayed beside the ninja. Drew stayed on Wade's right, standing between his friend and the two guys in common street clothes.

"Yeah, we followed y'all out here, but it ain't like we're *followin'* ya," Wade smiled, shaking a little to be sure the sarcasm could be read in his emphasis. "Nah, 's just that ah saw y'all takin' pictures in the direction of mah friends and I earlier, an' ah wanted t' know if'n ah could get y'all t' forward 'em to me."

The ninja blinked. "Wait, what?"

"You know! The pretty devil lady an' the pretty angel."

"Right, those bitches," the ninja said. He looked to the one in the zoot suit and gave a deep nod.

"Ladies," Drew and Wade corrected simultaneously.

Conversation halted for a beat, and then the strangers snorted and chuckled. "Why's that funny?" asked Drew.

"What, they got you whipped, *punto*?" asked one of the guys in bandanas.

Drew eyed him coldly. "That's not a nice thing to say."

"But you do know them?" asked the one in the zoot suit. "And their friends?"

"They were all at a table together," answered the ninja.

"Why, is that a thing?" asked Wade. "I'm sure we could introduce you if you wanted to come inside."

"No, no, we aren't interested in that," said the zoot-suited man. His voice was smoother and calmer than the others, and his enunciation came out slightly thicker than that of his companions. Wade chalked it up to the man's large canines. His theory was confirmed as the man offered the slightest of smiles and said, "We'd like to meet them, though. Lorelei and Alex Carlisle, right? You should tell us about them. Maybe go for a ride with us."

"Aw, now, Momma taught me not to get into big white vans with strange men like you," Wade demurred.

"We aren't asking," the zoot suit said. He gestured to his companions, who all either went for weapons or reached out to grab the two younger men, but Wade and Drew were both ready for it. The zoot suited man caught a faceful of Wade's drink.

Drew read his opponents fast enough to pick his first shots well. The guy closest to him jerked his shirt up to grab at the gun in his waistband. Drew's foot launched out just as the thug's hand came to the weapon. His kick connected with a loud "Bang!" and a burst of blood out to one side.

Drew didn't stop to assess; before his foot was back on the ground, his left arm swept out to clock the other thug in the face with the back of his fist. Screaming, Drew's first victim crumpled and slammed his head on the concrete floor.

Years of practice took over. Drew kept turning, his kicking foot now down on the ground allowing him to bring the other one up and around at the ninja. He only caught his opponent in the thigh, but contact was better than nothing. He hoped he and Wade could whittle the group down quickly. He remembered his last brawl with a vampire all too well to look forward to this one.

His companion had enough problems. It wasn't as if the drink had hurt his victim, who turned out to have strength to match his shocking speed. In the space between heartbeats, the man in the zoot suit had one hand around Wade's throat and then hoisted him in the air. He slammed Wade roughly into the side of the van. "Throwin' a drink in my face?" he snarled, his fangs now showing quite prominently.

Wade brought one hand up to grab at the vampire's wrist and try to relieve some of the stress on his neck. It also served to obstruct the view of his other hand, which came out of Wade's pocket to rest on his assailant's shoulder.

"What kinda *bitch* does that?" demanded the vampire.

He didn't hear the metallic clink of the Zippo, but it hardly mattered. The Everclear coating the vampire's face and neck caught fire instantly. He shrieked and flailed, throwing Wade away without a second thought. Wade fell across the shoulders of the guy in the ninja costume, bringing both tumbling to the pavement.

As Wade expected, the brief flash of burning alcohol was enough to set the vampire's flesh alight. Panicked, the vampire turned, ran straight into the side of a parked car and bounced off as he tried in vain to pat his flames out.

"Shit! Arturo!" blurted the ninja. He scrambled up off the concrete, only to have Wade grab one foot and shin and then twist hard. He fell face-first onto the concrete and then felt the brutal force of Wade's foot as it shot up between his legs into his groin.

After a brief struggle with Drew, the last standing thug lost control of his firearm before he'd ever gotten his finger to the trigger. The pistol clattered to the floor. Rather than dive for it, he put a fierce right cross into Drew's face. He followed up with a pair of shots to Drew's midsection, but then hesitated to assess the situations of his comrades. It was all Drew needed; his elbow came up at the thug's nose, crushing it instantly. "Aw, fuck!" the thug grunted, staggering back.

"Aaagh! Agh! My fuckin' leg!" wailed the other thug. Humiliation was as clear in his voice as pain. "I fuckin' shot myself!"

The shooter's screams were nothing compared to the vampire's. The smell of burning flesh and silk permeated the air as the flames consumed him, driving him further from any sensible reaction. His strong legs kicked right through both Wade and the ninja on the floor, knocking both men aside as the vampire ran out into the open only to trip over his own feet. He tumbled to the concrete, burning like a scarecrow in a bulky silk suit. His cries ended with his fall.

Drew brought back one fist, lined up his swing and stepped in to bring all possible force into his uppercut. One second more might have offered all the thug needed to recover, but he never saw the blow coming. The punch laid him out cold.

The vampire seemed finished. The other thug was down and clutching his wounded leg. Drew spotted his pistol and kicked it away, sending it under the van. That left only the ninja, who still tussled with Wade on the floor in a vicious ground fight. He lurched forward, wanting to help his friend, but the situation changed all over again.

"Freeze! FBI!" bellowed a loud, deep, commanding voice. "Hands over your heads, now!" The speaker moved in with his pistol drawn and pointed directly at Drew. Somewhere beyond the Glock was a dark suit and a blond crew cut, but the gun said enough all by itself.

He wasn't alone. Drew spotted two more figures, a white man and an Asian woman, also in business attire and also moving in with guns drawn. The woman pushed past Drew as her partner shoved him against the van. She stepped right into the still-struggling pile of Wade and the ninja, snatching Wade's wrist with her free hand and twisting it behind his back. She stomped down between the ninja's shoulder blades with one firm foot. "It's over!" she barked.

"Think they're legit?" Wade asked loudly.

"Shut up!" both of the male agents yelled. "Just shut up right now!"

Drew ignored them. "Hope so," he announced. The rougher push up against the van and the renewed chorus of commands fit his expectations.

"Sorry, man," grunted Wade.

"We said, shut up, or we will fucking gag you," snarled the woman who already had Wade half-cuffed. "Don't test us."

"Is it just them?" asked the blond man.

"Yeah, just the two of them," replied a somewhat muffled voice from behind Drew. "The others didn't seem to come out."

The blond grunted. "Good. This asshole over here needs bandaging, but he'll make it out of the garage first. Let's wrap everyone up and get out of here before this becomes a bigger scene."

"Bandaging? You ain't callin' an ambulance?" asked Drew. His only answer came as a gloved hand pushed his head up against the van. He felt another hand grab his wrist and twist it around his back and heard the sound of handcuffs emerging from someone's belt.

Drew let out a grim breath. Getting arrested by Spider-Man was not the way he'd intended to end his Halloween.

ONYX SHUDDERED at the touch of skilled fingers slipping under her skirts and over her hips. Given the intricacies of her outfit—bodice over blouse and leather belt over it all—she wouldn't have thought such a move possible. Yet the succubus pulled it off with ease and grace. Lorelei embraced her from behind, filling Onyx with anticipation. Onyx felt Lorelei's hands against her hips, and then over the creases between those hips and her thighs at her front, and then, briefly, teasingly, between her legs.

"You two mustn't become completely disheveled," Lorelei whispered, punctuating her words with a soft nibble of Onyx's earlobe. "The night is still young."

She felt the succubus hook her fingers around the top folds of her skirt and tug down gently, bit by bit, heightening her anticipation. Onyx opened her eyes at that first sensation of her skirts sliding down, torn once again between wanting this and not wanting things to go too far. Yet there was Molly, sitting on the bed right in front of Onyx, watching with wide, eager eyes.

Molly's outfit had been loosened up, too. Onyx gazed down at her lover's face, her exposed collarbones and the valley of her cleavage. She felt her trepidation fall away much like her skirt. Molly was here, and approved, and even slid her hands up Onyx's sides and gently over her breasts.

Lorelei read their relationship well. She knew which of her new playmates would dive into this sort of adventure, and which would need more reassurance. Neither young woman expected this, but as long as they were together, they could both enjoy themselves. Lorelei made sure Onyx had her lover's eyes in direct, easy view as she bent at the knees and slipped the skirts to the floor.

She smiled at the sight of the black thong panties over the pert ass in front of her. "Lovely," she murmured, remaining low as she brought one hand up along the inside of Onyx's legs. Her other hand reached out around those legs toward Molly's, gracefully slipping her fingers under the slit on the side of the sea witch dress.

Molly gasped, not expecting the touch, but instantly loving it. She bit her lip and parted her thighs encouragingly, and had no objection at all when Lorelei's fingertips gently discovered Molly's lack of panties. She looked up to Onyx, who knew the intimacies of Molly's costume, but found her lover's eyes closed. Lorelei's touch had moved from Onyx's inner thigh to her groin, cupping it gently and massaging it with a slow, slight ripple of pressure from the palm out along her fingers.

The succubus held the two in blissful anticipation, patiently probing each for their reactions and ensuring that their defenses were down. She pleased them and let their desires build. Her fingers between Molly's thighs became wet before long. Onyx, having a thin barrier of fabric between her flesh and Lorelei's hand, took slightly longer, but it was time well spent. When Lorelei curled her fingers over the top of those panties and pulled down, Onyx gasped but had no urge to resist. To the contrary, she wordlessly consented, stepping out of the lace as it fell to her feet.

"Will you indulge me?" Lorelei asked.

"Yes," hissed Onyx, who now felt Lorelei's fingers trace along her bared sex.

Molly let out a heavy breath. "You'll have to stop if you want us to give you any attention."

"Oh no, not yet," Lorelei smiled. "Soon enough. Right now, I want you to lie back together." She withdrew her hands long enough to rise and stand at Onyx's side. Lorelei reached out with the hand that had toyed with Onyx to trace against Molly's jaw, knowing the redhead could not resist tasting those fingers. It kept Molly distracted as Lorelei swept Onyx into a deep, slow kiss. The two pushed together, Onyx melting up against the succubus and losing the rest of her inhibitions.

Assured now that Onyx was utterly pliant, Lorelei guided her to lay back on the bed. She devoted one hand to Onyx's body, tracing across her chest and then down over her bodice to tease her groin and her warm and ready sex.

Lorelei's mouth, however, shifted to Molly, planting a slightly rougher, hungrier kiss on her other partner's mouth. The two made out fiercely, not quite struggling for dominance but sharing a hot intensity as Lorelei brought Molly to lie down beside her lover.

Onyx watched the pair kiss, wanting to be a part of it for either but also perfectly content to simply be a spectator as long as Lorelei kept touching her like this. For all the passion of the kiss, Onyx still enjoyed a gentle, skilled hand. Fingers slid across her wet labia, made a soft, circling pass over her clit and then slid low again to begin their tender, teasing invasion.

The succubus broke away from Molly, leaving her panting as she moved her mouth lower against the redhead's body. There was little point in a lingering trail of kisses, what with Molly still mostly clothed, but Lorelei had her crotch exposed by way of the slit in Molly's dress.

Lorelei's tongue came down just beside Molly's wet lips, teasing her wickedly as it moved up and over her vulva, then down the other side, her contact gentle but exciting. Simultaneously, Onyx gasped as Lorelei's middle finger sank into her to the knuckle, which skillfully kneaded her lips.

She coordinated her moves, escalating with both partners at the same moments. Her kiss between Molly's thighs became less teasing and more direct as her index finger pushed inside Onyx to join her middle. Her tongue made its first real caress of Molly's clit while her fingers gently curled up inside Onyx to stroke the most sensitive spot within her.

Both of the witches let out passionate moans. Each reached out for the other, with neither wanting to break contact from Lorelei or obstruct her in any way as she administered such pleasures to both but needing to do something as they rode out their pleasure.

Lorelei accommodated them expertly as they shifted closer and kissed. Her skills were more than up to the task. Her attention never waned on either partner. Their needful kissing grew rockier as Onyx began to shake and whimper and as Molly squirmed. They moaned and gasped their pleasures into one another's mouths, sharing lusty, physical satisfaction.

The succubus loomed over them at the foot of the bed as the two eventually sank down onto their backs. "Oh my God," Molly breathed. "That was... awesome."

"I do what I can in these restricted circumstances," Lorelei smiled.

Onyx laughed, looking from Molly to Lorelei, and then her eyes widened and her laughter died as she saw the succubus move over, just a couple of feet, bringing her head and those glorious lips toward her center.

Molly just watched and grinned as Lorelei planted her first, gentle lick across the intimacy that Molly had tasted so many times. Then she felt Lorelei's fingers slip between her legs, and knew she wouldn't be a mere spectator.

ALEX EMERGED from the men's room—and the line outside it—to find Jason and Amber there waiting for him. Amber looked perfectly pleasant; Jason looked a little annoyed.

Holy shit, Alex thought. He'd deliberately taken longer than Jason to give the pair a chance to break away. Alex held out his hands in apology and mouthed, "I tried, dude," before Amber spotted him.

Jason simply rolled his eyes. "There he is," he nudged Amber.

"Hey," Amber smiled as Alex rejoined them. "Haven't seen your date at all. Or your *other* date," she teased.

"I'm sure they'll turn up," he shrugged. "They'll find me when they want to. I've got my cell phone. You two should go out and have a good time. You don't need to keep me company."

"Aw, we've got all night," Amber replied. "Look, I know what it's like to be left all alone at a big party. We don't want to do that to you. Right, Jason?"

Her date immediately smothered his "fuck off, bro" glare before she looked back at him. Whatever Jason was about to say, Alex saw it die as soon as

Amber's eyes were on him. "Yeah, it's cool," Jason agreed, sounding entirely sympathetic and masking all of his annoyance. "Let's just roll back to the main rooms. We'll run into one or another of them sooner or later."

Amber put herself between them, linking up arm-in-arm with her date and his friend as they walked. "So you've gotta tell me how you swung that," she said.

"Swung which?" Alex asked.

"C'mon, now," she smirked. "I know Seattle's full of 'alternative lifestyles,' but *two* hot girlfriends? Seriously? You know that's not normal."

Alex half-smirked, half-frowned, and shot a look at Jason. "Oh, it's not?"

"Hey, my shit lasted like ten minutes," Jason objected. "They may as well have been sharing ownership of a pair of pants."

"Yeah, I already know about Jason and his blondies," Amber chuckled. "That's just what I mean, though. That was a fling. You think this is gonna last?"

"We're pretty committed," Alex said—and then he saw her. Tight white jeans, a black leather jacket over a black top showing off just enough cleavage to make a statement, and smooth, beautiful Latina looks on exactly half her face. It was the face that caught his eye, and the sultry, flirtatious grin as she crossed their path. That half of her face was lovely. The left half was chalk white, with swirling black lines coming off the corner of her red lips and a starburst pattern centered on her left eye.

Alex turned as she passed, his eyes on hers until she turned her head again. His arm slipped out of Amber's as his gaze trailed down to the Latina's backside. It was every bit as appealing as the rest of her. She looked over her shoulder once, turning the sugar skull side of her face to him and making eye contact again before she faded into a crowd of people at the other end of the hall.

He turned to find Amber and Jason waiting. Jason looked entirely oblivious. Amber watched him with a skeptical twitch in her lips. "Committed, huh?"

"Did you see the sugar skull? That was so tight!"

"Oh, so you were just appreciating her costume?" came Amber's cynical, mildly accusatory reply.

"Wha—well," Alex shrugged, "she's hot, obviously." He nearly complimented Amber on her looks, too, just to make plain that he didn't think she was chopped liver, and then stopped. *No. Jason's date,* he reminded himself. *Do nothing even close to flirting with her.*

"Did I miss something?" asked Jason.

"Nothing big. So, Alex, you were saying before? About your girlfriends?" Amber jerked her thumb over her shoulder toward the main ballroom.

He sighed. Sooner or later, he'd have to get used to this sort of thing. It wasn't like the subject was unreasonable. "What do you want to know?"

"How did this all happen? Where do you meet women like that? I know you swept in to rescue Lorelei somehow, but what about Rachel? C'mon, I want all the sordid details."

With most of the party guests still on the dance floor or at the bar, it wasn't too hard to find a table where they could all sit. "You really want to hear me talk about myself all night? I don't."

"Thank God for that," Jason quipped.

"Right?" Alex agreed.

Amber rolled her eyes. "Okay, fine. But does it ever get awkward?"

"Sometimes. It's work, just like any relationship, right? At this point we're all comfortable with each other. The biggest stress is me just trying to make all this fit in my head when the whole world says everyone's gotta be couples and anything else is icky and perverted. So there's that, and there's Rachel having to work crazy hours so she's never around at any consistent time. Plus I may never get used to living at Lorelei's financial level. It feels weird."

"Hey," Jason piped up, "how's your mom handling all this now? She cooler about Lorelei?"

Alex fidgeted in his seat under Amber's interested gaze and Jason's question. "That's not such a thing anymore," he explained. "She's not a hundred percent on us staying together, but that's because of the age and income gaps. At least she doesn't have anything against Lorelei at this point, y'know?"

"But...?"

"...but Rachel wants to meet her." He paused. "Mom still doesn't know."

Jason's eyes widened. So did his grin. Laughter quickly followed. "Oh wow, seriously? She wants to... oh man, can I be there for that?"

"What, would your mom not approve?" Amber asked. "Rachel seems more your age than Lorelei, at any rate. I mean I can see anyone being thrown off by the three-way thing. Or would your mom freak out by the girl-girl thing?"

"No, it's not that," Alex shook his head. "It's just me being involved with more than one person would be weird to... um... her." He saw the sugar skull pass by, moving through the room only a couple of tables away. Once again, they made eye contact until her path interrupted the connection.

He blinked it away. "Yeah. Mom had a tough enough time just adjusting to me being with an older woman like Lorelei, but explaining Rachel on top of that... I don't know if I could handle that conversation with my mom."

"I don't think many guys could," Jason laughed.

"What do you think you're gonna do?" asked Amber.

"I dunno," Alex sighed, "but I gotta figure out something by Thanksgiving, 'cause Rachel wants to be part of that. Ugh. Did I say ugh already? Ugh."

"What's this job that Rachel has?" asked Amber.

"She, uh... kinda works for the city? It's hard to explain. She supervises a whole bunch of people and so she's always on call." Alex looked away again as he spoke. Being this evasive was tough. Part of him wondered how Jason held up to Amber's curiosity, but the fact that she had so many questions indicated that he hadn't told her much. Alex felt the conversation getting away from him, though, and wished someone would come to his rescue.

Failing that, he needed to change the subject. "What's up with you and your family, though?" he asked Jason. "Anything getting better there, or are your parents still pissed?"

Then it was Jason's turn to sigh. He looked up at Amber. "So I haven't actually asked, but I don't suppose that you're a nice Jewish girl and it just hasn't come up?"

"Atheist parents, sorry," Amber shook her head. "Turned out the same way."

He nodded. "Figured." Jason's eyes turned back to Alex. "Yeah, they're still gonna be pissed at me."

"So speaking of which," Amber spoke up, "what was the deal with Rachel asking you not to start any theological debates?"

Alex winced. He'd tried, but here they were on the subject of his girlfriends again. Once more, he wished for a rescue... and then he saw a lovely half-sugar skull face approach him.

She leaned her hip against the table beside Alex's seat. He saw not a shred of shyness in her eyes. "Saw you lookin' back in the hallway," she said. "An' then just a minute ago. But you didn't come to say hi. Hope I ain't interruptin' nothing?"

If her good looks weren't enough to draw him in, her accent provided the rest of the lure. "No, not at all," Alex said. He sat up straight and found himself unable to take his eyes off her. Her natural confidence and smooth manner held his attention. "I'm glad you decided to come over and say hi. I just didn't want to get up and abandon my friends here."

She turned the natural side of her face toward Jason and Amber to casually say, "Hi," giving Alex another good look at her sugar skull make-up. "So you here alone, or is your date ditchin' you?"

"She's around," Alex said, unable to hold back a flirtatious grin, "but we don't have to be hand-in-hand or anything. We're not a jealous couple."

"No?"

His cellphone vibrated. "This might be her, sorry," he said, slipping it out to check it quickly. The message read: "Gonna b a bit. L says go have fun. --O." At that, Alex just smiled. "Nope. No jealousy issues at at all."

Amber leaned over to Jason. "Can you hear them?" she asked, unable to follow the conversation with the newcomer's back to them and the dance floor music still thumping.

Jason just shook his head. "Shit happens all the time with him anymore," he shrugged. "Minute Lorelei's gone, girls just flock all around him."

"She's not bothered by that?"

"You did catch on that she's kinda freaky, right?" he said. "Sometimes I wish I had his problems." Amber's hand came over his and gave him a squeeze, and he smiled at her for it. "But only sometimes."

"I like your problems better," she said.

"So what's your name?" the sugar skull asked, ignoring the pair behind her.

"I'm Alex," he answered. He saw nothing suspicious in the slight rise of her eyebrow and her tiny nod at his name. All he read from her reactions was a continued interest in flirting. "Who are you?"

"Rosario," she said. "I'm up from Las Vegas. Came to see my boyfriend, but turns out he's a drunk asshole so I'm single now, I guess. Figured I'd just have to find my own fun tonight."

"I like fun," Alex smiled.

"You look like it," she said. "Least you're dressed to be ready for it."

He snorted. "Well, this is an actual costume. It's from a book... y'know, whatever. Can I get you a drink?"

"The bars outside the dance rooms have shorter lines," she suggested.

He stood up and looked past her. "Hey, I'm gonna go get a drink with Rosario here," Alex said to his companions. "Looks like Lorelei's gonna be busy for a bit anyway. You don't have to have me tag along with you all night."

"Your friends can come, too," Rosario said loudly enough for their benefit, but then winked at Alex and dropped her voice to add, "or not."

Amber looked to Jason and found that his face had grown noticeably more serious. She rose as he did, leaning in to ask, "Is something wrong here? I mean other than the obvious?"

"Alex has a girl problem," Jason said, lowering his voice to ensure neither Alex nor Rosario could hear, "but it's not the kind you'd think."

They followed Alex and Rosario out of the ballroom, taking a couple of turns in the hotel's hallways. "I thought the bars were out the other way?" Alex asked, pointing down in the opposite direction as Rosario guided them.

"There's a second one upstairs from here," Rosario said, turning around and taking the loose ends of his bathrobe belt to tug him along. "We don' wanna have to deal with the crowd in the main lobby, right?" She walked backwards for a few steps, her eyes and her smile promising much more than idle conversation, before leading them around another corner.

Alex had no particular reason to suspect anything. He'd never seen Rosario before in his life, but that meant little. Women flirted and made passes at him all the time now. Lorelei was busy with the witches, probably doing exactly what he wanted to do with them. Rachel was nowhere to be found. A little time with a pretty stranger might lead to something unexpected and fun, or to nothing at all. He had nothing to lose. He followed.

Jason and Amber followed, too, suddenly feeling like a fifth wheel in all this. They both found themselves slightly uncomfortable when they passed a trio of large men in bulky black cloaks and generic monster masks at the corner of Rosario's next turn. "Uh, this just leads to a service exit," Jason observed.

"Yeah," Alex frowned, "are you sure—?" The rest of his sentence was suddenly smothered by the moist bandana Rosario shoved against his mouth and nose. She threw her other hand around his neck, holding on tight as Alex struggled and tried to spin away. The first involuntary whiff of the chloroform on the rag already had his head spinning. Rosario hooked one leg around his, throwing her hip into his midsection to bring him down to the floor as she clung to him.

Alex saw Jason and Amber grabbed from behind by the men in the cloaks. Another of them loomed over him, presumably to help Rosario, but that was about all his mind could process before he blacked out.

7

BLOOD DEBTS

He awoke on hard, flat ground. He lay either indoors on some stone floor or perhaps on a road. He felt the incredibly soft fabric of a blanket around him. The fabric was too thin to keep him warm but it was softer than any of his clothes... no. Not a blanket. These *were* clothes. Softer than wool, certainly softer than leather, and not nearly as warm.

It was hard to think.

He heard no birds or wind, just the echoes of voices and steady, far-off noises. He had to be inside somewhere.

His eyes would only open for the briefest of moments, and blearily at that. He fumbled about for something to hold and found only a flat, cold floor. *This is not Roman stone*, he realized.

Wait. Roman stone?

"I think he's waking up," said someone in a language he didn't understand, and yet he did. Why wouldn't he understand it, though? He'd grown up speaking English all his life.

English? What is that?

"Pull him up. Pull him to his knees," someone said. He recognized that as English. The Queen's English. Proper English. Like the captain, or the lieutenant.

Who? What in Juno's piss is a lieutenant?

Wait, Juno's what? Who the fuck is Juno? Who the fuck talks like that?

Strong hands grabbed him on both shoulders and pulled him upright, settling him—roughly—back down on his knees. He fought to get his eyes open. The light wasn't too bright, and clearly artificial—electrical lights, he now understood, and look how slick it all was!—and then he saw the concrete ceiling and the tan, smooth marble tiles of the floor. Green metal railing stood wherever a purposeful gap opened between the floor and the concrete walls. Signs saying "Westlake" and "Metro" could be seen here and there, along with what looked like advertisements for things he didn't recognize.

A great many people surrounded him in a crowded arc. Most wore black. *Where in Christ's name am I?*

His vision cleared. Several dozen people, mostly pale, watched him intently. Their garb tended toward dark colors, but the styles and fashions spanned centuries. Many bore weapons: swords hung on hips, or modern guns sat in holsters, and even one or two people carried genuine black powder pistols.

Signs and maps here and there offered directions to various streets or other destinations. He thought he might be underground somewhere. Perhaps in a subway tunnel? This one seemed nicer than the ones in Paris or Detroit... but when had he been to either city?

The war. He'd grown up in Detroit, but then he got drafted and went to Paris to fight the Cong and then Siobhan left him and he had that fight at the saloon, and then... *no. That can't be right.*

"Alex Carlisle?" asked a voice. That same voice with the proper English accent again. He placed it with a man toward the center of the group directly ahead of him. Standing nearby, amid men and women in dark clothing, was the girl with the sugar skull make-up on one side of her face. Rosario.

The Englishman gestured to him with his cane. He wasn't small. He wore a dark suit, made entirely of wool, with a silk pocket handkerchief, nice hat and all the trimmings.

He had Alex's wallet. He looked at it one more time and nodded to himself. "You are Alex Carlisle, are you not?"

"Yuh. Yeah?" Alex blinked. That sounded right. Alex Carlisle. This was one of the downtown Seattle bus tunnels, underneath a shopping mall and department stores. The buses ran one floor below—but he didn't hear them running now.

The Englishman looked at Alex's wallet one more time and nodded to himself. "Excellent. I suppose I should wish you a happy birthday, though in truth I am here to ensure otherwise," he said mildly. He handed the wallet to a pale man in an extravagant crimson toga with a laurel wreath on his head. "Lord Cornelius, once again you have earned the admiration of us all. I confess I expected this to take hours. Your people do excellent work."

Alex looked over his shoulder. There were more men behind him, too, though not all were pale like the rest. The pale ones wore '80s fashions that didn't seem intentionally ironic; the others dressed in ordinary street clothes. Alex saw guns in their hands. He also saw Jason and Amber stuck on their knees in front of the standing men, their hands on their heads as if awaiting arrest or execution. Neither looked particularly happy to be there.

"You okay?" Alex asked.

"Yeah," Jason grunted, "just holdin' out as long as we—"

"You shall not speak," interrupted the Englishman, loudly and forcefully but with notable calm. "You have already been instructed. Disobey at your peril."

Alex looked over Jason and then Amber, finding no obvious injuries or signs of panic. They both seemed to be holding up fairly well, but that did little to assuage his feelings. Anger bubbled up within him, quickly overwhelming his fear and confusion. Anger seemed the wrong response, given his predicament, but he didn't question it. Better to be angry than to panic.

Amber watched everything with a sense of great dread and creeping despair. She'd seen many of these faces on the sketch files kept by the task force. Most were from the west coast, but she recognized faces from New York and Miami and cities in between. Cornelius, in particular, looked exactly like his sketch. She'd thought the bit about him wearing a toga and laurel crown was ridiculous, but here he was in all his anachronistic glory. She saw the others give him all the deference suggested by his alleged lordship over Southern California.

They took her keys, her wallet and her phone when they grabbed her. Amber's prized prop replica assault rifle now lay in a gutter outside the hotel. *Thank God I didn't keep my badge in my wallet*, she thought for the third time, but that didn't resolve one bit of this predicament.

There had to be at least forty vampires here, give or take a few mortal goons. Nobody would be impressed if she identified herself and demanded they all surrender into her custody. She didn't think she could take even one of them out unarmed; the single vampire she'd arrested in LA weeks ago absorbed several gunshots like so many weak punches before he'd been brought down by sheer muscle and weight. The bullets that struck Kowalski's torso that night punctured and stunned him for the briefest of seconds, but beyond that he seemed indifferent to their effects.

She watched as Lord Cornelius moved over to Rosario and handed her the wallet. "You have done well, my dear," he said in a thick accent. "You must be rewarded."

Rosario nodded eagerly. "Thank you, my lord," she said, though the form of address sounded awkward from her mouth. "And my boys, too, right?"

Cornelius brushed a fond hand over her hair. She whimpered. "I know leadership when I see it," he said. His other hand touched her collar, then trailed down her chest and her belly without regard to propriety or privacy. Rosario seemed excited by it rather than put off, and shuddered as his hand kept moving lower until he lewdly clutched at her groin.

She inhaled sharply. Cornelius swept back her hair and placed his mouth on her neck. Rosario's eyes rolled back then and she surrendered to him as his lips spread over her flesh and then stiffened. A trickle of blood escaped his kiss to run down her front.

The crowd went silent. The distant echo of the bus tunnel remained, but aside from that the only sound anyone could hear was that of Rosario's blissful gasps. Her breathing became labored, and then raspy, and finally ceased. The other vampires and their attendants looked on, most with obvious lust in their eyes as Cornelius drained Rosario dry.

Cornelius released her with a flourish, holding his hands up and out wide as if expecting applause. She fell away from him, but a pair of pale, young-looking women in ancient dress caught her and gracefully carried her back. Scattered applause and a few calls of approval followed, but the reactions were not uniform. It seemed as if Cornelius had just violated some social taboo, yet was powerful enough to get away with it.

"Ah. Well," smiled the Englishman crisply. "We shall welcome her into the family, as it were, when she rises again."

"Ugh," grunted Alex.

The Englishman looked at him curiously. "I take it you disapprove?"

"Yeah," Alex fairly sneered. "Gross."

"You must have found her enchanting to have followed her so blindly."

"I did up until this," agreed Alex, "She's got the vampire herp on her now."

Cornelius became indignant. Blood still coated his chin. The crimson color of his robe made the stains hard to see except where the light reflected off the wettest spots. "Mortal chaff, have you any idea whom you address?"

"It sounded like you're the Great Cornholio? Did I hear that right?"

Though the word meant nothing to him, Cornelius recognized the insult for what it was. The Englishman held up a calming hand, though his head bowed somewhat in a show of deference. "Lord Cornelius, if I may," he said, and then raised his eyes toward Alex again. "Mr. Carlisle, you speak to Gaius Cornelius Vespasianus, Consul of the Republic of Los Angeles, one of the eldest of the society of night in this country. And I—"

"That name doesn't even make any *sense*," Alex spat without a second thought. "Nobody has people address them by their gens. Cornholio is either a poseur or an idiot."

Amber heard it all, but couldn't follow. "What's he talking about?" she hissed.

The other young man caught it as well. At first he just shook his head, but then understanding crept over him. "Oh, no."

The blood-stained face under the laurel crown screwed up in a rage. Cornelius tore a short sword out of a fold within his toga. "Impudent brat!" he snarled, "I will cut—!"

"Lord Cornelius, please!" cautioned the Englishman again. Two other vampires stepped out of the crowd, both of them rough, muscular men in dark leather and denim that seemed somehow just a bit off from what they should be wearing.

Alex looked at the pair curiously. Something about the long, scraggly blond hair of the one and the red beard of the other seemed familiar to him. He knew those rings on their fingers and the gold bands on their arms. They both carried large blades, one on his belt and the other over his shoulder. Both had small, light axes tucked in their belts.

If he'd been angry before, the mere sight of these two brought his feelings to a fever pitch. Old, simmering hatred welled up inside. Alex had never seen them before, couldn't know them from Adam, and yet his hands balled into fists and began to tremble. It was all he could do to keep control of it.

The Englishman sighed for effect and turned his attention back to Alex. "I am the Lord Mayor George Wentworth of New York. Like my friend and ally, *Lord Cornelius*," he said, emphasizing the words—though several behind him smirked at the sound of it—he continued, "I am a longstanding ally of the Lady Anastacia of this city. I believe you may have met her?"

"I might've heard that name," Alex growled, "but I don't remember."

"You would remember the Lady's grace and majesty," assured Wentworth.

"That's not how I'd describe you guys," Alex shook his head.

"Mr. Carlisle, we know you were the subject of a search by her court and by the Brotherhood of Apollo. We know of the involvement of demons from the Pit. You will find no salvation in being either evasive or insolent."

"What do you want?"

"Closure," Wentworth said, his calm returning once more. "We seek to resolve this issue and move on. It must be conducted in front of many witnesses so that no accusations of skullduggery or treachery live on after the fact." His arms spread wide to indicate the assembly of vampires around him. "Your opinions and motives are irrelevant... though we would like to hear whom you serve. The Lady also sought out someone named Lorelei. Lord Cornelius knows of a certain demon by that name. Is she your mistress?"

"I don't serve anybody," Alex replied, still holding his anger in check. His thoughts bent further and further toward violence, but he had friends here. He had to think of them first. Stalling offered the best bet for their survival.

"There was a party hosted by the Lady," Wentworth went on, "and now the home that held it is nothing but ashes and ruin. Do you know what happened there?"

"Your lady friend and her buddies kidnapped me. They wanted to hand me over to bad people. It didn't go so well for them."

Hisses and murmurs swept the crowd. Wentworth looked to Cornelius before speaking again. "Mr. Carlisle, is the Lady dead?"

"I don't know," Alex answered honestly. His eyes stayed mostly on the pair of long-haired vampires. He knew they were deadly raiders. He knew they were liars and scum. They'd ruined his life... when?

"You don't know?"

"Like I said, they were working for other people," Alex shrugged. "They got in the way. All I did was defend myself. I had no beef with them."

"Ah. Beef. How appropriate. Tell me, would your mortal courts recognize the self-defense plea of a cow after it had gored its butcher? I think not."

"...what?"

"You are mortal," Wentworth said. "You exist as servants and food. Chattel. If the Lady sought to give you to another, it was your place to be given. To be clear," Wentworth added with a shrug, "I explain more for the benefit of my associates than for you or your friends. Mortals are entitled to no explanations."

Alex let that process. His scowl remained. "Well, fuck you, clown."

"The wit of modern youth," spat Cornelius.

"Step up, Cornholio. I'll give you some modern wit right up your ass."

The remark caused an obvious stir among the vampires. "You challenge me?" Cornelius laughed.

"It is no formal challenge, my lord," Wentworth noted.

"His meaning is plain!"

"He is *mortal*. We should no sooner honor a challenge laid by a pig."

"It seems clear to me, Lord Wentworth," said the blond Nordic vampire. "Do not complicate the matter. We are here to see Lady Anastacia avenged, one way or another."

"But we should do so properly, Bjorn," pressed Wentworth, "and without dignifying this mortal trash with a trial by combat or a duel."

"Oh, just look at him, Wentworth!" snarled Cornelius. "What skill in combat do you think him to have?"

"We could ask those who were with Lady Anastacia," spoke up a short, pale Japanese woman in old, formal silks. "Perhaps a séance to speak with the dead? We might learn how many the boy has struck down."

"Other supernaturals were involved," Wentworth replied with a dismissive wave. "We know Lady Anastacia had trouble with mongrels in the area, and we know of her entanglements with sorcerers. Let's not jump to conclusions about this boy's relevance." Others murmured in agreement.

"No, no, no, I'm game." Alex piped up. He didn't understand vampire politics, but he recognized the opportunity. "I challenge. Sure. Whatever you call it. Me and Cornholio—"

"Stop saying that!" Cornelius seethed.

"—one on one. I take him out, you let us go."

"Alex," hissed Amber, "what the hell are you doing?"

"Fuck if I know," he grunted, lowering his voice. "Stalling mostly."

"For what?"

"The cavalry," Jason murmured. Amber turned to him with a questioning look. "It'll come," he assured her. "Just gotta hang in there."

Wentworth's brow furrowed and a sneer curled up on his lip. "You are here to be executed, Mr. Carlisle," he explained. "There is no trial. You have no rights. You will die tonight."

"Lord Mayor Wentworth," said Cornelius, "you have acted as our voice tonight, but as the eldest here, I claim the right to act as our society's hand. I need no proper challenge to justify myself in silencing this brat."

The Nordic vampires grunted in agreement. So did many of the others. No one seemed able to come up with a viable objection. Wentworth stiffened. "Very well, Lord Cornelius," he said. "As you say, he has no right to challenge, but no right to mercy or his impudence, either."

"Excellent," Cornelius growled. He stepped forward with his blade drawn.

Alex rose to his feet. Neither of the vampires at his side stopped him. Instead, they withdrew. "Wait, I don't get a weapon?" Alex asked. "What kinda crap is this?"

"It is your death, brat," answered Cornelius.

"You have no rights in our society," shrugged Wentworth.

"I call bullshit," Alex argued.

"Tell it to your carpenter god," Cornelius sneered, "after I've taken your head and drained your corpse of your blood."

Amber and Jason looked on as Alex began to shake. His hands remained balled up into fists, with his knuckles now running white. Neither knew how to stop this or how to interrupt. Jason thought to go down fighting with his friend if he could get up quickly enough.

"Oh, you fucking *wuss*," Alex snarled. "You're that afraid of a stand-up fight?"

Bjorn's bearded companion spat in disgust. "Would you cower from this mortal boy?" he asked Cornelius.

"No *vampire* has dared challenged me in centuries," Cornelius countered, his eyes narrowing. "I fear no one. You know this well."

"Then show us why," Unferth nodded, gesturing to Alex. "He has challenged."

"He has no rights—" Wentworth repeated.

Unferth held up his hand to cut Wentworth off. "We will not be called cowards by anyone, vampire or even mortal. It is not about him." Unferth jerked his broadsword from his belt and tossed it to Alex's feet. He looked at Cornelius. "It is about you. We would see you fight, Lord Cornelius. Even if only against a mortal stripling."

Debate ceased as Alex leaned over to take up the blade. He struck a ridiculous image, clad in pajamas and a bathrobe and holding a broadsword.

"Do you even know how to hold a blade?" Cornelius taunted.

"I played Dungeons & Dragons a few times," Alex deadpanned.

"You always played the wizard," muttered Jason.

"Whatever." Alex hefted the sword, swung it around, and gave no particular impression of having any real skill. It was balanced like a real blade, unlike the shiny pieces of crap offered in knife shops in the mall. The grip felt familiar, even if the metal seemed different. It felt like modern steel in an old, trustworthy shape. They'd given him a real weapon, not a showpiece.

The voices and memories in his head quieted in the face of imminent battle. Experience and training took over. He watched Cornelius laugh, turn to his fellows an offer a salute—a gladiator's salute. He didn't know Cornelius at all, but he knew his type. He'd seen this sort of thing before. Cornelius didn't take Alex seriously as a threat; he wanted to put on a display for his people. A long fight wouldn't suit his purpose. He'd want to end this quickly, and he'd want to make a show of it.

Alex set his stance and waited. Cornelius laughed, posed, and then gave an animalistic snarl, baring his fangs at Alex to frighten him before rushing in. Given the vampire's unnatural speed, Alex might not have been able to track him, but for the fact that Cornelius made exactly the move the young man's memories warned would be coming.

Cornelius crossed the distance between himself and Alex with startling speed. He made a playful yet frighteningly quick lunge for the young man's shoulder, thinking to hew straight through his body with a single mighty blow. Alex ducked and deflected the sword with a parry that took full advantage of the strength Cornelius put behind his swing.

The impact of the parry gave Alex's blade a boost of momentum. He spun in place with it, bringing his longer sword up and over in a wide arc that he buried forcefully into the back of the vampire's neck.

In the blink of an eye, Cornelius went from confidence and power to shock and helplessness as he wound up on his knees with a sword embedded halfway through his neck. Though most of his flesh died millennia ago, he still needed a working spine to carry the commands of his brain to his limbs. For all his speed and might, he'd been arrogant and even flamboyant—and his opponent made him pay for it with stunning skill. The fight began and ended in a single breath.

Astonished vampires looked on in complete silence as Alex jerked his sword free. Cornelius fell forward, his hands out onto the floor to keep him from falling onto his face. It seemed all he could make his body do. His head hung low, exposing a wound that gushed a steady stream of blood.

Completely given over to memories of battle, Alex didn't hesitate to follow through. He swung the blade down on the gap with a loud, bloodthirsty cry.

Murderous anger flared in his eyes as he chopped deeply into his foe's flesh, yanked his blade free and did it once more.

Amber watched in utter shock. She only barely tracked the start and finish of the fight, but she saw Alex finish his opponent. The head of her task force's most wanted suspect rolled across the floor in front of Amber and immediately began to crumble to ash.

Alex turned back to the semicircle of vampires and loudly demanded something of them in a language Amber couldn't understand. Some blinked in shock, and others in surprised recognition.

None showed greater understanding of the young man's words than the two Nordic vampires, who looked to one another with amazement. Unferth replied in the same language; Alex responded with obvious contempt and spat at his feet. Bjorn stepped forward, drawing a sword from his belt.

"Fuck me, I was right," breathed Jason.

"Jason!" Amber hissed. "Jason, what's happening?"

Alex kept shouting, pointing at one vampire and then another in what was obviously a series of challenges despite the foreign words and spittle that flew from his mouth. His whole body shook with anger.

"Shit's about to get crazy," Jason warned.

"*About* to?"

"Alex is havin' a freak-out," Jason said. "I dunno—aw, no," he groaned. Bjorn leveled his sword at Alex in a salute or a challenge. He came forward with less speed and more wariness shown by Cornelius, but with the same obvious intent to kill.

Again, Alex read the first swing almost before it came. His blade came up in time with the vampire's, only lower, and what initially looked like a badly misjudged parry smashed straight through two of Bjorn's fingers. The blade fell from his grasp in a bloody mess, but the vampire swiftly retaliated with a broad sweep of his other arm that sent Alex tumbling away.

Alex kept hold of his weapon as he hit the concrete. His vision had gone red with anger; rage and memory guided his movements and his thoughts. He owed this man a debt of blood. They went home and told Halla he was dead. She found another husband, who cast her out when Alex—no, Skorri— returned from the Danelands...

He had no time to sort through his identity. He couldn't think about what was Alex and what was another man. He needed that muscle memory, that skill and that rage, or he'd never live through this.

The vampire had to switch his left hand to wield his sword. He brought it down with such force that it bit a half-inch gouge into the concrete.

Alex kept rolling away. The sword came down again, this time closer to his head. He raised his own blade as he sat up to get out of the way. It was a weak parry against a vastly stronger opponent. The dodge saved Alex's life, but the parry cost him the sword as the force of Bjorn's blow tore it from his hand.

Alex spun on his hip then, hooking the vampire's shin with his right leg and then slamming his left foot hard on the side of his knee just like they'd taught him in basic, before 'Nam. The vampire stumbled and fell to the floor. Alex scrambled up again and rushed to the ashen remains of Cornelius.

Jason jumped forward. The men guarding him were too distracted by the spectacle to catch their prisoner. Jason snatched up the gladius beside the empty toga and tossed it to his friend, pommel first.

Bjorn's weapon slashed overhead again as Alex caught the gladius, fell forward and rolled. Unused to fighting with his left arm, Bjorn hadn't quite brought his sword back in time to defend against his opponent's retaliatory lunge. Alex stabbed the gladius directly through Bjorn's neck.

Painfully strong hands caught Jason's shoulders and arms. He was yanked back and spun by two pale men, one with thin '80s New Wave sunglasses and a ridiculous Mohawk, the other with a do-rag and an oversized, buttoned-down but untucked blue flannel shirt. Jason heard a loud boom behind him, but couldn't look to see what happened. All he saw were the fangs of his captors and hands reaching for his neck.

Then blood, bone and gore exploded out one side of the New Waver's head with another loud boom. A third boom went off half a second later, identical to the first except for the ringing in Jason's ears. More of the vampire's skull flew off to the side.

More booms split the air. Jason felt the hands gripping his arms fall away. The last hands on him, clutching his shoulders, released him with a soft, almost distant "splutch." Jason turned and saw Alex yank his sword out of the side of the man's neck. He wound up and cut loose with another swing to behead the staggered foe while Jason ducked and scrambled out of the way.

To Jason's left, Amber stood in a controlled, measured Weaver stance just like he'd been taught in his NRA classes. The vampire who'd held her in place lay at her feet, staring off at the ceiling with a confused gaze and a bullet hole in his forehead. She held his pistol in her hands.

"Holy shit," Jason blurted, "how did you—?"

"Jason," she barked, "get behind me!"

"Gun!" someone shouted, and then others joined the cacophony of warning. "She's got a gun!"

"Kill her!"

"Calm down. It's just a gun, you stupid cow!"

Jason looked right and saw the vampires in a confused crowd. Some drew weapons. Others shrank back. One pulled her bloody hand away from her dress, now with a large hole in it, and hissed with her fangs showing. A vampire needed a working brain, spine and heart; other organs weren't so vital.

Alex grabbed Jason and heaved him to his feet. The rage in his friend's eyes frightened him almost as much as the vampire who'd nearly bitten him. "Get out of here!" Alex snarled. "Run!"

A black wave of rushing bodies struck them both just then, knocking Jason to the floor again and carrying Alex away. So many of the vampires rushed in that they tripped one another up, each spoiling another's potentially fatal blow while Alex heaved himself up on one enemy's shoulders and hacked at another.

Jason coughed and rolled. One '80s reject lay beside him, stunned by the bullet through his brain. The other had clearly not been so lucky. His head wounds had apparently been enough to do him in, given the mix of ash strewn about within and beside the otherwise empty clothes on the floor. Bjorn lay face-down on the concrete, not beheaded but paralyzed by the hole through his neck.

Amid the closest remains, Jason found a large and unattended gun.

"Jason!" cried Amber as she reached him.

"Just get out of here!" he snapped back as he brought up the Mac-10. He'd never used one before; the closest thing was the semi-auto Uzi he'd rented for half an hour at a shooting range. But he looked to the mass of vampires mobbing Alex, aimed for a spot just past him, pulled the trigger and sprayed.

The vampires at the back of the crowd jerked and yelped, and some turned back on him with an annoyed look on their faces. Somewhere past that, Jason saw the flash of Alex's blade as his friend fought for his life.

Lights began cutting out with a series of small crashes. Fixtures went dark with the sound of shattered glass. The darkness was incomplete, but the spread of shadows changed the environment for everyone.

Something huge and furry rushed past Jason and Amber. It crashed into the horde of vampires with a blood-curdling howl. Screams erupted on the other end of the hallway as the vampires who hadn't charged at Alex found themselves similarly assaulted. Jason and Amber saw another such monster quickly claw its way across the ceiling and drop into the scrum.

More howls filled the broad passageways of the bus tunnel, followed by panicked shouts and screams from the vampires.

Alex hadn't a hope in hell of survival. Every second he remained alive seemed like a genuine miracle, but even so he did not go unscathed. A knife slid through his thigh. Long nails grown by supernaturally strong hands dug through his robe and his pajama shirt to carve bloody trails in his chest. Someone caught his left wrist, almost crushing it with a merciless grip and nearly yanking his arm out of its socket. Another hand grabbed for his neck; Alex swung his sword up in time to slice off all four fingers, then brought it up again and leveled it to jam the blade into the fanged maw that rushed at his face. He heard gunfire and howls, but it all just intermingled with the chaos threatening to overwhelm him.

He stumbled and fell back. Knives and swords and fangs and fists came at him, all too many for him to fight.

Two of the threatening faces suddenly flew back. Two more twisted and shrieked in agony. Attention turned from Alex. The hand on his arm went limp and then crumbled to ash. He heard screams of pain and panic and saw the vampires fall to fighting something big and menacing that came up from behind them. Several somethings, he realized.

Not all the vampires turned from Alex. A genuine off-the-rack creation of Hot Topic fashion and lots of hair gel kept coming. He crossed his pair of spike-knuckled trench knives against Alex's gladius. Alex parried, gave ground and saw nothing but brown fur and muscle behind his opponent. The werewolf broke through the ranks of the other vampires to snatch the faux-Goth boy by the head, its claws piercing his skull before the werewolf tossed him over its shoulder.

The monster rushed forward. Its head slammed into Alex's chest to knock him onto his back once again. It loomed over Alex, putting one huge arm down onto the concrete to Alex's left and then the other to his right with its lips curling back in a predatory snarl.

"Not an improvement," Alex grunted. His sword flashed up again, cutting straight through the werewolf's cheek. The monster's head jerked to the side with the blow. It yelped and batted the sword away, and then suddenly it shrank and the fur disappeared.

Alex found himself pinned to the floor by a naked brunette, who grinned at him despite the blood flowing from a small cut on her cheek. "All the trouble I go through for you," Diana smiled, "and this is the thanks I get?"

Fighting continued on beyond her. Though clearly outmatched for physical power, the vampires neither fled nor immediately fell to the werewolves' claws. Many fought back with skill and tenacity. The initial fury of the assault had scattered them and inflicted losses, but most of the undead rallied and made use of their superior numbers.

"Carlisle!" he heard Wentworth call out from somewhere amid the screams, roars and gunshots. "Do not let Carlisle escape!"

Diana ignored it all. She slid closer over Alex, propped up with her arms fully extended but with her legs and hips sliding up along his. The flow of blood from her cheek didn't seem to bother her. "Come on," Diana taunted, "don't I at least get a thank you kiss?" Her eyes closed and she puckered up her lips.

Alex punched her in the face.

Taking quick advantage of the distraction, Amber patted down the stunned vampire at her feet for ammunition. She and Jason could both see that the fight was by no means over, nor was its outcome certain. "Is this the cavalry?" she shouted as she reloaded.

His Mac-10 had already run dry. Jason's eyes swept the floor for another weapon, but between the damaged lighting and the rapidly shifting shadows he couldn't find one in easy reach. Then he spotted a black werewolf, hunched over the ashes and limp clothing of a fallen foe. It turned and eyed them hungrily.

"I'm gonna guess no," he said.

Amber drew down on it as the monster turned and crept toward them. "I'll shoot!" she warned, and when it didn't back off she did just that. The bullet sank into its muscular shoulder. Though it bled, the werewolf shrugged off the wound. She fired again, this time striking its skull. The monster's head jerked to one side, but when it turned back she saw little more than a deep, nasty abrasion.

Jason's mind worked fast. The werewolf was big and bulky up top, but—"Knees!" he blurted, pointing at its thin legs. "Go for the knees!"

She shifted her aim lower. Her first two shots missed, but the third struck the werewolf—not on the knee, but rather in its foot. The thing immediately slipped and fell with a howl of pain.

Jason pushed her to one side. "Go!" he yelled.

They got only a few yards, closing in on Alex and the strange naked woman who lay struggling on top of him before another furry monster rushed into their path. It reared up and let out a mighty roar, its claws extended with clear intent to kill them both.

Amber raised her gun again, looking for a target low on the thing's body, but its dark fur and the shadows of the tunnel blended too well to make for a clear shot... and then suddenly everything around her lit up.

The light seemed to literally float down through the ceiling. It came from a young woman in a revealing white skirt and top. The angel's broad, white wings were clearly not store-bought. Her tinsel halo was gone, replaced by the genuine article. Rachel hit the floor beside Amber hard enough that Amber felt it.

The black werewolf came straight at her. Rachel stepped into its lunge and threw her arms around the monster's head, moving every bit as fast as her opponent. Despite the thing's massive size and obvious strength, Rachel physically dominated the struggle from the start. Its arms wrapped around her and its claws dug into her sides, shredding her clothes and her skin, but she bore it all with a grimace and remained on her feet. For only a heartbeat, she stood her ground and locked in her hold on the beast. In the next heartbeat, she hooked her hands into opposite sides of its jaw and twisted brutally. The thing's head swiveled around on its shoulders with a bone-crunching snap. Then it fell limp at her feet.

If her wounds hurt, she gave no sign. She bled, but did not stagger. Rachel looked to Amber and Jason, gesturing to the largest concentration of brawling monsters. "Watch the rear," she said to the awed pair. Then she strode on toward Alex and his assailant.

Rachel grabbed a fistful of Diana's hair. The brunette was too surprised to react before the angel grunted, "No means *no*, chica." With that, she hurled the werewolf—using only that same handful of hair—up and over her shoulder and many yards down the subway tunnel. Jason and Amber both ducked reflexively as the naked body flew past.

"Wow, lover, you're a mess," Rachel frowned. She knelt beside Alex, put one hand around his head and softly put her lips to his.

The bleeding from his leg and chest slackened rapidly. His arm, nearly wrenched from his shoulder, still hurt but no longer felt useless. Her kiss did little to resolve his emotional turmoil or the chaos of his memories. She simply didn't have the time to spare for such concerns.

"Rachel?" he gasped.

"Yeah. It's me." She pulled him to sit upright, but could offer no further loving care. The angel walked past his companions, who stood guard only a few feet away. "Get 'em out of here," she said to Jason with only a quick glance. "Don't take any chances on what happens here; just get fucking gone. Prob'ly still gonna be some assholes guarding the street exits, so be careful."

Jason blinked in shock. "You can't get us out of here yourself?"

"Wish I could," she said with a shake of her head, "but I've got faith in you." She kept walking.

"What the hell is going on?" Amber demanded.

"I thought you had to protect him!" Jason pressed, pointing back to Alex.

Rachel tossed him a grin over her shoulder. "I do. Check out how I balance my personal and career commitments." She reached out into thin air with one hand. Her sword of flame grew from her palm.

Two werewolves leaped from out of the mob toward Rachel, crossing several yards in a single bound. The first came headlong into a broad slash of her sword. The werewolf caught fire instantly, engulfed from head to toe in the blink of an eye as it fell to the floor.

The other chomped down on Rachel's sword hand with its jaws. Though not as strong as Rachel, he was considerably larger and had her off-balance. She wrestled with the thing, trying to get leverage without having to drop her sword. The task quickly became entirely too complicated.

"Fuck it," she grunted, heaved the thing upright by her mangled arm. The angel punched at her attacker with her free hand, driving her fist up and in against its torso. Bones snapped audibly and its eyes bulged. Rachel punched again and again with blows so heavy that Amber and Jason could hear them as they landed. In just a few seconds of such treatment, the thing went limp against her. Rachel put her free hand against its nose and pushed upward to pry its jaws loose from her arm before it fell to the floor.

Jason finally answered Amber's question: "All this is pretty much exactly what it looks like. C'mon, help me with Alex." He gave her arm a tug, but didn't stop to see if she followed. Amber managed a backward step or two but couldn't turn away from the angel.

Rachel looked at the mangled ruin of her forearm. It began to heal as soon as it was free of the werewolf's mouth, but it hurt like hell just the same.

The angel let out an irritable sigh before she turned to face the ongoing battle.

If anyone else noticed the arrival of an angel, she saw no particular concern or change in attitude. Vampires fought werewolves. Werewolves fought vampires. At this point all of the mortal goons the vampires had brought along as servants or extra guns already lay dead. Rachel's eyes swept the grand hallway one more time just to be sure of that. "Nobody here but us freaks," she grimaced, figuring the three people behind her knew far too much to count as normals anymore. She stepped forward.

"Hey! Assholes!" she shouted. "Knock it off!"

The fighting carried on.

"*Helloooo?*"

A vampire flew through the air, ash trailing out of its shoulder from where its arm had been, and landed just over to Rachel's left. A werewolf quickly staggered past her in the opposite direction, flailing wildly to get the vampire off its back. The undead Japanese woman in the silk robe refused to give up, having sunk a pair of daggers into the beast's shoulder blades and now riding it for dear life.

Rachel couldn't believe this. Her exasperation drove her to blasphemy. "Motherfuckers, do you *not see* the goddamn *angel* right in front of you?" Then she blinked, rolled her eyes and looked up. "Sorry, sorry," she muttered.

A sharp, screaming battle cry came at her to herald her next attacker. It happened in an eyeblink; she hardly even got a good look at him. He was pale and Caucasian and dressed in an old tunic over a chain mail shirt, and he charged in with his longsword raised.

Rachel grabbed him by the neck, hoisted him into the air and then slammed him down onto the ground. The impact knocked the rest of his breath out of him. Rachel slammed her foot down on his face, crushing bone and rendering him immobile for the moment. She looked up to see if anyone noticed.

Nothing.

"Son of a bitch, seriously?" she sighed. It was at least as humbling a reminder of her limitations as the claws and teeth of the werewolves. She was an angel, and holder of dominion over the city, but she wasn't omnipotent. Being super obnoxious didn't make her super loud.

She'd have to resort to more obvious measures.

White light from her halo spread and intensified. Rachel illuminated every crack and corner of the tunnel, drowning out shadows and momentarily blinding anyone that looked directly toward her. Some shielded their eyes with their forearms; others couldn't help but turn away. The fighting quickly ground to a halt.

"Are we all listening now?" Rachel demanded loudly. The glare of her halo diminished. She strode to the center of the mess, where a small pile of struggling vampires and werewolves separated and crawled away from her in opposite directions.

No one spoke. Not a body came toward her. Weapons remained in hand, claws and teeth waited to sink into flesh once again, but no one moved. She seemed small and innocent compared to the horde of monsters and vicious undead, but they all backed away in trepidation.

"So, hi. I'm Rachel," the angel began, "and I watch over this city. And the surrounding area, so don't try to get technical with me about suburbs or some bullshit like that."

She heard a hiss from one side. Rachel turned her head to find the small Japanese vampire crouching low, still looming over the body of the werewolf she'd just slain. She clutched her daggers menacingly. "One would not expect an angel to bleed," she observed.

"Indeed," said Wentworth, who lurked several yards away behind a pair of bodyguards with swords drawn. "You strike an impressive visage, 'Rachel,' but I see nothing that could not be duplicated through mortal magic. Were you a genuine servant of Heaven, would not my own kind flee or crumble to ash in your presence?"

"Oh, whatthefuckever, dude," Rachel sighed. She blew at a lock of hair that dangled in her face, but it settled right back where it had been. "Don't buy into everything you read about yourself on the fuckin' internet."

Heads turned. "You don't sound like an angel," someone said.

"Yeah, I get that a lot. Believe what you want."

"I believe you're one sort of supernatural creature or another," replied Wentworth, "and you have just laid claim to this city. Presumably you wish to lodge that claim with us? And the mongrels, I would guess?" Wolfish snarls answered his last comment, but the vampire paid them no mind. His attention remained focused on the newcomer. "You seek to treat with us? What is your business?"

Rachel nodded. "Here's my offer: *Get the fuck out.*"

"Rend," growled a voice no human throat could produce. Rachel's eyes flicked to her left, where she saw a looming tower of brown fur and angry, blood-stained teeth move behind other forms. A bald patch on the beast's forehead gave a clue as to which one it was. The vampires in the foreground spread out and away from the monster; its packmates closed in. "Tear. Eat."

"Surprised you can say that much with a mouth like that," Rachel frowned.

The brown werewolf turned its head toward Wentworth, gestured toward him and then itself. "Hold," the monster managed to say, and then pointed with one clawed hand at the angel. "Kill."

Wentworth nodded darkly. "Agreed," he said.

Guns were locked and loaded. Fighters shifted into position. Rachel sighed and rolled her eyes. "Godless sonsabitches."

Like Alex before her, Rachel found herself faced with a mob of attackers rushing in from several directions. Unlike her lover, she was equipped to deal with it. The angel stepped into the oncoming assault with a broad swing of her sword. Bodies ignited and burned in its wake.

Amber watched with awe as the wave of monsters broke against Rachel and her blade. The angel left flaming men, women and monsters strewn in her path. She grabbed the nearest vampire with her free hand and hoisted him up as a shield against the teeth and claws of the werewolf behind him, then shoved his mangled body forward to knock the monster off its feet.

The monsters could hurt the angel—that much was plain from the blows she absorbed and the blood drawn by claws, guns and blades—but on the whole, she gave much better than she got.

Jason didn't bother to watch. He had hoped Rachel could intimidate the bad guys into letting them go, but once things descended back into violence he couldn't spare her much attention. "Alex!" he urged, snapping his fingers and waving his hand in his friend's face. "Alex, you with me, bro? We gotta bounce!"

Judging by the look in his eyes, Jason figured Alex could barely track his surroundings. He still had the short sword firmly in his grip, but gave few other signs of lucidity. Jason grabbed his shoulders and heaved him up.

"Rachel?" Alex asked.

"Yeah, Rachel's here. She's holdin' the bad guys off," Jason said. He made sure Alex could stand before letting him go. "Amber, you ready?" he asked, then saw her watching Rachel in awe. "Amber! C'mon, we gotta go!"

"Right!" Amber blinked and turned. "Right—no!" She brought up her gun toward the two young men and fired.

Her bullets flew past them into the three men who rushed up from behind them bearing guns of their own. One went down quickly, and then the other. Not every dangerous man down here was some crazed supernatural. The third, dressed in simple leather and denim, all but ignored the bullets that tore through him.

He didn't ignore the sword that came for his face as Alex snapped out of his reverie and charged in. Rather than shoot, the vampire brought his AK-47 up to block the blade. He struck back with his elbow, clocking Alex in the shoulder, but the fury of Alex's assault left the vampire no recovery time. Alex dropped low and slashed deep into the vampire's leg, cutting through muscles and tendons.

Amber kept her gun on the vampire, but with Alex in the way she couldn't get a clear shot. The young man had his free hand on the assault rifle then, grabbing it and turning it away in the sort of control move Amber learned at the academy—only no one in her class ever worked with swords. She kept them covered, ready to unload on the vampire, but in the end it wasn't necessary.

Before she knew it, Jason stepped in with a gun claimed from the vampire's fallen mortal companions. Heedless of the dangers of getting mixed up between Alex, his sword and the vampire's savage strength, Jason jammed the pistol against the vampire's head and pulled the trigger. Their foe jerked in reaction as the bullet passed through his skull.

It broke up the melee. Jason trained the gun on his victim again, still well within arm's reach, and fired. He let loose with a third bullet just to be sure. When the vampire fell, Alex stepped in and started hacking at his neck with the sword.

Amber looked down the hallway, eyes sweeping left and then right. The way out was clear. The other direction showed nothing but a fierce fight between an angel and an impromptu alliance that might crumble at any second—though neither of its factions would hesitate to tie up mortal loose ends.

"Okay, we're good," Jason said, snatching up a new gun just for good measure as Alex finished off the vampire. "We ready?"

"Go," Alex said. He turned back toward the fight and took a step forward.

Amber opened her mouth to object, but Jason did her one better. He tackled Alex to the ground. In light of all she'd just seen, she found that as crazy as the monsters deciding to fight Rachel.

"Let me go!" demanded Alex. He put his blade to Jason's neck.

"No! Alex, listen!" Jason countered forcefully. "Bad ass angel back there, right? Mere mortals here. Don't get in her way."

"I'll have their heads!" Alex snarled.

Jason saw the rage in his friend's eyes. He ignored the sword hovering close to his throat. "Alex, it's me, alright? It's Jason! I don't care who the fuck is in your head tellin' you whose ass to kick right now. You are Alex Carlisle and we been friends since grade school! You are not gonna stab me, so put the fuckin' sword down, bro!"

Alex wavered. His anger remained, but the blade turned an inch or two away. He pushed Jason back, but the other young man held on. "Get out of here," he growled, "I'll keep them off your back."

"Your girl's doin' that. Alex, you do *not* get to check out on me here. Not after all this bullshit." He thought quickly for a winning argument and swallowed hard. "Or are you just gonna leave us behind in this mess? Me and Amber, huh? Leave your people behind in a fight?"

Alex glanced toward the battle, then at Jason again and over his shoulder at the worried young woman in green fatigues with the pistol. "No," he grunted.

"Then get us out of here, soldier," Jason barked. He released Alex and pointed down the broad hallway, away from the fighting. "Exit's that way."

Alex nodded. "Fine," he said, "let's go."

Amber threw a questioning glance at Jason. He opened his mouth to speak and suddenly had a critical thought. "Shit! Our stuff!" he blurted. Jason quickly spun around, scanning the debris and bodies between them and the brawl up ahead. "There!" he snapped and ran off.

"Hey, get back here!" Amber demanded.

Jason crouched down beside a fallen body and the remains of a couple of vampires, now just dresses filled with ashes. Amber watched warily as he patted down the lifeless woman in white jeans and a leather jacket. She didn't immediately recognize her until her head turned to one side and Amber saw the sugar skull make-up on her face.

"Phone, phone, wallet," Jason muttered, quickly pulling items from her jacket pockets and placing them in his own. "Wallet, wallet... Dammit, where is it?"

"You wanted to flee," reminded Alex, suddenly speaking with a strange accent, "and now you wish to remain and loot the fallen?"

"Jason, we don't have time for this!" pressed Amber.

"We don't want them getting into our business later, either," Jason argued as he searched. "Maybe they could still find us anyway, but there's no reason to make it easy for—phone!" he cried out as he found Amber's plain black piece.

Alex released the magazine from his AK to check its capacity, then locked and loaded once more. His movements seemed completely proficient. The sword now hung on the cotton belt of his bathrobe, re-tied in a serious knot to keep it firm.

"I'm on point," Alex said, strangely affecting yet another new accent. "Don't bunch up, don't talk. Charlie don't need help findin' us." With that, he turned and hustled down the hall.

Jason turned his attention to Amber, only to find a demanding look on her face. The young man just shrugged and pointed one finger toward his own ear, twirling it quickly. "He kinda gets, like, 'Nam flashbacks an' shit, right?" he huffed. "We don't talk about it much." The young man wavered under Amber's disbelieving glare. "I try to respect his privacy, y'know?"

THE VAMPIRES GOT the point before too long. Rachel laid waste to every challenger—usually several at a time, as they swiftly realized none of them could stand against her alone. Their natural vulnerability to fire was enough to deter most of them, but even those who thought they might avoid her sword soon found that her strength and dirty tactics provided formidable additional threats.

The werewolves were another matter entirely. As the vampires withdrew from the fight, the furry monsters redoubled their efforts. Their bloodlust only grew with every passing second. Rachel dodged one by leaping up to stand atop its shoulders, flipping forward to slash her sword up along its spine before coming to ground, and then felt one of the werewolves catch her wing in its claws and tug roughly.

Typically, Rachel had to be immaterial or not; she couldn't have it both ways, couldn't interact with the physical world and let it pass through her at the same time. The wings of the angels and their demon counterparts were usually the exception to that rule, but as she was lifted off her feet, flung sideways and slammed into a wall, she learned that the werewolves apparently had enough of the touch of Hell in them to allow for such contact.

They could also hurt her. Rachel had gone toe-to-toe with demons of considerably greater strength and come away victorious, but she'd never faced fifteen such foes. As she bounced off the wall and hit the floor face first, Rachel understood why the werewolves hadn't been hunted down and eradicated long ago. Not only were they difficult to find, but it turned out that werewolves—at least in groups—could put up a real fight.

As she picked herself up off the floor, she found the werewolves closing in for another coordinated attack. They didn't communicate as far as she could tell, and probably didn't have to. Predatory instinct made up for that.

Still, these were not just predators. They were people, too, or at least they had been once upon a time. Rachel scanned the group until she found the large brown one with the bald spot. That one seemed to be the leader.

Rachel pointed to her and warned the others, "She's gonna cost you assholes everything." She kept her sword at the ready, still up for the fight despite being battered and bruised. Her confidence never wavered. "You know that, right? Shit creek without a paddle for any of you, and she's still not gonna get what she wants for it."

The lead werewolf growled. Rachel glanced back to confirm that Alex, Jason and Amber were long gone. Her eyes turned back on Diana. "You can't have him." She smirked a bit as Diana took an angry step forward. "It's not 'cause you're furry. It's not even because you aren't human. It's 'cause you're such a psycho cunt."

Diana reared back and howled. Several of the others did, too, which Rachel took for a final group psych-up before charging—but then one of the werewolves to her left rushed in just as the howl began. She was ready for it, sword up and level to impale the monster as it closed. With that, Rachel decided to play her trump card.

Guardian angels had the strength to defend their charges. Those who held Dominion carried the power to defend their cities. Without that strength, Rachel might not have survived this long into the fight. Without mortal witnesses, she could draw upon all might the Hosts had invested in her.

The werewolf on her sword all but exploded as flames burst from his body. The pommel of Rachel's weapon sent beams of light out in every direction. Clouds of fire followed, growing slowly at first but quickly wafting through the tunnel. Most of her opponents wisely fled. Those who did not died where they stood, engulfed in divine flame and wrath.

FURTHER DOWN THE HALLWAY, a lone figure in ash-stained white jeans and a black leather jacket stirred. The first thing she felt was a deep, almost painful thirst. She felt an all-encompassing coldness in her body, from fingers to toes, and if it wasn't uncomfortable it was still disconcerting. She felt thirsty.

The thirst had to be obeyed. The thirst, beyond all things. She knew that. She needed to drink.

Rosario's dead eyes fluttered open for the first time. She needed to drink. She looked around for something—some*one*, she knew instinctively—to feed upon. She needed to drink.

Then she saw the great, expanding ball of fire not far down the tunnel, and she came to understand another deep, overriding need as she scrambled to her feet and threw herself over the rails to the floor below.

8
———

THE AFTER-PARTY

They never saw him coming.

The escalators leading to and from the street above were separated by a wide staircase between them. The entrance was mostly enclosed by the front façade of a department store, while the overhang of the department store's second floor and the partial enclosure of its walls provided partial shelter. Two men in police uniforms guarded the top of the stairs.

He hugged the corner at the base of the stairs and held up an open palm to signal his companions to wait. Luckily, the enemy hadn't seen him peek around the corner. Now he had to watch their shadows against the wall of the stairway and wait for an opening.

Shooting these guys with his AK didn't seem like a viable option. That would give away their position to anyone else patrolling the street. He'd have to take them both out quietly. For all he knew, a dozen more such enemies lingered just out of sight upstairs, but he'd have to take the chance.

His slippers made too much noise, he figured, so he left them behind and waited for his chance on the cold concrete. The sentries looked outward, suggesting they served to deter anyone on the outside from coming in rather than staying in place to keep anyone inside.

One moved out of sight. The other one followed.

Alex leapt up the stairs, clearing three or four at a time in his rush. He was in it now, nothing for it but to push through and hope Charlie didn't waste him.

The first of the men in the police uniforms appeared again just as Alex reached the top of the stairs. He caught a brutal buttstroke from the young man's rifle across his head. Moving as he'd been trained, Alex followed up by thrusting the butt of his rifle forward again on his victim's face, knocking him to the ground. Then he spun and crouched, assault rifle trained on the second enemy before the guard had his gun out.

"Hands up, cracker. Now!" Alex hissed. He saw compliance and said, "Step back into here. Slow. Closer." He could hear Jason and Amber hurrying up the stairs after him. Emergency tape and no entry signs blocked the entrance to the bus tunnel. Alex gestured to the stairs. "Grab your buddy's ankles and drag him in with you. Steady, motherfucker, don't waste my time."

"Ohmygod, we're fighting cops?" Jason blinked.

"Listen, kid," the second sentry began as he obeyed Alex's instructions, "you don't know—"

"Wait, shut up," interrupted Jason. "Real cops would've gone in to check out all that noise from downstairs, right? Wouldn't they?"

Amber frowned and nodded. "Yeah, they would," she agreed, "but that doesn't mean... oh, man." Her mind raced. Monsters and angels and now assaulting men in uniform. It was way too easy to get on board this crazy train. She shook her head. "They might be fake uniforms or they might be the real thing on the take, but we can't just... Alex?" she asked. "You okay?"

"Long as the honky don't do nothin' stupid, he lives through this," Alex answered curtly. Once again, his diction and accent had changed. He kept his rifle trained on his prisoner.

Everyone else blinked. "Honky?" Jason asked.

"Whatever, man," grunted Alex.

"Hands up in the open," Jason said. "He's right. We're not into killing and we're not into kidnapping, so if you cooperate you both go home tonight. But you move one inch and he'll shoot you."

The prisoner faced a crazed young man in the torn, bloody bathrobe, with a sword in his belt and a gun in his hands. He made the obvious choice. "Anything you say."

Jason claimed the man's gun, then pulled the handcuffs out of his belt pouch and put them to use. Seconds later, the other sentry was similarly trussed up. Both sat on the stairs, though the one whose head Alex treated so roughly wasn't exactly upright.

Satisfied that neither of her companions were about to commit a murder,

Amber kept watch. She made note of the badge numbers in front of her. "Can't say this is a good environment for interrogating these assholes," she said, then bit her lip and hoped her comment hadn't revealed too much.

"No, probably not," Jason agreed.

With their prisoners sitting several steps below them both and facing the other way, Jason took another quick look at his phone. Nobody had answered his emergency text yet. "Dammit," he hissed. He poked his head up to see a deserted street. "We can't go back to the hotel for my car. They found us there in the first place, so they might still have people watching the party. Plus the first cop that sees us on the street is gonna arrest us on the spot... fuck."

"They'll only stop us for the guns," Amber reminded him. "We could just hide them and walk a few blocks. It's Halloween, who's gonna care how we look?"

Jason shook his head. "Your costume is enough reason to stop you 'cause you'll look like you *might* have a gun. And where'd you learn to shoot like that?"

"Hey, I told you, father-daughter bonding," Amber countered. "If anyone has a lot of questions to answer, it's you two."

"No, no, fair enough," he replied, holding up his hands. He glanced at the two prisoners and sighed. His eyes flicked to Alex. "How you doin'?"

Alex blinked hard and nodded, his weapon still on their two prisoners. Fresh air and a moment to breathe seemed to reduce his tension. "Getting there," he mumbled, then swallowed. "Familiar sights help. The street and stuff," he added, gesturing up a bit. "Modern clothes. The cop uniforms. It helps. I'm sorry. I was confused. I'm still confused." He paused. "I might start blubbering in a minute, too. Trying to hold it together."

"Don't worry about it, man," Jason said. "We got clear and Rachel took care of business. I'm sure she's fine," he added quickly. "She could leave that fight anytime she wanted, right?"

"Alex," ventured Amber, "is Rachel... is Rachel really an angel?"

He didn't answer at first, but then he nodded. "Yes. I'm not supposed to tell anyone, but you saw." His words came out slowly. Foreign urges and memories still echoed through his brain, telling him that it was crazy to hold a gun on police officers, and that this was war and nothing could be taken for granted, and that fleeing before Bjorn and Unferth lay dead in the snow was intolerable. He blinked all that away. He shouldn't tell Amber any of this, but talking about his life—his real life, not the memories of old ones—seemed to help.

"Yes. She's an angel." He kept his voice low.

"And she's your girlfriend?" Amber asked gently.

"Yeah," Alex nodded. He let in a deep breath, which shook on its way back out of him. "Rachel and Lorelei are both my girlfriends. Those were really vampires and werewolves. They were looking for me." He inhaled once more and blinked something back. "This wasn't Jason's fault at all. You shouldn't blame him. Only thing he ever did wrong was stick by me and save my life. Again."

Jason fiddled with his phone. "Like you wouldn't do the same?"

"If Rachel's an angel," Amber continued, realizing how shaky Alex had become in the last few seconds, "is Lorelei one, too?"

"No," Alex answered, shaking his head again.

"That guy said she's a demon. Is that true?" He didn't answer. Amber tried again. "Is she normal? I mean, human?"

"No."

Waiting a beat to see if Alex would volunteer the details, Amber finally asked, "What is Lorelei?"

"Awesome!" blurted Jason. He hit the answer button on his phone and put it to his ear. "Lorelei? Yeah, Alex is here with me and Amber. We're okay. Rachel came to the rescue but we're on our own now. We're at the entrance of the bus tunnel on Pine Street, between the malls." He fell silent, then looked at his companions with obvious relief. "Looks like we've got a ride."

***

"GONNA TAKE FOREVER for them to dig our cars out of this, even with the valet parking," Molly grumbled as she and Onyx followed Lorelei to the garage.

"I've taken that into account," Lorelei said. She scanned the garage entrance for threats or signs of trouble. Instead, she only saw a pair of bored-looking valets standing near a podium-style desk.

That a knockout like her would walk brazenly out into the cold of the garage in little more than tall boots and a bikini already made for a highlight of their night. Yet when Lorelei reached them, her face full of purpose and two fingers slipping into the side of her top, the two valets—now standing straight and perking up with interest—she put a whole new twist on things.

"This is my ticket. It's for the white Lexus in space 131. My friends here need their car as well. This," she said, producing several folded-up bills, "is a six hundred dollar tip. Every minute we wait for our cars will reduce this tip by one hundred dollars. You understand?"

"Y-yes!" blinked one of the valets. The other was smarter, and didn't waste time on idle conversation; he simply snatched the keys for Lorelei's car off the back side of the desk and took off running.

Lorelei smiled crisply at the remaining valet as Onyx fished her ticket out of her small leather belt pouch. "Forgive my curt manners. We're in a hurry."

"N-no problem!" the man said. He grabbed the ticket from Onyx and immediately shuffled through the rack of keys for the corresponding tag. He knocked more than a few to the ground, but couldn't have cared less. In seconds, he was gone.

Onyx pursed her lips. "Is this why you insisted on springing for valet parking on top of the tickets?"

"I've learned to treat my friends well," Lorelei said, turning her attention back to her phone, "and to prepare for emergencies. Please keep an eye out. We don't know who else might be on the prowl tonight."

The dark-haired witch gave a little nod, but said nothing more. She took Lorelei's meaning perfectly and turned her attention to their surroundings. Molly stood close, tense and ready to lash out at the first threat to appear.

"Fun party while it lasted," Molly muttered.

"I HAVE FOUR SUSPECTS, all under arrest under my authority. We need to keep them separate and isolated. You will remember that this entire matter is top secret. Do you understand?" Hauser expected the guard at the front desk to respond with a snappy "Yes, sir." When he didn't hear it, his eyes turned back from scanning the hallway for witnesses to the sentry.

The grey-haired guard's attention was less on the ID and badge presented by Hauser and more on the agent in the Spider-Man costume, also presenting badge and ID, standing directly behind him. They were the only people in the otherwise completely quiet and empty lobby.

"Wake up!" Hauser barked. "I don't care if all you ever see walk through these doors are Treasury lawyers and their secretaries. You are a sworn Federal officer and you will comply with interagency authority, you got me?"

"Yes, sir!" blurted the guard.

Keeley sighed and folded up his ID wallet. He moved to stow it on his person, and then remembered for the fourteenth time tonight that his super-hero costume didn't have any pockets. "I always hate going outside the Bureau for things like this," he sighed, watching the desk guard shuffle away.

"Well, you do look ridiculous, Paul," Hauser grunted.

Keeley blinked in shock. Hauser's tone conveyed no sense of self-aware-ness; Paul couldn't tell if his comrade was trying to be funny or not. He bit back his response in favor of staying on task. "I meant for custody and material support," he grumbled. "I figured Treasury would have someone more senior than a uniformed guard pushing retirement age here to meet us when you called ahead."

"They'll have someone here soon enough," Hauser shrugged. "Beggars can't be choosers. I'm not ready to trust the local Bureau office or the local cops yet, so this is what we've got for tonight. We'll need a better location right away. I'm going out to check on our guests. Wait here for the desk jockey."

"Why can't you wait for him?"

Hauser looked back over his shoulder with a disdainful frown. "You wanna go outside dressed like that?" he asked before he passed through the door and out into alley behind the Treasury building. A car, an unmarked Bureau van and a commandeered suspects' van waited nearby, along with several uniformed guards with assault rifles and his own agents. The car and Bureau van each had a single suspect inside. The suspects' ride held two more—their third buddy already in an emergency room under Bridger's supervision—along with a plastic bag of ashes and a burnt-up zoot suit.

"We doing okay out here?" he asked as Colleen and Matt stepped up to meet him. "Any troubles?"

"The Hispanics aren't giving any trouble," Colleen answered, "but that might be more about their concussions than anything else. The other two are sitting quiet and waiting." She paused before she added, "Can't say I'm crazy about bagging their heads like they're terrorists."

"They'll have more rights than terrorists get if and when they're indicted," grunted Hauser.

Whatever her argument, Colleen put it aside with a shake of her head. "Anyway, we've got bigger concerns. They're getting text messages. Urgent ones." She looked to Matt, who produced a pair of cell phones from his pocket for Hauser to see.

The lead agent scowled. "Jesus Christ, I can't read that teenage texting bull-shit. What the hell does this mean?"

"Cohen keeps asking both of these guys if they're still at the party and if they're okay. No reason why, just says he's urgent. He might know better than to put anything incriminating into a text message," Matt added.

"So if something went wrong at the party for everyone else like it did for our two guests, he might be trying to check on his friends," Colleen finished. "Anyway, the last message says L is coming to pick them up. Maybe that means Lorelei? I don't know. He says Amber's with him, so presumably she's okay, at least."

Matt lowered the phones. He and Colleen both looked at Hauser expectantly. "What do you want to do?" Colleen asked.

"We need more time," Hauser said, "and we don't know the capabilities of the people we're dealing with. We don't want them looking for these guys. Lanier, can you respond to these messages? Are the phones password protected?"

The other agent traded wary glances with Colleen, but answered, "I could crack one of them in just a couple of minutes."

"Do it. Then respond to say they're staying at the party and having a good time. Maybe use only one and say the other guy lost his or something. Go back through the previous messages to make sure you're using the same texting lingo these two use. You're a tech nerd, you understand this stuff."

He looked up quickly to see the door open again. Keeley appeared from within to give a thumbs-up. "We're set. Let's get this done," Hauser said before moving off to one of the cars.

Colleen and Matt traded uncomfortable glances again. "Tech nerd?" Matt asked.

"Yeah, I know. He says more about my looks than he does about my work," Colleen said. "Some people just can't help being dicks."

Her cellphone buzzed. So did Matt's. They checked, looked at one another and then both looked up toward Hauser... who had clearly received the same message.

"Keeley," Hauser barked, "get the Treasury guys to help you move our suspects inside." He quickly moved back toward the van and threw open the door. "Lanier, Nguyen, we're headed for the bus tunnels, *now!*"

THE MESSAGE REPRESENTED A SERIOUS RISK, but she covered for it well. Neither of her companions questioned Amber when she muttered, "Can't believe they could close off part of the bus tunnels like this. It's not even posted anywhere!"

Jason shrugged, standing far enough away that he couldn't see what she was really doing. "Money talks," he said. "Stories say vampires can get into peoples' heads. Even without that, we've seen the money they can cough up." He glanced up the staircase to Alex, who crouched just below its edge watching the street. "Guess they were more interested in revenge than we thought they'd be, huh?"

"Guess so," Alex shrugged. He still had the rifle in his hands and the sword in the belt of his bathrobe.

"You've gotta be freezing," Jason said. "You sure you don't want my jacket?"

"I've handled worse," answered Alex.

Jason threw Amber a troubled look. "No, he hasn't," he mouthed silently. Then it hit him: she was dressed for much warmer weather, too. Her fatigue pants and web gear made for slightly better insulation than Alex's lazy morning ensemble, but her tank top wasn't made to keep out the cold. "What about you?" he asked. The leather jacket was already off his shoulders before he finished speaking.

Amber quickly hit the last key to delete the text message she'd just sent to the task force from her history. "No, Jason, you don't have to..." Her voice trailed off as he put the jacket around her shoulders. She'd simply lumped her shivering in with all the other stress of the evening. The gesture meant more to her than the actual warmth. "Thanks."

"We gotta have a talk later," he said.

"Yeah, we do," Amber nodded soberly. "You've got a lot to explain here."

"It's a long story."

"Okay, straight to the point then: why would vampires and werewolves chase you and Alex?"

"We kinda killed a whole shitload of vampires last month," Jason shrugged. "I gotta say that doesn't feel nearly as cool to tell a girl as I thought it would."

"No?"

"No. Feels kinda douchey now that I'm in the moment."

"Okay, well, putting aside the how... *why* did you kill a bunch of vampires last month?"

Jason's eyes flicked up toward Alex, who wasn't looking at them. His friend gave no sign of approval or disapproval. "They kidnapped Alex," Jason said.

"Which was embarrassing enough the first time, right? I mean, y'know, vampires. That's lamer than Juggalos. But now it's happened to him twice, and—"

"Car," Alex hissed, and then followed with, "it's ours. Let's go." He waved his companions up, but held his position until they were beside him. The passenger side door to Lorelei's Lexus opened up, revealing her at the wheel. He paused and looked down the staircase, where the two men in police uniforms sat with their hands cuffed behind their backs. Both now sat upright and aware, but turned away. "We can't leave them like that," he said. "Give me the keys."

Jason blinked, but put the keys in his hand. "You want me to cover you while you uncuff 'em?"

"Not taking the chance," Alex muttered, and then called down the stairs, "Hey! Assholes!" He tossed the keys down to them. "We're leaving. Figure out how to unlock yourselves." His harsh tone diminished as he said, "Get in the car. I'm in last."

Jason moved first, venturing out of their cover ahead of Amber but waiting at the door for her to enter. Amber tumbled into the backseat behind Lorelei and waited as Jason unceremoniously joined her. Alex came last, his gun up and ready to return fire from whatever corner might hold an ambush until he was in the passenger seat.

The car took off immediately, just shy of squealing out of its brief parking spot. "Are any of you hurt?" Lorelei asked. She looked Alex over with a simple glance as her passengers grunted out their answers. "You must be freezing," she observed evenly. She put the heater on full blast.

"Someone's following us," Alex noted.

"It's Molly and Onyx," Lorelei replied. "We haven't seen Drew or Wade."

"I got a text from them a couple minutes ago," Jason announced. "They're okay, but they don't seem to know anything's wrong."

"If you can warn them subtly, do so," Lorelei told him, keeping her eyes on the road, "but put nothing in the open. We do not know how closely we've been watched."

"Way ahead of you," Jason said, typing out another message.

Alex let out a long, shuddering breath, leaning forward to put his face in his hands. His forehead rested on the dashboard. The sounds that accompanied his breathing were somewhere between loud shivers and sobs.

Lorelei reached out to touch the back of his neck with one hand. "You are safe, love," she said. Her eyes flicked to the mirror. "Has Alex acted strangely?"

"He kinda had an ass-whuppin' freak-out, yeah," Jason said. "Didn't always speak English. Got madder than I've ever seen anyone. He saved our necks, too, but still."

It was all Lorelei needed to hear. "Alex, you are with me, and you are safe," she told him again. "We are in a car headed home in Seattle. Let your sorrows go. They are not yours to bear." She kept one hand on the wheel and the other on him, lightly rubbing his neck and passing her fingertips through the hair on the back of his head.

Amber watched all of this with uneasy interest. For all the stress of the moment, Lorelei seemed perfectly calm. She took everything seriously, but Amber saw no worry or fear. Lorelei seemed completely confident in the face of vengeful supernaturals and a boyfriend going through a mental meltdown.

"You must stay with us tonight," Lorelei said, breaking Amber from her thoughts, "at least until sunrise. We have space. You are much safer with us than home alone."

"No argument," answered Jason. Amber just gave a shrug and a nod.

"Did they say who they were?" Lorelei asked. "Or what they wanted?"

"There were a few dozen of 'em," Jason said. "I think the ones in charge were a guy from New York and another one in a toga, said he was from LA."

"Cornelius?"

"You know them?" asked Amber.

"I've had my share of unpleasant encounters. He is quite dangerous."

"Oh," said Jason. "Well, Alex goaded him into a swordfight and killed him."

Lorelei's head tilted slightly. "Splendid."

"Website says this station was closed as of today, just after eight," said Lanier. He rode in the back of the van with his laptop open. Nguyen's driving made for some tricky work on the keyboard, but he was getting used to that. "I'd have to dig to see how far back this goes or when it was planned."

"I'm betting it wasn't at all," said Hauser. He sat in the front seat, strapping a black Kevlar vest over his chest. White letters emblazoned on both sides marked the piece as Bureau property. "Get your body armor on and lock and load. We don't have time to soft-shoe this one."

Lanier obeyed, closing up his laptop without objection. The Bureau van offered a pair of shotguns and an M4 carbine, the latter of which Lanier handed off to Hauser. Long experience had taught the task force not to go lightly when it came to firepower.

"Just park on the street, Nguyen," Hauser instructed. "We'll commandeer whatever local police turn up as soon as they arrive, but let's not call them ahead of time. We need to get the first look at the scene."

Nguyen pulled around the last corner and did just that. They saw nothing out of the ordinary. The street was quiet, with the occasional car passing by and a Metro entrance under a department store façade blocked off by orange traffic cones and yellow emergency tape. "Doesn't look like anything blew up here," Nguyen observed. "No smoke, no crowd, nothing."

She pulled up onto the curb as she spoke. Hauser was out of the passenger side door as soon as she stopped. Lanier followed quickly with his shotgun at the ready. They crept up to the entrance in smooth, trained movements. Nguyen hurried into her vest and grabbed the other shotgun, catching up before her teammates began their descent down the stairs.

They found a completely darkened tunnel and the smell of smoke, but no clouds to match. All three agents turned on the flashlights attached to their weapons and swept the hallway before moving in.

"Wow," murmured Lanier. The whole structure remained steady and firm, but signs of fire were evident a short distance down the broad hallway. Soot covered everything from floor to ceiling. The remains of burned and fallen chandeliers littered the floor. Here and there the agents saw smoldering piles of clothes and ash. Large fuming lumps of things that might have been large dogs or wolves could be found among the remains.

Two sets of footprints trailed through the soot, leading from the entrance on down toward the green ticketing booth at the end of the hall. From the wide spacing between each print, it seemed clear that the pair had been running. The field of soot ended well before the booth. It was difficult to see which way the runners went from that point.

Hauser held up one hand to halt his comrades. Then he reached into his pants pocket to pull out a simple, ordinary set of rosary beads. With his right hand still filled by the grip of his carbine, Hauser had to wind the beads around the fingers of his left hand with a swirling motion.

Nguyen watched him curiously. In her few years on the task force, Hauser had never struck her as the religious sort. She also knew just as well as her boss that the vampires had no special aversion to holy symbols. Yet as soon as Hauser had the beads wrapped up, with the cross on the rosary beads dangling from his palm, he brought his left hand back under the barrel of his carbine and got moving again.

"What the hell kind of fire burns like this but gives off hardly any smoke?" Lanier asked quietly. Nguyen just shook her head. The two followed Hauser.

He walked carefully and stealthily, sweeping back and forth with the light from under his weapon's barrel and taking in his surroundings. He paused briefly, tilting his head as if listening to something, and then turned off to the left, ignoring the trail of footprints. The other agents followed wordlessly.

At the landing of a nearby staircase, they found the body. The man lay face down on the stairs, clad in a leather jacket, jeans and boots. Blond hair spilled out on the floor all around his head. Hauser motioned for the agents to spread out as they approached. All three kept their weapons at the ready.

"FBI," Hauser declared. "You awake there?" He stepped forward, still ready to shoot, and kicked at one of the man's feet.

The leg jerked to one side as the formerly lifeless body started to twitch. The man seemed to want to crawl away, but could not rise or make his limbs work.

"Don't move," Hauser ordered. "Don't move or we'll shoot. Got me? We'll shoot you right in the head." The twitching stopped cold. Hauser looked to Nguyen and Lanier to coordinate, and then stepped forward to grab the man's shoulder and roll him over.

His head rolled limply on the ground as he was turned onto his back. Hauser and his agents saw angry eyes and a snarling face. The chain mail shirt under his leather jacket seemed somewhat suspicious. So did the ugly wound in the center of the man's neck. The horizontal gouge looked like it ran deep, but he bore only traces of red stains where his blood should have coated his whole chest and pooled out on the floor underneath him.

"Jesus, I don't think he can move under his own power," said Nguyen. "Someone must have stabbed right through his spinal cord."

"Yeah, but he's awake and aware," Hauser muttered, "which means he'll heal that mess with time. Get out your cuffs, people. We've got to get him secured before the locals show up."

"What about the tunnel?" asked Lanier.

"If we can get out of here before any cops check our van, we'll just leave it for the locals. It'll be interesting to see if they hush it up or if they react appropriately. That should tell us a lot about how much we can trust the department around here. Let's move."

———————

With Alex in rough shape, hospitality was not Lorelei's highest priority. She led him through the door to their apartment and relayed her welcome to her guests over her shoulder. "The guest bedroom has its own bath and shower. Don't hesitate to make yourselves at home, but please think twice before calling anyone."

"No worries, I'm in paranoia mode," Jason assured her as he and Amber followed. Onyx and Molly trailed behind, both of them watchful and serious. They closed and locked the door behind them. No one turned on the lights. Jason immediately went to the windows to draw the blinds.

Lorelei turned to the witches. "Any defenses you can erect are of the greatest importance," she said, her tone clearly marking it as a request rather than presuming to give orders. "If they knew we would be at the party, they may well know where we live. Whatever you need to move, whatever mess you might need to make, go right ahead. We trust your judgment." Then she guided Alex down the hall and into the master bedroom and called out, "I'll be out in a few minutes" before closing the door behind them.

"Wait," Alex grunted, turning back toward the door, "we shouldn't—"

"Ssshh, Alex, trust in our friends and our home," she told him softly, stepping in close. "We bought this place for more than just comfort. Molly and Onyx are as talented as any sorcerers I have ever met."

The bedroom remained dark. Lorelei stood near enough to brush her cheek against his. He felt her breath on his lips as she spoke. Her hands gently touched his arms, which stayed stiff against his sides to hold up the weapons he hid within his soaked bathrobe. "You remember Onyx, don't you? And Molly?"

"Y-yes. Yeah," he swallowed. Though the room was warm, as was the car ride over, the cold of the night and the wetness of his clothing kept him shivering.

"Do you remember me?" she asked.

His mouth wavered. He felt her lips upon his, gently providing a tender and effective reminder. It was only a simple kiss, but there was no mistaking her lips for anyone else's. The kiss warmed him.

"I feel like I'm about to die again," he confessed. "Any second. Like the fight's not over. I can't…"

"You are home with me, love," Lorelei assured him, her voice soft. Her hands moved from his arms to the center of his robe, opening it slowly. "You must relax." She reached into the robe, moving one hand across his chest until it came to the rifle tucked under his armpit. Her fingers slipped around the stock. "You have no need for this now. It will be close at hand."

He let it go. She took it from him slowly, slid the safety lever and then let it fall gently onto their carpeted floor. She remained close, softly kissing his cheek again. "You are not alone. You will not die again." Her lips pressed against his neck. "Not here, and not tonight, and not with me."

Alex swallowed hard. His voice still shook. "I almost died."

"Yet here you are. You fought and won. Jason stood by you. Rachel came for you."

She moved gently to take the sword. Hidden along his leg with no scabbard to cover its edges, the weapon had her just as worried as the gun. He kept the hilt pressed against his hip under his robe, separated from his thigh only by his thin pajama pants.

"Amber. Amber helped, too," he mumbled.

Lorelei held her first suspicious response to herself. "Yes. Amber, too." Her hand rested on the pommel of the sword, waiting for him to release it.

"I'm remembering," he said. She placed her forehead against his and held it there, listening to him. "I remember who everyone is. I remember where I am. I just… I remember so much more and it's all a jumble. And I can't turn it off. I don't want to lose my mind."

"You will not," Lorelei assured him. "I will not allow it. Trust in me. Trust in us. Let go, Alex. Let this go."

His pressure on the sword hilt eased. She grasped the handle slowly and took it from him, allowing it to fall away on the floor. Lorelei's hands moved up over his chest to push the bathrobe off his shoulders. "You are still cold and wet," the succubus said. She unfastened the two surviving buttons of his pajama shirt and slipped it off, deliberately touching much of his skin all along the way.

"You're so warm," he observed. "You're always so warm."

Lorelei slipped in close, pressing herself against him as she brought her arms around his back. "My world was cold before you," she whispered. "I will let no one take you from me."

His arms slipped up around her, holding her tight. She moved against him, reminding him of the comfort and luxury of her body. "Feel me, Alex," she said. "This is your life now. Not battle and lonely death. Those lives are done."

His shivering quickly diminished. Lorelei quieted his fears with her touch and her voice. "You have Rachel. You have friends, and lovers, and those who would be both... and you have me, Alex. We belong to one another." Her lips came to his neck, just below his ear. "Remember what you live for now."

His hands crept down her back toward her hips, coming to rest once they'd moved a bit lower than that. He felt her grin against his neck. "This is..." he mumbled, feeling his desires stir. "This is probably a bad time."

"I will never resist you," she assured him, her smile coloring the tone of her voice, "but we have company. If you wish it, I will love you without shame... but *you* may feel it a bit awkward to face our guests after the fact."

He let out another heavy breath. His body trembled anew, but in a vastly more pleasant way than before. He never knew how comforting her seduction could feel. "You know how to get through to me," he said.

"I understand the bonds we share. If I hadn't gotten through to you this way, I would have tried another. Now," Lorelei said, "you need a hot bath, and I need you to tell me everything that you remember."

JASON HAD THE BLINDS CLOSED. Amber found the controls for the fireplace in the living room and turned it on. She saw Onyx walk into the kitchen with a bag, taking up a spot behind the counter to work on something or another. No one seemed interested in turning on many of the lights.

Molly sauntered past Amber in her sea witch dress, carrying a plain brown paper bag and a hammer in one hand and a dining room chair in the other. She went to a corner nearby, set down her burdens and settled to a kneeling position. Amber watched curiously as Molly pulled a big black nail from the bag and then began murmuring. It sounded like a prayer, or perhaps a chant.

Curious, Amber stepped a bit closer to listen in. She looked to Jason, pointed at Molly and gave a quizzical look. Jason looked unsure of what to say.

Without ceremony or warning, Molly put the nail into the corner, right where the walls and floor came together, and started pounding it in with her hammer.

"Uh, hey," asked Amber, coming up closer, "what're you doing?"

"Home security," Molly replied.

"I'm sorry?"

"We planned on doing this in a day or two, but it seems kinda urgent now," grinned Molly. "We're gonna put some protections on this house in case we have any uninvited guests. Or people spying on us from outside."

"With a hammer and nails?" Amber asked.

"Yep." She gave the nail a few more whacks and then stood. "Magic."

"Seriously?"

Molly stepped on her knee-jerk response. "You got kidnapped by vampires and werewolves tonight, right? Anything else?"

"I saw Rachel."

"Sorry, I gotta be dodgy and vague here. When you say 'Rachel,' you mean—"

"Full-on wings and halo and sword on fire, yes," Amber answered. "I'm already contemplating serious psychotherapy."

"Won't help," Molly smiled. "Anyway, I'm Molly, and I'm a witch. Hi."

"Ah," Amber nodded. Her tone conveyed neither surprise nor belief.

"Onyx," Molly called over her shoulder, "tell her we're witches!"

Still behind the bar that separated the living room from the kitchen, Onyx held up a bundle of dried leaves on long stems in one hand and her ebony wand in the other. She calmly slashed the wand across the top of the bundle, which ignited with a flash of blue flame. Within a heartbeat, the flame died and the leaves were left gently smoldering in her hand.

Though startled by the flash, Amber didn't jump much. Her hand went to her gun but didn't pull it out. She forced herself to take a deep breath. Behind her, Molly began hammering the nail into the overhead corner. "That could be done without magic," Amber said.

"Yeah, probably," shrugged Molly.

"I'm just saying."

Molly gave the nail a few awkward whacks, irritated by the angle. "You saw an angel tonight. And the werewolves. And the vampires, for what they're worth."

Amber frowned. "And yet here I am wanting to argue with this 'magic' stuff."

"Sure," Molly nodded. "When you live your whole life believing you know how the world works and then you see direct evidence proving that wrong, it's tough to deal with at first. Ayn Rand fans have the same problem. But you'll adjust."

Amber watched as Molly stepped down from her chair, picked up her tools and moved to another corner. "Just sayin' I'd like more evidence than a stage trick," she muttered.

"Might not get a lot more of that. Most of the magic I'm gonna do tonight involves a hammer." With that, she turned back to her work.

Amber nodded, turned and found Jason in the living room. She pointed at the couch. "Okay, no more stalling," she said. "You need to explain. Everything."

ACROSS THE STREET from the apartment sat a dark, mostly empty office. A lone table stood near a window partially obstructed by curtains. Behind those curtains lay a pair of high-powered cameras, a laptop computer and an external hard drive.

All night the rig on the table had sat alone, left unattended in light of the Halloween party and the absence of the apartment's residents. It sat alone still, with the rig's owners now scattered and focused on more immediate concerns. Yet the rig was set to keep rolling all night, and well into the next day if need be.

There was little to record once the apartment's residents returned home and the blinds to all the windows were shut. Still, the rig kept recording.

Then a lovely young woman in Renaissance-era dress stepped out past the curtains, bearing a bundle of gently smoking leaves and soundlessly reciting words in old tongues.

Unbeknownst to her, the rig kept recording... until her ritual took effect, and the whole rig powered down on its own.

NEITHER HER TIME at UW nor the FBI Academy led Amber to rely solely on her memory. She tended to carry a notepad along with her iPhone and utilized both. As a favorite instructor at Quantico frequently told everyone, "Paper has a long memory." Investigations, interviews and interrogations had all emphasized the need to take recordings or notes whenever possible.

She had no chance to do that here. That happened all the time, but in such an event she would simply write her notes as soon as she could. Yet she was quite convinced from the start that she wouldn't forget a single detail of Jason's story.

"So we thought that was gonna be it from the vampires," he said, facing her on the couch with a somewhat penitent, hunched-over posture. "We were all pretty careful for the first couple weeks, but the more time went on, the more it looked like Lorelei had been right and they weren't gonna be out for revenge. She said predators don't look for prey that they know will fight back. But even so, it's just… what else should we do? Hide for the rest of our lives?"

Amber's brow furrowed. "But you haven't done anything to provoke them since?"

"No," Jason answered. "I'm pretty surprised by it all."

"They seemed to know who you were," she noted skeptically.

"Yeah, well, social media, right?" he shrugged. "The Internet's an archive. Everything lasts forever." The pair fell silent. The sound of Molly driving another nail into a corner elsewhere in the apartment carried through the living room. "I'm sorry about all this," Jason told her glumly. "I didn't know you'd be in any danger. But you can understand why I couldn't just be up front about all this, right?"

"It doesn't make me feel any better that you were keeping secrets from me. Stuff that could actually affect me, y'know? I mean it's not like you just didn't want to tell me about your action figure collection or something."

He frowned. "Okay, that's fair, but still."

"I'll grant you I don't know how you broach this subject," Amber continued, "because it sounds pretty strange to me and I believe every word of it. So I'm not sure how you tell people that your friend's girlfriend is an angel and his other girlfriend is a sex demon and you all just hang out."

"Y'know," Jason muttered, "now that I hear you say it, that sounds like kind of a crappy thing to call her."

"I'm sorry?"

"The sex demon thing."

"That's what she is, isn't it?"

"She's my friend," Jason shrugged.

Amber glanced around their surroundings, wondering whether to push this thought on him or not. She leaned in and dropped her voice lower. "How many people has she killed?"

Jason shrugged. "Bad people, you mean? 'cause from what Alex and Rachel have said, that's how it works."

"Uh-huh. Has it occurred to you that she might be manipulating all of you?"

"Sure."

"And?"

"I don't think so. She's never done anything to make any of us suspicious."

"Jason, you said it yourself. She's a demon," Amber pressed quietly. "She's, like, *literally* from Hell."

At that, he scowled deeply. "Maybe you should point that out to Alex. He might not have noticed. While you're at it, you can ask him if he ever noticed that his three best friends are a black dude, a country hick and a Jew. Or that those two chicks he met in his photography class are both dykes. Maybe he'll realize that's more important than how people actually treat him."

Words failed her. She tried to come up with some counter, but only felt worse for it. "I'm sorry," she said. "That's not what I meant at all. But you don't think all this is dangerous?"

"Well, yeah," he mumbled, bumping his fists together awkwardly. "So that's all there is to tell you. You can ask whatever of whoever you want now. You're in the know. But if you want to go, I totally understand. I mean not tonight. I'm not tryin' to kick you out or anything. I think you should stay the night with us at least. But after that, if you want to just get away from us and never see me again..."

She shook her head. "Stop it."

"I'm serious. You could've died tonight. Or worse."

"You didn't bail on your friend when demons were after him, did you?"

"Alex and I go back to elementary school. You only just met me. First real date and look how it turned out. Wasn't exactly romantic. Or chill."

"I think I found out my date's the kind of guy who stands by his friends even when the shit *destroys* the fan," Amber said, allowing a bit of a smile. "I can't say all this stuff makes me comfortable, but... no. I don't want to ditch you."

Tension escaped from him with a long breath. "Okay," he said.

"Okay."

He gestured toward the hallway. "I've gotta go hit the bathroom."

"I'll be here," she nodded.

Jason stood, hesitated, turned and bent over to kiss her on the lips. She found she wanted it more than she would've expected. Rather than shrink away or put him off, as part of her knew she should, Amber sat up and brought a hand to his face. She knew she shouldn't do this. Her body and her heart promptly overrode her brain.

It wasn't meant as anything more than a brief kiss. His lips brushed against hers, but quickly found them wanting more. Contact grew and spread, and then deepened as their tongues met. They had done this before, and enjoyed it, and now found it even more compelling than ever.

He didn't move away when the kiss broke. She didn't move far, either. "There's probably only one bed in that guest room," he said.

"We are *not* going all the way tonight," she replied, but grinned.

"Okay, but I note that you specify *tonight*...?"

"Don't you have to go to the bathroom or something?"

"Yeah. Sorry. Yeah," he mumbled before he walked down the hallway.

Amber watched him go. It wasn't until he stepped into the guest bedroom that she shook from her reverie and reproached herself for encouraging this. She reminded herself of all she had seen and heard, and thought back to her reaction to Alex jumping those two cops—which, she strongly suspected, was exactly what they were, rather than false uniforms over hired thugs.

Think. You're on an investigation. You need to keep your head clear, she told herself. *Prioritize. Get back into contact with the team or find a way to take notes or something.*

Her phone remained in the leg pocket of her fatigues. She could check it, send out a text with more info,or maybe try to provide at least some sort of update... but that would be risky. Any one of the people in this apartment might reasonably ask whom she communicated with at this hour, when her cover story emphasized loneliness and a lack of connections. She couldn't risk that yet.

She could duck into the bathroom once Jason was finished, though—or maybe now. The apartment was large enough that it might hold a bathroom unattached to a bedroom. She rose and stepped away from the couch, taking a look around her to decide where to go.

The apartment felt uncomfortably dark. The fire still burned, and a few lamps had been turned on here and there, but she still found more shadow than light. She couldn't hear Molly and Onyx at work anymore, either. Amber put her indecision aside and moved into the hallway.

Lorelei stood waiting. Startled, Amber stepped back. The other woman remained in her spot, watching her guest calmly. Her skin had returned to a human color; the wings had vanished, as had the horns and tail. The revealing ensemble had been discarded in favor of a full-length black silk nightgown. The garment flattered Lorelei's body to great effect. Even partly in shadow, her beauty stood out. Amber wondered if the demon had a single article of clothing that another woman might consider casual or plain.

Demon, she remembered, and her heart pounded. *She's a demon.*

"If I frighten you, I apologize," Lorelei said.

"Seems like a loaded statement at this point," replied Amber.

"I should ask how much Jason has told you, then. Or the ladies?"

"I wish I could say 'everything,' but I don't think we've had time for that," Amber shrugged, hoping she sounded friendly. She remembered what Jason had said: thus far, Lorelei had only ever hurt "bad people," and had done no wrong. Other than alter her memory at the pool hall, anyway, but she had to pretend she still didn't know about that.

Lorelei tilted her head slightly. "I would prefer not to make false assumptions tonight," she said. Her voice remained polite, but lacked warmth. "You seem guarded again. Perhaps more guarded now."

"Jason told me what you... sorry. That sounds bad. He, uh, explained that you weren't wearing a costume tonight."

"Tactful," conceded Lorelei. "I thank you for that effort."

"I'm not sure what else I would say?"

"It is less a matter of what you might say, and more one of what you might think or feel. Few mortals ever learn of my nature. Fewer still learn and remain with me, unless out of overriding lust or ambition."

Amber swallowed. Was that an accusation? A warning shot? "Jason doesn't seem bothered."

"No. Jason is dear to me. They all are. I have never had anyone to honestly call friends before I met the men you know now." She paused. "I owe them everything."

"You obviously think highly of them."

"I do. And you?"

Don't play this game with her, Amber told herself. "I like them."

"Jason's feelings for you continue to grow."

"Kinda not sure how I feel talking about that. No offense."

It seemed to Amber that Lorelei's eyes narrowed, but with the room so dark it was hard to tell. "You are still unsure of your feelings," Lorelei said, then tilted her head again. "No. You are not unsure of how you feel about Jason. Your conflicts have nothing to do with settling your desire, but rather with how you balance them with other concerns."

"Are you reading my mind?" Amber asked. She took a half-step back.

"I have not that ability," Lorelei said. "However, I understand desire... and I have walked this Earth for a very long time."

Silence fell between them. Amber held her tongue. *Journalists do this*, she thought. *You were trained to do this. Stay silent and watch the subject, like you expect them to say something, and sooner or later they say too much just to alleviate the awkwardness...*

"Is there anything I could do for you?" asked Lorelei. "Anything you wish to know, or anything I might provide?"

"Oh, I feel like I've got a lot of questions," Amber chuckled despite her nerves, "but I'm not sure where to begin."

"Anywhere."

"Okay... you've killed people?"

"Countless people, yes," Lorelei nodded. "I am not proud of it."

"Were you? Before all this?"

"To say that I did not take pleasure in what I did would be a lie. Pleasure has always driven me, but I have never been a thoughtless drone. I knew I existed only to serve another. There is no pride in being a slave. My victims all died for deeds that you would consider great crimes and sins. I do not mourn for them. But was I proud? No. Pride is only a recent gift."

"Because of Alex? And Rachel?"

"They gave me the opportunity, yes," Lorelei nodded. "I did not change for them. I am what I choose to be. But I would not have had that choice without them. I would not have either of them, nor would they have me, without Jason and the others."

"So you said."

"Understand, Amber, that I have every reason to be careful with my friends. I hope you can appreciate that."

"Are you worried about me?"

"I think you are intelligent, discerning and wiser than your years would suggest," Lorelei said. "You have entered a world you know you cannot yet understand, but you are quick to learn. And I know that in this chaos that erupted tonight, you stood in defense of those dear to me. I am in your debt, Amber. I truly hope we can be friends."

"I kind of thought we were on our way there already...?"

"That was before all you learned tonight. I would be hopelessly naïve to think that these events and the revelations they bring would not color your opinions.

"On that note, again, you are welcome here tonight. This home is guarded. No harm will come to you."

9

———

THE BEDROOM OF MISFIT TOYS

Blood stained the shirt, pajama pants and robe piled on the floor. Most of it came from his own veins. He sat in the warm bathtub, looking at his naked body, and found no scars. He had a few scrapes and abrasions, some matching the wounds he'd suffered and others from simple bumps and falls. Yet even the worst of it, like the gashes clawed into his chest, left nothing more than a few light scabs.

Rachel's kiss had fixed the worst of it all. Like the mottled coloring of the skin on his hands, which had been burnt to the bone before she fixed them, the visual remnants of his wounds gave no clue as to how serious they'd originally been. His body ached—he still felt like he'd been through a wringer—but he didn't look that badly off at all.

His heart and mind told a different story.

He heard the pounding again, quick and sharp and brief, and once again he jerked upright, partially rising, splashing water out of the tub. The pounding stopped. Eight blows this time. Last time it was five. Before that, it was seven.

Lorelei told him he would hear some hammering. That prevented him from reacting decisively about it. He didn't leap into action, but remaining calm provided its own challenge.

Bam! Bam! Bam! Bam! Bambambambam! ...Bam!

"Just a hammer," he whispered, easing himself back into the tub. Muscles in his neck and shoulders stayed tense. He knew he'd hear it again.

Alone in the bath, immersed in warm water and surrounded by white tiles and bright lights and marble countertops, Alex found himself staring at many things. He stared at the mirrors. The faucet. The water.

The lower-middle class boy in him felt mildly uncomfortable in this home, which seemed so opulent to the sensibilities of his upbringing. Memories of growing up poor in Detroit left him feeling even more out of place, as did thoughts of a life that ended only a few years before the one in Detroit began. Thinking of anything further back than that just made him feel like he must be in another world entirely.

He should be dead. Like so many times before.

He wondered when he would start shaking again. He wondered if the tub could stop an arrow or a bullet. He wondered if he shouldn't get out of the bath just long enough to go get the gun or the sword and bring them both into the bathroom so they'd be in easy reach. Others might think that crazy, he reasoned, and part of him agreed, but most other people didn't get jumped by monsters.

Bam! Bambamthump "Shit! Ow!" someone snapped. He knew that voice. Molly's voice, he realized. Again, he forced himself to sit back in the tub.

She just banged her thumb, he told himself. *Nobody's attacking her. She's a tough woman and a witch to boot. Just an accident with a hammer. Nothing to freak out about. She doesn't need your help.*

Bam! Bam! Bam! Bam!

See? Nothing to worry about. Right back to whatever the hell she's doing.

He heard the door open and shut. Once again he tensed, and then came the knock at the bathroom door. "Love? It's me. May I come in?"

"Yeah," Alex answered, somewhat hoarsely to his surprise. He swallowed hard and answered again, "Yeah," but the door had already opened.

She shut the door behind her, clad in that black nightgown that he liked so much. He liked everything she wore. He was fairly certain that was her highest fashion criteria, much as she might deny it.

Noticing the wet floor, Lorelei smoothly picked up a towel, ran it across the edge of the tub and then sat down on the now dry spot. Alex watched. His eyes drifted to her breasts when she bent over, and to her neck and her face, and when she sat beside him his gaze settled on her hip for a moment before rising once more.

She was fully aware of how he looked at her. She loved it as much as he loved looking, and told him often.

It didn't seem silly now, or juvenile, or shallow. It felt comforting. Intimate. He needed this, and her. Outside their home, his endless lust sometimes felt like a constant distraction. When his memories threatened to overwhelm him, it served as an anchor.

"Molly says she is almost finished," Lorelei told him. Her manner felt casual, but he recognized the deliberately calming tone of her voice. She was warm and reassuring without being patronizing.

"What's she doing?"

"Creating protective lines around our home. She drives iron nails into most of the corners to tie down a spell that will keep out the creatures of the night. Iron is of a time when mortal man found his way to fight back against the things that lurked outside the firelight. Man was no longer easy prey for the monsters after that. Iron is strong. Constant."

"Iron rusts," Alex replied quietly.

"Don't tell that to the nails," Lorelei smiled.

"It'll keep our problems out?"

"This is not the only protection that Molly and Onyx will erect. Never fool yourself into thinking any defense is impregnable. All told, though, this home will be as safe from supernatural incursion as any wizard's sanctum. It will be easily overlooked. Failing that, mere entry will be quite unpleasant for anything that isn't mortal... or an angel. I asked that Molly and Onyx ensure such an exemption. And one for myself, of course."

"Does she need to work in here?"

"As it turns out, no," Lorelei shook her head. "I thought it would be necessary, but Molly confessed that this room is already covered by other lines."

"Confessed?"

"I think she was hoping to get a look at you in the bath."

"Ah."

"She rides a high of anticipation and inevitability," Lorelei said. "On any other night, I'd have sent her in here and jammed the door shut behind her. She and Onyx look forward to what the future will bring."

"You seem like your anticipation's pretty high, too," Alex observed.

"It is." She reached into the tub to caress his leg. He heard as much seduction in her voice as reassurance. "They spoke to Rachel. They spoke to me. We have all come to an understanding about all this. Everything is out in the open."

Alex couldn't help but smirk. "You vetted them in advance of us hooking up?"

"No. They wanted to 'vet' Rachel and I," Lorelei smiled back. "Don't forget that this began to build before you and I even met. As usual my motivations were quite selfish. I adore them both."

Silence fell between them, but their gaze held. Both of them grinned a little wider. "You didn't," Alex said, "did you?"

"Only a little," Lorelei shrugged, though her nails gently trailed up his thigh. "I intended to devote myself entirely to you for your birthday, but then the opportunity came... and I'll note that the mere thought of what I did or didn't do with them clearly has you quite aroused, so don't expect any apologies from me."

"You're amazing."

"It takes one to know one."

Bam! Bambambambam bam! Alex inhaled sharply, but he didn't jump.

"That explains the water," Lorelei observed, glancing at the little pools on the tile and the wet spots on the bath mats. "Your tension will pass."

"Yeah. Well. It's easier with you here. Gives me something real and current to focus on. You kind of chase away the ghosts." He twirled a finger at his ear.

"Do you wish to talk about it?"

"No. It's the same as before. Same as the first time it all hit me. Usually with the dreams, it's just one set of memories or the other, but tonight it was all of them at once."

"Violence is obviously a trigger," Lorelei said, her hand lingering at his thigh. "I have paid attention to the comings and goings of your nightmares. But as you say, we can lay that aside for later."

"I just kind of have other things coming to mind. Seems like it'd help pull my brain the rest of the way out of this... whatever it is."

She tilted her head curiously. "What's on your mind?"

"When we first..." He paused, searching for the words. "Those first couple nights we had... I was afraid we'd never be able to have conversations like this. I had so much to get over with sex and with the bonds and hooking up with other women, but I think deep down what I wanted from the start was the relationship." He grinned at himself. "I was afraid I'd never measure up to you."

"You all but literally gave the shirt off your back to a friend in need. You made love to an angel in the middle of a crowd, danced with me just for the joy of it and took the head from a monster who stood beside Nero and watched Rome burn, all in one night," said Lorelei. "You have always respected me. Always seen me as nothing less than an equal. I will never lose my interest in you, Alex.

"Put me on my knees, ravage and use me as selfishly as you might. I will still feel your respect, your warmth and your love for me. I do not call you master, or put myself on display for you or offer myself to you because I am a woman, or because you are a man, or because I am a succubus bound to you through sorcery. I do it because we love one another and it feels good to us both."

She drew another smile out of him. "Well, as long as you know I respect you," Alex replied.

Though she chuckled a bit, Lorelei soon grew serious. Her voice remained low. "I gave great thought to what I might give you for your birthday. No material gift seemed appropriate. I knew you would be uncomfortable with anything expensive."

"I'm a twenty-year-old student living in a sweet downtown apartment with his hot, loaded, older girlfriend," Alex chuckled, "and his *other* hot, older girlfriend. I'm not even working now. I think I've got it pretty good as it is."

"You also have your hardships," she reminded him. "But that is beside the point. I pondered what I could give to the man who possesses me and all that I have." Knowing this would get an objection from him, she leaned in and put a finger to his lips before he could speak. "You do, Alex. You possess me. It gives me nothing but joy. I would have you embrace that tonight."

He sat up in the bathtub, unable to take his eyes off her. The finger on his lips moved away so she could caress his neck. Her voice remained calm despite the obvious desire in her eyes. "We lose nothing for acknowledging what already exists between us. Power exchange has always been a part of our romance. The only gift I wish to give you is one that you have had all along, but have been so reluctant to claim... master."

Only a month ago, such talk excited him, but that excitement was overwhelmed by its accompanying trepidation. He feared setting precedents. He felt guilt and shame over the arousal this gave him. All he wanted was an equal and a partner. He didn't want to give her the wrong impression.

They knew one another much too well to fear such misunderstandings now.

Alex shifted over in the tub, his eyes mostly still on hers as he reached for a towel and then stood. Lorelei rose along with him, stepping back to watch as he silently dried off. He stepped out of the deep tub, wiping off his wet calves and feet.

Lorelei sank to her knees in front of him. The stiff, erect manhood before her spoke to her lover's desires. As her hands came up his legs and then took gentle hold of his shaft, Lorelei's eyes turned reverently toward his. She stroked him smoothly, knowing exactly how to grasp him and how to please him. She knew he enjoyed this.

Her hands soon rested on her lap. Her eyes remained on his, looking up at him as her mouth opened and leaned forward. Alex sighed with immediate satisfaction and growing desire for more as Lorelei welcomed him into her mouth.

Hardly a night or day passed for them without such acts. Sex and sexuality dominated their relationship to their mutual joy. They tasted one another frequently, sometimes for hours, sometimes at several intervals on a given day. Tonight was not about all new acts; it was about exploring a new tone and context.

Lorelei made love to him with her mouth almost daily. At different turns, she would hold him prisoner, or provide easy satisfaction, or dominate him or simply shower him with affection, all through this one act. Tonight she did all that, but above all else, she served him with devotion.

Context made all the difference. Their lust rose. Lorelei brought her hands up again, clutching his ass as she bobbed back and forth. She coated his flesh with her mouth, unleashing her needs while seeing to his. They remained silent a long while, slaves to this shared pleasure.

Though she could learn his every desire through this act, Lorelei waited for his wordless cues. Her tempo rose and fell with his breathing and the gentle touch of his hands on her head. The soft, needful moans that accompanied her heavy, erratic breaths reminded him that this was just as good for her as for him.

Magic, Alex thought.

She withdrew only halfway as he came down from the high of near-orgasm and looked up at his eyes with the rest of his flesh still in her mouth. Both knew he was not ready for this to end yet. Lorelei did not allow her lips to spread in a grin, but her eyes glinted with agreement and approval before she slid her mouth back down his full length once again.

Alex closed his eyes and enjoyed her. His emotions swirled in a mixture of gratitude, ecstasy, love, and lustful potency. He felt power and possessive strength, knowing Lorelei fully intended this to stroke his ego as well as his flesh. He knew she would share that pleasure, too.

His eyes fluttered open. Her eyes were on him, hungry and devoted as before. Alex still had his hand on her head; his other hand joined it, and put a little more pressure on her, and he began to use her as she had offered. Lorelei could not speak, but gave every wordless indication of consent and eagerness.

Their motions grew rough, but neither experienced any pain. Alex began to grunt for them both, driving their pleasure every bit as much as Lorelei did. His hands clenched into fists in her hair while Lorelei's fingers dug into his hips. Their motion did not speed up, but contact deepened and sensation intensified until Alex could not hold anything back anymore.

She hungrily accepted all that he had to give. Every spasm of his muscles sent contractions through her body that were as delicious as his. She tasted his lusts, felt his needs, and satisfied them both along with her own.

Breathing heavily and trembling with bliss, Alex relaxed his grip. She stayed in place until his hands fell away, and then made a show of appreciating the size and feel of his cock as she released it from her mouth. As so often happened, it remained as aroused and needful as before, though now slick from her indulgence.

Lorelei's mouth spread into a grin. She exhaled, shivering out only two words: "Thank you."

He just looked at her, as enraptured as ever by her beauty. Whether her thanks were for the pleasure they shared through their bond, or for trusting her with this shift in the tone of their intimacy, or for giving in to selfish urges and using her like he had, he didn't know... but he knew she didn't want him to stop, and he could not resist.

Alex gently motioned for her to rise. She took his hand and walked with him out of the bathroom. They said nothing as they came to the bed. Alex slowly caressed all the curves that he knew so well, still clad in black silk and lace. She was a sensual work of art that he was privileged to enjoy by touch as well as by sight.

Lorelei melted and cooed under his appreciative stroking and kneading. She turned in toward his hands, offering up her hips, her belly, the valley between each thigh and groin. Her eyes pleaded with him as his fingers came to the thin strap over her shoulder. Alex passed it over, teasing her a little, his fingers slipping back down toward her breast to trace a soft circle over the erect nipple, still separated from his skin by the thin silk.

Lorelei's lip quivered. Her eyes fluttered open again, watching him in a state of near entrancement. "Master," she whispered softly, her voice full of appreciation, "I am yours to play with." She leaned in, shamelessly indulging his hands and his eyes along with her own desires. He knew he could bring her to a small climax just from this. It had happened before.

His hands slid up her chest to her collarbones again, then to the straps over her shoulders. Alex stepped in close, his cock sliding up against her groin. She moaned out louder at that, but remained still as he slipped away the fabric to reveal her full, alluring breasts. Notes of surrender and gratitude emerged from her throat as he caressed and teased her, softly pinching the nipple of one breast while palming and cupping the other.

"Oh yes," she sighed. Though he occasionally indulged in a firm grope, he understood that a light touch was key. His touch reduced her to whimpers, then beyond that, until she sank into the needful, rapid panting of orgasm.

No sight in his life was ever as beautiful as one of his lovers reaching climax through his affection. He watched her ride it out, knowing how it would drive him to undeniable needs of his own, and drank in the full experience until Lorelei leaned into him more for support than for indulgence.

She knew when she opened her eyes that she would be taken. The excitement drew her out of the afterglow of her climax. Lorelei whispered once again, "I am yours, master," and she looked on as Alex slid her dress down the rest of her body.

Her scent encouraged him to linger. Lorelei knew he would not reciprocate for her earlier oral attentions yet, not when she'd deliberately lured him to such a state of arousal. Still, she was unsurprised when he remained bent at the knees to softly kiss the lips between her thighs. The taste of her sex enthralled many before him, and indeed Alex took great joy in pleasing her thusly. She suspected there would likely be a good deal more of this later.

Alex stayed on this longer than she expected, stoking her desires even further. He didn't have to do this for her. He did it for himself, enjoying her taste and her scent and the feel of her sex against his lips and his tongue.

She grew wetter and weaker with every stroke of his tongue. Lorelei stayed still, sounding out her gratitude. Alex rose before she came to orgasm, leaving her in a state of ever-greater arousal and need, but she loved him for it. The succubus trembled as he guided her to the bed. Up until that minute, she didn't know if she would be on her knees or if he would simply recline and instruct her to pleasure him by his whims. She didn't know which appealed to her more. Yet when he put her on her back, with her legs hanging over the edge of the bed where he stood, she found it just as thrilling as any other alternatives.

Alex couldn't get enough of the way she looked at him. Lorelei and Rachel —and all the other partners he'd had since he met his two lovers—had awakened his confidence, but tonight brought things to a new level. He knew he could seduce the woman laying before him, and had done so many times before, but he'd never seen this degree of wanton submission from her. Alex knew all along that their bonds placed him in control; their relationship as master and servant was literal, though he preferred to ignore that. Tonight, however, she got him to embrace it.

His hands slid up her legs. He looked on her pleading expression, her quivering lip and her sinfully beautiful body and spread her at the knees, stepping in to brush his erection against one inner thigh. He teased her a bit longer, still touching her mostly with his hands while her spread legs now offered the rest of his naked body more contact.

The head of his cock finally slipped across the wet lips at her center, reducing her to helpless anticipation. Alex saw no reason to delay. He held Lorelei's left leg against his hip and probed her gently. Lorelei reached down to his cock, begging with silent eyes to be allowed to guide him. Alex didn't nod or give permission; he knew she could read his intentions just fine. Lorelei put the slightest downward pressure on his cock, keeping it at just the right angle as he first penetrated her. Then her hand fell away as she gave herself over to him completely.

"Ooohh," she moaned, eyes fluttering shut and her head tilting back as Alex invaded her. "My love." Alex pulled on her thigh as he thrust into her again, enjoying every willing inch of her. Ordinarily, such pleasure lured him into shutting his eyes. Tonight he could not stand to look away. The visual pleased him almost as much as the sensation.

"Say it," Lorelei whispered. "Tell me."

He fucked her slowly and possessively. "You're mine," he said.

The demon gasped. "Again!"

"You're mine, Lorelei," Alex hissed. "All mine."

The fullness of him within her testified to the truth of his claim. Lorelei felt her meltdown begin, set off as much by his words as by his relentless thrusts.

She threw her head back again, letting out loud, uncontrolled moans as she came for her lover as if for the first time.

Alex drank it all in. This would go on for a long while, he knew. Neither his virility nor stamina were entirely natural, but he never felt the least bit guilty for that. He wasn't the only one to benefit.

"THAT ROBE LOOKS GOOD ON YOU."

"I feel weird wearing her clothes."

"It's just a bathrobe. Just for tonight."

"Yeah, but..." Amber frowned, looking at herself in the mirror. Nothing about the robe was out of the ordinary; it was black, terrycloth, comfortable and clean. It covered her up just fine from neck to ankle. It didn't magically push her breasts up and together or draw the eyes directly to her ass. "I just figured she wouldn't own anything that wasn't all about showing off."

As she spoke, she noticed Jason's reflection in the mirror. He sat on the bed, looking at her... or, more specifically, her backside. Amber's eyes rolled as she turned to face him. To his credit, his gaze turned up toward her face. "It's nice to see I'm not chopped liver by comparison as far as some people are concerned, though."

"Oh, you lying two-faced bitch."

"Excuse me?"

Rachel turned to face Theresa with a sour expression. Her outfit was still in tatters, with ugly scars running across her skin at her arms, her shoulders and even her neck. "You heard me. That bitch is just playing him."

"You know that's not true," Theresa said, adding with a mutter, "at least not entirely."

Rachel sat on the dresser right beside the mirror, still haggard and torn up from the fight. To one side of the bed stood Theresa; on the other, near Jason, was Daniel.

"Still. Like I said," Amber grumbled, "just feels weird wearing someone else's clothes, y'know?"

"Loaded statement for the fail," quipped Rachel.

"Right?" agreed Daniel.

Theresa shot him a look. "You're not helping."

"Yeah, well, this isn't the first time I've had to wear Alex's gym clothes," Jason replied, and then blinked. "Wow, that came out wrong."

"Locker partners?"

"Something like that, yeah," he shrugged.

"Gotcha. Nobody ever wanted to partner up with me," Amber said as she came to sit down on the bed with him.

"Can't imagine why," frowned Rachel.

"That is unfair!" snapped Theresa. "Amber has always been a wonderful young woman. Her peers never gave her a fair chance."

Rachel glared at Theresa. "Well, fuck. *I* wouldn't have a *clue* what that kinda bullshit is like!"

Theresa opened her mouth to retort, and then promptly closed it again.

"So listen," Amber told him. "About tonight."

"Still really sorry," he nodded.

"No, I don't mean earlier. I mean now. The rest of the night."

"On the bright side, she totally wants to fuck him," noted Rachel.

Theresa shook her head. "It won't happen."

"Why not? He's a cute guy. Might be more than she deserves."

"Agreed," sighed Daniel.

"Don't you start again," Theresa told him.

"I could go sleep out on a couch," offered Jason.

"What?" Rachel blinked. "No, Jason, don't do it!"

"No, you don't have to do that," Amber demurred. "I'd rather not be alone here. I'll feel better if you're with me."

"Tap that ass, Jason!" cried Rachel. "Jump on it and ride it like a horse that's never been ridden!"

"I can appreciate that. Honestly, I'd rather not be alone tonight, either."

"That's the spirit! Strip 'er and split 'er in half, buddy!"

"Rachel!" gasped Daniel.

"Oh, suck it."

"I'm just saying," Amber continued, "I can trust you, right?"

"Laaaaame," Rachel groaned.

"You hold no love for her, yet you would see her lie with your friend?" asked Theresa. "Why?"

"Sure," said Jason, "but that's why I offered to go sleep in the living room. I mean if you feel weird, anyway. I can keep my hands to myself."

"Oh, please," Rachel said with a roll of her eyes, "it's just sex. She's got her hooks in him already anyway, he might as well at least get laid in the deal."

"That would only make things worse," Daniel pouted.

"You sure about this?" Amber asked. "We can just go to sleep?"

"What, you're not wiped out?"

"Physically, sure, but after everything I've been told tonight? I'm kinda wound up again. I want to lay down, but I don't know if I'll fall asleep."

Jason shrugged, stood, and pulled the sheets back. He gestured for her to get into the bed. "It's not gonna eat us."

"You sure? You don't think any Satanic sex stuff has gone on in here?" Amber asked, only half-jokingly.

He winced. "I think they've got a bigger bedroom for that—"

"And the living room, and the kitchen counter, and the balcony," Rachel smirked.

"—and it's not something I want to give a lot of thought."

"Dining room table," Rachel continued, seemingly distracted by the personal memory exercise, "that one time in the closet, the shower, the bathtub, the other shower..."

"Could you please stop talking about that?" Daniel asked.

"What? It's my home. You don't like what goes on here, then GTFO, buddy," Rachel grumbled, jerking her thumb over her shoulder.

Amber crawled into the bed, still wearing the robe. Jason turned out the lights and got in beside her. To the angels, the room hardly darkened; there were shadows now, but the light shed by their halos and their natural radiance remained.

"You seem quite proud of your sex life," said Theresa.

"Yeah, maybe I am. Maybe I'm thrilled to be in the relationship I've found. But I don't go putting it in anyone's face—'cept right now, 'cause you two uptight bitches are sitting here in *my home* pissing and moaning about a couple of people maybe getting it on. When the hell did we all get so fucking uptight about fucking?"

Jason and Amber settled in. They shifted a bit. "Comfy bed," observed Amber.

"Better than what I've got at home," nodded Jason.

"Angels fuck. Angels fuck all the time," Rachel continued, ignoring the renewed wince on Daniel's face. "When did we all get wound up? I mean we don't have orgies in front of everyone or anything, but nobody ever felt ashamed about it."

She turned to look at the pair of mortals laying on the bed. "She totally wants to fuck him," Rachel said again. "Wow, look at her. Staring at the ceiling fighting with herself over it. That's a whole big bag of conflict there." She turned to Theresa. "So I get the guilt over building this whole relationship on a foundation of bullshit, but what's her other damage? She's already gone this far with him, what difference does it make if they bump uglies?"

"Amber does, in fact, suffer from a guilty conscience," Theresa answered.

"That can just make it hotter. Worked for me the first time with Alex."

The other two angels glared at her, fuming with wide eyes. "There is also the matter of her professional standards," Theresa continued rather than engage with Rachel's over-sharing. "Ordinarily, fostering this sort of a relationship with the subject of an investigation would destroy the case, get her fired and quite possibly even sentenced to prison. Those rules likely do not apply here, though. She is not entirely comfortable with that, or with what she has already done... and her superior refuses to clarify the matter."

"Wow," Rachel frowned. "Sucks to be her. And poor Jason."

"Tell me about it," Daniel sighed.

"Do you think Rachel's really an angel?" asked Amber in the darkness.

"I think she's something that we would call an angel," said Jason, "but what an angel actually *is* may not be what we think."

"What's that mean?"

Like Amber, Jason stared up toward a ceiling he could not see. "Think like a scientist. You can make observations, right? She's got wings, and a bright ring of light around her head, and she can do amazing things, right?"

"Yeah, Jason, I'd pretty much call that an angel."

"Okay, but when you see a big animal in the ocean with tentacles and huge eyes, do you automatically think 'sea monster?' Maybe you would've a hundred years ago. But now you know better, and so you might think, 'Oh, maybe that's a giant squid.' You only know better, though, because other people have taken the time to make the observations and study them over time and gather evidence.

"Now, we both *know* that all this supernatural stuff is real. I've seen demons and werewolves and shit now, right? But that just means that I can study them —theoretically, anyway, 'cause I don't want to make a habit of this shit—and then I can figure out what they really are. And then they go from being a 'monster' to being a specific kind of animal.

"I've known Rachel for like a month. I can say offhand that she's an angel because she fits a popular image, but to be rational about all this, it's not like I have a firm, scientific explanation of what an angel actually *is*."

"You said Alex went to Hell."

"I did, but again, that's just a convenient term. I know he got pulled into some other dimension, or maybe he got transported to someplace that exists in this dimension but we can't normally get to it. But do I know that was Hell? Do I know that's really where bad people go when they die? How do I know I'm not jumping to conclusions about something that could be rationally explained if I had more data?"

"Know what I like best about Jason?" asked Rachel. "He's smart."

"So you say," Theresa frowned. "After all he has seen and experienced, he still doubts. I would not necessarily call that intelligence."

"Not givin' up on being an atheist then, huh?" Amber mused. "After all this?"

Jason nodded. "Anytime God wants to come out and prove to me that he exists, I'm happy to hear him out. But it might be a tough thing to manage." He smiled at Amber's snort of laughter. "Is Rachel an angel? Sure, I guess, but I don't know what that actually means. I just know she's my friend."

"Aww!" Rachel blushed. She stepped forward. "I wanna hug him! But now I can't! Dammit... Amber, hug him, you cold-hearted deceitful—"

"I like being your friend," Amber said.

"Aww," sighed Rachel. "Dammit. She meant that. Bitch."

"Even with all the crazy supernatural bullshit?"

"Yeah. Even with. You handled it well." She took his hand and squeezed it. "The world went crazy and you kept your head. Your friend might be a bad ass with a sword and Rachel might be an angel, but you were the one who made me feel like I might get out of that alive."

Rachel blinked and stood back. She watched as Amber leaned in closer to him, her hand moving from his chest to slip around his neck. "Wow," she said. "She meant that."

Jason propped himself up on his elbows, meeting Amber's lips with his. The two kissed softly, but hungrily.

"She did," Theresa agreed quietly. "Oh, my Amber."

Their kiss deepened. Whatever her nervousness over her mission and regulations, Amber found her immediate needs and emotions more pressing. After all she had learned, she was surer than ever that Jason was one of the good guys. She still didn't know her real boundaries. Perhaps this was okay. And perhaps, even if it wasn't, there simply wouldn't be proof...

She broke off from the kiss then, her forehead leaning against Jason's. "I'm not ready yet," she confessed.

Rachel groaned loudly. "Well, they're in for the night, I guess. Up to you two whether you're gonna stand around and gawk like a couple a' fuckin' pervs or go check on your other charges or whatever, but I'm late for a three-way." She stepped through the bed, pausing only to look at Daniel. The angel looked on at the pair on the bed with both hands covering his face, though his fingers spread enough to allow him to see. "Daniel, seriously? C'mon, she just red-carded herself. It's over."

"Rachel, you could stop this from going any further!" Daniel protested, pointing at the bedmates.

"So could either of you," she shrugged.

"But we can only drop hints! Give them signs that they will likely ignore! You could show yourself and tell them to stop!"

Rachel gasped in blatantly feigned offense. "Daniel! How could you even suggest that? What sort of angel would I be if I were to interrupt something as intimate and beautiful as this? What sort of *lady*?"

With that, she strode right through the wall, leaving Daniel and Theresa behind to wring their hands or whatever they might do. Rachel moved through the dark hallway with only a single step, intending to move straight to the bedroom, but her sense of responsibility got the better of her. Wildly pleasurable sensations continued to run through her body as the mystic bonds between herself and Alex shared the joys of his night with her. She wanted nothing more than to join in.

It might be difficult, she realized. No matter what sort of front she put up before Daniel and Theresa, her heart remained troubled. The secrets she had to keep from her lovers seemed to only multiply... and whereas Alex might not have a clue about Amber, Lorelei already held suspicions.

This conversation might well require an investment of time. If she had to run out in the middle of it, matters would likely only get worse. Best to ensure she had the time. Rachel needed to double-check on her city. Rather than going straight to the master bedroom, Rachel turned and walked through the other guest bedroom.

She heard whimpers and the sounds of kissing. A bed frame, though bought specifically for its sturdiness, gave up an occasional creak. Rachel turned toward the sound and found two young women, naked and intertwined on top of the sheets.

Rachel sighed at the glorious moment. They were trusting, faithful and madly in love. However they might stray in the name of curiosity and fun, the two were a solid match. They were also dead sexy.

"What kind of lady indeed," Rachel muttered. She smacked Onyx on her tight, pert butt. The resultant yelp of surprise followed Rachel and her playful grin out the window.

SHE LAY atop her lover with her legs spread for his mouth, freely reciprocating the pleasures he lavished upon her sex with her own kiss. They forgot all about time and gave little thought to their troubles, escaping for now in this solace. They enjoyed the taste of one another and the shameless intimacy of this act.

Lorelei released him from her mouth when she sensed the new arrival. Nothing about this development inclined her to apologize or cover herself up. Were it not for the earlier events of their evening, the succubus wouldn't have even paused until the newcomer joined them.

Guilt and worry rarely appeared on Rachel's face. Nor did she often look hurt.

She stood near the foot of the bed, out of Lorelei's reach with her arms crossed over her chest. The signs of the night's battle still marred her clothes, but the scars on her flesh continued to fade. "You two feel so good," she said with a quiet, plainly apologetic tone.

"Alex," said Lorelei. The sensuality and submission vanished from her voice.

Nearly smothered between her legs, Alex broke off only long enough to correct her: "Master," he grinned.

She shifted her hips. "Alex, my love," she said, turning her body to roll off him. The succubus sat up straight on the bed, glancing at her somewhat surprised lover. "Rachel is here."

Her tone preempted any sort of smile from him. Alex sat up. "Rachel? Oh my God, are you okay?"

She nodded as he stood and moved to her. "I'm fine. Or at least, I will be. It's not as bad as it looks. I mean yeah, I feel pretty beat up, but I'm moving around fine. Just the cost of doing business with fucknut monsters. Gotta take a few hits if you wanna dish any out, y'know? I'll be fine."

The shimmer of tears in her eyes as she turned to Alex left him in doubt. He put an arm around her shoulders. "You don't sound fine."

"It's not about getting a little scratched up," she said. "I'm sorry I couldn't be here with you."

Alex looked over to Lorelei and found her still sitting on the bed, watching silently. He felt surprised that she wasn't at Rachel's side even quicker than he was. "I feel bad about carrying on without you tonight," he confessed. "I mean, I know you don't want us waiting on you, but after tonight—"

"No, Alex, it was the right thing," Rachel interrupted, shaking her head. "You needed it. We all did."

"I still feel bad."

"This was necessary," Lorelei said. "This, or something like it. I had to bring you out of the chaos of your memories and the stress of your abduction. I took advantage of our intimacy and our bonds to do so."

"I don't—I'm not saying I feel bad about tonight, just that I don't want Rachel to think we forgot about her."

"I'd never think that," Rachel said. "That's not what bothers me." She let him guide her to the foot of the bed, where they sat down together. Rather than moving to join her lovers, Lorelei remained where she sat.

"Then what is bothering you?"

She let out a fretful sigh. "Too many things. There's so much I can't tell you. I don't even know how to explain it." The angel looked over at Lorelei. "I'm sorry."

Emotion vanished from Lorelei's face. "Did your concerns have anything to do with the attack tonight?"

"No! No, if it was about that, I'd have been able to *do* something. I had no more warning about that pack of assholes than you did. I wasn't with him because I had to go find out what's up with... this," she shrugged. "If I had known the supernatural goat dick brigade would show up tonight, the rules about intervening wouldn't apply."

"Do they still?"

"Yeah," Rachel answered. "I'm sorry, but they do."

"Lorelei," Alex broke in, his arm still around the angel, "are you mad at her?"

"Rachel knows some troubling information," she frowned, carefully choosing her words in response to the blonde's pleading look. "Were she to tell you, she would violate the trust that the Hosts have placed in her regarding her relationship with you, or regarding her responsibilities for this city. I am unsure which, because she hasn't shared this information with me... though I have my suspicions."

"Lorelei, you know I love you," said Rachel.

"But you do not trust me."

"That's not—Lorelei, I didn't even have time to process anything. I'm not omniscient. You were standing right there and I was just catching on. I couldn't say anything in front of—!" She stopped and turned to look at Alex. "Oh, fuck, you're already figuring shit out, aren't you?"

"Was this something that came up at the party?" Alex asked.

"For fuck's sake, Alex, can't you just be dumb for a couple minutes?" Rachel pleaded. She stood up. "And put some pants or a blanket on or something, you've been driving me nuts with that thing all night. Both of you. I'm out of my mind right now and you're both still buck naked."

Blushing, Alex looked back to Lorelei, who handed him a pillow without comment. Her eyes went back to Rachel as he put the pillow over his groin. "Have you had time to consider the matter, then?" Lorelei asked. "We could speak privately. You know that I do not wish to jeopardize Alex with knowledge not meant for mortals any more than you."

Rachel shook her head. "Lorelei, I can't tell you if you'll act on it, and I don't see you just blowing this off."

"Then my suspicions are only further aroused. As is my ire."

"Lorelei, I can't!" Rachel protested. "It's not that I don't trust you. The two of you mean everything to me."

"Not everything," countered Lorelei. "You serve a cause that you place higher than your concern for Alex and I. You serve Heaven."

"That doesn't make either of you mean any less to me."

"Does it not?" Lorelei asked. "You are not a slave. You are not subject to supernatural compulsion to obey your superiors. Whatever obligations you feel, they are a matter of your own choice. Do you think I would ever place anything above my lovers? Do you think Alex would?"

"Lorelei, she's got a job to do," Alex interrupted. He didn't snap, nor did he raise his voice. All pretense of being master of anything or anyone vanished. "We've all had to compromise. We've all got boundaries."

"What if this endangers you?"

He turned to Rachel. "Could it?"

"I can't answer that," said the angel. "I will always do everything I can to protect you, Alex. And Lorelei, and our friends. But there are times when I just can't interfere. I can support you, I can love you, but... I've got rules. It's bad enough that we're together at all, as far as Heaven is concerned. The second I step too far out of line, that's the ball game."

Her eyes flicked over to Lorelei. "You're right. I care about my job. I love my job, but not as much as I love you. It's not about losing my post. If it came to a choice like that, I'd hand the job back to my bosses with a doorknob shoved up its ass. This is about keeping you us all together. The moment *you* start giving the other angels a real reason to say you're a threat, all three of us are in a world of shit. Nobody expects you to be a saint, or even to be nice, but I can't put you in conflict with them. That would fuck over everything for all three of us."

Lorelei did not respond. Alex looked down at the fresh scars on Rachel's legs and belly. He had seen her fight demons before, but beyond that, he didn't think anything could hurt her. He also knew that she was even more powerful now than she had been back then, when she was—"It's something mortal, isn't it?" Alex asked.

Rachel winced. "Lover—"

"The problem is someone who's mortal, and who still has a guardian angel with them," he reasoned, "because if they didn't, there'd be no conflict with Heaven."

The angel sighed. "Motherfucker."

"Unless it was some angel just being an asshole," Alex continued, "but if that was the case, you wouldn't have to keep your mouth shut."

Again, Rachel just shook her head. "Please stop."

"There are reasons we both love this man," Lorelei reminded her quietly. She shifted on the bed, moving closer to them both at the edge.

"Yeah? There are reasons I love you, too, y'know."

"Okay," said Alex.

"Okay what?"

"Okay, whatever. If that's the problem, then we deal with it whenever it's out in the open like normal people. We never thought life would be easy street all the time. It's not always good guys versus bad guys. Sometimes there aren't any of one or the other."

"Well, you're pretty definitely a good guy," Rachel muttered.

"Look, the point is, if that's the dividing line between when you can help me and when you can't, then I've got nothing to cry about. I gotta just live life at some point, right?"

Rachel didn't respond. She looked to Lorelei. The succubus let out a long breath and nodded in concession. "You have confirmed nothing and denied nothing. I had hoped to draw more detail out of you. Having failed at that, though, it is possible that there is no direct or intentional threat at all, but perhaps some other matter that concerns you."

"It's true," Alex nodded. "I could wipe out on my bike tomorrow."

"I was kinda hoping to make sure you couldn't walk tomorrow," Rachel said. "It's still your birthday."

"Kinda long past that, actually," Alex noted.

"Fuck that. Your birthday's over when we say it's over." She looked to Lorelei. "Are we okay?"

"I will not be able to forget my suspicions," Lorelei said, "but I think I understand your concerns now." She reached out to take Rachel's hand. "I would burn all of Heaven to the ground before I allowed us to be driven apart."

Rachel just laughed. "Don't. Don't tempt me right now."

Lorelei let the issue drop with a sly grin. "I would tempt you toward much more pleasurable things tonight."

THE DOOR OPENED LOUDLY, breaking the silence of an otherwise undisturbed conference room. Its sole occupant sat before the table with his arms behind his back. Each wrist had been cuffed to one of the chair's back legs. The room's lights had been on the whole time, but the young man still tried to doze off. With the arrival of newcomers, he raised his head.

"Woah, waitasecond," a voice said, "you've had him sitting like this since we dropped him off?"

"But you said—"

"Goddammit, this is not what I instructed," a third man said. He came closer to the chair as he spoke, with the sound of keys in a ring. He ducked down behind the chair. "Listen, I'm gonna take off the cuffs. Just take it easy."

There was a tug at the bonds. His left arm was freed first, then his right. The aches in his back and shoulders did not ease so much as they shifted, now that he could finally move after an indeterminable amount of time stuck in the same uncomfortable position.

"Get your ass down to the other rooms and make sure the other guys aren't being treated this way," said the first voice. "This isn't Guantanamo Bay."

"Are you okay? You look like you can move your arms," he heard the man behind him ask.

He turned his head this way and that, rolled his shoulders and put his hands on the table, but said nothing.

The door shut and locked once more. The two new arrivals, both dressed in suits, moved around the table. One of them set a plastic bottle of cold water from a vending machine in front of the prisoner. He then sat down on the other side of the table, laid aside his manila file folders and said, "I'm Paul." He gestured to the man with the blond crew-cut, who remained standing. "This is Joe."

Paul waited for a response and heard none. "We can arrange a trip to the bathroom if you need, it's okay," he said, striking a mildly friendly tone. "No cuffs or anything like that while you're in there."

Again, he heard no response, so he continued. "Your name is Drew Jones. You just turned twenty-one, you live in an apartment off Aurora Avenue North and you've enrolled at the UW for the winter quarter, yadda yadda," he said, and then paused. He tapped one of the manila folders. "Is the yadda yadda good enough? I could go on, if you need me to make more of a point of it."

Again, silence. "Drew, do you know why you're here?"

"Explain it to me," Drew said calmly.

"You and your friend Wade were involved in an altercation tonight with several other individuals in plain view of an undercover Federal agent. One of those people you fought with died on the scene."

"I'm under arrest?"

"What do you think?"

"I haven't been told that 'til now. Ain't been advised of my rights. I don't know who you are other than 'Paul' and 'Joe.'"

"We're with the FBI, Drew. Who were those men you fought with tonight?"

"You still ain't advisin' me of my rights, dawg," Drew said, his voice strong but his demeanor serene.

"Drew," Paul sighed, "do you know those men had connections with a Mexican drug cartel?"

"I know that *Miranda v. Arizona* says you are required to advise me of my rights."

Paul smiled. "I imagine anyone who can cite the full name of that case knows his rights well enough without having them read to him from a card."

"Do I get my phone call?"

"Not gonna happen, sorry," Paul shook his head. "And yes, that's legal. You stepped in something deep and messy. You know that, don't you? The man you and your friend set on fire burned straight to ashes. You know that isn't natural, right?"

Drew's eyes shifted from one man to the other and back again. "I want to talk to my lawyer."

"You heard what I just said, right?"

"Yes. I want to talk to my lawyer."

"This isn't a television show."

"I want to talk to my lawyer."

"Drew, you're in serious trouble. It's in your best interests to cooperate."

"I want to talk to my lawyer."

"Drew, cut the crap. Your buddy Wade already told us everything. He's still a loyal soldier deep down."

The conversation halted. Eventually Paul spotted the quiet grin as it slowly spread across Drew's face. "Then why you even in here talkin' to me?"

"Because we need to verify what he said," Paul shrugged, seeming reasonable and calm, "and because we need to know if you'll cooperate, too."

"I want to talk to my lawyer."

"Drew," grunted Paul, "there could be a way out of this if you cooperate now."

"I'll cooperate with my lawyer," Drew said.

"What do you think we're doing here, Drew?" Paul asked, maintaining his conciliatory tone. "Who do you think you're dealing with?"

Drew gave a slow shake of his head. "I want to talk to my lawyer."

"Do you work for anyone, Drew? Did you fight with those men on behalf of someone else?"

"I want to talk to my lawyer."

"Where'd you get all the money to rent an apartment and buy a car?"

"I want to talk to my lawyer."

Joe spoke up: "Has she been sleeping with you, Drew?"

At that, Drew's gaze shifted. His jaw clenched for a brief moment. "I want to talk to my lawyer."

"Oh, bothered by that, are you?" Joe smirked. "Is that because she has, or because she hasn't? Or because she's sleeping with one of your other buddies, huh? Maybe more than one of 'em?"

"I want to talk to my lawyer."

"Not gonna stand up for yourself?"

"I want to talk to my lawyer."

"Must be rather emasculating, is all, I would think."

"I want to talk to my lawyer."

"Alright, fine, fine," Joe said, waving his hands. "Hell with it. You sit and chew on your situation for a while. You're with us for the duration, anyway. While you're in here alone, you should consider who you've been running around with, and what they've gotten out of you. 'cause all you've gotten is a heap of trouble for yourself."

The agents stood. All they left was the plastic bottle of water.

"Hey, wait," Drew said before Paul shut the door.

The agent leaned back in. "Yeah?"

"You still haven't advised me—"

Paul shut the door and locked it. He walked several steps away before he spoke. "That got us nowhere."

"He might need time to stew on things some more. It's fine. You know how all this goes, Paul. We've gotta let him be the first to drop the 'v-word.'"

"Yeah, well. You still want to take the lead with Reinhardt?"

"Yes. Hang back. If he thinks you're the one in charge, that's fine."

They came to another small conference room and looked through the window before opening the door. Inside, they found Wade sitting at a table, rubbing his wrists.

"I'm sorry about the restraints earlier," said Joe as he came in. "That wasn't what we wanted done. It was a screw-up and it'll be dealt with. I had them come in and release you the moment I found out. Your buddy, Jones, too."

"Uh-huh," Wade nodded, watching him evenly. He still wore most of his steampunk outfit, though with all the gears and metal pins removed from his vest and shirt he just looked like a poor, hatless cowboy.

"You want some water? Need a trip to the bathroom? We can arrange either of those right now."

"Ah'd like t' hit th' john, yeah," Wade replied.

"Okay, we'll get there in just a minute," Joe nodded, taking a seat at the table opposite Wade. This time he had the files. "I'm Joe, this is Paul—what's funny?"

"Nothin'," Wade said, smothering his grin. "Paul an' Joe. Go on."

"Do you know why you're in here?"

"Reckon ah oughta let y'all explain it to me."

"You and your buddy got in a hell of a fight tonight," Joe said. "Lit a man on fire. Killed him. Beat up a couple other guys, all with serious criminal records. And you did it all in front of a Federal agent."

"So y'all are Feds?"

"Mm-hm."

"Whut branch?"

"Federal Bureau of Investigation. So, you want to tell us what happened?"

"Y'all don't already know?"

"We'd like to hear it from you."

"Ah'm not sure ah'm interested in talkin'."

"No? Why's that?"

"Ah can think of a dozen reasons," Wade shrugged. His expression remained perfectly pleasant, even friendly.

"You know, Wade, I have a feeling we're all on the same side here," Joe said, also remaining mild. He tapped his manila file. "You served in Afghanistan, right? Airborne?"

"Reckon if y'all got files, there ain't no reason to ask the questions."

Joe nodded. "Sure. Sorry, rhetorical is all. I served in the Marines, earlier than you did, of course. But yeah, I've read the file. You graduated high school a semester early and went straight into boot camp, then served with the airborne in Afghanistan. Not too many guys your age with a record like yours," he said. "Expert Infantry Badge. Bronze Star. Silver Star," he added, his eyebrows going up. "Your friends even know about that silver? Your family? Whole bunch of pats on the back in there, too... and then the last month or so of your record is sealed and marked Secret. Everything but the medical record on your wound, which doesn't seem like the sort of thing they cut a guy loose over. Why's that?"

"Well, that 'Secret' mark kinda does what it says on the label there, Joe."

"Oh, I understand. But I can ask."

He received no answer.

"You never made E-4, Wade. You weren't even halfway through your enlist-ment. So I have to ask myself, how's this guy wind up with his record sealed and a ticket home for a relatively superficial wound? You're probably not even limping anymore, right? And, you know, I'm with the FBI and I'm on an investigation, so I had every reason to look." He paused, waiting for a reaction. "What happened on that patrol, Wade?"

Wade tilted his head curiously, but said nothing.

"See, I've got this trail of sealed, secret documents, all about some patrol you went on. And your platoon leader, Lieutenant Stamp got sent home three days after that patrol to sit behind a supply desk. Hell of a thing to happen to a senator's son."

He paused. Watched Wade. Saw a twitch of his grin. Something about this amused the young man. "That happens, and there's virtually no report of what happened on that patrol... and then a week later you take a bullet in the butt that should've been fine within a couple of months, but instead they give you a medical discharge. Best man in the platoon, hell probably even the whole damn company, and they pat you on the head and send you home for that. So what happened? What did you do? Or what do you know? Did Lieutenant Stamp have the same problem?"

"Stamp got rotated out on a medical," Wade said.

"Yeah, says here he got severe trench foot?"

"Really?" asked Wade, his knowing smirk still strong. "Ah heard it wuz a dental problem."

Joe's head turned slightly at that. "Is the Lieutenant missing a few teeth?"

"Pro'ly not anymore," shrugged Wade. "But that's jus' speculation. Ain't none o' mah business. Ah'm a civilian now."

"See, I think they'd only send someone like Stamp home if he'd screwed up so badly that nobody would follow him anymore, but he was connected well enough that nobody wanted him to take the fall he deserved," Joe mused. "So the question is, which side of it were you on? Given your record and the smile on your face, I'd have to guess it wasn't Stamp's side. But if you were cashiered, there had to be some reason. So maybe it wasn't just Stamp on the wrong side of it, was it?"

Wade shrugged. "Couldn't say. That's all apparently marked Secret, right? Ah'm jus' a poor dumb hick grunt. Ex-grunt, anyway. Ah don't know any secrets."

Joe just nodded. "I can respect that. Couple guys got hurt on that patrol, though, I can see that much. Roadside bomb. They recovered okay, but it reads like nobody was sure it'd turn out that way. You were in this little village... did it even have a name?"

"Hell if I know. Prob'ly ain't even there no more."

"Oh, it's there. I can show you the satellite from three days ago." He paused. "Is it still there because of you, Wade? You and the Lieutenant's sudden dental problem? He freaked out and you kept him from blowing up a village full of innocent Afghans, didn't you?"

"Sounds like a pretty good secret there," Wade shrugged. "Shame ah can't confirm it for you."

"See, that's what I thought," Joe grunted, "and you know I wouldn't put all that out in the open unless I had already confirmed it through other means, right? So yeah. I think you're one of us, Wade. I think you're one of the good guys."

"That so?"

"Yes."

"You're the good guys?"

"We are, Wade," he said. "But I gotta tell you, I've got some doubts about the people you've been running around with. I'm not sure they're up to the sort of thing you want to be involved in, and I don't—"

Wade slammed his hands down on the table and interrupted, with a triumphant grin, "Fear Down and We Know All."

Joe blinked. So did Paul. "What's that?" asked Joe.

"That's your approach. You spent a couple minutes tryin' to develop a rapport, 'cuz you knew a stern posture would be dumb, so you went for a sympathetic tone, an' then you made your interrogation approach. You're blendin' the 'Fear Down' approach with 'We Know All.' Took me a second t' figure it out, 'cuz ah was lookin' for just one approach, but y'all went and blended two an' came at me with both of 'em." He pointed to the files. "Izzat folder stuffed with blank papers? Or totally irrelevant stuff, like th' manual suggests? Wait, no, ah'm sorry, y'all are FBI. Probably got y'all's own manual. Y'all don't use the Army Intelligence and Interrogation Handbook, do ya? Ah got mah copy at Barnes & Noble."

Joe stared at him, his friendly demeanor vanishing. He took in a long, slow breath. Paul looked at him with more concern than he intended to show.

"An' y'all still can't process whut jus' happened, 'cuz all y'all can think is that this kid talks like a dumb-ass redneck, so he's gotta be an idiot, am ah right?

"So whadda we do now?" Wade asked. "Ah don't really need t' go t' the bathroom, by the way. Ah jus' figured you'd offer an' then pull it away from me t' put some extra stress on me, but really, ah'm fine. This is fun. It's like that time Mr. Choy pulled that pop quiz on us all in civics an' didn't think ah studied. What's next?"

EVEN ANGELS SUFFERED FLAWS.

That they enjoyed an existence free of many mortal limitations was never in dispute. Ageless and powerful, they lived without many of the needs of humanity. There was no hunger, nor deprivation, nor fear of disease. Apart from extraordinary circumstance, death would only ever be temporary. Their hierarchy and society reached for lofty goals. They dedicated themselves to compassion and honesty, to the defense of the weak and service to the divine.

For all that, they were imperfect, and as uniquely made as any living being. Arrogance abounded, though often muted in its expression. Though they did not suffer the influence of the mortal body, whose queasy stomachs and trembling nerves could exacerbate the impact of fear, an angel's courage could still fail.

Angels could miscommunicate. They could be cliquish. Insecure. Judgmental.

Rachel had always faced her flaws and her fears head-on, openly in front of all of her peers, and thus never quite fit in among her own kind. In the beginning there were only the angels, and their world was perfect. Then came the Fall, when those who could not rise above their flaws turned against the rest and tried to overthrow the divine order. The faithful accepted that they, too, were flawed, but vowed to overcome their faults, and soon comforted themselves with the belief that they largely succeeded. Admission of imperfection became a polite conceit—but, being the direct servants of the divine, those imperfections were never considered significant.

Rachel had never accepted that. She was flawed; perhaps not quite as badly as the fuck-monkeys who created and inhabited Hell, but just the same, she knew she was broken. She could name some of her faults and knew there were others she could not see in herself. Every other angel had such faults, too, and they all knew it, but Rachel—not uniquely, it must be said—refused to pretend to perfection.

And so it passed that Rachel did not fit in, which inherently marked her among her peers as genuinely, obviously flawed.

Angels loved. They enjoyed deep friendships, and close bonds as warm and accepting as mortal families, and passionate romances... all among their own kind.

Rachel once loved another angel. She experimented with others, engaging in dalliances and trysts, but only once did she fall in love. Their peers saw chiseled perfection, and for a long time so did she, until he burdened Rachel with his flaws more severely and more thoughtlessly than he could ever recognize. She left him, to the shock and sharp judgment of her peers, further exposing her many flaws.

Angels could be imperfect, and stubborn, and honest, and terribly lonely.

That loneliness, at least, was now a thing of the past. Rachel lay atop her dangerous, seductive lover, who kissed and manipulated Rachel's body with hunger and skill. The demon knew that Rachel was flawed, and did not judge, and loved her.

Rachel trembled in ecstasy, writhing over Lorelei just as the succubus intended, bathing in sensuality and acceptance. Seductive fingers stroked her sides, taunting her sensitive breasts and more while her kiss occupied the angel's mouth.

Mortal hands slid up her back, warm and lustful and loving. Rachel's breath quickened as Alex moved in behind her. She broke her kiss with Lorelei, looking down through dangling blonde locks at her lover's wicked smile. The succubus spread Rachel's legs open with her own. Rachel put up no resistance.

He was, in so many ways, every bit as flawed as Rachel—and, being mortal, had many more burdens to bear. Rachel saw those flaws. She also saw his strengths, and his charm, and the light of his soul. She knew truths about him she could not share. He held complete faith in her judgment, and she loved him all the more for it.

Rachel's breath shook as she felt him tease her, probing gently to ready her for the coupling she now desperately wanted. She looked down at Lorelei, her lip quivering and her brow knit together in a pleading expression, almost apologizing for this, for wanting him as much as her. Balancing multiple lovers was never easy, nor something one could take for granted. Entering this relationship, Rachel hadn't known how things would work out. She didn't know it could be this good.

She felt his cock slip between her and Lorelei. She pushed her hips down, capturing his length between herself and her other lover just to enjoy the intimacy the three shared.

In the eyes of many of Rachel's peers, Alex and Lorelei vindicated all Rachel had ever done and had ever been. In the eyes of others, the pair represented glaring evidence of just how broken Rachel truly was.

Fuck 'em. She knew she was flawed. She knew she made mistakes. She also had love, and if it was not the love of other angels, that suited her just fine. She had it much better here in the Bedroom of Misfit Toys. She had made love with angels before, but those angels had never loved her for her flaws as well as her strengths... and not one of them had ever fucked her like this.

She gave in to them both, to a demon grown tired of evil and the mortal who'd never given a second thought to being anything but good. Rachel soaked in Lorelei's embrace while Alex penetrated her, filling her and bringing her to complete surrender.

Alex took it slow, indulging her in a rhythm that would inevitably build with time. His lips trailed up and down her back as he worked his hips, holding himself up from the bed with steady arms. She felt him enjoy her deeply, and knew Lorelei could feel it, too. They stared into one another's eyes, sharing him through the bond that first brought them together.

Rachel's lust for him rarely abated. She wondered, sometimes, how Lorelei could stand it, when she was created to feed on her prey's lusts and his pleasures. If Rachel longed for him so badly, how much more would a succubus want?

She moaned with pleasure as Alex thrust into her, pushing back against him and needing more and more. She respected his struggle for self-control. Adored him for it. But she adored his lapses, too, and enjoyed them without complaint.

Her head swam with pleasure. She gave herself up to her lovers, and they reciprocated in kind. Alex became relentless, and she with him, spiraling further and further into shameless, intimate rutting until they found mutual release.

Rachel cried out. So did Lorelei, in much the same tones and much the same reaction. The angel's hold on the flesh within her tightened and rode out his climax, mingling it with hers. As their voices fell to heavy breathing, Rachel's mouth came down on Lorelei's, drawing her into a long, deep kiss. She felt Alex relax on her back, still within her but momentarily spent, leaning in to catch his breath.

"I'm such a slut for you two," Rachel murmured against Lorelei's neck. She smiled, glad Alex had not left her yet and already looking forward to having them—and being had—again soon.

"Mutual," said her man, kissing the nape of her neck. He read her mood. "You have to go?"

"I should," Rachel nodded. "Monsters on the loose. You'll both keep the party going for me?"

Lorelei glanced up at Alex and smiled. "I will defile him in your name, love."

She let out a grunt of approval before she extricated herself from their embrace, slipping in a kiss for her man. "Don't be in such a hurry to find a new job," she smiled. "I'd rather you have more time for this."

He sank down onto the bed, with Lorelei rolling over to drape herself along his body possessively. They watched the angel rise, shake herself and pull a fresh white dress from out of an armoire before sauntering through the balcony door. Then their home was quiet again.

"Thank you," Lorelei murmured. "I may be the most needful of us, but sharing her with you is always beautiful. You've become a wonderful lover. You get better all the time."

"I should hope so," he smirked.

"I do not say this idly," Lorelei pressed, caressing him with one lazy, affectionate hand. "You've learned to read your partners. Help them lower their defenses. You have confidence without arrogance. You know you are desirable, and you know why."

His head turned in toward hers. He kissed her forehead, holding her closer. "And the fact that you do not try to downplay this with a self-deprecating remark tells me you know I'm right," Lorelei smiled.

"Older and wiser, huh?" Alex asked.

"Yes," Lorelei nodded. "Show me."

10

IT'S CHEAPER THAN THERAPY

Alex awoke to the stroke of an affectionate hand across his chest. He shifted and stretched, slowly opening his eyes to find Lorelei sitting beside him in a blue top and a short black skirt. Muted daylight pushed through the drapes. It had to be past eight at least.

"What's the plan?" he asked.

"I would look into certain matters regarding last night," Lorelei answered. "It will be easier for me if I do so alone."

"You've been thinking about this all night, huh?"

"Only since you drifted off to sleep. You and Rachel occupied my full attention before then."

"You two are good now?"

"We're fine. I am irritated by the situation, not her." She paused. "Our original plan was to spend the entire day ravishing you. As she said, your birthday is over when we say it is. I hope you will allow for a rain check."

"I haven't been spoiled enough already?" he asked.

"Not remotely... master," she added with a sultry wink.

He chuckled. "Well, you've been thinking all this through and I just woke up, so I guess I should trust your judgment. Is there something I could do to help?"

"Remember that you are hunted," she told him. "I know better than to ask you to remain here, but a little paranoia is surely in order. Be wary. Think twice before speaking to strangers or putting yourself in a vulnerable spot. I would strongly suggest that you be home again before nightfall. This home is hidden and protected against those who attacked you."

"Fair enough," Alex nodded. "Getting kidnapped blows. Think it'll be safe to go to my classes tomorrow?"

"I hope so. Our enemies have every reason to believe you are protected now. Last night couldn't have helped their resources. And as always, the more public the setting, the less power any supernatural creature can employ. We creatures of the night prefer to act in the shadows for good reason."

She stood and took her leather coat off the plush chair nearby. "Also, it would be good of you to play the host for our guests. None are up quite yet."

Alex sat up and rubbed his eyes as she left. Getting out of their large bed, Alex rolled his shoulders, stretched to touch his toes and found everything in working order. He wandered to the bathroom, got the water running in the shower and looked groggily in the mirror. The young man staring back at him looked much the same as the one he'd seen there the morning before, though with a few new scrapes and bruises.

Mindful of his houseguests, Alex kept his shower short. Cleaned up and dressed in jeans and an old t-shirt, he roamed out into the living room and then the kitchen. With only one mortal in residence, the apartment's larder was not exactly well-stocked. He rummaged through the refrigerator and cabinets for anything he might have to share.

"So I have to ask," came a voice from behind him, "who keeps this place so tidy? Rachel doesn't seem like the housecleaning type, but then neither does your other girlfriend." Alex looked up over his shoulder to find Amber standing behind the counter in Lorelei's black bathrobe. She looked perfectly awake.

"We only moved in here a couple weeks ago," he shrugged, dropping a few apples into a bowl that he placed on the counter. "Haven't settled into any sort of patterns yet, but yeah… Rachel's kinda bad about cleaning up after herself," he smiled. "It's mostly me."

"See, I figured anyone living in a place like this would hire a maid."

"Yeah, we tried that already," Alex confessed with a wince. It was too early in the morning to dodge or hide anything, particularly in his own home.

"Did that go poorly?"

"Nothing like last night. Just a bunch of awkwardness. You want anything to drink? I should warn you there's no coffee. We're bad Seattleites. But there's a building concierge and they'll bring up something from the coffee shop on the corner of the building if you want. Normally I feel like that's way too one-percenter to even consider, but after last night I'll totally make the exception for you."

"Just water, thanks," she said. "Are you not comfortable living the high life?"

"I'm still getting used to it," he said as he grabbed a glass and poured. "Getting used to a lot of things, I guess. You'd think all the crazy supernatural bullshit would make all the little stuff like income gaps seem irrelevant, but it turns out life goes on. Even when people around you have wings."

"I imagine," Amber nodded.

"Is Jason up yet?"

"Yeah, but he went straight into the shower."

Alex just nodded. "I owe you an apology. Jason didn't tell you before last night because... well, he couldn't, y'know?"

"Yeah. I'm good. I get it. No worries, at least as far as that goes. Jason gave me the low-down last night. Lorelei talked to me a little, too."

"I don't think you'll wind up being a target in this, by the way," he said, "but I can't guarantee that. I'll do whatever I can to make it go away. They want me, and none of them seem to do the whole 'hurt your friends to get to you' thing, but I wouldn't pretend to know how any of them think."

"What if I keep seeing Jason?" she asked. "You guys aren't gonna stop being friends, right? So there's always going to be something like this... isn't there?"

His shoulders sagged. He leaned on the countertop. "Yeah. Probably."

"Didn't mean to be gloomy on you."

"No, it's something I've thought about before. I'm just not sure what I can do about it besides trust Lorelei and Rachel. And my friends." His eyes came up to hers. "You should know I'd be dead without Jason. Several times over. And I don't want to think about what would've happened to Lorelei. He's... he's a great guy."

"I've kinda caught on to that."

"He's way smarter than me. I mean I know he's kinda goofy—hell, I'm goofy, too, just different—but like I said, he's not the type to leave anyone hanging, or—"

"Alex, is there some reason you feel like you have to play wingman for him?"

That made him blink. "Is that what I'm doing?"

"Yes."

"Um."

"I like him a lot. I did just hint that I'm gonna keep seeing him."

"Okay."

"So is there some reason you're worried about it?"

"No, I just..."

"I mean, I'm not out here to hit on you or anything."

"Oh, thank God," Alex blurted, and immediately regretted it. "I'm sorry. It's not that I assumed you were. I just... um... it's been weird."

"What, with the crazy sex demon and the witches and all the girls that you've hooked up with in the last month? Yeah, Jason told me. Relax. I'm not interested."

"You have no idea how glad I am to hear that. No offense," he added hastily, "it's not like you're—"

"Stop," Amber said, holding up a hand to halt him. "I'm not offended. What, you think because you're hooked up with a succubus every woman just magically wants to get into your pants?"

He glanced around the apartment, suddenly feeling sheepish. It sure sounded stupid now that he heard another woman say it. Best to deny it as firmly as he could: "...no?"

"I mean, I grant that you're an attractive guy," she said as gently as she could, "but maybe you shouldn't let all this go to your head, y'know?"

"Wow."

"I'm sorry, that came out really bitchy, didn't it?"

"No, I just..." Alex almost laughed at himself. "I feel so validated right now."

"Huh?"

"Nevermind. So I'm thinking I could maybe do pancakes?" he offered.

"None for us. I'm in the shower as soon as Jason gets out, and then I think we're gonna go get my car. After that, I don't know what he wants to do. Or tomorrow. How the hell do you just go back to school after this, y'know?"

"Want my advice? Just go to class. Seriously, you may be kind of distracted while you're there, but when all this shit started happening with me it turned out that going to school or work helped adjust. Like I said, life goes on."

Amber considered it. "That's what you're doing? Trying to lead a mostly normal life?"

"Kinda. What else am I gonna do?"

"I figured fighting vampires and werewolves and stuff would be a full-time job."

"I'm not looking for fights," Alex said. "I've had enough of fighting. Way more than enough of it. I don't really know what I want to do with my life. I've got a list of things I *can't* do, but I haven't put together a list of what I can. Regardless, I'm not interested in any crusades. I've done enough of that. Literally."

"Fair enough," Amber replied, smothering a bit of a frown. "I feel like I've got a lot of questions."

"I don't mind talking, but I'm not sure how many answers I can give. I just don't have 'em. Knowing an angel doesn't mean she'll explain the universe to you. There's stuff ordinary mortals aren't meant to see, I guess. It might drive us nuts."

"You mean like going to Hell? Wouldn't that drive a person insane?"

"Well, to be fair, I only saw like one room," he shrugged, "and I was only there for five minutes, tops. It's not like I got the full tour."

They heard a door open down the hall. Both looked over to see Molly wander out wearing loose black pajamas. She rubbed her eyes as she shuffled to the kitchen. "Gimme coffee," she mumbled.

"You got pajamas?" Amber asked, and then turned back to Alex. "There were spare pajamas?"

"I brought my own. Extra clothes, too," Molly answered. She glanced at Amber and shrugged. "I got invited to an all-night birthday party with a hot guy and his demon seductress girlfriend and their other bugnuts angel girl-friend. I'd be crazy *not* to pack an overnight bag."

Amber rolled her eyes. "Well, if I'd known..." she joked.

"Anyway," Molly said, "I need coffee."

Alex just smiled and moved toward the phone. "Lemme guess, black? Would Onyx want anything?"

"Oh, if you're calling for coffee delivery, I want something complicated and girly. Onyx likes it black, though. Wait, you've got a landline? Seriously?" she asked, struggling to believe her bleary eyes. "Who has a landline anymore?"

"Call me old fashioned," Alex shrugged.

"You're twenty," noted Amber.

"Yeah, so about that," said Molly, "what're you doing today? Anything?"

"I didn't have any plans yet."

"We've been talking about your little problem," Molly said, twirling one finger at her ear without the slightest concern for tact. "Maybe Onyx and I can help you get your head straight."

In Doug Bridger's defense, he had been up for over twenty-four hours. He'd gone from staking out the suspects' apartment to watching the Halloween party, and from that fiasco to securing a wounded suspect's hospital treatment and then straight to running a ritual to cloak the presence of Wade, Drew and the others arrested that night, and then back to the morning stakeout shift outside the residence.

Academia, the pursuit of the occult and the Bureau had all taught him discipline. They taught him mental stamina. He could do this. He could sit in a car for hours as Downtown Seattle woke up and began a lazy Sunday. He could watch the traffic peak and recede, take note of a mostly clear sky and listen to the news while never losing focus of the building and his subjects.

The text message from Amber provided a helpful nudge. "Leaving, old red Civic," was all she said, but it was enough. Bridger pulled away from the front of the building to its side garage, nabbed a parking spot and waited.

He spotted the car as it emerged from the exit. His eyes darted this way and that, ensuring he had a clear path out of his street parking spot to follow the Civic. He saw the driver of the car signal, threw on his turn signal and checked the crosswalk to make sure he was clear.

Then he saw those legs. Mystic wards against mind tricks and the evil eye aside, Doug was only a man. He couldn't help but notice those long, slender, perfect legs that reached all the way up under that tight miniskirt and the shapely, attention-grabbing ass underneath it.

Nor was he the only one to notice her as she walked by. Why she threw off her coat at that particular moment, striding across the street in those heels, most would never know. Doug figured it out, though, as soon as traffic around him went all wrong. Brakes squealed and fenders slammed together. His car was struck at the front as he pulled out, bashed at the left corner by an SUV whose driver swerved right to get a better look at the raven-haired woman.

Doug cursed. The Civic evaded the whole mess with its occupants probably none the wiser. He looked at the two men in the SUV, who craned their necks around to see the woman rather than looking first at the damage they had done.

Frowning, Doug looked, too. He saw her get to the corner, already putting her long coat back on. Her body language shift dramatically. In one moment, her walk commanded the attention of everyone around her; in the next, she was just another pedestrian on a blustery street. Then she was gone.

He sighed, looked up at the SUV and waited for it to pull back enough to allow him to exit his car. His hand reached for his phone to hit the speed dial. "This is Bridger. I lost 'em. But I can at least confirm that Lorelei isn't a vampire."

LORELEI WALKED AGAINST THE WIND, her coat whipping around her legs until she had it secured once more. She couldn't know whether or not the vampires knew where Alex lived. If they did, however, they likely employed mortal surveillance during the daytime. The spells erected by Molly and Onyx would turn attention away from their apartment, but not the whole building. That meant people staking out the exits, probably a car ready to follow Alex as he left... and that meant distractions were in order.

She would have preferred more solid information, but for now she had to run on educated guesses—both about her enemies and her friends.

Nothing in Amber's conversation with Alex hinted at any particular agenda on her part. Lorelei observed the whole thing, having never left the apartment in the first place. She held to the corners and the shadows as her lover and their guests got themselves together, unnoticed by all thanks to her supernatural talents. Even Onyx, who had already demonstrated that she could see through Lorelei's illusions, seemed to detect nothing. As she suspected, neither of the witches were exactly morning people. Either Onyx had the best poker face Lorelei had ever seen, or she simply didn't have her mystic "eyes" open before breakfast.

She waited through their morning shamblings and chatter. She listened for clues from Amber, who ultimately dropped none. And then she stayed ahead of them as they all left in Molly's car to ensure a clean getaway—at least from whomever the vampires might have watching.

The other faction probably had someone watching, too.

Lorelei strode down the block, glancing around for a convenient setting. With the city's obsession with convenient, overpriced coffee, it was just a matter of finding a shop with the right amount of customers. She found a likely spot, turned and looked around at the street with a welcoming smile for anyone who might still be watching her, and went inside.

Minutes later, as she sat at a tall table with a paper mug in her hand, her gamble paid off. The leather and denim ensembles on the two newcomers contrasted sharply with the hipsters and casual wear of the rest of the coffee shop's customers, but in Seattle such contrasts were often the norm. They revealed themselves less by their clothes and more by their posture and body language. Few people entered a room and took subtle sniffs in more than one direction.

She waited and observed. That two of them would appear surprised her, though on reflection she knew it shouldn't have. They operated in packs as often as loners. The man was tall, well-muscled and serious. His companion, a pretty if rugged blonde, gave every indication of following his lead.

They took in their surroundings, turned toward Lorelei and approached her without a word or glance at one another. The succubus waited. "I apologize," she said mildly, gesturing to the other side of her small, round table. "I have only the one empty chair."

The tall man sat in it, staring daggers at Lorelei while she smiled back at him with obvious interest in her eyes. His companion looked around and spotted a nearby table where a man sat facing a chair that held a friend's jacket. The blonde took the jacket off the chair and put it on the table before picking up the chair, daring him to object with her eyes. He risked no protest as she placed the chair at Lorelei's table and sat in it.

"You allowed us to see you," the man said, his voice deep and gravelly. "You obviously wish to talk. We will wait for one other first."

"I have time to wait." Lorelei smiled charmingly, leaning forward a little as she asked, "Would I have escaped you if I'd wanted otherwise?"

"No. You reek of him."

"Naturally. I have claimed him. What do I call you?"

The blonde put her hand over his before he answered. Lorelei noted it with a raised eyebrow. Her smile did not diminish as she leaned back once more, sweeping her hair back with a hand. As she intended, the male's eyes never left her. "We will wait for one other," the man repeated.

Even Lorelei's mild disappointment came out with a sultry look. "Very well."

They didn't wait long. Lorelei recognized the werewolf by her confident posture and her purposeful stride as soon as she walked into the shop. Such short hair was well out of the ordinary; most werewolves let it grow out, rather than buzzing it down so close to the scalp. Then again, her kind could grow a full head of hair in days. Perhaps she had something to fix.

The woman looked over the shop much as her packmates did before coming over to the table. The blonde relinquished her chair without a word and quickly found another one, giving an instant clue as to the pecking order.

"You are the demon," the newcomer said.

"I am Lorelei. Are you Diana? We only saw one another in passing, and under terrible circumstances." Receiving a nod of confirmation, Lorelei then glanced to the male once more. "And you?"

Diana held up one hand. "Has she spoken to you or tried anything?" she asked the man beside her.

He shook his head slowly. "She only asked our names. I did not allow more."

Lorelei pursed her lips with mild amusement. "You gave orders not to speak with me," she surmised.

"I know what you are," said Diana.

"Do you worry I might seduce your male right here in the coffee shop?" asked Lorelei. "Ah. Yes, you considered it. You ensured he would not come alone," she said, nodding toward the blonde, "and you arrived as quickly as you could. Perhaps you believe I'll throw some demonic enchantment over him? All magic is inhibited by the presence of many mortal witnesses, Diana. Mine as well as that which enables your shifting forms."

The blonde scowled. "Demons lie."

"That we do. And worse. Just like your kind. Again, what should I call you? Feel free to lie about your names. I won't hold it against you."

"I'm Jared," said the male. "This is Sally."

"Excellent. Can I get you anything?"

"Alex," said Diana flatly.

"Straight to the point, then," Lorelei nodded. "You want him. I have claimed him. You know that he is protected."

"The angel surprised us," Diana conceded, "but we tasted her sweet flesh. My pack would be happy for more. Another clash would not go so well for her."

Lorelei glanced to Jared. "Tell me, how many of your pack have you lost in this endeavor already?"

"Seven," he answered.

"Jared," said Diana.

Lorelei's attention turned back to her. "Is Alex worth that? Is he worth more?"

"You tell me," said Diana, her eyes narrowing. "What do you want for him?"

"You wish to bargain?" Lorelei laughed.

"I am a practical woman."

"You are most plainly not," the succubus replied, still quite amused.

"I suspect you aren't as strong as the angel," said Diana. "You are an obstacle. I will remove you one way or the other. In the end, I will win."

"No, Diana, you won't," said Lorelei, still entirely at ease despite Diana's intensity. "You have already lost the endgame, or you wouldn't be here now. Neither I, nor the angel nor Alex make any difference in that."

Diana's eyes narrowed. "I'm afraid I don't take your meaning."

"I know how all this turns out for you. I've met the demon that created the first of your kind. You're Hell's stray pets, set loose to sow chaos in the neighbor's yard."

Silence fell between the two. Lorelei saw the tiniest crack in Diana's façade of self-assurance. She decided to widen it.

"You were born a normal girl, Diana. I imagine you had a family, but at some point you did something more than a little naughty. Something vile. Hit and run accident, perhaps? Knowing abandonment of a friend in dire jeopardy? Or maybe you skipped straight to murder, but it was surely someone who didn't deserve it." She saw a blink, but didn't acknowledge it. "The particulars are of no concern to me. They're not my business. But *you* know the details.

"The one who brought you into your pack knows them, too, I'd wager," Lorelei continued, casually pouring a packet of sugar into her coffee. "Is he still around? She? Someone came into your life and started pushing you. Perhaps it was with honeyed words and a seductive, predatory grin, or perhaps it was more intimidating than that. Whatever their technique, someone taught you that it was easier to look at people as prey rather than as equals. Someone guided you down a bloody, ugly path."

None of her audience spoke. Diana maintained a stern, patient demeanor, but Sally's breath seemed to deepen as she listened. Jared continued to stare at Lorelei. She didn't even need to look to know. Instead, she continued.

"Your sins grew worse. You broke from your family, perhaps in a gruesome fashion. Whether the killing started right from the beginning, or if it came later, it doesn't matter: at some point, you became a killer, and you *liked* it. You hungered for it. The further you got from polite society and conventional morality, the better. Mercy, guilt, ethics—those are all the silly illusions that make people into sheep, aren't they? You feel no remorse. That feeling died well before your first shift. Before the first time you ate human flesh and found that nothing was sweeter."

"Your angel friend tastes sweeter," Diana taunted.

"An appropriate segue," observed Lorelei. "Haven't you ever wondered why the one who brought you into your pack couldn't just bite you in the first place? Has anyone ever explained all this testing and initiation as anything but 'tradition,' as if that's an answer? Do you think the older ones even know?

"You met the reason why last night. Once upon a time, Diana, you had an angel. You were under the protection of Heaven. The angels can't be around to protect mortals all the time, of course, and they can do little to protect mortals from their own choices. There *must* be free will, you see, because without free will there could be no faith, and nothing is so important to Heaven as faith. You can't have faith without free will, and you can't have free will if humanity knows the angels will intervene in every little genocide, hm? Bad things happen to good people all the time, Diana. Angels let good people suffer. They *have* to, otherwise Heaven's whole scheme loses its charm.

"All those crimes, all the little atrocities you committed on your path to becoming what you are now? None of that was to condition you. None of it was to test your worth. All of that was done to drive away your angel, Diana. You may think you were abandoned by Heaven's light, but to your angel's thinking, it was the other way around.

"It's the same with the vampires. You'll never meet one that didn't want to become what they are. Oh, some of them piss and moan about lost humanity, but pin them down on it and you'll find the truth. Only the worst sorts of people rise again after all the blood is drained from them. The good ones? Those drained by a vampire while still under Heaven's light? They just die. The angels make sure of that. And it's the same for your kind.

"Evil doesn't come *from* the touch of Hell, Diana. Evil *invites* that touch."

Lorelei smiled sweetly at her new acquaintances. "You can't talk to mortals about these things, you know. It removes the suspension of disbelief. It ruins that whole con of faith and free will that I spoke of before. The angels become quite cross about that. There's no reason you can't know, though. The fate of your soul is sealed. But don't worry," she smiled warmly. "I'm not one to judge."

Silence fell between them. Lorelei noticed that Jared's face was still set in stone. Sally looked disturbed, but held her tongue. Diana's eyes placed her reaction somewhere between the two. "Demons lie," she said, echoing Sally.

"That we do," Lorelei agreed. "But sometimes we must tell the truth, too, or it would be too easy to disbelieve everything we say. You'll have to decide for yourself whether I was lying to you just now, or if I decided to tell you the truth —one monster to another."

"Why tell us all this?" asked Diana.

The succubus casually picked up her mug again. Her manner remained almost insultingly pleasant. "You asked what I might accept in exchange for Alex. I wanted to show you that you have nothing of value to offer me. You bargained that away for a fur coat and frightening claws long ago."

Diana drew in a long and slow breath. "So it's war, then?"

"I don't know," Lorelei replied after another sip. "Knowing what you know now, is he even worth fighting over? Do you look forward to seeing the Pit so soon?" She let the threat sink in. "Or would you rather have someone to put in a good word for you once you arrive? Because you will be there, sooner or later, and my good word is something I will offer in exchange for peace. Antagonize me further and even the rest of the damned will pity you."

Lorelei waited for Diana to formulate a reply. Instead, the pack leader stood and stalked out of the coffee shop without another word. Her packmates rose to follow, though Lorelei caught noticeably different moods in their eyes.

Sally ventured a final exchange. "You said that Hell cannot touch a mortal who still has an angel's protection."

"Correct."

"Then why does he still have an angel over him?"

"I'm not sure if you noticed, but that particular angel is quite insane."

MATT LANIER WOKE up to the sound of the apartment door opening. He sat up on the couch, rubbing his eyes and feeling guilty for sleeping. He'd gone to the apartment with that in mind, but it was difficult to rest while everyone else was working.

Amber came in and closed the door behind her. "Hey," he said, "we've been worried. You okay?"

"Physically? Yeah. Listen, where is everybody? We've gotta talk. We read this whole situation all wrong."

"They're all out running around," Matt mumbled, rubbing the sleep out of his eyes. "Doug and Paul had stakeout duty. I guess something went wrong with the surveillance gear last night, though."

"Yeah, you can tell them to pack up the cameras and come back. Lorelei knew the apartment was being watched. She just didn't know by who, but she had some friends of theirs do some magic to hide everything, so that's probably a wash. What about Hauser?"

"He and Colleen are both out, too. Amber, what's wrong?"

"Oh, y'know," Amber said, nervously crossing her arms over her chest, "got kidnapped by vampires, shot a bunch of people, had my whole world-view turned completely upside-down. And I stood by while Alex and Jason assaulted and handcuffed a couple of cops last night."

"Yeah, we know about that. They weren't cops. Hauser got 'em. Amber, listen, we all know what a crazy situation we put you in. Nobody's about to throw any stones—"

"And I've been making out with a suspect."

"...oh."

"Yeah. So, I'm gonna tell everybody the answers to a bunch of deep questions about the true nature of the whole universe," she said, crossing her arms uncomfortably, "and then you guys can all decide whether to put me in handcuffs or a straightjacket. Either way I'm pretty sure I just lost my job."

Matt knew wouldn't be getting to sleep after that.

"I'M TOTALLY ABOUT to put my foot in my mouth here," warned Alex. He kept his voice low so as not to draw too much attention to himself in the open, brightly-lit store. Before him was a row of large white bins, each with clear plastic lids over them. He held a clear plastic bag open beside one of them as Molly scooped out some of the bin's contents with a plastic trowel.

"You do that a lot with us," Molly smiled, pouring the white flakes into the bag. "Are we special? Or do you do that with everyone?"

He considered his answer. "Yes."

"Go ahead."

"This is not how I expected magic to work."

"How so?"

"We're in a store, buying materials out of plastic bins and putting them into plastic bags."

"How else did you think we got our materials?"

"I dunno, I just figured it was more labor intensive than this. I figured you had to go out into the world and gather stuff by hand or something. What? Don't look at me like that. *Obviously* I don't know what I'm talking about, that's what I'm saying. I only know magic from fiction, and that's not a reliable source. I just figured you had to, I dunno... gather your stuff yourself instead of buying it all in a store?"

"Who says this wasn't gathered properly?" Molly grinned. "You think we're shopping at McMagic's?" She took the bag from him and sealed it shut with an ordinary twist-tie, then wrote a bin number on it with a marker as she spoke. "Half of learning to practice magic is simply learning to *believe.* After a while you get the hang of identifying other believers and separating them out from the pretenders and the dreamers and the quacks. And the scammers."

Alex glanced up at the woman behind the counter. She wore a black apron over her faded sweatshirt and busily typed away at her iPad. Onyx stood nearby, providing a visual contrast as she focused her attention on a display case of jewelry. Though Onyx carried a cell phone, drove a car and went to college, Alex hadn't had the slightest hesitation in believing the Gothy girl he'd always seen in black silk and lace was a witch. The woman behind the counter, however, might as well have been working at a hardware store. "So is she a believer?"

"Who, Cheryl? No. But she's open-minded, and that's enough. For most of her customers, this is all just aromatherapy and meditation aids. It has perfectly ordinary uses. That's how she thinks of it. But she also knows it has religious uses. She's not the sort who thinks that the five major faiths are the only legit ones."

"This is religion for you?"

Molly nodded. "Practicing magic means understanding the nature of the world and how to live in it. You learn it to make sense out of life. What else is religion but that?"

"Makes sense," Alex conceded. He followed Molly and helped her gather more bits of powders and crystals from the bins.

"We call ourselves witches 'cause that's the closest term, but we're not true wiccans. We do stuff differently. We're pagans, and not fluffy-bunny pagans, either. They're who I meant when I mentioned pretenders and dreamers.

"We don't go to church on Sundays, or any house of worship on a specific day of the week. We don't have idols. We hardly ever do what you'd call praying. But we have our ethics and our taboos. We have a strong sense of spirituality." She paused, considering her words carefully. "We have a belief as to what happens to us when we die."

His eyes had wandered down to a rack of merchandise as she spoke, but they came up to meet hers again. Molly had vibrant green eyes. "Do I fit in with that?"

"You're kind of walking proof, actually," she said. "Most people would freak out over meeting an angel or a demon, 'cause it'd kind of confirm things they always believed but *knew* they'd never see proven, right? Didn't freak us out one bit. You, though..." Molly shook her head. "It's one thing to meditate or cast a spell to try to get in touch with a past life. You're a whole 'nother level.

"Our Practice holds that souls can come back, at least sometimes. That's part of why we think we can help you. But we're not a hundred percent on that. The spells we want to use... they're not designed for your specific problem. We're gonna have to tweak them a little."

"So my issue isn't common enough that someone already made a spell for it?"

Molly shook her head. "Like I said, we'll have to tweak what we know. On the bright side, you're already a believer. Accepting that magic is real is critical. You don't have to follow our Practice or any other. Magic works fine on non-believers, but it's much easier and more effective on believers. You've already had more than enough experiences to overcome your doubts."

"I know the magic is real," Alex nodded. "I'm just not sure I can accept that there's a spell to just make all the problems in my head disappear. Seems too easy."

"Wait for it," Molly smiled, and not without sympathy.

"Okay, we need eleven hundred bucks," said Onyx as she rejoined them.

"Huh?" blinked Alex.

"Eleven hundred. That's how much the jewelry's gonna cost."

"Jewelry for what?"

"The ceremony. We need silver. The kind you eat off of won't make the grade."

"What, are we melting them down to make bullets or something? I thought we were gonna work on getting my head straight."

"We are. We need a bunch of small, pure bits of silver," Onyx explained patiently. "And we gotta throw it all away when this is done."

"You were saying about this being too easy?" Molly asked. He pulled out his wallet with nothing more than a rueful smile as she poked him. "Anyway, Lorelei will cover it. It's her money, right?" Then she saw him grimace. "What?"

"Not sure I want to talk about it," he mumbled.

"Alex," Onyx said, putting a hand on his shoulder. "Full disclosure. You've gotta trust us with absolutely everything if we're gonna do this. We have to bring down every barrier we can. You've gotta be ready to bare your soul here."

"That's a two-way street, though, right?" he asked. "We keep talking about me and my issues. I don't want to sound ungrateful, because the fact that you two are even trying is a lifesaver here. I was just kinda hoping the first time we got to hang out wouldn't be the All About Me Show."

She tilted her head curiously. "What do you want to know?"

"Lots," he shrugged. "Molly just told me that this is religion for you. What is it that you believe? How did you two get together? All of it."

Molly looked at Onyx and didn't even need to see a nod to read the consent in her eyes. "Playing 'Twenty Questions' is fine, but it's not exactly the way to build the sort of connection we need."

"I'm not sure we can take shortcuts now, though," Molly replied.

"No, but at the same time... I mean, y'know?"

Alex had looked from one to the other as they spoke. "I don't know. Whatever it is that you two know, I don't." He watched Molly turn her head this way and that, taking in the whole shop with her vision. So did Onyx. That had him doing it, too. Farther back in the store were a couple of customers, but none within a direct line of sight. The store manager, several rows of merchandise away, seemed completely disinterested in them. "What's going on?"

"The thing is, Alex," Molly began, "if you hadn't backed off on us, we probably would have already built the sort of intimacy we need. We're not afraid of sharing anything with you. It's just that right now, things really kinda *are* all about you. We know how to open up. We need you to be able to do it, too, at least to us."

"Okay?" he asked. Like Onyx, his eyes kept sweeping the store. He heard Molly fumble with something.

"Gimme your hand," she said softly, stepping closer to him. "Hold it open." She took his right hand in hers, and guided it down. He felt the fabric of her shirt at first—and then her belly, and the satin of her panties, and the soft hair and warm, tender flesh beneath them.

Easily aroused as always, Alex felt his body come alive at this sudden turn of their conversation. Molly met his surprised look with a naughty smile. Onyx seemed not the least bit bothered; the grin on her face indicated that she found this amusing, but beyond that she didn't look their way. She kept watch to enable this.

"This is the level of intimacy we need with you, Alex," Molly said quietly. "You know we want you, and you want us, and not just as a fling. Maybe it'll turn out that way in the end, but I don't think so."

Her breath grew heavy, as did his. She put the smallest of kisses on his lips. He knew this was rapidly arousing her, too. "Is this part of what we need to do?" he asked, hoping she'd say yes.

"Not to fix your head, no," Molly told him, warming to his touch. "*This* isn't a magic thing. It's not part of our beliefs. It's just to make a point."

"What point is that?" His voice was just as low as hers. Molly had his heart pounding in his chest.

"This *will* happen," she said, pressing a bit on his hand to encourage his touch and, shamelessly, to heighten her own enjoyment. Molly gasped a bit as he moved his hand gently, palming her flesh with all the practice she'd hoped he would demonstrate. "We're already on our way emotionally. It's just timing. All three of us, naked, in bed together. No secrets, no barriers. No inhibitions. Wow, you feel good."

"So do you," he nodded. They breathed all the same air. "So this... is this how Practitioners bond?"

"It's one way they can," Molly winked. "There are lots of others, but this gets the job done if you open your heart along the way. We don't want to be your live-in girlfriends. We do want to be intimate with you."

"But we want you to have your head straight when it happens," Onyx told him, stepping in close. "We want you without all this baggage weighing down your soul. You're loaded with grief and anger and confusion. You're scared of losing your identity. That's not a healthy place to start."

"Can you get there, Alex?" Molly asked him. "We can't bring you there with magic. This has to be genuine. But can you accept that we're already in a close, stable and sexual relationship? That we can share anything, including each other?"

"We have no problem with who you are, Alex," said Onyx. "We're not asking you to change. We're asking you to open up to us."

"Even if it involves other people? There's stuff I'm just plain not supposed to tell anyone."

"If it's about you, then yeah. Even if it involves Lorelei or Rachel," Molly nodded. She gently drew his hand out of her pants then, letting out a heavy breath as she cooled down.

"Do you think either of them have a problem with you talking to us about anything?" Onyx pressed. "They don't seem terribly inhibited."

"What do you want to know?"

"Right now? Nothing. Anything," shrugged Molly. "Tell us one of those things you've been carrying around that you're afraid to talk about. Something about Lorelei's money bothers you. Tell us."

He knew she just wanted him to answer the question for himself. His eyes came to hers, and then to Onyx. "Depending how you look at it, it's my money. It's my apartment, and Lorelei's driving my car."

"What, you mean like it's all legally in your name?" Molly asked.

"No," Onyx answered quietly before Alex spoke. "No, it goes deeper than that, doesn't it?"

"It's been part of us since the beginning," he shrugged. "I'm not even sure how to say it, 'cause honestly, I'm kind of ashamed. More than kind of. I feel like I should object more or something, but Lorelei gets talking, and she's always perfectly comfortable with it, but even so..." He looked at the floor, frowning and trying to come up with the right words. "This is one of those things I'm afraid will make you think I'm a total creep."

Onyx smirked. "I didn't think you were a creep when you told me you had a girlfriend who's okay with you sleeping with other women. We both kind of figured things would only get weirder when we found out your girlfriend's also a demon."

"Yeah, but we're not just boyfriend and girlfriend," Alex said. "We're master and servant. Or slave, if you want to get blunt." He let it hang there for a moment, waiting for the pair to look at him in disgust. They did not.

"It's not just the ritual bond," he explained. "She says it's part of being a demon. They've all got masters. And Lorelei loves it, at least with me. She doesn't go there when other people are around, but when it's just her and I— and Rachel, a lot of the time—she calls me 'master.' We go back and forth on this a lot, and she says she has all the freedom she could ever want with me.

She's... kind of built to get off on this, but she could never let go and enjoy that before now 'cause everyone else she's been with before me was complete scum. It used to be humiliating. It's not with me."

"Then why does it bother you?" Onyx wondered.

"Because it's wrong, isn't it? Shouldn't I be trying to fix that somehow? Give her *real* freedom? I mean, I don't treat her like a slave. I don't order her around or humiliate her or anything like that, but it's still there, and last night... last night we both got really into it. Truth is, I like it. And I know I shouldn't."

"Part of you is turned on just thinking about it right now, aren't you?"

Alex nodded. He looked at the two again. "Like I said. Creepy."

"Sounds like informed consent to me," Molly shrugged. "Everyone has their kinks. I can appreciate that one."

"We're not gonna judge you on it," said Onyx.

"How could you not?" asked Alex.

"Do you expect all your relationships to be like that?" nudged Molly.

"No, of course not."

"Does Rachel have a problem with it?"

He snorted. "No, of course not."

"And you never treat her like that around other people?"

"Never."

"Then I think it's pretty hot," Molly grinned, "and I'd love to hear all about it. Slowly," she teased.

Alex blanched. As he cooled down, he became increasingly aware of his surroundings again. "Not here?"

"No, not here," Onyx said, poking Molly. "But are you willing to tell us?"

"It's not even so much the knowing as the openness," elaborated Molly. "Even if you don't give us all the salacious details, it'll make the same difference if you're just genuinely willing to tell us." Then she bit her lip, fighting a grin. "Although the best way to cross that bridge is to actually tell us."

"I went into Jason's apartment with him to make sure it was safe," Amber told her team. They sat or stood around her in a semicircle while she leaned forward in a large plush chair. "I hung around a bit and we talked, but I told him I needed to go home and check on things. Then I came right back here."

Silence hung over the group as they considered her words. Amber sat waiting for the hammer to fall. "And you don't think they suspect you of being up to anything at all?" Hauser asked in a thoughtful tone.

"Oh, I think Lorelei suspects *something*," Amber shrugged, "but I can't tell exactly what. Jason still thinks I'm legit. Alex, too, I think. And I have no clue what Rachel thinks. She seems kind of removed from the group as a whole. I think she mostly only talks to Lorelei and Alex and keeps everyone else at arm's length. Friendly, but distant, I guess."

"And you're sure you were sober and sound all night?" Colleen spoke up. She had her poker face on, betraying neither anger nor concern. "No chance anything was slipped into your drink?"

"I'm as sure as I can be. I can't guarantee nobody used any sort of magic on me, 'cause I wouldn't know in the first place, right?" Amber looked to Doug Bridger.

Snapped from his thoughts, Doug shook his head. "No, you wouldn't," he said, "but I can't find any residual energy on you. That doesn't mean nothing happened. I'm already sure those two 'witches' you talked about are the real deal, and they're better than I am. But as far as I can tell, you're clean."

"Right. So no guarantees," Amber sighed. "No guarantee I'm not just ready for the loony bin, either."

"Could all of that angel business have been faked with magic?" wondered Hauser. Like Colleen, his eyes turned to Doug.

"Someone could have cast spells on Amber to make her *think* she'd seen all this, sure. I don't see any evidence of that, but it could happen. But as for actually creating all those effects at once? Going toe-to-toe with werewolves physically, and being able to fly and blast out all that fire? Plus all the other effects she described?" The occult expert shook his head. "There's a lot about magic I just don't know, but all that added together goes so far off any scale I'm familiar with that I've gotta say no."

"And Lorelei?"

"She's another matter. So far all Amber has described is some illusory magic. I couldn't do that, but there are plenty of people who can."

"Agent Maddox," Hauser said, "what's your read on what they do next? The whole group?"

"I dunno," she shrugged, "probably find a way to get the vampires and the werewolves off their backs and then go about their lives." She had forced herself to look Hauser in the eye when she told him how far things had gone with Jason, but had stared mostly at the floor since then. Only now did she look up once more. "Like I said, I think we had this whole group pegged wrong from the beginning. Jason, Alex, even Lorelei... they're the good guys."

Hauser snorted. "By her own admission, this Lorelei woman is a murderer. It doesn't matter who she's sleeping with now or how much she claims she's changed her stripes. She's a criminal. End of story."

"Demons aren't exactly part of our mandate, Joe," Keeley pointed out.

"No? How aren't they? We're here to handle crimes committed by creatures that science doesn't even know exist. Seems like she fits the bill to me.

"Jones and Reinhardt murdered a man in a parking lot in full view of Bureau agents. Amber saw Carlisle and Cohen commit felony assault and kidnapping."

"Sir," Amber said, "they can't exactly dial 911 and say vampires are trying to kill them."

"Nobody gets to play vigilante, either," Hauser scowled. "And nobody gets to turn an American city into their own little warzone."

"What were they supposed to do?" asked Amber.

"These are *crimes*, Agent Maddox. If they wanna prove they're the good guys, they'll get their chance. Lanier," he said, shifting his attention. "We need a better place to hold our prisoners. And we need to get a tac support team up here as soon as possible."

"Joe, I think we've got something else to work out first," reminded Paul.

"What's that?"

Paul nodded toward Amber. "She's compromised the whole case, Joe."

"No, she hasn't," Hauser frowned.

"Joe, she got romantically involved with a suspect in an investigation!" snapped Colleen. "The case is blown! We can't bring any of this to a prosecutor, let alone in front of a judge."

"We're not the regular FBI, Agent Nguyen," Hauser replied flatly. His eyes turned back to Amber, ignoring the shocked looks on everyone's faces. "Agent Maddox, did you have sex with him?"

"Wait, what?" Amber blinked. "No! But—"

"Did you offer him sexual favors in exchange for information? Was any of this foreplay done on a *quid pro quo* basis? Did he intimidate or blackmail you?"

Her jaw fell open. "No, of course not. This all just spiraled away from me. I started to tell you this could happen days ago, but I couldn't get clear guidelines out of you. That's no excuse, though, and I know it. I should've been more explicit. I accept full responsibility for what I did, and I'll face whatever conse-quences—"

Hauser held up a hand to stop her. "I'm not suggesting anything like that. This is not a problem for our case. That's my point."

"The hell it isn't!" objected Colleen.

"That's enough, Agent Nguyen!" Hauser barked. "We are *not* under stan-dard FBI regulations. Agent Maddox improvised and came through with infor-mation and evidence we may never have gotten through any other approach. I wouldn't give a damn if she *did* fuck him. That's her call. We are not going to close the investigation, we are not going to go home, and we are not going to turn a blind eye to the laws that have been broken here.

"Agent Maddox? Are you still with us?"

"Sir?" she blinked, still in complete shock.

"Cohen is only one of the people at risk here. He might get off with a plea deal when this is all over, but we've gotta see it through to make that happen—unless we want to just abandon this whole matter and let him and his friends and God only knows who else die at the hands of two different groups of super-natural criminals loose in this city. Do you want that?"

"No, sir. Of course not."

"Then we need you to stick with this. You need to stay on Cohen. Go back to his place and try to steer him away from looking for Jones and Reinhardt." He turned from her then, pacing across the small living room as he thought. He seemed completely oblivious to the shocked looks he got from Amber, Colleen and the others on the task force. Nor did he notice the discomfort as they looked at one another.

"Lorelei and Carlisle are the keys here," he said. "We'll need a lot of leverage on her. But everything we've seen points to Carlisle being a stand-up guy and a boy scout..." He scratched his chin and frowned. "We're just gonna have to put that to the test. Lanier."

"Yeah?"

"I need to see Carlisle's class schedule again. And a map of the campus." He sat down on the couch beside Matt, looking over his shoulder as the agent typed away on the laptop. Then he looked over at Amber. "Like I said, we need you to stay on Cohen. Get on it, Agent."

Still shocked to have her job, Amber rose and slowly walked out. She made it halfway down the hall before she heard the door open and shut again.

"You know you screwed up, right?" Colleen asked her without venom but also without pulling any punches. "Doesn't matter what Hauser thinks of it. This is flat-out bad."

Amber shook her head. "I know, Colleen. I'm sorry. I don't know what else to say other than that. I screwed up bad and I'm sorry and maybe I *should* lose my job."

"That's obviously not happening now," Colleen shrugged, "and as mad as I am at this, I knew it was way too soon to put you on an undercover assignment. There are agencies who probably wouldn't bat an eye at this, but they don't handle domestic law enforcement." Her face held its frown of displeasure. "Do you think you could've gotten this info without going about it the way you did?"

"Yeah. Probably. I don't know... Jason would still have been interested in me, but I probably could've held it to 'just friends' if I'd really tried."

"Then why didn't you?"

She feared the question would come up in front of everyone. Alone in the hallway with Colleen, it seemed no less daunting. "Because I like him. Probably more than any guy I've ever met. But I should be able to keep all those feelings separate from the job, so... maybe that means I'm not fit for it." She took a deep breath. "But that's where we are, and we gotta follow through, so how do I make this right?"

Colleen's frown turned to a scowl as she looked over her shoulder toward the closed door. "At least you're owning your bad calls. You're not the one I'm worried about right now."

"Yeah, I'm a little..." Amber's voice trailed off. "Is it just me, or did he want me out of the room? And did you think it was weird that he brought up the possibility of Jason getting out of trouble on a plea deal?"

At that, Colleen turned back to her. "You may not be right for undercover work," she said, "but don't start drafting your resignation letter just yet."

MAGIC, as it turned out, involved an awful lot of running around buying stuff.

It seemed they went to every florist in town, picking up dozens of lilies and as many of the darkest roses they could find. They bought wine and whiskey and sake. They went to a cemetery on the north end of the city and bought from the groundskeepers a couple of the small American flags sold for the graves of veterans on patriotic holidays. After two fruitless stops, they found a coin dealer whose wares satisfied Molly, and there they bought three silver coins.

Alex paid for it all.

"There are rules against working magic strictly for profit," Molly explained at one point in their drive. "Sometimes it's okay and sometimes it's not. Last night with your apartment? That's fine. Lorelei came to us offering payment of her own volition. We tried to turn down her money and do it for free. She insisted. We went back and forth with that three times, and she knew to keep pushing until we said yes. She doesn't practice our kind of magic, but she knows the customs. That's why it was okay to let her pay us. This situation is different."

"How so?" he asked. He sat in the back seat of Molly's car, with Onyx riding shotgun. "I don't want to rip you off."

"You're not," said Onyx, looking back at him. "Don't try to argue that, either. It's not fair now. We told you how it works, so that'd be a dodge. We can't charge you for magic now."

He cocked his head curiously. "Ever?"

"Pretty much," Onyx nodded. "Wouldn't anyway."

"Why not?"

"Because we're a thing now." She looked him in the eye as she said it, letting it sink in and smiling a bit. "It may be too early for labels, but we're a circle of one sort or another. You'd come running if we ever needed help, right?"

"I haven't come to your rescue ever," he pointed out. "This isn't the first time for you, though."

"It'll come," chuckled Molly. "Besides, do you and the guys keep score?"

"Point," Alex nodded. "But it's okay for me to pay for the materials?"

"That's kind of a requirement in this situation," said Molly. "You're gonna do a lot of the set-up grunt work on this, too. It'll mean more that way. This is kind of all about you paying back what you owe."

He frowned a bit. "Y'know, from what memories I've got, and from my dreams and all that... I don't feel like I owe anyone anything." He paused. "Except for maybe a couple of apologies."

"It's not like that," Molly told him. "You didn't borrow or steal anything from anyone; the people who put you in this condition did that. But the way to resolve your problem involves paying back the guy they stole it from. Remember, magic is all about symbolism. What you see and what we do isn't necessarily how death and the afterlife actually work; it's just symbols we understand. Anyway, who do you owe apologies?"

"I don't remember a whole lot," he said. "Just snippets. Sometimes I think I mix up the names, and sometimes I wonder if I'm not just making stuff up. I can't always tell what's an actual memory and what's... I dunno, something I saw on television once." He paused. "Every time I get talking about this stuff, I worry that I'm droning. Plus it's all kind of sad."

Onyx stayed twisted in her seat so she could keep her eyes on him. "Talk," she told him, more as an invitation than an order.

He nodded, looking out the window as they drove. "I think there was a lady named Siobhan that I was in love with," he said. "I think I said some shitty things to her, and she left me... and I think I never had a chance to say I was so sorry."

It was much as Molly warned him. He did a lot of grunt work.

The first tasks were simple, such as sweeping the bare concrete of the ritual room in their small two-bedroom apartment. He poured rosemary into four small mortars, each of them placed at the four cardinal directions—conveniently marked out by tacks placed in the ceiling. Given the positioning of the building, the directions were a bit counterintuitive, but none of the architects had considered calling the corners when they designed the apartment.

When he was done, Onyx lit the rosemary with a long match and murmured words in a language he almost thought he knew, but couldn't identify. She came over to him and softly said, "Remember everything you can. Don't fight it and don't think about your life now. Think about your life *then*, and how you died. Try to remember names. Your names, other names. Lovers, friends, enemies. Write them on the concrete, outside the circle. It's okay if it hurts. It's okay if you get mad or if you cry. You need to grieve... and it's okay to grieve for yourself."

She kissed him on the cheek and then left him alone, closing the door behind her. They had studying and planning to do, they had said. The grunt work was all about him.

He picked the petals off the bouquets of roses and lilies, using them to completely cover the outer ring of a circle that looked like it had been etched into the foundation concrete with a Dremmel tool. It was painstaking work and murder on his knees.

At first he thought little of his fragmented memories of past lives. Too much of the present occupied his mind, with monsters hunting for him and two lovers from very different worlds all working to share one another and find balance. Onyx was only a year or two older than he, and Molly only a couple of years beyond her; to be in this apartment that they paid for themselves made him think of his lost job and his dependence on his lover's wealth.

Eventually, though, the memories came. It was the pain in his knees that took hold first, reminding him of calisthenics on hard concrete. He remembered basic training, which took different turns and different shapes as two lives who'd served in the same Army blended together and pulled apart. One ended bitterly, in a jungle after an act of sacrifice, buying time for one comrade who stuck with him through thick and thin and another who'd just as soon have spit on him as talk to him. The other ended on a spring day, on his back, looking at the sky with an old woman holding his hand as he bled out, thinking of the woman who'd been his wife for only a handful of months, and most of those spent miles apart.

The first tear fell.

He stopped, found a pencil, and wrote "Marie" outside the circle. Then he got back to work on the petals.

The longer he breathed in the scent of burning rosemary, the easier the memories came. They remained a jumble, never complete and often without context or even a specific emotion. His tears were not constant.

He wrote "Aidan" and "Tinney" and "Chelsea," unsure of who was who. He got back to work for only a moment, and then stopped again and wrote something else in very different letters.

Then he wrote more. Foreign letters came to him naturally. He remembered people being surprised that a goatherd could write. He'd gotten that all his adult life, short though it was. He remembered some of the people who'd laughed at his runes, and tried to carve their names into the flat, bare stone.

The pencil broke.

Molly and Onyx found him on his knees, staring furiously at the markings. His arms shook with rage. The two shared a wary glance, both amazed at the scrawlings all over the floor. Most weren't in English at all.

They took to his sides, crouching down to his level. "Those are Viking runes, aren't they?" asked Molly, her voice low and gentle. She didn't understand his response, which came through gritted teeth in a language she'd never heard. The two witches shared another look before she asked, "What does that say?"

"Skorri."

"Who is Skorri?"

Again, his first response didn't sound like English. He swallowed. "Me."

"Who are they?" she asked, pointing to the last runes he had drawn.

"Unferth," he grunted, pointing at one and then the other. "Bjorn." He took a deep, shaking breath. "I'll have their heads."

Onyx put her hand on his back. "They're gone, Alex. Maybe a thousand years gone."

"No. I saw them last night," he growled. He looked over at Onyx, staring at her until recognition crept back into his eyes. "I saw them. With the vampires."

"Wow," Molly blinked. "What're the odds?"

"Do you remember them being vampires before?" Onyx asked.

"No. No, they were... they were on my side. Mostly." His voice became normal once more, though the anger remained. "Oarmates? Is that a word? Or is that from a book? It's hard to remember little stuff."

"What's the big picture, then?" Molly asked. "Why do they have to die? Other than being vampires, right? It sounds personal."

He nodded, and stared at their names. "They left me to die. They sailed without me. Left me with the... with the Danes, for a whole winter. We were on a raid, and it went bad and we had to flee. They got to the boats before I did and left me. I could've died. I should have died. I made it through the winter and found... I found my wife carried another man's child.

"He cast her out. I took her in, but there was... shame for her. Men scorned me as weak for taking her back. We left for another village, and... and she was murdered there. I avenged her... yet none of that would have happened to her but for Unferth and Bjorn."

"Alex," said Onyx, placing a hand on his cheek. "You don't seem to me like the type to get hung up on revenge."

"What are you—of *course*, I want revenge, I—what did you call me?"

"Alex," she repeated. "You're Alex."

He stared at her, then closed his eyes and let out a shuddering breath. "I feel a little freaked out by this."

"Yeah, I would be, too," Molly agreed. "It's okay. You need to *feel* everything."

"What's happening?"

"You need to grieve," Onyx told him. "You need to mourn, and face all this baggage from all these lives, and then you need to let it go."

"Will I forget everything?"

"A lot of it," she nodded. "This is all a part of you. It's who you are, deep down. But you won't feel it so much, and that's what hurts you and confuses you. It's not the memories, right? It's the emotions."

"Don't the memories cause the emotions?"

"They won't once you're ready to let them go."

"Why can't I just forget it all?"

"Because you need it, Alex. Because this," she said, pointing to the runes, "all this is you. Skorri is you, but you're not living that life anymore."

"Wouldn't it be easier?"

"We talked about this when we came up with this plan," continued Onyx, taking his hand. "You're a great guy with a big heart and we like you that way. We like you a lot. But your life is *crazy*, Alex. You grew up in a stable home and a nice, safe city, and now you live in a world with monsters.

"Part of you shot and stabbed your way out of a house full of monsters once, Alex," she said, looking him in the eye. "You *need* that part. It saved your life twice now. Grieving isn't about forgetting. It's about releasing emotions and moving on."

Molly took his other hand. "Hold still," she instructed as she produced a marker. She wrote on his hand, painstakingly copying the runes that spelled out his name in Old Norse.

"The circle isn't done yet," she said, "but I think we can help you with the rest."

HE KNEW this would be weird. He trusted the women who brought him here and who told him what he needed to do. He desperately wanted his nightmares and all of his nameless heartache laid to rest. But it was still weird.

Alex lay in the center of the ritual circle, still inhaling the rosemary smoke. He felt cold, given the bare concrete underneath him and the lack of a shirt or shoes. His companions sat inside the circle with him, one at his feet and one at his head, both chanting something he could almost recognize. He couldn't see either of them, or anything else. His eyes were covered by two of the silver coins they'd bought that morning. He held the third in his mouth.

He needed the coins, they said, to pay off the boatman—with interest.

The words they chanted seemed so familiar. Alex had scraped through two years of Spanish in high school. That was the extent of his foreign language skills. Yet listening to the witches, he could swear he knew half of those words. They used words like "love" and "death" and "memory" and "obols," which he knew to mean "coin" but had never heard or used in his life.

These weren't proper obols. They weren't even close. He knew that, too, and had a clear idea of what an obol should look like. These were silver coins, and maybe that was close enough for sorcery, but they weren't actually obols.

He remembered all sorts of strange things, too. He remembered lying on less comfortable surfaces than this, like the rocky ground on the road to the Holy Land and the slave pen in Rome. He remembered toiling in fields and shivering through cold nights outside Danish villages, waiting for people to go to bed so he might slip in and steal some food.

Molly and Onyx shifted from his head and feet to each take up a spot kneeling at his sides. They took his hands.

He remembered lying on a field in the spring, staring up at the sky with his belly in a terrible twist of pain and wetness. He remembered a woman who knelt beside him and held his hand as he died. Even with the coins over his eyes, it was as if he could see her clearly.

Except instead of the old Roma woman, he saw Onyx. Molly was there, too, kneeling at his other side... but now in his mind he couldn't tell Onyx and the Roma woman apart.

They kept chanting. They each took up one of his hands, holding them palms-up to the sky in supplication. At first, his hands bore the same uneven discoloration and faint burn scars that they had for a month. Then he saw the blood and blisters from building Halla's funeral pyre on a cold morning all by himself, and feared he might never be able to play the piano again.

No. Not the piano. Not anything. He hadn't played a musical instrument since that time he and Wade got busted for sword-fighting with their recorders in music class in the fifth grade.

Conflicting images and sensations from his body and his mind left him feeling much like this was a vivid dream from which he might awaken any moment. He lay on his back but stood; had his eyes closed, but saw his surroundings. Molly and Onyx gripped his hands and lifted him up in the dream world, which now bore no resemblance to the springtime meadow of before, and... "Onyx," said Molly.

"What?"

"Your clothes."

Alex looked. She wore the clothes of the old Roma woman. Molly appeared as she always did. None of Alex's clothes changed, either.

The two witches exchanged a long, thoughtful look. Whatever their thoughts, they did not share them with Alex. Instead, they turned to the task at hand.

They stood on a rocky riverbank. Fog stretched all around them, thin enough to reveal the waters beyond but little more than that. Alex thought to look up. He felt as if he might be underground somewhere. That led him to wonder where the light came from. With the coin in his mouth, he couldn't ask.

The witches led him by the hand. "This is Acheron," explained Molly as Onyx resumed the chant. "We need to find the boatman."

Alex turned his face to her, wanting to ask something. He couldn't speak. Molly shrugged. "We've never been here before, either."

They walked. The witches took care not to step near the water. Alex looked to it as they moved and felt his sorrow rise. He felt loneliness. He felt betrayal. He could remember the names.

For a time, all he heard was the chant held by Onyx and the sound of their footsteps on the cold rocks. Then he heard the soft sound of something pushing through the water. Soon, they saw the source of the sound.

The build and curves of the boat stirred old memories for Alex, but the boatman seemed familiar only as a figure out of stories told by old men. He seemed like a poor man, long unshaven and dressed in red and brown rags. Everything about him spoke of power and vitality despite great age. He pushed his boat to the shore with his ferryman's pole and waited.

Alex watched from his spot on the shore. He felt the coins removed from his eyes as he lay on the floor in the apartment. Onyx took the coin from his mouth, both in the apartment and on the shore. She placed them in his hand, and then the two witches took hold of his wrists and guided him up to kneel on the concrete. His eyes stayed shut there so that he might continue to see the river and the boatman.

"You need to pay him," said Molly in his ear. "It's only one coin for you, but two more for what was taken."

His eyes didn't turn to meet hers. "Won't that mean stepping into the water?"

"Only for a few seconds," she told him. "You need to do that, too. But don't stay long. Don't get in the boat."

"Do I say anything?"

"No. He knows."

Swallowing his dread, Alex took the first few steps slowly. The boatman waited, not looking up and seeming utterly indifferent to the young man that approached him. Alex felt the pull of the current even at the edge of the cold water. It looked peaceful, but standing in the river he now felt its strength. Barely in the water to his knees, he feared it could sweep him away.

"Where is your angel?" the boatman asked in an aged, severe voice. Alex froze in place for a moment, shocked somehow that the boatman spoke at all. "He should guide you. He has been with you all the other times, after the first."

Alex didn't know what to say. The witches hadn't prepped him for this. "You know me?" he asked.

"I know every soul who passes," said the boatman. "You are not special for this. I know your companions, too. Where is your angel?"

Thoughts processed as the boatman spoke and Alex stammered. "I'm not... he isn't with me anymore," Alex said. Rachel hadn't explained much more than that, but it wasn't the sort of conversation he'd forget. "I don't have a guardian now. But I'm not here to cross."

"Why do you come?"

"To pay you back for what was stolen."

He held out the coins. Slowly, the boatman reached out an open hand and waited until Alex dropped his repayment. Then he looked down at the coins in his hand and gave a satisfied nod.

His task complete, Alex turned to go. A thought occurred to him. He turned back. "It was the same angel every time?"

"Your first was a woman," said the boatman. "After her, it was always the same man."

The boatman said nothing more. Alex felt no desire to linger and every need to leave. Walking out proved difficult, though. The undertow of the river fought him with each step. He jabbed his ankle on a rock under the water, gasped in pain and found his eyes watering.

Everything about this hurt. It had hurt all along, but something about this simple, stupid jab at his ankle punctuated it all. After all he had endured, this last bruising proved too much. Pain shot through him, and with it came a first, unbidden and completely unnecessary tear.

Alex picked up his foot and stepped forward again, cursing himself. The pain wasn't enough to cry over, certainly not in front of friends. It wasn't like being shot or beaten. It wasn't like losing a lover. He'd been through all that.

He'd been through a lot of that.

A second tear fell, and then a third. Molly and Onyx came to the edge of the water and reached out to him. They took his arms and pulled him the rest of the way out of the water, and knelt with him as he fell to his knees weeping. He felt Molly push gently at his shoulders, indicating that he should lean forward.

Onyx put something in his hand, both in the dream world and the apartment. He held the small silver ring tightly as he sobbed. "Who are you crying for?"

His eyes fluttered open for a brief moment. His tears fell into a bowl placed at his knees by Onyx, whose chanting had ended. "Marie," he huffed.

"Why?"

"I never came back to her."

She fell silent, letting him cry a moment longer, and then took the hand that held the ring. "Let it go," Onyx said, bringing his hand to the bowl and turning it over. "She knew you wanted to come back. She knew you loved her. Let Marie go."

He let out a heavy breath and opened his palm. The ring fell into the bowl to lie amid the drops of his tears. Though he did not wail or thrash around, his weeping only increased.

Another ring came into his hand, this one from Molly. She watched more of his tears roll down from his cheeks to fall into the bowl. "Who are you crying for?" asked Molly.

"Siobhan."

"Why?"

"I said such awful things. She didn't deserve any of them. She left me and I can't blame her," he shuddered, "but I'm still so sorry."

Molly went through the same motions as Onyx, bringing his hand over the bowl. "She knows now," Molly said. "She knows you loved her. Let Siobhan go."

The ring fell into the bowl. Then it was Onyx's turn again.

"Who are you crying for?" she asked as she placed an earring in his hand.

"Stephanie."

"Why?"

He inhaled sharply. "Fuckin' bitch shacked up with fuckin' Ted from the drugstore," Alex mumbled with obvious anger. "Took my money from 'Nam and married another man behind my back."

Neither Molly nor Onyx could miss the shift in his pattern of speech. Even amid such ritual and magical power, they couldn't help but share an amused grin. Molly quickly got a grip on her mirth. "Let her go," she said, turning his hand over to drop the ring in the bowl. "Just let the bitch go."

They remained with him on the shores of Acheron and the floor of their apartment, hearing of loves lost to tragedy or, just as often, to treachery. They ignored the passage of time and hoped only that their supply of silver jewelry would hold out.

PLASTIC WRAP COVERED the bowl in his lap so none of the tears would splash out. Alex didn't believe it had all come from his eyes. Onyx explained that he'd had a lot of mourning to make up for, but he suspected some other magic might have been involved. Regardless, the simple practicality of plastic wrap and a rubber band over a big ceramic bowl offered a brief point of amusement amid his grief.

He held it in both hands in the back of Molly's car all the way to the Montlake Cut, which linked Lake Union to Lake Washington. Parking so close to the university was always a challenge, but with perseverance they found a space. Alex carried the bowl from the car to a spot halfway across the drawbridge that spanned the cut. The two witches walked beside him.

Traffic crawled by as they came to the center of the bridge. The sun had set an hour earlier, coinciding with the end of their ritual. Most of the time since then had been spent allowing Alex to come down from his emotional ordeal. He felt better now—he understood that this matter was unfinished even before Onyx told him of the next step, but his anguish had quite clearly been productive.

Molly and Onyx seemed pleased with their timing and how much they had accomplished before dusk. Alex had little sense of how much time such rituals usually took, but even he felt surprised that it was still so early.

"Samhain's a good night for this sort of thing," Molly told him while he unwrapped the bowl on the bridge. "The best night, really. 'bout time you caught a lucky break."

He looked at her with a bit of a grin. "I'd lose track of the lucky breaks in my life if I started counting 'em," he said. "You both count for a bunch."

"Yeah, well, sounds like you've had some crappy luck to make up for in your previous lives," Molly shrugged. "Consistently crappy. Maybe the universe owes you this one."

"It is kind of weird how consistent all that is," said Onyx. "Dying from violence every single time. Always checking out young. It's not weird to see parallels and patterns, but that's just... more than weird," she finished, buttoning up her long black coat against the breeze.

"Do you remember much now?" asked Molly.

"Less than before. I know it's there, but now it's more like remembering books rather than experiences. Feels more distant."

Alex faced the rail of the bridge, looking out at the water below. He cradled the bowl with his left arm so he could use his right hand. "Is there anything I'm supposed to say or do?"

"Anything you want. Whatever feels right. You could say goodbye or sorry or whatever again," Onyx suggested, "but you kinda said all that already. It's invested in the jewelry."

"You're not sending gifts to the afterlife," added Molly. "For all we know it works out like that on the other side, but mostly the silver is just a carrier."

He reached into the bowl, drew out a silver bracelet and looked at it for only a moment before he tossed it into the water below. The lack of ceremony seemed odd to him after all the ritual chanting and procedure, but he trusted the guidance of his friends. If they gave no instructions, he must not need any.

On occasion, he looked at a particular piece and said, "Goodbye." At other times, he did not. He had no conscious thought as to which piece represented what, or why he would need to say anything at all. He simply did what felt right.

Finished, he upended the bowl over the side of the bridge to let the remaining water out into the canal. Alex let out a long sigh and closed his eyes.

"How do you feel?" asked Onyx.

"Better." He considered her question further. "Relieved." He ran his fingers along the bar of the railing.

He'd fought in Vietnam, and against the Saracens. He'd raided against the Danes. He'd had a wife leave him for a wealthier man, and another sell him to slave dealers, and another cheat on him with the village priest. It was all there, but no closer at hand than thoughts of middle school or the bike he'd ridden in fourth grade until it was stolen. He remembered losing Halla, remembered losing Siobhan, but he couldn't be sure of their names. Memories of being cut from the football team during tryouts were much clearer. "It's all in pieces. Is that normal?"

"We don't know if there is a normal with this," Onyx reminded him.

He nodded slowly. "I feel like I'm me again, but... but it's there. I know things happened, I know it kind of shapes things, but I couldn't tell you accurate stories."

"That's probably for the best," Onyx considered. "Let it process. The important thing is you feel like yourself, right?"

"Yeah. Thank you." He turned to face the couple. "What now?"

"Depends," Molly shrugged. "You feel like you're all right in the head now? No shame if you just want to go home and go to bed or see your ladies or whatever."

He didn't answer out loud immediately. It would be difficult, looking back, for any of them to remember whose face cracked with a mischievous grin first, or whose eyes first glinted with a wordless invitation. But they would all remember who broke the tense, eager silence.

"I'm starving," Alex said coolly. "Can I take you both to dinner? Go someplace nice? Anything you want."

Onyx smothered her grin and nodded. "I could eat," she admitted.

Molly's jaw dropped. "Motherfucker."

"What?"

"You're gonna be like that?" she said, exasperated and trying not to laugh. "All this bullshit and now you're gonna play coy with us?"

Though his good mood was obvious on his face, Alex masterfully held his cool composure. He stepped in close to Molly and gently took hold of the lapels of her leather jacket. The redhead said nothing and let it happen, her eyes wide with surprise as her body stirred. The bridge was no longer a cold place.

Alex gently pulled her close and kissed her, softly at first but soon building with lust and desire. Molly's hands remained at her sides, but she could have melted. When her eyes finally opened as their lips parted, Alex gave a little nod.

"I'm worth it," he assured her, and then stepped away.

Onyx let out a half-irritated, half-amused sigh next to her lover. "He really is," she grumbled. She took Molly's arm and tugged the bewildered redhead into motion back to her car.

11

TRUST

Matters of safety and security remained unresolved. The day's activity revealed only partial information, providing her with little that she could act upon decisively. She had planted a few seeds that might or might not germinate and followed up on leads that, while going nowhere, at least eliminated possible complications.

Enemies still stalked the city for those dearest to her. Mystery and mistrust still dogged her from within her small circle of friends.

For all that, Lorelei felt quite satisfied as she relaxed in the large bathtub. Water hot enough to scald a mortal surrounded her, along with bubbles and the soothing scent of her candles. She had lived in homes more opulent than this—palaces, even—but for the moment, the succubus was beyond content.

Desire ran through her—not just her own endless desire, but specific lusts and longing from her mortal lover, now fully embraced. The simplest, most obvious of Lorelei's schemes stood ready to come to fruition. She relished in his lighter, more spontaneous trysts, but those that came through deep and genuine affection were always much better. For all its ease, her sense of anticipation and accomplishment at helping this along left her feeling quite smug indeed.

Light from a dearly familiar source chased away the shadows. Lorelei's eyes opened and turned to the door, which had never opened. As usual, the angel simply stepped right through. The aura of light from her halo and her body remained muted and timid, more likely a result of her mood rather than a result of deliberate consideration. For all the passion of the previous night after their brief argument, Rachel knew not all was settled. So did Lorelei.

"Hey," Rachel said.

Lorelei's quiet, self-satisfied grin remained. "My love," she acknowledged.

"I feel weird. Good weird."

"You've felt this before."

"Yeah, I know, and... and Alex isn't here."

"He is not."

"I mean I figured he wasn't with you, 'cause I can recognize *those* fireworks," Rachel explained.

"Oh? We've fallen into a routine?" murmured Lorelei.

The angel smirked at her. "More like you're the only one who takes it off the charts every time."

"I am not," Lorelei said mildly, her eyes meeting Rachel's with meaning. "I know full well what you two share."

The blonde huffed. "Yeah. Well. Point being, this is... uh..." She shuddered and couldn't keep the grin off her face. The demon in the bathtub felt it, too, though her outward reaction was not so obvious. "Is he with the witches?"

"Yes." Lorelei reached out of the bathtub to briefly slide her hand against a towel hanging nearby before picking up her cell phone. A single push of a button revealed a brief text conversation. "They have helped him lay to rest the turmoil of his past. I know no details as yet, but if one reads between the lines it is clear that his situation is vastly improved.

"He has taken them to dinner," Lorelei continued, looking meaningfully at the angel, "and plans to stay the night with them."

"Hhhhuh."

"This is no spontaneous tryst," warned the succubus, "nor is it a matter of lust alone, though I feel an abundance of that, as well. Two young women, both of whom mean a great deal to him, and both of us connected to his pleasures... and you know his other connections to me."

For once, Rachel was at a loss for words. She stared at her lover.

Lorelei's smug grin remained. "If there were ever a night to hide away from the world and have me all to yourself..."

"They went to dinner?" Rachel asked, her voice shaking.

"They have only just arrived, and likely haven't been seated. If you have affairs to put in order, you have perhaps an hour." She paused thoughtfully. "I could ask him to stall, if you like?"

"Nonono!" Rachel blurted. "An hour's good. Fuck it, I don't even wanna wait an hour, I'll just—shit, I gotta find someone to keep watch, and—"

"May I be of assistance in some way?" offered the succubus, still relaxed and smooth in the face of the angel's obvious excitement.

The thought broke Rachel from her rush of thoughts. "Tell him thanks for the warning shots?"

"I shall convey your love."

"You're the one gettin' all of *that* tonight," Rachel quipped before she dove through the closed door once again.

———

"THE CHALLENGE here is to not eat yourself into a food coma," Alex grinned as the waiter collected their menus and moved off. "I've only been here a couple times, but as far as I can tell everything's awesome."

"I refuse to go home sluggish," said Onyx. "You can take us here again sometime and I'll pig out on lobster. Not tonight."

"You come here with your girlfriends?" asked Molly. "Do they actually eat?"

"They eat when they feel like it. I'm the only one who needs food." He paused, his eyes still on the redhead. "We've been talking about me and my life all day long."

"What's wrong with that?" she asked, sipping her beer with a grin. "We're interested. You're an interesting guy."

"I'm not a narcissist."

"Wow, check out the five-dollar words," chuckled Onyx.

"No, seriously. This is back to the conversation in the shop today. I don't know Onyx nearly as well as I'd like—"

"Got to know her pretty well already from what I gathered," quipped Molly.

"—and I've spent more time with her than I have with you."

Molly swallowed another pull of her beer. "Are we dating?" she asked. "Is that what this is? A date? Are you dating both of us?"

He grinned back at her. "That's for you to decide. Tell me tomorrow."

"This sure is an attitude change after dodging us for a month," said Onyx. "Is this the new you or something?"

"I'm... feeling a lot better. About everything. I don't even know where to begin." He paused. "How different do I seem?"

Onyx fell silent and openly stared. Alex knew she saw things ordinary men and women could not. She shared a look with Molly as if to silently compare her impressions to her partner's. "You're still you. Whatever changed from everything we did today, it didn't turn you into a player." She paused. "We can both still take you at your word."

"I owe you more than I can say for today, but that's not why I'm so interested in you. Both," he added, glancing at Molly.

"Does that take effort?" Molly asked with obvious amusement.

"What?"

"Splitting your attention like that. Two women at once."

"Hey, I'm not gonna pretend I'm a pro at this," Alex shrugged. "It's only been a month, like you said. Rachel and Lorelei are full-on serious about each other, too. It's not an act just to get me turned on."

"Does it?"

"Hell, yeah!" The ladies laughed. He continued. "Ever since Lorelei and I got together and my sex life got crazy, I've felt like there was something wrong about it all. Like I'm doing something awful by letting sex take such a priority between her and I, or for fooling around with other women. I keep wondering if something's just *wrong* about all this. But then I think, 'Says who?' Society? Strangers whose opinions I shouldn't care about anyway?

"Hurting people is bad. Lying is bad. Everyone has to take responsibility for themselves. Past that... nobody has a lock on how people should handle all this. Nobody has *the* right answer. It's all just a matter of opinion. I'm interested in you. It seems mutual. My girlfriends are fine with it. Why should I give a damn what anyone else thinks?"

"You don't have to justify for us," shrugged Molly. "Our Practice holds that sex is morality-neutral. Like you say, it's not how much you hook up or with how many people. It's about the context and the way you go about it."

"Still kinda playing with fire, though," Onyx noted. She glanced at her girlfriend. "We got away with it once. Doesn't mean we won't get burned."

"I have faith," Molly told her. "Like you said... he's still the same guy we scoped out in photography class. Creepy stalker behavior in cemeteries aside."

"Do you always scope people out like this?" Alex asked. "Like with the aura-reading thing?"

"I have to concentrate a little," answered Onyx with a shake of her head.

"It's not hard, but I have to think about it. If I saw everyone's auras all the time, I'd probably go nuts. Or at least stagger around like I'm stoned."

"I have to concentrate more," Molly admitted. "She's better at that than I am."

"But you've been doing this longer, right? You're a couple years older than Onyx. How long have you been working magic?"

"Practicing," the ladies both corrected. Molly grinned more. "You're determined to make this conversation about us, aren't you?"

"Yeah, but I'm not trying to dodge questions. Ask me anything," he said, "but I asked you first."

Molly shot Onyx a curious look, and got only a shrug in response. "I already got a first date out of him."

"You got lunch at Dick's and an afternoon shagging," Molly countered, "and everyone can make their own stupid puns in their heads without sharing out loud."

"Just sayin' he already knows me better than he knows you."

Molly's eyes turned back to Alex. "You realize you're scoring all kinds of points with the way you look at me, right?"

"How am I looking at you?" Alex said. He kept looking at her the same way.

"You *know* you're doing it!" she accused playfully. "You know you've got a look."

"What's it say?"

"It says 'rawr,' mostly," Onyx muttered with a grin.

Alex laughed, looking down at the table for a moment to control his brief blushing, but his eyes—and his look of controlled, intense interest—came back up to Molly once more. "It's still your turn."

"I'm from a big family in Phoenix. They disowned the living hell out of me when I came out of the closet. I thought I was fully lesbian, later figured out I'm bi, but whatever. I realized I wasn't a good Christian on top of all that, so yeah. That was the boot. Friends weren't much help, either. The only family I had who didn't freak out on me was my uncle—"

"Her hot uncle," Onyx chimed in.

"—who lives up here in Seattle," Molly finished as she poked Onyx. "He took me in, helped me finish high school and get on my feet. I was nineteen when I met Onyx. She was almost done with seventeen." She gave a little grin. "And just for the record, *she* made *me* wait."

"I wasn't ready yet," explained Onyx without a shred of guilt.

"Nothin' wrong with that," said Alex. "Still. That couldn't have been easy."

"Fuck no, it wasn't," Molly huffed. "You see how hot she is. Hell, you've seen her naked."

"Mostly," he corrected. Molly's eyebrow went up. Onyx just waited for Alex to finish. "She didn't take off her bra."

"Oh, man," Molly grinned widely, "you're in for a treat."

"He lives with Lorelei," Onyx reminded her. "Like anyone could compete with that. Except maybe an angel, right?"

"It's not a competition," Alex replied. "I don't look at it like that."

"I'm not worried," Onyx told him. "I'm just saying."

He shook his head again. "Hey, I know I'm a letch. I'm a horrible letch. Always. But I don't rate women's looks on a scorecard. It's not like that. I'm either attracted to someone or I'm not. I don't have a minimum acceptable height and weight ratio or any bullshit like that."

His pair of dates shared another heavily loaded look. Both had wry grins that spoke volumes to one another. Onyx twirled the mixing straws in her drink. "So your relationship with Lorelei and Rachel is permanent as can be, right? Not just because of magic, but because that's how you all *want* it?"

"Yes."

"And anything else that takes place outside that relationship is secondary to you and the two of them, right?"

"Yes," he nodded. "Not to short-change anyone, but yes."

"No, honesty is good," Onyx said. "Perspective is good. Do they have veto power in your extracurricular activities?"

His lips pursed. "Yes. They haven't claimed it, but yes."

"Would you put up with whatever boundary-setting bullshit Molly and I had to do in order to keep ourselves happy with each other?"

"Yup," Alex told her.

"Even if our expectations were inconsistent and we kept changing the boundaries?"

He made a face. "What, you don't have a manual ready to go for this?" he laughed. "Yes. I understand. We're all just making this up as we go along, right?"

Onyx fell silent as she stared at him. Alex didn't look away. Molly waited until she couldn't anymore. "Does he mean it?"

"Yup," Onyx said. "He's meant every word he's said since he sat down."

"Huh? What, are you running some sort of lie detector spell on me?"

"Yup. You may not be a player at heart, but you've got all the talent for it, and you have succubus cooties all over you. Girl's gotta be careful."

"And he's not even mad," noted Molly.

"Nope," said Onyx.

Alex waited, saying nothing.

Again, Molly waited until she couldn't. "What do you think?"

"I think we may have a winner," Onyx solemnly declared.

ANGELS NEEDED NEITHER FOOD, nor drink, nor sleep. They lived without material wants. The guardians, in particular, were largely defined by their responsibilities. Most came to love their charges, seeing their work as a pleasure and comfort rather than a duty. Socialization with their own kind happened in a haphazard manner, as friendships developed in conjunction with the relationships of guarded mortals. And while duty never ended, the simple facts of mortal life sometimes allowed a guardian to step away from time to time with no danger to his charges.

Yet it was not until the dominion of Seattle fell under its newest management that any guardian angels could enjoy something as revolutionary as "time off." To Rachel, everyone deserved a day off now and again—even if they'd never felt the need for one before.

"Annalise, Jordan, Christopher, Malik: you guys have Cassandra's work load 'til sunset tomorrow. Split it up. Be good. Brian, Bob, Sara, Dave: you're pickin' up for Boris tonight. Don't give him any shit, either. He's burned out."

"Why do you keep calling me 'Bob?'" asked Robert.

"Because you look like a Bob." Rachel turned from them to the next small clutch of angels standing atop the skyscraper. Others glided by overhead, listening for updates or instructions. The Columbia Tower stood taller than · any other building in the city, and therefore offered a wonderful vantage point for planning.

"Is that it for coverage issues? Anyone else gotta take a coffee break?"

An angel raised his hand. "Uh, do we actually schedule *coffee* breaks, too?"

Rachel opened her mouth to deliver an incredulous answer, then closed it. She shut her eyes tightly and pinched the bridge of her nose.

"Sorry!" someone else yelled. "Stan's new here! We'll take care of him."

"A'right!" Rachel carried on, addressing everyone. "We already have a much cleaner shithole than we had a month ago, but it is *still* kind of a shithole! Remember that I trust your judgment and I encourage you to take the initiative when you see a problem. We will observe the right of free will and we will not overstep our bounds, but that leaves us with a fuck-ton of leeway to do some fuckin' good, you hear me?"

Many cheered. While all remembered Rachel's old reputation, they also understood how much she had accomplished in recent weeks. Many greatly enjoyed her management style. After untold centuries of observing the balance and simply holding ground, it felt good to be proactive once again. Not every angel cared for Rachel's demeanor, but they at least appreciated the chance to act with a free hand. A few others rolled their eyes at her coaching, but they didn't object to her instructions.

"Again, we still have a shitload of out-of-town monsters fuckin' around in this city. Do not feel constrained to any of that 'cycle of nature' bullshit. They are fucking monsters. You see fangs or a trench coat with tentacles or some jackass with two legs and a tail, you are weapons free! Don't give 'em any breaks. No free dinners in my city. *Miracles are authorized.*"

Again, her orders received a scattered cheer. Rachel turned away, but then turned back. "But watch out for the fake fangs! You're in Seattle. Don't go Flame On just 'cause you spotted some aging Capitol Hill Goth boy, okay?"

"Rachel, we got this!" called out another angel. "Go take your night off!"

The words of appreciation surprised her. Rachel's face broke out into a smile.

Angels floated or dove away on broad white wings. Others, having farther to travel, all but vanished in a flash of light. Still others remained; not everyone at the impromptu briefing had a pressing engagement.

A few waited for a private meeting with the boss.

"You appear to have this well in hand," said Lawrence, who stood beside Rachel throughout her brief check-in. "I suspect I will have little to do tonight as your stand-in." The dark-skinned angel favored her with a cool but genuine smile. "It is already a better city than it was just a month ago."

The smile just wouldn't come off Rachel's face. "You'll make me blush," she warned him. "I can't thank you enough for this."

"No, I understand. This is only one of many things that Vincent did poorly, yet no one felt justified in complaining about it. Everyone just dutifully soldiered on. It is only fair that you, too, benefit from policies you set and maintain for everyone. I don't mind filling in again, especially as your plans to take last night off were so badly disrupted." He paused. "I suspect I would regret asking what you'll be—"

"I'm gonna get fucked outta my mind," Rachel answered through gritted teeth as a handful of angels approached.

"...yes, my suspicion was correct," Lawrence sighed.

"You're cool?"

"Chill out," he smiled. "I've got this." With that, he turned and walked away.

That left Rachel with one further meeting. She moved over to speak with the newcomers. Two of them she knew quite well; of the others, she had only met the brunette just last night.

"Jon. Marvin," she nodded to the familiar faces. The pair returned her greeting by way of curt nods. She didn't take it personally; they all got along just fine most of the time, and she knew the source of their irritation. Rachel turned her face to the brunette. "Theresa, could you introduce us?"

"This is Patrick, Elizabeth and Sergio," said Theresa, her demeanor perfectly professional despite the obvious undercurrent of tension. "The others couldn't leave their charges to be here just now."

"I may have to go soon, too," added Sergio. "This is a long way from most of the people I watch over."

"Gotcha," Rachel nodded, perfectly ready to take everyone at their word. "So I gather that Jon and Marvin's boys are being held by some of your people?"

"They have not been harmed," said Patrick, "nor do I see much reason why they would be."

"They're being held in secret and without due process," grunted Jon.

"You're an angel and a lawyer?" asked Elizabeth.

"I know how mortal courts work," Jon replied sourly.

"Not this court," muttered Sergio.

"They slew a vampire at your Halloween party, Rachel," said Marvin.

"They broke the law," Elizabeth shrugged.

Rachel held up her hands. "Woah. People. Peace. We're all good guys here. My mortal buddies are good guys, too. You all know that. You say your guys are the Feds, you say this is a matter of law... are all those Feds working in good faith?"

Furtive glances flashed between the newer angels. "More or less," Theresa answered with a sigh, "though no one is perfect."

"Your '*mortal buddies*' have held their tongues," said Elizabeth. "This does them no favors, but so far has doomed them to nothing, either. Thus far no one has had just cause to intervene on either side of the... dispute."

Rachel's eyes flicked to Jon and Marvin. They both shrugged, clearly annoyed but knowing they had to concede the point. She wanted dearly to ask Elizabeth why she said 'mortal buddies' like that, but decided to set an example. "Nobody's leaving the city, then?"

"No."

"No phone calls home, either," noted Jon. "Drew's family is bound to get worried in a day or two."

"You'll have to cross that bridge when you come to it," said Elizabeth.

Theresa put her hand over Elizabeth's. The other angel withdrew hers quickly, looking to her comrade with sudden annoyance. Theresa ignored it. "Rachel, as you say, no one is leaving your dominion and no one has come to serious harm. This is a trying predicament for Wade and Drew, but it isn't fatal and it isn't born of evil. The same can be said for Jason."

"Is he with Amber right now?" asked Rachel.

"Yes. They are safe. I will look in on them again as soon as we depart."

"It concerns me," Elizabeth spoke up, "that your sorcerous 'predicament' puts you into such close contact with these mortals that you would take this personal involvement in their matters."

At that, Rachel dropped her professionally pleasant expression and stopped trying to fight her scowl. "You wanna check the fuckin' attitude, princess? Some nasty supernatural motherfuckers have come into my city lookin' for mortal scalps, and these three guys are damn sure on their hit list. Friendship or not, *that* makes all this my business. And you don't know how many conversations I have with my other guardians about the mortals they watch over every fuckin' day of the week, so maybe you wanna watch and learn before you judge, okay?"

Her eyes swept the group. Jon and Marvin's frustration remained. Theresa closed her eyes to hold her temper in check. If anything, Sergio seemed to show some sympathy for Rachel's concerns.

Elizabeth just turned her head down and looked away. "As you wish, Dominion."

"Oh, for fuck's sake, we're all on the same side here last I checked," grumbled Rachel. "Look, I don't wanna take up any more of your time. You all got shit to get to. Just stay on your toes and don't be a stranger to the other local angels. We've got good communications going around here finally and we need to make use of them. If it looks like this is going to go supernaturally pear-shaped, I need to know immediately, capeesh?"

"We'll give a yell," nodded Sergio.

Elizabeth couldn't hold it back. "Do you plan to tell your succubus? Or your mortal lover?"

"I plan to stick to my fuckin' duties and keep the fuckin' faith with my fellow angels," Rachel said through gritted teeth. "Hope everyone else does as well. We through?"

"Yes. We're done here," Theresa answered quickly. She turned to Elizabeth and Sergio. "Come on."

Rachel blew a lock of her blonde hair out of her face as the trio left. She turned her eyes to Jon and Marvin. "How bad is it?"

The pair looked at one another with slight discomfort. "It's ugly," Marvin said. "The leader of this investigation doesn't have the soundest judgment. He's not after Wade or Drew, though. He wants the vampires. And the werewolves. Our boys are just a means to that end."

"As far as we can tell, anyway," added Jon. "Our concern is guardianship of our charges, after all. It's not our place to follow the agents around."

"They haven't spoken to either Wade or Drew since last night, either," Marvin nodded. "At the moment, they're both being kept isolated. The most harm they have suffered since last night has been from boredom and worry. They're tough. They've come through okay this far."

Jon snorted. "You'd probably be proud of them, actually."

"Always am," Rachel said. She let out a heavy breath. "Okay. Thank you. Find me and let me know if this goes wrong, okay?" She gave each of them a slap on the arm and then strode off the side of the building.

Marvin and Jon exchanged frowns. "You didn't tell her about Hauser's angel."

"You didn't, either."

"Of course not! I didn't want her to punch me."

"Well, she'll find out sooner or later... just hope I'm there to see it."

"And hope she doesn't punch both of us afterward?"

———

Anticipation built throughout the short drive back to Onyx and Molly's home, muting the friendly banter and laughter shared in the restaurant. Streetlights flashed past as Molly drove. Though she normally kept the stereo on, tonight she opted, without conscious thought, to leave it off.

None of them missed the change of mood.

Sitting in the back of the car, Alex found himself staring at his companions. He could only see so much: arms, shoulders, their necks and hair. He wanted to see more, of course. His body and mind often reacted this way to attractive women... but in the case of these two friends, it went beyond that. There was much more.

He broke the silence: "When do you have to be in class tomorrow?"

"We both start at nine," Onyx answered.

"Yeah, we didn't think about that," grumbled Molly. "You gonna be okay without stuff from home?"

"Sure. I'll just buy a notebook and a pen from the bookstore before class."

Again, they drifted into silence. Alex accepted it, sensing that no one found it uncomfortable. That alone bode well for them.

They arrived. Parked. Exited the car in the ever-present light rain, still in silence. Onyx found Alex's hand with hers and held it as they walked across the small apartment complex. Molly unlocked the door and opened it, looking back over her shoulder with a quiet smile. She discarded her leather jacket as Onyx closed the door and threw all three of the locks.

Alex took his cue from Onyx: like her, he hung his coat up on the rack beside the door.

Despite mutual hopes and desires, none of them knew who would or should make the first move. Every experience had its own mood and context. He didn't feel the least bit awkward, though, and much like the silence in the car he found that promising.

"What do you think?" Molly asked Onyx, still smiling quietly.

"Oh, you know what I think already," Onyx said, blushing a bit in spite of her comfort. "The question is what do you want?"

Molly glanced thoughtfully at Alex, then back at Onyx. "Yeah. I'm there with you. Might not be the wisest thing, but it feels right."

Alex waited. Onyx turned to him and explained. "Two things. First, our bedroom is kind of a disaster, like the rest of this apartment. We didn't expect company. There are dirty clothes and books and disorganized bits of make-up everywhere."

"'I'm shocked,'" Alex deadpanned, "'shocked to discover that gambling is going on in here.'"

"Shit, he just quoted *Casablanca*," Molly blinked.

Onyx couldn't help her grin. "Told you he was cool."

"What's the second thing?"

"Witch stuff. We need a minute. You can watch, if you want. So, uh... that time we got together... I was being careful. I had my defenses up."

He cracked a grin. "Okay, I know this is gonna sound like a total line, but the whole thing with Lorelei means I'm sterile and I can't catch any diseases," he said, scratching his head.

Molly and Onyx both erupted in laughter.

"No, it's true!" Alex laughed back. "Succubae aren't meant to spread misery —at least, not like that. I mean they spread all sorts of hate and drama anyway, but that's about scheming, not..." The ladies kept laughing. He sighed and said, "Look, the point is, whatever you want me to do to be 'safe,' I'll do it. Condom, magic spells, whatever. I don't need it, but I don't expect you to *believe* that."

The laughter abated. "Wait, wait," Molly chuckled, waving her hands. "So all these women you've hooked up with—"

"You realize I can still at least count 'em all on my fingers, right?"

She paused to laugh again. "They do expect you to wrap it up, right?"

"They usually don't even think about it," he admitted, looking at the floor. "It's a succubus cootie thing, I guess." Eventually the laughter from that died off, too. "Again, though," Alex pushed on, "anything you want me to do—"

"Not you," Onyx interrupted, putting a hand on his chest and bringing herself to a measure of calm again. "Us. I mean it's good to know that you've got the birth control and the STD protection covered," she giggled, "but I'm not talking about that. I'm talking about the other stuff with your, um... demon cooties."

"I don't understand."

"We want to be naked with you," she told him, perfectly serious despite her mirth. "Totally naked. Full disclosure, kind of. We want the whole you. And if there is anything different about you because of Lorelei... we want that, too."

His brow knit with concern. "I thought you said that it wasn't really a thing?"

"Oh, I didn't say that," Onyx corrected. "I said it's not mind control. Nobody's going to do anything with you that they wouldn't do with another guy they found really attractive. That doesn't mean I wasn't horny out of my mind just sitting next to you without my defenses up the other night. It might've been even worse for me 'cause I know what I've been missing."

"Still gonna get back at you for that," muttered Molly.

Onyx rolled her eyes before looking at Alex again. "We want to be just as vulnerable as you are, otherwise this isn't fair."

"Y'know, I'm not used to talking things out ahead of time," Alex said.

"Different strokes," Molly shrugged. "The way we see it, you shouldn't do a thing if you can't talk about it."

He nodded. "No, it's not a complaint. Anyway. What do you want me to do?"

"Nothing," Onyx said. "You wanna watch, go ahead. Just give us a minute."

The pair walked into their ritual room—no more than four steps away from the living room. Alex saw them join hands as they moved, which seemed equally casual and solemn. He had never given much thought to personal rituals until he'd fallen in love. He had seen Rachel pray, though, which had the same quality. It was at once second nature and still a conscious choice.

They faced one another in the center of the ritual circle, now holding both hands. Alex watched from the doorway. "Perfect love and perfect trust," said one, and then the other.

The words struck a chord for him. It sounded lovely. He also realized there was probably much more to it than he heard on the surface. It was something for a later conversation.

Molly turned to one shelf, reaching into it without stepping outside the ritual circle. She drew water from a jar with one cupped hand, allowing it to drip through her fingers without concern. Alex noticed her murmuring something quietly in a language that sounded faintly familiar to him. She turned back to Onyx, who stood waiting, and raised her cupped hand to let the water drip from between her fingers onto Onyx's head.

Onyx had her eyes closed until Molly was finished. Then Onyx repeated the ritual for Molly with equal grace.

They looked to one another, and then turned to him. Alex stepped back out of the doorway to allow them to exit, with Onyx coming up first to place her hand on his firm abdomen. Molly slipped around his other side, standing enticingly close. He could feel her nose brush up against the side of his neck as she inhaled deeply.

"Can't actually smell anything different about him," she murmured. The redhead was close enough that Alex felt her t-shirt brush against his forearm—and her breasts pushing gently against his bicep.

Onyx worked her hand under his shirt to touch his skin. "Yeah, I can't tell any difference, either," she said. Alex felt a welcome, almost electric sensation at her touch, but couldn't say it was different from any time she'd touched him before.

They pulled away then, leading him into their bedroom. As they warned him, there were clothes strewn about and other ordinary signs of life. He'd have been intrigued, were the moment not so charged.

Standing at the foot of the bed, they turned back to him one at a time. "So we've talked about this," Molly grinned, surprising Alex with the hint of shyness in her expression, "but you're the only one here who's ever been in a threesome before."

"Not this threesome," he noted, and found himself again surprised—this time by his own confidence. He closed the distance between them again. "Every situation is different."

"Still," Molly nodded. She looked him up and down, searching for words and finding none, and liking it in spite of her verbal frustration.

Alex caught on. "So it's important to pay attention to both of your partners," he said, coming around one side of Onyx, "unless everyone's straight, but I haven't been in that situation before." He brushed back the hair that dangled over her neck and slipped one hand around the front of her waist. "But in a situation like this, I figure a fair way to get started is to sort of... team up on someone." He beckoned to Molly with one finger as his lips fell softly against Onyx's neck.

She inhaled sharply, her eyes widening as Molly stepped up to her with an eager grin. "Hey, wait," she protested without actually objecting one single bit, "Molly is the one who—" Onyx was interrupted by her lover's kiss, which she accepted gratefully. Their mouths and tongues slid together, finding comfort and excitement as always, while they both felt Alex's hands moving between them up and down Onyx's shapely body. When Molly finally let Onyx speak, the younger witch said, "Molly got left out last time."

Undeterred, Molly slid down the shoulder straps of Onyx's dress and smiled at her. "I'm sure everyone will make that up to me tonight."

Onyx felt Alex bring his hands down across the front of her hips. "Ohh... but shouldn't we start with you?"

She felt a grin against her neck. "Nobody needs to take a number," Alex reassured her. "You just move where you feel right. But to be honest," he said, glancing up at Molly with meaning, "you're the one wearing the complicated boots."

"Huh?" Onyx whimpered.

"Point," Molly nodded.

Alex came out from behind her, and together with Molly guided her to sit down at the foot of the bed. Then he and her girlfriend both knelt in front of her and each took up one of her boots and got to work unlacing.

"These things are complicated," added Molly in a loving complaint.

"Seriously," Alex agreed.

Onyx watched, reveling in her growing arousal. "You didn't complain last time I left them on."

Alex stopped. He looked at Molly, who kept unlacing. "She leaves them on?" he asked with obvious interest.

"Sometimes," the redhead grinned. "Not tonight." She tugged one boot off and ran her hand up her girlfriend's leg as Alex finished his work.

"I'm spoiled," said Onyx.

"Wait for it," both of her partners replied.

As soon as everyone was barefoot, Alex knelt on the bed at Onyx's side. She looked up at him as he unlaced the back of her dress, and then to Molly as she, too, came up onto the bed on her knees at her other side.

Overheating despite losing clothes, Onyx turned to grab at Molly's belt. She unbuckled it with practiced hands as Molly swept off her t-shirt, revealing a black satin bra and smooth, inviting skin.

Onyx let out a little gasp as she felt Alex gently sweep one hand over her naked shoulder and across her collarbone to her chest, just above the valley between her breasts. It seemed such a simple thing, just a hand on her skin, and yet it felt so good. She felt his leg and hip against her back as he shifted himself up, strong and steady enough for her to lean against. Her head tilted backward and up, allowing her to watch as Alex locked lips with her girlfriend in a mutually hungry kiss.

She saw Alex slide his hand along Molly's arm and then run his fingers through her short red hair, just the way she liked Onyx to do it. She noticed the way Molly's body moved, and saw her breath quickly grow heavy, and knew her girlfriend would not be the one to break off that kiss. Even while arousing Molly like that, Alex had the presence of mind to slide his fingers between Onyx's breasts, gently stroking her and making her want more. The sights, the sounds and the sensations of it all left Onyx panting.

She dimly remembered something about a two-against-one sort of strategy to this, but he must have just been trying to reassure them. Alex seemed able to occupy both of them at once just fine.

RACHEL MOVED through the glass and drapes of the balcony door without a sound. She discovered a trail of rose petals leading across the apartment toward the bedroom. Scented candles provided soft illumination for their home. Without thinking about it at first, Rachel's eyes glanced to the wine rack, spotted a particular empty slot, and took in a shaky breath.

Lorelei was going all-out tonight.

When it came to mortals, Rachel could see love and devotion as easily as an ordinary man or woman could see shapes or color. She felt every bit as much love from Alex in the throes of raw, dirty, bent-over-the-couch passion as she received from him in their most tender moments. Yet when it came to Lorelei, Rachel was just as dependent on faith and trust as mortals were with one another.

She knew Lorelei loved her. She knew that what they had was real and honest. She knew that she and Lorelei would be together millennia from now.

She also understood that what she "knew" about Lorelei was no more certain than what she "knew" about the Almighty. In the end, it was still faith.

Lorelei didn't have to romance Rachel like this to make the angel feel loved or appreciated... and had to know that. She didn't have to shower Rachel with all this girly stuff that the angel damn well adored despite her normally crass disposition. The effort meant even more because it was so unnecessary.

Any time now, Rachel knew, she would start feeling the shared sensations of their other lover's hot shenanigans. Thinking would be hard. Between that and the attentions of a wicked seductress, Rachel knew she might very well be pleasured out of her mind. Her comment to Lawrence had been no idle boast.

She realized, standing there with a trail of rose petals leading to the bedroom, just how vulnerable she was to Lorelei.

Sharp teeth brushed against her neck. Strong, taloned hands seized her from behind, grabbing her from under the arms and tugging her close. Rachel gasped as she was lifted off her feet.

The teeth at her neck quickly retracted into a deep, sucking kiss. Rachel gave in to it, moaning in appreciation. She felt Lorelei's breasts at her back, their skin separated only by Rachel's thin white dress and whatever Lorelei wore. The succubus smelled amazing as always, and felt as warm as ever. Rachel wanted to just give in, to go limp and surrender... but could not.

"I hope you have no plans to go anywhere tonight," hissed the sinister voice of her lover in her ear. "I have no intentions of letting you leave."

"No. No one will look for me tonight," Rachel answered. Ordinarily she could abandon herself to this. It wasn't as if Lorelei didn't have her heating up already. Yet Rachel's reply was about more than sex play.

Lorelei sensed it. She let Rachel back down to her feet but did not release her. She remained behind the angel. "You are troubled tonight," Lorelei said at Rachel's ear. Her tones still dripped with sensuality and power.

Rachel's breath grew heavy. She nodded, feeling the talons that were once Lorelei's fingernails trace up and down her arms and her sides. She felt the demon's tail slip up and down her leg. It all felt so good. Rachel was far stronger than Lorelei; the succubus could indulge in the full range of rough play, but far more went into these dynamics than who could overpower who.

"Some secret shame, hm?" Lorelei whispered. Again, Rachel nodded. "Look at you. Dominion of a city. Slayer of demons. Yet here you are, longing for pleasures that would shame any other of your kind. Able to pitch me through the wall at your whim," Lorelei said, her talons reaching around to trace down the angel's throat, "but the moment you and I are alone, you're reduced to this."

One hand remained at her throat. The other slipped down her backside, over her ass and then up under the hem of her dress. Lorelei's touch glided up along Rachel's inner thigh until it came to the wet warmth between her legs. "Oh yes," the demon murmured, "I think we know who holds the real power here."

Rachel's turmoil increased. Lorelei could get anything she wanted out of her. She knew that before she came back in here. There was love and trust between them, but also the deep love of what Lorelei could do for her, and to her... and how the demon could read her. Lorelei knew something troubled Rachel, and now here they were, captive and captor. No negotiation. No calm, reasonable conversation. Just this sudden test of trust between them. "Lorelei..."

"Yes, my love?" the demon murmured, straightening up to nibble at her ear. That hand remained between Rachel's legs, toying with her. Rachel's eyes fluttered with pleasure at her touch. "Do you have something to confess?"

Rachel's mouth quivered. She wanted to tell Lorelei everything. Power games aside, this was the love of her life—Lorelei and Alex, and he had as much of a right to know as she did.

Then a wave of pleasure swelled up within them both as their absent partner sank onto a bed with his new playmates. That undercurrent had been there for the last minute or two, Rachel realized, but now she felt a phantom kiss grow deeper and hungrier from miles away. It left her that much weaker in Lorelei's hands.

The succubus behind her let out a sultry note of approval. "Mmm. We've taught him well, haven't we, Rachel?"

More sensations hit her. Lorelei continued to toy with her as Alex's passions grew. He had two lovely women with him, whom he'd longed for since before Rachel had ever laid eyes on him. It felt beautiful and lustful and so very near.

The talons at her throat traced down to her chest, and then to the top of her dress. They began to tear through the fabric with ease. Rachel felt all the more defenseless for it. The remnants of the garment hung at her hips. She felt weaker, and hotter.

"As we were saying," Lorelei said, "you have something to confess?"

"I know something," Rachel whispered, trying to find her voice, "that you want to know."

"Is this something new?"

"It's about—"

Lorelei's hand snapped back up to Rachel's throat, closing around it with shocking speed but without pain. "I asked a yes or no question, love."

Rachel gasped. A finger intruded within her, its touch highlighting Rachel's arousal and Lorelei's expert touch. The talon was gone completely, leaving nothing but soft and pleasing skin. Alex continued to enjoy the embrace of two others, sharing every sensation with Rachel whether she liked it or not—and she did like it, perhaps too much if she were honest with herself. It felt so good to put herself in Lorelei's hands like this, too. "Mostly."

The hand between her legs withdrew only long enough to give her a sharp swat on the ass. Rachel whimpered again. And then the fingers were back at the sensitive flesh of her sex. "Not a yes or no answer, but a fair one, I suppose," the demon mused at Rachel's ear. "Is this the same matter we discussed last night?"

"Yes," Rachel breathed. As she expected, her straight answer was rewarded with greater pleasures. The finger in her sex continued to stroke her, but now Lorelei's thumb gently teased Rachel's clit. It wasn't the first time Lorelei had played this game with one of her lovers in one capacity or another.

"Don't we have that settled?" Lorelei taunted.

Dammit, she would have to ask a question like that. "Do we?"

That wonderful hand at Rachel's center moved away to roughly tear away the last shreds of her ruined dress. The other hand remained at Rachel's neck to hold her in place. Then she felt an even harder swat against her naked ass. She could withstand far more punishment than that, of course, but the pain wasn't what made her yelp. It was the helplessness.

Her body's needs and the vulnerability of her heart left her completely at this demon's mercy. The fact that Lorelei could work her over with such sensuality only made it harder to think clearly. Nor did Alex's shenanigans aid her resolve.

"Tell me this, at least," Lorelei hissed, bringing her fingers back once again to tease Rachel's pussy. "Is this something that could lead Alex or our friends to harm tonight?"

"No," Rachel answered honestly. Then she swallowed. *Hell with it,* she thought, *the spanking feels kinda good, too.* "Not tonight."

Swak!

"Incorrigible," murmured Lorelei, and then she pushed two fingers much deeper into Rachel than before. The angel moaned and bucked against them. "But I suppose I should reward honesty."

"Oh, Lorelei," she moaned. "I'll tell. I'll tell anything."

"You would?"

"Yes," Rachel confessed, her head sagging somewhat as Lorelei's hand released her neck to roam across the angel's naked chest. "I can't... I love you. I'm yours. I feel so bad. About this. Ohhh."

"Rachel," Lorelei murmured, licking her ear while she groped and penetrated her and further pleasures aroused her from miles away, "do you trust me?"

"Yes."

"With everything?"

"Yes. Oh fuck yes."

"You would tell me about Amber? About all of this?"

"Yes," Rachel answered hoarsely. "Amber's—"

The motion that interrupted her was rough, but it silenced her in time. Lorelei withdrew her hand and turned the angel to allow for a kiss. Lorelei invaded Rachel's mouth with her tongue, kissing deeply and scratching Rachel's skin as she drew her close.

By the time Lorelei released her, Rachel had all but forgotten what she was about to say. Then she felt a hand between her legs once again, and a finger on her lips.

"I owe you just as much trust, my love," Lorelei told her. "I know what it is to keep secrets for another. I know your love for our friends. I will trust you, as you trust me."

Rachel's eyes went wide. The fingers within her continued their work, but the words from Lorelei's mouth and a single, directed stroke of one fingertip inside the angel combined to send her off on her first meltdown of the night. Rachel leaned into Lorelei, resting her head on her lover's shoulder as she came, loudly and in complete surrender.

There would be more. She knew this would only be the beginning, given their history and the situation they shared that night. But the conversation made this as much an epiphany as it was a climax.

Lorelei held Rachel close as the blonde settled down from that first peak. "And we should perhaps establish some sort of safe word before long, my love."

Rachel let out a long breath, relaxing in the demon's embrace. "Holy fuck, you sure know how to romance a girl."

———

THEY HAD Molly on her back, stripped to her mismatched underwear and an appreciative, slightly nervous grin. Alex lay propped up on his elbow at her left, gently running his right hand over her body and kissing her neck and her shoulder. Onyx loomed over Molly's right on her hands and knees, similarly reduced to her lingerie.

Alex couldn't get enough of either one. Just as she had a month ago, Onyx dazzled him. Her black lace only enhanced the allure of her natural curves and pale skin and complimented her long, curly black hair. Molly was only a little less shapely, but she was fit and soft to the touch and no less feminine or appealing.

He felt some of Onyx's black curls fall against his face as he continued giving Molly such attention. The other woman claimed a kiss from Molly's mouth, dragging one hand along their male companion's shirtless side but mostly focusing on the redhead.

"Okay, now I feel spoiled," Molly said without a hint of complaint.

"Good. It'll get worse," Onyx smiled.

Molly brought up one hand to put around Onyx, only for her lover to snatch it by the wrist and place it firmly back on the pillow. "None of that yet," Onyx scolded lovingly. The other witch opened her mouth to protest, but instead inhaled sharply as she felt Alex run his hand down her chest and over one breast, gently squeezing it just to see how she'd react.

Seeing a favorable outcome, he gently played a little more, his hand moving from one to the other. Molly began to writhe under both of them as Alex explored and Onyx continued to kiss her. Pinned and helpless, Molly could only run her bare legs against her partners' to reciprocate.

He watched Onyx reach down, still lip-locked with her lover, to the front clasp of Molly's bra. She snapped it open and slid back one cup to expose Molly's firm breast. A brief swirl of her fingers around the nipple gave Alex all the hint he needed. Molly's breath grew heavy as his lips trailed toward it until finally his tongue replaced the other woman's fingertips.

It left his hands unoccupied. There was plenty to touch, of course, but Alex felt the desire to escalate. His right hand trailed down Molly's belly as she received their attention. If her breathing became even heavier when his hand slid over her panties to press lightly against her crotch, he couldn't tell... but the way Molly parted her thighs showed approval. He felt heat against his palm, along with a slight dampness to the fabric.

Releasing Molly from their kiss, Onyx freed her lover to be more vocal in her appreciation. Onyx smiled as she shifted down on the bed to join Alex, her mouth coming to Molly's other breast. She, too, spared a hand to roam over Molly's body, though Onyx also employed the light scratch of her nails.

They took their time with her, allowing Molly to reach out for their heads and necks. She tried for a light touch, not wanting to give the wrong message and disrupt what they were doing for her. "So good," Molly huffed, gratefully accepting the favors of two partners. "God... I'm going crazy."

Her words didn't deter Onyx or Alex. However, Alex felt a slight nudge from his other partner, and when he looked up he saw Onyx with Molly's nipple in her grinning teeth and open eyes looking at him. As close as they were it was hard to track, but the sight of it was delicious. Then he realized what Onyx wanted: he felt her tug down on Molly's panties.

Wordlessly, Alex helped.

Molly cooperated by lifting her hips up off the bed. Alex leaned back, releasing her breast from his mouth so he could pull the panties the rest of the way off. His hands came up toward her center then, exploring her legs by touch while he parted them further.

Crowded together like this, Onyx had little trouble tracking him through touch. His hands occasionally reached out to her fondly, but she knew already how much he wanted her. She was glad to see there was no particular imbalance here... at least, none other than the one she wanted to see addressed.

Molly's eyes fluttered open to see her lover above her. Once again, she almost said something only to be interrupted by a new pleasure from their new partner. This time, it was the soft, gentle downward brush of his tongue against her sex. "Oohh hey," Molly announced involuntarily.

"No?" asked Alex.

The redhead panted. "I just... well..."

Onyx reached down, ran her fingers through his hair, and pushed his head down between Molly's legs. She smiled warmly as Molly let out more moans in response to the tongue and kiss that went to work on her.

"Too much about me," Molly complained unconvincingly.

"No, we're making up for lost time," Onyx said. She went to work pleasing Molly's upper body as Alex focused on Molly's center. Onyx knew how good Alex was with his mouth. She wasn't the least bit surprised by how quickly he had her on the edge of orgasm, particularly given Molly's long warm-up period.

She reached down to Alex again. "Not yet." Obediently, Alex withdrew, despite the consternation in Molly's breath. Onyx looked over her shoulder at him, glanced meaningfully at his boxer briefs, and nodded.

Flush with heat and need, Molly panted, "Why'd you make him stop ohmygod wow," she blinked as Onyx moved out of the way enough for Molly to see.

Onyx shifted back into a kneeling position. Her hands lingered over Molly's arms and her side. She watched as Alex moved in between her lover's legs.

She knew how good this felt. For a month, she had felt guilty over this; regardless of Molly's soothing reassurances, it haunted Onyx. Now it stoked nervous feelings that had only teased her in her fantasies. Irrational thoughts ran through her mind as she looked on: What if Molly liked this too much? What if this forged some intimacy deeper than what Molly and Onyx shared?

She put it out of her head. This had to happen. Change was inevitable. She couldn't live with the questions hanging over her head. She had to know. She also, despite Molly's sentiments to the contrary, couldn't deny to Molly what she'd enjoyed for herself.

Sexual tension and fascination only intensified her emotions. As much as

Onyx worried about the potential consequences, she wanted to watch this happen.

Molly felt him move up against her thigh. Her heart raced as the head of his tool brushed against her wet lips and up over the soft patch of red hair above them. She had tried guys a couple of times; intellectually, she knew she wasn't exclusively into girls. Her previous experiences with men left her unsatisfied, though, and in looking back, she should've known ahead of time. She didn't care for the expectations her male partners carried or the priorities that drove them.

This was different. The way he looked at her and his smile, and the way he talked to her even before his life went nuts had always appealed to her. She felt like she could talk with him about anything... and so she did.

"Why me?" she whispered without even meaning to. It just fell out of her mouth.

He paused. He knelt between her legs, upright and about to go for it when her mouth interrupted. For the first time ever, she even felt embarrassed in front of Onyx—but only for a moment. Alex brought one hand to the side of her head, brushing her cheek with his fingers. "Because you're so strong," he answered.

It could've blown everything. Alex was a sensitive, caring guy; this was just the sort of thing that would put the brakes on his moves. Molly couldn't get the words out, couldn't tell him he'd answered perfectly and that she wanted him more than ever now, or how much it meant not to hear some bullshit about her looks... or just how beautiful he'd made her feel. She wanted to tell him not to stop.

Instead, she felt him between her legs again, and gave up trying to speak. He read it in her eyes, perhaps, or maybe like Molly he was just too horny to stop for anything but a red flag. Any further thought about it was drowned by the wave of pleasure slowly forced into her as they joined.

Onyx watched Alex sink his cock inside her lover. She saw Molly's instant ecstasy and saw the two form a new bond that neither would forget. Her heart pounded in her chest as she knelt beside the pair, watching Alex make his first few soft but strong thrusts into Molly and listening to Molly's moans. With all her magic laid aside for tonight, Onyx couldn't see their auras, but she hardly needed a spell to recognize the gravity of this. The carnal beauty of it had her mesmerized, but in the back of her mind she still heard warnings.

Then she felt them both reach for her. Almost simultaneously, she felt

Molly reach between her legs, just to gently stroke her and convey wordless affection, while Alex rested his hand on her hip. She blinked and looked from one to another. Molly was much less composed, but no less aware. Alex seemed a little swept away, too.

"You're beautiful," he murmured, and pulled her in for a kiss.

She heard Molly sigh with pleasure. He kept thrusting slowly and smoothly while he drew Onyx close and brought her mouth to his. Onyx melted into it, leaning on his strong shoulder and on the feminine thigh between their bodies. She felt Molly's hand roam over her, and though weak and shaken by obvious distractions it was no less reassuring.

Anatomical practicalities aside, no one had forgotten this was a threesome. Onyx was still an equal party. She felt Molly tug at her panties, felt Alex slide his hand down to her other hip and help Molly's efforts along by selfishly stroking her ass. She grinned into his mouth.

Soon there was a hand between her legs. She honestly didn't care whose it was. "Give it to her," Onyx hissed. "Harder."

Alex obeyed. Molly gasped. Onyx pulled back, wanting to settle this matter of her panties and access to her body while Alex settled the scales between herself and her girlfriend. She made room for Alex to lay against Molly and then slipped up beside them, heedless of the bumping of the bed and the loud noises coming from the recipient of Alex's attention.

"Feeling guilty at all?" Onyx grinned beside Molly's ear.

"Unnh... yeah!" Molly confessed with a moan.

"Good," smiled Onyx. "Enjoy that, too."

Molly let out a whimper of gratitude for her girlfriend's understanding, and then gave up a longer series of moans as Alex fucked her. She bucked her hips against his. Molly brought her legs up around his waist, encouraging him to go as hard and deep as he possibly could. She could think of little else.

Committing himself to his partner completely, Alex let his possessive instinct run free. It only ever came to the fore in moments like this. He wasn't the jealous type, nor was he comfortable with territorial attitudes in relationships. But with the moans in his ear and the occasional kiss on his neck or bite on his shoulder, and when he felt the embrace of Molly's thighs on his hips and her hands on his back, and with the silken grip of her sex around his as he thrust again and again, Alex had no worries about respect or propriety.

Their bodies came to an understanding. All else took a back seat.

Molly lost control first. She gasped out her lover's name and his. She dug her fingernails into his sides and pushed up with her hips against every thrust. Alex fucked her straight through orgasm, moving his head aside enough that Onyx could plant yet another reassuring and understanding kiss on Molly's mouth.

Her partner relaxed his rhythm. Alex looked up at Onyx to make sure she didn't feel left out. Onyx just grinned. "How're you doing?" she asked.

"Onyx, your girlfriend is insanely hot," Alex breathed.

"Yeah? I think so. Haven't had enough of her yet, have you?"

"Not really—"

"Ooooh, god, 's mutual," sighed Molly.

"—but we don't want you left out anymore," Alex huffed. He kept moving his hips, still going in and out of Molly. She felt too good to stop.

"Yeah, love," Molly agreed. "You need... ooooohh... some attention, too."

"Sure do," said Onyx. "You just keep doing what you're doing. Something seems unfinished here. I can tell," she winked. "But, now that she's had a little relief..."

Onyx shifted around on her knees once more, this time throwing one leg over Molly's shoulders so she could kneel directly over Molly's face. Onyx put her hands on their other partner's shoulders to help settle in her balance.

Alex heard Molly let out a note of approval. "I'll just be down here, then," Molly giggled, and then Onyx purred with appreciation for the first lick of Molly's tongue against her lips.

The dark-haired witch leaned on Alex's shoulders, smiling up at him as her eyes fluttered. "Hi there."

She had never seemed more beautiful than now. Alex kissed her hungrily, all his self-control falling away once more as two women indulged him in such intimacy and affection.

"Mh. Hey. Wait," Onyx said, shifting back a bit from him. He watched as she tried to steady herself, which didn't really work out until Molly stopped licking. Onyx chuckled, reached behind her back and unfastened her bra. Her eyes met his as she let the lace garment fall away.

"Molly was right," Alex smiled with a shake of his head. "They're beautiful. Like the rest of you."

Onyx rolled her eyes and then leaned back against him, letting Molly resume her naughty work. "Shut up and grope me," Onyx sighed happily.

The need to keep a steady pace for Molly only intensified his need for release. It was a long, sensuous road to orgasm for him, and for Onyx, and on the way to Molly's second. None of them finished together. All three were happy to keep at it until the scales were even.

"I HAVE BETTER sex than any angel ever," the breathless blonde declared to the ceiling. Spread out on her back and utterly ravished, Rachel's body bore everything from hickies to bite marks to slight red trails of blood from Lorelei's talons. Only the bottom sheet of the bed remained; the rest sat on the floor in a torn and slightly wet pile. There were still a few candles lit, but the well-loved angel gave off more than enough of a glow to illuminate the room.

"I could say much the same for myself," murmured Lorelei. She returned to the bed with a pair of champagne flutes, kneeling beside the angel to offer one glass and clinking it in a silent toast before she took a sip of hers.

Rachel sat up only long enough to down her glass in one move. She tossed it over her shoulder lightly enough that it landed on the carpet without breaking it. The succubus put her hand on her chest then, shoving her down onto her back again and straddling her at the hips.

Lorelei towered over her. She kept her glass in one hand and claimed one of Rachel's breasts in the other. The angel just arced her back to meet Lorelei's grip. "Mh. You're amazing," Rachel sighed.

"I had help tonight," admitted Lorelei.

"Help that you trained," the angel grinned.

"I find the role of mentor delicious," Lorelei mused after another sip. "But we shouldn't discount his own natural talent. Or his passion. Or your influence."

"Hah! If it was just me and him, it'd be wham, bam, thank you ma'am every night and... well. Whatever."

The words faded away from her. Lorelei looked down curiously. "What is it?"

"I don't like thinking of it being just me and him," Rachel said. "I wouldn't give him up for anything, but... I could never give you up, either."

"Nor I," agreed the demon. She looked at Rachel with thoughtful affection. "Sometimes I almost forget which of us is older."

"Age and mileage, right? You've been through a lot more than I have." Rachel paused. "You've endured more. Overcome more. I like thinking of you as the older one. The one with more experience. I don't think you're ever gonna know how much I look up to you."

"We all hold one another in a certain degree of awe. All three of us."

"Yeah. Yeah, we do."

Lorelei fell silent for a moment. "You would have told me everything."

"Yes. Still would. Y'know, with the right persuasion."

"You must not. *This* is unconditional," Lorelei said, gesturing to the disheveled bed. "*I* am unconditional. For you, and for him."

"I know. I get that now. I'm just sayin'... I'd put myself in your hands anytime. For as long as we're both still around." She slid her fingers along Lorelei's arm.

"Even if I play rough with you?"

"Oh, especially if you'll play rough with me," grinned Rachel. "You had me goin' with the roses and the candles."

"Tonight has been no less romantic for me," shrugged Lorelei. "There is trust. Intimacy. Pleasure." She tossed her empty flute onto the pile of torn sheets. Lorelei laid down atop Rachel, wrapping her in a warm embrace and intertwining her legs with her lover's.

The soft kiss they shared contrasted sharply with the raging needs of the last few hours. Rachel trembled as Lorelei brushed her fingers through blonde hair. "Can I be underneath you forever?" Rachel asked.

"I've much too deep a submissive streak of my own to be on top forever," smiled Lorelei, "but we could surely alternate every century." She saw a troubling thought pass over Rachel's eyes. "No, Rachel," she said soothingly before her lover spoke. "I will not let him go of old age, either. We will find a way."

"Might have to be naughty about that."

"You've never struck me as the type to adhere well to every rule."

"No. Maybe not." They sank into another kiss, but Rachel could not hold it long. She broke off in a loud moan of surrender. "Oooh, holy fuck they're at it again," she grinned joyfully.

"Did you think this was finished?" smiled Lorelei.

"I thought *they* might be. I knew we were just taking a break. Damn, this is like being in bed with four people all at once."

"In a way, we are."

Rachel breathed heavily and writhed against Lorelei, feeling every bit as good as if their other lover was within her. "You knew this was coming, didn't you?"

"I did. You receive only his pleasures. I gain this, but also feel his desires."

Rachel shuddered. "Who is it now?"

"Onyx. Again. They are making... arrangements."

Rachel's hands slid down Lorelei's back to clutch at her ass. "Luckiest angel ever."

BEAUTIFUL AS ONYX was from the front, Alex found the view from above and behind perfectly appealing. She had a great back, after all, and an even better ass. She pushed it back against his hips, taking his full length inside her and sending his heart pounding again.

The view of Molly pleased him, too. She lay on her back, her head in a pillow and her panting face in an expression of ecstasy as Onyx licked and kissed between her legs. Her eyes fluttered now and again, alternating between total surrender to her lover's intimate kiss and eager delight at the carnal visual of Onyx being taken from behind right in front of her.

By now, they all shared some measure of satisfaction. This new session was less about need and more about opportunistic indulgence. The ladies delighted in their new playmate's stamina and were glad to take full advantage. Given what they could offer, Alex was quite happy to cooperate.

He held back in his thrusts, savoring Onyx and allowing her to concentrate on her task. He watched the rise and fall of Molly's pleasures, smiled as Onyx shifted one hand up to clutch at one lovely breast, and like Molly occasionally closed his eyes and simply enjoyed the beauty between them.

While she knew Onyx was enjoying the hell out of her other partner, Molly had no complaints at all about the favors she received. Familiarity and shameless love coupled to provide a wonderful bout of oral service. Onyx went gently at first, knowing how well-attended Molly's pussy already was tonight, but she also knew when to get serious. Molly let out a grateful, somewhat breathless moan when Onyx pushed her tongue into her, relishing the intimacy as much as the sensations. She whined in the brief moment it took Onyx to replace her mouth with a couple of fingers, but when those digits turned upward and began gently stroking exactly the right spot within her, Molly found herself off to the races again.

Her climax was almost as loud as before, though without quite the same tone. After hours of play and several orgasms drawn from her by both partners,

Molly was close to exhaustion. "Lay there and take it" had been Onyx's instruction, and at this point it was all she could do, anyway. She happily rode out her body's spasms and let Onyx stimulate her all she wanted to extend her bliss.

As she so often did, Onyx followed up her ministrations with soft kisses and caresses all around Molly's center. For a moment, Molly even forgot they had extra company. Then, as the pleasant fog cleared, she sensed the rhythmic movement of her lover back and forth against her legs and hips and remembered why.

Her eyes opened. Onyx remained on her knees and elbows before her, grinning lustily as Alex slowly fucked her behind. Molly had only one problem with that, and it was the "slowly."

"Hey," she sighed, "you can be rougher with her than that now."

She saw the flutter in her lover's eyes as Onyx heard her words, and noticed that the way Onyx rocked back and forth against Alex had already become more pronounced. Molly also saw Alex grin a little. "You sure?" he asked.

"Yeah," Molly grinned back. "Impress us."

"Uunnh," was all Onyx had to say about it. Without Molly to attend, she found less and less reason not to focus on his delicious penetration. Her lover had already taken care of anything else she wanted to communicate, anyway.

His thrusts built in intensity and in tempo, slowly at first but working his partner up to a needful frenzy. Molly watched as the two gave up all pretense of romance or tenderness and just fucked. Her hand eventually snaked down toward her well-pleased sex, unable to resist stimulating herself just a little to go along with the show right on top of her.

Onyx felt like she might lose all control. It scared and thrilled her to be taken like this. He was a good guy, and would never once hurt her, but she liked this so much... "Molly?" she gasped.

Her lover squirmed and scooted downward. Alex hooked his hands around his partner's shoulders to lift her up and make room. It interrupted his rhythm, but Onyx still felt him deep within and felt all the more intimate for letting him control her body like this. When he lowered her down again, she found herself laying against a familiar, welcoming body.

Then that cock picked up the pace again, threatening to consume every bit of her attention. "Molly?"

She felt a light embrace that still allowed her body to move in reaction to her other partner. She felt a kiss against her cheek. "Wrong name, lover," Molly hissed. Onyx whimpered out a protest, but Molly shushed her. "We're both here for you. You can say it."

"Unh," Onyx grunted repeatedly. She felt her body build to a great climax. He didn't let up.

He *never* let up. He wanted her. Adored her. Wanted to trust her with everything and keep her and her secrets safe. Wanted to make her happy. Just like Molly.

"Alex," she shuddered as the first spasms rippled through her. She felt Molly kiss her again in approval. Felt him relentlessly pushing her to greater pleasure. "Oh, god, Alex, yes!"

Her orgasm stretched out long enough to bring him into his. Onyx felt her body release tension and stress, felt relief and pleasure wash over her as Alex kept pounding and Molly kept approving. She felt his release within her and shuddered in delight, knowing Molly experienced the same thing tonight.

She felt loved.

He didn't pull out as they settled down, merely holding himself upright on his knees as Molly soothed her. Onyx felt a couple of tears run down her cheeks, which Molly kissed away as she always did. She looked up over her shoulder and let out a nervous laugh, but knew Alex would only smile and comfort her.

He did.

They lay together with Onyx in the middle and the others close enough to reach over her and touch. There was a good deal of that as they cooled down. Onyx felt Alex up against her leg and grinned. "I'm not sure I can do anymore with that tonight if it gets hard again," she exhaled.

"Yeah, I might be done, too," nodded Molly. "You gonna be okay?"

"It's a curse," he smiled, plainly not regretting anything. "I'll be fine. Just don't tease me unless you're actually up for more. I'm kind of easy and you're both naked and incredible."

"Mm. Should we put on clothes?" asked Onyx, happy to be in the middle. "Please don't."

"Hah! Okay." She let herself just soak in the moment, but eventually opened her eyes up to Molly's.

"Hey," Molly said, "would you mind hopping in the shower?"

Alex blinked. "Oh, wow, do I—?"

"No, no," Onyx interrupted. "We need to talk about you behind your back."

He just laughed. "Okay. I can do that." He hefted himself out of bed, staggered out and closed the door behind him.

The two women stared at one another in the candle-lit room. They kissed with tenderness and passion, and then stared again.

"We're okay," Onyx declared quietly.

"Yeah. We are. Maybe better than ever."

"Thank you for this."

"Hey, I wanted it, too," Molly shrugged. "Remember?"

Onyx grinned. "Glad you aren't disappointed."

Molly's eyes widened and she let out a heavy breath along with a shake of her head. "Hell, no. But listen, Onyx, you've never been with a guy before Alex. I'm sure you already know this, but he's—"

She stopped as she heard a warning knock at the door. Alex came in with a tall glass of water and towels from their closet. "Thought you might want these," he smiled, setting the towels down at the foot of the bed and the handing the water to Onyx. Without another word, he left and closed the door again.

Stunned, Molly turned her attention back to Onyx. "Okay, that dude is *not normal.*"

"That was sweet!" Onyx protested, quietly so Alex wouldn't hear. "I've brought you a towel or water after sex before."

"I know! That's what I'm saying." She helped herself to a gulp of water and then put the glass on their nightstand. "I get why you're so hung up on him, though."

"You like him, too."

"Yeah, I do, but..." Molly let out a sigh as she stared at the ceiling. "So I like him. I'm down with this. I just don't like him as much as you like him, and I don't want that to be an issue."

Onyx shifted on the bed to curl up against Molly's side. "I don't like him as much as I like you."

"Not an issue, love. I know. I just want you to know where I'm at with him and with you and him being a thing."

"We don't have to be," Onyx offered.

Molly shook her head. "You totally do. And I'm not saying I'm not interested, either, because I am. Now more than ever. We're just on different levels. Nothing wrong with that, right?"

Onyx nodded against her. She let her thoughts unfold. "So... we're both interested?" she grinned.

"Yeah," admitted Molly, pretending to be much more chagrined than she actually was. "Yeah, I guess I'm not ready to totally write off all guys after all. But look: we don't need to put a label on this, right? We don't need to arrange for regular visitation rights or anything goofy like that?"

"No labels," Onyx agreed with a shake of her head. "We just stay open to this. Just call it 'serious friends' and go wherever it takes us."

Molly held her grin back, but only for a moment. "You know I'm gonna fuck him a lot, right?" she taunted. "Probably even when you're not around?"

"Oh noes," Onyx sighed.

"Maybe his girlfriend, too, if I get another crack at her."

The other witch patted the redhead's chest. "You mean if she takes another crack at you."

"Semantics." She moved over to face her partner. "And this is gonna make me seriously mushy about you for a good long while."

WHEN ALEX RETURNED to the bedroom door, he listened for conversation, heard nothing and knocked softly. Hearing a murmured "Come in," he opened the door and poked his head inside. Molly and Onyx lay on the bed, still on top of the sheets and still wonderfully naked, wrapped in one another's arms.

"Am I interrupting anything?" he asked, reading some obvious signals in their body language. "If you need more time, I can crash out on the couch...?"

"No," said Onyx. She and Molly released one another, with both shifting back on the bed to make room between them. Onyx beckoned to him with a single finger. "C'mere."

12

CUFFED AND STUFFED

Molly grabbed him by the collar and jerked him close, claiming a kiss before she turned and headed into her next class. Her rough assertiveness didn't bother him one bit. Their lips soon parted, and then she pushed him back again, somewhat more gently than she had drawn him in.

"I expect a flirty text message once in a while," she warned, and then turned to give Onyx a brief and tender hug. A passerby wouldn't have noticed their kiss. Alex saw it, though, brief as it was.

"Go be mushy or whatever," she grinned at her girlfriend, and then turned to walk through the classroom doorway.

"Wow," Alex blinked, still a bit bewildered.

"Yeah, I know," smiled Onyx. "C'mon."

Neither of them actually spoke of who would walk whom to where. They simply started across campus and headed for the music rooms where Onyx was due for class. Onyx held her books close to her chest. All Alex had for the day was a brand new thin notebook and pen from the campus store.

"She's kind of amazing," said Alex.

"Yeah. I know. Believe me, I know."

"I didn't expect, um... that," he smirked, jerking his thumb over his shoulder.

Onyx just shook her head, but he could see the way she beamed with happiness. "Molly's all fire and raw intensity, but she's also the warmer one between her and I. She's a badass chick on the outside and a teddy bear inside. A bear with teeth and claws and bear muscles, but still."

"You're not exactly ice yourself."

"No, but she says I'm all… I dunno, discipline and resolve. Mostly comes out with the magic and with tense situations. She's hard on the outside and soft on the inside. I think I'm kind of the opposite."

"I can see that," he smiled. "Iron fist in a velvet glove." They kept walking, mostly ignoring the other people around them as they moved through the campus of concrete and stubborn greenery.

"I can't thank you enough for everything," he said. "For not letting me go. For all the help with my crazy. And, y'know, last night."

Onyx came to the words she'd been searching for all along. "I'm not looking for a full-on boyfriend. I figure what happens, happens, but I just want you close," she said. "I have since I first met you. I don't want you all to myself or anything like that. Even if I give you shit for fooling around, I don't actually care. You've got your loves and I've got mine and I'm happy for all that. I just… felt like you're important to me."

She squeezed his hand at her side. It was only then that they realized they'd been walking hand in hand. They smiled it off and kept walking.

"Music theory," she grumbled as they arrived in the room. "Such a mistake."

"You're saying I should cross this class off my list?"

"It's the professor," she said, her voice dropping. "She's a pinhead."

She kept talking, but Alex missed a few words as his eyes came to rest on the upright piano against one wall. It was black and unassuming, with no exceptional craftsmanship or decoration to make it unique. There were likely clones of it elsewhere on campus.

Focused on sorting out the materials in her book bag, Onyx didn't notice right away as he moved off. "Thing is, I usually take an extra class or two and drop one if it looks rocky, y'know? But I didn't catch on right away that this lady was such a freak, and…" She looked up. "Alex?"

He sat on the piano bench, looking the keys up and down. Everything was clean and polished. There were a few nicks and scratches here and there, but nothing to complain about. He was used to instruments in much worse outward condition than this…

…except Alex had never played the piano in his life.

"Alex?"

He tapped a couple of keys. It was an ordinary piano, one just like thousands of others, and it sounded clearer and prettier than anything he was used to playing.

He tapped a few more, playing out just a few measures of "Camptown Races."

Onyx stood beside him, watching his hands—mottled and discolored, but healthy and strong—hover over the keyboard.

His foot tentatively slipped up over the pedals. His fingers found new keys without initially pressing them. He tested out a couple more melodies.

And then, without warning, he began to *play*.

It wasn't her kind of music, but any fool could recognize his skill and talent. This was some old piece, with some name Onyx would never remember on a test but would probably impress her theory professor. Over the course of minutes, without talking to her or looking up or even breaking concentration, the music picked up in tempo and complexity, rose and then picked up again. She recognized patterns and wondered if he added personal flourishes.

Smooth and confident movements from his fingers brought out the full sound of the instrument. To Alex, the piano in front of him was a work of wonder. It had an engraved factory logo noting its mass production, but it was still so much better than anything he'd ever played on before.

His eyes widened and his chest rose and fell with excited breath. He chuckled. He played. He *winked* at her.

He made this look easy.

"Alex," she said, no longer afraid of snapping him out of some Zen piano trance after he winked at her, "what... what is this?"

"Haydn," he said, still playing. "Sonata 46. I think. Not completely sure."

Onyx just stared at him. "You're playing a sonata."

"Yeah."

"You didn't tell me you played piano."

His grin widened. "Well, I'm only doing the first movement."

"Fine, be mysterious," Onyx sighed, nudging him. "I can't say I'm surprised. You have a musician's hands."

He stopped cold, staring at the piano. His face turned to her, but his thoughts seemed distant. "What did you say?"

"I said you have a musician's hands," Onyx repeated. "I've always thought so. Why, is that weird?"

He blinked, trying to grab hold of the memory that teased at the edges of his conscious mind. Something about springtime and burning diesel...

He shook his head. Turned back to the piano. Tapped a few more keys. And then his grin returned. "Can you do me a favor?" he asked. Alex pulled his phone out of his jacket. "Can you video a few seconds of this?"

LORELEI STARED up at the ceiling, feeling content and enjoying the loving mouth and affectionate hand roaming her body. The sun had been up for some time now, bringing enough light to the closed blinds to illuminate the bedroom. Lounging on their bed, Lorelei soaked up the lingering afterplay of her lover. Everything about Rachel's body language and touch spoke not only of devotion, but veneration.

"I needed this, Rachel. I needed you," she said, stroking the angel's hair. "Thank you for last night. This morning. Now."

"Totally mutual," Rachel murmured. "I should probably get going, though. Let you get on with whatever you have to do today."

"I've no plans as yet," said Lorelei. "I could enjoy this high indefinitely."

Rachel's physical affection paused. "You know as far as I'm concerned the same rules for Alex apply to you, too, right?" she asked. "I'm not worried about you doing any crazy soul-stealing tricks or abusing people. We all know those days are done. As long as I'm not shut out or neglected, you can do whatever you want. Tramp it up all over town. Have a ball. No reason to hold back on my account."

"Rachel... I have had my own dalliances," Lorelei told her.

"Yeah. I know."

"How did we never speak explicitly on this before?"

Rachel just sank back down against Lorelei's chest. "Didn't need to, obviously. I knew what you were when I jumped into bed with you." As Lorelei's head reclined back onto a pillow, Rachel's teeth dragged against her nipple just enough to draw out a reaction. "If it gets you hot to think of it as cheating on me, though, I totally understand. I'll even demand make-up sex."

"Mmh. I've come to appreciate love and loyalty... but a little treachery now and again would still be delicious." Her fingers ran through the angel's hair. "You are perfect, you know."

"Angel. Can't help it."

"You'll pay for that remark," grinned the succubus, who then jerked again as Rachel's teeth teased her other nipple.

They heard her phone ring. Lorelei reached out to put a pillow over it.

"You sure about that?" Rachel asked.

"He'll forgive us."

"Yeah, but there are still baddies out there."

"A fair point." Lorelei rolled away from the angel, rose sensuously to her hands and knees to taunt her partner more, and then picked up the phone. She looked curiously at the screen and played the video message.

And then her heart began to pound.

"Hey," Rachel said, now laying on her back and staring up at the ceiling. "That's Haydn, isn't it?"

"No." She swallowed hard. "It's Alex."

Her partner rolled up on her knees and moved to look over Lorelei's shoulder. She could feel the renewed heat and arousal in her lover. As soon as the clip ended, Lorelei immediately replayed it. "You know," she breathed in awe, "he worried, when we first came together, that he would bore me before too long."

Rachel looked up at her lover's awed expression. She knew Lorelei's passions and interests. She shared a few, though perhaps not as intensely. Rachel couldn't help but grin. "He's pretty good on that piano."

"*Very* good."

"I mean, he's not like a virtuoso or anything, but that's some skill there."

It was a long moment before Lorelei said anything. Rachel waited. "Lover, I gotta get going."

Lorelei nodded. "I think I may have to meet him on campus."

Rachel's grin widened. "Just make sure I have enough warning to brace myself for that."

"Now I will repeat this, because I can't emphasize it enough: I know he may not look it, but the suspect is exceedingly dangerous. He may be armed. He's fought his way out of captivity before." Hauser looked out at the dozen uniformed officers in the room, searching for any signs of doubt.

Pictures of Alex Carlisle and a map of the college campus covered the presentation screen of the conference room. All the officers were fairly familiar with the campus already; it was, ultimately, only a couple of blocks away from the precinct headquarters. One of the diagrams had positions and numbers listed to make sure all the bases were covered for the arrest.

"We all know our positions. We all know the plan. Are there any questions?" Hauser asked.

A black officer near the back raised his hand. Hauser read his nametag. "Officer Johnson?" he asked.

"Yeah, if this guy is so dangerous, why are we picking him up in the middle of class on a campus? Wouldn't it be safer to pick him up somewhere else? Like his home?"

Hauser nodded. "That's a fair question. Everything in our psych profile and our direct observation shows that he's less likely to put up resistance in public. If he perceives a threat to other people around him, he'll back down. If we try to take him in private, he'll probably resist and someone will get hurt. I know that's a little counterintuitive—"

"So wait," spoke up the fit, young officer beside Johnson with a skeptical frown, "we don't want anyone to get hurt, so we're gonna use a bunch of innocent people as a deterrent?"

"I figure the twelve police uniforms will be the real deterrent, Officer Murray. Any other questions?" Hauser asked. He winced when Johnson and Murray glanced at one another and Murray raised his hand again.

"I'm sorry, I just wanna get this part straight: we're the good guys here, right?"

"Murray, Johnson, outside," sighed Sergeant Barnes. "I'll talk to you in a minute. Everyone else, are we all ready to go?" he asked as the pair of officers headed out of the room. "No? Okay, good. Let's roll on out and wait for the go order from Agent Hauser."

Watching the room clear out, Hauser turned to the lieutenant by his side. "Is there going to be a problem with those two?"

"No," the lieutenant shook his head. "Just a little attitude, and they have a point. But they'll do their jobs. I got 'em transferred up from South Precinct for just this sort of thing. Believe me, if this guy does put up a fight, you want Johnson and Murray there to end it."

It wasn't the answer Hauser wanted to hear, but he decided to roll with it. He hit his cell phone and brought it to his ear. "We still have contact?" he asked.

"Yeah, we spotted him. He walked with the Goth girl to some other classroom not on his schedule, but now he's headed to class. Dancing."

"Dancing?" Hauser blinked.

"Yeah, sort of. I mean not like a full musical routine, or anything, but he's boppin' along all happy-like. Not a care in the world. Looks like swing to me, maybe?"

"...swing dancing?"

"Can't tell if it's East Coast or West Coast. I'm out of practice."

Hauser pinched the bridge of his nose. "Keeley—"

"He's in the classroom now. We're good to go."

"Okay. Let's move out."

———

HE PUT the date on the first page of the notebook. Class names didn't matter; he'd recognize the subjects later just from whatever notes he wrote down. The notebook was only meant to get him through the day, anyway. He'd probably just tear out the pages he used and put them in the pockets of the leather jacket hung on the back of his seat on his way off campus later that day.

"So for the next few weeks, we'll be tackling selected short stories from your anthology," explained Professor Mayfield. She leaned against the table at the front of the classroom, holding up the thick text just in case anyone was confused. "This anthology was put together by some of the greatest minds in literature today."

Alex tried to listen. Instead, his mind wandered as he looked at his pretty professor. Lorelei had taunted him over her, suggesting that he could woo her into a much less academic or professional relationship. He'd had a crush on her, sure; she was intelligent, educated, mature, pretty... all things he admired greatly.

Then she forced the class to read *The Glass Menagerie*. Emotional cruelty like that was unforgivable.

"These stories," she said with almost breathless reverence, "contain a wealth of human emotion and human experience. These are what we mean when we call something *literature*."

"So you'll put together a double-entry journal for each story, like so," she said, holding up an example. "You draw a line down the center of the page, and when you find a particular passage moving or if something strikes a chord within you, quote just a little of it on the left and then write your reaction on the right."

He'd done these before. He wrote "short stories" on his notebook page and drew a short line down the middle. On the left he put, "Quote tale of human misery and helplessness here," and on the right he scrawled, "Write down anger and disgust at assignment here."

"Now, I have some slides to show you examples," continued Mayfield as she moved back around the table for her laptop, "if I can just get the projector to work right again…"

Alex stared at his paper. He had no idea how he'd be able to focus on this sort of work. Creatures of the night hunted him, he'd just started up another wild and unusual relationship, fragments and echoes of past lives were still settling in his head, and as if all that weren't enough, there was still Rachel and Lorelei.

He felt a tap at his shoulder and looked over to his side. Dylan Jorgensen leaned in from the next desk over. "Didn't we do exactly this in Ms. Uribe's class?"

"Yup," nodded Alex.

The burly classmate in the Twelfth Man jersey smirked. "I think I liked maybe *one* of those stupid short stories in that class," he huffed. Alex gave the briefest rise of his eyebrows in acknowledgment, but said nothing. Dylan added, "Think I was baked in her class most days, too."

"Yeah," Alex nodded quietly. He could believe that.

"One time I cut that class to hook up with Jocelyn."

Alex bit his lip. *That* he did *not* believe.

Someone in a suit came into the classroom to speak to Professor Mayfield, distracting her further. He had another man with him, also in a suit, looking calm and collected. Mayfield seemed surprised by whatever they told her. Alex faintly heard the door at the back of the classroom open, but didn't look back. He sensed nothing wrong. Besides, not laughing in Dylan's face required concentration.

"You know she hooked up with, like, eight guys at the end of our senior year, right?" Dylan added.

His first thought was to ask why that mattered. Dylan seemed to think it scandalous. Alex hardly saw anything wrong with it at all, even if it weren't ridiculous. Jocelyn simply didn't operate like that. Then he decided the conversation just wasn't worth having.

He spared Dylan a glance. "I'm kinda over high school, man," he smiled gently.

Before Dylan's frown turned into a retort, he was cut off by a suited man who stepped between their desks. "Alex Carlisle?"

Alex looked up and immediately recognized trouble. Broad shoulders, a near flat-top haircut and a serious look that spoke of readiness for violence all added up to bad news. He realized then that the second suited man stood on the other side of his desk, also right in front of him—and that two uniformed cops loomed over him at either side from behind.

He didn't answer. All four of these men meant business. The suited man on his left kept one hand out of sight, maybe holding pepper spray or maybe something worse.

Strong hands smoothly and firmly took hold of Alex at each shoulder, tugging his arms back in a compliance hold. "Oh, shit!" blurted Dylan. Other students voiced their surprise as well. Alex said nothing.

He couldn't fight this. Not here. Legitimate or not, there was nothing he could do. Resistance could get bystanders hurt if things got crazy. He grimaced as the cops tugged him out of his desk chair. He should have seen this coming.

"Alex Carlisle, you are under arrest for assault, arson, kidnapping and conspiracy," said the blond with the near flat-top.

"Please, folks, just remain calm," said one of the other cops in the room as Alex was guided into a standing position. The uniforms just seemed to multiply with each passing moment. "Everything's fine, we have this under control."

"Spread your legs apart. More."

"Don't do anything stupid."

"People, just settle down, stay seated, everything will be fine."

"We've got him. We've got him. Pat him down."

"Get his notebook. And his jacket. Make sure we have everything."

"You got any more stuff here, dude?"

"No weapons down your pants, right? I'm not gonna get cut on anything?"

Alex stared straight ahead as he was held in place, patted down, cuffed and patted down again. The cops took his wallet, phone, keys and even the twenty-six cents in change from his pocket. Everything went into a plastic baggie held by one of the suited men.

"Okay, make a path, please," bellowed another of the cops. "Make a path!"

Holding his tongue and doing his best to hide his reactions, Alex still couldn't help but look around as he was moved out of the classroom. The last thing he saw on his way out was Dylan Jorgensen and his cell phone.

"Holy shit," Dylan babbled, "I am tweeting the *fuck* out of this."

"You have the right to remain silent," said one of the suited men as soon as they were outside the classroom. Alex meant to listen, but his eyes went out across the normally empty and dreary campus of wet, bare concrete. He saw faces and cell phone cameras in many of the windows. "Anything you say can and will be used against you in a court of law..."

They marched him down the concrete walkway, down the stairs and out to the parking lot. The suited men held his arms while the uniformed cops moved out to the sides. Several police cars sat waiting, along with a couple of other unmarked vehicles. None of the officers taunted him. No one did anything out of the ordinary from what Alex knew of arrests and police behavior—most of it learned from television, of course, as he'd never been arrested. But so far, everyone played it perfectly straight.

He hoped, briefly, that this might be an honest, actual arrest rather than some move by any of the various creatures of the night out to get him.

They brought him to a van. Its side door rolled open. Inside, a man in a sharp, subtly pinstriped suit with a goatee leaned forward toward Alex with an open palm full of salt crystals and a wooden wand in his other hand.

Alex lashed out with a crescent kick that curved up into the man's face. It was a great kick, one that would have made Drew proud. The force of the blow sent its victim tumbling to the floor of the van.

He didn't get any further licks in. The other two suits expertly bent him at the waist and slammed him face-first onto the floor of the van. He felt an elbow dig into the small of his back. Someone's leg wrapped around his, preventing him from kicking. Both of these guys were larger and heavier than Alex, with leverage and the skill to use it.

"We got him!" someone barked over Alex's back. "We've got him. Just watch for crowd control."

"Bridger, you okay?" asked the other.

"Unf. Yeah. Yeah, I'm... I'm okay." Alex heard him shuffle up to his feet again, still having to crouch inside the van. "We're not here to hurt you, Alex," he said. "We're the good guys."

"Doesn't fuckin' show too well," Alex growled. A strong hand held his head down on the floor.

"Carlisle, we do *not* want to hurt you," a voice growled right back in his ear, "but you are wrapped up in all kinds of bad news and we can't take any chances. We are not letting you go and we will not tolerate resistance."

"Yeah, that sounds like good guy talk," retorted Alex. Still, something inside him asked, *What if that's true? How else are they supposed to handle this?*

"Do your thing, Bridger," said the other suit.

Alex heard a language that sounded at once familiar and alien. Between his struggling and the voices of the other men present, he couldn't make out specific words. He felt salt crystals fall across his head, and a moment later he felt a small splash of water on his scalp.

"We need to move."

"I'm done," said Bridger. "Let's get him in and go."

"Help us get him in the van," grunted Hauser. His eyes darted over his shoulder to make sure the local cops wouldn't hear as his voice dropped. "Gag 'im and bag 'im as soon as the door's shut."

"Jesus, you think there's been a shooting?"

"Hope not, with all of us standing here at the windows."

"Yeah, we're being kinda dumb, aren't we?"

"People, can you please return to your seats?" asked the annoyed professor. "I realize some of you are only just out of high school, but you should be past this sort of silliness by now. I'm not here to manage you."

The crowd of students remained glued to the window. Only a few other students, mostly the older ones, stayed at their desks. Molly sat among the latter, happy to take advantage of the distraction. It gave her a chance to close her eyes and prop her chin up on her hands.

Sleepy though she was from the previous night, she couldn't complain for a second. That was a good time. She looked forward to a repeat. In the meantime, the class of mostly kids who saw community college as the thirteenth grade of high school could ooh and aah about cops on campus all they wanted.

"Oh, hey, they've got a guy."

"You know him?"

"No, but shit, they aren't screwing around. That's like six cops there."

"I think I've seen him before."

"Yeah, ohmygod, he's that hot guy with the motorcycle."

"You think he's hot? Seriously?"

"Yeah, you know, it's this thing called sex appeal? That stuff you *don't* get from wearing saggy pants?"

"Hey, shut up, I look swag."

"Mm-hm."

Molly sighed. Stupid clueless teenagers.

Then her eyes snapped open. She burst out of her chair without warning, one hand clamping down on the strap of her book bag. Her desk wobbled in her wake, sending her abandoned notebook tumbling to the floor. The students crowding the open door never knew what hit them as she shoved her way through.

Both her classroom and her quarry were on the second floor of their respective buildings, separated by an empty and lonely courtyard and a lot of inconveniently oriented walkways. She spotted only the backs of a pair of cops as they rounded the corner of the building opposite hers and descended its open staircase, headed for the parking lot.

Molly ran, cursing to herself all the while. Her boots weren't bad for running, but they weren't track shoes, either. With so many people still out watching or looking through windows, she couldn't risk anything remotely flashy in the way of magic. Even if it worked at all, the number of witnesses would greatly weaken such a spell. The only thing she could think of in her rush down the stairs and across the quad was a brief prayer for luck.

Doubtlessly, she knew, there was probably a better spell to cast, and she would think of it ten minutes after it was too late. She ran.

Rounding the corner into the parking lot, she saw a couple of the police cruisers pull away. A van rolled on out into the street just as she got there, just behind a patrol car. Only one police unit remained. Her luck held.

"Kevin!" she shouted. Her thirtysomething uncle and his partner both paused, blinked and looked around. "Kevin! Tyrone! Hold up!"

"Oh, hey," smiled Kevin Murray. His partner's face brightened a bit, too, but only until Molly's expression was easier to read. Both cops waited for her to close within conversational distance. "What's up?" asked Kevin.

"That guy you arrested," Molly huffed, "who was it?"

"Uh," answered Kevin, glancing uneasily at his partner.

Molly shoved him on the arm. "Dammit, Kevin, it's important!"

"Hey! Chill out! We're good," Kevin grumbled. "Why do you want to know?"

"You think you know him?" asked Tyrone.

"Yeah, and I think it's probably some seriously dirty bullshit, so who was it?"

"Guy's name was Carlisle," Kevin finally answered. He saw Molly wince. "That would be exactly what you didn't want to hear, huh?"

"Where are they taking him?" Molly asked. Again, the two cops exchanged glances. "Oh, come on, if he was just arrested like any other asshole you could tell me he'd be at the county lock-up or whatever, right?"

"We could," Kevin frowned, scratching the back of his head, "if he was arrested on state or local orders..."

Molly processed the implication quickly. "Oh, you are fucking kidding me."

HE WOULD FORGIVE HER. Knowing Alex, he likely wouldn't even be irritated. He would express a little frustration at having his mundane commitments interrupted, but any such protests would crumble under her touch. Long and regular indulgences from two lovers had her at the height of her powers.

Piano music from a small, portable speaker dock filled the bathroom. Lorelei exited the shower feeling every bit as aroused and energized as she had been with Rachel just a few hours before. She hummed along, resisting the urge to dance in favor of quickly readying herself to leave, find her lover and mercilessly ravish him.

There would have to be a talk, afterward, about his newly awakened—or re-awakened?—talent and his selection of composers. Lorelei appreciated Haydn, but he had never been a particular favorite. Still, a man who could play like that could play any number of other pieces.

She couldn't stop smiling as she dressed in stockings and garters, knowing he would get an extra little thrill when he felt them under her dress. There was more than just the musical talent on display in that message. There was a glint in his eye, a strong hint of confidence and seduction. He knew this would turn her on.

Now half-dressed, Lorelei reached for the phone to replay the video. She knew she was about to fall in love with him all over again.

The phone rang in her hand. She saw Molly's name on the display. "Hello?"

"Lorelei, I'm at school. Alex just got hauled away by the Feds. They know about the fight after the party."

Her passion and excitement came to a dead halt. Lorelei's eyes flared with anger and understanding.

SHE SAT WAITING on his futon for him to get out of the shower. There was little to keep her company besides worry and guilt. The text message from Hauser five minutes earlier confirmed that she wouldn't be able to put this off any longer.

Jason emerged dressed and ready to go. His good cheer only made her feel worse. "You wanna grab anything to eat on the way?" he asked.

"No. Jason, listen... we have to talk. Sit down?" she requested, gesturing to the futon.

His happy mood immediately diminished. He sat, leaving a little space between them and keeping himself turned toward her. "What's up?"

"I wanted you to know... well, a lot of things. I wanted you to know that I've felt bad about the way I've been with you. I've been jerking you back and forth and it hasn't been fair at all. This is two nights now that I've slept next to you but not *with* you and that's... well, that's kind of how it's been all along, y'know?"

"Amber, I'm not in a rush," he said. "I mean I know how I feel about you, but I don't expect anything—"

"You should, by now," Amber interrupted with a shake of her head. "With the way I've been acting, you totally should have expectations. Not 'cause you bought me dinner and I owe you sex or anything stupid like that, but the way I've acted with you..." She paused. "I've wanted to, Jason. You're an incredible guy. I've wanted to, and I can't."

His voice held steady, but gentle. "This sounds like a break-up talk."

"I wish it were that simple," she sighed. "I haven't been straight with you."

"Please, God, tell me you're not a werewolf," he said.

"I'm not, Jason. I'm not a werewolf or a demon or anything like that." She held the grin off, not wanting to sidetrack the moment with levity. She didn't have the time. "I am older than I told you, though. I'm twenty-four."

His expression held. He obviously knew to expect more from this, but so far he had no reason to flip out. "Okay? So that's an age gap, but it's still a single digit. I know people dealin' with four figures. I know that means a lot between us right now, but in a year or two it'll mean less..." he frowned. "Wait. I've seen your ID."

"Fake."

"Why would you need a fake ID when you're twenty-four?"

"Jason... I've had other relationships I didn't tell you about, too. The last guy was... he was Ivy League and rugby and handsome and everything you'd want on the boyfriend resumé, and you blow him out of the water. You're the smartest, sweetest guy I've ever met. You're brave, you're tough, you're funny, you're not afraid to be who you are... and I honestly think the age difference might not really be that big a deal in the end. You're more mature than any guy I've ever dated, too, when it comes down to it."

"...but you're not interested? Is it the weirdness factor? All the crazy?"

"Not even that," she shook her head. "And that's the worst part. Even with the weirdness factor, I think: 'Y'know? All he did was stick with his friends when they needed him. Who wouldn't want that?' But I can't."

"Why not?" he asked quietly.

Her hand went to the pocket of her jacket to fish out her wallet. "I'm sorry. I'm so sorry."

The badge and the ID card marked "FBI" all but stopped his heart.

"You've been under investigation since before I met you. I have to take you in, Jason," Amber told him. "There are two cops right outside your door. Please don't make this harder than it already is."

Completely stunned, Jason wanted to ask if this was a joke but the question died on his lips. He didn't know where to begin or what he could say.

Amber stood. "I need you to hold out your hands, please."

He closed his eyes, now knowing far too many things he could say but too smart to let any of them fly. "How do I know you're not working for the bad guys?"

"I did everything I could to protect you the other night. That was real. I had no idea that would happen." She waited. He stared at her. "Jason, this goes way beyond just you and me. Getting away from me won't change anything. You'll just be a fugitive."

Holding on tight to his anger, Jason rose and held out his wrists. "This hurts."

"I know," Amber said as she pulled out the cuffs. She put one on his right wrist, then guided his arm around his back before putting on the other one.

"No. You don't."

"Please don't say that." He heard her rustling something out of her jacket. "In fact, right now you might not want to say anything." She paused. "It's Amber. I have Jason cuffed. He's coming peacefully." Then, with the phone back in her pocket, she asked, "Where are your keys? Jacket pocket? We'll lock up on our way out."

"What, no search warrant? Or did you already do that while I was asleep?"

"We've got the warrant," she answered with a mix of patience and guilt, "but the search comes later."

"Great. Front left pants pocket."

She patted him down, taking his phone, wallet and keys from his pockets. Then she gestured for him to walk toward the door. "Like I said," Amber told him, "it's better if you don't say anything for now."

Amber had the door only half-open before the hand clamped around her throat. Her eyes went wide as Lorelei stepped in through the doorway, her face set in a controlled rage, and pushed her back with an iron grip. The other woman's glare was terrifying; her strength doubly so.

Lorelei snatched the gun from Amber's shoulder holster with her free hand. She ejected the clip, pressed the safety and then dropped it to the floor in a few quick and practiced moves. "Jason, are you all right?"

"Lorelei, no! Don't hurt her! She's a—oh, holy shit!" Jason blinked further as he looked outside his door. Slumped to the floor in the hallway were two uniformed police officers, both with their eyes closed and smiles on their faces. "What did you do to the cops?"

"They'll live," Lorelei declared in a grim tone, "provided I am not given cause to end them. Are we alone here? I saw no other police present."

Amber gasped for breath and swung forceful blows at Lorelei's elbow and shoulder, hoping to break her grip. It worked, but Lorelei quickly reasserted control. She snatched up Amber's wrist and bent it backward and around, swiftly bringing the younger woman into a hold that put her on her knees. Amber couldn't believe Lorelei's strength.

"Lorelei, it's just us," Jason answered quickly, "but you can't hurt her! She's not one of the bad guys!"

"That remains to be seen. We must bring the officers in here before someone sees them. Can you do this? No, you are restrained. Come here." She maintained her hold on Amber with one hand, while fishing her key ring out of her jacket pocket with the other.

Despite the urgency of the moment, Jason spared a heartbeat to roll his eyes. Of *course* Lorelei carried around handcuff keys out of habit. He stood near her and turned around. The first of the cuffs came loose in just two seconds; she then gave him the keys to let him take care of the other himself. "Drag the policemen inside, please," she instructed calmly after taking the cuffs from him.

"You're making a huge mistake," grunted Amber.

"That also remains to be seen. Whom do you serve, Amber? Or what else should we call you?" Lorelei immediately went to work putting Amber in her own handcuffs.

"Amber's really my name," she answered. She managed a look over her shoulder to see Jason drag the first of the cops into his apartment. "I'm an agent with the FBI. Jason's under arrest." She glared up at the other woman. "So are you."

"Indeed. Will it shock you if I am not willing to take your legitimacy for granted? How am I to believe you are truly what you say rather than an errand girl for some animated corpse? Or worse?"

"They attacked me, too! I fought to get us all out. Jason saw, Alex saw!"

"It would not be the first time the corpses sacrificed some of their number to create a credible misperception," Lorelei scowled. Though she had Amber cuffed, she maintained her hold on the other woman.

"Lorelei, she's not going anywhere," Jason said as he shut and locked the door. He stepped over the two unconscious cops. "You don't have to hold her like that."

"Did you resist arrest? No? And yet she put you in handcuffs. Were our positions reversed, Amber would not let me go unrestrained. Would you?"

"That's not—that doesn't fix anything," Jason pressed. "Lorelei, I believe her."

"They have arrested Alex," Lorelei told him. "They took him from his classroom at school, in full view of the campus."

"What?" Amber blinked.

"This surprises you?"

"That's... doing it like that is crazy. You people are hunted. Why...?" She fell silent then, remembering not to think out loud in front of suspects.

"Yes. Why, unless someone is supposed to know that Alex was arrested?"

Amber swallowed hard. "It might've been done to get the vampires off his back. They'll know they won't find him at home or with his friends."

"You sound unsure."

"It's because I *am*."

"Are Drew and Wade also under investigation?" Lorelei asked.

"They're—" Amber hesitated. She wasn't sure whether or not it mattered now. She couldn't help but notice, though, that rather than reinforcing her grip to inflict pain, Lorelei merely held her in place and waited. "They're in custody. My team arrested them on the night of the Halloween party."

"What?" burst Jason. He wheeled around to look Amber in the eye. "But I've had text messages back and forth with..." a scowl fell across his face. "Oh, that's just some dirty pool there."

"It's not strictly illegal," Amber muttered, "depending on the circumstances."

"Oh, what, circumstances like ours? Nice."

"I hope for your sake they are unharmed," Lorelei warned.

"They're in Federal custody, not a dungeon," retorted Amber. "We're not your enemy here."

"Yeah, you keep saying that," Jason said. "What'd you arrest them for?"

"I wasn't there," she dodged. "But you're charged with assault, arson and conspiracy," Amber winced, and then glanced over to the two unconscious men on the floor. "And kidnapping police officers now, probably. Jason, this is only going to get worse."

"What is your team's agenda?" demanded Lorelei.

Amber bowed her head. "I can't answer that."

"Why," said Jason, "because it's all bullshit?"

"Jason, I know you're one of the good guys!" Amber snapped. "But you've broken the law. A whole lot of laws. This mess doesn't get cleaned up by you going around breaking even more laws. Either of you."

His eyes came to Lorelei's. She could read the conflict in his heart.

"Jason," Lorelei said, "there is only one woman in this room who has never lied to you or used you as a tool against those you care about most."

He took a deep breath and looked back to Amber. "She's got a point."

13

EXTRAORDINARY MEASURES

"I don't blame you if you're angry. You're obviously in a bad spot. We haven't explained much of anything. We've been a little rough. See, we're dealing with some serious, ugly business, Alex—business you're familiar with— and we don't have the advantages you have. We don't have the allies you've had. So we have to be extremely careful, and yes, a little rough."

Alex sat opposite Hauser at the conference table. Handcuffs secured his wrists to the armrests of his chair. Two other agents, whose names he'd learned were Keeley and Nguyen, stood nearby with their eyes trained on him. Two armed guards lurked on the other side of the closed door, too. His back still hurt from the scuffle at the van. He said nothing.

The room felt old and long unused. It felt musty. Some of the paint sagged. The light fixtures worked, but Alex suspected this room hadn't been used in at least a decade or more. He wondered where they'd taken him.

"So I imagine you'd like that explanation now?" Hauser asked, sitting down in the chair across from Alex. Hearing nothing, Hauser put a small stack of manila files on the table. He opened one in front of Alex and drew from it a series of close-up pictures of various people, each attached to a standardized form. Other than the fact that these were all primarily facial pictures, there was little to unify them. Some were old, some relatively new. Most of the subjects were fairly young. There seemed to be an even spread of men and women.

"Do you recognize any of these people, Alex?"

He looked over the photos. He glanced at the text on the files. It all seemed to be personal information: name, date of birth, physical description. Most were from the west coast. Many were from Seattle or its neighboring towns.

"Am I supposed to have a lawyer for this?"

"We can arrange that, but it'll take time. Until then, Alex, I need to know: have you seen any of these people? Because it would help put a lot of fear and pain to rest if you have."

"Why don't you try explaining all this to me instead?"

Hauser leaned forward in his seat. "Everything I've seen and heard of you says you're a stand-up guy, Alex. Everything says you're one of the good guys. Law-abiding, honest, compassionate, patriotic... up until recently. Then things got weird. Are you still a good guy, Alex?"

"Are you?" Alex asked. "Were you ever?"

"Oh, yes," Hauser nodded. "You weren't kidnapped. You were arrested. We're not thugs. We're the FBI."

"Cops can be bought."

"Yeah, they can," Hauser agreed. "I've seen it. I'm not bought. Alex, if I were a paid tool for the people who are after you, I wouldn't keep the act going this long. Those kinds of people would just strap you down on a table and hurt you until you talked. You already know what that's like."

Alex stared at him, his eyes narrowing. "Explain."

"I'm with a special task force formed under secret national security orders to deal with supernatural crimes," Hauser said. "If that sounds crazy, you should ask yourself how crazy it would be if there *wasn't* such a task force, because you know the kinds of things that are out there in the shadows. You know they get sloppy. You know what modern technology and organization can do.

"We've been around since the nineties. Before that, it was just independent agents and individuals in local law enforcement all feeling like they were alone. Like nobody would believe them or help them with the shit they knew was out there. We answer to proper, designated officials within the Department of Justice. We have real judges that handle all of our trials. Everyone gets his or her day in court. Or night, for most of our suspects."

"Supernaturals," Alex frowned.

"Yes. Vampires. Werewolves. You've fought a few. You've taken on a couple of demons, too, and that's a step up from anything we've dealt with as far as we know. How you tell a demon from your garden-variety monster with delusions of grandeur I really don't know, but I'm hoping you can help us with that."

"What happens to these supernaturals you catch?"

"Like I said, when they commit crimes, they go on trial."

"Supernaturals get trials? Terrorists don't always get trials."

"This task force and the courts we answer to didn't get set up under the same circumstances that brought us the war on terror. That gets played by different rules. We got set up before that, so we have to adhere to constitutional rights and legal code as closely as possible."

The younger man's brow furrowed. "And that never changed?"

"The existence and functions of this task force was never, ah, fully disclosed to the Bush Administration. It kind of ran on its own until 2009."

"You're shitting me."

"Hey, would *you* have told those guys about all this?"

"You don't look like a Democrat to me."

"I'm not," Hauser admitted with an uncomfortable frown, "but it wasn't my call." He waited for the skeptical look to come off Alex's face. It never left, so he continued. "Alex, we're trying to bring down murderers and organized criminals with powers most people think exist only in fiction. They do real harm, though. You know that."

He tapped one of the pictures in front of Alex. "These people are all missing. We have reasons to believe they are all victims of various vampires whom we haven't caught yet. So I'm asking you, have you seen any of these people?"

Alex looked down at the pictures again. He tried to keep his face clear of emotion, but his breath deepened. "What does all this have to do with me?"

"C'mon, Alex, don't play dumb," Hauser said patiently. "You kicked one of my guys in the face today because you knew he was going to cast a spell on you."

"I kicked a guy who came at me with a wooden stick and a handful of some sort of powder," Alex replied. "Lotta different ways to read that."

"So I haven't made it obvious enough that I know what's going on with you?"

"Seems kinda stupid to admit or deny anything without talking to a lawyer."

Hauser reached into another file folder and slid out a detailed, high-quality sketch. "Do you recognize this woman?"

Alex glanced down at the face of Lady Anastacia—twice, though he didn't mean to. He brought his eyes back to Hauser's. "Should I?"

The agent pulled a glossy sheet of paper from a third file folder. This one contained several different pictures of the same man from various angles and ranges. "Have you met this man?"

Alex looked down only once this time. He knew instantly that he shouldn't have even done that much.

"You're no bullshit artist, Alex," Hauser said. "You might know when to keep your mouth shut, but it takes a lot more than that to throw a guy like me off a scent. You've seen Kanatova before, and you've seen him. I can tell by your face.

"This man is Carlos Medina, and he's not a vampire. He's been missing for over a month. He comes from Ciudad Juarez in Mexico, and he's a high-ranking member of a large and nasty cartel of drug traffickers and murderers. They sent him up here and he disappeared along with his wife and two of his thugs. When a guy like that goes missing, all sorts of bad things happen."

The younger man's eyes fell away. He stared at the table, then off to one wall.

"I need to know what happened to Carlos Medina, Alex. People could get hurt. Innocent people. Cops. Federal agents. People with families. I need to know."

It could all be bullshit, Alex thought. *It could all be bullshit and this could all just be a long con to get something out of me.*

A voice he couldn't actually hear said, *You can't take that chance. People could die. Can you live with that?*

"Alex, this is bigger than you. You need to talk to me."

He's right. It's bigger than you.

Alex swallowed hard. "He's dead. You won't find a body."

"Do you know who killed him?" Hauser asked, his voice easing further.

Tell him. Tell him everything. He needs to know. People could die.

"Am I being charged with something?"

"That depends," said Hauser. "Right now, I've got you on kidnapping and assaulting two people with a deadly weapon, assault on a Federal agent and resisting arrest. That's just the stuff I can sew up in court right now. It gets much worse once the prosecutor hashes out all the charges that come from waging some wild-assed secret vigilante war in the middle of an American city. You don't get to blow up houses and bus tunnels and plead self-defense."

"But you'll let me off if I talk, I suppose?" Alex frowned.

"That depends on a lot of things. It depends on how cooperative you are. I already know a lot. I have plenty to go on from here without you, but it makes a big difference if you can corroborate things. But you have to tell me everything. You have to tell me about the vampires and the demons and Lorelei and Rachel. All of it."

Alex looked up at him then, a sense of dread growing inside as he considered Hauser's demands—and where they could have come from. Some random Seattle vampire might have coughed up Alex's name in some moment much like this one, but it seemed unlikely that they would know the angel's name...

"Who talked to you?"

"Your friends rolled over on all this when they got into trouble of their own."

"Right. Pull the other one."

Hauser let out a sigh. "No, I haven't had any luck with that line on them, either," he admitted. The agent took a sip of his coffee and leaned back in his chair. "That's a tight group of pals you have there. To be honest, though, they've all got their own legal problems at this point. Might help them to know they didn't have to keep silent on your account."

Alex stared, his mind racing through conclusions. The pieces quickly fell into place. He winced, feeling an emotional jab that would probably be much worse for someone else. "Damn," he muttered. "Poor Jason."

"Yeah, poor Jason," Hauser nodded with something akin to sympathy.

"You son of a bitch," Alex hissed.

"Alex. I'm telling you. I play rough because I have to, not because I enjoy it. I'm one of the good guys."

He didn't know any better, said the voice in Alex's head. *He doesn't know you or the others. How could he have done anything differently?*

Alex looked down at the table once more, wishing the voice he took for his conscience would shut up and leave him alone. Forgiveness and logic didn't make him feel any better for what his friend would have to endure—if it wasn't upon him already.

"I'm gonna go out on a limb and suggest one last time that we could all dial this back a few steps," Amber spoke up from the back seat of the parked car. She sat with her hands still cuffed behind her. Her voice remained calm as she looked up at the tall trees outside the window. "We're not the bad guys. I know you're not the bad guys. We could all just talk this out if you'd ease off from this."

The woman in the driver's seat was unimpressed. "You might have started by opening a dialogue rather than making arrests."

"I wish I could've. I don't see how."

"No?" Lorelei asked mildly. "After you saw the danger Alex and Jason both faced, you could not have come forward and explained yourself and your agency's concerns?"

"You know it's not that simple."

"The same could be said for our position. I do none of this without regret." Lorelei turned to Jason, who sat in the front seat wearing a naturally troubled expression. "Can you do this?" she asked him with considerably more empathy than she showed Amber. "You have every right to step aside or object. I will think no less of you for it."

"You're still gonna go in and get him anyway, right?" Jason shrugged.

"I would not put you in the middle of it."

He glanced over his shoulder at Amber. It didn't help his glum mood or his worries. "I've come this far. You're not leaving me here to protect me, are you?"

"I would never doubt your courage or your wits," Lorelei shook her head. "I am simply much stealthier on my own. We may need Amber before this is over, and someone must stay with her. But I am worried about you. It would be natural for you to question me, and all of this. It would even be natural for you to still feel torn over Amber. I know what it is to manipulate someone as she has done. I know how lost and conflicted you must be. This is no test of your loyalties. Not on my part."

"Hhff. That's a good line," grumbled Amber.

Lorelei ignored her, focusing her attention on Jason. "You mean that, don't you?" he asked Lorelei.

"I have walked this world for three thousand years, Jason. In all that time, I have made fewer friends than I have fingers to count them upon." Lorelei's hand came to his. "You are one of them. There is no crime I would not commit nor any foe I would not face to keep you safe."

He smiled a little. "Alex is a lucky bastard."

"He has been since he met you, and he knows it. I have been similarly blessed. Fear not," she said, leaning in to kiss his cheek. "You will not be alone for long."

Lorelei stepped out of the car. She stood at the side of the closed door and put on her sunglasses. The car sat to the side of a small park trail surrounded by tall evergreens and bushes. "I rarely look for your kind these days," she said quietly to the otherwise empty trail. "You do not often concern me."

The two angels standing beside the car concealed their surprise. Demons of Lorelei's stature could sometimes see their kind if they exerted enough effort. It was a rare trait, though, and easily forgotten.

"I will say nothing of your presence to them. I would do nothing to harm Jason—and I will be quite satisfied to resolve this without harm to Amber, despite her trespass against me and mine."

She saw nothing but a stern, wary frown from the female angel, who was a stranger to Lorelei. The other had never spoken with her, but Lorelei had seen Daniel before. "I sense you have something else to say...?" he asked.

"Yes. As I said, I mean no harm to Jason or Amber. Should you wish to ensure no one else is harmed in all of this, I suggest you find the angel in dominion over this city and bring her here. Immediately."

In the car, Jason watched Lorelei pause and look around, but thought nothing of it. She knew what she was doing.

"So you realize how bad this is, right?" Amber asked. "I mean not just trying to bust Alex out, but what she did to those cops?"

"They're fine," Jason muttered.

"You call that fine? Whispering sweet nothings into their ears to make 'em forget the whole morning of being knocked catatonic and dragged into a strange apartment is 'fine?' That's still gotta be like felony brainwashing or something. Probably a law that applies there somewhere."

"Better than leaving them tied up at my place," Jason shrugged.

"Is that why she did it to me that night in the pool hall?" Amber asked. Jason blinked, turning to face her. "Yeah. I know about that. The question is, how do you know she's never done it to you?"

He didn't answer right away. "She's my friend."

"Sh'yeah, soon as she tells you so with that *voice* of hers and a flirty touch. How can you ever trust someone who can do something like that? How would you even know any better?"

"How do any of *your* friends trust you not to run their names through your FBI records every other day? Or take their fingerprints? Or keep files on 'em?

Oh, wait, I forgot. You don't have any real friends, right? Wasn't that part of your story? Is that something you made up to get me feeling sympathy for you, or is that one of those little true facts about yourself you slip in like your real first name to minimize the number of lies you have to keep straight in your head?"

Amber sucked in a long breath and bit her lip. "I guess maybe I deserved that. You've got every reason to be mad."

"You know why I'm fuckin' pissed?" Jason fumed. "It's not the undercover bullshit. It's not that you thought I might be up to somethin' greasy. It's the fact that you keep droppin' hints that I shouldn't trust people who've had my back from square one when they could've written me off and ignored me as just another random jackass. Like I should bail on them when they've never once bailed on me."

"That's because I'm used to having to look out for myself rather than waiting for people to abandon me or stab me in the back!" she retorted.

He glared at her, but as he watched her, his face softened. "Yeah," he sighed, "maybe you haven't had a whole lot of real friends after all. Otherwise you wouldn't make a play like that, huh?"

"So ARE you ready to start talking?" asked Hauser.

"I'm not ready to blindly trust you, if that's what you're asking."

"I understand that. But let me ask you something: am I being less straight or less real with you than the demon lady you've moved in with?"

Alex just stared. "You did not seriously just say that."

"I did. Hey, look, I get it. She's gorgeous and rich and I have to imagine she's wild in bed, and she doesn't care how many other women you fool around with, right? Even encourages it, from what I understand? What twenty-year-old guy wouldn't jump right into bed with that?"

"Impersonating my mother isn't going to get you anywhere with me."

"No? I'm sorry, is your mother not a smart lady?" Hauser asked respectfully. "My profile on her says she is. Alex, I don't want to insult your intelligence. You're clearly a guy with a big heart. But have you ever considered that Lorelei's entire approach is tailor-made for a guy like you? I mean, what part of 'fix all your problems and cater to all your fantasies' doesn't sound a *little* too good to be true?"

He has a point, the voice within Alex conceded. *You've known that all along.*

Alex scowled. "We're not exactly having this conversation on equal footing."

"Can't be helped, pal."

"Don't call me pal."

"Alex, I'm trying to help. You're a good guy. That *means* something to you. Decency isn't a punch line for you. Responsibility isn't, either, is it?"

You know that's true.

"What's he doing?" Alex asked, nodding toward Bridger at the end of the table. The other agent remained in a semi-meditative position, his fingers curled in a strange fashion.

"Keeping out unwanted eyes and ears," Bridger answered in a murmur.

"How do I know you're not getting in my head?" frowned Alex.

"Won't hold up in court," shrugged Hauser. "At least as far up as we've been able to appeal it. Can't get the Supreme Court to rule on the constitutionality of using magic to read minds or compel confessions. Anyway. How'd you lose your job, Alex?"

"All this stuff you already know and you have to ask that?"

"I do if I want to hear your side of it. C'mon, we can't throw you in jail for anything there. Not like your old company wants to press charges. So what happened?"

"My boss wanted to jump me. I wasn't into it. She held my job over my head and I said no, so she fired me for sexual harassment."

"Your boss is an attractive woman," noted Hauser. "Your girlfriends don't have a problem with that sort of thing from what I understand. Why did you?"

"I'm not into bondage," Alex scowled, and then tugged meaningfully on the cuffs securing his arms to the chair.

"Yeah, sorry about that, but you have to understand our side of this. Taking down a single vampire is serious business for us. You fight 'em in groups and wake up the next morning with hardly a scratch. Back to the point: why didn't you go along with her?"

"It wasn't right."

"See," Hauser nodded, pointing at Alex with a pencil, "I figured it was that. You could just live on your rich girlfriend's dime and party it up, but you don't, because you want to pull your own weight, right? Maybe keep yourself grounded in reality? So you keep that job, and you keep pushing papers twenty hours a week and you keep going to school... until that gets taken away from you, and you become that much more dependent on your girl-friend. That girlfriend who just magically makes all your problems go away, right?"

He isn't wrong.

"You're the ones telling me magic is real," said Alex. "Hunting werewolves and vampires and shit, right?"

"Sure. I'm asking if you honestly think magical bullshit makes your life better without any price or any consequence. Or does all that sex and all that material comfort seem natural to you?"

It's not.

Alex grimaced. He wished he could stop thinking things like that. He wished it would stop making sense.

"Am I getting through to you, Alex? Do you see what I'm saying? I'll grant that you know her better than I do, but doesn't any of this make you just a little uncomfortable?"

"WE'RE HOME NOW. Onyx is running another dowsing spell on him now that we're sitting with our tools and our circle, but..." Molly's voice cut off on the line for a moment as she listened to her partner. "Yeah, the direction she's pointing lines up with Magnuson Park, but she can't get a solid feel for where. He must be under some sort of concealing magic. I'm sorry. I thought we'd do better here."

"No, you've told me a good deal already," Lorelei assured her. She stood at the edge of a tree line, looking out at several old brick buildings and scattered cars in long-neglected parking lots. The park had once been a naval facility, with many of its buildings leased and repurposed by other groups. Most of the sprawling property served as a public park, but the buildings still stood. The university had several operations across the sprawling property, as did a few community charities and some government research labs. A few other build-ings remained unused—and therefore likely candidates for government opera-tions that required privacy.

"If this area lines up with what you were told," said Lorelei, "then I am likely on the right track. I know now that I am looking for powerful magic. That should narrow my search significantly."

"Well, it's not necessarily powerful," explained Molly. "It's not always a matter of matching power with greater power, or skill. Onyx kicks ass at this sort of thing, but even a competent novice could block out this technique."

Lorelei nodded to herself as she considered the ramifications. It was not lost on her that Molly and Onyx were more forthcoming about their Practice than most sorcerers she had ever encountered. Even those she had thoroughly seduced in the past at least tried to evade giving up much information. These two readily volunteered details. Not for the first time, she considered the weight of genuine friendship.

"That is helpful, thank you," Lorelei said, "but regardless, at least I know now that I am looking for some trace of sorcery. I can usually sense that much. It is far easier than checking every room in the building."

"You sure you've got the right one?"

"This is where the police intended to bring Jason," Lorelei said. "The agents may have had plans to move from here, but it is what I have to go on. I should be on my way now."

"Say the word, we'll be down there to help," Molly offered.

"It may come to that. If you could be nearby in case I have need later, it would help. But if this genuinely involves mortal authorities, I am loath to involve you directly. The complications could quickly spiral out of control and they could last a lifetime."

"We're on our way in a minute," answered Molly. "Give us a call whenever you need. Don't even think twice about it."

Her eyes closed. *Brave girls*, she thought. Just a few months ago, she likely would have seen them as little more than useful and lovely tools. "Thank you." With that, she hung up the cheap, disposable phone, detached its battery and put both pieces back in the pocket of her black leather coat.

She considered how to best handle this as she walked briskly toward the tall glass doors at the entrance. She also considered how her lovers would want her to handle such a task. It was one thing to abandon the cruel habits she had learned over three thousand years. It was another thing entirely to actively concern herself with minimizing harm to others around her when such restrictions brought such inconvenience.

Lorelei cloaked herself in several enchantments, rendering herself easily ignored to all but those she spoke with directly. Cameras would not likely record her approach to the building. She found the door locked. Its electric call box looked long dormant. She rapped her knuckles against the door and waited.

The man who eventually answered it wore a simple janitor's suit, but he immediately struck her as nothing of the sort. He seemed fit and aware, clean cut and somewhat severe. Lorelei promptly noted the slight bulge under his left arm.

"Excuse me," she asked, and then stood slightly within his personal space. His training warned him to step back, but his desire got the better of him. The succubus poured subtle power into her words. "Can you *help me?* You work here, don't you?"

"Ah, yes, I do, miss," blinked the janitor. "What can I do for you?"

Lorelei gave a tight-lipped smile, putting on a skillful blend of professional demeanor and flirtation. "I work for the city as a building inspector," she said. Even the thinnest of cover stories would be enough; her approach was not meant to appeal to the intellect. "Oh, there's no trouble here," she then smiled disarmingly. "I ran an inspection here some time ago, and that's when I misplaced some files. I know, it all sounds a bit dodgy, and I hope you can *overlook* that. *It's nothing to do with you.* I'm just trying to fix a mistake *without anyone catching on.* But it's urgent and finding these files would *help me* so much. I would be *so grateful.*"

She watched his breath deepen and saw his eyes flutter, occasionally flicking down toward her cleavage and up to her gorgeous face again. His desires distracted him from both the obvious holes in her story and the violations he was about to commit. "I'm not... supposed to let anyone in here," he blinked.

"Oh, it'll be a quick in and out," Lorelei assured him. "*No one needs to know.* What's your name?"

"I'm Dean," he said. The little twitch of his eyes that followed told Lorelei he knew better than to share such information.

"Like I said, no one needs to know," she whispered. "I won't tell if you don't."

Dean's common sense and professional responsibilities fought a losing battle with Lorelei's smile and the cut of her coat. He gestured for her to step inside and closed the door behind her. Then he produced a small radio from his belt. "This is Dean," he said. "We're clear. Just someone scouting the building for a rental." Dean winked at Lorelei and hissed, "Let's make this quick."

"You have Drew and Wade?" Alex asked, keeping his emotions in check.

"We do."

"They're here?"

"I'll ask the questions," scowled Hauser.

"I want to see them."

"No way. Not without you showing a lot more cooperation."

"What's your name again?" Alex frowned. "Hauser? You want to show me you're one of the good guys? Let me see my friends. Prove this isn't all bullshit."

"I'm not the one with something to prove, Alex. I'm not the one facing a couple centuries of prison time. You are."

He has a point. Consider his perspective.

No, Alex countered in his head. *Fuck that.* "You haul me outta class and chain me to a chair with this bullshit story about vampires and demons and fairies—"

"Oh, I didn't say anything about fairies," Hauser pounced. "There are fairies? Tell me about fairies."

"Fuck if I know," sneered Alex. "Anyway, you want me to start believing you? Step up with something other than pictures. Put my friends in front of me. Let me talk to them. Prove this isn't all bullshit."

"And that'll get me what, exactly?"

"It'll prove to me that you haven't killed them. It'll prove you haven't hurt them. Because if you have, my silence is gonna be the least of your problems."

Hauser leaned in, his eyes narrowing. "You're making a lot of demands for a guy who has nothing to bargain with."

Bridger's eyes snapped open. "Something is here," he declared in a murmur that could not fully disguise his fright.

"What did you say that was about, Dean?" asked one of the two uniformed men she found at the top of the stairwell. Both wore body armor and carried serious weaponry, but seemed calm and relaxed. "Something about wanting to rent the building?"

They saw only Dean. "Yeah, some department from the college or something," he grumbled. "They still questioning the suspect?"

"Yup. Been in there for a while now."

The woman they did not see standing behind Dean murmured to him, *"Forget me. Be on your way."*

Dean nodded. "Guess maybe I should stay downstairs, then."

She slipped around Dean as he turned back, smoothly liberating his keys from his belt along the way. She was out before the stairwell door closed. Fully under her sway after a few minutes with her, Dean never even noticed.

Lorelei sensed the mystic wards on this floor as soon as she came off the stairs. To her partial relief, she could tell they were not demonic in nature. Despite such fortune, the wards presented their own problem: she had no way to tell if she had fully evaded detection.

Her answer came when both uniformed guards raised their hands to their earpiece receivers. One urgently moved to the staircase.

The succubus gently rested seductive fingers on the neck of the other. *"Relax,"* she whispered into his ear. *"Sleep."*

Instantly, the first guard turned to her. His eyes went wide at the sight of his partner slumping over on his feet as if leaning on an invisible friend before falling to the floor. Suddenly the remaining guard felt himself kissed fully on the mouth.

Stunned and swept away by the instant ecstasy, the guard only blinked once before he, too, heard an undeniable instruction to take a nap.

Lorelei stepped away, knowing she couldn't remain. Dean said there were only a handful of people present, but the uniforms and gear on display attested to their general discipline and vigilance. At any second, she would have company, from upstairs or perhaps down the hallway—

--and then she jumped back from the stairwell door. "Fuck, finally, there you are," Rachel blurted, and then looked down at her feet. "You—! Oh. No. You didn't. Okay," she sighed in relief. "I was afraid you were gonna start whacking people."

The succubus frowned. She turned and walked down the hallway to the left, figuring it was as good as any.

Rachel followed. "Lorelei, talk to me," she urged.

The succubus merely placed one finger over her lips and kept walking.

"Oh, c'mon, talking without being noticed is just a little more effort! Dammit, fine, whatever," Rachel rolled her eyes. "Okay, yes I knew Amber was fucking five-oh, but I couldn't *say* anything. You know that, right?"

Lorelei turned to her with a quizzical expression. "Five-oh?" she signed with her fingers.

"Yes! Five-oh! The heat! You know, undercover cop, pig in a blanket?" the angel made several hand motions to go along with her strange slang. Lorelei just shook her head and continued on. Rachel chased after her. "Lorelei, seriously, I didn't want this clusterfuck to happen. I did everything I could to stop it, which I grant amounted to a paper sack of piss, but I tried. You know my hands are tied over mortal affairs. Believe me, I was all over Amber's guardian angel's ass like a bad case of hemorrhoids." Lorelei paused and made another face of obvious distaste. "It was all I could do!"

The succubus made a broad gesture with her hands and mouthed the words, "Where is he?"

Rachel gave a pained expression. "I can't. If I could, I'd bust him out myself. I'm sorry." She walked with Lorelei. "Are you mad at me? You're wearing your poker face again. I can't tell if it's because you're just focused on the job or because you get all quiet and inscrutable when you're about to murderface some poor fuckers or if you just don't want to talk to me 'cause you're pissed."

Again, Lorelei stopped, this time to hold one finger up over Rachel's lips. The angel fell silent.

Footsteps resounded through the hall behind them. "Jacobsen! Gutierrez! Can you hear me? Hauser, we've got men down. They're alive and I can't tell if they're hurt, but they're unconscious."

The succubus glared. The angel pleaded silently. They both moved on.

ALEX WATCHED Hauser receive reports over his earpiece. "Get everyone moving and sweep the whole floor," ordered Hauser. "Guns out. Take this seriously." He turned his attention back to Bridger again. "Talk to me."

The other agent shook his head. "I can't get a sense of anything other than the fact that there's a presence here."

"Only one?" Hauser demanded.

"Stealthy. I wouldn't even be sure, unless..." he frowned. "It's hard to explain."

"Hauser," spoke up Nguyen, who thus far had been silent, "we still don't have Maddox yet with her suspect."

"Shit," Hauser grimaced. "Call her." He looked to Bridger. "Can you find Maddox with your magic or whatever?"

Bridger let out a frustrated breath and shook himself from his trance. "Yeah," he muttered, flexing his fingers, "yeah, I can try."

Hauser put his finger to his earpiece again. "Dammit, we've got men down." He rose out of his seat.

"Let me talk to her," Alex spoke up.

Hauser stopped. He glared at Alex. "You know what's happening? Who is it? Who is 'her' that you want to talk to? Is it Lorelei? Rachel?"

Chained as he was, Alex gave what little of a shrug he could. "I can think of about five different women it *might* be. One of them isn't my friend at all, and if it's her, she's probably going to kill people unless I can stop her." He paused. "She might kill me, too, so it's not like she's here to do me any favors if it's that one. But I won't know until I find her."

They heard people rush past the door. Someone shouted outside.

"You won't try to get away?" Hauser asked.

"I don't want to live on the run, no," scowled Alex. Hauser moved over toward him, handcuff keys in hand. "But after this, you let me see my friends. Otherwise I ain't doing a damn thing to help with the *next* person that comes looking for me."

Hauser hesitated, but let out a grumbling breath. "Fine."

ABANDONED offices stood as a silent testament to government inefficiency. Lorelei found old yet perfectly useful desks, chairs and even office equipment left behind almost every door. She suspected that the office had been repurposed more than once since the Navy ended operations in the building, but even those later occupants left much behind.

She moved through the hallways swiftly and silently. Rather than invest the time in picking locks—Lorelei had to admit to herself that she was a bit out of practice—she noted the doors she could not open and continued her sweep through the building. Better to get a sense of her surroundings and eliminate the larger spaces first and then narrow down the more complicated tasks. She needed to know how many agents and guards occupied the site, their capabilities and their priorities. She also needed to maintain as much of her stealth as possible.

Uniformed men with body armor and drawn weapons moved in pairs, hoping to locate her. To her relief, her powers of stealth seemed more than adequate for the task. They knew she was here, but could not actually spot her. The demon let patrols pass without disruption.

The occasional guardian angel with said mortals, however, was another matter. "Rachel," demanded one, "what is the meaning of this?"

"Oh, un-wad your fuckin' panties, Jerome," Rachel snapped. "I got this shit. She didn't kill the other dudes, she's not here to hurt anyone else, okay?"

"You mean to chaperone her, then?" the other angel frowned skeptically. His charge, and the mortal partnered with him, continued on down the hall. Jerome stayed behind as they passed the unseen intruders.

"What the—Jerome, *when* have I not been cool with you? Has there been a single moment since I took over where I let this city backslide?"

Lorelei shook her head and moved on. Rachel and Jerome continued to bicker as they trailed behind her. It was a distraction that Lorelei could ignore, but apparently not something that Rachel could simply shut down.

She rounded a corner, heard a door open around the next and pressed herself against the nearest doorway. With at least one sorcerer at work among these mortals, ordinary practices of stealth meant as much as her supernatural abilities. She paused and listened.

"Aw, fucking seriously?" complained a familiar voice down the hall. Lorelei recognized the sound of handcuffs being fastened.

"You aren't getting out of my sight or out of my hands," said another. "You take off running and I will shoot you like any other fleeing felon, got me? Let's go."

Lorelei waited. She watched as Alex came around the corner and toward her, his hands restrained at his back. He was flanked by two uniformed guards and a husky, fit blond man in rolled-up shirtsleeves and a loosened tie. Her love looked irritated, of course, but unharmed.

"So what's your plan?" asked the agent behind Alex.

"Walk out into the open and hope I can talk everyone down," Alex answered. "You got anything better?"

"Hauser," said someone back from the group, "Bridger thinks he's got a bead."

"Go," grunted the blond man. Whomever he spoke to rushed back the way they came.

Lorelei watched. The group passed her by. She fell in behind them. As she suspected, Hauser had his pistol out, but it was pointed straight up rather than into her lover's back. Hauser's other hand stayed firmly clamped in a control hold between Alex's handcuffs.

"Well?" demanded Hauser.

Alex sighed. She knew that tilt of his head; he was rolling his eyes. "Hello?" he called out loudly. The tinge of sarcasm in his voice almost made her grin. "If you're there, it's Alex! I'm here and I'm okay! Please don't break the FBI!"

"That's it?" demanded Hauser. "That's your fucking plan?" The two guards looked this way and that, ready to shoot.

"C'mon out and talk to me," Alex asked, ignoring Hauser. "Please."

Assured that her moment would not get better, Lorelei moved around the group again. She reached out briefly to caress her lover's neck, revealing her presence to him alone. Her eyes remained set on the man holding him.

"Lorelei, don't," Alex said quietly. "Just hold off."

"You see her?" Hauser pressed. Lorelei slipped in behind him, undetected by the two uniformed men at his side.

"No. Chill."

"You think this shit is funny?!"

"Lorelei, we can't fight our way out of this," Alex announced, his eyes cast down to the floor. "I don't want to spend my life hiding from the cops."

Her hands shrank back from Hauser's neck. She slipped back around him to stand in front of Alex. "What would you have me do?" she asked. Her voice dropped so low that only he would likely have heard her even without her enchantments. "I cannot leave you here."

"We have to work with these guys," Alex said. He tried to speak louder than necessary, not wanting to give away the invisible woman's position. Lorelei's hand came up to caress his chest, but he didn't look at her. "They've got the guys, too, but I don't think they want us. They say they want the vampires."

"You are too trusting," Lorelei warned. "Police and courts can be bought and manipulated. *You* can be manipulated. Your altruism makes you vulnerable."

Other guards appeared down the hall and at the corners. "What's happening?" asked Hauser. "Is she talking to you?"

"Well, duh," Alex scowled.

"Tell her to stand down and show herself."

"I can get you out of this, Alex," Lorelei assured him, calm and cool as ever. "Just let me handle it."

He shook his head. "I think these guys are the real deal, Lorelei. This is bigger than you and I. It's... I need to help them. People could get hurt."

"Have you not sacrificed enough for others already? This man cares nothing for you and your little life. Can you not see the ambition in him? He will only use you. He threatens all that we have."

"I have to try," he shrugged. "I'm sorry, but I have to try."

She looked upon him with a gentle, forgiving frown. "I fear you are being played, love."

"Maybe. I don't know. Look, just get out of here. It's okay."

"No," Hauser barked. "Carlisle, you tell her to show herself right now." He holstered his gun, but his tone and expression gave no hint of a relaxed attitude. His other hand remained on Alex's cuffs.

"You know I cannot abandon you," murmured Lorelei. Then she gasped in pain and horror.

Hauser's hand was up again, holding a simple, cheap rosary. To everyone else, the hallway remained as it was. For Lorelei, it erupted in an unbearable white light. The holy symbol dropped her to her knees. "Show yourself!" Hauser demanded.

The light scoured her enchantments from her like a hot wind. Lorelei fought to face it and saw not only her tormentor, but the silhouette of an angel that stepped up from behind to place his hand over Hauser's.

Someone else shouted. It might have been Alex. She couldn't hear over the two voices—one mortal, one angelic—who ordered her again, "Show yourself! Show your true self! Let mortal eyes see you stripped of the favors of Hell!"

Lorelei screamed. She felt her body warp and shrink. One of her legs all but buckled and she felt her back twist. Her eyes no longer tracked as they should—as if one of them had gone lazy.

"No!" someone protested. She could see people struggling—Alex, she realized, and Hauser's two minions trying to restrain him. She couldn't help. She couldn't even stand.

"Heaven will burn away your lies," said the voices in tandem, "and then it will burn away your foul presence from this Ear—"

"Mother*fucker*!" she heard Rachel shout behind her.

Lorelei looked up again. The light and its power faltered, if only for a moment, and then Rachel swept past the fallen demon. She saw the angel beside Hauser look on with fear and a protest that came too late. Before he could utter another syllable, Rachel's fist plowed into his face and sent him flying back down the hallway.

Hauser remained. He seemed oblivious to the actions of the angels. The light from the rosary diminished considerably, but Lorelei remained weak and vulnerable.

She turned her head to one side and saw Alex there, still coming up short in his struggle with the two guards. Their eyes met—or at least one of Lorelei's met his, for her other eye would not focus. She read the shock in his eyes and knew exactly what he saw.

"Get a good look, Alex," Hauser said. "That's who you've been with all this time. No magic, no bullshit. *That's* who she is."

"Hauser, put that thing away!" Alex demanded. The guards had him pinned and barely able to even see her. "She's not hurting anyone!"

"You're right about that," Hauser replied. "Not on my watch."

Alex saw Hauser lower his hand, but he didn't put the rosary back in his pocket. It remained out and at the ready. He turned his attention back to the small, terribly thin woman on the floor beside him. "Lorelei," he said, "look at me."

"Leave me, Alex," she replied, her voice now little more than a croak.

He shuffled closer to her, still on his knees and still restrained by his handcuffs. She felt his presence and shrank further from it. "Lorelei, look at me."

Though the bonds between them should have left Lorelei unable to disobey a direct command, Lorelei felt no such pull. It was not her master's control that turned her head. She merely heard desperation in his voice and responded, despite her urge to hide away.

He saw the crooked lip that covered unsightly teeth. He saw a nose that had been broken and never properly set. Her hair was scraggly and thin enough to reveal bits of her scalp. Her back seemed misshapen. He saw scars from sickness and badly-treated wounds on skin that had been worn by the elements and malnourishment. No trace of her former beauty remained.

He saw eyes that had only ever known rejection and scorn—and the terror of feeling it again.

"Okay, get him up," Hauser grumbled before Alex could speak. "Get them both up. Put that fuck-ugly thing in cuffs and lock her in a room under watch."

"You son of a bitch!" Alex snarled. "What did you do to her?"

"You don't get it," Hauser shook his head. "That's who she really is. She's a monster and a murderer. This is my job. I'm here to save you. Guys, get 'em up."

THE MERE SIGHT of the angel filled Rachel with rage, just as he feared it would. He had hoped to avoid her detection, at least until the most vital part of his mission could be finished. Instead, she caught him in the middle of that task.

Rachel's punch would have pulverized the skull of a mortal man. Though he was intangible to the mortal world, he had no such defense against one of his own kind. She hit him hard enough to lift him off his feet and send him flying back through the far wall.

He landed inside an empty office. He tried to recover quickly, but knew he would be too late. Rachel appeared again through the wall and immediately swung her leg up into his groin. He braced himself just in time to keep from being knocked through the building itself, but that did little to save him from the pain. He let out a low grunt and doubled over, and felt yet another blow as Rachel's strong left hook came into his cheek and knocked him to the floor.

"I told you to fuck off and *stay* away when you were *fired*, Donald! Do you remember that? You remember sulking away in shame after being fired for cowardice? Do you think my being promoted means you get some kinda fucking parole?"

The angel at her feet groaned out a couple of incomprehensible words. Still seething with anger, Rachel reached down to hoist him to his feet and then wrapped her left arm around his neck. Dragging him along with her, she poked her head through the wall. She saw Hauser's men haul Alex and Lorelei away. Lorelei looked hurt—but she would survive.

Rachel also saw Hauser put the rosary back into his inner coat pocket.

"Son of a bitch," Rachel hissed. She shoved Donald back into the empty office. "You better talk fucking fast, asshole! Where do you get off empowering a mortal like that?"

Donald rallied, standing up straight and stepping up to her. "You dare strike a fellow ang—"

She slapped him hard enough to turn his head to the side. "Ask me that again, shithead!"

"You have no right to strike me!"

"The fuck I don't! This is my city you're fucking around in, and you know damn well that you are not welcome here."

"My charge led me here," he protested.

"Alex isn't your charge anymore, asshole. Remember? I just asked you if you remembered that. You lost that job because you fucked it all up."

"Not Alex. Hauser. He fights against servants of the Pit and their spawn. *He* still walks under the protection of Heaven. It is my duty and my right to aid him."

"By empowering him with divine wrath?" Rachel burst. Her eyes narrowed as the implications caught up to her. "You set all this up."

Donald raised his hands as if to call a halt to her accusations. "Hauser and his people learned of the demise of this city's vampires all on their own. Jason's computer picture gave them the connection they needed."

"Jason's what?" Rachel blinked. "You're telling me they found a picture on the fucking Internet and that brought 'em here? One fucking picture? How'd they even *find* that, Donald? They just happened to be looking at random pages? Do you even know how the Internet works?"

"Well, I... it matters not!" scowled Donald.

"I told you to leave Alex alone," she said. "Have you been talking to him? You have, haven't you?"

"Alex is no longer under the protection of Heaven! I will speak to him if I must in pursuit of my duties."

"He's under *my* protection, jackass. He's not your pawn anymore."

"He was never a pawn," Donald sneered indignantly. "How dare you. I made him a hero, time and again, until he began to resent me. I never should have let that filthy Roma witch touch him."

"You abandoned Alex!" Rachel gasped, taken aback by the gall on display. "You abandoned him and you abandoned me!"

"Who do you think unlocked the door to that chapel?" he protested.

"Yeah, and then you ran like a bitch! You left him there on his own when you should have helped him."

"Alex showed me none of the fire and prowess of his earlier lives. How was I to know how that fight would have turned out?"

"So you just pissed yourself and bailed. I know this story."

"What would you have had me do? Expose myself? Like you did?"

"I'd have had you do your fucking job, asswipe! I had no control over being in that chapel! You know that! Those assholes had magic that worked on angels!"

"And I had no right to expose yet another angel to it!" replied Donald, jerking his thumb at his chest.

"Oh, you seriously expect me to believe that's why you ran away? Have you even convinced yourself?"

"It all seems to have worked out for you quite well regardless," Donald huffed. "You and Alex both walked out of there and right into a bed with that demon whore."

Rachel's fists clenched hard enough for her knuckles to crack. Donald blinked and took a step away. "Hauser," she seethed. "You're here as Hauser's guardian, and he's after vampires... but you know damn well he doesn't need you empowering him with a rosary just to take on vampires..."

Donald swallowed hard. "I have my duty!"

"Yeah. Duty." She stepped forward. "What did you call her again?"

Donald stared into her eyes. He then blinked, took a deep breath, and fled through the window.

"How long do we sit waiting in the car?"

"You realize that telling you anything now is kind of a problem for me, right?"

The question would have drawn a frown out of Amber, were one not already entrenched on her face. "Does it mean anything if I tell you this sucks for me, too?"

"What, sitting in a car in your own handcuffs? Yeah, I bet it does."

"That, too," Amber muttered. "I meant what I said before. I feel awful about this. And about hurting you."

Jason looked back over his shoulder at her. "Believing anything you say now kinda has the same problem as answering any of your questions," he said.

"Yeah. Yeah, I guess it does," she sighed. "It's true, though. For what it's worth. And I'm not mad at you for this. It's just that I didn't want to see you both make so much more trouble for yourself. Especially you."

"Especially me? What, did Lorelei do something to you to make you feel less bad for her, too?"

"Lorelei isn't the one who made me feel special," ventured Amber.

Jason felt that one. "*Wow*," he winced. "Yeah, you're not making me feel any better with this. Kinda makin' it all worse, actually. And—" he turned back to look at her again. "You kissed me."

"Yes," Amber nodded.

"Like, a *lot*."

"Yeah. I liked it." Her eyes flicked up at his, then down again. "Sorry."

"How's that—how's that even *legal*? I mean how are you supposed to build a case on that?"

Amber's frown returned. She was genuinely tempted to tell him how likely she was to lose her job over it. Training and dedication held on. "How's anyone build a legal case about a demon and her boyfriend fighting vampires? You'd be surprised what my group can get away with."

Jason sat back in his seat, facing forward and feeling glum. He glanced through the trees and saw three people in business attire, one woman and two men, all approaching with guns drawn.

"Oh, you gotta be kidding me," Jason grumbled, but put his hands up on the roof of the car as instructed.

14

UGLY

They left her alone in the room, chained to a chair and flanked by cameras and lights. One set of her chains was made of cold iron. Another seemed to be inlaid with silver. The sole decoration of the room was a crucifix set in the wall beside the door. She considered, absently, that the mortals employed every plausible myth and superstition that did not explicitly cross the boundary between Judeo-Christian faith and sorcery.

Lorelei would have preferred the latter. Sorcerers could present significant challenges, but it was a rare practitioner indeed whose power and guile matched hers at every level. It had been a long time since Lorelei had crossed a vessel of faith that could genuinely harm her, though—and never had she faced one like this. Had she not been at full strength, the encounter might have ended her.

Moments after Hauser and the rosary in his pocket left the room, Lorelei felt the chains constrict. Her normal visage steadily reasserted itself. Lorelei slowly grew back into her usual statuesque figure and height. For a brief instant, Lorelei felt a wave of relief. The effects of Hauser's rosary were only temporary, or perhaps contingent on his presence. He cut her powers and muted her enchantments, but he did not completely unravel her. She was weakened, but that would pass.

That understanding did not erase her feelings of humiliation.

.   .   .

HALF THE CITY turned out in the market that hot summer's day. Anyone free to leave their homes or their duties came from villages far and near. Only so many men came to participate in the auction, and few of them had the wherewithal to bid upon the greatest prize. Some came knowing they would be outbid, but wished to make a valiant go of it. Some knew that they would profit from the overreaching of their competitors. But most came simply to watch, and to dream.

The beauty, Amata, was finally of age to marry.

"I do not know how my voice will hold out today," said the crier, an older man in a robe with a graying beard and a kindly face, "but I will do my best. My son will take over for me if I cannot last the day." His eyes swept the group of young women, all of them freshly bathed and primped as best they could be. Amata was not the only lovely girl, but her flawless skin and her shapely figure stood out even among the other pretty girls waiting near her. Some were excited. Many could not hide their trepidation. A few could barely hold back tears.

"Remember to smile," the crier told them all. He turned to the gaggle of prettier girls, all off to one side from the rest. "Wealthy men have come today. Very wealthy men. Shine." The crier held out his arm, gesturing for the girls to walk out into the open space cleared for the auction. Amata led the group out, plainly being the prettiest of the bunch.

The crier's smile remained as the passing girls—one by one, two dozen this year— became less and less comely. Then came one with her large nose. One with her ugly scar and her limp. He smiled at them all.

And then came the last, shuffling, older than the rest. Her head hung low.

The crier took her thin hand and smiled encouragingly. "This time, Beletsunu," he told the small girl. Her lazy eye refused to look at him, but the good one met his gaze. The other girls had helped with her black hair, sweeping it back and around to cleverly help it look thicker on her scalp. They used powder to smooth out the pox scars on her cheeks. Nothing could be done for the crook in her nose, or the crook in her posture, or the shape of her jaw. She knew better than to part her lips when she smiled.

"You are kind, sir," she told him, and meant it.

"No, Beletsunu. I am not kind. I am certain." He squeezed her hand again. The other girls could put all the powder and flowers on her they wanted, but he knew that nothing could do more to help an ugly girl shine than hope.

There was reason for it this year. He would begin with the prettiest, taking competing bids for the beauty, Amata from men who had longed for her—and what a struggle that would be! Yet the losers would also surely pay well, once Amata found a husband, to take home a bride who might not be as beautiful but would still be lovely enough to assuage their loss.

As tradition held, the prices won by the pretty girls would then be offered as dowries for those who were not so pretty. Hope could help an ugly girl shine; a handsome dowry could help her even more. The crier had more pretty girls this year than not, and among them was the beauty, Amata.

In all his years, the crier had never been left with a girl unable to fetch a husband until Beletsunu. She had remained standing, three years in a row, while the crowd dissipated and mocking jokes echoed through the marketplace at the end of the auction. But not this year.

He had reason to hope. So did Beletsunu.

"Do not speak," said Milkilu as they entered her new home. He was a wealthy man. Tall. Fit. Handsome. It was the second time he had given her such instructions.

The crowd in the marketplace had not scattered once Beletsunu stood alone and unclaimed. They remained, out of curiosity and mirth, to see how great a dowry the crier would have to offer so that Beletsunu could finally find a husband.

No one expected Milkilu to step forward, though as the dowry grew quite high few could blame him. He'd barely lost out in the bid for Amata's hand in what became a close and bitter contest. No one expected the kind smile on his face as he spoke out, though, or the way he effortlessly took Beletsunu's hand and kissed it, right there in front of everyone. Beletsunu expected it least of all.

He offered his surety to follow through with the marriage. He spoke with her parents. Made arrangements. Gave her hope.

And then, leading her from the ceremony to their home, with its opulent gate and its spacious gardens and its servants, he said only three words: "Do not speak."

She shuffled behind him, trying to keep up with his long strides. She naturally wanted to ask if she had done something wrong or offended him somehow, but did not want to disobey her husband on her first night as a wife.

The home was spacious. Opulent. Most families had only one room to their home; Milkilu had many. She passed a sitting room, and a kitchen, and a storage room with a pallet where one of the servants could sleep. Beletsunu followed her husband, awaiting instructions and hoping for a chance to make amends for whatever transgression she might have made.

She saw their bedroom then, with its lush cushions and soft blankets and comforts she had never known.

She saw the naked, painted whore who waited in the center of the bed.

"Wait here," grunted Milkilu. He pointed to a space just outside the door and then walked inside. She saw him shed his tunic and leave it pooled at the entrance, and could not bring herself to watch as she heard the sounds from within.

Beletsunu stared at the corner. She stood close to it, close enough that she could see little to either side, because it meant that no one could see her ugly face. She had done so since childhood, and did so now, and then as now tried to control her tears. She put her hands over her ears to block out the grunts and moans and wet noises from her husband's bedroom.

"Beletsunu!" she heard him call harshly. "Come!"

She wiped her eyes and shuffled in, trembling, knowing not what she could do but obey. She looked up at her naked, handsome husband, who stood by the bed glistening with sweat and with his manhood coaxed to readiness by the nameless woman's touch.

"Ugh," he groaned, looking away. "No. I cannot do this. Not even if I close my eyes and have a real woman to help me. If you are asked, we laid together on our wedding night and you took ill." He shook his head, and then pointed out of the bedroom again. "There is a pallet in the storage room. That is where you will sleep. Try not to make noise. My servants will show you your chores in the morning. Go."

Her mouth quivered. Her voice refused to come, but she managed in a whisper, "Husband...?"

Milkilu pushed his whore aside to step forward and slap Beletsunu across the face, driving her with a single blow to her knees. "Do not call me that," he snarled. "Do not ever call me that. I married you for the dowry. Nothing more."

Beletsunu looked up at him in horror. She should not have been shocked, and she knew it. There had always been the concern that he was only interested in her large dowry. It seemed so obvious. But there were his words, and his smiles, and his polite gestures toward her family. She had allowed herself some hope that he would, at the very least, be kind.

Instead, he slapped her again, harder this time. And then again. "Do not make me look at your vile face!" he roared. "Cover it up! Wear a cloak or a sack or something if you must show yourself, but get out of here now. Go."

Beletsunu wanted to cry herself to sleep that night. The tears came, but sleep did not. She had always been an insightful girl. It occurred to her, as she sobbed and her husband grunted and his whore called out his name, that the man who'd taken the ugliest bride in all of Babylon had, in doing so, become a much wealthier man.

There was some chance that her family would look in on her. That they would see his kindness for the sham that it was, and that they would have the marriage annulled and force him to return both his bride and the dowry. There was some small chance that her family would care, but she did not allow herself to hope again.

She was an insightful girl.

"You must try not to anger him," counseled Hunzuu. He wiped away the blood from Beletsunu's nose with a rag. Of all the servants, Hunzuu was the kindest—or, rather, the least unkind. He at least paid attention to Beletsunu, and showed her what her husband expected in his house. He corrected her mistakes. He explained her husband's wrath after the storm passed.

"I do everything he asks," Beletsunu protested quietly. "I avoid him. I stay out of his way. I clean his bed and replenish the incense and leave out the water and the wine—"

"You mix in too little water with the wine," Hunzuu said. He sat with her in the storage room. "I have shown you before. He beat me for the same, until I learned how he likes it. I will show you again."

"He has beaten the other servants?" Beletsunu asked.

Hunzuu frowned. "The master, your husband, is a good man," explained the older man. "But he has his ways, and when they are denied, he is angered. Yes. He has beaten the other servants. All masters do."

Beletsunu watched Hunzuu with her good eye and listened closely to his tone. She heard what he did not say. That angry masters beat servants was not unheard of, or even considered shameful. Hunzuu had no need to cover for him, yet there was hesitation in his voice. "Has he killed?" she probed. "For what?"

"I must go," Hunzuu replied. He kept the rag in his hand. "The master will send me to fetch a woman for his bed tonight. It is always this way when he has been angered."

She put her hand on his wrist. "Tell me, Hunzuu," she pressed. "Please. I do not... I wish to understand his anger, that I may not incur it. What happened?"

"It is nothing you need concern yourself with," Hunzuu shrugged. "It was merely the boy who tended the horses. He was careless with the feed. There was mold, and a horse died. The master was... angry," he finished. "As I said. He will want a woman tonight. Make sure the lamps and the incense are ready. Do not trouble about the wine. I will handle that."

"He killed the boy over a horse?" Beletsunu asked.

"Horses do not come cheaply," Hunzuu shrugged again as he left.

Had he paid attention, he might have noticed that Beletsunu did not ask out of shock, but rather a need for clarity.

———

SHE WATCHED him with his women.

He preferred to have the bedroom brightly lit and gently scented. He preferred his wine cut with water. He paid little heed to the pleasure of his partners, but expected them to praise his prowess.

Some were whores. Some were servants. A few, spread over the course of months, were other men's wives. Adultery was a crime for women, but not for men... and if Milkilu could buy a husband's silence with his gold, then there would be no accusation to worry about.

When all was well, he settled for cheap satisfaction. When troubled, or angered, he would pay for good company to relieve his tension. He enjoyed scented oils, on himself and his women, and paid to have plenty on hand.

He liked to find quick, early satisfaction, and then to let a woman try to coax him to readiness again. His second bout would always last much longer, driving him to distraction. He was loud and careless. He would kneel on the bed, facing away from the door, and usually for his second coupling he preferred to take his women from behind.

A woman could sneak into the room while he rutted this way. Even a woman with a crooked back and shuffling feet could do it.

———

"TWO HORSES!" Milkilu roared, striking Ubar with the shovel again and again. His young servant gave up any attempt at prostration or pleading for forgiveness. Ubar curled up and covered his head, absorbing the blows as best he could with his arms and his back. It didn't help much.

"You stupid fool! How could you be so careless?" Ubar jerked with each blow, sobbing but too frightened to defend himself or flee—and now too injured in any case.

"*Master!*" *came a voice. Milkilu spun, finding Hunzuu there on his knees. "Master, mercy! The boy made a mistake. He has been punished, and will learn better."*

The rage did not abate. Milkilu strode forward, swinging the shovel at Hunzuu now. "And who should have taught him?" he roared. He struck his faithful servant across the shoulder, and then in the hip, and more. "You know better! You know to have the feed sifted and checked!"

"I did, master," Hunzuu cried between his gasps and grunts of pain. "I did! We both knew! We both checked! I am sorry, master. We are both so sorry."

Milkilu struck Hunzuu again, breathing heavily as he tired from the exertion of beating his servants. The blow landed across Hunzuu's ankle, awkwardly but painfully. Milkilu tossed the shovel aside, letting it fall across Ubar's back. He stomped away, past the dead horses at the edge of the stable.

It occurred to him that Hunzuu should have been out in the fields. He wondered how Hunzuu even knew that Milkilu was in the stables, or that Ubar was being beaten. No matter. One more thing to discipline Hunzuu for later.

His intervention hardly did any good. Ubar would likely die from his injuries. Milkilu had seen it before. And now most of the other servants were gone on business. Hunzuu would not be running errands for a day or more. Milkilu fumed, striding through his home, wondering who could fetch—

She knelt in the kitchen, her head bowed to the floor and covered by the hood of a cloak. "Beletsunu," Milkilu growled.

"Yes, master?"

"Do you know the way to Gemeti's house?"

"Yes, master."

He grunted. Subjecting Gemeti to Beletsunu's face would not be the best way to summon her, but he could soothe any insult with more gold. "Take money. Go to her and tell her to come here tonight. Then get back here and prepare the bedroom."

"Yes, master," Beletsunu replied, and waited until he had passed to rise.

Milkilu let out a sigh. At least his wife was good for something. Convenient, he thought, that she was there in the kitchen when he needed her.

THE WINE WAS STRONGER *that night. The incense, too. Milkilu failed to notice either change, consumed as he was by his company. In truth, both the wine and the incense had grown slightly stronger each night for months, bit by bit, carefully measured so as to escape his detection.*

Milkilu didn't notice. Nor did the whore, Gemeti. She stayed on her hands and knees as he required, moaning loudly at his magnificence. Their bodies gleamed in the candlelight from the scented oils that covered them both.

Even with the loss of the horses, Milkilu considered that he could practically buy Gemeti now. They could come to some arrangement and he could have her live here in the home with him, or at least come to him most nights. He gave it a moment's thought, gulping down his wine while he held her hip with his other hand. No. Better to look into who might be available for marriage soon. He had the money for a sizeable dowry, should anyone desirable be offered.

At this point, he'd been married to Beletsunu long enough that an accident would not seem so suspicious. It was about time he got rid of the stupid, ugly cow, too. The thought of freeing himself from her drove him on. Gemeti's moans became commensurately louder.

He never saw his wife until it was too late. The kitchen knife slid across his neck, cutting deeply, robbing him of his voice. He gasped and pitched forward, blood spraying all around as he collapsed on top of Gemeti.

Beletsunu grabbed the whore's hair with her free hand. She stabbed the screaming, naked woman without a second thought. Beletsunu didn't know what had driven Gemeti to prostitute herself and didn't care. All that mattered was her silence. Beletsunu murdered the young woman on her husband's bed, and then turned her attention to her flailing, gasping husband.

He tried to knock her away with one hand, keeping the other on his neck as if to stop his bleeding. Half-drunk and disoriented by pain, though, Milkilu couldn't land much of a blow. Beletsunu ignored it. She stabbed him several more times, giving special attention to his legs. She jerked and carved with the knife, just to ensure that he could not run.

"Your servants will notice how your screams have ceased," Beletsunu said as he collapsed back onto the bed. "Hunzuu or Ubar will come to your aid. They may be on the way now. But they will not move quickly tonight after the beating you gave them both."

His eyes were wide with panic. He stared at his wife, gasping for breath that came now with a sick gurgling noise.

Her one good eye looked on without pity. "I will be distraught when I am told that you did not escape the fire," Beletsunu told him, her voice entirely flat. "I will weep for you, husband. I will grieve. Everyone will see, and take pity."

She slipped toward the table and knocked over the decanter of scented oils onto the rug, and then the candle with it.

"Master?" called a weak and weary but concerned voice from outside.

The flames roared to life. Milkilu flailed weakly, pleading for mercy with his eyes.

"Hunzuu?" Beletsunu answered with a fearful voice. She scurried from the room as the fire quickly spread. "Hunzuu! Hunzuu, come quickly! Please!"

Milkilu saw her disappear behind the smoke.

SHE WEPT *outside the walls of Milkilu's burning home, driven to her knees by her grief. Everyone saw. Everyone took pity.*

Most gave her space. There was little to do for her just yet. The immediate concern was for salvage of property and livestock. Two servants had already perished in the flames, and still more stood at risk. Such a simple, stupid accident. Such a tragedy.

"You weep with talent."

Beletsunu looked up with shock. Her good eye and her mouth conveyed her horror. The fire illuminated the night outside her home. Standing over her was a tall, broad-shouldered man in a dark, rich tunic.

The dancing lights of the fire allowed her to see his handsome face and his short, well-groomed beard. The dark pools of his eyes would surely have unsettled her, had she not already been so unsettled as she was.

"How dare you?" she gasped. "My husband is dead! Our faithful servants! You come here to mock me?" Her voice cracked as she spoke, her words punctuated with sobs.

"Excellent," chuckled the stranger. "Most guilty women would immediately deny any implied accusation, but you know better than to show that you recognize it. You skip straight to indignation. Parry and attack. Very good indeed. Don't worry. No one will hear us. Your secret is safe with me."

"What secret?" Beletsunu asked, looking around to see if anyone could shield her from this cruel man's taunting. No one seemed to notice them at all now.

"The knife hidden in your dress, for one. It still carries blood from your husband and his whore. You washed it from your hands quickly, but the knife is not yet fully cleaned. Should I go on?"

Beletsunu did not respond. She watched, waited, and listened.

"He had it coming," the man continued. "Don't worry. I will not expose you. I have waited some years for that one to die, and I appreciate the manner of his death. Killing the whore was a nice touch, though," he smiled thoughtfully. "And the servants in the fire. I would not be able to speak to you openly had you not been so thorough.

Though I have to say, it was the thoroughness that I appreciated most. You have talent."

"You're mad," Beletsunu countered. "I am a small woman, and weak. I could not—"

"But you did, and we both know that you did," he said, still smiling. "You are a small woman, and strong, and resourceful. And now a widow, all alone. Where will you go?"

Beletsunu's eyes narrowed. "Who are you?"

"I am Baal," the man told her as ashes began to fall around them. "I come to make you an offer."

———

"Babe, are you okay?" Rachel asked.

Lorelei's gaze drifted away. Regardless of her appearance, she did not feel fine at all. She felt Rachel's hand on her knee, felt the angel's pleading eyes on her, and eventually shook her head. "No."

"They're not gonna hurt you again," Rachel assured her. "I won't allow it. I won't leave you." The succubus let out a bitter, skeptical breath. "I mean it, Lorelei," Rachel said. "I can't and I won't."

Only then did Lorelei look up, her eyes taking in the room once more in a practical assessment. There were cameras, which surely had microphones. They were not likely set merely to record. Someone was probably watching her, ready to sound an alarm if she did anything remotely suspicious. Speaking openly seemed unwise.

She hung her head again, considering her options. Mortal men watched her every move... but they were only mortal men. She knew languages that died out centuries ago. No one else understood her, but an angel might.

"These walls have ears," Lorelei murmured in Beletsunu's native tongue.

Rachel blinked, not immediately understanding. Then the light bulb seemed to go off. "Right," she said. "Sorry. Good plan. Shit, I haven't heard that language in forever. Lorelei, I'm so sorry."

"You saw me?" asked Lorelei, still keeping her voice low. "You saw what happened?"

"Yeah, a little," nodded the angel. "It wasn't just the rosary, or the guy. They aren't special. There was another angel there, too. I separated them. Wish I had fucked him up a bit more, but he ran."

"I thought I was safe from your kind," said Lorelei. Her voice, even this low, did not come to her without effort.

"You're supposed to be," Rachel frowned. "I thought he'd never set foot in this city again. This shit is way deeper than I ever realized."

"Who?"

The blonde did not answer immediately. Lorelei watched the brief conflict in Rachel's eyes. "His name is Donald," Rachel said. "He's... he's a guardian angel. For Hauser. And for Alex, before we all met. Yeah. Way too convenient, I know," she added sourly as she saw Lorelei process the information.

"You told Alex that his guardian abandoned him."

"He did. He popped the lock open on the chapel where Alex met us, but even so, he ran before the action started. He's got his own bullshit justification for it. Nobody likes to admit cowardice, especially to themselves. The thing is, all this stuff with Alex and us... I think it blindsided Donald. He didn't see any of it coming. He thought Alex was just a big old failure, but he's clearly been investing in Hauser for a long time."

Lorelei frowned. Her language didn't have a proper term for that, so she repeated it in English: "Investing?"

Rachel sat back on her butt in front of Lorelei, drawing her knees up to her chest and wrapping her arms around them. It was rare that her young face held such a grim expression. "Guardian angels aren't supposed to play favorites. They have rules, but they also have lots of autonomy. No guardian can be everywhere at once, so they have to make judgment calls and prioritize. Most of 'em do it in good faith. Hell, normally I'd say that all of them work in good faith. They're angels.

"But angels aren't perfect. You know that. I know that. They fuckin' *hate* to admit that, but it's true. Anyway, if you look at one given guardian and you get real critical and start peeling away every little decision and look at it, sometimes you see patterns that don't exactly indicate complete impartiality, y'know? Like a parent who plays favorites." She gave a little shrug. "Vincent got that way before he took on dominion here. It's one of the things that drove us apart.

"Mortals make their own decisions. Angels give hints and leave signs and sometimes they whisper encouragement or warnings or whatnot, but in the end it's supposed to be all about the mortal's choices. Free will, right?" she asked with a smirk, and looked up to Lorelei's steady, piercing gaze. Her smirk faded. "Yeah. Yeah, I know. Anyway. I think there's a good chance that

Donald's been giving a lot more guidance to Hauser than he probably should."

"How do you know this?" Lorelei asked, reverting to far older words again. "Did Donald confess it?"

"No. I couldn't pin him down that long. I'm making an educated guess. I mean Hauser's here, doing his thing, and he's using a rosary, and..." Rachel's words turned to a mumble. She chewed on her lip hesitantly. "And Donald has a pattern."

"How long have you known Donald?"

"Only met him twice now. Once after the first shit went down with us and Alex, when he got held to account for it. And then just a couple minutes ago."

"Then how do you know his pattern?"

"Because a friend looked into things she's not supposed to," Rachel mumbled. "You remember Hannah? She was Alex's guardian once, a couple millennia ago. Then he had a new life, and a new angel... and then a pattern started." Her shoulders rose and fell with a heavy breath. "Guardian angels are judged on a lot of factors, but the biggest is a matter of how their charges live their lives. Whether they're good people or bad, whether they're brave or cowardly... whether they're virtuous or if they're corrupted.

"Turns out you get a lot of bonus points if someone you watch over is a hero. More if they die that way."

Lorelei just stared. "There was a pattern?"

"Nobody ever gave it a second thought. It's part of who Alex *is*, y'know? He's a brave and unselfish soul. No bullshit about that. It's why we love him. It's why he loves a couple of freaks like us." She paused. "But that's not enough to explain why he died young in some sacrifice play every fucking time. Nobody ever gave it a second thought," she repeated bitterly. " 'cause Donald's an *angel*, right?"

"Where is Donald now?"

"I don't know," the angel shrugged.

"Could he be with Alex?"

"He might be. I hope not. I told him not to go near him, but he obviously only gives a shit what I say if I'm about to fuck him up."

"You must go to Alex now," Lorelei hissed.

"Nuh-uh. No can do."

"Rachel, he needs you."

"You need me," Rachel countered, looking at her firmly. "Fuckhead Donald might come back in here with his fuckhead mortal tool and that rosary. Like I said, Hauser doesn't have the juice to really work that thing. It's just a cheap trinket. But if he's got an angel channeling through it, they could kill you."

"They must want more here than me," Lorelei argued. "Too much is at stake."

"Lorelei—"

"He knows how to manipulate Alex. They both do, or I would not be here now in chains. What happens to him?"

"What happens to you if you die?" Rachel snapped. "I know what happens to Alex. He dies and we weep and then he goes to Heaven and I find him and we sort shit out. We lose him until either he comes back or we find a way to fix things for all three of us, and it hurts like a motherfucker but it's not the end.

"If *you* die, what happens? Your soul returns to Hell and you, what, get regenerated in some lake of fire and crawl out into the welcoming arms of your bros down there? Who's gonna foot the bill for your recovery, huh? Belial? Fuckin' Lucifer? They all know you don't play for their team anymore, babe. You go to Hell again, you aren't gonna be a jailer this time. You'll be an inmate. It'll be full on damnation with a big fat helping of personal grudges on top.

"And if you die under the sort of scouring Donald and Hauser are packin' there, you're *gone*, Lorelei. Like for really reals. No reincarnation, no sliver of hope that maybe someday I can get you out of Hell somehow. You'll just be gone forever. I won't let that happen."

Lorelei listened and bowed her head once more. She shut her eyes tightly. "I never thought..." She paused, trying to hold her voice steady rather than allow it to quiver even in such intimacy. She had nothing to hide from Rachel, but the cameras and microphones were another matter. Regardless of her language, she didn't care to betray anything through tone. "The difficulty of loving more than one person is that one cannot always be there for both in all times. I never thought you would choose to be with me over Alex."

Rachel's face softened. She reached up to wipe away the tear on Lorelei's cheek. "I said I love you and I meant it."

Lorelei turned her head enough to kiss Rachel's hand. "What of your post?"

"Fuck it," Rachel shrugged. "I've done more in a month than Vincent did in a century. If a couple days is all it takes for this city to backslide deeper into the shitter than it was with him in charge, I guess I shouldn't hold dominion, anyway." She rose to her knees, placing her forehead against Lorelei's. "I've got my priorities."

Lorelei nodded, pausing for only a moment to bask in her lover's touch. Then she turned her thoughts to the situation at hand. "My strength returns slowly, but I do not know if I will be able to slip all of these bonds. I presume you cannot simply free me, or you would have done so already."

"That's the sort of thing that could get us into even bigger trouble than this," came Rachel's grim agreement. "I can justify defending you from Donald, but the rest of this shit..." she shook her head. "It's one thing to be here at your side. It's another to intervene directly with mortal events. There are rules."

"I know," Lorelei whispered. "You bend them for me all the time. I am forever grateful."

Mechanical noises broke into the quiet tone of their conversation as the locks on the door opened. Rachel stood and slipped around Lorelei. The angel leaned on the back of her lover's chair as the demon sat up straight to face her captors.

Hauser entered first, with one hand held low while he clenched the bit of holy symbolism that gave him such an advantage. Two more agents followed. He gruffly introduced them as they entered. "I'm Special Agent Hauser, FBI. These are agents Nguyen and Bridger."

Two others followed them, though the mortals were unaware. Lorelei didn't see them, either, but Rachel made plain that her captors were not alone. "Oh, good, you brought a witness," she said. "Donald, you even *whisper* to that fucknut with the rosary and I'll send you back to Heaven carrying your jaw in your hand." Her eyes slid briefly to Sergio. "Quote me on that all you want."

The angel beside Nguyen blinked. "We seek only to protect our charges." He turned his eyes on Donald with obvious concern. "The rosary is meant to counter her power."

"Bullshit. Donald tried to use jack-off here to smear Lorelei into the carpet earlier. It's not gonna happen again."

Her answer only heightened Sergio's expression of unease. Donald didn't look at him. "I will not have this demon whore use her magics on these mortals!" he protested.

"She doesn't need any magic against these guys," Rachel said, placing her hands on Lorelei's shoulders. "So I guess you get to just stand there and shut the fuck up."

"Do we call you Lorelei?" asked Hauser, oblivious to the other conversation.

"That is my name," replied Lorelei. She heard Rachel, but the other angels did not reveal themselves to her. Still, she trusted her lover to handle them. Lorelei had to focus on the mortals.

"Not the only one, though, right?" Hauser smirked. "I'm sure you've had other names over the years?"

"Lorelei is the most appropriate name."

"You seem to have recovered quickly from what happened out in the hall," observed Hauser, twirling his finger as if to indicate her face. "You didn't look like that when we brought you in here."

Lorelei took in a long breath and smiled faintly at his tone. "This is familiar," she said. "You consider yourself a righteous man, and me a demon, and thus you use suspicion and disdain as your shield. I have met 'good' men such as you before. You have already condemned me."

"You did break into a Federal facility and put down my guys," Hauser pointed out. "Seems some suspicion might be in order. And here you are trying to look like a glamour model again like that's gonna sway me."

"This is my natural state," said Lorelei.

"Sans the wings and so forth? Seems more likely that what I saw earlier was the truth."

"Truth is subjective. I owe you no explanations for my appearance."

"Yeah? You owe one to Alex?"

"I would, of course, be glad to speak to Alex," Lorelei replied evenly.

"Because you're in love with him, is that it?"

"Yes."

"And you came here to rescue him from me?"

"I did."

"He thinks *he's* saving Alex from *you*," said Rachel into Lorelei's ear. "Alex and the guys." Her eyes slid irritably toward Donald. "Can't imagine where he got that idea."

"You—I can't believe you!" burst Donald. "You threaten me if I aid my charge, but you counsel that demon right in front of us?"

Rachel gave him the finger and added for Lorelei, "That's not Hauser's main mission, but it's on his list."

"What's your agenda with Alex?"

"What 'agenda' would lovers have?" Lorelei asked Hauser. "Are you not familiar with the concept?"

"Right. And his friends, huh? The one's you'd face anyone and commit any crime for?" Hauser paused for dramatic effect. "We picked up Jason Cohen and freed Amber a few minutes after our little altercation out in the hallway. So now that we've got you and all your boys in—"

"You make a mistake in calling them 'boys,'" Lorelei interrupted quietly.

"That's what the inmates in Federal prison will call them," Hauser snapped with no small trace of menace. "They're all facing serious charges with serious penalties. I will goddamn guarantee convictions, and the judge that'll preside over their cases isn't the sort to go for the minimum sentences.

"You're a savvy woman. I figure you know where I'm going with this. They're in enough trouble to ruin their entire lives. You claim to care about them. You even claim you're in love with one of 'em. Presumably that means you don't want any of them in prison until they're old and grey, which is exactly what's going to happen. So if you want to help them, you'll have to help me and answer my questions."

"And where do those questions and answers lead me?" asked Lorelei.

"You're in your own heap of trouble, lady," Hauser grunted. "Cooperate and it might not be so bad for you. More importantly, those guys will all walk. The question is whether you care enough about them to take that deal."

Lorelei arched an eyebrow. "You can guarantee their freedom?"

"Sure. Four well-meaning, naïve guys practically just out of high school fall under the sway of a wealthy demon seductress? It's not like they murdered innocent people. I can see the score there. You talk, they walk."

"But if I do not cooperate, then those four well-meaning, naïve young men rot in prison for decades?" Her eyes flicked briefly to his companions. "One wonders why so many Americans do not trust people in your profession."

"If you don't talk, I'll do what it takes to uphold the law and safeguard the public. Now: Are you really a succubus?"

"To answer that, we would have to establish a common definition. I doubt you understand what a succubus is."

"Are you a demon?"

"What is a demon, Agent Hauser?" asked Lorelei. "What power did you employ in the hallway? Why did it work? Do you understand it? Does the sorcerer at your side?" she asked, tilting her head toward Bridger. "Do you understand the magic that he practices?"

"Do you want to help Alex and his buddies or not?"

"Of course," Lorelei nodded calmly. "You haven't told me what you want."

"I want answers." Hauser folded his arms across his chest, his scowl never wavering. "All those questions you just threw back at me? *You* answer them. I want to hear everything you know about all this supernatural bullshit. The vampires. The werewolves. Demons. Rachel. I want the truth. All of it."

"Oh?" Lorelei asked, her lips almost slipping into a grin. "Is that all?"

Rachel's eyes went wide. She glanced at Donald in shock, but the other angel looked on with his face set in stone. Rachel quickly clamped her hand over Lorelei's mouth. "You can't," she hissed.

The agents didn't see Rachel at all. Their mortal minds ignored the momentary impression the invisible angel's hand made on Lorelei's skin. "Seriously, Lorelei, you fuckin' can't. I'm beggin' you. I know you want to wreck this dude, but it's his *soul*."

Lorelei made no effort to reassure her companion. She simply waited for Rachel to remove her hand and then explained, "I do not profess to know all there is to know of the lesser vermin, but I may possess knowledge valuable to you. We can barter for that information. Hunt the mongrels and corpses all you wish. I will be glad to see fewer of them."

"And the rest?"

"Those answers would only weaken you."

"How so?"

"Again, Agent Hauser, what power did you use upon me? How does it work? You cannot answer these questions, but you have faith—and you knew that faith would be enough, didn't you? Consider the difference between knowledge and faith, and how the one might impact the other."

She watched as Hauser's eyes narrowed. Rachel leaned in close. "Somebody's been fucking with him," the angel said. She looked at him intently. "He's had a piss-poor success rate with his interrogations lately and it's grating on him."

"So now you're concerned with my success and my safety?" Hauser asked.

"You asked for my cooperation," said Lorelei. "Your questions are far more complex and carry greater danger than you realize. Would you prefer that I simply lead you astray and let you suffer? That does not strike me as cooperation."

"It's the guys," Rachel said. "Drew and Wade. They've been fucking with him."

Hauser folded his arms across his chest. "What about Rachel?"

"She is quite beyond you," Lorelei answered, shaking her head slightly. "Put her out of your mind."

"I might've thought before this week that a demon would be beyond me."

"Do you plan to subdue her with the great power of your Christian faith?"

"Motherfucker," Rachel muttered. "He wants me to help him deal with all the vampires and bullshit." Her eyes turned to Donald. "That's what all this is, right? Just a chance to get me to intervene here, make your guy look good, and I take a fall for getting hip-deep in mortal bullshit?"

"One could argue that you are already far deeper than that," said Donald sourly, "but as I recall, you didn't want me to speak."

"We can talk of the monsters you hunt for some time," said Lorelei. "We can speak of their organizations and their habits and weaknesses. I can explain what transpired here in Seattle that led us to this current debacle. Will you let us all go in exchange?"

"It's a start."

"What more do you want?"

"He wants all the monsters," Rachel said, looking to Lorelei meaningfully. "All of them. Including you."

Hauser reached for the papers on the manila folder and turned over the top sheet. He revealed an autopsy photo of a young, fit black man and an accompanying report. "This guy look familiar to you at all? His name is Damon Demetrius Bell. You murdered him just last January."

Lorelei glanced down at the papers only once. "What proof do you have?"

"Mostly circumstantial evidence. I've got witnesses that can put you with Bell shortly before he died. Given what I know about you now I can construct a plausible story. It won't be good enough for a conviction, but I don't need anything more if you make a full confession."

"He wants to get you away from Alex for good," Rachel grimaced. "Because *someone* told him it was the right thing to do."

"And then?" asked Lorelei.

"And then Alex and his buddies can go free. No charges."

"What if I do not?"

"Then I put you and everyone else away on the stuff that *will* hold up in court and I move on to the next bad guy while you *all* rot in prison."

"You do not offer a compelling bargain," Lorelei replied dryly.

"It's the one you get. I'm not leaving that kid in your hands regardless. He's better off in prison than with you."

"I somehow doubt that he will agree. Agent Hauser, you have me here now only because Alex wanted to give you a chance," Lorelei explained. "You used force against me in spite of his cooperation. Do you sincerely believe you will have his trust now?"

"I doubt he'll be so interested in *you* anymore after what he saw," snorted Hauser. "He's a twenty-year-old kid and you've led him around by his dick for a month. Maybe he'll wise up now that he's seen what a fuck-ugly hag you are underneath your magical illusions or however it is you create that face. If he talks and you don't, then I've got no reason to give you any breaks at all."

Lorelei smiled. Hauser didn't like it. "What?" he asked.

"You mock and deride me for my appearance. You presume to split lovers apart because you do not approve of their relationship. You bargain with the freedom of others to serve your ambitions. Perhaps you have not considered this, but to wear the righteous armor of faith, one must actually *be* righteous.

"Bring forth your little trinket and pray at me again, o' mortal man. Let us see if you still wield the same power you did mere minutes ago... or if you have already cracked that armor you wore so confidently."

She gazed intently at him as she spoke, watching his face for any sort of tick or tell, and then she saw it: his narrowed eyes twitched just a bit with sudden realization.

"Tell me, Agent Hauser," Lorelei asked in tones that might have been soothing in another context, "do any other sins weigh upon your conscience?"

Rachel gave her shoulder a slight squeeze. "You're good," she breathed.

"Uh-huh. Guess we're already at an impasse," Hauser sighed. "It's natural for a suspect to get combative once she realizes she's cornered. I'll let you chew on this for a bit." He rose from the table. "Think it through. There's no way I could let you go even if I wanted to, but if you cooperate we can make all this easier on you."

He opened the door to leave, with Nguyen and Bridger following in his wake. The pair of angels beside them also withdrew. Sergio's gaze stayed on Donald rather than Rachel or Lorelei.

"He blinked," grinned Rachel.

"He did," nodded Lorelei, "and he did not. He knew I would not crack in his first attempt. Leaving me here to think on his offer was always part of his plan."

Rachel came around to face her. "What's wrong?"

"It is as he said. I never wanted either of you to see me like that."

"You know I don't give a damn."

"No," Lorelei nodded quietly. "Not you."

OUTSIDE IN THE HALL, with the doors secured and several paces away, Hauser and his team regrouped. Keeley appeared from another room to meet with them. "The mics picked up just fine," he said. "Nothing seemed distorted. I'll have to listen again to be sure it recorded, but I don't think we had any interference."

"She didn't pull any magical tricks on us, either," Bridger nodded. "Nothing that I could spot, anyway. And now that I know to look, I can still see the wings and the horns and such. And the tail. I don't know how we can secure a tail, but I don't think she can reach anything useful in there with it and even so I don't know how prehensile it—"

"Yeah, good," Hauser grunted. He rubbed the bridge of his nose and then his eyes. "I figure that went about as well as could be expected."

"You okay?" asked Nguyen.

"Fine. Just irritated. First those two punks, then I thought I was getting somewhere with Carlisle, and now..." He jerked his thumb at Lorelei's room. "We'll break her. I don't care if she's a demon or if she's from Mars. We'll get there. Anyway, how's Maddox? She holding it together?"

"Just making a written report while it's still fresh," nodded Keeley. "Why?"

"We need to put all four of those guys in a room and confront them together, Paul. I need you to do that."

The other agents looked at one another with obvious surprise. "Uh, Joe," Keeley said, "none of them have actually confessed. Why would we put them in the same room where they can—?"

"Look, I told Carlisle that he could see them," interrupted Hauser irritably. "If she's right, and I think she is, I gotta make good on that. Otherwise I'm lying and that might be a weakness if I flash the rosary again."

"Joe, where did you even get that thing?" asked Nguyen. "Why didn't you tell us? What do you know that we don't?"

"I knew we'd be facing a demon, so I went to a church," Hauser snapped. "You need to know more than that? Is it time for us all to have a sit-down chat about our religions? I had an idea and it worked. What more to you need to know?"

Keeley and Nguyen frowned, both glancing at Bridger. The occultist shrugged. "It's possible Lorelei's right. Confidence is a huge factor in matters of magic and... well, faith. If Hauser doubts his ability to keep Lorelei in check, then he won't be able to do it. Even if she's lying," he added pointedly.

"Joe, this is a bad idea," Keeley pressed. "Jones has been a brick wall and Reinhardt just treats all this like it's a game. You put the two of them together with the others and it could be a disaster."

"So don't let it happen!" snapped Hauser. "They're all loyal to each other, right? Use that."

"You don't want to be in the room to do it?"

"No. I'll watch. I'm in no shape to do a second interrogation right now. We'll have Amber with me so she can corroborate anything they say, but it has to be you." With that, he stomped off down the hallway.

Nguyen threw Keeley an uncomfortable look. "At least he knows his limits," Keeley shrugged.

15

ALEA IACTA EST

They sat Alex down in a new chair and a larger room with a conference table at its center. Like the rest of the building, Alex saw signs of disrepair and age. Someone had drawn the curtains back from the window, allowing for some natural light and a view of the trees. That alone made the room nicer than his improvised cell, which was little more than a cot in a locked closet.

Getting handcuffed to yet another chair wasn't so nice.

They left him in the room with a single agent, who sat at one end of the conference table with his laptop open. His jacket hung from the back of the chair. His tie, loosened but still hanging from his open collar, looked like a hated nuisance. Alex watched him. The man didn't look up from his work.

"Please tell me you're writing an angry blog post about how my civil rights are being violated," Alex said.

"Mm-hm," the agent murmured.

The door opened. A uniformed guard came through, leading in two familiar faces and a couple more men in suits.

"Hey, guys," Alex sighed grimly.

"Oh, man, I plead the Fifth on anything this fool says," Drew announced as he stepped through. He still wore the same suit from the party, minus the tie. His hands were cuffed behind his back.

"Your mom pleads the Fifth on anything I say," replied Alex.

Drew paused and blinked. The guard behind him pushed him along as Drew muttered, "Can't believe you finally got me."

"Aw, y'all wanna have us a group discussion now?" said the other prisoner. Like Drew, Wade still had his Halloween clothes on, though the gears had been stripped from his outfit and his hat and belt were gone. Also like Drew, he was still cuffed.

"Hi, Wade," Alex said.

"Alex." He looked over his shoulder. "Hey, if y'all're gonna do 'im like that, you oughta go all the way an' get him one a' them leather masks. He's a biter."

"Just sit down, all of you," said the agent at his computer. He gestured to seats at the table, to which the guards guided their prisoners. With the group seated, the agent who had led them in found himself a spot at the end of the table.

"You guys okay?" asked Alex.

"Wondered when someone was gonna realize we were gone," Drew frowned.

Alex scowled. "Yeah, well, we all thought we had texted back and forth with you a few times already," he said.

"Shit, really?"

"Wouldn't make that one up," shrugged Alex.

Drew turned his gaze on the agent. "Hey, so for the twentieth time: does my family know I've been arrested?"

"Nope," the agent shook his head. "Sorry. National security trump card."

"Is that why we ain't actually been charged with nothin' yet?"

"We're about to get to all that," the agent said. There was a knock on the door. "C'mon in," he called out.

The door opened again. Jason was led in, handcuffed like the rest, by Nguyen and another agent. As his eyes swept the room, he let out heavy breath. "Sorry, guys."

"What're y'all sorry for?" asked Wade.

"Turns out Amber's an undercover Fed."

Drew shot the other agents a glare. "You sent someone in to play him like that? Man, that's just *low*."

"They're pretty good at going for the low blow," said Alex.

"Yeah, I can't blame you guys for being mad," sighed the other agent. "These are Agents Lanier and Nguyen," he said, gesturing to each in turn, "and

I'm Agent Keeley. We're with the task force that has been investigating your group and your shenanigans."

"Is this everyone? Where's Lorelei?" demanded Alex. "Where'd you put her?"

"Woah, they got her, too?" asked Wade.

"Shit," Jason winced.

"These assholes hauled me out of class this morning. She came in here to get us out and I tried to talk her down, 'cause I *thought* these might be the good guys," Alex said, glancing resentfully at the other agents. "Then the asshole in charge took her down with some magic bullshit and they carted her off. She looked completely fucked up and I don't know where she is."

"Lorelei's in custody and she's fine," Keeley nodded. "Alex, guys, I gotta tell you: I don't think you've been able to see her objectively. Her face is back to the way you're used to it, but what you saw out there is the real deal. She looks like that naturally. I mean, she's a demon, right?"

Alex glared at Keeley, trying to control his anger. "That's your plan? Sweep in here, arrest and fuck up everyone I care about and then tell me I don't understand my own life?"

"Hey, hey, dial it back, Alex," Keeley said, holding up his hands. "We don't have to be enemies here. Like we've been trying to tell you, we're not the bad guys. You're in a lot of trouble. We want to help you out of it.

"Now, normally we wouldn't let a group like this all see each other like you're doing now. We've been watching you, though, and the more we piece things together, the more we think we can give you this chance. And you've all been pretty firm about protecting one another. Alex, Jason, these are some tough friends you have here," Keeley continued, waving his pen at the other two young men. "Been here about thirty-six hours, interviewed three times—"

"Interrogated," Wade corrected.

"—and they haven't cracked."

"You seem pretty cheerful about all this," observed Drew.

"I don't take this personally. My boss might, of course. But I don't see any reason to bluster or get mad. Just a waste of energy. Gets me stressed for no good reason. Anyhoo," he shrugged mildly, "this whole deal isn't about me, right? It's about you.

"And the first thing we've gotta do is make sure we're all on the same page so we can drop all the denials and the diversions and move on." He turned his eyes to Alex. "Look, I get that you're mad. If I saw something like that happen to my significant other, I'd be pretty pissed, too. But you gotta understand, we can't take any chances. And, well," Keeley shrugged again, "you saw her with your own eyes, buddy. She never told you about her face, did she? Doesn't it make you wonder what else she hasn't told you?"

Jason watched Alex carefully, noting the building anger in his friend's eyes and his breath. "What is it you guys actually want?" he asked, remembering Alex's rage in the bus tunnel. He didn't want Alex to explode.

"Full depositions, for starters. We need answers. A whole lot of answers. And they'll be better when they're corroborated by other witnesses and participants," he said, gesturing around the table.

"About what?" asked Drew.

"Everything. Lorelei, Rachel, your pool hall, your witch friends, and especially the night you guys apparently blew up most of the vampires in Seattle. We've got everything Jason told Amber, but we need to know more. We'd like to hear it from all of you."

"I'd like to hear from our lawyers," Drew scowled.

"Yeah. I hear that," Keeley nodded with feigned sympathy. "Turns out we've only got one lawyer for this case, and he's both out of town and down with the flu. We don't have anyone else to spare just yet. National security rules, guys. Sorry. But if you don't want to talk, you can wait for him in your rooms. Alone.

"Listen, guys, we already know, right? We know everything Jason told Amber and we already know everything she saw, from Rachel right down to your two witch friends doing their thing in Alex's apartment—and they're gonna have to talk to us before this is all over, too."

"'Doing their thing?'" asked Jason. "You mean Amber saw two girls redecorate an apartment in the middle of the night? When did that become illegal?"

Keeley frowned. "That's for later. Let's start with Rachel: what's her deal?"

"No," Alex answered flatly. "Not a subject we'll discuss."

"I can't play it that way, guys. I'm sorry."

"Too bad."

Keeley looked to the others. "Is she really an angel?"

"Couldn't tell you," Drew shrugged.

"I ain't sure who you're talkin' about," replied Wade.

Keeley tried again with Alex. "Does she come to your rescue when you're in trouble?"

He looked around the room. "Don't see anyone rescuing me right now."

"Rachel who?" pressed Jason. "I've known a bunch of Rachels."

"Even if this is the make or break issue?" Keeley asked. "Even if it could keep you out of going to prison for the rest of your life?"

"Yep," nodded Alex.

"Can you tell me why you won't talk about Rachel?"

"Nope."

"Why not?"

"Can't tell you. Sorry."

"Okay," Keeley sighed. "What about the rest of you?"

"Y'all ain't even told us what we're in for," said Wade.

"Ah. Right," Keeley nodded. "For you two, we're looking at assault and battery on several individuals also in custody—"

"Self-defense," Wade and Drew intoned simultaneously.

"—you think that'll hold up?"

"We didn' go out there with any weapons. Ah'm bettin' those assholes got criminal records longer'n any paper I ever wrote in school. Drew an' I ain't got nothin' worse'n a couple parkin' tickets between us. An y'all claim you saw the whole thing. That means y'all saw them hit first. How's that not self-defense?"

"You also committed murder in that fight, Wade. Of a vampire, no less, which is kinda hard to do without premeditation."

"A vampire," Jason repeated.

"Yeah. Guys, Amber saw an angel fight monsters. We've got a demon in custody. We can drop the denials, okay? You admitted to an undercover agent that they exist, and you've both seen and fought them in person."

"Doesn't mean there was one in the fight with Drew and Wade," said Jason. "You got a body?"

"Jason," Keeley said, "I know you want to defend your friends here—"

"You got a body?"

"—but you weren't even there, so how about you not make speculations about it that won't make any difference in court?"

"You got a body?"

Keeley frowned. "Do vampires leave bodies, Jason?"

"Not to my knowledge," Jason said, "they just leave ashes."

"Right. And we've got that."

"Right. And do you know the chemical composition of dead vampire ashes?" He paused, calmly waiting for Keeley to answer. "Do you know how to prove in court that those ashes are vampire ashes? Or from any kind of person at all?" Again, he waited a beat for a reply. "Do you know what vampire ashes look like under a microscope, Agent Keeley? 'cause I do, and I know that you can't prove to anyone that those ashes came from anything organic."

Keeley blinked.

"Say it with me," Jason deadpanned: "Oh, snap."

She wanted to cheer.

Before that moment, she wanted to crawl under a rock and die. She sat beside her silent boss in a mostly empty office, watching the interrogation unfold on a computer screen as the camera on Lanier's laptop relayed it. Aside from a curt query regarding her well-being, Hauser said nothing to her. They sat forward in their chairs, listened and watched with growing trepidation.

They had a solid case against the crew. They had physical evidence, they had surveillance and an airtight timeline. Hauser planned to offer the guys immunity in exchange for depositions and testimony. The guys were all smart enough to know it was their only way out.

Amber also knew how far Alex had already gone to protect Lorelei, more than once, and how far Jason had gone to protect them both. Her heart sank ever further as she watched Jason endure the conversation, knowing he under-stood just how ugly this would get. Every time Amber felt like she couldn't feel more guilt, she found herself proven wrong.

And then, in that brief flurry of words, Jason tore the whole thing apart.

Hauser sat beside her. He leaned further forward. She leaned back, hoping he wouldn't turn his eyes to look at her as she bit down on her fist to prevent herself from laughing or crying out.

Does Hauser even understand? Amber wondered. She looked at the back of Hauser's head as he watched. Her eyes turned to the screen again. She caught sight of Keeley's face. *He gets it,* she realized. *Keeley gets it. He won't tell them, but... Oh my god. Jason.*

Minutes later, the ill-conceived group interrogation broke up. Hauser rose and stalked out of the room without a word. That suited Amber just fine.

She turned off the video, stared at the blank screen, and wished she could high-five the guy who would probably never speak to her again.

HAUSER FOUND his agents standing at the end of the hallway. Nguyen looked out the window, arms folded across her chest. Lanier had his back to a wall, his head tilted up to the ceiling. Keeley had his hands up on the back of his head as he looked at the floor, walking in something between a circle and a strange pacing motion.

"They're all locked up in their holding rooms?" asked Hauser. "Are they secured? Carlisle?"

"Yeah," nodded Lanier. He didn't look at his boss. "Yeah, they're all good."

"The whole program's screwed, Joe," said Keeley. He put his hands down and looked at Hauser. "We've fucked it all up."

"No. We continue the investigation. I knew it was a mistake to put them together, and I take full responsibility for it. But one bad interrogation doesn't mean we're sunk. We keep them all on ice for a while, we try again—"

"Joe, do you not understand?" Keeley pressed. "We gotta cut 'em loose."

"What are you talking about? We're not cutting anyone loose."

"Oh, for Chrissake, Joe!" snapped Nguyen. "Jones and Reinhardt! We have to let them go. That Cohen kid is right. We can't convict them for killing someone who we can't prove ever even existed."

"Chemical analysis," muttered Lanier, his eyes still on the ceiling. "My God, how did nobody ever think to do that?"

"We never investigated a murdered vampire before," Nguyen answered, "and if we did, we never even knew. We didn't have time to analyze the sample we got from their arrest. Amber could've done that for us, but Hauser had her with Cohen every waking second," she added, waving her hand at him absently.

Hauser ignored the critique. "He could be bluffing."

"He's not bluffing," frowned Keeley. "Go look that kid in the eye. He knew exactly what he was talking about. The second they talk to Lopez, he'll demand a full chemical analysis of all the evidence and that'll be the end of it."

"There are still the other charges—"

"What, for getting in a fight with some two-time losers with gang ties in a parking lot? You think they'll make credible witnesses? Jones and Reinhardt will demand a jury trial, and you know the jury will sympathize with them. Lopez will demolish us in court and then they'll walk. And that one-hundred percent conviction rate will walk right out the door with 'em."

"To say nothing of how many times Jones has demanded to see a lawyer,"

Nguyen put in. "And now that he's heard his buddy Cohen go off, he'll know exactly what to say when he finally gets one."

"Fine. They walk. Who are they going to tell?" Hauser shrugged. "We've still got Cohen and Carlisle over a barrel if they don't talk."

"And what if they don't?" asked Nguyen. "They're both ready to take the fall for Lorelei. You know as well as I do that we can't convict her unless she confesses, and she'd have to be an idiot to do that. Christ, all we've got is a babbling idiot convict as a witness and a year-old dead body. You think we'll find a pathologist who can prove she screwed someone to death?"

"That's enough, Agent Nguyen," Hauser snapped. "That *thing* broke into a Federal operation and assaulted Federal agents with intent to free suspected felons. Between that and what she did to Maddox and those cops—"

"Without a single injury?" interrupted Keeley. "Come on, Joe! She'll get a slap on the wrist and be out in a few years, and it's not like deporting her for her sketchy citizenship is going to be more than an inconvenience for her."

"This whole program rested on nobody knowing about it. Now we have to cut two guys loose, we don't even know where their witch friends are, and sooner or later we'll have to let Lorelei out and God only knows what she'll do then. And we still don't know anything about that Rachel person!"

"We're not spooks, Joe," Nguyen pressed. "We don't do any indefinite hold bullshit. We have to let them go."

"Get ahold of yourselves," Hauser ordered. "All of you. We're not letting anyone go yet. We're not throwing in the towel and going home. This was never about those four guys. We keep them under lock and key and we keep our eye on the ball while we come up with a new way to win this."

"What are we trying to 'win' again?" murmured Lanier. His eyes came down to rest his gaze on Hauser. "Didn't we come up here to find out what happened to the local vampires? I mean, we found that out, right? It looks like they're all dead. What else was on the agenda?"

Hauser glared at him and then stormed off down the hallway.

Lanier glanced from Keeley to Nguyen. "Did that seem like an unreasonable question to either of you?"

———

It cannot end like this.

Hauser sat in his temporary office—just an old chair, an older desk, some cabinets and thankfully a working radiator—and stared out the window at Lake Washington while the sky grew dim. Since arriving a week ago, Hauser continually forgot how much earlier in the day sunset came this time of year, so far north of Los Angeles.

All those monsters out there, laughing at the law. At the people they prey upon. Laughing at this nation and everything it stands for.

Laughing at you.

The thoughts kept running through Hauser's head, popping up continually no matter what he did to blot them out. Writing notes and starting up a report didn't help. Staring out the window didn't help. Seeing the release papers Keeley had drawn up for Jones and Reinhardt absolutely didn't help.

They all hunt Carlisle, and you have him. They can't be far. There will never be a better opportunity.

Hauser turned back to his laptop, moved the mouse to open up his email and check it for the tenth time—and without intending it, as if some invisible force had bumped his hand, opened up the file holding Maddox's reports.

There has to be an answer somewhere, said the voice in his head. *Don't give up. Look. Look again.*

He couldn't wish for better results than Maddox delivered. That she went far out of bounds in getting romantic with Cohen was indisputable, at least from the standards of the FBI. Even though he signed off on everything she did after the fact, Hauser had to worry about her emotional state. Either Maddox hid a heart of stone under that innocent face, or things had gotten away from her and all this would probably tear her up inside.

This isn't a normal investigation. We have to take risks. We can't follow every rule. Sacrifices must be made.

Hauser glanced over her reports, but he returned once more to the fight in the bus tunnel and, in a second window, the explanation Cohen gave her. He read and re-read, wishing he knew how to get any of the prisoners to talk about Rachel. She seemed like the key. She stayed aloof, but when Carlisle was in danger, she came to the rescue... and, according to Cohen, there was a pattern there. An obligation. Something.

Rachel faced down a mob of vampires and werewolves and kicked ass. Maddox saw it. She'd have died there without that intervention.

She'd do it again, wouldn't she? Hauser thought. *She didn't protect Carlisle from us, but we're not monsters... maybe that's the difference?*

He stared at the report, waiting for it to come to him.

title

Look higher. Scroll up.

Hauser followed the silent advice, moving back on the report to the part before Rachel appeared. He read and re-read Carlisle's exchanges with the vampires. Their posturing. Their declarations. The tension Maddox saw between them, and her sense that they shared some obligation avenge Kanatova.

They have to kill Carlisle, or their social compact breaks down, something told Hauser without ever being heard. *They have to kill him.*

He considered explaining that to Carlisle—and maybe even Lorelei. Maybe that would be enough leverage to pry their mouths open.

A second, unbidden thought overrode the first: *Rachel must protect Carlisle. They must kill him... and she cannot allow that.*

We must take risks. Sacrifices must be made.

The room grew dark as he stared at the screen. The words repeated in his head over and over, drowning out other thoughts and objections until the unthinkable seemed rational, and even necessary:

We must take risks. Sacrifices must be made.

Hauser blinked and rubbed his eyes, looked out the window and then checked the clock. He closed his laptop, stood, and opened up the cabinet that served as the team's improvised evidence locker. Personal belongings confiscated from Carlisle, Jones and the rest sat in marked bins.

One particular bin held a leather jacket, a roll of cash, a pair of axes light enough for throwing, some old Nordic jewelry, and a partially dismantled cell phone. Hauser pulled out the latter, put the pieces back together and reactivated it.

Potentially, the owner's friends had enough connections that they could track the phone as soon as it turned back on. It seemed unlikely, though; while they weren't Luddites, they didn't catch on quickly to all the opportunities of modern technology. The organization and minimal usage of the phone in Hauser's hand testified to that. It did, however, have a mapping application.

Hauser scrolled through the contacts list. Few of the names meant anything to him. One name stood out for him, though he didn't think too much as to why.

Hauser opened up a text message to Unferth. He inserted a link to the mapping application... and paused.

Everyone knows the risks. Sacrifices must be made.

He hit the send button and then turned off the phone.

The angel speaking at his ear stepped back. Donald's hands slipped off Hauser's. His shoulders sagged as he experienced a bout of weariness normally unknown to his kind.

Guardian angels offered suggestions and guidance to their charges all the time. It required imagination and finesse, but little effort. Direct manipulation such as this—something Donald had never attempted before—drained him much more than he expected.

It would be worth it, though. It was all for the greater good.

BELLEVUE OFFERED a number of posh houses, but even this one wasn't remotely as opulent as Wentworth's Manhattan home. The area likely boasted grander lodgings, but as in any matter of travel as this, one had to weigh stealth and discretion over comfort. Claim too great a home and the neighbors and friends of the owners might notice the changes in their behavior. The less wealthy the resident, typically, the easier it was for new occupants to go unnoticed... but Wentworth had his standards.

Wentworth awoke shortly after sunset, moving swiftly from oblivion to full awareness as he usually did. In his breathing days, he would shift and stretch and groan about the earliness of the hour or whatever noises his servants made. Now his eyes simply snapped open, suddenly marking him as an animate corpse rather than an ordinary dead body in a bed.

He found the lady of the house and her adult daughter kneeling before his bed—no longer the mother's or her husband's in his mind—dressed in nightgowns just as he had instructed. They waited for him to drink from them, happy to be made of such use. Any vampire could bestow pain and terror or addictive, mind-bending euphoria through their bite. To Wentworth, the latter seemed the obvious choice. Terrorized servants always harbored thoughts of escape or rebellion, both of which bred inefficiency. Well-rewarded slaves, like his host family, gladly opened their homes and threw familial obligations to the wind in hopes of enjoying the brief ecstasy of his fangs.

Wentworth fed lightly upon them both, leaving them on the bed in a state of bliss while the man of the house dressed him. Satisfied, he ventured out of the bedroom to check on his staff and allies. His mortal servants from New York would have been up through the day, monitoring events in his home city and the local news here in the northwest. One waited outside his door to hand him a copy of the New York Times as he walked through the halls.

His eyes stayed on the paper as he moved, but his mind wandered. Tonight would see a final meeting of his allies and an assessment of their quest for justice. If he could not demonstrate his ability to find Carlisle again, the coalition would fray. All understood the need to kill the boy. Regardless of Anastacia's fate, Carlisle's existence was simply intolerable after what he had said and what he did to Cornelius. But first he had to be found, and clearly his guardian presented a formidable problem. Wentworth counseled patience and recovery as his allies licked their wounds, but he worried that inaction would weaken his position of leadership.

He descended the stairs as he read the headlines. Rounded the landing and shuffled down the hall. Reconsidered his support of a candidate for mayor. Pushed open the door to the kitchen. Passed by the sliding glass door and the deck overlooking the backyard. Glanced up at the gaggle of strangers staring at him from the other side of the glass. Crossed the kitchen to the dining room to double-check seating plans for the meeting tonight.

Stopped. Turned. Looked again.

A collection of roadside trash stood on the deck, all looking into the kitchen. A man and woman wore the denim and leather chaps of bikers. Two or three of the others, dressed in ordinary faded jeans and t-shirts, immediately struck Wentworth as truckers. The tall woman at the front of the group with her hair cut down to a short brown stubble looked like some hippie hoping to hitch a ride on the freeway... except for the intensity in her eyes and the cocky attitude of her grin.

She reached up to tap on the glass with her fingernails and then gave a small sarcastic wave.

Though vampires did not need to breathe, Wentworth maintained the habit to keep up appearances. He evaluated the newcomers and the overall situation in the time it took to inhale and let the air out again with a disgusted grumble. Then he stepped forward to unlock and slide open the glass door.

"I trust you have not slain or unduly harmed my sentries?" he asked irritably.

"Not at all," the woman replied in a mildly defensive tone. "We came to talk."

"Yes, I know." He noted the quizzical rise of her eyebrow and gestured for her to enter. "Even if you had overwhelming force, your instincts would still compel you to attack with stealth and surprise. This assembly is meant to impress me with the strength you have chosen *not* to use," he explained, gesturing to the others.

The woman stepped inside and offered her hand with a smile. "I am Diana."

"Wentworth, Lord Mayor of New York," nodded the vampire. He took her hand, then dropped it to eye her companions. "I presume you will want someone to accompany you inside?"

"I wouldn't want to fall prey to your hypnotic stare," she said, her lips pursed with amusement. "Billy. Come in, please," Diana gestured to the scruffiest of the bunch. To his credit, he removed his ball cap and held it in both hands.

Wentworth didn't look at him long enough to allow for introductions. He gestured to the table and chairs at the breakfast nook, not waiting for his guests to take a seat before he claimed one for himself with a clear path to the exit. Diana pointed to a chair for Billy before she took her own.

"I take it you're the alpha wolf?" Wentworth asked, doing his best to smother his unpleasant mood.

"That's not a term we use, actually," said Diana. "The concept of alpha wolves came from studies done solely on wolves in captivity. They don't act like that in the wild." She fixed him with a steady gaze. "And whatever our animal natures, we are not mere animals. We are still people with human brains."

"Indeed," Wentworth said. He gave a curt nod of acknowledgement. "Then I would ask if you lead this group, or if instead you speak for the leader? I had thought the packs of this area answered to one called Caleb?"

"Caleb is dead. I have succeeded him. The packs answer to me."

"Excellent. You are already far more poised and pleasant than any other of your kind I have met." For a brief moment, Wentworth considered his further questions and the value of small talk. He promptly decided to forego all of that. "What do you want?"

She tilted her head to acknowledge his forthright manner. "Apparently I want something I cannot have." She waited to see if he understood the implication and then explained, "You and yours meant to kill him the other night."

"Carlisle," Wentworth said darkly.

"Yes. I only arrived as things got out of hand there. A packmate observed you and the rest for a short bit before that, but he didn't quite understand what was going on. You blame him for what happened to the vampires of Seattle?"

"We do," confirmed Wentworth, "though likely not Carlisle alone." He considered his next words carefully. "We are aware that the Lady Anastacia held you prisoner at the time."

"Yes," Diana nodded. "I escaped as a result of all that happened, though I don't claim to understand all that went on or why. I first met Carlisle while we were both prisoners. We helped one another escape, though his associates came to his rescue at about that same time. You met one the other night—the angel."

"Do you know if he killed the Lady Anastacia?"

Diana shook her head. "I don't know for sure, but I don't think so. I don't know who specifically killed her. Alex had other matters on his mind at the time. Anastacia and her court were a complication for him, not a focus. You are aware of the demon?"

"I am aware of *a* demon, yes," Wentworth emphasized deliberately. "We have not met. Cornelius recognized her name and perhaps knew her, but he did not elaborate. Now he is gone, at Carlisle's hands and in front of many witnesses. Even if he did not murder the Lady, there is blood on his hands that cannot be ignored. Your kind may be our enemy, but none would question the practicality of calling a truce, or at least talking like this. Carlisle is mortal. He is livestock."

She smiled faintly. "I see. If you let that slide, what's next? They'll let women vote and allow blacks to use public restrooms?"

"Precisely so," Wentworth agreed, "and then—!" He stopped himself, his mind only then catching up to his mouth. He frowned. "Cute." He paused to consider his next words. "You intervened before he was killed in the bus tunnel, but you also fought the angel. You say Carlisle is something you cannot have?"

"He would have made an excellent mate," nodded Diana, "but I see now that those two whores have ruined him. The angel and the demon," she elaborated when his eyebrow rose. "I won't bore you with the details."

"You're too kind," Wentworth deadpanned. "So if that's the case, then why haven't you and your pack moved on? Oh, no, wait. Don't tell me," he said, holding up one hand. "If you can't have him, no one will?"

"That is one way of putting it, yes. Mr. Wentworth, does this amuse you?"

"Somewhat," he mused, tapping idly on the table. "You have such poise and diction. You're clearly educated. This blend of post-graduate sophistication and trailer park murder motives is quite striking."

Silent until now, Billy all but choked. Diana's eyes narrowed. Neither reaction seemed to bother the vampire in the slightest. "Mr. Wentworth," she asked, "why is it that your kind and mine don't get along?"

The vampire snorted. "We like to see ourselves as unchallenged masters of our territories. We're predators and we don't like threats or competition. The same goes for your kind. Naturally, we don't like anything that unsettles those perceptions."

"Is there no deeper reason than that?" Diana pressed thoughtfully. "You come from a society of people who live for centuries. Surely there are stories of how all this conflict originated? Where your kind and mine came from?"

Taken aback by her question and her earnest expression, Wentworth found himself at a loss. "This not a turn I expected in our conversation," he said, "though I didn't exactly expect to talk to you tonight at all. We might do best to stick with one subject at a time."

She sat back in her chair, looking disappointed. "Fine. You lost many of your fighters the other night—some to my pack, a couple to Alex and his friends, but mostly to the angel, correct?"

"Correct," confirmed Wentworth.

"And you plan to pursue your vendetta?"

"We must."

"Then you will face the angel again. Your forces are not up to that task." She waited for him to object, but he did not. "We hurt her."

"Did you now?" Wentworth asked mildly.

"Yes," said Diana. He couldn't help but note a glint of bloodlust in her eye. "We were distracted by your fighters. We were unprepared to face her. But given a second chance, without such complications? We would end her. I am sure of it."

"You've come to offer an alliance?"

"I came to offer a deal, anyway. We help you against the angel—and the demon, who will undoubtedly get involved before this is all over—and you cede Seattle to me. It's rather shy on resident vampires these nights, anyway." Again, she offered a friendly smile. "You'll be a hero among your kind. Peace with a werewolf pack, vengeance for your lost associates, and the statement that not even Heaven itself can strike at you without being paid back in kind. And you'll have the chance to see Alex dead—by your hands or by our claws, what does it matter?"

Wentworth considered her words. She offered a better deal than she knew.

"I have to wonder why you don't simply go after all this on your own if you're so sure of your power?"

"Two reasons. First, we have the strength, but we have lost the scent. Your kind always has greater resources than mine."

"And the other?"

"As much as I might want to snuff out Carlisle and his friends," said Diana, "I *could* walk away from all of this. My rage does not outweigh my interest in survival. I come to you offering aid and alliance because you have something to offer."

Wentworth's eyebrows rose. "And that would be...?"

"Immortality."

The proposal shocked him. It plainly shocked her companion, too, but he could not even form words to voice an objection. A single glance from Diana ensured his cowed silence.

Wentworth paused to let the implications catch up. "You understand that you would not become some hybrid powerhouse?" he asked. "Those are myths. You would become like us, but the beast within you would die in the transition."

"Your kind is not without power," said Diana. "Certain conversations have lately convinced me that longevity is preferable to primal might for souls like ours."

Again, Wentworth took the moment to think. As much as he wanted to take her up on her proposal, the truth was that Carlisle's trail had gone cold.

Then the kitchen door opened. Unferth walked in carrying a cell phone in his hands and murder in his eyes.

16

SHADOWS

Normal children feared the dark. They knew monsters lurked in the shadows, waiting to pounce. Darkness hid mundane dangers, too. One could so easily trip over something unseen, or get lost, or tumble down a hole. Nobody liked it when they couldn't see. But children understood that darkness could hold more than just loose toys or tree roots. Children knew that monsters preferred the darkness.

That had been Onyx's first clue that she wasn't normal. She liked being alone in the dark just fine. If monsters could hide there, so could she.

It helped that her sight and hearing had always been so sharp. Onyx often sensed trouble before it found her. She didn't recognize this talent until later in life, when her fascination with fictional magic led her to real research, and then dabbling and one day actual practice. Onyx learned to use senses beyond her eyes and ears, but she also learned to make the most of those natural gifts.

She could deal with a cloudy, moonless night. She could handle wet grass and tall trees. She could handle fog, too... even if it had been summoned up by her companion.

Molly followed close behind Onyx, partly distracted by the need to maintain her hold on the fog. A month ago, this would have been much more difficult. Neither woman expected that an exodus of most of the other Practitioners of the city—those that survived the fight at Kanatova's party—would make it easier to work their own magic. They couldn't complain about the outcome.

Fewer Practitioners in a given place meant more power for those who remained.

As always, mundane effort made magic that much more effective. Onyx and Molly dressed for the task in dark pants and black jackets. They moved with care and deliberate stealth. They avoided the roads, the parking lots and trails that ran through the park.

Beyond the tree line stretched an expanse of unkempt grass. Past that lay a parking lot, and on the other side of that stood a broad, three-story brick building. Onyx pointed to the building, then put her hand in Molly's and whispered in her ear to briefly share the supernatural acuity of her vision.

"Occupied," Molly murmured softly. It was obvious enough. Several cars sat outside the building. There were lights on, too—but in each window, drapes or blinds covered the lights.

"No signs on the building, either," whispered Onyx. "UW and NOAA marked all the buildings they use. All the other old Navy buildings got boarded up or..." Onyx fell silent, placing a hand on Molly's shoulder. She turned her head toward sounds Molly couldn't hear. Her hand gripped tightly in sudden alarm.

Molly already had her wand in hand. She twirled it in her fingers to hold it pointing down, pushed herself and Onyx back against the nearest tree and plunged the tip of her wand into the soft, wet earth. Slowly and silently, the tree branches bent lower around them. The grass at their feet grew higher, and with it the stems of rhododendrons that had never gone into bloom. The bushes rose almost a foot with each breath the women took. It was imperfect cover, but in the darkness they didn't need more than that. They only needed something to break up the sight lines.

Another breath passed. Then another. Eventually, Molly heard the soft padding of footsteps from behind them. Her eyes turned right and she saw what Onyx had heard: a huge grey wolf, over three feet tall at the shoulder, sniffing through the grass. Molly kept one hand on her wand. The other gently reached into the pocket of her jacket to pull out a few leaves. She inhaled from her right and exhaled to her left, dropping the leaves to her left.

Onyx watched intently. She felt the breeze shift, bringing them downwind of the wolf. She heard it sniff and watched its ears twitch, but the beast seemed to relax its vigilance. It sat to look over its shoulder and let out a soft whine.

It waited. Molly and Onyx could do little but watch and listen. Each could deal with a mere wolf. Neither one thought for a second that it was that simple.

Onyx heard the others before Molly did. A silent gesture and a squeeze of her shoulder told her partner how to shift the wind again to give them the best chance of remaining undetected. Molly did so with some effort, knowing that she would soon lose her hold on the fog as a result of all this. It seemed a small price to pay when the other wolves appeared to their left and to their right, sitting or standing in wait uncomfortably close to their tree.

Even Onyx barely heard the arrivals that followed before she could see them. Human shapes in black clothing of wildly varying styles emerged from the darkness. Some carried weapons. Others appeared empty-handed. With her sharp eyes and even the minimal light from the building, Onyx could see the wolves' breath. As near as she could tell, these people didn't breathe at all... and they were many.

A LOUD, pounding fist on the door snapped Lorelei and Rachel from their silent embrace. Lorelei still sat in her chair, with her arms restrained behind its backrest by several pairs of handcuffs. Rachel knelt beside her, arms still wrapped around Lorelei's waist. The angel was indifferent to the cold, hard tile. Lorelei lifted her head from Rachel's shoulder. Rachel turned to look back at the door as it opened a mere inch.

"Hey in there," a man asked, "do you need food, or is that not a thing for you?"

"Yes," Lorelei answered. "I hunger."

"Sandwiches okay? Or do you have crazy demon dietary requirements?"

"I will take what I can."

"Is it my imagination," asked Rachel, "or were those loaded statements?"

"If Alex cannot sate my needs, I must tend to them myself," Lorelei murmured with her eyes still on the door. "You always please me, but I draw more strength from mortals. My power returns too slowly. I grow bored with this place."

Rachel's eyes widened as she slipped back from her lover. The sinister tone in Lorelei's words sent a wave of desire through the angel. "Woah, wait a fuckin' sec here," she stammered. "You're not gonna—I mean—oh fuck, you are, aren't you?"

"My opportunities are dictated by who comes through that door. The women of this group would not be susceptible. Much as I would love to ruin

Hauser, he is undeserving." Lorelei's head tilted curiously. "I suppose I have changed more than I thought."

"Yeah, but... I mean... uh..."

"They could always refuse me."

"Name one mortal who ever turned you down?"

"Alex."

"Yeah, for like a *day*," Rachel noted.

Lorelei nodded solemnly. "It was amazing." Her eyes turned to Rachel's. They all but left her melting. "To be fair, I was in much worse shape at the time. Don't worry. I'll be gentle."

"Gentle?"

"I may plant suggestions and reassurance, but the fun is in the temptation. Blunt mind control is for brutes and amateurs." She grinned wickedly. "They have to give in willingly in the end if either of us are to enjoy it."

The door came unlocked again. First to enter was one of the guards, still clad in black BDUs and body armor. Following him was one of the agents carrying a simple fast food bag and a drink.

Lorelei smiled. "Agent Bridger. I hoped to see you again. Who is your friend?"

Bridger hesitated. So did the guard. It lasted only a heartbeat, but Lorelei saw it. So did the invisible angel in the room.

"I'm Theo—"

"I'm not sure we want to get into all that," Bridger interrupted.

"Must we be so extreme?" Lorelei asked. "You no doubt wove spells to defend the both of you against malevolent influence. I can only talk to you, and I mean none of you harm. Please, Agent Bridger, Theo, *relax. Do not fear me.*"

Standing against one wall to bear witness, Rachel winced. She knew that tone and the effect it could have. Sure enough, she saw a slight change in the stance and body language of the two men. They didn't let their guard down completely, but it was enough to signal Lorelei's success. Bridger's sorcery wasn't strong enough to block out Lorelei's supernatural influence. Neither man appeared capable of ignoring her natural charms, either.

Oblivious to the angel, Theo took up a spot beside Lorelei. He rested his hands over his belt buckle in a ready stance. He then adjusted his pants while no one looked—no one except the angel on the other side of the room, at least, who covered her face with one embarrassed hand.

Bridger stood directly in front of Lorelei, his expression still one of wariness and professionalism. "I'm a little surprised that you need food. Everything I have read about succubi says that's not the case."

"Succubae, Agent Bridger," Lorelei corrected. She stared up at him, leaning forward as much as her bonds allowed. Her choice of outfits hadn't focused on showing off any of her assets, but posture alone conveyed the proper message. "You may find the accuracy of your research is mixed. You must *open yourself* to personal experience if you wish true mastery of a subject."

Bridger's eyes fluttered. "What's inaccurate?"

"I don't presume to have read all there is to read," Lorelei said, "but I imagine your sources paint me as a dangerous woman eager to fuck men to death for my own enjoyment?" No objective observer would miss the seductive tones and slow, enticing cadence of her voice. Again, she glanced at Theo, wanting to make sure he felt engaged in this conversation. "I cannot harm anyone in a *single, casual tryst.*" She smiled. "Sometimes it's *just for fun.*"

"We just came in here to give you a dinner break and go," he said, swallowing hard. "It's not an interrogation or anything."

"Does it have to be an interrogation for us to talk?" she asked. "I'm much friendlier in private settings."

"Shit, the door," Theo muttered. He stepped over to close it.

"What are you...?" blinked Bridger.

"*Relax,*" Lorelei repeated. "It's just us. No one needs to know. *No one will know.*" Once again, both men lost some of their wariness. Their eyes fluttered. Every word carried alluring notes. Her lips spread in a smile subtle enough to seem natural despite the setting. "I cannot hurt you. I am bound. If I were able to escape, I'd have done so before now, wouldn't I?"

"She's got a point," said Theo.

Bridger shot him a look. "Let me do the talking, alright?"

"Oh, we don't have to be like that," Lorelei said. She glanced to each of the men standing over her, feeling her power rise as their willpower and common sense waned. "I can accommodate both of you."

Rachel slapped her other hand over her face.

ALEX STOOD and held out his hands as instructed. A guard came in and cuffed his right wrist, and then his left—but this time the cuffs went on with his hands in front rather than behind his back. Alex looked down quizzically at his bonds and then up toward the door again. He found the answer in the form of a sandwich and a soda in Keeley's hands.

"Have a seat," Keeley gestured to the cot. It was the only furniture in the old office. Keeley stepped inside and held the food out to Alex once he sat down. The guard left, closing the door behind him. Keeley leaned up against it, folding his arms over his chest and taking up a relaxed stance. "How are you holding up?"

"I'm not sure how to answer that," said Alex. Given the handcuffs, he fumbled around a bit as he unwrapped his food. "I figured if I got food at all, you'd probably just handcuff me to another chair and spoon-feed me. Or put me on a liquid diet."

"Hey, like Hauser said, you've got some crazy skills. I figure you haven't practiced fighting in handcuffs, though. Not many people do. Y'know, we have the story Cohen told Amber, but you're the one with all the memories, right?"

"What is it you want to know?" Alex asked. He opened up the sandwich to see what was in it, just to make sure it wasn't drowned in some foul dressing. Something inside said to eat it regardless. Those fragmented memories Keeley hinted at all agreed that he should never pass up an opportunity to eat or nap while in trouble like this.

Keeley huffed. "Hell, everything. Anything. I'm a history buff."

"I don't remember things clearly," Alex shook his head. "A lot of it is a jumble. It's like I can't be sure what I actually remember, what I'm imagining, and what I piece together between bits of memory and stuff I've seen on TV or read in books."

"I gather it's not pleasant?"

Alex chewed on his sandwich. "No," he said, then gulped hard. "Mostly not."

"Do you feel older and wiser since all those memories came along? Or do you still feel like you're twenty?"

"A little of both," Alex shrugged. "The memories aren't solid." He wondered where the agent wanted this conversation to go. "I feel like I just left behind a few hundred miles of emotional baggage, okay? I'm not eager to go delve back into it. You'd get more out of talking to a historian than you would out of me, 'cause I'd only know my own experiences. I'm pretty sure I did a lot of farming. Anyway, have you talked to the others already tonight? Or am I the first?"

"You're the first. Seems like you're the key player at this point. Alex, you get what we're trying to do here, don't you? I mean, I understand if you don't like Hauser. Hell, Hauser understands if you don't like Hauser."

"Good for him," Alex said abruptly.

Keeley shrugged it off. "Monsters are out there preying on people. We can't just expose them to the whole world. You know how crazy things would get. So we do the best we can here. You could help us do it all a lot better with what you and your friends know."

"We talk, you let us go, right?" Alex asked. "What about Lorelei?"

"Yeah, I figured that would be the catch for you, huh?" His smile faded. "She's a murderer, Alex. We don't get to let that go. We know about one guy she killed for sure, and you and I both know there are more. We've only begun investigating all that. She has to answer for her crimes. Whatever has happened between you and her, that doesn't go away, y'know? I mean, do you think she has told you everything she's ever done? You really think she's completely honest with you?"

"No demon has ever lied to me as often as my government."

"Point," Keeley snorted. "You've got me there."

"She's not what you think," Alex said. He felt too weary and glum to get upset talking about it now.

"She's not a demon?" Keeley asked. "Not a succubus?" He watched the younger man sigh and take another bite of his sandwich without answering. "I know you love her and I've heard what you've been through together, but does that make up for murder? Can you tell me why she shouldn't be punished for all that?"

Alex considered his words as he chewed and swallowed. "I've met the sort of people she used to answer to," he said. "I've seen where she came from. I don't think you or I know the first thing about punishment."

"You know, we told her that if she comes clean, we'd let the rest of you go. Clean slate for all four of you, no further trouble from us. Think she'll go for that?"

"Why are you asking me?"

"Because you live with her. Because you're in love with her."

"I think she's smart enough not to get suckered by that kind of logic. Sorry."

"Even so," Keeley pressed gently, "you've seen what she really looks like now. You know she hasn't been honest with you about everything. You don't have any doubts about her?"

Alex paused. He lowered the sandwich from his mouth, staring off into space thoughtfully. "You know what's tough about this relationship?" he asked. "You know what the biggest problem is in being with someone like Lorelei?"

Keeley said nothing, but gestured for Alex to continue. He leaned in to listen.

"All the fucking people trying to *invent* reasons for me not to trust her."

"Mostly I hoped to talk to a man who might understand me a little better than ordinary mortal men," Lorelei said to the increasingly interested agent before her. He couldn't help but notice how she said 'man.' No one in the room could.

"Oh, I understand you, babe," grinned Theo, hoping to catch her eyes.

He failed at that. Lorelei only had eyes for Bridger. "I'd like to understand you much better," the agent said, feeling his confidence build.

"I believe you could," she smiled back approvingly. "Mystics like yourself have so few of the hang-ups and preconceived notions of modern society. You're already free from so many social mores. So many silly taboos."

"Well, y'know," Theo tried again, "it ain't just mystics who are open-minded."

"Theo, take a break," Bridger said, his eyes still on Lorelei.

"*Yes, Theo. Take a break,*" Lorelei repeated, holding that gaze. "*Cover for us, will you? And turn off the cameras while you're away.*"

The last vestiges of Theo's common sense and self-control rallied one last time as he blinked. "The cameras...?"

"Yes. That way we'll have some privacy when you come back to me. *Later.*"

"Oh," Theo agreed. His spirits soared as his willpower crumbled. "Right." With that, Theo stepped out of the room and shut the door.

"Well," grumbled Rachel, "that's one less pissy guardian angel I'll hear from over this—" Then she stopped. One less angel. The moment was down to Lorelei and Bridger, the dabbler in sorcery... who by definition had no guardian angel.

"Wow," Rachel blinked. "That was damn considerate of you."

"I thought we might have more fun if things were one on one," said Lorelei.

"I shouldn't have done that," Bridger said without a trace of regret. "Now I'm all alone in a room with a demon."

"I think you know better than that," Lorelei said, working him over with her eyes and voice alone. "I think you know these bonds will hold me. Your sorcery protects you. I'm rather more at your mercy than one might expect."

"I think you're right," Bridger nodded, coming closer. "I think you like it, too."

"It helps that you're nice to look at," she conceded.

"Am I, now?"

"Yes. And no ring on that finger. No Mrs. Bridger at home? No girlfriend?"

"Not a lot of time for romance," Bridger shook his head. "Not in my lines of work, anyway."

"Such a shame," Lorelei tutted. "So much to offer. So much to appreciate. You have a nice face. I'd love to see more of you."

"Does that go both ways?"

"Of course," Lorelei breathed onto his lips. "We were talking about under-standing one another better, weren't we?"

Rachel watched Lorelei kiss Bridger and felt a deep, lustful shudder over-take her. Part of her hoped Alex wouldn't get too upset over this. Most of her just wanted the show to continue.

One wish came true right away.

———

"WE'RE on the wrong side of this, Paul," Nguyen declared as Keeley stepped into the old, barely-furnished break room.

"Y'think?" Keeley frowned. He looked to Lanier, who sat beside Nguyen at the table rubbing his eyes. "Where's Bridger?"

"Theo says he's in the bathroom, wasn't feeling well," Lanier grumbled. "They took demon chick her dinner and that was that. Theo took over for me on the security set-up so I could come talk to you."

"No problems there?" Keeley asked.

"I didn't see any. Red Bull and Starbuck's won't make for eternal vigilance, though," sighed Lanier. "I'm sure it's fine."

"Well, I wanted Bridger to be here, but I don't want to sit conspiring all suspicious-like for long."

"This might sound dumb," Lanier put in, "but do we want Amber here?"

"No," Keeley shook his head. "No way. She's too close to all this as it is. I don't want to drag her into this if it blows up in our faces, either."

"I already talked to Bridger," said Nguyen. "He's of the same mind as us. We have to call. Hauser might bite our heads off for jumping the chain of command, but I can't see a way around it. Oswalt needs to know what's happening."

"Matt?" Keeley asked, looking to Lanier.

"Yeah. We gotta call."

"Agreed. Okay." Keeley let out a long breath. "I'll do it."

"It might be a long call," said Nguyen. "What do we tell Hauser if he asks for you?"

"Know what? I'll just go on a Starbuck's run for Lanier," Keeley grinned. "I can't shake the feeling that something's creeping up on me here, anyway."

LORELEI SANK down onto Bridger's lap with a grateful moan, savoring the first moments of penetration. She rocked against him for a few moments, closing her eyes to enjoy herself. Her arms were still restrained by multiple handcuffs, but they hardly prevented her from getting what she wanted.

Bridger's hands felt good on her naked hips. His lips on her neck pleased her, too. She hadn't lied to him about his looks. He would be even more attractive when she was done with him, too. Unlike Molly and Onyx, Bridger's magical wards didn't block the beneficial changes she made on the bodies of her partners. The hard flesh thrusting into her made that abundantly clear.

She felt glad for it. Not only did it enhance her pleasure, but it seemed the least she could do to make up for his inevitable feelings of regret. Once again, Lorelei was reminded of her soft spot for good guys.

She was also reminded of how good it felt to be genuinely naughty.

Her eyes opened to see Bridger's face overcome with passion. She swam in his feelings of lust and pleasure, drawing strength and power with every passing second. Her lips came down onto his, kissing him hard and invading his mouth with her tongue.

Behind the chair, Rachel watched breathlessly. She didn't feel jealousy, but no display like this could leave her without at least a little envy. Her commentary died on her lips. She didn't want to spoil the moment.

"Unbutton my shirt," Lorelei breathed against Bridger's cheek.

"Mh. You uncomfortable?"

"No," she grinned fiercely, "but you'll like what you see."

Bridger grinned back. He had no doubt of that. Lorelei leaned back and kept working his sex within hers, demonstrating the incredible strength and control of her lower body to his immense pleasure as his hands fumbled with her shirt. The sight of her breasts encased in a black lace bra gave him an extra thrill. He ran his hands over her belly and up her sides before he unfastened the bra at its center.

Glad for the lustful hands on her breasts, and then for the mouth that followed, Lorelei let out a sigh of pleasure. Bad enough that she'd had to skip right to this with so little foreplay. It was a shame to reduce this to so brief an experience.

Catching sight of Rachel behind her partner, though, Lorelei focused on her true goals. Pleasant as Bridger was, she had greater lovers to be with.

"Give in to this," she hissed into Bridger's ear. She leaned forward, eagerly crushing her body against his. Her hips kept moving, masterfully crushing his self-control. "We haven't much time. Give in to me. Let go."

"Why... why rush?" he asked.

"We can't get caught," Lorelei reminded him. She fixed him with a wicked smile. "If we are caught, we can't do this again."

Bridger liked the sound of that. "I feel like I could go any moment."

"Then let it happen," she encouraged him.

"But... you?"

"Don't worry about me. I'm not like other women. I will be satisfied. Give in to your urges, Douglas. Give in to your lusts. *Give in.*"

He didn't need the extra encouragement, but it brought out his basest desires just the same. Bridger claimed her hips again with his hands and moved them in tune with his most selfish needs. His breath grew louder as orgasm drew near. Bridger's eyes opened to the sight of the most beautiful woman he'd ever met swept away by passion. He'd wanted her ever since he first looked at her. Anyone would, he thought. Now he had her in his lap, at his mercy and loving it.

Carnal joys brought him past the point of no return before he knew it. Bridger watched as Lorelei came in the same moment as his glorious release. They shared a long, passionate climax that forced his eyes shut once more.

The rush subsided. His body began to relax. His eyes fluttered open once more. His eyes drank in the sight of Lorelei's mostly naked body. She rolled her shoulders as if to work out a kink. He felt her tense against him.

With a rippling sound of snapping metal, Lorelei pulled her arms apart. Links from each set of handcuffs went flying through the air behind her.

Bridger's eyes went wide as her hands swiftly wrapped around his head. Her lips came down onto his for one last deep, forceful kiss that stole his breath away.

"*Relax. Rest. Sleep.*" She stroked his cheek soothingly. "You were great."

Bridger slumped in his seat. Lorelei stepped around him to come face to face with the lover who stood behind him. "Sssoooo," Rachel managed. "Need an after-fuck drink? Vodka martini, shaken, not stirred?"

She shook her head, taking hold of the angel's hands. "Thank you."

"Thank... me?" Rachel blinked. "For what?"

"For understanding. For trusting me. For accepting me for what I am."

"I'm not the one we need to worry about here."

"No," Lorelei agreed. "You are not." She turned to get back to business. Rachel tugged on her hands.

"You *are* gonna make it up to me later, though, right?"

"COFFEE RUN," muttered Keeley.

"Another one?" asked the guard.

"I know," the agent grumbled back, "I'm turnin' into a native. Want any? Gotta be tough sitting here in the dark like this."

The guard station was just inside the first hallway intersection near the side entrance. Frank had a large, old wooden desk to sit at, but his only light came from the laptop that showed the security cameras ringing the building. The sub-machinegun on the desk and Frank's body armor would likely provide a good visual deterrent to any trouble, but he wasn't there for deterrence. "Nah. Caffeine will just keep me up all night after my watch is over. I'm good."

Keeley snorted. "Suit yourself. It's the only way I ever got through stakeouts."

"Doesn't that leave you peeing in a bottle in your car all night?" the guard asked as Keeley walked away.

"Nice. Thanks for reminding me of all those good times." He waited for Frank to buzz the newly-installed security lock on the old, heavy door, then stepped outside.

Nighttime in November was cold, wet and extra dark. Keeley understood why Amber moved away. He shoved his hands in his pockets as he headed to the parking lot at the building across the road from his own. All he heard was his feet sloshing through wet grass left to grow wild.

The figures stalking him from three different directions never made a sound.

Keeley walked to his car with a heavy heart. He wondered if he was about to end his friend's career. Either way, this would surely damage that friendship. Hauser was gruff, direct and often unsympathetic, but Keeley knew his boss was also a dedicated agent and a good man. He'd just lost perspective. It happened in the job sometimes. That was why the system had so many checks and balances.

Arriving at his car, he found himself face to face with a pretty Latina in dark jeans and a leather jacket. She seemed to appear out of nowhere. Her icy blue eyes stared into his. "Hey there," she said with a cool, friendly smile. "I'm a little lost. Can you help me?"

His eyes threatened to close, but he managed to keep them open. Even so, Keeley's vision blurred around the edges. As if in a dream he knew would turn to terror at any moment, Keeley felt his chest constrict and his shoulders tense. In the back of his mind, he knew he should cry out, but he couldn't. He wanted to snap out of his reverie, wanted to flee or seize the situation, but his body wouldn't respond. He couldn't look away from her hypnotic eyes.

"What're... what're you doing out here?" he managed. His voice seemed just as weak as his muscles.

Other shapes moved at the edges of his vision. Human shapes. Humans and... dogs? Big dogs. Huge ones.

"Looking for a friend. I like you, though. Will you be my friend?"

Someone stepped up behind him. Firm hands took hold of his arms. The Latina moved in close, intimately sliding her hands up his chest. Keeley wanted to object, but his mouth wouldn't work. She brought her fingertips to his cheeks, then turned and tilted his head. Just like whoever held him from behind, she seemed surprisingly strong. Her body pressed up against his as she put her lips against his neck.

He felt the bite. Felt her drain him. Wanted to resist, wanted to fight back, but he couldn't. The sensation felt so good it frightened him, and left him hating himself for even feeling that. His breath came out in short, shallow gasps as she took and took and took.

"Not too much, Rosario," someone counseled. "Just enough to break him in."

"We could try the other way," growled the man holding Keeley in place.

"I'll take it under advisement."

"Don't test me, Wentworth. They have my brother."

"And we will resolve that," said the calmer and wiser voice.

"Nuh... not gonna... no," Keeley gasped as the kiss pulled away from his neck. Already his clouded mind longed for more. "No, don't... no..."

"You can have more if you want it," said Rosario as she stroked his face, "but you have to help me and my friends. Look at me, baby. Don't resist. What's your name?"

"Paul. My name's Paul."

"Hello, Paul. You're going to be mine from now on, okay? You're going to be mine and you're going to help me along tonight."

Paul's shoulders slackened. He felt lightheaded and confused. He asked, trying to make his objection plain in his tone, "How... what do you want me to do?"

"You see, Unferth?" asked Wentworth. "She's a natural. Cornelius chose well."

"What's this?" Rosario asked, pulling the gun from Keeley's shoulder holster. She patted around his pockets, found his wallet, opened it and held it out to Wentworth. "Is this what it feels like?" she asked, her eyes still fixated on Keeley's.

"Damnation," Wentworth hissed. "This was only a matter of time."

Keeley heard more dogs approach. Someone walked with them—a woman, he could tell, wearing a long skirt and a coat. It was all he could tell from his peripheral vision. Rosario's blue eyes still held his focus.

"I'll not share my kill with the bitch," Unferth hissed beside Keeley's ear.

"The bitch has good ears, you know," the newcomer said. "Who have we here?"

"Proof that this situation is as complicated as I feared," answered Wentworth. "Mortal authorities are involved, and doubtlessly aware of whom they hold. The entire operation must be seized. We cannot simply smash down the door."

"Oh, I'm sure any one of mine could get through those doors," mused the woman, "or at least the windows."

"Not without alerting those inside," Wentworth countered. "They may call for help before we have taken the whole building. We must keep this isolated."

"I'll not put my brother at risk for your hurt feelings," Unferth added curtly. "I came here to get him out."

"Peace, please," Wentworth broke in. "We can work together on this. We all have a role to play, and we will all get what we want. Freeing Bjorn must come first. That requires stealth, not just brute force."

"You have a plan for that?" asked the woman.

"Paul can help us," said Rosario. "Can't you baby?" her cold fingers stroked his neck again, teasing his flesh where her fangs had been. "Is there a way inside?"

Keeley held his tongue. He couldn't tell her. He couldn't.

"There's a keypad on the outside that door," someone said.

"Aw, is that so?" Rosario asked. "Tell us the code, Paul."

"No," Keeley said.

Rosario raked his sensitive neck with her nails. The pain was so sharp he couldn't even cry out. "Maybe you didn't hear me the first time," she said, her voice still distressingly hypnotic. "You're mine now. You don't say no to me. 'No' is for people who can make their own decisions. You can't do that anymore... can you?"

Keeley's eyes watered. His body trembled with fear. He felt so weak. "No."

"How long will this take?" asked the other woman.

"Not long, I think," said Wentworth. "Rosario seems to be a natural at this."

Rosario's eyes wouldn't let Keeley go. She wouldn't even let him have his own thoughts.

———

AMBER KNOCKED on the door and waited for an answer before she entered. It seemed like the right thing to do. She was still part of the team, officially, and had as much right to be in the break room as the others, but at this point she wouldn't take anything for granted.

One of the tactical support guys answered the door. Amber offered up a polite but awkward smile and stepped around him into the makeshift break room. The tactical guys—those not on a watch, at least—seemed to all sit at one table. Two of her teammates sat at the other.

"You wanted to see me?" Amber asked Nguyen.

The older agent looked up from her book at Lanier rather than at Amber. "Did you tell her I wanted to see her?"

"You said to text her," shrugged the other agent across the small table.

"I said to invite her."

"Yeah, by text."

Nguyen rolled her eyes, then turned them toward Amber. "We're bored. I've got a deck of cards. You want to play?"

Amber's first instinct was to decline. This couldn't be more than a token effort. Maybe Hauser or Keeley put them up to it. Though they would never say so, both agents probably hoped Amber would just say no and leave so they wouldn't have to go through with this.

Grown-up Amber told downtrodden teenage Amber to take a hike. "Sure," she said, opting to see if there might be more to this. She pulled out a chair and sat down. "What's the game?"

"Just ordinary cards," answered Lanier as Nguyen pulled the deck out of her coat pocket. "Nothing fun or anything."

Nguyen raised an eyebrow as she shuffled. "What other kind of cards are there? You hoping I carry around a trivia deck or something?"

"Colleen here is one of those people who hears 'board game' and immediately thinks of Monopoly or Risk," Lanier smirked.

Again, Nguyen looked at the two like she didn't understand. "Matt knows I'm a geek like him," explained Amber.

"Yeah? And?"

"And geeks have better games," Amber shrugged. A smile twitched at her lips. "With, y'know, fun in them."

"I could throw these across the room and you two could play fifty-two card pick-up like my kids," Nguyen suggested.

"No, I'm good. Regular cards is fine." She paused as Nguyen dealt. "Thanks for inviting me."

"Yeah, well, I figured I know what everyone else is up to except for you," said Nguyen, "and I didn't want you sitting in a room alone staring at the walls."

Amber looked to Lanier. "How many cameras have you set up here, anyway?"

Lanier blinked. "Not that many. I'm not even watching them. She made me close up my laptop, see?"

"We've got a security watch going. You needed the break. Both of you," Nguyen added meaningfully.

"Well, anyway... thanks. I kind of was just staring at the walls, honestly."

"Feeling like you aren't really part of the team?" ventured Nguyen.

"Kinda, yeah. I've screwed up enough."

"No, you haven't," said Lanier as he sorted and righted his cards. "It's a crazy case, and it's your first assignment like this. We're all still making this stuff up as we go along."

"Pretty sure what I did was bad," Amber frowned. "And what I didn't do. I'm the one who turned up here in the back of someone's car with handcuffs on."

"We got our suspects in custody and nobody on our side got hurt," said Nguyen. "You're the only one here who's gone one on one with a demon woman, so I figure none of us have any right to throw stones. Things go wrong even with normal perps. And we're not here for the normal ones.

"Besides," she added, "this all went wrong when we arrested Reinhardt and Jones. You didn't have anything to do with that."

"What do you think will happen with them?" Amber asked.

"We'll have to let them go one way or another," shrugged Nguyen. "There's no way to prosecute them on the evidence we've got. It's just a matter of when Hauser gets that through his head. But that's kind of why we wanted to talk to you. I figure you've been walking around with everything hanging over your head, and it's time to tell you that this isn't your screw-up. You made some mistakes, but *you* didn't botch the case. We all did that without you. I figure by the time all this gets worked out, any of your goofs will just get rolled into the whole big ball of 'oops' and it won't even seem like that big of a deal."

"I'm ready to own my mistakes," said Amber.

"We know. That's part of the point."

Amber's eyes came up to Nguyen's. She understood then that Nguyen held back something significant in her reassurances. "What do you mean?"

"I'm just saying don't be in any hurry to start checking the want ads. This isn't over yet." She paused. "And you're not in the doghouse with any of us."

Silence held long enough for the three to look at their hands. "So you didn't call me down here to play cards."

"No," Nguyen sighed, "I don't even know what we're playing."

"I might have a different card game in my laptop bag," Lanier volunteered, "but I should warn you it's pretty offensive."

Amber's eyes lit up. "Do you have any of the expansions?"

KEELEY'S shuffling feet brought him to the door, but his remaining will fought to reassert itself. He felt so little control… or, really, so little of anything. His numb body moved slowly as he screamed and shouted inside to stop himself. Nothing seemed to work.

Others walked with him, but the cameras wouldn't see them.

He saw the door come closer. His hand rose toward the keypad. Trembling fingers stretched out to the buttons, inputting the proper sequence.

The system beeped. The door unlatched. Keeley's hand moved to the handle, but then it stopped. He refused.

He couldn't know how much strength and courage it took to assert himself even that much. He only thought, over and over, that he couldn't do this.

Rough, impatient hands shoved him aside. Unferth pushed past him and threw the door open. Keeley slumped against the doorframe, opening his mouth to cry out a warning, but all he could let out was noiseless breath.

Down the hall, Frank stood from his desk. "Forget somethin'?" he asked.

Moving with practiced skill and unnatural speed, Unferth drew one of the thin throwing axes from his belt and hurled it down the hall. With a sickening crunch, the blade of the axe landed inches deep in Frank's forehead.

Keeley watched him fall dead at his station as the vampires pushed past. His mind cried out an objection that his voice couldn't carry. Strong, familiar hands hoisted him up from beside the doorstep. "Come on, Paul," said Rosario, "keep it together. We might still need you."

"No," he whispered. She didn't hear him, which let him escape punishment. It also gave him the courage to say it again: "No."

———

IT WASN'T all about magic. Sometimes it was simply about body language and paying attention to who stood with whom. The magic certainly helped, though. Without it, Onyx could never have kept track of so many naturally stealthy creatures in a dark, rainy parkland.

The rain, though, had more to do with Molly. Working the weather like this was only a pipe dream a month ago. Now if Molly wanted fog, she brought it up from the lake. She wanted rain, and so she convinced the clouds to let go. Magic like that took serious concentration, though, so everything else fell to Onyx.

She had to maintain their spells of stealth, holding that power in the raven's feathers and opals wrapped in bay leaves clenched in her left hand. She served as the pair's eyes and ears. Molly's preoccupation also left Onyx relying on her own judgment as the vampires and werewolves came to the exterior of the building, spread out and then sent some of their own inside.

The pair remained hidden by virtue of the tree and the unnaturally large rhododendron bush. Onyx watched and learned, noticing the way the wolves and those who walked with them shied away from the vampires. They seemed impatient to Onyx, too, but animals were Molly's thing. Werewolves were far from natural, but that still meant that Onyx was no expert.

Yet she could read people just fine. Sometimes she could read small groups. The group of vampires clustered at the edge of the parking lot returned to the spot close to the witches' hiding place as several others guided their apparent captive to the side entrance and then inside.

Onyx wished desperately that she could do something for that poor guy the vampires had grabbed, but had to let it go. He was simply out of her reach. Any overt display of magic would only get her killed, and none of her subtler tricks seemed likely to work, either.

Given a few moments to hide, watch and think, Onyx hit on something practical. She fumbled in her pocket for a small plastic bag of ground black pepper and poppy seed. She murmured words in Greek, opening the bag to insert the tip of her ebony wand and then twisted it thrice. Onyx pulled her wand out and pointed it at the vampire in the suit and hat.

He looked around strangely, his head turning as if unsure of his surroundings or perhaps hearing things that weren't there. The vampire scratched his head and stepped back from his spot, looking to those around him with a questioning posture. He soon recovered—at least, outwardly—for he took on a confident posture and met those who came to him with strength and poise.

Onyx took what she could get. A leader with a clouded mind had to count against the group somehow. She watched the group for more opportunities, listened for trouble coming her way, and hoped she and all her friends would live to see the sunrise.

"CARLISLE IS in the janitor storage closet on the... third floor on the... on the corner." The words came from Keeley's mouth slowly and painfully. He tried to keep them in, but his mouth wouldn't do what he wanted. Thinking became harder and harder.

Unferth snatched the keys from Keeley's hands. "Which ones?" he hissed.

"Marked them," Keeley mumbled. "Red for the vampire. Green for... for the kid. No." The last word fell out so softly that no one heard it, even pressed together in the dark hallway. "No."

"Stay here," Unferth told the others, keeping his voice low. "I'll be faster and quieter alone."

"Wait, Unferth," Rosario urged. "We're just supposed to scout and report back, and only grab your brother if it looks easy."

"And I shall do that," he said, pushing past.

"Then why did you ask about—dammit!" she fumed as he rushed down the hallway. She turned her eyes to the other vampires in the hallway intersection. "He's gonna fuck up everything, ain't he?"

"Would you like to tell him no?" asked one of her companions. Francois had been one of Cornelius's favorites. Rosario had no clue why. He seemed like a reject from some Goth-wannabe version of the Three Musketeers, complete with frilly and lacy poet's shirt and black cloak. At least he didn't have a stupid hat.

"A little late now," shrugged another vampire. His English accent, pencil-thin mustache and beret did little to impress her, but his World War II fatigues and his old-fashioned machinegun denoted a certain level of competence. At least he seemed to understand how to work in a team.

Rosario let out a little sigh. Every one of these fucks was much older than her, but Wentworth decided she was in charge. Some shit about being the last scion of Cornelius or something. She could never tell if he was actually trying to show respect or if he just wanted to passive-aggressively bust her ass.

She shook her head and tried to take control of the situation again. "Okay, we gotta wait Unferth out a bit an' see if he can find his bro on his own, I guess. Maybe we need to get out of sight?"

"No one has appeared so far," noted Francois.

"We shouldn't be too worried. They have the demon locked up. How many of these blokes are there?" asked the soldier. He nudged the dead guard on the floor.

"Yeah, I guess," Rosario frowned. "I mean, you said there's the four guys, the demon an' your five FBI guys, right?" she asked Keeley. "So how many does that leave with this asshole dead? Four more pigs?"

"No," said the trembling man nearby. He winced as if he'd said something he didn't mean to say. "I... can't... no."

Rosario's brow knit as she caught on. "Wait, are you tryin' to hide somethin' from me?" she asked, stepping forward. She saw his fear as she drew close. "Four other agents, right? Is that all? Who else is there?"

"T... tac... no..."

"C'mon," she said, tracing her sharp nails against his neck as a warning. "Who else? Tac what?"

"Tactical... s-s-squad for sup... support. Security."

Rosario's eyes widened. "Oh, what the fuck? Seriously?" she asked. Her hand tightened around his neck. "How many of those? Are they like this guy? They're well-armed, right? How fucking many, *puto*?"

"S-s-suh six," Keeley mumbled. A tear welled up in his eye. "Six. Five now," he added, gesturing weakly to Frank on the floor.

"Aw, shit," Rosario winced. "We should warn the others."

"Should I go?" asked Francois.

"No," she said, pulling her cell phone out of her pocket. "I got it." She called up the screen and her messaging program.

Keeley looked down at her, and her phone, and his gun sticking out of her waistband just in reach. She didn't seem to notice him anymore. Standing still so as to be left ignored, his eyes went from her to Frank. Keeley barely knew more about him than his name. Now he was dead.

Keeley would be dead soon, too. Dead, like all his friends, because he couldn't think. Couldn't say no in anything more than a whisper. Couldn't fight back.

His eyes turned back to Rosario, and her phone, and his gun in her waistband.

His trembling hand reached up, slowly, to the gun. His muscles felt weak. Just moving like this took such effort, as if fighting against some invisible resistance that he knew was actually his own body and his own mind—

No. Not his own mind.

He'd die at least owning that.

Keeley's hand found the gun. His finger hooked the trigger before Rosario noticed. He managed two shots, sending bullets through her upper leg. Her femur snapped just below the hip joint before she fell. "Aagh! Fuck!" she screamed.

The gun stayed in his hand. It felt heavy, too heavy to turn and use, but also like salvation. His strength seemed to return in the form of the gun in his hand.

Then the butt of a rifle slammed into his head. A sword stabbed through his chest. Keeley fell to the floor beside Rosario, who roared in anger and reflexively went for the nearest source of fresh blood. This time, her kiss and her fangs were not kind.

He hadn't the strength to aim his weapon at anyone, but his gun was loud. It would at least warn his friends. It would disrupt his enemy. Paul Keeley died pulling the trigger of his gun until there were no bullets left. The flash of his muzzle lit the darkness with each shot.

He died fighting.

17

BY THE SWORD

Sleeping alone felt strange.

Alex lay in his cot under a pair of old, stiff Army blankets. The room was too cold to sleep without his shoes on, but he figured he could manage. Something about the blankets and the cot felt familiar. He'd slept like this before, in another life, or maybe in more than one. For once, the thought didn't bother him. He'd made his peace with all that yesterday, and last night.

Two women he adored helped set his head straight last night, and then invited him into their bed. Were it not for his interest in them—and his ridiculous and completely unnecessary effort to find an icebreaker—he wouldn't be here now. He wouldn't have Rachel and Lorelei in his life.

He wouldn't be lying here, thinking that it suddenly felt strange to sleep alone when he'd done exactly that for all but the last five or six weeks of his life.

He wondered if Lorelei would sleep tonight. He wondered where they kept her and when he might see her again. That brought unpleasant, unbidden thoughts.

You know what she looks like now. What she truly looks like.

She's a murderer. A monster. She's led you on for all this time.

Alex stared at the darkness above him, wishing he could silence the unwelcome voice in his head. He accepted Lorelei's past. He knew she had things to hide from him. If she wanted to hide her scars, was that wrong? Were they his business?

Life with Lorelei was nothing short of amazing.

She only wants to corrupt. She uses you. This fantasy life of easy sex and luxury is all distraction and manipulation. What does she do when you aren't looking?

She'll want other men. She'll whore around behind your back, if she hasn't already. You think you indulge her, but she fucks other men and laughs at you.

Alex scowled and rolled over on his side. That was a stupid thought. They'd had that conversation, and inevitably would again when the time came. The notion of Lorelei getting with other guys didn't turn him on. The idea that they would both live honestly and freely together meant the world to him. Jealousy seemed like more of a burden than a right.

This isn't right. It isn't natural, and you know it. Living with Rachel isn't natural or right, either. She's mad. You can see she's mad.

What angel *would allow all of this?*

That seemed dumb, too. Alex only remembered tiny fragments, but Rachel answered to her peers for everything. She went before them, with Alex and Lorelei, and the other angels allowed it.

More broken memories. How much of your mind can you lose? How much can you let them steal? Demons and witches and lunatic angels?

What if Hauser is right?

Ugly feelings churned in his stomach. Not Hauser. Fuck that guy. He didn't have to hurt Lorelei like that. And the guys—

He hurt Lorelei with holy power. Righteous power of good. What does that say about him? About her?

If Rachel loves you so much, where has she been since then?

His frown deepened into a scowl. Why were all these dumb thoughts coming to him now? Rachel had so much more to deal with than Alex and his problems, regardless of how bad they got. Alex took a long, deep breath, trying to calm himself and silence his worries.

Then he heard the pops of a gun.

He held still, eyes open to the darkness as he listened. Two shots, then a pause, then a sustained series of shots from a semi-automatic. Nothing more came. He was on the third floor of the building, and to his impression that put him far from any of the other improvised cells. The noise might have come from a different floor, or perhaps he just heard the echo... but those had to be gunshots.

He heard hurried footsteps, too. Alex pushed the blankets away and sat up as he heard keys jingle. One of them went into the lock on his door, and then the door opened.

Hauser stood there with his gun drawn, wary for any ambush from within the room. "Turn around and put your hands behind your head," Hauser ordered quietly.

"Did you hear that?" Alex hissed.

"Shut up, turn around and assume the position, kid," Hauser snapped. Even with his temper flaring, he kept his voice low. "You're the key to all of this. I'm not letting you out of my sight or letting you pull any tricks. And if somehow you do get away, I swear to God I'll have you on the most wanted list so fast your head will spin. Now turn around!"

Holding his own anger, Alex did as he was instructed. It wasn't until Hauser had the cuffs on him that they heard the angry roar of multiple guns downstairs.

EVERYONE in the break room went for their weapons at the first sounds of gunfire in the hallway. Amber and the other two plainclothes agents carried only pistols. The trio of tac guys at the table closest to the door had considerably more on hand. The tactical team leader—he'd introduced himself before, but Amber could only remember his first name was Miguel—snatched his MP-5 off the table as he rose from his chair. He glanced toward Amber and the other agents and gave a couple of hand signals: Wait. Check the window.

Amber and the others crouched low while Miguel turned out the lights. By then the gunfire outside ended. Nine shots in quick succession and then nothing. She looked to Nguyen and Lanier but found her fellow plainclothes agents inclined to follow Miguel's lead.

Pistol in hand, Lanier slipped up to the window and risked a peek outside. "Shit," he hissed, jerking his head back down. He promptly reached for the old, heavy drapes and pulled them shut. "There's gotta be two dozen people creeping around out there!"

"We can't stay in here," said Nguyen. Open laptop computers at the tables offered some ambient illumination, but with the overheads out and the curtains drawn the room was dominated by shadows.

The tactical guys pressed themselves up on either side of the door. Miguel took the lead, his weapon at the ready. He checked his men, threw a readying look to Nguyen and her agents, and put his hand on the doorknob. It opened inward, which didn't allow for Miguel to use it as cover, but the tac leader moved like he knew what he was doing.

Within a single breath, Miguel's MP-5 went off at whatever he spotted down the hall. Sudden urgency filled his eyes as he fired, as if trying to hit something too fast to pin down. It all happened too quickly for anyone to help or react. One second he stood in the doorway shooting, and the next he had a rapier through his chest.

At first all Amber saw was a black shape, a sword, and a staggered comrade. The attacker moved with incredible speed and power, shoving Miguel against the wall and then tearing his blade free in a torrent of blood. He spun back to face the room, fangs bared and his black frock coat swaying dramatically.

Then the vampire spotted the other people around him. "Aw, shit," Francois blinked as five fingers squeezed their triggers. The vampire was fast, but not fast enough to outrun bullets.

Flying lead ripped through him from hip to shoulder. Flung against the wall as gunfire pulverized bones and shredded muscles, Francois held his mind together just long enough to wish he'd stayed on the other side of the room. He slumped against the wall, knowing well enough to play dead until his undead flesh mended.

Amber knew better. She took careful aim at his head from only a few yards away and fired—and then fired again and again until there was hardly anything left.

With the threat down, the other two tac officers swung around the doorway, one high and one low, fully prepared to fire on another threat. They had a target, but they also had a small, round object flying through the air at them—and then it exploded before landing. The tac officers barely got off a shot before the grenade blast sent both men tumbling to the floor.

Though shaken by the blast, Amber caught none of its shrapnel. Nguyen and Lanier were both down, too, though she couldn't see blood or other obvious injury. In the darkened room, she couldn't even tell if they might be moving. Amber shrugged off the fog in her head and the throbbing in her ears to scramble forward, staying low with her weapon at the ready. She moved off to the right, hoping to ambush anyone who came in the room.

Too much blood and gore covered the tac officers to hold out any hope for them. Their bodies still carried much better equipment than anything the agents had. Amber reached for Miguel's tac vest, pulling open a Velcro pouch soaked with blood from his savaged chest. She had time to grab one vital bit of gear.

Automatic gunfire started again, this time right over her head. The new threat came around the door to sweep the room with bullets. With every one of her comrades down, Amber had little time to think or plan. She simply acted. Amber raised her weapon and fired at point blank range, putting bullets into the gunman's chest. He staggered and fell against the wall, still moving but momentarily stunned.

Run, said a voice in her head with all the speed of thought. *You can't defend your friends alone, but you might lead the enemy away from them. Run.*

Amber heeded the advice, believing it to be her own idea. She pushed herself up and toward the door, coming to it just as another foe appeared. In a flash of memory, she recognized her as the sugar skull girl from the Halloween party, but that hardly mattered.

She didn't feel her guardian angel's hand on hers. She didn't think about how quickly she moved, or that the vampire seemed ready for her. She simply pointed her weapon and fired. The bullet went straight through Rosario's cheek, disorienting her and giving Amber the chance to shove her way past.

Rosario collapsed to her hands and knees on the floor. Her companion shook off the last effects of Amber's shots, lurched back toward the doorway and over Rosario. He made it just in time for Amber's flash bang grenade to land at his feet with a blinding white light and a deafening boom.

Amber ran for the stairs at the other end of the hall without looking back.

The effects of the grenade wore off faster on the undead than they would on the living. "Bloody hell," the Englishman sputtered as he rubbed his eyes. "What was that thing?"

"I'mma fucking *eat* that bitch," Rorsario seethed. She picked herself up off the floor and gave her companion a shove. "See if any of these assholes are alive and get 'em back to Wentworth if they are. I want fucking blood."

"WHERE THE HELL IS YOUR GIRLFRIEND?"

"Probably wherever you put her, douche. Look, uncuff me and I'll help!"

Hauser ignored the offer. "Not her. The other one. How do you summon her? Is there a prayer or a spell or something like that? Do you just call out her name?"

Pushed along down the hallway by the agent behind him, Alex turned his head over his shoulder to throw a sour look. "Yeah, I point my magic sword in the air and I call out, 'The power of Christ compels thee.' Are you nuts?"

"Is it just straight-up danger?" demanded Hauser. "Is that it?" He shoved Alex toward an open doorway leading to a broad, old office. Long-abandoned desks and old chairs occupied the room, along with rolodexes, desktop phones and computer monitors that had been obsolete when Alex was in grade school. Along the far wall stretched a wide bay of windows.

"Hauser, people are in trouble down there!" Alex argued. "What the hell are we still doing up here? We've gotta help!"

"I am helping!" Hauser growled. "I have a plan!" He pressed up against the wall beside the window and looked out at the grounds below. "They're all here. All the vampires hunting you. And now all we need is for your angel to show up and take them out for good."

Alex looked at him like he'd grown another head. "Are you out of your fuckin' mind? Did you *want* this?"

"How does it work? Dammit, tell me! Do you have to get hurt?" he fairly snarled, drawing back his gun as if to pistol-whip his captive. Alex made ready to kick Hauser away, but then Hauser stopped. "No, she'd probably just come after me, right? Stupid." He looked around the forgotten office, then out the window again, and came to a frantic decision.

Hauser fired a shot through the glass, then smashed the rest out with his pistol and pointed down at the grounds. Dark shapes ran here and there, some human and some not. Hauser took only a second to draw a bead before he fired.

Return fire crashed through the rest of the window a second later. Hauser knew to duck in time. He looked at Alex expectantly, but the younger man just watched Hauser in shock.

"Where is she?" Hauser shouted at him. "She could destroy them all!"

"What the fuck is wrong with you?" Alex snapped back. He jerked free of Hauser's grasp, backing away as best he could without stumbling. The more he saw and heard from the frantic agent, the surer he was that Hauser had somehow lost his mind. Alex reached for any way to reason with him, or some other plan to deal with Hauser.

Alex tripped over a large, heavy lump on the floor behind him. He rolled to his knees and came face to face with one of the tactical support officers—Alex thought his name was Theo—who lay with his lifeless eyes staring at the ceiling. The man's M4 lay next to him, but with Alex's hands bound behind his back the carbine would do him no good. "Oh, shit," Alex breathed. Before he could act, a pair of strong hands grabbed his shoulders.

Inhumanly strong hands.

Alex flew off his feet, lifted like a rag doll and slammed down onto a desk by his assailant. He heard Hauser shout and fire off a couple more rounds, followed by a crash.

Even without the lights on, Alex recognized his assailant. He still had that same red beard and scraggly hair, the same towering figure and the same runes worked into his mail shirt. The leather jacket he wore over his armor made little difference. The blade in his hands was doubtlessly modern steel, but it held to a pattern set centuries ago.

A bullet burst through Unferth's chest from behind, doing little more than causing him to jerk a bit and snapping some rings of his mail.

"Back off!" Hauser shouted.

"Bjorn," grunted Unferth.

Alex saw another dark shape sweep by, heard another couple of shots from Hauser's pistol and then a crash. Alex rolled off the desk out of Unferth's reach. He dodged around the other vampire, rushing to get to Hauser. As he suspected, Bjorn already had the agent's arms in a tangle. Bjorn's mouth opened wide, fangs bared.

Throwing out a low, sweeping kick, Alex struck Bjorn right at the knee. The vampire's leg buckled and he stumbled. Unferth's hands grabbed Alex from behind again, throwing him backward onto the floor.

"Drink, brother," Unferth told the other vampire. "I'll finish this."

"Just like you to fight a bound man, Unferth," Alex snapped. He twisted and scrambled to get to his feet again, still handicapped by the cuffs on his hands.

The pair froze at his statement. Bjorn momentarily forgot about his meal. He lifted Hauser off his feet and threw him into a set of file cabinets against the wall, which collapsed under the strain.

"You know us," said Unferth in a tongue Alex barely recognized. He understood the words only because they were so simple. "How?"

If either vampire felt the slightest surprise, it didn't show. They were fighting men, though, accustomed to focusing through distractions and unexpected developments. Neither would let their guard down over the words of a cornered and unarmed man.

Just looking at the pair caused his blood to boil. He only remembered snippets. "You left me to die," Alex growled. "I came home to find my wife carrying another man's child because she thought I was dead, and then everyone called her a whore. She suffered because of *you*."

"Skorri," gasped Bjorn in recognition.

Alex blinked. He knew that name. He couldn't remember his face, or his voice, or his home, but he remembered what happened. He remembered how Skorri and Halla died.

He remembered what Skorri—what Alex—could do if his hands were free.

Unferth and Bjorn closed in from two sides, backing Alex toward a corner of the office. He leapt up onto a desk, scrambling to move away, but the vampires were too quick. Bjorn snapped his sword up to slap at Alex's ankle with the flat of his blade, tripping the young man and leaving him tumbling to the floor.

"My neck hasn't healed yet," Bjorn managed in a raspy voice. "Must we keep him alive?"

"Feed on the other one," said Unferth, jerking a thumb over his shoulder. He loomed large in Alex's field of vision as the young man hurried back to his feet again. Behind him, Bjorn turned his attention toward Hauser—and the sudden white light that flared through the room from his direction.

"Back!" Hauser ordered. Though winded and bruised, Hauser walked toward the two vampires with his crucifix held forth. The pair shrank away, arms held up to shield their eyes. Alex saw that the light wasn't from Hauser himself. Some came from his crucifix. Most of it came from a tall figure behind him, with broad white wings and a halo bright enough to chase away the shadows.

"There you are, you fucking asshat!" shouted a familiar voice from the hallway.

The angel behind Hauser turned his head toward the voice with a snap. So did Hauser. So did Alex.

Rachel shot over the rows of desks at the other angel in the blink of an eye. She tackled him straight through the wall, instantly plunging the room into darkness once more.

Bjorn recovered his wits quickly. He rushed toward Alex, grabbing him by the shoulders and forcing him to his knees. Looming over Alex from behind, Bjorn snarled at Alex with his fangs bared as he leaned in to bite.

Then he let go with a sudden jerk. Alex scrambled forward to get clear and then turned to see Lorelei with her hands on the vampire's arms, bending them back in a struggle of raw strength. Bjorn's hips jutted forward under the strain of Lorelei's knee at the small of his back. Alex could hear the cracking of bone inside Bjorn's torso.

She let go of Bjorn's arms to take up his sword and a fistful of his hair. Lorelei tugged his head to one side to expose his neck and brought the blade clean through it in one brutal, bloody swipe.

"No," came a choked cry from Unferth. "No!" He snatched up the thin axe from his belt and hurled it at Lorelei, planning to follow up with a charge—but faltered when he saw the axe strike against her cheek and fall away.

The blow did hardly more than to briefly turn her head. Lorelei calmly strode toward the vampire. Unferth drew his sword, met her gaze... and backed away, step for step as she approached, until he leapt out the window.

Alex watched in awe, unsure of what to say. She turned back to him then, moving with deliberate speed and purpose. "I have keys," she said. "Let me get you out of those things."

"Stop!" someone demanded. Standing only a few feet away, Hauser drew down on Lorelei with his gun in one hand and his crucifix in the other.

"I just saved your life, Agent Hauser."

"For the sake of whatever angle you have, sure," he huffed. "You're just as bad as those—"

He'd have fired if he saw the slightest threatening move, but the tail didn't appear in his vision until it snatched the gun out of his hand. Lorelei followed up with a hard backhanded slap that sent him to the floor. Hauser's head slammed into a desk on his way down, knocking him unconscious.

With that, Lorelei turned her attention to Alex, absently taking the gun from her tail with her left hand as she walked. She stepped around Alex, deftly releasing him from his handcuffs. "Our friends are in danger," she said. "This place already smells of death."

"What happened with Rachel just now?"

"Hauser's powers of faith are counterfeit. Rachel is dealing with the source. It may take her some time. Are you well? Can you fight?"

"I think so. Thanks for the save. That was..." he paused, looking down at

Bjorn's ashes. "This guy ruined my life. A long time ago. Him and the other one."

Lorelei held out Bjorn's sword. "You are my love, my partner and my first and best friend. Your debts are mine to pay."

SHE ALMOST LOST HIM. Donald squirmed and struggled against Rachel, doing all he could to break from her hold as they tumbled through the air. Her wings kept them both aloft. Donald beat his wings against her as he slipped out of her grasp. Three seconds of panicked effort bore fruit as he worked out of her arms and soared into the sky.

He hardly made it three yards before Rachel escalated to fighting dirty. She snatched at the bottom edges of a wing and yanked hard. Donald fell back with an unmanly squawk.

Then she grabbed his hair with both hands. Donald shrieked as she pulled him downward again. The two fell through the air, but only Rachel had any control. She landed on her feet. He landed on his head and back—hard. The fog in the air had just begun to give way to rain, but none of that made for a softer impact.

"Mother*fucker*," she snarled, "did you think I was finished with you? After the shit you pulled?"

"What—Rachel, no! Don't hit me!"

She punched him in the face. Rachel then grabbed hold of his wrist, twisting it and refusing to let go. The pleading noises in his grunts and gasps disgusted her. "Do you cry like this every time you run into someone who can act on your level?" she asked. "Is this why you push all your charges into becoming fucking heroes? Does it make up for your total lack of guts?"

"Stop—no!" denied the battered angel. "It's not like that!"

It was only then, glaring at Donald and waiting for him to explain himself, that Rachel noticed the pops and booms of gunfire. In the sudden rush to nab Donald, Rachel had abandoned her situational awareness. It came rushing back to her now with new and distressing revelations.

All around the building lurked dark shapes, many of them firing guns or moving in with blades drawn. She heard screams from inside.

"You can't fight me and save lives at the same time," huffed Donald.

Rachel jerked on his twisted wrist. "How did—how are you so quick to point that out?" she demanded. "Did you see this coming? *What did you do, Donald?*"

Someone else cried out in pain. "Is beating me worth letting mortals die?" asked Donald.

Again, Rachel looked to the building, but then something blocked her view. It emerged from the shadow of a tree, eight feet tall and covered with fur. She couldn't hear the sniff of the werewolf's nose over all of the gunfire, but its body language was quite plain. The monster gave several quick yelps as it moved in, circling close but apparently unable to see the angels just yet.

Others appeared from several directions.

"Why are there werewolves here?" Rachel asked. "Why aren't they fighting with the—Donald, what the fuck is going on?"

"How should I know?" Donald shot back. He tried to scramble away, less from Rachel than from the predators now forming a ring around them. Rachel held him in place.

Her mind raced. She couldn't trust Donald to help, but she couldn't count on him to run, either. The vampires presented more than enough of a danger to the mortals all by themselves. A pack of werewolves this large made for a much greater threat. If they were actually working together as it appeared...

The pack had their scent. The ones in wolf form reared up on their hind legs and grew into monstrous humanoid shapes. Those already in such a form crouched low as if ready to pounce.

She couldn't take herself out of the fight by pinning Donald down, but she couldn't let him run free, either.

"Time to be a guardian, Donald," she grunted. Rachel heaved him up and yanked him around again.

"What—wait, what are you—?"

Donald let out a shriek of helpless terror as she literally threw him to the wolves. He tumbled into two of them, who turned on him with teeth and claws.

Rachel's sword of flame erupted from her palm. The rest of the pack saw her immediately and shifted their focus on the new prey.

"Dammit, Wentworth, give the order!"

"No," the other vampire murmured, his head slowly shaking. "No, we mustn't rush in. Something is... strange here." His gaze drifted all along the building façade. Questions and concerns teased at his mind. Details of the plan flitted out of his memory. He couldn't remember the names of his companions.

"You heard the gunfire inside," pressed the man beside him. Wentworth knew the man's name—or knew he should. The brace of black-powder pistols in his fat leather belt seemed familiar. Wentworth imagined him in ancient sailor's rags, but those would have fallen apart long ago, which must have led him to this ridiculous set of cut-off black jeans and his tight shirt. "There was more on the other side of the building just now, and—are you even listening to me?"

"Hm? What?" Wentworth blinked, tearing his gaze off the sailor's shoes. "Of course I am listening! I am trying to listen for clues as to what transpires inside, if you don't mind."

"There!" blurted out the fallen Catholic priest to Wentworth's right. Wentworth couldn't quite remember his name, either. The priest pointed, somewhat melodramatically, to the front of the building as the main entrance flew open. A single figure staggered out, carrying one body and dragging another with him. Wentworth frowned. Didn't they send five people in? Or more?

Rosario. That was her name. Rosario and... Rupert? Where was Rosario now? Wentworth saw a great deal of blood smeared across Rupert's chin, neck and chest. So sloppy. And those bullet holes through his shirt and jacket did him no credit. "What have you to report?" asked Wentworth.

"Stronger resistance than expected, sir," said Rupert. "Unferth ran off alone in defiance of orders, and then we got into a scuffle with these ones and some others." He dumped the bodies of Nguyen and Lanier at Wentworth's feet. "They have a SWAT team or some such inside, sir. I'm not sure how large. We lost Francois and Rosario ran off after one mortal who escaped the fight. She ordered me to bring these two out as she ran off."

"This much trouble from mortals with guns?" sneered the priest.

"Begging your pardon, sir," Rupert frowned, "but if you'd like to experience a firing squad like Francois met, I'm sure it could be arranged. I'd be in awful shape myself but for the three freshly dead inside there to drink from," he added, nodding back to the building.

"This does present something of a problem," Wentworth mumbled. "We should—er—that is..." His voice faltered in tandem with his mind. Why was it so hard to concentrate?

"We should go in there and slaughter them all!" snarled the sailor.

"He's right," nodded Rupert. "They can do a nasty number on one of us with focused fire, but with enough numbers their guns won't make much difference."

"Yes, we should—wait. Let's not be hasty," Wentworth said.

"Wait for what?" demanded the sailor.

"It could be a trap."

"A trap?" snorted the priest. "How? We know their numbers."

"There's still the angel to worry about," noted a pale girl in a black flapper dress.

"Yes," Wentworth nodded in sudden thought, "that's absolutely right, erm —miss," he agreed. Damnation, but why couldn't he remember names? "We must not rush in and be left facing the angel."

"That's why we brought Diana and her mongrels," sneered the sailor.

"Diana?" blinked their leader. "Ah, yes, but, you see... we haven't seen them in action yet. We must wait and make sure they can do the job." That sounded good enough, he figured.

"The wolves and the angels are engaged," growled a familiar voice. Heads turned as another vampire approached from the shadows off to Wentworth's left. Unferth emerged from under the trees looking filthy and wet, but what caught everyone's eyes was the broken bone jutting out through the skin of the vampire's left forearm.

"Where in the hell did you go, mate?" snapped Rupert.

"After my brother, as I said." He pulled on his left arm with his right hand, wincing with the effort and some degree of pain as the bone gradually returned to its rightful place within his flesh. His eyes turned back to Wentworth. "The werewolves fight with two angels now, both on the other side of the building. It seems like an even match, but that gives us time to act."

"What of your brother?" asked the sailor.

Unferth shook his head. "I freed him, but we ran afoul of the demon before we could get outside. Bjorn died in battle with her."

"Hrm. The demon," Wentworth frowned. "We'll have to consider that complication."

"Consider my ass!" the sailor pressed. "Send a group around back and hit the enemy from both sides!"

Wentworth almost took him up on his suggestion, but hesitated. Everyone else seemed to have something to say, too. It all seemed like good advice, but much of it contradicted the rest.

He wished his people would stop confusing him.

AMBER MADE it up to the second floor, out of the stairway landing and a few precious yards down the hall. She didn't even know where to go. She simply knew there were other prisoners up here, perhaps ones that could help fight off the monsters—if she could figure out where Hauser had locked them all up. Amber slowed only to reload her pistol.

She ran and stumbled in the shadows, wishing a few of the lights would come back on. Bad enough that her ears rang so badly from the fight downstairs, but finding her way around in this darkness would be next to impossible.

A hand caught her arm as she ran, heaving back and bringing her to the floor. A brutal kick to her side drove the wind from her. The same foot to deliver the blow then kicked her gun hand hard, knocking the weapon from her grip.

"Fucking whore," Rosario barked. She spat blood onto Amber's face, looming above her with a facial wound that would have incapacitated if not killed any ordinary person. "I'll rip out your heart and fucking eat it for doing this to me," she shouted, much louder than necessary, as she pointed to her cheek.

Amber wheezed out a defiant reply, or at least tried.

"What the fuck ever, bitch," said Rosario. "I can't fuckin' hear shit right now 'cause of you, anyway."

Looking around for her weapon, refusing to simply give up, Amber saw only shadows, Rosario's feet—and a pair of sneakers behind the vampire.

An obsolete computer monitor crashed down on top of Rosario's skull, enveloping her whole head as glass and internal components shattered. Jason twisted and heaved on it, putting one leg behind Rosario's to worsen her loss of balance.

He wasted no time. Jason swept up Amber's pistol, pointed it at the monitor before Rosario could wrench it off her head and fired repeatedly. Rosario jerked from the first shot, and the second and third, but not the fourth. He paused for a heartbeat, then another, and finally kicked Rosario's lifeless shoulder.

It burst into ashes. The rest of her slowly began to crumble.

"Jason?" asked Amber.

"Yeah. So listen," he said, turning to her to help her up. "I ain't even mad, okay? I mean you had a job to do and you didn't know me and then you were stuck with the whole undercover thing. I get it."

"What?" Amber blinked.

"I'm just sayin' I'm not mad. But, like, I know who you really are now, and you know about me and what I've got going on, and obviously I'm not seriously going to jail for all this shit," he went on, gesturing with his gun to the crumbling body behind him, "since I'm clearly one of the good guys, right? So can we still date?"

"Jason, are you—how'd you get out of your cell?"

"You mean how'd I get out of an old locked office?" he frowned. "You know how many YouTube videos I've seen for that?"

She needed no further explanation. It seemed perfectly plausible out of his mouth. "There are vampires attacking the building!"

"I kinda caught up to that point already."

"And you want to talk about dating me?"

He shrugged defensively, gesturing again to Rosario's corpse with Amber's gun. "Like I'm ever gonna get a moment like that again?"

Amber shook her head as if to clear out the topic and move on. "Do you know where the others are?"

"A couple, yeah. Here, you should take this." He handed the gun back to her as he moved to another door. "You're a way better shot than I am. Wade, you in there?" he called out.

"Yeah!" came the muffled reply. "What th' fuck's goin' on?"

"Bad guys!" answered Jason. "Amber, do you have the keys?"

"No," she shook her head.

"Shit," Jason spat. "Wade, I gotta kick down this door!"

"Aim for just below the doorknob," Wade advised, "and give it all you got."

"Right, stand back," huffed Jason.

"Hey," Amber counseled, "I don't think—"

He didn't wait for her advice. Jason's foot came up at the door in a strong, solid kick that succeeded only in creating shooting pains from Jason's ankle all the way up his leg. "Owww, fuck, fuck," Jason winced, spinning around and hopping on his good foot.

"You alright?" asked Wade from the other side of the door.

"No, that fucking hurt!" Jason snapped. "Did I at least budge it a little?"

A heartbeat passed. "Sure," Wade plainly lied.

"Oh, son of a bitch," Jason grumbled. "Just gimme the gun."

"Wait, what?"

A hand rested on Jason's shoulder. "Allow me," its owner said. Lorelei put her foot into exactly the same spot Jason had tried. The door flew open.

"Oh, thank God," Wade sighed when he saw Lorelei.

"Did you thank Him for putting you here in the first place, too?" she asked with a wry frown.

"Where'd you two come from?" Jason blinked.

"Upstairs," said Alex. "Do you know where Drew is?"

"He's in that one over there," answered Wade as he stepped out of his room and pointed. Lorelei followed his gesture without pause.

"Amber," said Alex, "we all need to be cool with each other if we're gonna get out of this, okay?"

She nodded in agreement. "No, I get it now. I'm sorry for everything. Look, I think they killed a bunch of my team and at least half of our tac support squad, too."

Whatever else she might have said was cut off by the crash of Drew's door as Lorelei forced it open. The pair moved to rejoin the others. "I don't know how many vampires there are," Amber went on, "but like I said, they've already taken down a bunch of my people. I don't know where Hauser is."

"He's upstairs, but he's out cold," Alex said. "Something's wrong in that guy's head. I think he wanted this to happen. He figured Rachel would have to come to the rescue and wipe out the bad guys."

"Is he right?" asked Jason.

"Not exactly," Alex replied.

"Rachel faces a greater problem for now," said Lorelei, "leaving us to face the threat we already know."

"We need a plan," Wade spoke up, "and I need a—oh, thanks, Alex," he said as Alex put the M4 carbine and its spare clips he'd taken from Theo's body into Wade's hands. Wade turned his attention back to Amber. "Tell me y'all pack them anti-vampire bullets? No? Shit."

"We'd never even heard of such a thing until we met you guys," she replied.

"Why haven't they just bum-rushed this place yet?" Drew wondered. "They gotta know we can't hurt 'em easily."

"They may suspect the agents here have countermeasures ready for their kind," Lorelei suggested. "We can't expect the delay to continue. We have no hope of negotiating our way out. They cannot tolerate this operation. They *must* capture or kill everyone here. Their social order demands it."

"Do we try to fight our way out?" Jason suggested.

"Dark buildin', dark woods, us against sneaky-ass vampires?" Wade shook his head. "We'd get eaten alive. This buildin's too big to hold with just us. We gotta find a spot we can defend an' dig in until we find some better option. Need a place where we can see what's goin' on outside, though."

Alex pointed up toward a corner of the building. "Upstairs. You can see out in two directions and there's enough old furniture to make some barricades. Better than nothing, anyway."

"Stay together," warned Lorelei. "I will try to draw off some of their numbers. I am far more suited to such a task than any of you."

"I'm with you," Alex said, falling in step with her as soon as she turned to go. He waited for her to argue, but she merely took his hand.

The others would have watched them disappear down the shadows of the hallway but for Wade urging them to move. "We gotta go. Amber, y'all keep anybody else on this floor?"

"No," she shook her head, following the rest. "No, it was just you guys."

"Most of the doors are open, anyway," Drew murmured, "except this one here." He turned to it suspiciously, sizing it up for a kick.

"Oh, that's where we kept—" she winced as Drew slammed his foot into the door with a precise and powerful kick. "Lorelei," she finished.

Inside, they saw only a chair, a lamp hanging from the ceiling, and a snoring man on the floor with his pants and boxers crumpled in a pile beside him.

Four pairs of eyes bulged. "Bridger?" Amber burst.

Though initially as stunned as the others, Wade quickly recovered. "Okay," he said, "don't lie. There ain't *one* of us who didn't see this sort'a shit comin' a mile away."

EIGHT FEET and seven hundred pounds of teeth, fur and claws all clamped onto a girl's sword-arm made for a bitch of a handicap.

Though stronger than her opponents, Rachel still had to contend with their size, ferocity and superior numbers. The monsters knew how to fight as a pack, too. As soon as she batted away the lunge of a grey wolf-monster, a black one would leap in to exploit the opening. Its claws slashed down her shoulder and chest, and though she withstood the wounds and kicked the thing away, it gave the red wolf a chance to dart in behind her and chomp down on her left ankle.

All the while, the black werewolf clawed and clung to her right arm to keep her sword out of the fight. He couldn't hold her in place, and in fact found himself repeatedly lifted off his feet and flung around, but his claws stayed on. She felt them scrape agonizingly through her flesh.

Somewhere in her haze of pain and anger, she heard Donald's scream. Rachel caught sight of him across the clearing from her. His sword flailed in wild circles to keep his foes at bay with fire trailing in its wake. He backed away all the time, and clearly wanted to simply flee, but then she saw why he couldn't: one of the beasts had already done a vicious and bloody number on his wing.

Even when walking in the mortal world, few things could touch an angel's wings. They simply faded through everything, living and inanimate alike. Yet they were real, and an angel couldn't fly without them.

The first werewolves had been bred to hunt angels. Rachel knew little of that history, but every angel knew how dangerous they could be. Whoever created the first of their kind ultimately abandoned the effort, finding them too limited or too hard to manage. Yet the legacy lived on and, at the moment, quite literally bit Rachel in the ass.

"Oh, you little shit!" she shrieked and slammed her left fist down on the mutt's head. The force of her blow flung him off, sending the wolf to the ground, but once more another came in from the same side. She couldn't get a grip, couldn't find her footing and knew she'd be in just as much trouble as Donald before long.

"Aw, man, they've got those other FBI agents," murmured Alex. He crouched at the window set into the main entrance doors with Lorelei beside him. They found no enemies to fight on their way through the halls, but they did find the bodies of Keeley and the other tac officers.

"Do not let this display fool you, love," Lorelei warned. Nguyen and Lanier knelt with their hands on their heads, facing the building with a gun-toting vampire in a suit watching them both. "They mean to kill us all. At best, they will hold captives only long enough to extract all possible information." Her eyes slowly swept their field of vision to take in as much as she could. "I count fifteen, but they would be foolish not to have the other exits covered."

"Better eyes than mine," he grunted.

"I see quite well in the darkness, but I would not underestimate their talent for stealth."

"What do you think they're waiting for?"

Lorelei shook her head. "I cannot say. Most often what hinders their kind is internal politics and suspicion. I believe one of them rules the vampires of New York, and I see another from Las Vegas. This is a greater concern for them than I ever would have guessed."

"How many of these guys do you know?" Alex asked.

"I have known a fair number, though I have generally avoided them. Of all the curses to afflict mortals, theirs is one of the most easily spread," she grimaced. "That in combination with their longevity makes for a good number of such vermin."

Alex considered it with a frown. "Well, we should give the guys a couple more minutes to get set before we do anything," he said. "No telling when or if Rachel can handle her side of this on her own, either, right?"

"I would not hazard a guess when she might aid us. We may have to resolve the rest of this before she is able to help."

"What's she dealing with, anyway?"

He saw her stiffen slightly at the question. Her answer came slowly. "I believe Rachel would rather I not say."

"Hrm," he grunted, his eyes turning back to the window.

"She only wants to protect you, love," Lorelei said. "Admittedly, I am torn on the subject myself. I would tell you all, but Rachel..."

Alex shook his head. "It's fine. I understand. I'm used to it," he added.

Her hand reached out to his. "You seem accustomed to crisis, too."

"Do I?" he murmured. "I guess it's just... familiar. Molly and Onyx helped me a lot yesterday. Kind of put everything into perspective. It's a long story."

"You carry a new confidence in your eyes," Lorelei observed, "but you are still yourself. Still the Alex I have known. I like it."

Alex glanced at her smile and couldn't help but grin back and blush a little. He suspected she would always be able to get that reaction from him. "You don't have to hide anything from me, you know," he said. "Your face. Any of it."

"This is my natural face," Lorelei told him. "At least, it is my natural face now. You saw an echo of the past. Nothing more. It takes no effort to look like this."

"Hauser and Keeley both figured I'd turn on you after I saw that," Alex shrugged. "I figured they'd tell you the same thing. Didn't want you to wonder."

She squeezed his hand. "I never doubted you."

"I'm just saying. You don't have to hide anything from me, ever."

"There is much to tell you, but now is not the appropriate time," said Lorelei. He gave a nod of agreement, turning his eyes out to the window once more. She came to a decision. "Rachel faces one who engineered much of this, if not all of it," she explained. "To look upon him, you would not think to call him one of your personal demons... but no term would fit better." Lorelei gave a small shake of her head then, indicating she would risk telling nothing further. "Rachel loves you. Trust her."

"Loves us," he corrected with a slight grin. "Okay, we can't wait forever. We have to do something to help those agents out there."

"We might find a way to slip out of this building undetected," suggested Lorelei. "I cannot open doors without being seen, but we may find a broken window or the like."

Alex considered it but shook his head. "If they spot us pulling any tricks, they might just kill their hostages on general principle. This whole mob came out here looking for me, right? Maybe we should just give 'em what they want."

ONCE UPSTAIRS, Wade split his group in half to secure the floor in what little time they could spare. He took Amber with him to the corner office while Jason and Drew hustled down the hall to jam the doors shut at the far stairwell. The pair gave only a quick peek into each room they passed on the way, repeating the process on their way back.

"Wait up," Drew said at the double doors of the main center office pool. "Saw some light out there."

"Where?" Jason hissed.

"Outside window. Looked weird. C'mon." Drew moved as quietly as he could, keeping his head low and watching for any odd danger the office might provide. He and Jason passed through the rows of desks, noting the wreckage from Alex's earlier fight in the same room.

They crept to the windows, risked a quick look, and shared a gasp of surprise. The grounds below flashed with the orange lights of flames and the bright glow of two halos as a pair of angels—one quite familiar and the other a stranger—battled against a swarm of wolves and wolf-like monsters.

Rachel appeared to hold her own, but not much more. She struggled against two and three at a time, battering away one beast only for another to jump in and take its place. The other angel flailed and struggled to pry a wolf off his back as its jaws sank deeper and deeper into his shoulder.

"Can we help her?" Jason asked.

Drew turned to look around the room, but found no options. "Not unless you think shooting with that pistol will help. There ain't even nothin' here I could throw worth a damn. 'sides, we gotta stick with the team. C'mon," he said. Drew gave Jason a slight tug on his sleeve, heading out of the room again, and then came to a stop.

"Aw, shit," he grunted. "It's Hauser."

"Well, Alex said he was KO'd up here," Jason frowned.

"Yeah. Suppose it ain't right to just leave 'im. Help me get him up."

The pair shared the older man's weight between them, each taking one of his arms across their shoulders before hustling out of the room. They moved quickly down the hall, passing Theo's dead body before reaching the corner office. They found Wade and Amber there slowly and gently pushing up one window.

"Found your boss, Amber," Jason huffed.

"Ssshhh," she warned. Amber spared them only a glance as the two guys settled Hauser down on the floor.

"What's goin' on?" Drew asked.

"Looks like a couple of Amber's buddies're still alive after all," Wade said in a deliberately low voice. With the window now halfway open, Wade crouched low beside it and picked his M4 up off the floor.

Amber took up a spot beside Wade to look outside. Bridger followed. "I can't believe they're alive," she breathed. "This is so bad."

"You don't think they might've been turned into vampires already, do you?" suggested Drew.

"No, we saw that happen in the bus tunnel," answered Jason. "They wouldn't be up and moving already. It takes a little time to process, I think."

"We have to do something," said Amber.

"Well, ev'rybody's standin' still," Wade murmured. "Think I can pop that asshole behind 'em as long as nobody's movin', but I dunno what good that'd do." He quietly drew a bead on the vampire just the same, figuring he made for a higher priority target than any of the others.

"Are you sure?" Bridger asked. He looked from Wade to the agents and back again. "How good are you with that thing?"

"Pretty good," he said, "presumin' y'all crazy black helicopter CIA types keep y'all's weapons sighted in properly."

"Rachel's on the other side of the building fighting a bunch of werewolves," said Jason. "Her and another angel. I can't tell which side's winning."

"Sounds like that's above our pay grade," Wade decided. His eyes stayed on his target. "Lorelei an' Alex said they're fixin' to start some shit down there. I reckon if they do, I better be ready to nail this one asshole here. Maybe Amber, Bridger and I can provide coverin' fire for their buddies t' make a run for it. You two down with that?"

"Yeah," Amber nodded, taking up a spot beside him.

Bridger moved to another window, his pistol drawn and ready. "On it." He didn't bother asking why Wade had suddenly taken charge. The younger man had plainly been through more training and firefights than Bridger and Amber together.

"What do we do?" asked Jason.

"Watch the hallway an' the other window," Wade instructed, gesturing to the other corner. "If one of us goes down from a gunshot or whatever, take care of it. But mostly ah figure they ain't gonna settle f'r one angle of attack. We need to be able to put up some sort of defense, so that's y'all. Hopefully they don't think t' just send in someone downstairs to shoot up through the floor," he added.

Drew and Jason shared a grim look. Amber felt much the same way. She glanced back at them, and at her boss. "How does Hauser look?" she asked.

"Out, but he's breathin'," said Drew. "Don't worry. If he wakes up, I'll just punch him out again."

Amber opened her mouth to object, but then couldn't think of a reason why.

"Molly, I gotta let the leader guy go," Onyx whispered. "Those two hostages gotta take priority here."

If the redhead heard, she gave little indication. Onyx didn't dare break

Molly's concentration, either. Not at this point in her spell. She frowned, shifting her tools in her hands for another round of confusion hexes on her new target.

Onyx shivered in the cold. Bundled up for a night in wet woods or not, the night only grew more unpleasant under Molly's magical guidance. Eventually, Onyx knew, adrenaline would kick in and she'd forget about the cold, but until then it was goddamn freezing out. Rather than blocking out the rain, the tree above them served only to collect the water into great big drops that fell across them both.

"You about ready for showtime?"

Molly kept murmuring. She gave the slowest of nods, holding up two fingers, and then dropped back into meditation again.

Two minutes, Onyx thought. *Please let this all hang on for just two more minutes.*

"PATIENCE, PLEASE," Wentworth urged his companions. "I have heard everyone out. Fear not. This impasse will resolve itself."

"Impasse?" scowled Unferth. "What impasse?"

"The one with—ah, that is—I mean our tactical quandary." He gestured to the pair of FBI agents kneeling before Marco and his gun, and the building beyond.

"Sir," Rupert broke in, "there's no impasse. We simply need you to give the order to attack."

Murmurs of agreement rose around Wentworth. He found more agreement than he expected. In fact, he couldn't find a single dissenter. His eyes went back to the darkened building before them. Sure, there was still the fight on the other side, but that was planned. That was the whole reason he agreed to work with the mongrels in the first place.

Why not attack?

"Hey, uh, boss?" asked Marco as he turned his back on the hostages.

"Marco, turn around!" Wentworth snapped. "Keep your eyes on the prisoners!"

"Oh, right, sorry," Marco blinked, shifting his attention again. Then his head tilted curiously. "Um, but, boss...?"

"Very well," said Wentworth to his allies. "If they wish to hide, we'll just have to dig them out. Unferth, Rupert, each of you will take four—"

"Boss!" called Marco again.

"What?" Wentworth growled. He turned once more to Marco, only to see the other vampire pointing toward the partly open door to the front entrance.

Guns and other weapons came up at the ready. Wentworth held out his hand to signal for readiness. "Hold," he warned.

"Hey out there!" came a voice—Carlisle's voice. "Don't shoot! We're good. Just want to talk." The door remained only partly open, affording no one a view of the speaker behind it.

"Show yourself!" demanded Unferth.

"I'm kinda not in the mood to get shot," Carlisle replied. "And someone other than Unferth should do the talking."

"I will speak," called out Wentworth as he stepped forward. "Where is the demon, Lorelei? I would treat with an equal."

"That's too bad. I'm all you get."

Wentworth's eyes narrowed. He looked to his compatriots, but found no one offering a helpful sign. Surely a demon would not hide behind a mortal boy like this. Perhaps she fled when she saw the numbers arrayed against them?

"Then you know what must happen here," said Wentworth. "Our quarrel is not with the demon, but you concern us greatly."

"Yeah, I guess. You don't need to involve all these other people, though. You don't have to hurt anyone else."

"That remains to be seen, Mr. Carlisle," Wentworth said. "Many have been hurt on both sides of this conflict. Only you can put an end to this."

"Pretty sure I'm not gonna like how that goes."

"You will enjoy it less if we must come in there to get you. That way ends only in pain and death for everyone. Surrender yourself and I give you my word we will not hurt anyone else. Your lover and any of the others inside will be free to go."

"Are you mad?" hissed Unferth. "Let's just go in and get them all!"

"You already tried that, remember?" Wentworth murmured. "We know he is dangerous in his own right. We know little of what else lurks inside. If we draw him out, we may eliminate him before taking the rest. Better to fight our enemies piecemeal than all at once."

"What if this is a trick?" Unferth pressed. "What about the demon?"

"I should hope everyone here is watching for treachery, Unferth," Wentworth answered. "Wouldn't you at least prefer to deal with it on our own terms?

"Still. Curious that it's Carlisle speaking," Wentworth mused. "One would expect the agents holding him to take the lead. Or the demon. Perhaps this is her plan of escape?"

He called out again, "Mr. Carlisle? What say you to my offer? Shall we let the rest of these poor folk off the hook?"

"Let one of them go first!" came the answer. "Show me some good faith and I'll come out."

"I'm afraid that would be unwise on my part, Mr. Carlisle. If I give you one, I'll have only the other to bargain with." He gave a rueful smile and a single shake of his head. "That is not good strategy for me. You'll have to accept my word."

"For what that's worth," Rupert snorted quietly.

"Mortals," Wentworth sniffed. "We owe them nothing."

"Alright, fine!" Alex called out, waving one hand from behind the door. "I'm coming out. Don't shoot!"

"We wouldn't dream of it," assured the lead vampire.

The door stopped opening. "Not funny!"

Wentworth sighed. "Mr. Carlisle...?"

As he emerged from inside, the vampires all around tensed. They'd seen him take down one of their luminaries already. None would be so careless with him ever again. Wentworth nodded to individuals on his left and right. Blades and guns came out as five of the vampires crept forward, spreading in an arc around the lone young man. They watched his empty hands come up in surrender.

Tellingly, Unferth stayed in place. "This feels wrong," he growled.

"We'll sort that out soon enough," said Wentworth. He raised his voice for the others as he said, "Let him come out into the open!"

"Boss?" asked Marco, still in place behind the prisoners. "Did you want me to go out there, too?"

"No, damn you! Just stay with them!"

"Sorry," Marco mumbled. He turned back to his job, but found himself still a bit lost. He had a gun, right? Why wouldn't they want him in the group surrounding whatshisname there? That's what they were here to do, right? What he traveled all the way to Portland to do?

Wait, Portland? Was that it? Or Vancouver? Was he in Canada? Why couldn't he remember?

Carlisle. He remembered Carlisle's name, anyway, 'cause it came up again and again. Alex or something. There he was, anyway, walking out into a welcoming party of five other vampires. He didn't look like much. Just some punk kid in a leather jacket and jeans.

That, and Carlisle's twin brother suddenly appearing right behind him, throwing something in the air. *Hey, wait,* Marco thought, right before the axe blade landed in his face.

Flames exploded from the mouth of the first Alex Carlisle as he crouched and swept the field before him. Screams of pain and terror split the air. Two of the vampires caught fire instantly. Another scrambled to get out of the way, but even his supernatural speed wasn't enough to save him completely. Most of his body evaded the blast, but even one burning leg was enough to send him flailing away in full panic.

Marco missed the show. Too many things happened to him at once. He jerked backward from the axe in his head and immediately felt the sudden shock of bullets tearing through his upper chest and neck. His one good eye caught just a glimpse of the two mortal prisoners scrambling forward to get away from him before he could shoot.

It was the last thing he ever saw.

The bolt of lightning from the clouds above annihilated Marco where he stood. Its accompanying clap of thunder shocked everyone. As the air split with light and sound, more than a few of the vampires flung themselves to the grass.

Long experience with artillery and airstrikes carried Alex through the sudden distraction. Though just as surprised by the lightning as anyone else, he'd opened up this fight and was already focused on following through with it. Alex slipped Bjorn's sword into his right hand on his way to the two agents. Nguyen and Lanier both lay face first on the grass, having gotten only a few yards from Marco before the blast.

Lorelei, too, recovered quickly. Dropping her illusory disguise, she turned on the nearest vampire still standing after her ambush. Talons replaced her fingernails as she tore into her victim's neck.

Gunfire from the upper floor of the building behind them added to the chaos. Though little of it struck any particular target, the vampires still scattered and leapt for cover out of reflex if nothing else.

Only the most disciplined of fighters among the enemy held themselves together. Rupert turned his gun on Lorelei, firing at her in short, controlled bursts that knocked her to the ground. It made him a target for more of the gunfire from above. Unlike most of his fellows, Rupert knew the sting of bullets well enough to shrug off all but the most jarring strike.

Alex had his mind on other things. "Up!" he urged Lanier and Nguyen. With one hand on Nguyen's arm and his other trying to hold both sword and Lanier's coat, Alex heaved up to help the pair to their feet. The two agents made it to their knees, at least, shaking off their disorientation. "Go for the building!" Alex yelled. "Just go!"

His eyes came up in time to spot the nearest oncoming threat. Unferth ran straight for the group. Alex had no time to think of anything fancy. He simply got between the vampire and the agents, brought up his sword and went down in a heap as Unferth tackled him to the ground.

HER SECOND WIND arrived shortly after the lightning bolt, which she knew for the magic that it was. She didn't stop to analyze it—with all the monsters fighting for a piece of her flesh, Rachel didn't have much time to think about anything—but she felt a surge of strength just the same. It reminded her of a rainy night in downtown and that first flight into the sky after being grounded for days because some fucknut had cut off her wings.

That wouldn't happen again. Not even with these fucking asshat wolf-people trying to bring her down. She still had the one mangling her sword arm, and another biting her leg. A grey wolf made a new lunge for her side. Rather than swatting it off, Rachel grabbed at its neck.

She bent at the knees, spread her wings and leapt straight up into the air.

The grey managed a yelp of helplessness as she soared higher and higher. His packmates missed their chance to let go in that first second of flight, and rather than working together to keep the angel grounded now found themselves hanging on for dear life.

Rachel's grip on the grey turned vicious as she flung him into the towering monster clinging to her right arm. "Mother! Fucker! Get! Off! Me!" she yelled, slamming the grey into the beast with each word. Bones cracked as she battered the pair senseless. Finally, the black werewolf on her arm lost its grip and fell away, plummeting back toward the rooftop of the building hundreds of feet below.

She dropped the grey, leaving her with only one remaining passenger. While it still clung to her with jaws sunken into her hip, the wolf's eyes looked up into hers with sheer desperation.

As if driving her sword into a sheath at her hip, Rachel stabbed right through the wolf's head. The flames didn't hurt her at all. The beast fell lifelessly away.

Alone in the air now, Rachel looked down at the ground below. On one side of the building, she saw Donald still struggling to hold off the rest of the werewolf pack. On the other, she saw numerous shapes dart this way and that, with flashes of light and a few smoldering spots in the grass. Someone fired guns out of one window.

She saw the larger werewolf crash through the roof of the building not far from the shooter's corner. Two others of its kind on the ground saw the crash and jumped up onto the side of the building, rapidly climbing up after its packmate.

Rachel let out a bitter sigh. "Aw, balls."

THE WEREWOLVES MOCKED HIM.

Donald swung his flaming blade at each and every one as it approached. His hurt and bloody wings attested to what they would do if they got hold of him again. The beasts surrounded him eagerly, forcing him to turn in circles that would have left any mortal dizzy. They kept their distance, with each of them making feints and lunges to keep Donald frantic.

They laughed at him, too. He heard it in their yips and whines and saw it in their eyes.

In all his many centuries as a guardian, Donald never fought such foes. Direct conflict like this could never be in the interests of his charges. How much good could he do for the other souls in his care if he perished defending just one of them? In the few instances where Donald's charges fell into such danger, they did so with courage and honor that did both themselves and their guardian proud—and he was proud, when they fell, to meet their souls and take them to their reward.

None of which he could do if he became lunch for some Pit-spawned mongrel.

Yet here he was, fighting for his skin against monsters whose teeth and claws dug into his flesh even when the angel could pass right through everything else in the world around them. They could hold him down, grapple him and hurt him. And though he knew his death would be but temporary, the thought of it still chilled him to the core.

He had to escape. Rachel could deal with all of these monsters. With her in the fight, Donald could just concentrate on protecting his charge, and—

—no. Joseph. Rachel will know as soon as she looks upon Joseph. She'll know how far I've gone.

Donald's eyes flicked over to Rachel as she soared into the sky with three of the vile beasts. He couldn't pull the same trick now. Too much damage had been done to his wings. But at least she was clear for the moment, granting him a chance to escape her. At least she'd taken some of the enemy with her.

Even this momentary distraction proved fruitful for his opponents. Both of the werewolves pounced at once. "No! No!" he shrieked, darting in one direction to escape only to run into the waiting arms of another looming threat. Grappled and held firm, Donald panicked. He fought to break free, found his strength, and instinctively drove his sword into the closest beast.

None of his opponents could have been as surprised by the success as Donald himself. He wasted no time in following up on the opportunity. Donald poured his divine will into the dying beast, immolating it from the inside out. Heat and flame burst from its body until it suddenly exploded, enveloping the air around it in fire.

Donald seized the opportunity to flee. He rushed past the other werewolf in a mad dash for the building beyond. Shaken and momentarily blinded by the blast of flame, none of them pursued. Donald's eyes rose to the skies long enough to see Rachel fling down one foe and then another. She still had one left to deal with.

He prayed that it would distract her long enough.

ANOTHER BOLT of lightning split the air in front of the building. The flash and its accompanying crack of thunder put an end to the duel of gunfire between Wade and Amber in the corner window and the vampire in the World War II fatigues. They saw nothing left of their foe beyond a patch of scorched ground and a pair of smoldering combat boots. With that settled, they shifted to other targets.

Bridger took up the next window over, firing with his pistol whenever he had a decent target. He couldn't risk shooting into the melee between Alex and his opponents, but there were others to go around. "I think Lorelei's still alive!" he shouted over the gunfire. "She's still moving!"

Amber withdrew from the window to reload. "Worry about someone besides your booty call!" she snapped at Bridger.

"Look, I said it was dumb, alright?" he retorted. "I just got carried away in the moment!" He glanced over his shoulder at the other guys, who kept watch at the window in the other corner of the office. "Don't tell me you guys wouldn't!"

Drew and Jason shared an uneasy look. "No way, man," Drew vowed.

"Never," Jason shook his head.

"I mean, she's like an older sister to us."

"Yeah. We *respect* her."

"Totally, dawg."

Bridger scowled. "Oh, you are so full of—!" Bullets crashed through the window behind and above him. Bridger dropped to the floor.

"You're the occult expert here," Amber said. "Don't you have anything mystic you can do to help?"

"I'm not that kind of occultist."

"Oh, what, did you use up all your mojo with Lorelei?"

Wade pulled back from the window to reload. "Kids," he said, "can we let that go f'r now? Ah ain't got much ammo, an' this fight may go—"

The crash down the hall grabbed everyone's attention. Drew slapped Jason's shoulder and moved away from the wall with his buddy in tow. "We're on it," he grunted.

"You've only got one gun between you!" objected Amber.

"Probably won't do us any good, anyway," Jason muttered as they left.

They didn't have to go far. Staying low and sticking close together, they found flashes of orange light against the far wall from the broad office pool and heard accompanying swearing and growls. Jason looked back to Drew. "Rachel?" he asked.

The doors burst open as a mass of brown fur crashed through them and into the opposite wall. It slumped to the floor, shaken and bloodied.

"Shit! Werewolf!" blurted Jason. His gun came up as the thing reared its ugly head and snarled at them.

Then a heavy old typewriter flew through the air to slam against the werewolf's head, banging the other side of the monster's skull into the wall once more. Keys and other components scattered everywhere. The thing went limp on the floor.

Drew moved in for a closer look as the fighting inside continued. Jason stuck with him, keeping his gun trained on the fallen beast.

They found Rachel inside, leaping from desk to desk to kick and throw abandoned office equipment at the trio of werewolves trying to corner her. Desktop monitors, old lamps and staplers became dangerous projectiles in the angel's wake. She made an obvious effort to stay out of reach from her opponents while still delivering pain and distraction.

The guys bore witness to her prowess and grace, but also to her injury. They saw the blood on her dress and the nasty wounds to her arm and her side. She dodged and danced, evading one attack after another until she spun and met a lunging werewolf with a downward slash of her sword. The flames cut straight through the monster from shoulder to gut. It let out a final cry of anguish.

One of the others caught Rachel in a bear hug from behind, pinning her arms to her sides. Its companion rounded a pair of fallen desks to charge in with both claws up for a vicious and potentially fatal blow.

It never landed. Drew launched himself across the office, delivering as solid a tackle as he'd ever managed on the field in high school. His shoulder and upper arm caught the werewolf and brought it tumbling to the floor with him.

Practice and training won out over animal dexterity. Drew made it to his feet first, spinning around for a sweeping kick across the werewolf's face. The heel of his foot slammed right into the thing's eye.

His luck couldn't hold out for long, though, and in the next instant he was bowled over by the much larger and stronger foe. It tore into Drew with a single rake of its claws, eliciting a scream of awful pain.

Bullets slammed into it from across the room. Jason fired repeatedly into the thing's mass, drawing blood and causing harm but not nearly as much as a gun should. The thing looked to Jason once, and then to Rachel—and found the angel breaking free of its packmate's hold through sheer brute strength. She swung backward with her flaming sword, cutting the werewolf behind her down without a moment's look back.

Her last enemy in the room had just enough time to turn and run, but by then it was too late. Rachel caught the werewolf by the scruff of its neck, heaved it up and slammed it down to the floor before driving her sword straight down into its heart.

"Drew!" Jason called, rushing over to him. His heart broke as he came to his friend's side. There was simply too much blood, too much rent flesh and broken bone. Drew's eyes tracked him, looking up with desperation, trying to say one last thing.

Rachel dropped to her knees beside him. "No, no, no," she said frantically. "You're okay, Drew, you're okay." The fear in her voice didn't match her reassuring words. Tears welled up in Jason's eyes as he watched her put her hands on his ugly wounds.

Jason dropped to his knees at their side. "Can you help him?"

"Hold his hand," Rachel said, looking at Drew with intense concentration before closing her eyes. "Just hold his hand and talk to him, okay?"

"*Joseph, you must awaken.*"

Hauser lay on the floor without stirring. Neither the erratic booms of gunfire mere feet away nor the occasional blasts of frighteningly close lightning and thunder roused him. His chest moved up and down as he steadily breathed, though no one else in the darkened office could see it.

Donald saw it all. He understood severity of Hauser's concussion at a glance. He knew that Hauser would recover just fine, medical attention or no, but that he wouldn't be roused for some time yet... without intervention.

Bullets came through the window, punching cracks in the ceiling tiles and causing drywall to burst. Donald had no fear of such threats. He ignored the bullets, and the mortals at the windows who so bravely fought back, and the action outside. All of it would be for naught if his charge did not take part.

"*Wake up, Joseph,*" Donald whispered. He placed his hands on Hauser's head. "*This is your battle. This is your destiny. Awaken.*"

Hauser's eyes snapped open. He looked left and right, taking in the situation around him with startled breath. Hauser felt for his gun, found it missing, and picked himself up off the floor.

"*You have all the weapon you need, Joseph,*" Donald continued, closing his hand over the rosary still wrapped around Hauser's left hand. "*You know what must be done.*"

Hauser loomed up behind Wade, Amber and Bridger as they fired out of the windows with their dwindling supply of ammunition. Hauser saw dark shapes and flames, muzzle flashes and clashing steel.

"*See the monsters. See your duty. The monsters and the demon are still out there. You must destroy them. Hurry.*"

Without a word to the others, Hauser rushed out of the room. Down the hall lay a fallen man and the flashing lights and crashes of another fight inside one of the rooms. It wasn't the way he needed to go. Coming to the stairway entrance, Hauser quickly worked to clear away the old and broken furniture jammed up under the doors. He had to get outside.

He had a way to fix this. He could still come out on top.

ALEX MET Unferth's offense head on, stepping in close to change Unferth's line of attack. He parried away Unferth's sword and stepped right onto the vampire's foot all in a single move, bringing his left elbow into his opponent's side and shoving him to the ground.

Neither fighter relied on flashy moves or spectacular grace. They'd learned to meet and break an opponent quickly, so as to move on to the next opponent to arise. As Unferth stumbled and fell, Alex spun off his foot to face the vampire behind him—some pudgy old priest or friar clad in a dark mockery of holy vestments. Alex ducked low under the slash of the priest's sword, putting his own blade straight through the vampire's leg just below the knee. His foe collapsed with a yelp, clearly more startled than hurt, but it put him down just the same.

Others rushed in from either side. Alex picked the Confederate cavalryman on his right and slashed. That left the other attacker unchallenged, but Alex had nowhere else to go. His parry deflected the rebel's saber, but rather than suffering an attack from behind he heard a scream of agony. Alex stepped around his opponent, found Lorelei at his side with blood trailing from her taloned fingertips and then saw her tear into his opponent's chest. The cavalry-man's voice went from the rebel yell to the high-pitched cries of a helpless victim as she quite literally tore out his heart.

Alex spared no time to watch the horror. He turned just in time to meet

Unferth again, parrying and dodging savage blows. Others moved in on Alex at the same time, trying to take advantage of his distraction, but Lorelei stayed with him. He heard more than he saw, but even focused on Unferth he still caught glimpses as Lorelei fought and ended a violent parade of pale anachronisms.

Despite all of this, Unferth pressed on. He came in high, but Alex ducked. He stabbed for the midsection, which Alex parried away. Unferth's blade cut slightly into the Venetian courtesan that moved in to aid him, and then the pair of foes wheeled away while Lorelei blasted her with a breath of flames.

"Where's the rage, Skorri?" Unferth goaded. He made one attack after another, never tiring but knowing his opponent must. "Where's your righteous anger for all you lost?"

Alex had other things on his mind. This ground was terrible. Too much loose mud, no place to get a firm stance. He gave way to Unferth's swings. "Didn't you get banished for your stunt?" he shot back.

Unferth's lips curled back in a sneer. "They cursed us for cowards and cast us out, yes," he said, "but in the wild, we found power—or it found us! I have walked this world for all those centuries!" As Unferth shouted and snarled, his fangs stood out. "And what of you? Do you think we didn't hear what became of you? You and your whore wife?" Unferth kept swinging. "Nothing to say about that now?"

Thunder rolled in the air. Another lightning bolt blasted something near the tree line, disrupting the remaining gunfire there once more. Alex stayed focused on his opponent. He backpedalled and dodged and eventually found his footing. He waited for another swing, parried it hard to get Unferth's sword clear, and then punched right at Unferth's mouth. The steel hilt filling his hand added weight and mass to the blow, costing Unferth several teeth and even one of his fangs.

Falling victim to the mud and slick grass, Unferth slipped and flopped onto his back. Alex seized the initiative to snatch Unferth's sword arm at the wrist with his empty left hand. He brought his blade down in a decisive overhand arc he'd learned fighting Gauls for Rome's legions to hew Unferth's arm off at the elbow. Unferth let out a shout of shock and pain, which Alex silenced with a kick to the jaw.

He followed up with a wicked slash across Unferth's neck. The vampire's eyes went wide as he fell back, but Alex didn't let up. He slashed back again, aiming for the same point and striking true. Unferth's head dropped off his shoulders.

"I'm kind of over it," Alex grunted. "And you."

He had no time to catch his breath. A black mass of fur tackled Alex to the ground without warning, laying him out on his back. Large, clawed hands slammed down on his left shoulder and right forearm, pinning them both, but the worst danger came from the jaws that opened around Alex's neck. He felt the thing's sharp teeth against his skin, but they didn't close. They simply stayed in place.

"Hold, or he dies!" someone shouted.

Everything ground to a halt. The guns ran silent. The thunder ceased. Only the rain continued as it had.

Alex looked around as best he could for some escape. He saw Lorelei nearby, with her two surviving opponents backing off to circle her with blades ready.

He saw bare, feminine legs walk past the wolf-monster at his throat.

"Is the lightning the work of the angels?" Diana asked in a loud, calm voice. She stood in human form, naked and unashamed in the middle of the battle-field. "I should think electricity would not be the way to save poor Alex here. And I grant the angels are powerful and fast with their swords, but not faster than Jared's bite."

Lorelei didn't respond. Alex saw her eyes on him, but then realized he misjudged. She didn't look at him. She looked at the monster holding him down. "We can bargain if he lives," Lorelei said. "I will trade much for him."

A pair of wolfish feet padded up beside Alex opposite Diana. He glanced up at the towering monster. The thing paid him little mind, focusing instead on Lorelei.

"The angels," Diana replied. "Can you call them to us? One of them scampered off, but the other one—the girl, Rachel—was inside, last I saw. I don't hear anyone fighting up there now, but I don't see my packmates out here, either. I don't like the implications of that."

"I cannot call them, no," Lorelei said. Her eyes never left Jared's. "They wish no harm to Alex, either. The angels will honor my bargain."

"Then how important is he?" asked another voice. Alex glanced off to its source. Wentworth and several others ventured out of the tree line, guns and blades at the ready. Most kept their eyes on Lorelei.

"He is important enough to give anything," said Lorelei. Her voice dropped to a meaningful tone. "Anything."

Diana gave a snort at Lorelei's words. Wentworth scowled. "You know we've come for more than just Carlisle."

"I know what you desire," Lorelei said. She still looked directly at Jared. "Leave this place with Alex and I unharmed, and I will give you what you want."

Alex felt the teeth slowly ease up.

"The angels will appear, then," demanded Wentworth. "The angels and any mortals hiding inside. All of them. They will surrender themselves immediately."

"Little vampire," Lorelei said without looking his way, "I do not bargain with you."

"No, no, he's got a point," said Diana. "I think we can all... wait." Diana turned to look at the monster beside her, then to Lorelei and her packmate once again. "Jared?" she asked.

Jared didn't look at her. His jaws came off Alex's neck, and he uttered one of the few words his wolfish snout and jaws could manage in an animal growl of lust: "Deal."

"Jared," Diana repeated, this time with a stern tone.

Lorelei favored Jared with a cool, charming smile. "I believe Diana objects," she said. "Will she be a problem for us?"

Jared looked on Diana with murderous thoughts plain in his eyes. One of his clawed hands pulled back from Alex's arm. He let out a low snarl.

Diana stepped back, ready to shift. "Jared, you cannot believe anything she says! She is a demon!"

The other two werewolves backed away, suddenly unsure of the loyalties of their comrade. One whined plaintively, reaching for Jared, but he ignored her completely. Jared turned in a crouch, orienting himself toward Diana. He remained in place over Alex, but now none of his limbs held his prisoner.

"Diana," said Wentworth, "control your man!"

"Shut up!" Diana barked. Locked in a staredown with Jared, Diana's shoulders came forward and then back in the beginning of her shift into a larger, monstrous form. She let out a growl that Jared matched, escalated to a snarl, and then met Jared's lunge with teeth and claws as the two fell into a vicious tangle.

Everyone moved. Alex heaved himself up to grab at his blade. Lorelei rushed toward him. The other two werewolves, silently watching the tension between Jared and Diana until now, snapped out of their fascination. One darted for Alex. The other turned toward Lorelei.

"Carlisle!" Wentworth yelled. "Get—argh!" Bullets from the building's corner window punctured his dead flesh and bone, doing little serious damage but driving him to the ground through force alone. The gunman to his right fared worse, taking a pair of rounds through the head and collapsing in a twitching mess.

Sword in hand now, Alex rolled out of the way of the first swipe of werewolf claws to come at him. He brought his weapon up to meet the second, slicing into the thing's hand. It jerked the hand back, but Alex saw little blood.

He saw Lorelei beyond it as she rushed in, meeting the other werewolf who rose to meet her with a blast of fire from her lips. The thing shrieked as much in surprise as pain. Lorelei shoved the thing aside, still intent on aiding Alex. He knew his role instantly: Alex flashed his sword up at the werewolf's face, backing up and keeping it distracted. Lorelei leapt up at the thing from behind, plunging her taloned fingertips into its eyes.

It crouched and turned, flailing blindly in Lorelei's direction but touching nothing. Alex slashed low for the thing's knee. Again, his sword dug only a shallow cut in the werewolf's fur and muscle, glancing off bone rather than doing real damage.

"How do we hurt this fucking thing?" he asked, jumping back when the beast slashed in his direction. "Do we need silver bullets or what?"

"Give me the sword," Lorelei urged. Alex tossed it to her, blade upright, allowing her to catch it in a smooth motion. She raised it high in both hands and drove the sword down into the werewolf's chest. It reared back and let out a yell of agony. Lorelei jerked the sword handle left and right, driving it to its knees and then to the ground.

A lone, smoldering wolf rolled in the wet grass to salve its own hide. Wentworth scrambled off toward the trees under the assistance of several of his remaining people. Though their numbers were diminished, Alex knew they were still a threat. He turned his eyes back to Lorelei as she rose from her gruesome work. Lorelei wrenched the sword back out of it, doing even more damage, but the beast lay still. "Silver is a helpful weapon," she said, "but in the end one just needs enough force."

"We gotta find cover," Alex warned.

"Stay close to me," Lorelei replied, taking his hand in hers. She drew him into a low crouch. With no one looking their way for the briefest of moments, she saw the opportunity to escape the center of battle. "I will conceal us," she explained.

Alex and Lorelei turned their attention to the landing in front of the building, where Jared and Diana fought in a savage tangle. Broad and powerful strikes gave way to brutal grappling with tooth and claw. Each bit into the other's shoulder in an effort to reach the neck. Then the black werewolf got enough of a grip to rise up on his legs, slamming Diana down onto the concrete steps.

"I know we talked about other guys," Alex huffed, "but I am *not* okay with that deal you just made."

Every bit as weary as her lover, Lorelei gave a tired nod. They watched Diana deliver a frightful swipe of her claws across Jared's face, turning his head and drawing no small amount of blood. "As I said," Lorelei noted, "he must walk out of here first." Jared stumbled back as Diana followed up with a slash across Jared's chest. "You must give me *some* credit, love. I have my standards."

In spite of everything, Alex huffed out a laugh. He looked at Lorelei, sharing a smile with her in the middle of the insanity, and then felt a surge of panic as white light washed over them and twisted her face and her body before his eyes.

Screams of terror from the vampires in the trees intermingled with the howls of the wolves. Alex heard little of it, frightened as he was to see Lorelei crumple into a ball and cover herself with wings that hadn't been visible a moment before in a vain attempt to shield herself.

Just as before, the light was harmless to Alex. He rose to his feet, snatched up the sword and ran for the man with the glowing rosary.

A large, inhuman shape loomed between Hauser and Alex. The werewolf's form trembled with the effort, with smoke rising from its fur, but the beast came on in defiance of its pain.

"Get back!" Hauser commanded. "Back! Why won't—back!"

Focused on catching up, Alex didn't notice how the light wavered and diminished with Hauser's doubt. He saw only the monster raising its arms, and the threat beyond it, and had to find a way to resolve both.

Alex covered the distance just as the monster raised its arms for a murderous lunge. He reversed his grip on the sword, heaving up with both hands to run it through Diana's hide from behind. Desperation and a running start gave Alex added force, while the light of Hauser's rosary depleted Diana's strength. The sword plunged into her back and out her chest. The werewolf expired instantly, falling onto her side still impaled by the blade.

Someone yelled out, "No, don't!" but it wasn't Hauser. The agent had no time at all to react before Alex drove a right hook into his jaw. Hauser fell back onto the concrete. Most of the light went out with him.

That brought Alex face to face with an angel to weakened and frantic to conceal himself from mortal eyes.

"HE'S GONNA MAKE IT, isn't he?" Jason asked, holding Drew's hand tightly. "He'll be okay, right?"

Rachel's hands remained on Drew's chest. She never wavered in her focus. As she felt his ribs slide slowly back into place, the angel gave the slightest nod. "Yes," she said, every bit as relieved as either young man. She leaned in to kiss Drew's lips.

Hard.

"Uh," Jason blinked.

Rachel pulled back from Drew. The young man was covered in his own blood and a shredded ruin of a suit, but at least none of his internal organs were still exposed. He looked back at Rachel in shock. "He'll be—oh, no," she gasped.

"What?" Jason demanded. His head turned toward Rachel, and then followed her gaze out of the room and to the office across the hall. He saw the flickering white light outside but had no clue what it meant. "Rachel, what?"

The angel leapt to her feet and hurried out. Jason blinked at the sight of Rachel vanishing through a solid wall and noticed that the light outside had gone out again.

"Did that just happen?" Drew asked. "Did Rachel just kiss me?"

"I think she did!"

"What the *hell* with those women tonight, man?"

"I dunno, dude," Jason shook his head. He grabbed Drew's wrist to help him to his feet. "Maybe Alex is losin' his game?"

"Naw, don't say that."

"Bro, you just kicked a *werewolf* in the *face!* Maybe Ray's turned on by that shit?" He looked Drew over from head to toe. "You feel okay?"

"I feel great!" Drew shrugged. Then he made a face. " 'cept for that smell, anyway." He and Jason both glanced around, now aware of the smoke and flames of two burning corpses in the room, one of them quite close by. "Ugh," they shuddered. Together, the pair turned to go, but came to a halt as they looked out the broken double doors.

The werewolf on the floor shrank before their eyes, steadily shifting into a naked, hairy, overweight white man with three days of stubble and a tattoo of a Mac truck flying a Swastika flag on his shoulder. He groaned loudly, muttering something about a fucking bitch, murder and his cock.

Drew and Jason shared a single, decisive look.

Billy's eyes snapped wide when the hands clamped down on his wrists and ankles. "Woah, hey, waitaminute!" he blurted. Injured and exhausted, he could put up only weak resistance to the two guys who heaved him off the floor and carried him back into the smoky office. "Lemme explain, you guys," he tried, "I'm just a truck driver, I never wanted any of this! No! No!"

They flung him onto Red's fiery remains. He slipped and struggled to get up while boiling juices and burning flesh clung to his body. Billy screamed in pain and terror. He couldn't get it off. He couldn't shift. He couldn't heal.

He managed to get to his feet, but by then the purging flames set by Rachel's blade spread to his own flesh. Billy rose, staggered back and beat at the flames in panic.

Drew waited until he was lined up with the broken window to deliver his best roundhouse kick. He sent Billy out the open window to fall three stories to the ground outside, where he landed on a concrete sidewalk and continued to burn.

Neither Drew nor Jason needed to look at one another for the fist-bump on the way out of the room.

As soon as he could move, Lord Wentworth ran for his life.

He refused to give up the battle until the white light washed over everything. Though he saw allies and acquaintances he'd known for centuries die in seconds, the consequences of failure still loomed too large to ignore. Neither the lightning nor the demon and her mortal lover could kill everyone instantly. They could be overcome. If he could just rally his forces, if Diana and her people would get their act together, if they could find whoever or whatever directed that lightning... if.

But then the divine white light appeared, frightening him to his core. It lasted only a few seconds, and yet the vampires closer to its source than Wentworth fell and crumbled to ash where they stood. Wentworth's own skin felt ready to burst into flames.

He admitted defeat. He'd been outmatched. As soon as the light vanished, he rose and ran. He didn't get far.

The girl in black appeared out of nowhere. She tripped him with a simple and almost childish sweep of her tall boot, sending him sprawling under the trees. He hit the firm root of a tree with his nose. Hurriedly rising once more, Wentworth's eyes turned to the girl just in time for her to smash a hand mirror into his forehead, shattering it into a hundred little pieces.

It startled him much more than it hurt. Wentworth looked upon her with some surprise. She stood tall and proud, with long and curly black hair framing a lovely face that showed an almost insulting lack of fear.

"You're the one in charge," she said.

Wentworth held his tongue. Whoever she was, he owed her no explanations. He got to his feet, brushed the glass from his forehead—some of it would require a bit of plucking—and collected his nerve. "What do you want?"

"I want you to get the fuck out of this city. Forever. Don't come back. Don't send anyone else here. Just go now and forget all about this."

Wentworth bristled at her tone. He brushed off his jacket. "Indeed."

"This," she said, holding up the remains of her hand mirror, "is far worse than a threefold curse. It's all dependent on your actions and your intentions. If you want to survive it, I suggest you leave now, go home, and don't even so much as think about hurting anyone."

"Little strumpet," Wentworth snarled, "if you think—"

Her black wand came up at his face, causing him to jerk back. "Or we can skip right through the conditional stuff and go to me melting your brain. Or we can see if my partner can put her lightning between the trees yet."

Though appalled by her arrogance, Wentworth knew better than to push his luck. He'd already decided to flee. With a last rally of his pride, the vampire spit at her feet, turned to walk away and promptly tripped over another tree root to fall on his face.

"Like I said," Onyx smiled, "you might want to keep those nasty thoughts in check." She spared a last glance to watch him rise and scamper off before returning to Molly's side. The other witch remained under their tree, her full attention still on the scene in front of the old building.

"We good?" asked Onyx, touching her partner's shoulder.

"I can't see any bad guys still up," murmured Molly. Her tone and stance made plain the effort spent on maintaining her hold on the weather. "Lorelei's still alive, but I think that messed her up. I can't tell what's going on with Alex and that angel."

Onyx hardly needed the narration. She saw it all for herself. "Is it just me," she asked, "or is Alex about to punch him?"

"WHAT DO YOU MEAN, 'NO?'"

The angel bore blood and bruises from his fight. His wings were in tatters. He looked at Alex without answering his question, then stepped straight through the young man as he moved to Hauser's side. "Joseph," he said, crouching beside the fallen agent, "you must rise. This is not over. The monsters still live."

Alex glanced over the battlefield. Lorelei remained crumpled in a ball, alive but not moving. He saw Molly and Onyx emerge from the tree line, watching him and the angel. Not a single vampire remained in sight. They could be hidden, Alex thought, but by now they would likely have taken some shots. The werewolves all lay still where they fell—Jared torn up and bloody at the base of the steps, Diana just beside him with the sword through her torso.

"I don't see any monsters moving around here," Alex said. He watched the angel warily. "Why do you seem familiar?"

Hauser heaved himself to his hands and knees, shaking his head to clear the cobwebs. His eyes swept the concrete until he found what he needed.

Alex saw it, too. He stomped down on the rosary before Hauser got to it. The cross snapped under his foot. "How do I know you?" Alex pressed, still focused on the angel.

Memories raced by. He'd seen this face before, while lying in a field in springtime, and in the dirt outside a saloon, and in a dirty, blood-strewn room in Antioch. Every time, Alex remembered looking up to see this man standing over him.

He couldn't remember the angel's words, but he remembered praise... and apologies. Or excuses.

He remembered the angel's voice. "That was you in my head tonight, wasn't it?" Alex asked, and had his answer in the surprised, guilty expression that washed over the angel's face.

"Dammit," Hauser snarled, "who are you talking to?" He looked over his shoulder, saw the angel, and stumbled in shock.

"Joseph, no!" the angel blurted out, but it was already too late. He looked over to Alex. "Why wouldn't you listen to me?" he demanded. "They're monsters, Alex! All of them! Especially that Roma witch and that demon whore," he added, pointing past Alex, but whatever else he might have said was cut off by Alex's fist in his mouth.

He didn't hurt the angel much. The strike made Hauser wail oddly, but if Alex caused the angel any pain, it was all emotional. That seemed entirely plausible, though, judging from the look on the angel's face.

"Aw, fucking dammit, no," someone gasped from the doorway. Alex saw Rachel there, looking at him and the angel with despair. "Alex, you can't—!" She stopped herself. Her head tilted. "You aren't freaking out."

"I feel a little freaked out," he assured her, his eyes back on the other angel.

"Yeah, but you should... you should be worse." She stepped close to him. Her hand came to his shoulder. "You know who this is, don't you?"

"I don't," Alex shrugged. "I've never met any other angels than you and the ones we ran into together. The only other one you ever talked about was... was Donald," he remembered.

Images of battlefields and dirty streets flitted through his mind, all of them the last sights he'd ever seen. In each of them stood Donald, reaching down to lift Alex to his feet again. He thought back to the boatman's question. "Was it always Donald?"

"Yes," Rachel said. Her eyes searched him. "Every time. He wanted you to be a hero every time."

"It was only for the greater good!" Donald protested.

Alex shook his head. He glanced toward the witches, who drew closer with their wands ready. "I'm over it," he said. "Shouldn't I be?"

"Shit, I wouldn't be. But mostly I worried that you'd freak out like Hauser here," she huffed sadly. Her gaze fell to the stunned agent with pity... and then her eyes went wide with horror.

"You didn't," she breathed.

"Didn't what?" asked Alex.

"Rachel," Donald began, holding his hands up defensively, "I can explain!"

"You son of a bitch!" Rachel snarled. Righteous fury consumed her as she turned to face him again. "You *possessed* him? How *could* you?"

Donald didn't make it out of reach before she nearly lifted him off the ground with a kick to his gut. She slammed the palms of her hands against his ears, grabbed hold of his hair and threw him past Alex onto the grass.

Then she got mean.

"Are those angels?" someone asked beside Alex. "And are they fighting?"

He glanced over to Nguyen and Lanier, who stepped out into the entryway with him. Though disheveled and bloody like everyone else, they seemed okay enough to walk. "Yeah," Alex nodded. "Looks like."

"Stop hitting me!" Donald yelled.

"Stop being a bed-wetting fucker!" Rachel yelled back louder before hitting him again.

"That's Rachel," Alex added needlessly.

"What's wrong with Hauser?" asked Lanier. The others glanced down to see the lead agent huddled against one wall, watching the angels fight in a state of shock and distress.

"I think, uh... I think he saw something he's not supposed to see?" said Alex. He scratched his head awkwardly, turned back to watch the brawl, and then saw the black monster on the sidewalk stir. "Oh, shit," he grunted. "Tell me you guys have a gun on you."

"We were looking for some inside," Nguyen said, watching the werewolf rise with understandable alarm, "but we couldn't find any."

Alex dropped to his knees and grabbed at the sword imbedded in Diana. He gave it a hard tug, found it stuck fast, and put one foot against her hide as he strained to pull it out.

Jared pushed himself up with one ragged but still mighty arm, then another. His eyes seemed to glow with rage as they fixed on Alex and the agents.

"Get back inside!" Alex barked at them. "Grab Hauser and go!"

He felt someone step past him then, moving entirely the wrong way to avoid trouble. The loud boom of a shotgun followed. Alex found Wade standing over him, racking in another shot and firing again. Blood erupted from Jared's torso as the second blast hit. Wade stepped up closer, pumping and firing until Jared fell back. With only one shell left in the weapon, Wade stepped close and let it rip into the creature's chest. For all the werewolf's resilience, the relentless point-blank assault of shotgun blasts was more than Jared could take. He collapsed in a bloody heap.

Alex watched in awe. Wade turned and shrugged . "Ran outta bullets f'r the other guns," he explained. "Figured we'd come see whut wuz goin' on down here."

The rest of Alex's friends came outside along with Amber and Bridger. They looked on in wonder at the final fight playing out on the grass. Jason looked to Alex curiously. "Why's Rachel kickin' that other angel's ass?"

"I dunno." Alex threw up his hands. "Something about wetting the bed?"

"That's awkward," grunted Drew.

"I know, right?" Alex replied. He left the group to walk over to Lorelei, who had not yet picked herself up off the ground. Alex saw her wings and tail again, but they seemed to fade as he reached her. The woman on the ground before him had thin, scraggly hair and a misshapen curve to her back. He saw scabs and bald spots on her scalp.

Alex knelt beside her and put his hand on her shoulder. "Lorelei?" he asked.

"Leave me," she hissed. "Just... give me time. I will recover."

"Lorelei, you don't need to hide from me."

"Alex..."

"Look at me, Lorelei. Please."

Reluctantly, she consented. Her hand reached out for his. Alex saw pox scars and ugly, jagged nails. He held her hand gently and waited until Belet-sunu's face turned to look up at him.

Alex leaned in and kissed her. His arms came around her small, weak shoulders as he drew her close.

"This will pass," Lorelei hissed. "I just need a little time."

"I don't care," Alex told her. "I love you."

The others watched as the ragged and bloody angels brawled. After the loud chaos of the battle, this last struggle seemed almost quiet and anticlimactic, though it was plainly quite serious to the two combatants.

Donald managed a few blows and blocked a couple of Rachel's punches and kicks, but he simply couldn't put up a fight to match Rachel. For every swing he threw, Rachel landed three. Eventually Rachel knocked him to his knees and swept up with a kick to his face that sent him sprawling on his back.

She let out a heavy breath, turning around to survey the field. "Is the rest of this fight done now?" she called out.

"Looks like," Wade answered. "Reckon we're all good. Watch yer boy there!"

Rallying in desperation, Donald rolled to his feet away from Rachel, stood and reached out one hand to ignite his sword of flame. "Enough!" he cried. "I will not allow you to—"

Lightning and a deafening crack of thunder silenced him. Everyone blinked at its brilliance. Donald fell to his knees, charred and stunned, his blade extinguished once more.

Rachel threw a tired wave toward Molly and Onyx. "Thanks," she huffed.

Molly lowered her wand. "My pleasure," she replied. "Does he really wet the bed?"

18

FALLOUT

He followed the light.

Strange feelings washed over him. He'd forgotten his pain and his fear, but he knew, intellectually at least, that he should feel both. Paul Keeley saw darkness all around and instinctively moved toward the light.

The hallway seemed familiar. None of the illumination came from the overhead lamps, though, or from any window. It all shone from a beautiful brunette in a white dress, whose halo and broad wings cast light all around. She looked on Paul with a sad smile.

The mere sight of her comforted him. He didn't know her, and yet he felt as if he always had. She reached out her hands, which he took.

Paul looked around at the hallway. He saw shell casings and several bodies lying on the floor. He saw himself on the floor. It all clicked.

"I'm sorry, Paul," said the angel.

His breath shuddered. He wondered, suddenly, if he even needed to breathe at all now. What was the point? "Who are you?"

"My name is Elizabeth," she said. "I have known you and loved you all your life. I have watched over you since you were born, and I will take care of you now."

She had a friend, apparently. Another angel stood there, somewhat shorter and seemingly younger but no less beautiful. "You did good, Paul," the blonde said. She reached out to squeeze his wrist briefly. "I'm Rachel."

463

"What happened?" asked Paul.

"You fought back," Rachel told him. Tears welled up in her eyes, but he saw as much pride as sorrow. "You saved the day. You saved your friends. And you saved pretty much everyone I love."

"It didn't feel like fighting," Paul confessed. "It felt like weakness."

"No, Paul," Elizabeth shook her head. "It took great strength to overcome the power that held you. I only wish I could have aided you. The sorcery on this building left me unable to see you, and I had others to watch over. I could not come to you in time. I am sorry."

"It's what happens," Rachel added. "It's how all this works. We do the best we can. Elizabeth did the best she could." She glanced at the other angel, who only had eyes for her charge. "She helped you become the man you are. I'm grateful for it."

"What happens now?"

"Now we leave this place," explained Elizabeth. "You will have no more fear, no more pain. You will leave behind who you have been, and you will once again be who you *are*. You will have answers."

"And if you want to come back here someday, that'll be your choice," said Rachel. "This life is over now. But if you want another, you can have it."

"We should go," Elizabeth said.

"Thank you for waiting for me," Rachel told her.

Elizabeth just nodded. "Donald is dealt with?"

"Jon and Marvin took him," Rachel confirmed. "He'll be dealt with later, but at least he's under wraps for now." She gave Paul's arm another squeeze. "Thank you."

Rachel left the other two to their journey. She passed Paul's body in the hall, and Miguel's and those of his comrades, and brought her hands to her face.

Knowing what rewards awaited those men made little difference. The dead still deserved to be mourned, even by angels.

Rachel wept.

"LOOK, I'll take the fall for what I did. It was selfish and stupid and I'm not one to cover up my mistakes with bullshit. She didn't control my mind or anything."

"Bridger!" Lanier hissed.

"What?" Bridger whispered back.

"Shut up!"

Bridger shut his eyes tightly and nodded by way of apology. Like Lanier, he wore a body armor vest over his shirt and was now much better armed than he had been during the fight. With shotgun and carbine at the ready, the two agents positioned themselves on either side of the next closed door, counted off, and quickly pushed inside. The pair swept the room with their eyes, ready to blow away anything that moved.

Nothing stirred inside Hauser's temporary office. The room lay perfectly still, occupied only by the old desk, chair, some of Hauser's belongings and their improvised evidence locker.

Their posture relaxed. This room made for a clean sweep of the building. "I'm ready to call it a night," Lanier sighed.

"Yeah, I wish," Bridger agreed.

"I'll bet."

"Okay, I deserved that. Probably a lot more before it's over, too. I get it."

"I just don't get how you're so sure she *didn't* do some sort of mental magic on you or something," said Lanier. He walked around the desk to examine Hauser's laptop, still sitting open and ready. "You just seem so much smarter than this. It's bad enough that you banged a suspect in custody, but a *sex demon*? What part of that seemed like a good idea? Unless she did get into your head?"

Bridger ran a hand through his hair. "My warding spells all held. I know they did. And I knew it was seriously dumb, but..." he shook his head. "If she got into my head, she didn't do it with magic. There's all that sex appeal, and then there's the occult curiosity, and—"

"Occult curiosity?" Lanier blinked. "Seriously?"

"You ever commune with spirits?" Bridger scowled. "You want to know the sort of things I've studied?"

Lanier held up his hands. "Nope. I'm good. Don't need to know. You just do your occulty thing and I'll do my tech stuff and..." He paused with a frown, looking at the phone beside the desk. "Hauser had a five," he said.

"Huh?"

"This isn't Hauser's," Lanier muttered. He picked the black phone up off the desk and activated it, finding it unlocked. He instantly recognized the screen layout. Tapping the icons, Lanier found an active message trail—or at least a series of messages from the same source in response to a single outgoing message. Checking the time stamps as he read, Lanier's face grew pale.

"What is it?" asked Bridger.

"I think I know how they found us."

"I SHOULD'VE JUST FOLLOWED your lead the second you showed up," sighed Alex. He walked hand in hand with Lorelei under the trees, ostensibly to sweep the area around the building but mostly just to catch a minute alone. The familiar beauty of his lover's face and her normal figure had returned, as she predicted. "I just had one of those moments where I figured your priorities and mine are pretty far apart, and I didn't want to cross a point of no return."

"You were not wrong to hesitate," Lorelei told him. "A further escalation would likely have had lasting consequences for our lives even after we escaped. It would have affected our friends, too. I had thought to free you and then we could address the details later, but I don't blame you for not wanting to jump off that particular cliff."

"Yeah, I guess," he shrugged. "Still. You wouldn't have been put through all of... that," he frowned, tilting his head back toward the building. "Whatever Hauser did to you. Lorelei, you know... if that's your true face, you know I'm not—"

"It is not," she assured him. "I am not wounded. I do not hide my true face with an illusion, as Hauser and his people suspected. My body was molded into what you see now—or, rather, what you see when I let my demonic features show. This state also feels perfectly natural. You saw an echo of my past. I did not always look as I do now, but as I mentioned before... I was made into a succubus. What you saw is how I looked before that transformation."

Alex nodded. "You didn't want to talk about it," he said gently. "I'm not going to pry. I just wanted you to know it wouldn't freak me out one way or the other."

Her expression softened. "Your patience means so much... but no. I am not averse to telling you the story. Not now, after all we have shared and endured. I did not want to tell you that night when you asked because you were already burdened with your own ugly memories. I know I can share my past with you. I can share anything with you."

He nodded. "Yeah. You can."

"Alex," she said, coming to a stop. He felt the tug of her hand and faced her. "I must make a confession. This may be neither the time nor place, but I refuse to leave this matter hanging over our heads. It concerns the manner of my escape tonight."

He watched her attentively, giving a little nod to encourage her to go on. "The power Hauser and Donald used weakened me. I could not simply batter the door of my cell down or burn my way out. I had to wait for our captors to provide an opportunity, and I had to be somewhat more ruthless than you may have liked.

"I seduced one of the agents in my cell, Alex. I overcame his inhibitions, I used him and I left him passed out in my chair when I left. I cannot and do not claim that I had no other options as any sort of excuse. There were other possibilities. That was the one I chose."

His eyes slowly widened. His mouth fell open with astonishment. "Jesus Christ, Lorelei!" he blurted. "What the hell? With that lead up, I thought you were gonna say you murdered somebody or something."

"No. I have never been the sort for casual violence." She watched and waited for him to say more.

Alex frowned a little as the revelation settled. "We talked about this," he said.

"We did. Talking about it and knowing it has happened are different things."

"Sure," he nodded.

"I need to know how you feel, Alex."

"How am I supposed to feel?"

Lorelei shook her head. "This is not about expectations. I don't want you to arrive at some preconceived outcome. I want to know where you truly are."

"What am I gonna say? I mean, how many other women have I been with?"

"You have my encouragement and support in that," Lorelei countered. "I have enabled your other trysts for a number of reasons—many of them quite selfish," she noted soberly. "But I never obliged you to reciprocate. There have never been conditions, nor will I ever set any."

"No, but you want your freedom."

"Not remotely as much as I want you and your love. I need to know if we can do this. If we cannot, we—I—will have to adjust somehow."

"I don't want you to be someone you're not," Alex said. "I've never wanted that." He pushed through his hesitation. "Who was it?"

"Bridger. Their occultist."

"Are you attracted to him? Or was this more about convenience? I'm not mad, I just want to understand."

"Both concerns played their part. I find him attractive, yes, and convenience played a role."

Alex caught the tactful choice of words. "There's more to say there."

Lorelei conceded his point with a nod. "Initially, he was accompanied by another guard. I considered seducing them both, but it seemed inconvenient and so I sent the other man away."

Alex blinked. "Huh." He paused. "Did you *want* to get with both of them?"

"Only in the abstract," Lorelei conceded. "My goal was our freedom. I enjoyed the tactics I used, certainly, but that enjoyment was a means and not an end." She took his hands. "You don't seem to be building toward anger or rejection. Are you hurt at all?"

His next questions were clearly rhetorical: "Do you still love me? Do you still want me?"

"Of course. As much as I might enjoy other men, I will always want you more. There is no competitive angle to this." She paused. "I don't need to elaborate on that, do I?"

Alex shook his head. "You'll never lose me."

"Nor will I ever want anyone the way I want you. I am a creature of lust. I enjoy what I am, and I make no apologies for it. I want to play with other men from time to time, but my desire for you runs much deeper. As I said when we first spoke on this, what binds you, Rachel and I together is far beyond magic."

He took in a deep, thoughtful breath. "We still need to set some actual rules. I need boundaries."

"We both need boundaries." Lorelei turned to look toward the building and an approaching white light as she spoke.

"Can it wait 'til after my bullshit's finished?" Rachel asked wearily. She strode into their arms, resting her head on Alex's shoulder.

"Sure," Alex said, glad to be of comfort. "Is there anything we can do?"

Rachel sniffed a bit, squeezing both him and Lorelei. "No," she sighed, "just deal with the mortal stuff here and let me deal with fuckheaded asshat Donald. And I would appreciate it if you'd go home and cuddle or sixty-nine or something until I'm back," she chuckled. "The good vibes would help me through this."

"Well, if it's a chance to be supportive..." Alex grinned at Lorelei.

"Donald is in some manner of captivity, I presume?" asked the succubus.

"Yeah, he's gone. Marvin and Jon offered to take care of it." She didn't bother to explain who they might be. "This is such a mess."

"We will handle the mortal aspects of this," Lorelei assured her, stroking her hair and her shoulders. "Do what you must. Know that we are always here for you."

"This has you shaken up pretty bad, doesn't it?" Alex observed.

"People died," Rachel nodded. "Donald pissed all over his duty and his power and that's horrible to see, but people died. Hauser may never be the same. And he tried to kill you," she said to Lorelei. "He wanted to come between all of us."

"He failed in that," Lorelei replied. "Go and deal with what you must. Come to us when you can."

Rachel nodded, hugged them close one more time and then turned to walk away. "Oh," she said, turning back, "Alex, listen, I don't want you to freak out or anything, but I kinda got carried away with a moment and sorta put my tongue down Drew's throat. I mean it's not like I wanna fuck him or anything, I was just all hyped up and... what?"

Alex buried his face in his hands, and then peeked out toward Lorelei. "Okay, so boundary number one..."

THE HELICOPTER MADE ONLY a couple of passes before withdrawing, moving on to keep watch over the main entrances to the park. Its spotlight ran over the building and its immediate surroundings only once before abruptly cutting out. The group watched it from the third floor, occupying a large office not quite as shot up as the one used in the fight.

Alex broke the silence between them. "Am I crazy for feeling responsible for all of this?"

"Yes," came the unanimous answer.

He expected it from the guys. He didn't expect it from Lorelei, though, which left him grinning a little in spite of himself. "I'm just saying you guys go through a lot of shit because you're my friends."

"Shit happens," Wade shrugged. "Ain't like you picked these fights. 'sides, we all hadda eat Gefilte fish that one time 'cause we're Jason's friends."

"One time!" Jason protested.

"An' we'll never forgive you," maintained Wade. "Ever."

"We definitely need a do-over on our birthday this year," Drew decided. "We couldn't have been at that party for even two hours before it went to hell."

"I'm with you," Alex said, and then paused. He glanced at Lorelei, who merely raised one curious eyebrow. "Wait, no. I can't back that up. I missed most of the party and I didn't enjoy having a psychotic episode or whatever, but past that I can't complain about how my night turned out."

Drew rolled his eyes. "Okay, maybe *you* had a good night, but it sucked ass for Wade and I. We need a do-over."

"I'm sure something could be arranged," offered Lorelei. She saw the pair of friends smile, but noted Jason's glum expression. Her hand reached out to take his. The younger man looked back, nodded in appreciation, but said nothing.

Footsteps broke the silence. They looked toward the door to find Nguyen approaching, her weary face set in a frown. "I hate to say this, but I think you were right about Hauser being controlled somehow, Lorelei," Nguyen began. "Someone sent messages from our captive vampire's phone to one of the others relaying our location. No one besides Hauser had access to it. The time stamps add up. I can't confirm it yet, but it looks like he's the one who told them where we were." She looked around the room curiously. "Where'd the other two go?"

"Bathroom break," Jason grunted. "Down the hall. They'll be back in a few."

"Where is Hauser now?" asked Alex.

"Handcuffed to a radiator downstairs. He's still not in good shape."

"He may recover with time," said Lorelei, "but he is clearly the victim of crude and clumsy mental domination. The experience usually inflicts some trauma. He was not ready for the revelations he experienced earlier, either.

"Unfortunately, you and the others will likely forget much of what you saw of that angel and rationalize the rest into terms and images you find more comfortable. Written or recorded accounts will become muddied or vanish, as well. You will remember that Hauser was manipulated. You will not remember the details."

"So we're just going to forget Rachel?" Nguyen asked.

"No. Rachel is a special case because of the bond she and I share with Alex. I recommend that you not dwell upon her, though. Heaven keeps its distance for good reasons."

Nguyen let out a frustrated breath. "That's gonna make writing these reports a joy. At any rate, local police are cordoning off the area now—hopefully while obeying our orders to stay out and leave this to the Bureau. My bosses have more task force agents rushing out to help clean up this mess, but it'll be a few hours. We all appreciate you staying around. It looks like we can get you all on your way home shortly."

"So, that's it?" Wade asked after the group exchanged a round of glances. "We just go home and call it bygones?"

"That's how I plan to play it, yes," Nguyen confirmed. "I'm closing this case as soon as I can. I've got concerns and I've got questions," she said, eyeing Lorelei meaningfully, "but in the end, we never had solid cases against you and you weren't our primary target to begin with. Everything we could reasonably charge you with seems to have been a matter of self-defense. So for the record, I just wanted to say that we're square here.

"However, I'd love to interview you all on a less adversarial basis," she continued. "You have experience with supernatural matters that nobody on our task force can match. You might provide a lot of valuable insight for us going forward. That's not going to happen tonight, though, or tomorrow. We'll make arrangements, if you're willing."

"Seems fair," Alex shrugged.

"Of the vampires, the werewolves and some others, I can speak," said Lorelei, "but my advice on other matters will be sparse at best."

"Strictly voluntary," nodded Nguyen. "I'm not talking about subpoenas here."

"But that's it, then?" Drew asked. "Just do an interview and it's cased closed?"

Nguyen pursed her lips. "I need to speak with your other two friends, but they aren't in any trouble, either. As far as you're concerned, though? Just the interviews. Nothing more. Move on with your lives and call us if you run into trouble in the future. Maybe we can repay the favor you did us here."

Drew let out a sigh of relief. Lorelei leaned her head on Alex's shoulder. Wade sank into a chair.

Jason quietly walked out of the room, his eyes cast down to the floor.

"I'm sorry I haven't introduced myself until now. My name is Colleen Nguyen, and it looks like I'm the agent in charge now," she sighed wearily. Stress and exhaustion showed on her face as easily as all the dirt, but none of it looked likely to put her down soon.

The hallway offered no place to sit, but it beat speaking outside. The three stood under one of the hanging lights. It hardly offered complete privacy, but Agent Nguyen wanted at least a little space from the others for this.

"I'm Onyx," nodded one of the young women.

"Molly," said the other. She made a little wave with one hand before folding her arms across her chest once more.

"First off, I wanted to thank you for all of your help here tonight, both with the rescue and hanging around until now. On a less pleasant level, I'm obligated to tell you that this entire incident and everything you know about my task force is one big national security secret. If you tell anyone, by act or omission, you'll be arrested, tried and probably put in prison. Again, that's something I have to say. I don't want to be the bad guy. We owe you our lives... and that leads me to the real reason I wanted to talk to you.

"You're obviously talented sorcerers. I'm told that's the proper term to use in a conversation like this. Anyway, I've heard at least a third-hand account of everything you did last month with this crew, and I can see what you've done here in this incident. I wanted to ask if you'd be interested in helping us out in the future?"

Neither of the younger women expected that question. "You want us to join the FBI?" Onyx blinked.

Nguyen shook her head. "No. Well. Not immediately, anyway, but I'm sure the option would be open once you met our recruiting standards. Neither of you have a college degree yet, as far as I know. But like I said, I'm the agent in charge of a very special task force with special rules and resources. I can't just recruit new agents out of the blue. I can, however, hire outside consultants."

"You mean the kind you pay money, right?" Molly asked. "Like, paid consultants?"

"Absolutely," nodded the agent. "You'd have to pass the background check, of course. Do either of you have criminal records? Are you both American citizens?"

The pair snorted out a laugh. "Yeah, we're good there," Molly nodded. "What sort of work are we talking about here?"

"I'm not talking about full-time responsibilities, and I don't want to put you in the line of fire. I'm talking about a case-by-case relationship. It may only come down to providing expert advice. But we pay for that," she added for Molly's benefit.

"How much of this has to do with keeping track of us?" Onyx ventured.

"That's a concern," the agent shrugged, "but outside of you turning up here to save our asses, I don't have much to pursue with you two. I plan to wrap up this case and put it to bed. I'd be a lunatic to try to charge any of you with much of anything after all that's happened. At any rate, it's too late to keep our task force a secret from you. I'd rather have you on our side. I'm more than willing to show you two that we answer to actual judges and real courts. This might be a big government secret, but it's also under strict supervision.

"So, what do you say?" asked Nguyen. "Should I give you a call in a couple days?"

Neither Onyx nor Molly needed to look at one another to know the answer, but they shared a grin anyway.

"I AM NOT DRUNK! I am not high on some drug! As I have already said, hooligan teenagers hijacked my automobile at gunpoint and left me marooned here! I simply need to return to my lodgings."

The pair of police officers watched and listened to the protest with skeptical frowns. The lights of their patrol car offered enough illumination for the gathering, but everything else around them was still dark. "Sir," said the one called Murray, "I'm gonna ask you again. Reach out with both hands, close your eyes, and touch your nose with your right hand."

Wentworth stared daggers at the presumptuous mortal, but held his wrath in check. After all he'd been through tonight, he did not need further violence. He had to find shelter before dawn, and he needed to get far from this scene as quickly as possible. Bad luck put him in the path of these cretins as soon as he'd made it from the Magnuson park property to a major street, but at least the police officers had a vehicle.

Letting out a grumbling breath, Wentworth acquiesced. He touched his nose with one finger. "Are you quite satisfied?" he asked. "Or must I recite the alphabet again?"

"Well, sir, I'm satisfied that you aren't drunk," Officer Murray shrugged.

"Excellent. Now *take me to my lodgings downtown*," he urged, staring deeply into the officer's eyes.

Murray blinked. He shook his head a bit, looking toward his partner. "Yeah," he murmured, "I think we can give you a ride."

"Thank you," huffed the vampire. He tugged his filthy and disheveled shirt into place.

"Kevin?" asked the other officer.

"We can take him downtown, right, Tyrone?" Kevin Murray shrugged.

"Well," frowned Officer Johnson, "we need to pat you down before we put you into our car. Put your hands on the roof of the car, please."

"I—wait, what?" blinked Wentworth. "You already checked me for weapons! I'll not submit to another such search! *Take me to my lodgings downtown*," he urged the other officer, employing a similar stare.

"Yes sir, we'll be happy to," Murray told him. Now behind Wentworth, he took hold of the vampire's shoulders and pushed him into the side of the car.

"Now, see here—!" Wentworth protested, but his words fell on deaf ears. The pair worked together seamlessly, overcoming his great strength through teamwork, leverage and swiftness as they each took hold of an arm and swept one of his legs out from under him. His knees landed painfully on the pavement. Before he knew it, Wentworth was in handcuffs.

"Shit," grunted Murray, "this dude's really strong."

"Double-cuff him," said Johnson. "Grab mine. We'll get his ankles, too."

———

THEY LEFT SHORTLY before dawn with little in the way of fond farewells. Nguyen offered a lift to Lorelei and Molly's cars, which lay across the many acres of parkland and through the police cordon. It seemed the only decent thing to do.

Alex and the others followed Lanier out to a minivan in the parking lot. Not too far away, Bridger and Amber worked to photograph all the remains from Rachel's battle with the werewolves. Amber looked up only once. Alex thought she made eye contact with Jason, but then she turned her back on the group. Jason kept walking, though his head bowed somewhat. Alex thought to pat him on the back or something, but it seemed patronizing.

Then Alex glanced over to the pair of agents one more time. He gave Lorelei's hand a squeeze. "That guy?" he murmured.

She nodded, and then looked to him curiously. The couple fell a step behind their group. Her eyebrow rose. "You wouldn't mind?"

"It's entirely up to you," Alex shrugged. "You always accommodate my shenanigans."

Lorelei pursed her lips with amusement. "I'll remember your choice of words," she said as she broke off from the group. The others noticed her change of direction as they piled into the minivan, but none came up with reasons to stand there watching with Alex.

Lanier lingered. Alex gave him an accusing look. "She's not gonna jump him in the open for everyone to watch, ya perv," he said with feigned irritation.

"I am pleased to see you made it through the night unscathed," Lorelei said to Bridger. She didn't quite smile, but her words sounded genuine enough.

Bridger rose from his work, unsure of what to say. "I'm not sure that's the word I'd use to describe it," he shrugged, "but I'll be okay. Does your, uh, boyfriend there, um... Am I in for another kick in the face?"

"No. We have an understanding," she smiled. "Thank you for asking. And you? I would imagine your superiors will not be pleased."

He threw a guilty look toward Amber, who pointedly kept her eyes on her camera and the ground. "I think I'll be alright, all things considered," he said.

Lorelei gave a little nod. She stepped closer to him, producing a small black business card from nowhere and slipping it into his shirt pocket. "Call me next time you're in town. Perhaps I'll be able to make it up to you."

With that, she walked away, leaving him watching in awe.

Lanier had already slipped into the driver's seat, wanting nothing more than to get on with this. "Shall we depart?" Lorelei asked Alex as she joined him.

"He's got a goatee," Alex observed.

"Yes."

"I thought you didn't like facial hair."

"I don't care for it, but it's not a deal-breaker. You kicked him?"

"Yeah," Alex nodded. "When they arrested me."

"He remembers."

Alex paused. "Are you telling me that to soothe my ego?"

"Perhaps. Does it need soothing?"

"Well," he grinned, "you did fool around behind my back."

"I intend to make up for it," she nodded with a solemn smile. She accepted his hand as she stepped into the minivan.

Alone among the group, Jason looked back as they drove away.

"I DEMAND to speak with your superiors! And my attorney! I'll have both of your heads for this!"

"Christ, I'm seriously havin' second thoughts about not gagging him," Tyrone grumbled. He sat in the shotgun seat with his arm propped up against the door, resting his cheek against his hand.

"Cruel and unusual, buddy," replied Kevin. He had to raise his voice a bit over the shouts of their prisoner, but past that he kept his calm.

"This is intolerable! Where are you taking me?"

"I told you, we're taking you downtown," Kevin shrugged. "Soon. Meantime, we need a bite to eat. The cliché kind," he added with a snort.

He pulled the patrol car around the back of the donut shop, rolling past several parking spots until he got to the side driveway between the shop and the tall concrete wall separating the property from the nearby apartment block. "Chill out here for a while, buddy," Kevin grunted as he turned off the car and got out.

"What? You mean to leave me here?" Wentworth fairly shrieked.

"It's a safe neighborhood," Tyrone shrugged. "You'll be fine."

Wentworth watched in horror as the pair strolled around the corner toward the donut shop. He could see them through the building's side windows as they entered.

"We need to start eating healthier," Tyrone said.

"Huh? What do you mean? Oh, hi, Orion," he smiled. "Nice to see you."

The skinny, curly-haired young man at the counter looked up at the two officers and froze long enough to let out a slow, annoyed breath. "Hello, officers," he muttered.

"Could I get a maple-bacon and a chocolate glazed?" asked Kevin.

"Just a bearclaw for me," said Tyrone. "And a mocha, no whip."

"Sure," Orion grumbled. He put down his guitar and rose from his stool to retrieve their orders.

"You know what I mean," Tyrone said to Kevin as soon as Orion was out of easy earshot. "You ever do a calorie count on this stuff?"

"Just work it off at the gym," Kevin shrugged.

"I'd have to live there to work this off. I can't do that. I've got a wife."

"Oh, sure, rub my bachelorhood in my face."

Behind the counter, Orion rose with bearclaw and maple-bacon bar in hand to look out the window at the thrashing, panicked figure in the back of the patrol car. He shook his head in annoyance.

"You might try dating someone sane for once. I'm just sayin'."

"Oh, are you calling Officer Esposito crazy?"

Tyrone shot him a deadpan stare. "Yes."

"Okay, fair enough," Kevin grumbled.

The pair then cringed and looked out the window at the sound of a terrified, strangled cry. "Jesus, he's got some pipes on him," Tyrone blinked.

"I know, right?" asked Kevin. "I mean, all this distance *and* through two windows? Wow."

"Hey, you ever tell anyone about the kinda freaks there are in this town?" Tyrone asked.

Kevin gave a little snort. "Seriously? Who am I gonna tell?"

"I don't know. Your niece, maybe?"

"I'm not worried about her," Kevin shrugged. "Molly and that girlfriend of hers have their act together. They're not gonna fall into anything crazy."

"Uh-huh."

"Mostly, I just wish more of the department knew. Or other agencies. I mean, it'd be nice if we could get FBI support with these assholes or something once in a while, y'know? But they'd just think we're nuts."

A second scream drifted across the counter as the first rays of the dawn came through the entrance of the donut shop. Kevin and Tyrone looked out the window involuntarily, but their attention was tugged back to their surroundings once more as Orion slapped their plates down on the counter.

"Okay, guys, I put up with a lot because I want to be supportive," Orion said, frustration boiling to the surface. "But could you quit bringing every stupid vampire you catch to my parking lot for their suntans?"

Over his shoulder, smoke and flames drifted out of the windows of the patrol car. "Aw, shit," Kevin blinked, "he actually caught fire! How are we gonna explain that?"

"I LIKE THE ROSE PETALS," Alex said as he discovered the red trail leading to their bedroom. He walked barefoot through their home, his shoes and socks discarded in the foyer with his jacket.

"They were for Rachel," explained Lorelei with a smile.

"Yeah, her torn dress by the balcony kinda gave that away," he grinned back. He came to a halt as he stepped into the bedroom. Ripped sheets, broken glasses and knocked-over bedroom furnishings decorated the room. "Wow. You two had a good time, didn't you?"

Lorelei looked upon the disheveled chamber with a cool, pleased smile and not a shred of shame or embarrassment. "Passion occasionally brings a material cost along with its blessings. I don't believe apologies will be forthcoming."

"It must've been spectacular to see."

"I doubt we would have allowed you to stand aside and watch, had you been present," she mused. "Still, it is good to devote time solely to each other. We are as committed to one another as we are to you."

His smile deepened, but he couldn't hold back the yawn. "I'm exhausted," he confessed, "but Rachel had a request."

"She did," agreed Lorelei. She stepped in close, hooking one hand around his neck to entice him with her fingers on his skin. "My needs may even run deeper than hers." Her face came close, favoring him with a kiss and a long, tender caress of her cheek against his. "I feel your desire for me, love. It is flavored by your fatigue, by your doubt... by your longing. You are still unsettled that I have strayed. Yet you know we will work this out. You love me and want me now in spite of this change. You feel the pull of the inevitable." She paused and confessed into his ear, "Forgive me, love, but it is delicious."

His arms slipped around her waist. "Desire comes in flavors?"

"Yes," she nodded, lips trailing along his neck. "Context is everything. I draw power from the desire and the pleasures of my victims. The feeling is different with each individual, but even beyond that, my own pleasure differs with circumstance. It depends as much on the situation as the partner."

Caressing fingers turned to unfastening buttons and buckles. Their breath grew heavy. "Tell me about it," Alex murmured into her ear.

He felt her smile against his neck. "I am a wicked woman." She paused. "That concerns you, and it excites you at the same time."

"Yeah," he said. He pulled the open shirt from her shoulders, revealing her black, lacy bra and the beauty it shaped. He felt Lorelei tremble with appreciation as his touch roamed her sides and her chest. "This is nice."

"This is for you. I am for you, Alex," she told him. "I put it on for you yesterday after you sent that video. I had plans. I needed you badly." She pulled his boxer briefs down to free his erect need. Her fingers went to work, gently caressing and teasing his flesh as she spoke.

"Instead, I eventually satisfied myself with another man. I seduced him against his better judgment while bound and while Rachel watched. He put his career at great risk to sate his desire for me. He felt guilt and worry, but his desires overran all that. He *had* to have me. And I thought, with every passing second and with every pleasant touch, that I would have to answer to you for what I did... and even *that* felt good. All those details, that unique blend of conditions... I enjoyed it greatly."

Lorelei kept his hands above her hips. He couldn't slip her pants off without taking full control, and he didn't want to do that. Not while those fingers came ever closer to much more sensitive and needful flesh. "Is this the moment to talk about that?"

"It is," she nodded, "because you must understand why I enjoyed it, and why I will inevitably stray again... and why I will always come back, eagerly and of my own free will. Why no matter how few or how many partners we both have, at our core we will still belong to one another."

She curled those fingers over his shaft, pushing his remaining garment the rest of the way down his legs. "We share so much, Alex. We tend to one another's lust. We keep our secrets together. We make love as much as we *fuck*," she hissed teasingly into his ear.

"Love and sex are not the same, but they become so much better together. You and Rachel love me. I feel it in *every* context. We share an intimacy that will never be matched."

"Drop the illusion," he murmured. "Show me the real you."

He felt the tail snaking along his leg before he saw her red skin and her demonic wings and horns. His heart quickened at the sight of her.

"I love you, Lorelei," Alex murmured. "I love you... and I trust you."

She let out a note of curiosity, but her lips were on his neck.

"You're worn out. You were hurt. You need this, don't you?"

Lorelei paused in her affection to nod. "I am weakened, yes," she said. "I am drained, and hungry. I need this."

Alex nodded. He drew her up gently by her shoulders to face him and then kissed her tenderly. "I don't have a job to be at today," he reminded her, excitement and eagerness building as he spoke. "No place to be 'til tomorrow morning... we could spend all day and night on your recovery. Or just plain gluttony."

Lorelei's eyes glittered as her hands moved over his chest. "You would put yourself at my mercy?"

"I trust you," he nodded. "With my life."

Before she could speak, Alex seized her by the shoulders and pushed her back onto the bed behind her. He advanced, stepping out of the pool of his clothes on the floor to grab hold of her pants.

The red demon grinned as he roughly stripped her from the waist down, not stopping to note the lace over her sex before he tugged it off. "What of your exhaustion?" she taunted. "Didn't you want a shower?"

Alex pushed one of her legs apart from the other with his knee, resting it on the bed as he bent over her. She felt the head of his cock tease at her inner thighs, but his attention was on the rest of her body as his hands roamed. Elated at the look of possessive hunger in his eyes, she stretched and bent into his touch.

"We'll get to the shower," he said. He grabbed a fistful of her hair close to her scalp, tilting her head back. He'd gotten good at that, causing only excitement and no appreciable harm. His mouth came down on her neck as he added, "You can take over when I'm too weak to lead."

She let out a laugh of physical and emotional excitement as he attacked her. Pinned to the bed, she surrendered eagerly to the hip that pressed against hers, the hand that knowingly cupped her breast and pinched at her nipple, and the mouth that claimed kiss after kiss. Her body responded to his lust as it always did, readying her to accept him well before he actually laid his claim.

Writhing underneath him without shame, Lorelei begged him to take her in wordless sighs and whimpers. She gyrated against him, coating his cock with her wetness and challenging his will to hold out.

Her mouth quivered at the first push of his invasion. Lorelei raised her legs in a soft embrace around his hips, spreading herself to welcome him into her. Together they savored a long and slow initial penetration, and then Lorelei yelped with delight as he withdrew and speared her.

Alex rose slightly. The hand on her breast moved up to her shoulder at the neck, where he pushed down gently but possessively. He thrust into her roughly again, noting the appreciation in her eyes and the lewd and eager spread of her legs. The sight of her beautiful face and body surrendering to him only drove him on. Alex fucked her in smooth, selfish strokes.

Lorelei reveled in her lover's complete surrender to his lust for her. She felt both the triumph of her seduction and the joys of those submissive strings buried deep within her that only Alex could pull. She felt him embrace his desires and knew it would grow even easier now to get him to indulge them in the future, both with her and with others. All he'd truly needed was a sense of equality.

For that, she loved him all the more.

THE TEXT MESSAGE tone roused him, but in truth he hadn't yet fallen asleep. He crawled into bed after making it home, figuring he was in no shape to do much else, anyway. Screw classes. The hell with homework. Fuck going out.

Fuck everything right now. He'd deal with the world tomorrow.

Still, Jason reached out from his blankets and pillows to fumble for his phone. The message was exactly what he expected: "You hungry?" Drew had asked. Another text quickly followed: "Wade and I are up for whatever."

Jason let out a sigh. He knew what brought this on. He had good friends. "No, I'm good. Just sleeping. TTYL," he texted back, and then dropped the phone off the side of his bed. It thumped onto the carpet with a sound much like a doorbell.

Wait. Doorbell? I have a doorbell? It rang again, confirming its existence. *Shit,* he thought, *might as well see who it is.*

A hope teased at the edges of his mind, but he pushed that aside. He plainly didn't have that kind of luck. Clad in gym shorts and an old t-shirt, Jason rolled out of bed and shuffled to the door.

"Hi," said Amber.

Jason blinked at her and then looked out the door to check the hallway. She stood there alone, hands in her pockets and an unreadable expression on her face. He stepped on his urges to say anything mean. For all he knew, she'd walk away right then and there. "Hi. What's up?" he asked.

"Can I come in?"

Again, he stopped himself from saying anything witty. He stepped aside to let her in and closed the door behind her.

"Did I wake you up?"

"No, not really," he yawned. "Drew took care of that for you."

"I couldn't talk to you before," she said. "After the fight, I mean. Or before it. Not after the arrest and everything."

"Seemed like you didn't want to talk."

"No," she shook her head, "I did. I just had a lot to do. I've still got a lot to do. I thought about just calling you, but the phone seemed... cowardly."

Jason didn't bother to hide his frown. "You kinda gave me the let-down spiel right before you put the cuffs on me." He saw the pained look on her face and shrugged. "I'm just saying if that's what you're here for, you don't need to be. I get it. Don't repeat it. The first time was enough."

"That's not it," Amber said. "At least that's not why I wanted to come over. It's not like I wanted this to play out the way it did, and…" She rubbed her eyes. "Look, I'm exhausted and good people I knew are dead and I got an official 'for the record' reaming for how things went down with you and I. If shit wasn't so crazy, I'd probably have lost my job over how I handled things with you. Bridger's in just as much trouble, too, actually. But with the task force so chewed up like this, I guess they just want to hang on to what they've got, and let us off with… sorry," she sighed. "I'm babbling."

He said nothing.

"I'm babbling, and you're still listening to me. After everything."

"Does that not happen to you much?"

"No. Actually. Not like you."

Jason shrugged. "I'm listening. Kinda said all I had to say last night after I saved your life."

"I saved your butt a couple times in the last week."

"Sure. Not saying you didn't."

"I could've taken that freak last night, too," she frowned.

"Yeah, I know, you're not a damsel in distress, and I'm not the hero," he shook his head. "I'm just the sidekick."

"Jason," she said, "who's the real hero in *Lord of the Rings*?"

"Samwise. Duh. Why?"

"Don't call yourself just the sidekick. Ever. Your friends wouldn't, and neither would I." She paused. "You know the answers to questions like that, and you *listen* to me when I talk. Jason… did you mean what you said last night?"

"Yeah," he nodded. "I thought you didn't believe me. Or didn't care."

"No. No, I didn't exactly hear it, because my ears were still ringing and everything was crazy, but it sounded like you said you weren't mad and you're still interested in me."

He thought back. "I'm pretty sure it sounded smoother than that at the time."

"Listen, I know I'm on this big secret task force thing, but it's not like I want this to be my whole life, y'know? I plan to stay on, but it's not because I want it to be like this all the time. I don't envy your friends or anything. I want to come home to a normal guy and a normal relationship."

"There is no such thing as normal."

"No, I know," Amber nodded, "but do you get what I mean?" She searched his eyes for understanding. "I don't need you to be a big hero. I know you're a hero. That might be great when things hit the fan, but really I just want someone I can trust and who will listen to me and be supportive and fun and be... you."

He read the tension on her face and in her voice as she spoke. For all Jason had said and done, Amber knew better than to think she could just come in and sweep him off his feet after all that had happened. She seemed as ready to have her heart broken as he was.

Rather than prolong it, Jason stepped in and gently kissed her. Whatever else she might have had to say vanished under the tentative brushing of their lips, which soon built into an embrace and heavier affection. Excitement and hope banished her fatigue as her body came alive with his touch.

"This is going to be seriously complicated," she warned him.

"We're smart," he said. "We'll figure it out."

"OH YES BABY justlikethat fuckyes pleasedon'tstop mnh, mnh, mnnnhhh."

"Rachel?"

"What?" she blinked with a gasp, looking up at the sound of her name. She sat alone on a bench outside the cathedral, where she hoped no one would notice her heavy breath or the way her body trembled. Fearing she'd been busted, Rachel stood and faced her new company.

Hannah tilted her head curiously. "Am I interrupting anything? I thought you might be in prayer from the way you were whispering."

"Hah! Um. Well," she scratched at her head, relaxing somewhat once she saw that Hannah was alone, "I wouldn't call it prayer, but it's certainly a kind of communion. Uh..." she stepped in closer and whispered, "Remember how I told you about how I kinda share things with Alex?"

"Yes," said the other angel, not quite blushing but unable to stifle an amused twist of her lips. "You need not elaborate—"

"Alex and Lorelei are fucking each other out of their minds," she all but squeaked.

Chagrined, Hannah sighed. "Will you be alright?"

Rachel nodded. "I feel fucking great. I'm afraid that's the problem!"

"I imagine this happens quite often? You haven't had a problem controlling this before."

"No, and I'm pretty proud of myself for keeping it together right now, too, but that doesn't mean it's not a challenge." Rachel stopped, took in a long and quivering breath that she let out with a shudder.

Hannah watched and waited through that long breath, and the next. "Better?"

"Yeah, that's not remotely the end of it," warned Rachel.

"The others are assembled," said Hannah, turning the conversation toward the business at hand. "Lawrence and I have already spoken with Donald. His defense rests entirely on the premise that his actions served a greater good at the expense of his charges, but... well, I already know that will hold little weight with the assembly. I don't believe Donald's previous reputation as a fine guardian will save him, either, in light of how all this calls his past accomplishments into question. This hearing will not provide the sort of surprises yours held. You have only to walk in and lay the charges. I suspect you will not even need to stay for the whole proceeding if you have other things to do."

Rachel shook her head, though a note of excitement escaped her throat. "No," she said, "I'm here for the long haul. Not gonna rush out on my job to jump into bed." She paused. "Which only makes me more pissed at him."

"His offenses are indeed egregious," Hannah deadpanned. "Though I meant to suggest you might have other *duties* to attend."

"Right! The job. Dominion. Yeah. Think that's under control right now, too. I made the rounds earlier. I'm good. Seriously."

"You're ready, then?"

"Yeah."

"Nothing I might do to help you through this?"

"I'll love you forever if you'd pull my hair and spank me a little before we head in there."

Hannah rolled her eyes and turned away. "I suspect your love for me will endure if I decline, dear."

"But Hannah, you're my confidant!" Rachel pleaded sarcastically. She followed her mentor into the cathedral, hissing, "If I can't turn to you in my moment of need, who else is there?"

"The burdens heaped upon you are truly unfair."

"C'mon, we've been intimate before!" Rachel quipped. Hannah turned, gave her a dry look, and then continued on her way. "You could at least tell me I'm a dirty girl or something."

"On that note," Hannah said, "please remember that this is a chance to set an example for your dominion. A little eloquence and propriety would serve you well."

Rachel dropped the rest of her teasing pleas as they entered the main chamber. Somewhere off beyond the altar, a mortal swept and cleaned with only the light through St. Mark's windows and a couple of overhead lamps to guide him. He knew nothing of those assembled, neither hearing nor seeing the glory of hundreds of angels packed into the pews and hovering overhead. The light would have blinded him instantly.

Standing before the altar, Donald watched Rachel's approach with all the composure he could muster. Others stood nearby, but the disgraced guardian angel wore no chains or other restraint. He couldn't escape this.

All eyes turned to Rachel as she strode down the aisle. "Rachel of Seattle," called Lawrence, looming beside Donald at the altar, "you have called this assembly to address charges you have laid against this guardian. We will hear your case, we will hear Donald's defense, and we pass judgment. Please begin."

Rachel took a spot beside Donald, glanced at him once in obvious disdain, and then turned to face the assembled angels. She could have heard a pin drop.

Time to be eloquent, she thought, and then her body shuddered in time with her far-off lovers. Rachel's mouth opened and promptly shut to stifle a moan.

The assembly waited. The words she'd worked out to begin her case flitted away from her mind. *Fucking dammit, you two*, she thought. *I had something for this moment! Shit! Shit! Everyone's staring! Dammit!*

She jerked her thumb at Donald. "This motherfucker is a complete twat-waffle of a guardian," she began.

"HOLY SHIT, THIS *IS* COMPLICATED."

"It's just a bra."

"Yeah, but damn, y'know?"

Standing with Jason's arms wrapped around her inside her unbuttoned shirt, Amber let out a playful sigh and reached back to help him. "You just have to unhook the clasps," she told him.

"You say that like I wasn't trying to unhook. That's not a normal clasp."

"How familiar are you with women's underwear?"

"Do you really want me to answer that?"

"Not if it'll spoil the moment."

He answered her with another kiss, full on the mouth, as his hands reached up to massage her back now free of her bra. She hummed appreciatively at both aspects of his affection, letting him walk her slowly backward into his bedroom. To his credit, he'd happily dragged out their foreplay in the living room until she couldn't stand anymore.

She stopped as soon as she felt the corner of his bed against her legs. "Wait," she said, and claimed another kiss before she went on, "I have to ditch these."

"What?" he asked.

She reached around to get rid of the handcuffs behind her hip. Her gun already sat on his coffee table, quickly discarded to prevent any accidents. "Don't get any ideas about these," she said, holding up the cuffs. "They're not comfortable."

"Yeah, I noticed earlier."

"No, I mean even in bed."

Jason scowled in protest. "So, what, you and whatever guy you were with just jumped right into the bondage stuff the same day they gave you your first pair of handcuffs, didn't you?"

"Well, yeah," Amber snorted. "What do you think happens? Hey," she said, her hand coming up behind his neck as he rolled his eyes, "He's not here now. He lost."

"I wasn't worried about it."

"Besides, I'm still sore about being put in my own handcuffs. That was pretty messed up. I didn't even get an apology."

"Maybe I can make that up to you?"

Amber's grin broadened. "Maybe," she hissed, and then tugged him down onto the bed beside her. She pulled his shirt up over his head, tossing it aside before running her hands down his chest. His fingers went to the button and fly of her slacks. Her hips rose to aid his work.

"Tell me you've got condoms," said Amber. She immediately noticed his slight hesitation. "Oh, you're kidding me. I just didn't want to spoil the moment before, so I figured I'd ask later, but—"

"No, I've got condoms, we're cool," he grinned.

"What, you don't like wearing them?"

Jason shrugged. "I'll wear a condom. No big. I was just thinkin' I've got a clean bill of health from the clinic sitting on my dresser there. But I'm cool, they're right over in—"

She stopped his hand as it reached for his nightstand. His eyes came back to hers to find a naughty gleam. "Tubes are tied," she said.

"You sure?" he asked.

"Well, I was under sedation at the time."

"No, I mean... okay," he smiled broadly before the two fell into kissing again.

Amber put off removing his gym shorts until he had her in nothing but her panties, wanting to get some sort of parity going before the moment came. Touch alone told her that he wouldn't disappoint, but more and more she noticed how well they synched as they played. She loved his attitude, his easy manner, and his patience.

He knew how to take it slow. He also knew when to get naughty. The hand that slipped up under her breast to gently knead and stroke her while he hooked his other thumb under her panties proved that.

Such a good catch, she thought approvingly, *except...*

"I don't want a long-distance relationship, Jason," she said in his ear.

He slowed. Her panties didn't come off. "Wait, is this a one-night booty call?"

"No! No, it's not that either. Did you think it was?"

"Well, I'll take what I can get, but it's not what I want."

"I live in LA, Jason," she told him. "I busted my ass to get out of Washington. I need the sun."

"Is this something we need to work out now?"

"What if it is?" she grinned, plainly not meaning it.

"Fuck it, I can transfer," he grunted as he tugged her panties free.

Amber sighed at the feeling of his hands all over her hips, welcoming him to go on playing as long as he wanted. Her appreciation grew more vocal as she felt his gentle fingers move between her legs to explore the wet flesh there. He stroked her lips and tenderly probed, drawing out both moans and more welcoming warmth.

Ready to stop fooling around now, Amber pushed him over onto his back and grabbed for his shorts. They came off easily enough, treating her to her first sight of him fully naked. She smiled with approval as she straddled him. "Oops. Look who wound up on top."

"I can handle that."

"Sure you can," Amber said, and then gasped as his hands firmly guided her hips into place. She reached between them to guide his shaft, wanting to tease herself for only a moment more before claiming him.

She'd never felt so beautiful. Other guys had flattered her before, wanting to get where Jason now was, but Amber knew Jason was much more genuine than that. He felt so good within her and looked at her with such affection. Amber lay down on top of him, wanting to feel as much of her partner as possible as he began to move to their mutual pleasure.

"You mean it, don't you?" she breathed against his ear.

"Huh?"

"Everything."

"Yeah! I'm just... I'm... not really a talker," he grinned, pushing into her again with his hands possessively wrapped around her ass.

"Me, neither," Amber smiled, and abandoned the rest to just enjoy the ride.

ALEX LAY ON HIS BACK, overcome with both fatigue and pleasure. Almost every muscle from his legs to his shoulders all but trembled with exhaustion. His body refused to go completely limp—not when the seductress above him demanded more from him—but where he'd begun with her this morning as a lustful and dominant aggressor, nightfall arrived to find him a helpless but willing victim.

He'd bent her over and had her crying out his name. He'd lain side by side with her and made love until they'd shared whispers and tears. And now he lay underneath the demon, mustering only enough power to push up with his hips as she rode him through another shaky orgasm. Her curse refused to let his sex wane in its potency, but its enhancement of his stamina had limits. Eventually, the mortal had to let the demon take control. He knew only the sight of her beauty and the constant pleasures of her sex. Everything else had been gloriously exhausted to leave them focused on this one ecstasy.

Countless men and women had died with Lorelei like this. He fully understood why. This wasn't the first time they'd taken one another to extremes. He sometimes caught himself arranging his calendar to allow for this... and, after all that had developed between them and within himself in the last few nights, Alex saw no reason to hold back on that anymore.

Lorelei's hips gyrated back and forth over his, her fingers lewdly rubbing her labia to enhance the sensations of her climax until they abated. She enjoyed his gaze on her body enough that she turned the lights on when it grew dark. Riding him through this last satisfaction, Lorelei's eyes opened again with a cool, serene smile. "Thank you for this," she said.

"Thank you," he rasped.

"You need water again," she observed.

"I need you," he corrected, though his voice remained just as dry.

"The night is yet young," Lorelei chuckled, "and there is no escape from me now... master." Lorelei rose from him, indulging him with a long look at her body in her full glory as she strode out of the bedroom.

Alex smiled up at the ceiling. He couldn't feel the least bit guilty about that term when she had him at her mercy like this. He likely couldn't get out of bed now if the building caught fire.

That thought occurred to him as the light in the room flickered and brightened. He knew that effect. Alex turned his head slightly toward the angel who slipped in through the wall. She came to him with a breathless expression, moving with deliberate slowness as she laid down against him and planted a soft, gentle kiss on his lips.

He felt his strength return in a rush. Rachel banished his fatigue, leaving him feeling as if he'd just slept and shaken off the burn and aches of his strained muscles. Alex embraced her and kissed her back, knowing what she wanted of this. His hands pulled up her dress as she brought her hips in line with his and wordlessly drew his flesh into her.

They shared breath as well as pleasure. Rachel's eyes opened with his. "Wow, have I needed this all day," she groaned with relief.

His hands drifted to her hips, working her into a slow and steady grind. "I figured you'd feel it all day."

"The connection's wonderful," she said, her words stretching out along with her muscles as she writhed against him, "but it still leaves me wanting the real thing. Every time. Didn't even want any foreplay after today."

"And now I need not be gentle with him for the rest of the night," smiled Lorelei as she returned, glass of water in hand. She set it down on the nightstand rather than passing it to Alex. It wasn't as if he needed it now. Lorelei slipped onto the bed, crawling up close to the two. She welcomed the touch of both of her lovers as she came within reach.

"I wasn't worried," Rachel sighed, "just horny. Thanks for... mmh... making me a panting tramp in... in front of my... oh, fuck 'em."

"We'd rather have you," Alex replied.

Rachel giggled. "Dirty boy."

"I might be, yeah," he confessed. Rachel looked at him curiously as their grind continued, but Lorelei already knew. She'd tasted it on him. "It's like you said. Time to drop all my baggage and have some fun."

"Yeah?" Rachel grinned broadly.

"I still remember all the bad stuff," he said, his breath equally charged by their connection, "but it's kind of put to rest now. Seems like a sin not to enjoy all the good stuff in my life, too."

"That is much the way I have always seen things," Lorelei agreed.

Alex glanced over toward her, with one hand caressing her body while the other stayed on Rachel's hip. He knew full well how good he had it, and wanted his partners to know it. "I'm still at your mercy tonight," he reminded her.

"I'll get off 'im if you need," offered Rachel. "Soon."

"You know I enjoy this," Lorelei answered. Her words came out in the same long, breathless tones as Rachel's. "I would not interrupt."

"No," Alex said, drawing her closer, "but you could still join us."

Rachel leaned back on Alex, allowing her and Alex to draw Lorelei close. Their union did not break, but their hands and their mouths became devoted to their other partner as the demon straddled his chest.

Lorelei sighed with contentment. Her lovers got better all the time.

ABOUT THE AUTHOR

Like many Seattleites, Elliott Kay is a Los Angeles transplant. He is a former Coast Guardsman with a Bachelor's in History. Elliott has survived a motorcycle crash, serious electric shocks, severe seasickness, summers in Phoenix and winters in Seattle.

Other books in this series include *Life in Shadows*, *Personal Demons*, and *Past Due*, as well as short stories in *Small Victories* and the related book *Days of High Adventure*. His other works include the military sci-fi series *Poor Man's Fight* and the sword and sorcery series *Wandering Monsters*.

To join Elliott's notification list for upcoming releases, send an email to elliottkaybooks@gmail.com

Short stories and sneak-peeks of coming work appear on his Patreon page at https://www.patreon.com/elliottkay

Website is at www.elliottkay.com

Twitter: @elliottkaybooks

Made in United States
North Haven, CT
04 March 2023

33527226R00274